Clocktower Books

The Rx Pharmacy Sleuth Trilogy

A Cozy Mystery Classic

by

Renée B. Horowitz

Starring Pharmacy Sleuth

Ruthie Kantor Morris

Here For the First Time in One Volume:

Three Fabulous Mystery Novels

Rx#1: Rx for Murder

Rx#2: Deadly Rx

Rx#3: Rx Alibi

Rx Pharmacy Sleuth Trilogy

by Renée B. Horowitz

Rx

Pharmacy
Sleuth
Trilogy:

A Cozy
Mystery
Classic

STARRING

RUTHIE KANTOR MORRIS, R.Ph.

Contents

Book I: Rx for Murder

Ruthie Kantor Morris, R. Ph.
Pharmacy Sleuth Series
created and written by

Renée B. Horowitz

MEDICAL CENTER

NAME _____ AGE _____
ADDRESS _____ DATE _____

R

#1

Rx for Murder

SIGNATURE _____
LABEL
REFILL 0 1 2 3 4 5 PRN NR

Rx for Murder (#1 in the Rx Pharmacy Sleuth Trilogy)

The Rx Pharmacy Sleuth Trilogy

Print and Digital editions available.

Cover Design: John T. Cullen, Clocktower Books. Photos: iStockphoto [woman: dishapaun];[prescription: arenacreative];[green bottle: pzAxe].

Dedication

For the memory of my husband, Arthur Horowitz, Registered Pharmacist, and to the memories of both our dads:

Hyman Braunstein, Registered Pharmacist

and

Sam M. Horowitz, Registered Pharmacist

Acknowledgments

Many thanks to John T. Cullen, Kathi George, Janice Steinberg, Teresa Chris, and Lyssa Keusch

Author's Note

To the best of my knowledge, there is no supermarket chain called Food Go. I also coined the name Food-Fed for the store brand of a decongestant that plays an important part in this story. Many drugs that required prescriptions at the time of this novel (such as Rogaine, the hair regrowth treatment and Nicoderm, the nicotine patch) no longer require prescriptions but now can be bought "over the counter." Others, such as Seldane D, have been discontinued. Such changes in status are a pharmaceutical constant and may affect other drugs before you read my Rx series. Also, I chose to refer to Viagra although this drug was not available when *Rx for Murder* takes place. In an earlier version of *Rx for Murder*, published by Avon Books, the hormone Oreton was prescribed instead of Viagra. Some of the restaurants mentioned in *Rx for Murder*, as well, are no longer in existence in Scottsdale.

For the sake of the story, the author has also ignored the change in Arizona law that now requires a pharmacist to counsel new prescriptions.

From The Folly of Being Comforted (Poem)

One that is ever kind said yesterday:
"Your well-belovèd's hair has threads of grey,
And little shadows come about her eyes;
Time can but make it easier to be wise
Though now it seems impossible, and so
All that you need is patience."

    Heart cries, "No,
I have not a crumb of comfort, not a grain.
Time can but make her beauty over again:
Because of that great nobleness of hers
The fire that stirs about her, when she stirs,
Burns but more clearly. O she had not these ways
When all the wild summer was in her gaze."

O heart! O heart! if she'd but turn her head,
You'd know the folly of being comforted.

"The Folly of Being Comforted" by William Butler Yeats
From *The Poems of W. B. Yeats: A New Edition,*
edited by Richard Finneran (New York: Macmillan, 1983*).*

Chapter 1.

Five customers were waiting at the pharmacy window, and Joey had gone on break. I needed a break, too, but there was no way I could leave.

"Miss, when will the pharmacist be back?" A woman about my own age peered through the window at me. She wore a bright paisley blouse with clashing pink shorts and pink tennis shoes.

"I'm the pharmacist," I said. "May I help you?" My smile was forced. I could see she wouldn't accept me as a professional—but, I reminded myself, it was worse thirty years ago when I got my pharmacy degree.

"No, I mean the fellow who just left. The pharmacist."

She was ready to believe that Joey Franklin, my 20-year-old technician, was in charge. "I'm the pharmacist," I repeated more firmly, straightening the lapels of my white lab jacket so she could read the words on the name tag, "Ruth Kantor Morris, Pharmacy Manager." She never looked at it, but did hand over two prescriptions.

While I tried to clear the backlog, more people lined up at the window. I waved and said, "Be with you in a minute," but one waiting customer walked away. People want instantaneous service today. I try not to let it bother me when I lose business for my company, Food Go, but it's frustrating. And not just because I'm in the employee stock plan.

It was hot even with the air conditioner blasting away. Summertime, I wear my hair short to cope with the desert heat, but my forehead was uncomfortably damp. With the back of one hand, I brushed a lock of auburn hair, tinted nowadays, out of the way and rushed to help more waiting customers.

Joey returned from his break and pitched in. His dark eyes, always sharply intelligent, seemed animated with suppressed excitement, but we couldn't talk until a pause in the flow of customers about an hour later.

"Do you remember that old guy who comes in for his Viagra? The one with the pretty blonde wife." He waited while I handed out a prescription and cautioned the customer not to take it with dairy products. "You always say that's why widows like you don't have a chance. Because the old guys marry young gals..." Joey looked stricken. "I didn't really mean old," he said.

I remembered him all right. Harry Stokes. Another one who thought Viagra would help him keep a young wife. "Was he in for a refill today? It can't be more than a few days since the last time."

Joey's excitement was at the bursting point. "He won't need Viagra now."

"What happened?" I asked.

"He's dead."

I felt a pang of sadness. Harry Stokes had been good-looking and polite. I always remembered the polite customers. And I appreciated the way he respected my professional judgment—often asking my opinion about nonprescription drugs.

"And that's not all," Joey said. " I think he was murdered."

I had no chance to question him. Someone was tapping on the pharmacy window to get my attention.

"Excuse me. Where's the rubbers?" It was a teenage girl.

"Just over there, on the left." In my day, women never bought condoms, and certainly girls didn't. Even men were embarrassed to ask for them. Thirty years ago, they'd come into Dad's store and wait for me to walk away from the counter. After a while, I learned to busy myself elsewhere so they could talk to Dad alone.

A customer left three new prescriptions at the window, and I had no time to talk or even speculate about Joey's bombshell. He looked like he wanted to say more but had to get the phone, one call right after the other. He was a dependable technician, who wanted to study medicine someday, and was always asking questions. Although pharmacy law required me to check his work, I rarely found an error.

By the time Joey's shift ended, half a dozen people were waiting for their medications, and I barely had a chance to wave goodbye to him. I had no opportunity at all to think of Harry Stokes.

But I like to keep busy, and the night schedule works best for me since Bob died. It's that much later till I have to go back to my empty house. Nearly two years, but I still can't get used to being alone. My friends tell me, "Come on, Ruthie. It's not like you can't manage. You're different than the other women of our generation. Most of us didn't have careers."

Then they talk on, letting me know how lucky I am to have a profession, to have always worked, to make a good salary, to have no children. I stopped communicating my feelings and fears after the first bewildered months of loneliness. No one wants to hear the truth, anyhow.

They ask, "How are you, Ruthie?" and I say, "Fine." And most of the time, I am fine.

I guess it's getting better because I don't cry myself to sleep very often any more. And about a year ago, I started noticing good-looking men like Harry Stokes. He was a little older than Bob, and his expression wasn't so serious. Bob always seemed to be working out a problem in his head, maybe because of his engineering background. Friends considered me the outgoing one and Bob the introvert. But then again, I deal with people all day long, and he worked with machines.

Don't misunderstand me! Nothing was the matter with Bob's sense of humor. Sometimes it seemed to take him forever to get to the punchline of a joke, but I'd give anything to hear him tell one again. I wouldn't get impatient either.

Harry Stokes was different. He smiled more and he kidded with Joey or with me whenever he came in. Not about the Viagra, though. We didn't dare joke about it.

I knew he'd been a widower for some years because Denise Seaford from the Food Go coffee shop had pointed him out to me. Denise was a divorcée, about 10 years younger than me, and she was interested in Harry Stokes. She lived next door to Harry and knew all about him. In fact, I remembered the day last October when Denise told me he remarried.

"She's after his money."

I laughed. Denise thrived on melodrama. "After all the times you've told me how much you like him," I said. "Maybe she feels the same way."

"That's different. I'm old enough to appreciate a man in his sixties. But she's only half his age." Then Denise leaned over my table and spoke softly, as if confiding a secret. "She's just a couple of years older than his children. Could be the same age as the married son, now that I think of it."

Denise had to leave to refill someone's coffee. My shift in the Food Go pharmacy over, I sat there thinking about Harry Stokes and his young wife. I had never told Denise that I sometimes daydreamed about Harry. He'd see me standing behind the pharmacy window, nibbling on some danish and gulping down coffee between customers.

"Let me take you to dinner," he'd say. "You look like you need to relax."

"Wonderful idea," I'd answer. My imagination worked very well with the details: what I would wear, when he would call for me, where we would eat, and what we would say to each other. We'd find that we laughed together and talked a lot. I could work out the conversation in the restaurant, but after that my imagination faltered. It had been too many years since I'd dated, if they even called it that today. I had no idea how to act after dinner or whether Harry, who was from my generation, would expect me to be uninhibited like the younger women I talk to and read about. Well, now I knew. He had skipped a generation in choosing a new wife.

Denise returned and started to tell me that her neighbors all figured the Stokes children were unhappy about the marriage. "When so many years went by and he didn't remarry, the kids thought they were safe."

"Safe?"

"It's like a TV soap. There's money. Lots of money. And the son and daughter are used to having whatever they want."

I thought Denise was probably exaggerating. Most of the young people I know want their divorced or widowed parents to remarry. That way, they don't have to worry about them. Or if they're less selfish, they want the parents to be happy.

Denise went away again to microwave a slice of pizza for someone. When she came back, we occupied ourselves comparing schedules. We were looking for a night when we were both off and could go to the movies together.

Since then she'd kept me up to date about Harry Stokes and his wife, Betsy. I knew they honeymooned on Maui, and I heard when they redecorated Harry's home. Denise told me Betsy was pretty, but a stereotypical dumb blonde. "And you should see her clothes. She never wears the same thing twice."

"How do you know?" In Scottsdale, we don't see much of our neighbors. We all live behind our block fences and, although we spend a lot of time outdoors, it's usually on our own patios or in our own swimming pools.

"I see her getting into her BMW, the new one he bought for her. Or walking out to the mailbox."

Denise seemed envious. I knew she was struggling, even though she had kept her house as part of the divorce settlement. Not for the first time, I thought what a nice bit of gossip it would make for Denise if she learned that Harry Stokes was taking Viagra. But of course I wouldn't reveal anything about a customer's prescriptions.

Now, instead of the details of Harry's new life with Betsy Stokes, I would be hearing about his death and funeral. I shivered as I began my closing procedure for the pharmacy, wondering whether Joey was right about murder.

I connected the order machine to the telephone and began to transmit 40 or 50 items from the order book. The pharmacy closed at nine, although Food Go stayed open all night. That made it hard to get out of the place, because last-minute customers could come into the store while I tried to finish up. Sure enough, while I was printing a copy of my computer's Rx record for the day, a woman came in with a prescription for birth control pills.

"Why couldn't she get here sooner," I grumbled quietly as I filled her prescription. "They never remember until they start to think about bed."

At least I didn't have to back up the entire day's prescriptions the way they did in some pharmacies. All Food Go stores were linked to a mainframe computer at the central office, and they ran the backups.

I took off my white jacket, put it neatly on a hanger, locked the door to the pharmacy, and went to sign out. Yes, we have to punch a timecard even though we're supposed to be professionals. That's one disadvantage of working for a chain of supermarkets. Dad would have been upset if he'd lived long enough to see me working for Food Go. I remember the bitterness in his voice whenever he talked about the "chains" and the way their competition was forcing him out of business.

Thinking about Dad and how pharmacy has changed over the years, I reached in my handbag for the canister of Mace that I always carry, and walked out of the store. Employees are supposed to park at the outer perimeter of the lot and leave the closer spaces for customers. And although the Food Go parking lot is well lit, occasionally there are assaults and carjackings around town. It doesn't hurt to be careful.

Just as I pulled into my driveway, I remembered I'd wanted to look up Harry Stokes's prescription record. I was curious to see what other medications he'd been taking.

Chapter 2.

When I work nights, I often have lunch in the Food Go coffee shop before signing in. On Tuesday, I got there early enough to visit with Denise. Always ready to say what was uppermost on her mind, she began speaking even before I pulled out one of the green plastic-covered chairs and picked up a menu.

"Did you hear about Harry Stokes?"

I mumbled the usual sympathetic words, trying to discern at the same time if Denise looked the way she always did. Despite the heat, her makeup had been carefully applied. As usual, her eye shadow, lavender today, dramatically emphasized pale gray eyes. I saw no sign of tears or a sleepless night, and her makeup wasn't heavy enough to hide any traces of emotional outpouring for Harry Stokes. But I couldn't interpret the slight difference I did read in her expression.

After that quick glance to assess Denise's reactions, my first thought was a selfish one: good, she wasn't really in love with him. I don't have to treat her like a mourner.

Denise leaned over the table to take my order and retrieve the menu, although we both knew that I always had the same tuna salad and iced tea at this time of the year. We were in the middle of the Arizona monsoon season, with temperatures hovering at the 110-degree mark and unusually high humidity. But under pretense of taking the order, she could spend more time talking to me.

"You'll never believe what's happening," she said. "The children want an autopsy."

I stared at her, startled at the news despite Joey's comment. She smoothed the frilly green apron that served more to identify her as a Food Go waitress than to protect her clothes. Denise, always immaculate no matter how busy the coffee shop was, wore a multicolored, slightly flared skirt in shades of violet, orchid, and lavender. Her sleeveless blouse picked up the same lavender as the skirt, both exactly one shade darker than her eye shadow. Although Denise was no taller than my own five and a half feet, with hair the color we used to call dirty blonde, she made me feel nondescript in my pale yellow shirtdress.

Denise clearly enjoyed my surprise. "Betsy won't allow it. Don't you think that's suspicious?"

"You've been reading too many Sue Graftons," I said. "Any wife would be distraught at the idea of an autopsy. I was terrified they'd insist on one for Bob."

"That's different. You told me you couldn't allow an autopsy for religious reasons."

"Even so," I said. "An autopsy's the last thing a new widow wants to think about."

A young couple, in matching khaki shorts and T-shirts advertising a walkathon, went to a table at the opposite end of the coffee shop. While Denise waited on them, I thought about autopsies. Didn't the need for one simply mean the cause of death hadn't been clearly established?

It was just like Denise to dramatize everyday events. Well, maybe a neighbor's death wasn't exactly an everyday event, especially a neighbor she'd wanted. And you, I asked myself, weren't you also looking at him that way? But I told myself that was different because I'd never mentioned my daydreams to anyone; they served only to pass the time.

I was still thinking about those daydreams, unwillingly comparing them to reality, when Denise returned with my sun tea. "Why do people always sit as far away from each other as they can?" she asked. But she was smiling when she said it. Denise never got upset with her customers, even the demanding ones, and I often wished I had her patience.

I didn't comment. I was more interested in the Harry Stokes drama than where people chose to sit in Food Go's coffee shop. "Do his children suspect murder?" I asked, thinking about Joey's suspicion.

Again, I saw something indefinably different in her expression. "Now, who reads too many mysteries?" she asked me.

Although we were talking about the death of someone we both cared about, I found myself grinning at Denise. "It's a natural question. Why else would they want an autopsy?"

"They claim she drove their dad to suicide."

"Suicide!"

"It's not as farfetched as murder."

"Yes, but it seems unlikely when they've been married such a short time."

"I don't know about that," Denise muttered before she left to take care of her other customers.

I sat there, sipping my sun tea and thinking about Denise's comments. Would a seemingly well-balanced man like Harry Stokes commit suicide? What if he remarried and then discovered he'd made a mistake? Even though Arizona is a community-property state, divorce seemed more likely. Denise had told me Harry Stokes was wealthy. Surely, he would have insisted on a prenuptial agreement to protect his children.

Denise returned with my tuna sandwich and I told her what I'd been thinking. "Some people don't want to look foolish," she said.

"Suicide is a rather drastic way to avoid looking foolish." But as I ate, I remembered Harry Stokes' prescriptions for Rogaine and Viagra. Surely a man who was planning suicide wouldn't be getting refills to control baldness and increase his sex drive. I'd have to look up the computer records and see when we'd last filled those scripts.

My watch showed that it was time to get going. I paid for lunch, lost the battle of the tip again—Denise always refused to accept one from me—and went to punch my timecard with five minutes to spare.

Tim Barnard, my staff pharmacist, was working the day shift. He was planted at the computer while Joey took care of customers at the window, answered the telephone, and handled the cash register. I knew from experience that Tim would not move away from the computer unless I forced the issue. He considered it an assault on his professionalism to touch the telephone or the register, and didn't like talking to customers unless he had to.

I got a "Thank God, you're here" look from Joey and a shrug in Tim's direction. Tim, about a dozen years older than the technician and a registered pharmacist, didn't treat Joey very well. For that matter, he was often obnoxious to me, too. He'd been with us about a year, and Joey and I both wished he'd never transferred from a Food Go pharmacy in Tucson.

The day's order from our drug warehouse had come in but wasn't unpacked. I knew better than to expect help from Tim, so I asked Joey to begin while I took over the window. Between customers and phone calls, I went back and worked with Joey.

"You'll never believe what's happening," he said, echoing Denise. He seemed even more disturbed than she had been, but maybe he was just excited about the unusual situation. I wondered if I seemed different, too.

"I know. The Stokes children want an autopsy."

Joey deflated. "Oh, you had lunch in the coffee shop and Denise told you."

I admitted this was true and repeated my reaction to Denise's suppositions. The phone rang five or six times, ignored by Tim, who didn't seem to pay attention to our conversation either. He, at least, was acting the way he always did.

Since I was the responsible pharmacist, I picked up the phone and took down a Vicodin Rx from a local dentist. I handed it to Tim at the computer.

"Someone ought to report that dentist to the State Board," Tim grumbled. "He prescribes too many narcotics for his patients."

Tim was probably right, but I didn't say anything. He complained enough without encouragement. I returned to the back of the pharmacy to work with Joey, who had already unpacked and priced out the over-the-counter items. "Thanks for finishing the OTCs," I said to him.

"But I've been waiting to tell you the really great news. My brother-in-law is working on the Stokes case." Joey's excitement surfaced again.

"How can it be a case if it was a natural death?"

"That's what they're trying to find out. And I'll be in on all the details because of Frank."

Joey's older sister was married to someone on the Scottsdale police force. I hadn't really paid much attention when he'd talked about Frank Moreway and the cases he was on. Dad had so imbued me with the necessity for professional discretion that I found it difficult to understand people who gossiped about privileged information.

"You must never repeat anything you hear behind this counter," Dad told me long before I entered pharmacy college. "You'll learn who's pregnant when they come in for prenatal vitamins. You'll learn who has pneumonia. You'll learn who's using birth control. But all that information is privileged." I still remember how upset Dad was when Winston Churchill's physician wrote a book about his famous patient.

"And it's not just an autopsy," Joey was saying. "Harry Stokes's family has filed some kind of complaint with the police. I don't understand exactly what it is, but they want his death investigated."

This was something new to think about. I stored it in my mind to look at later and returned hurriedly to the pharmacy window to help a customer. Her little boy was crying loud enough to disturb everyone in the store.

Chapter 3.

A few days later, Joey told me that an autopsy had been performed on Harry Stokes, but he didn't know the cause of death. Either he hadn't seen Frank since the autopsy, or his brother-in-law was no longer disseminating professional information. Most likely, it was too soon for the results to be in.

I thought about the mysteries I like to read when I can't fall asleep. Sometimes, preliminary post mortem results show up quickly, but not always. It varies with the author's need to deliver red herrings before facts get in the way.

Half a dozen plots went through my mind. In a whodunit, I'd be doing some amateur detecting to catch Harry Stokes's murderer. I smiled at the thought. Which fictional sleuth would I be? I could easily identify with a V.I. Warshawski or a Kinsey Millhone. But, I thought wryly, other people would see me as Miss Marple or Jessica Fletcher. The age-old question went through my mind. *Why was I, a woman who still saw herself as a thirty-five-year-old, doing in a fifty-five-year-old body?*

With a sigh, I remembered that I couldn't be the amateur who brilliantly solved the Stokes case—not because of age, but because common sense told me Harry Stokes had probably died of a heart attack. He wasn't the first man who married a young wife and... Well, there were plenty of jokes along those lines. They invoked images of the fox and the sour grapes, and that was not the way I wanted to see myself.

I looked up to find Denise at the pharmacy window. She was wearing a black-and-white geometric print with a red venetian-glass necklace and matching earrings. I marveled at the way she'd found lipstick of the same red shade. In spring and fall, she wore the same dress with a flowered scarf, a deeper red, draped over one shoulder. She had *that* shade of lipstick, too.

"You looked so busy, I didn't want to interrupt," she said. "Do you have a minute to chat?"

"Actually, I was just daydreaming. But don't tell anyone or they'll say I don't need technician hours and cut Joey back."

Denise still seemed different, but I decided it was because she was quieter than usual. She must have cared more for Harry Stokes than I'd guessed. Maybe I should suggest going out together after work so she wouldn't go home to brood about might-have-beens. Mall hopping sounded like a good idea, and we could cool off at the same time.

Some of my long-time friends find it strange that Denise and I socialize outside of Food Go. "But she's a waitress," they say. "What do you talk about?" Then they focus on the differences in our education and background.

At first, I explained that Denise is fun, and I need to be around someone with her lighthearted outlook. Eventually, I decided I was buying into their condescending attitude when I tried to justify our friendship.

Denise and I hadn't spent much time together before Bob died, but afterwards her matter-of-fact emotional support did more than all the bumblings of my other friends. Although her marriage had ended in divorce rather than death, she understood my early shock and inability to function.

She had married young and been divorced at the age of 40. When they divided the community property, Denise got the house and her ex-husband got everything else. After twenty-two years of marriage, she found herself alone—with no skills, no children, and no relatives in Arizona. But Denise felt fortunate to get the waitress job at Food Go that my other friends scorned. And she never told me how lucky I was to have a profession.

"Will you come to the funeral with me?" Denise suddenly asked.

I hesitated. It would be awkward because I didn't really know the Stokes family other than as customers. Then I remembered what I had been thinking about. Denise was there for me when I needed her. If she had really cared about Harry Stokes and needed support at the funeral, I wouldn't let her down. I would go with her even if I had to change shifts with Tim. And that was something I usually tried to avoid.

"When is it?"

"Monday morning. Nine o'clock. At Messinger's."

At least I was off next Monday and wouldn't have to deal with Tim's reluctant consent to any kind of change. "Okay. Will you drive?"

Denise said she'd pick me up at eight-thirty Monday morning. I wanted to ask about mall hopping tonight but couldn't decide if this was the right time.

"Can I come along with you to the funeral?" I hadn't realized Joey was listening to us, but he rarely missed anything that happened in the pharmacy.

Denise arranged to pick Joey up, too, and then drifted away when both phones started ringing. A doctor was on line one, returning my call. I'd phoned because his patient brought in a prescription for Prozac, an antidepressant, and the dosage seemed too high.

"Yes, doctor. I'm checking on that script for 15 Prozac capsules. You wrote for one cap TID." I gave the Latin abbreviation for three times a day. "The recommended dosage is one QD, one daily."

"You're right, but I want to try the higher regimen for a short time. That's why I only wrote for 15 caps." I'd expected an argument for questioning his intentions, but he thanked me for checking it out.

"You're welcome, doctor," I said, pleased to be treated as a fellow professional.

We were so busy for the rest of the day that I was surprised when Tim, on nights this week, came in at four to begin his shift. We overlapped for an hour, not usually the most pleasant hour of my day. But today, I was glad to relinquish the computer to him and concentrate on customers at the window.

A young woman, carrying a baby who looked no more than six months old, handed me a prescription for prenatal vitamins. A toddler hung onto her mother's leg with both arms. I felt sorry for the mother, but warned myself not to jump to conclusions. Maybe she wanted this third child.

When the baby started crying, I held up two lollipops, making sure only the mother could see them, and raised my eyebrows in a question.

"Wonderful!" she said, as she unwrapped and delivered one to each child. "Now Terri Sue, thank the nice lady for the sucker," she told the little girl, who released her mother's leg to grab the lollipop. Meanwhile, the baby stopped crying and the mother smiled happily at me. Mother and little girl both said, "Thank you."

I gave the prescription to Joey, who took the vitamins off the shelf, handing script and bottle to Tim to generate the paperwork on the computer. Then Joey went on break so he could be back to help Tim when my shift ended.

My next customer, also with two small children in tow, had the opposite viewpoint. She was there to refill her birth control pills.

"Do you have the number?"

"Number?"

"Prescription number."

She had no idea what the number was or what kind of birth control pills she used, but I got her name and asked Tim to find her in the computer. It's easier if we have the number because then I can quickly locate the hard copy of the prescription. Otherwise, we've got to sort by name on the computer. If the name is a common one or if the computer is in process of spitting out records and labels for someone else, it takes that much longer to help the customer.

I offered lollipops, again out of the children's line of vision.

"Don't you know how bad sweets are for children?" she asked. "You ought to be ashamed of yourself."

Can't win them all, I thought, and apologized. Half an hour and five scripts later when my shift ended, I was glad to check out.

Denise was clocking out at the same time, and we walked into the Food Go parking lot together. A blast of hot, humid air contrasted sharply with the highly air-conditioned interior of the store. My relatives back east think we have a dry climate and, most of the time, they're right. But not in August.

"Any plans?" I asked Denise.

"Just to get home and collapse. We ran out of chocolate ice cream at three o'clock. And then everyone wanted chocolate and only chocolate."

I made sympathetic noises. Then I mentioned my idea about going to the mall.

"Which one?"

One thing about Scottsdale—we've got malls. Some of them are in adjoining cities and towns, but still only minutes away. Denise suggested Paradise Valley Mall, which was actually in Phoenix, but not too far from home for either of us. We agreed to meet in front of Dillards and got into our respective cars.

I took the sunshade off the windshield of my white Accord and folded it away. Then I removed the bath towel from the steering wheel and inserted the ignition key. I turned the air to its strongest setting, but the bath towel hadn't helped much. The steering wheel was so hot, I could barely force myself to get going.

Denise drives faster than I do, so I'm used to arriving after her whenever we go out together. I found her right where she said she'd be, and we walked into the mall, savoring the cool air.

"Are you looking for anything special, or are we window shopping?"

"I guess I just didn't feel like going home yet," I said.

Although we both stood on our feet all day at work, walking around the mall seemed to relax us. But we still hadn't made the transition from the workday. Denise was detailing her manager's incompetence. "He knows it's hot and it will keep on being hot. And he knows chocolate is our best-selling ice cream."

Since the Food Go coffee shop only offers chocolate, vanilla, and strawberry, I could see her point. Besides, I had heard this complaint before. Denise, who worked hard to keep her customers happy, hated it when she had to disappoint them because of her manager's failures.

"You'll never believe what happened today, Ruthie. I was so angry, I finally asked why he didn't order more chocolate since we always run out. You know what that guy said?"

She didn't wait for me to guess but smiled, looking more like herself than she had since Tuesday. "He said, 'If I order more chocolate, I won't sell the other flavors.'"

We were passing a toy store when Denise grabbed my arm. "Look." She nodded toward the shop without slowing her pace. "There's Betsy Stokes."

I barely had time to wonder what a widow of three days was doing in a shopping mall toy store, when Denise whispered, "Slow down. I want to stand here until she comes out."

"Denise, I don't think that's a good idea."

"I just want to see who the old guy is."

"What guy?"

"Don't you see the man with her?"

I glanced through the shop window. Betsy Stokes, whom I hadn't been able to picture when we talked about her, now looked familiar. But then so did the man at her side. They were standing at a display table of windup plush animals, all in motion. The man seemed to be in perpetual motion, too, picking up each toy and inspecting it in turn.

As we watched, Betsy scooped up a toy elephant and took it to the cashier at the front of the store. When she turned, I got a better look at her. She was a tall blonde with crimped hair; even through the shop window, I could see how attractive she was. Now that I saw Betsy Stokes, I remembered that to me she always had seemed the archetypal blonde.

I hadn't filled many prescriptions for her. When she picked up Harry's various medications, my few attempts at friendly conversation had met with brief responses.

Until the moment that Betsy approached the toyshop counter, I wasn't sure if the man was with her or just another shopper. But now I saw him hurry to her side and take out his wallet to pay for the elephant. Betsy was shaking her head and reaching in her purse, but he put his hand on her arm and smiled at her.

The smile made my pulse race, and I couldn't figure out why. "I know him," I said aloud. And then quickly, again without knowing the reason, I thought, *and I like him.*

Denise had pulled me over to a bench opposite the toy store, where we could seem to be in casual conversation when Betsy and her gentleman friend exited the store. "She sure likes them older," Denise muttered just as our quarry came by.

For a moment, I hoped they hadn't seen us. But Denise was determined to be noticed. "Betsy. Betsy Stokes."

Betsy turned toward us. She had green eyes that now mimed surprise. "Oh, hello Denise," she said without enthusiasm.

I remembered that they were neighbors, but maybe Betsy was embarrassed to be seen at the mall so soon after her husband's death. Denise nodded toward me and reminded Betsy that we were acquainted. "You know Ruthie Morris, from Food Go."

"Yes, of course. I'm sorry. I didn't recognize you without your white coat."

I couldn't tell if this was a putdown. *Don't be so sensitive, Ruthie*, I thought. *People do associate you with the white-jacketed figure behind the pharmacy window. You know they rarely look at you as an individual.*

It was absolutely necessary to come up with words of condolence, shopping mall or no shopping mall. I summoned up appropriate sentiments, and Betsy thanked me graciously. She was not so gracious about introducing the gentleman with her; Denise's maneuvering, embarrassing as it was to me, seemed to be in vain. However, he held out a hand to each of us, saying, "Michael Loring."

And then I knew. Was it only a few hours ago that I told myself I felt like a thirty-five-year-old? Now I was twenty again.

Michael Loring. And even without consciously recognizing him, my reaction had been the same as it was all those years ago, down in Tucson at the University of Arizona. His eyes were the same electrifying blue. As I looked into them, I thought, *I should have recognized him by that overwhelming vitality, as though he were bursting with energy.* He hadn't even changed so much in physical appearance. I saw some gray at the temples, but since his hair had always been light, it blended well. His face had lines that hadn't been there when we were young. They made me realize how much I'd aged, and I quickly looked away.

I wondered if I should say just two words: "Ruthie Kantor." Did I want to remind a man who was only three years older than me, a man who was with an attractive young blonde, that I was Ruth Kantor?

Two widows, I thought ironically. *But what a difference.* And then I was ashamed because I realized I was feeling sorry for myself, and I'd vowed never to do that again.

Denise was talking. The elephant had evidently been difficult to wrap, and its trunk stuck awkwardly out of the shopping bag. "Is that for one of Harry's grandchildren?" she asked.

"No, it's for me."

I could see Denise struggling to hide her surprise, or maybe she was trying to think of a response to Betsy's unfathomable comment. Was it possible that someone would go to the mall to buy herself a toy three days after her husband's sudden death? In my religion, the bereaved didn't even leave the house for seven days after the funeral. I had no idea what Betsy's beliefs were. But I remembered Michael Loring's religion. Oh yes, I remembered.

Denise sketched an awkward goodbye and I mumbled something, too. I couldn't concentrate on anything but my own turbulent thoughts. I hadn't seen Michael in thirty years. Closer to thirty-five years. And now he was escorting a young widow whose stepchildren believed had caused their father's death.

Chapter 4.

Somehow I got through the evening of window shopping at the mall and kept up my end of the conversation when Denise and I stopped for a snack. But for once, I couldn't wait to get home and be alone with my whirling memories. During all the years that Bob and I were married, I rarely thought about Michael. He never showed up at the few class reunions I attended and, because Bob and I were happy, might-have-beens had no place in my life.

After Bob's death, I was surprised one day to find myself wondering about Michael. It happened at a low point, before I started trying to pull myself together. I was sitting at the kitchen table in a housecoat, eating a cheese sandwich that I'd thrown together. No lettuce, no tomato, no mayonnaise. I hadn't even sliced the cheese—just pulled off a chunk and stuffed it between two slices of bread. Suddenly, a spasm of self pity jolted me and I was stunned to find myself thinking, *if I'd married Michael, I wouldn't be alone now.* But just as this idea came into my head, I realized what I was doing to myself. I remember now, my resolve to get on with life began that day. But this new determination didn't stop me from thinking occasionally of Michael.

When we first met, Michael Loring and I were both in our second year at the pharmacy school in Tucson. Only a handful of women studied pharmacy in those days, and I was asked out so often by male students, I could easily have gone to movies or college dances every night in the week. But I lived at home—most young women did in those days—and I was allowed to date only when I had no classes the next day. In our family, that meant only Saturday nights.

Fridays, when the sororities and fraternities partied, we attended synagogue services and then sat down to a sabbath dinner. My mother and father liked to invite out-of-state students to these Friday night dinners, but they reserved this traditional hospitality for Jewish students. And Michael Loring was not Jewish.

In the 1950s, rebellion might mean wearing too much lipstick or staying out until one A.M. when your parents insisted on a midnight curfew, but for most of us, it didn't include intermarriage. When Michael and I started seeing each other, parental objections surfaced.

"We're only going to a movie," I would say. "We're friends. We're in all the same classes. We study together."

But I knew it was more than that, and I'm sure they knew it, too. Michael and I saw each other every day that semester, and we spent hours walking and talking. I had stopped dating anyone else; in the language of the Fifties, we were going steady. Unofficially.

At first, I tried to keep the arguments with my parents from him. Michael called for me every Saturday night, and I was always ready to leave when he arrived at my house. I wanted to minimize the time he spent under my parents' scrutiny. They were so coldly formal, it surprised me that Michael took so long to realize something was wrong.

"Your parents don't like me," he said one evening as we left my house.

At nineteen and not very sophisticated, I didn't know what to answer. "Oh, Michael," I said and burst into tears.

"What is it? Tell me what's wrong."

Michael was only three years older than me, but he had spent two of those years in Korea. He had grown up in Boston where his dad was an attorney, and Michael also might have studied law if the army hadn't made him a medic. So, I'd always considered Michael much more cosmopolitan and mature than I was.

"Tell me," he repeated.

"It's not you; they like you." I took a deep breath and blurted, "It's your religion."

"My religion! They don't even know my religion." We had gotten into his car and were riding along Speedway. "You and I have never even discussed it."

"It doesn't matter what religion. Just that you're not a Jew."

Michael quickly pulled over to the curb and turned to look at me. "I don't understand."

"Jews have very strong feelings about intermarriage," I told him. "In some traditional families, they mourn a child who marries a non-Jew as if he or she had died."

After a long silence, Michael reached over and took me in his arms. We had never talked about marriage before, and I began to be afraid that my frankness would turn him away.

"I don't think either one of us is ready to rush into marriage," he said, caressing my hair. My hair was longer then and lighter, ginger not auburn, and I wore it curled under in a pageboy style. "We both have to graduate first," he added.

"I know that."

"But I do love you, Ruthie. I tried to be patient until you were sure, but I've known my own feelings since the day I met you."

"I am sure," I said. "But it's impossible."

"It's not impossible."

My sadness was overwhelming because I'd known it would be this way. "You don't understand."

"No, I guess I don't. Your parents seem so... so modern."

"You mean because my father doesn't have a beard or wear a skullcap. Because mother and dad dress like anyone else."

Michael took a deep breath. "Don't link me to that kind of stereotyped thinking. You know better."

I folded my arms on the dashboard and rested my head on them. I couldn't speak. Until now, I hadn't worried about prejudices on Michael's side. I was too absorbed with those of my family.

"Look at me, Ruthie. We have to trust each other to move beyond this problem."

But even though we continued to spend time together until Michael went home that summer, we couldn't get beyond it. And in the fall, he transferred to the pharmacy college at Fordham University in New York.

* * * *

I thought about Michael all weekend, between filling scripts at Food Go on Saturday and cleaning my house on Sunday. *Will he be at the funeral? How does he fit into Betsy Stokes's life? And even more important, should I tell him who I am?*

My mind produced a collage: the young man I'd loved in pharmacy college and the Michael I'd met in the mall Friday night, crow's feet softened at the corners of his eyes, which the harsh artificial light had revealed. I made promises to myself that I had no intention of keeping. Everything I did around the house became compulsively related to Michael: as I cleaned out the garage... Michael recognized me; as I dusted all the miniblinds... Michael walked up to me at the funeral home and said...

This is sick, I told myself, and five minutes later, I was throwing everything that didn't move into the washing machine and imagining another conversation—at the funeral home: Michael walked up to me and took my hand.

"Ruthie," he said in my daydream. "I recognized you the minute I saw you at the mall, but I didn't want to say anything in front of Betsy and your friend."

His eyes were as blue as I remembered them, and in my imaginings, the graying hair I had noticed at the mall was as blond as it had been years before. "I couldn't forget you," he said. "That's why I never married."

I wanted to ask him about Betsy Stokes, but that could wait because Michael was holding my hand. He smiled gently at me, "You look exactly the same as you did in pharmacy school."

The daydream reminded me of the way I felt at my twentieth birthday party when Michael took my hand and told me he was leaving Tucson for good. That bounced me back to reality. Despite my strange state of mind since meeting Michael again, I couldn't avoid the truth of our situation. I was no longer nineteen or twenty and, romantic imaginings aside, it was nonsense to suppose Michael wouldn't know the difference. I tried to comfort myself with the undeniable fact that Michael was also thirty-five years older—but like the musings of the poet Yeats, I knew the folly of being comforted. As brief as our meeting in the mall had been, I could see the same intensity behind the blue eyes and the same energy that had attracted me to Michael all those years ago. But this Michael was seeing a beautiful young blonde, a woman whose husband had just died under suspicious circumstances.

Chapter 5.

When Denise picked me up on Monday, Joey was already in the car. It was obvious that all three of us had dressed carefully, toning down the bright colors of Arizona summer wear. Denise wore a turquoise and white dress with a straight skirt and large white-and-gold buttons. But her turquoise eye shadow was understated today and her lipstick paler than usual.

"Joey was just telling me the police questioned everyone in the Stokes family," Denise said.

"That's right," Joey added. He was wearing dark gray pants with a pale gray shirt. A dark blue, discreetly patterned tie, must have been borrowed for the funeral because I'd never seen it before. "My brother-in-law says they know it wasn't a heart attack."

"I hope they really zeroed in on Betsy." Denise said. "She's the one I suspected all along. And when Ruthie and I saw her at the mall... Shopping, for heaven's sake. I would have been home crying my eyes out."

"People grieve in different ways," I reminded her. "That doesn't mean she drove him to suicide. And it certainly doesn't mean she murdered him."

"You never want to believe anything bad about people, Ruthie. But I've told you all along that she married him for what she could get. Harry's kids think so, too."

"How do you know?" Joey asked.

"I overheard them talking the other night. Everyone else was indoors, but Richard Stokes—that's the son—came out to smoke. His wife must have followed him outside." Denise was quiet for a few seconds while she concentrated on finding an opening for a left turn. "I guess they didn't realize I was on my patio. They were right near the fence between our yards, and I could hear every word."

Although I was curious, I couldn't bring myself to ask about the overheard conversation. But Denise didn't wait for questions. She told us Richard sounded agitated as he assured his wife the police knew something was wrong and that they suspected Betsy.

"Frank never mentioned that," Joey said.

We were pulling into the parking lot at the funeral home. "I'll tell you all the details, later," Denise promised.

Before the memorial service began, while I looked around the chapel, Denise whispered the names of the various family members to me. They were all sitting in the front row. "Richard Stokes, the son I talked about in the car. He's the first guy on the left. The one with the bald patch on top. His wife, Nancy, is next to him. I guess they figured the grandchildren are too young to take to a funeral." She stopped and shook her head at the thought. "And Harry's daughter and her fiancé are on the other side of Nancy."

But I was no longer listening. My eyes had focused on Michael Loring sitting just past the others, next to the widow. Denise must have noticed him a moment later, for she drew in her breath and was about to speak when the memorial service began.

It doesn't make any sense, I thought. *Denise accounted for all the relatives. Why is Michael sitting with the family?*

The minister spoke with feeling about Harry Stokes and his contributions to the community. I gathered he'd been an active and well-respected member of his church. Although I'd liked Harry, this picture contrasted in my mind with the man who had married someone half his age and then relied on Viagra to feel young and Rogaine to fight baldness.

Perhaps I was unfair. They used to say that no man is a hero to his valet. Pharmacists may be the modern equivalents of valets. We know who's on Micronase for diabetes and who's using Anusol HC for hemorrhoids. We know who's on Antabuse to combat alcoholism and who's taking Lithium for manic depression. Like other members of the health professions, though, we usually keep our mouths shut and our thoughts sympathetic.

The memorial service ended and all of us filed out of the chapel. We stood around the parking lot waiting for the cortege to the cemetery to form. "Look," Joey said. "There's Tim Barnard. Wasn't he supposed to be working today?"

I turned in time to see my staff pharmacist getting into his green Buick Riviera. Many of the young women who worked at Food Go seemed to be interested in Tim, though I could never understand why. Today, though, he looked particularly handsome in a dark, summer weight suit. And for once, he had neatly brushed his thick hair back from his forehead.

Tim hadn't said a word about attending the funeral, and I was surprised to see that he cared enough about a customer to pay his respects.

Out of sheer curiosity, I made a mental note to bring up the subject tomorrow at work.

Joey had drifted away, and Denise was talking to a couple of neighbors she introduced as the Brandens. They were discussing whether to go to the cemetery or to meet at the Stokes house afterwards.

"I don't know what's customary," Denise explained. "I'm Catholic and they're Protestants of some kind."

Raymond Branden, a short stocky man in western shirt and bolo tie, assured Denise that most people would join the mourners at the Stokes home after the burial. His wife explained why they weren't going to the cemetery. "I started a roast before I left this morning," Verna Branden said. "When I get home, I'll finish cooking it and take it over to their house."

Unlike the Brandens, Denise wanted to join the funeral cortege, but Joey and I talked her out of it. She agreed on condition that I visit the Stokes home with her that afternoon, and I promised, knowing I wanted to see Michael again. As we talked, I was watching him help the widow into one of the black limousines and get in beside her. I figured the chances were good that he would still be with her after the burial.

None of us said much on the way back. I had expected to hear comments from Denise, but she was quiet again, the way she had been for most of the past week.

* * * *

Joey lived with his parents in one of Scottsdale's lovely condominium complexes, and Denise drove past towering palms to a guarded gate and stopped. The guard peered into the car, saw Joey, and waved us through. Alternating pink and white oleander bushes, neatly trimmed, lined the driveway, leading to a huge three-tiered fountain shaped like a wedding cake, but surrounded by stone coyotes. Many Scottsdale condos boast ornate fountains, but this one was an outstanding sculpture. We dropped Joey off in front of the fountain.

"See you at the store later," he said, waving goodbye to both of us.

Thinking about the store made me wonder who was working in Tim's place. Maybe he had changed shifts with the relief pharmacist who worked on our days off.

"We've got a few hours to kill until we join the crowd at the Stokes house," Denise said. "I don't want to walk in empty-handed. Why don't we order a fruit basket for the family? Then we can go out for something to eat and, if it's still too early, we can wait at my house."

"I should get home and change first," I said, thinking of Michael.

She glanced at my navy print dress. "You look just right."

"It's sticking to my back. In this heat, I'll soon look like I slept in it."

"That's what you get for wearing silk when it's a hundred and seven degrees in the shade. Don't worry about the creases, Ruthie. You look great." She smiled at me. "A friend once told me creases show the integrity of the fabric; I guess she meant they tell everyone your dress isn't polyester."

"Polyester has its advantages."

I was glad that Denise seemed more like herself, and I agreed to her plans. Besides, despite my misgivings about eavesdropping, I really did want to hear more about the conversation between Harry Stokes's son and daughter-in-law.

Denise didn't say anything about the Stokes family for a while, and I asked no questions. Now that she had emerged from her quiet spell, she appeared to go out of her way to be amusing. We chatted about work. She told me about the customer who always gave precise instructions on how he wanted everything served and then mixed it all together on his plate. I told her, without mentioning names, about one of my customers who had insisted on a description of everyone ahead of him. He intended to look for them in the store and ask them if I could fill his prescriptions first.

By the time we went to lunch at the cafeteria, we were both chatting the way we usually did. Then, Denise suddenly got serious again. "I started to tell you earlier about Harry's children. His son, Richard, was going on and on about the will. He said he was pretty sure that Harry hadn't changed it."

The details of the conversation she'd overheard seemed to substantiate what Denise had believed all along. "Betsy's in for a big surprise," Richard Stokes had told his wife, Nancy.

"You think she was surprised when Dad died?" she had replied.

"That's not what I meant. I told you the police questioned her for hours. If there's anything to find out, they'll get it out of her."

"Can we count on that? They wouldn't even have questioned her if you hadn't called with your suspicions."

Richard didn't respond for a moment, and the only sound Denise could hear was the chirping of crickets on the patio. *Probably puffing away*, she thought, as she caught a whiff of cigarette smoke. Embarrassing as it was to eavesdrop, she couldn't go back into her own house now, even if she wanted to; they would hear her.

"I wasn't the only one who spoke to the police," Richard continued. "Sheila called them, too."

"Your sister? I can't believe it. I thought she was too wrapped up in her new boyfriend to notice anything else."

"Listen carefully, Nancy, and try to think for once. I told the police Betsy married Dad for his money. But if he never changed his will, that takes away her motive." He paused. "And it gives us one."

"Richard, what are you saying? No one could think *you* killed Dad."

"Or you. Or Sheila. Or her new guy."

Nancy shrieked and her husband shushed her and said, "Do you want everyone to hear, you fool?"

"You're the fool! You're the one who got the police started investigating in the first place." Then her voice rose again.

"Can't you quiet down?" he hissed at her.

"No one can hear us. They're all inside, and the air-conditioning is blasting away."

"Well, shut up and listen to me. No one knows I lost my job last month. They all think we're well off."

"You can't keep it from the police," she said.

"Why not? They won't check with my boss. I mean my ex-boss."

"Well, what did you tell them?"

"They asked me my occupation. I told them I'm an aerospace engineer." Now his voice got louder. "Damn it, I am one even though I was laid off."

Again, there was silence for a while. Denise couldn't see into their yard because the block fence was too high, but she imagined Richard was puffing on his cigarette and thinking. Then she heard, "Richard, what are we going to do?"

"Nothing."

"But what if they question us again?"

"We've got nothing to hide. After all, if Dad hadn't remarried, there'd be no question about the money."

Nancy murmured something that Denise didn't catch. But she heard Richard's answer: "No, we don't have to wait long. I explained it all to you before. Dad had everything in a living trust, so there's no probate. We'll get the money very soon."

They went indoors then and, after a few minutes, Denise had returned to her own house. She hadn't slept well that night because the overheard conversation kept running through her mind.

"What do you make of it?" she asked now as she finished recounting the details to me.

"I don't know, but I think we'd better leave it to the Scottsdale Police Department." I was appalled to realize that Denise had eavesdropped on so private a conversation.

"Well, I don't have much confidence in the police. After all, they never questioned me."

Sometimes, I thought, *Denise carried things too far.* "Why should they question you?"

"You know I wanted Harry for myself. The truth is I hate Betsy for taking him away from me."

If Denise's aim was to startle me, she had succeeded. I decided laughter was the best reaction. "Denise, in that case, you would have killed Betsy. And, as far as I could see this morning, she's still very much alive."

"It may sound funny to you, but maybe I brooded all these months about being scorned."

I took a different tack. "Why do you want to be a suspect? We don't even know yet if Harry was murdered?"

"*She* murdered him, but I don't mind being a suspect. Not if it leads to an investigation. I just don't want them to say suicide and close the case."

I had no answer to that and changed the subject. We picked up the fruit basket we'd ordered before lunch and drove to Denise's house. Although I had been there before, I had never seen her neighborhood in the daytime. She pointed out the Stokes house next to hers on the east and the Branden house on the west. I'd wondered why someone as wealthy as Harry Stokes was reputed to be would live next door to Denise. Even though she and her ex-husband had been comfortable, they certainly had not been rich. But when I saw the Stokes house, I understood.

It was on a corner lot, at one end of a cul-de-sac, and it was much larger than the other homes on the same street. From its Spanish-tile roof to the freshly painted block exterior, the house, with its spacious, well-kept grounds, looked luxurious.

"That was the original house on the property," Denise explained. "Years ago, the owners sold off the rest of the land for development. But they kept the house and about half an acre for themselves."

Denise pulled into her carport and led the way into her own house. "Harry and his first wife were only the second owners. Of course, they did a lot of remodeling."

"Did you know the first wife?" I asked.

"No, she died before we moved in, at least nine or ten years ago. That's why everyone was so surprised when he suddenly married again. After all this time, we thought he wasn't interested in remarriage."

We were sitting in Denise's kitchen, overlooking her patio and pool. The pool was kidney-shaped, a very popular type in Scottsdale. My own pool was a rectangular one, designed for swimming laps in a relatively small area.

From the air, the swimming pools look like little turquoise jewels. Tourists always comment about them when they fly into Sky Harbor Airport for the first time. But when they land and confront the desert heat, people begin to realize why backyard pools aren't considered luxuries here.

"But Denise," I said. "Even if Harry's remarriage surprised you, nothing you've said so far means that Betsy drove him to suicide or killed him."

She suddenly got up and loomed over my chair. "Well, I live right next to them, and if I told you everything I saw and heard over the last few months, you'd believe me."

Chapter 6.

When we walked next door to the Stokes house, I was surprised at the striking black-and-white decor of its contemporary interior, which contrasted sharply with the southwestern exterior. A buffet lunch was set up in the formal dining room, and people walked about with plates of food in their hands. The crowd was large enough to spill over into the living and family rooms.

"Too bad it's so hot outside; their patio is beautiful," Denise whispered. "And be sure to notice the kitchen. They just spent $30,000 remodeling it."

I was too busy scanning the crowd for Michael Loring to care about the patio or the kitchen. Richard Stokes was talking to some people in one corner of the living room. His back was toward me but I knew him by the distinctive bald patch. Unlike his late father, the son didn't seem to be using Rogaine to grow hair again. Maybe his wife liked the bald spot; some women did.

For the first time, I got a clear view of Richard's wife, Nancy—I recognized her by the mauve dress she'd been wearing at the memorial service. Although she couldn't have been much older than Betsy, her stepmother-in-law, her short brown hair was starting to gray. She was a thin, tired-looking woman, in sharp contrast to Betsy, who had seemed bursting with vitality when we saw her at the mall.

Harry's daughter, Sheila, had changed to white tennis shorts and a T-shirt that said "Scotty's Groupie" in large purple letters. I knew her by her long French braid and reflected how different all of them had looked from where I sat, eight rows back, in the chapel. The only people I could be sure to recognize were Betsy Stokes and Michael Loring, and when Denise pulled me along to the newly remodeled kitchen, I finally saw them.

The kitchen, starkly sophisticated with its black granite counters and stainless steel built-ins, wasn't too crowded. They were sitting at the table, a huge granite slab, and Michael seemed to be talking earnestly to Betsy. She nodded her head occasionally but, whenever people approached the table, stopped the conversation to speak to them. I guessed some of the earliest visitors were taking leave of her, reiterating their condolences, while she was thanking them for coming.

Although I'd made up my mind to talk to Michael today, I found I couldn't interrupt. *Ruthie, you know that's just an excuse*, I told myself, but I left the kitchen without a word to anyone.

Denise seemed restless but remained at my side, and I knew I didn't want to speak to Michael until she was busy elsewhere. As we stood at the buffet table, helping ourselves to fruit salad, Mrs. Branden came over to point out her roast to Denise. I drifted back to the kitchen.

I leaned against the silver-and-black refrigerator, holding my paper plate and pretending to eat, while I waited for someone to distract Betsy so I could talk to Michael alone. In my mind, I worked out ways to reveal my identity. Maybe the subtle approach would be best. "Do you ever reminisce about pharmacy school?" or "I haven't seen you at our reunions." No, that was too coy; I would be direct. "Do you remember me, Michael? I'm Ruthie Kantor Morris."

After a while, a young couple came over to talk to Betsy, and I quickly went to Michael's side of the kitchen table. He had stood politely at the couple's approach and now turned his full attention, along with that forceful blue gaze, to me. I hesitated.

"We met at the mall the other night," I began.

"Yes," he said. "I see you no longer spend Friday nights at the synagogue."

I couldn't hide my surprise. "You recognized me."

"Not right away," he admitted. "But before you and your friend walked away, I knew."

"You didn't say anything."

"I didn't want to upset Betsy. She has enough on her mind."

I was silent. He took my arm and led me from the kitchen to a quiet corner of the formal dining room, opposite the laden buffet table. My mind was racing, but I could only think in clichés. "Well, it's certainly been a long time" or "How strange to meet this way." A saying of my mother's, "We should meet at a happy occasion next time," nearly made me giggle, and I realized I could easily make a fool of myself if I didn't control my nervousness.

Michael was still staring at me, but I couldn't read his expression. I wanted to ask how he'd recognized me, but I didn't dare. He surprised me again.

"You were sporting your serious look. That time just before your birthday, you looked at me exactly the same way."

I remembered every detail of that afternoon because I'd relived it hundreds of times. And I felt the same pain now that had overwhelmed me so many years ago.

It was close to the end of our second year of pharmacy school. I didn't know yet that Michael had applied for a transfer to a pharmacy college in New York.

Arizona weather in May can be pretty hot even in Tucson, although Tucson, with its higher elevation, is slightly cooler than Scottsdale. That day, the day Michael and I knew we'd soon part, was comfortably breezy and we were walking on campus between classes. The scene between us could have come from one of my favorite books of those days, *Marjorie Morningstar* by Herman Wouk.

Michael led me to a shady spot under a grapefruit tree. "Let's touch down here," he said. Even his choice of verbs reflected his boundless energy. Michael never told people he intended to go somewhere; he said he would dash upstairs or rush over. That crackling vitality had first attracted me. It never moderated, even in the Arizona heat.

I leaned against the tree and watched Michael. He seemed unusually quiet.

"We need to talk about our future," he said.

"Why can't we stay as we are?"

"Because I don't want to run home for the summer and leave you here."

I looked up at the tree. The season was over; most of the fruit had been picked or fallen to the ground months ago, but a few grapefruit clung tenaciously to the highest branches. "There's nothing we can do."

"Damn it! There are plenty of choices, Ruthie. But you have to be willing to make some hard decisions."

"You know we're both still in school."

"I've figured it out. I can get close to full-time work on nights and weekends during the school year. If you're willing to work part time, we can afford to get married."

Married to Michael. How I wanted to shout, "Yes, let's forget everything else and do it." But although I'd be twenty years old in a few weeks, girls brought up in traditional middle-class homes didn't give up their families so easily in those days. We were less sophisticated than today's young women; even the fact that we were called "girls" then, and lived at home until marriage, underlines how different the times were.

Now, in Betsy Stokes's dining room, Michael gently touched my shoulder. "You're thinking about those two kids under the grapefruit tree in Tucson."

"Yes," I admitted and turned away from his intense gaze.

"How have the years been for you, Ruthie? I know you're married because your name is different."

I couldn't bring myself to tell him about Bob. If I say that I'm a widow, I thought, *somehow it will sound all wrong. And what about Betsy? I couldn't compete with her, even if I wanted to.* Later, when I got away from the force of Michael's personality, I would have to look closely at that last thought.

Michael must have noticed my reluctance to answer, for he started to tell me about himself. He had married right after graduation from Fordham, but the marriage had not lasted long. He changed to a less personal topic.

"Are you a practicing pharmacist? Where do you work?"

That was an easier subject for me. I told him about Food Go, and we discussed the changes in pharmacy over the years. We laughed about the ointments and suppositories we'd learned to compound in school and how unlikely it would have seemed then to dispense only prepackaged medications.

"Remember when we were supposed to make peppermint water in the lab and ran out of time?"

My awkwardness and unease vanished for the moment and I smiled warmly at him, delighting in the memory. "You were the one who decided to dissolve a peppermint Lifesaver in the mixture."

"Well, the professor thought it was the best peppermint water he'd ever tasted." Michael's lips curved upward and his eyes caught fire the way I remembered, the way that once made me want to be with him forever. But forever had been only one academic year.

It was odd that I'd just been thinking about *Marjorie Morningstar*, because the fictional Marjorie and what she represented had influenced my breakup with Michael. The family in the novel was like mine, even though we lived so far from Marjorie's New York City. And when she rejected her first love and later became engaged to someone else, I agonized with Marjorie as she confessed the early affair to her fiancé. Her guilt was overwhelming because in those days "good Jewish girls" were expected to be virgins when they married.

The part of Herman Wouk's novel that had affected me most was the reaction of Marjorie's husband-to-be to her confession; he never again mentioned the subject, but he never again wore the same joyful look. The double standard was very real in the 1950s, and I knew I was not going to disappoint my husband like Marjorie Morningstar. That's why, after I turned down Michael's marriage proposal, I also turned down his plea to go east with him anyhow.

Michael must have noticed that I'd stopped laughing and was looking serious again, but I didn't want him to know which tape my mind was running on its multimedia screen. He, too, became serious.

"Ruthie, were you Harry Stokes's pharmacist?"

"Yes."

"I must talk to you. There are too many unresolved questions about his death, and I need to know what prescription drugs he was taking."

"Don't the police..." I started to ask. As I spoke, I could see Betsy crossing the room toward us. Michael was watching her, too.

"They seem to suspect Betsy," he said quickly. His voice caught and he cleared his throat to cover it. "I have to help her."

Chapter 7.

Seeing your first love after thirty-five years should be comic, I thought, *not traumatic*. After all, even when the years are kind, how can any of us live up to the memories and retouched photos in our minds? But again, I identified with the poet Yeats who knew the folly of being comforted. And I, too, wasn't finding it easy to be wise, because the years had only intensified the impact of Michael's vibrant personality.

I reminded myself I knew nothing about this Michael or the kind of person he was now. What was his relationship to Betsy and why was he so concerned about her? And most of all, if Michael walked into Food Go, would I tell him what he wanted to know? I resolved to look at the patient profile for Harry Stokes the first thing next morning, so that I'd know what prescription drugs he was getting before Michael asked for the information.

I had no opportunity to call up the record on the computer. Food Go, like many supermarket chains out here, is open twenty-four hours a day, although the pharmacy has shorter hours. When I got there on Tuesday morning, Michael was waiting for me. He was inside the store, pacing in front of the pharmacy window.

"I didn't know your schedule, so I thought I'd just come in." He looked toward the coffee shop. "I'll jump out of the way while you open up. See you in a few minutes."

I unlocked the door, flipped on the lights, stepped onto the raised floor of the pharmacy, and started my opening procedure. Nowadays, we depend on the computer just like other businesses do. I turned on the monitor and keyed in my password. Then, I quickly initialized today's disk and was ready to begin.

The main office had relayed two messages overnight, and I printed them. One warned about someone forging Rx's for Vicodin, a painkiller with hydrocodone. The forger had a clever modus operandus—he first asked for a generic drug to allay suspicion and then for Vicodin. I smiled at the description—between 5 feet, 7 inches and 6 feet, 1 inch with either light hair or dark hair—and wondered how we were supposed to recognize him.

The other message reminded us that inventory was scheduled in three weeks and asked that we cut down our orders as much as possible. I put both messages on the small bulletin board for Tim and Joey to see and looked up to find Michael watching me through the glass windows. When I slid them open, he handed me a cup of coffee and a pastry from the coffee shop.

"I hope you haven't lost your craving for cheese danish," he said.

"No, but they still call them breakfast rolls out here."

"So they do." Michael leaned over the counter and put his own coffee cup down.

"Share?" I asked, moving the pastry back toward him. Then I wanted to pull the word in because it brought the past reeling back.

"Share," Michael agreed and grinned so warmly at me that I had to grip my side of the counter for support.

Any minute now the phone will ring or customers will come to the window and rescue me, I thought. *You can hold on long enough, Ruthie. Don't be a fool.*

"Does it sound odd to say the last few days have had some of the saddest and happiest moments," Michael said. "When I woke up Friday morning, I never dreamed we'd meet again before the day was over."

"It was a shock for me, too." I had meant to say 'surprise,' but the word 'shock' escaped before I realized it.

"We didn't get to talk much yesterday. Do you have to be home right away or can we meet after you finish here?"

"Five o'clock," I said and excused myself to help a customer at the window.

Unlike some of my friends who hang around and talk while I try to work, Michael quickly stood aside and waited for me to be free again. When I was, he returned to the window.

"Ruthie, I need to know what prescription drugs Harry Stokes was taking."

I hedged. "You know I haven't had a chance to look up his record."

"Could you do it now?"

"Why?"

Michael sounded impatient. "It's important. I told you all about it yesterday."

It was my turn to be brusque. "You didn't tell me anything, Michael. Anything that would justify my breaching patient confidentiality."

"Patient confidentiality! The patient is dead."

"As far as I'm concerned, that doesn't make any difference," I flared. "Haven't you ever done any continuing education in pharmacy ethics?"

Michael's eyes flickered, but I could see he was trying hard to control himself. "This is not idle curiosity. I need to know what Harry was taking."

"After you talked to me yesterday, I thought about it all evening. I don't see how I can give you that information. But I'll be glad to give it to the police."

"The police," Michael exploded. "All they want to do is railroad Betsy. They can't believe that a young woman could marry an older man for anything but his money."

"I'm sure *you* want to believe it was love," I said and then was ashamed at my sarcastic tone.

"What's that supposed to mean?"

"Just what I said."

He stared at me for a few seconds. "You certainly have changed," he said and walked away. I could see the doors leading into the parking lot from the pharmacy window and, after a moment, Michael's tall figure hurrying out of the store.

My face felt flushed, and I was so shaken that I had to sit down. I couldn't believe Michael and I, meeting again after so many years, had quarreled. It's a matter of principle this time, too, I insisted aloud, but there was no one to hear. I asked myself whether I was being self-righteous to mask jealousy. If Michael hadn't been spending his time with the young widow, would I have given him the prescription printout? I didn't know the answer.

From time to time during that long day, I had to choke back tears. My identity as a professional helped as it had during Bob's long illness and death. I was here for people who needed their medication, not to indulge in self-pity. So I concentrated on filling prescription after prescription. When Joey came in at ten o'clock, he looked solemn as he told me his brother-in-law was going out to the Stokes house again to talk to Betsy.

"Why?"

"I only know what Frank said. They have some questions for her."

Maybe Betsy did drive her husband to suicide, I thought. After all, she had Michael waiting in the wings. I wanted to ask whether the police thought it was suicide or murder, but that seemed too melodramatic. Anyhow, it wasn't right to pump Joey when he shouldn't have had the information in the first place.

The day dragged along. Even Joey was quieter than usual, as though he'd sensed my mood, and for once I was looking forward to Tim's arrival.

One hour after he comes in, I'll be able to go home, I thought. Then I can let go. But I found I no longer wanted to cry; I wanted only to search my heart and see what meeting Michael again really meant to me.

A few times, Joey started to talk to me and seemed to change his mind. *I really must lighten up,* I thought. *It's not fair to him to make his workday miserable, too.*

"Joey, I know I've been a bear today, but it's not anything you did. You don't have to tiptoe around me."

"It's not that," he said. "I need some advice, but I didn't want to bother you."

The telephone rang before I could reassure him. Simultaneously, two customers appeared at the window, and I went to help them while Joey grabbed the phone. *As soon as we're both free again,* I promised myself, *I'll find out what's on his mind.*

Just before four o'clock, we had some breathing space. Joey left the computer and walked over to the counter where I was working on the reorder list. Usually when he wanted advice, it was about his plans to go to medical school. I waited, noticing how drawn the young face looked. I saw shadows under the dark eyes and blamed myself for not talking him out of summer courses at ASU. It was hard enough to work and go to school full time during the rest of the year.

"About two weeks ago," Joey began, but was interrupted by Tim, who walked into the pharmacy and muttered a hello to me. For Joey, his only greeting was a raised eyebrow and nod toward the ringing phone, uncalled for because Joey already had his hand on the receiver.

"For Mrs. McCullough? Her hydrochlor... what? Do you mean HCTZ?"

I listened approvingly while I did some paperwork that was due before I could leave for the day. Joey was a good technician, and I could trust him to handle refills.

"What strength, twenty-five milligrams or fifty? Did she give you the prescription number? That's okay; we'll find it." Joey hung up the phone and said, "I hope the original really was filled at this store." He started toward the computer to look it up, but Tim pushed him away.

"I'll take care of it. You go and unpack the order."

I suppose I should have put a stop long ago to Tim bullying our technicians, but Joey and I both try to ignore it rather than turn the place into a battlefield. Luckily, Joey doesn't seem to hold a grudge; any other technician would have quit after one week.

"Saw you at the funeral," he said to Tim. "We didn't know you were going to be there."

"I knew the family in Tucson."

Before I had a chance to ask Tim about that, two people appeared at the window to pick up their prescriptions, and both phones began to ring. We were too rushed for conversation during the next hour, and my shift ended before I had time to clock watch. In fact, we were so busy that I clocked out twenty minutes late.

I walked into the parking lot, relieved that my work day was over, and I no longer had to put up a professional front to hide my personal turmoil. Now I could relax and consider what to do about Michael. In immediate contradiction to this thought, I saw him approach from the tree-shaded part of the lot. As Michael walked toward me, the sunlight accentuated the blond strands in his graying hair and, from the distance, he looked exactly the way I remembered him. "Your well-belovèd's hair has threads of grey," as a friend had told Yeats. When I saw Michael approach that afternoon, I realized how sorry I was that I'd sent him away again. I knew once more that time had not made me any wiser than the poet.

I didn't move until Michael reached me. Even though I was still up on the sidewalk and he was in the parking lot, he was a head taller than me. Michael took my hand, and the gesture was so natural that I stepped down and followed him without a word. He unlocked the door on the passenger side of his car, a silver-and-gray Lexus, and held it open for me, then went around and took down the sun shield. It must have been 140 degrees in the parked car, so I kept my door open until he started the air conditioning.

"I found an interesting Mexican restaurant not too far from here. Is that all right with you?"

In Scottsdale, it's easy to find any kind of restaurant you want, so I was curious to see his choice. We pulled in front of Marilyn's First Mexican Restaurant, a place I'd never tried. Michael always had a knack for discovering restaurants with good food, even when we were students with limited funds. But I wondered whether he'd lost his touch. This place was too pretty; it seemed like part of the tourist scene rather than a restaurant serving authentic Mexican food.

We went through the brick patio with its chairs and tables covered in bright primary colors. As we waited to be seated, I watched a young woman in Mexican dress rolling out tortillas at a counter just inside the entryway.

The restaurant, with it high-backed booths upholstered in blue and its red and yellow seats, had a relaxed atmosphere. When we were seated and had ordered our beverages, Michael smiled at me. "How little you've changed."

And how different that statement was from his angry words in the pharmacy. "I was thinking the same about you," I said aloud. My reading glasses were on now as I scanned the menu. "Maybe that's why nature dims our sight as we grow older."

"You know, Ruthie, I've thought about the past all day today. And I made up my mind that I wasn't going to give up so easily this time."

I didn't know if he meant our relationship or his demand for Harry Stokes's prescription record. The waiter approached, so I could avoid a reply while we scanned the menus. Like many Arizona restaurants during the off-season, Marilyn's offered a "sunset menu" with considerable savings. I was careful to choose spinchada from the specials, but Michael ordered beef chimichangas, which were on the regular menu. Spinchada was a dish I'd never heard of, but it was vegetarian and the description intrigued me. A spinach enchilada in a white sauce, topped with almond slivers.

"I blame myself for not fighting for you," Michael said as soon as the waiter walked away.

Had he been that unhappy? My own misery was overwhelming at first, but when I met Bob Morris about two years later, I was ready to fall in love again. Once in a while, I wondered about Michael, but Bob and I were happy and those thoughts were fleeting.

Now, I looked across the table at Michael. Despite the heat, he was wearing a white shirt with thin burgundy stripes, a burgundy tie with a navy and white pattern, and navy slacks. I couldn't remember if he'd been dressed more casually that morning, so I didn't know whether he'd changed for dinner with me.

My own gold and white print dress, polyester and cotton today, was a compromise between the demands of my long workday and the expectation of seeing Michael again. I searched my mind for a more comfortable topic than our breakup and realized we hadn't yet talked about our lives since pharmacy college. He must have been thinking along the same lines.

"Tell me about yourself, Ruthie. All I know is that you're Mrs. Morris now."

I took a deep breath and told him about Bob, not my first love—but my love just the same. I didn't say that, of course. When I got to Bob's death, he reached across the table and lightly touched my hand for a moment. The shock of his touch was so intense, I dropped my eyes like a nineteenth-century heroine to hide my reaction. But I think he felt it, anyhow.

"There's something I want you to know," he said. "I'm not wining and dining you to get the Rx printout."

I pointed to my iced tea. "Hardly wining."

The waiter brought our tortilla chips and salsa. By the time we'd each helped ourselves, I'd decided how to ask the main question on my mind. "Why are you so anxious to help Betsy?"

"I thought I should be here for her for as long as she needs me," Michael said.

His words struck with such force, I had to work to keep my teeth unclenched. I felt like chewing my nails, something I hadn't done since childhood. More than that, I wanted to rage at the unfairness of it when we had just met again after so many years apart. Luckily, Michael didn't seem to expect a reply because I had none to give.

"She has no one else," he continued.

"What about her stepchildren?"

"Unfortunately, they haven't tried to know Betsy as a person. She needs friends now, but they haven't given her a chance." Michael's voice rose slightly. "She's too decent to complain, but I know how badly they've treated her."

I bit my lips, willing myself to silence.

"That's why I'm trying to spend as much time as possible with her," he said. He was holding a tortilla chip in midair, obviously too agitated to eat it.

He certainly can rationalize, I thought cynically. It's not her long blonde hair or her green eyes; he's just helping her out.

"You see," Michael continued, "her mother remarried and moved to London after our divorce. I'm the only one she has now."

"Oh," I said, drawing out each word, ashamed of my thoughts but relieved at the same time. "Betsy is your—your daughter."

"That's why I want the police to stop bothering her. I know they always suspect the spouse when they can't explain a death, so I've got to unearth what really happened. Before it's too late," he added.

"But how will the prescription record accomplish that? What was the cause of Harry's death?"

"He went into a diabetic coma and his heart failed."

"That shouldn't have happened. His diabetes was under control."

Michael put the chip down uneaten and added more salsa to it. "I'm convinced he took something that caused a reaction. But what could have interacted with his other prescriptions?"

"How can you be sure it was a fatal interaction?"

"Listen, Ruthie, we *know* he didn't commit suicide. He and Betsy were happy. Very happy," he emphasized.

He didn't meet my eyes when he said that, and I wondered briefly about his insistence. Was he holding something back?

"If Harry was taking two drugs that were contraindicated, we would have known it when we filled the second script. Didn't you find the vials?"

"We found Micronase, Lopressor, Viagra, and Rogaine."

I ran them over in my mind. Micronase for his diabetes and Lopressor to control his blood pressure. I remembered he'd been on those for quite a while. He'd been taking Viagra since his marriage. The same was true of Rogaine to grow back hair. No interactions there at all. "Maybe he had something filled elsewhere," I said.

The waiter materialized with two large platters. One taste of spinchada and that was the end of my reverse snobbery about upscale Mexican restaurants. This was gourmet cooking, which didn't stop me from pouring the rest of the salsa over everything on the plate.

"It's possible, of course, that he went to more than one doctor and more than one pharmacy, but we haven't found anything else except OTCs."

I doubted whether anyone could commit suicide with over-the-counter drugs, but even aspirins can be fatal if you take enough of them. We were both silent for a while as we worked at our dinners, but it was a comfortable silence this time.

"I'm sorry about the way I behaved this morning, Ruthie. I don't want you to compromise your ideals."

A quick glance at Michael's face showed me that he was not being sarcastic. "And I'm sorry I lost my temper," I said.

"No, you were right. I realize now you didn't even know Betsy is my daughter."

I hoped we weren't going back to the sticky topic of patient confidentiality. Was a father-in-law entitled to the records of his deceased son-in-law? And how much privacy was left to Harry Stokes? His wife and Michael now knew what he may have carefully hidden from them: he was using Rogaine to suppress baldness and Viagra to restore potency. I was sure from what I had seen of Harry and his careful grooming that he would have guarded this information while he was alive. On the other hand, I doubted that he could have concealed his diabetes and high blood pressure.

"Here's what I've been thinking," Michael continued. "I won't ask you to give me a printout since you consider that unethical. But could you scan the record and tell me whether you see anything that we didn't find, anything that would interact fatally." He stopped me before I could speak.

"Don't answer now. Think it over and I'll be in the store tomorrow afternoon."

We talked about Michael's job; he was the pharmacy director at one of the Tucson hospitals. We talked about the differences between Tucson and Scottsdale. We talked about everything except whether we were going to pick up where we had left off so many years ago. But the conversation flowed as if we had known each other forever and, in a way, we had.

Just before we finished our dinners, Michael asked how I liked my spinchada. He seemed hesitant, and I couldn't understand why. After a pause, he went on, "I was wondering if you ordered a vegetarian meal because you still observe the dietary laws?"

I remembered how curious he'd always been about Jewish traditions. "Bob's family weren't observant Jews," I explained, "so I gradually became less religious after we were married."

Michael looked surprised. "I thought it meant so much to you."

"It did. I suppose if we'd had children, I would have continued my own family's ways."

"Only for your children, not for yourself?" His eyes held mine. "It's rather ironic, Ruthie. I would have encouraged you to keep your traditions."

Chapter 8.

I was on the day shift again on Wednesday, and I arrived at Food Go early, resolved to look up Harry Stokes' prescription file right away. Although our pharmacy doesn't open until nine in the morning, customers often show up as soon as I turn on the lights. So this time I went through my opening routine in the dark to avoid interruptions. Then I typed in Stokes, Harry and looked at his prescription history. At first, I found just what I expected to see. On July 29th, only four days before his death, he had renewed his Rogaine and Viagra prescriptions.

The previous entry showed Micronase, 5 milligrams, which I hadn't remembered at that dosage. Well, no wonder; Tim had filled it. Up until June, Harry was getting 2-1/2 milligrams for his diabetes but, in July, his doctor had increased the dosage. It looked like Harry hadn't been controlling his diet and exercise. His doctor had also increased the Lopressor, and the higher strength indicated Harry's blood pressure must have been climbing.

I sat there in the dark and thought about what the little screen showed. Was Harry worried that his health was deteriorating? Was depression a possible side effect of his medications? I would have to read the package inserts and remind myself about any side effects.

But then I got up and looked at those white letters on my blue computer screen again. Would a man who was depressed and about to commit suicide care about growing more hair? He had refilled his Rogaine prescription only a few days before his death. It didn't make sense to me, but it wasn't enough to build theories on.

I looked up at the clock and saw I still had twenty minutes before opening, so I thought about Michael. Should I discuss the record with him? He already knew about all four prescriptions, and he must surely have seen the fill dates on the vials. But did he know about the increased dosages, and had he considered the psychological implications?

Someone was rapping on the pharmacy window. I looked at the clock again; it was still too early to open, but I told myself that the customer is always right and stepped over to the light switch.

This customer was wrong. He wanted his wife's Premarin refilled, and he wanted it now. "I have to get your doctor's okay," I told him. "But he doesn't take calls before nine."

"You're the only one who has to call the doctor," he told me. "The other lady never bothers me."

"The other lady?"

"Yes. She just fills it and doesn't give me all this crap."

"Sir, I'm the only woman at this pharmacy."

"Don't tell me that. I want my wife's medicine."

"Sir, I'll try to reach your doctor and have it for you as soon as possible." I suppressed a sigh, hoping this encounter didn't presage a difficult day. "Do you have some shopping to do elsewhere in the store?" I asked him. "Why don't you try us again at about nine fifteen?" I turned away and picked up the phone before he could say anything else, but I could hear him just the same.

"Damn lady druggists," he muttered.

Can't win, I thought, and held the phone through a recorded message that told me the doctor's office would open at 9:30.

When Joey arrived two hours later, I had filled about a dozen prescriptions and had five more lined up on the counter, waiting for him to run them through the computer, print the labels, and stack them with the scripts ready for me to fill. He was shouting to me as he came through the door to the pharmacy.

"They arrested her!"

"Oh, no," I said. "Not Betsy Stokes." *Poor Michael*, I thought.

"Not her. Denise."

"What?" Now I was the one to raise my voice. "How could Denise have anything to do with Harry Stokes's death?"

"I don't know the details," Joey said. "But Frank told my sister, and she called me just before I left for work."

I sat down, my mind racing. Denise lived next door to the Stokes house, and I knew she'd been infatuated with Harry. I certainly had heard enough diatribes against Betsy after the marriage. But murder ? I thought about Denise and how she had looked and acted since Harry's death. Subdued, yes, but that seemed natural enough in light of her infatuation. Denise had not been acting like someone with murder on her conscience; in any case, I was convinced she couldn't commit murder.

The stock comment of parents, friends, and acquaintances everywhere: I don't believe it. She was kind, quiet, a good person—you name it. And yet, I really couldn't believe it.

I remembered our conversation after the funeral when Denise seemed to be complaining because the Scottsdale police hadn't questioned her. She'd admitted hating Betsy, but what did that have to do with Harry's death?

For the rest of the day, I tried to concentrate on doing my job without making mistakes. I triple-checked each prescription because I knew I wasn't thinking clearly.

Michael had said he'd be in that afternoon, but he hadn't shown by the time Tim arrived to relieve me. We had no overlap today, and I didn't wait; I removed my white jacket, hung it neatly on a coat hook, clocked out, and walked over to the coffee shop.

As I did, I tried to remember Denise's schedule for this week, but hers was more confusing than mine. Then I mentally formed questions for the other waitress to extract information without giving anything away.

Even before I reached the coffee shop, I could see a chubby young woman resetting one of the tables. What was her name again? Ellen, and she didn't want to be called Ellie.

"Ellen, has Denise left for the day?"

"Left? She hasn't even been in. They called me early this morning." Her round face took on an aggrieved look. "I wasn't supposed to be here until four, but I had to get the kids to the sitter and rush over here."

"Is she sick?" I asked cautiously.

"What do I know? My manager told me it was an emergency, and I'd better get to the store right away. So I did."

I tried to sound casual. "Oh, well. I'll catch her tomorrow."

Ellen was still talking as I walked away. "Didn't even say please. Just wanted me to drop everything and work two shifts."

All the way home, I wondered whether to call Denise. Ordinarily, I wouldn't have hesitated. I'd phone to see how she was feeling and whether she needed anything. But after Joey's news, maybe it would be better to reach Michael and see what he had heard. No, he might think I was looking for an excuse to call him, and I didn't want that.

I arrived home without reaching a decision. Kicking off my shoes, I turned the air down to 70 degrees and went into the family room to check my answering machine. The light was blinking, and the digital readout showed three messages. After pitches from two salesmen, evidently not deterred by the machine, I heard Denise's voice.

"Ruthie, I know you'll be tired and hungry when you hear this, but I need to see you. Please come right over."

I was so relieved to realize Denise must be at home that I put on my shoes and rushed out the door. It didn't take long to reach her house. Despite my concern for her, though, I couldn't help wondering about Michael again as I passed the Stokes's place and saw his Lexus in the driveway. I pulled into Denise's carport.

Denise answered the door within seconds after the chimes sounded. She was wearing a T-shirt, white shorts, and running shoes—the summer uniform in Arizona, except on the job. It's also the winter uniform, but only for tourists. Her long hair, usually so carefully curled and brushed, looked uncombed. No eye shadow today and no earrings. Her eyes were red, but I couldn't tell whether it was from fatigue or from tears.

"Thank God you're here," she said. "I didn't know who to turn to."

She led me from the small Mexican-tiled entryway into her living room. Denise's furniture, unlike Betsy's, brought the southwestern style of the house indoors. I sat down on her sofa, trying to make myself comfortable against a trio of throw pillows with sandpainting motifs.

"What happened?" I thought it better not to repeat Joey's story that she'd been arrested.

"The police were here at seven this morning. I was getting ready for work and they waited while I finished dressing. Then I had to call Food Go to say I wouldn't be in." Denise stopped and her face reflected the surprise she must have felt. "They wanted to question me." She sounded indignant rather than upset.

My role should have been to dispense sympathy, but I was so relieved to hear she hadn't been arrested that I blurted, "Well, only the other day you complained because they hadn't questioned you."

"People say a lot of things when they're upset."

"Yes, I know."

"They started questioning me, and they sounded like they thought I killed Harry. So, before I realized what I was saying, I told them they were wrong. That I loved Harry."

Uh, oh, I thought.

"Then the questioning got worse. Hell hath no fury and all that."

"It got worse?"

"They asked me how long Harry and I had been sleeping together."

I gripped the carved wooden arms of the sofa in shock. Could they be right? Then I was angry at myself for doubting Denise. My expression must have revealed that first reaction.

"It's not true," she said. Her voice was stiff.

"I know."

"But you wondered if there was fire along with the smoke. Ruthie, if you doubt me, what chance do I have with everyone else?"

She was right, and the knowledge made me uncomfortable. We were friends; but for a brief moment, I'd thought the police must have evidence of an affair. How odd that Joey's news didn't make me believe she could commit murder, but this had nearly changed my mind.

"Fantasies are one thing," Denise said. "You know about them. I used to talk to you because you were so sympathetic."

"Yes, I remember." I also remembered my own daydreams about Harry and was glad I'd never mentioned them. Suddenly I had a terrible fear that the police would suspect me of an affair with Harry. Would they believe my denials any more than Denise's? I could feel the throw pillows digging into my back and reached behind to adjust them.

"They questioned me for hours," she said. "I could have called a lawyer, but I know I haven't done anything wrong. I work too hard to throw money away on a lawyer."

"I still don't understand why they suspect you."

"Could be someone told the police I hang around the pharmacy a lot. They think I had access to something."

"What?" I was outraged now. Yet an inner voice reminded me that I could be suspected for the same flimsy reasons that had momentarily made me doubt Denise.

"They wouldn't even tell me what drug. I said I've never gotten anything from you without a prescription."

"Of course not. They must know I can't just hand out drugs to my friends."

Denise looked away as if to gather her courage. She was sitting next to me on the sofa and had thrown one of the pillows on the floor. Picking it up now, she pulled at the piping, getting more agitated by the minute. "I don't know about that. Don't you remember the day I forgot my hay fever pills? You know which ones I take. You gave me two to tide me over."

"Seldane. Yes, I remember now. But it doesn't mean anything. We do that all the time and when the prescription comes in, we just deduct the two tablets we advanced to the customer."

Denise ran her hand through her long hair in a nervous gesture. No wonder she looked unkempt today. "They questioned me about that day over and over. After a while, I started to feel guilty. Then they got me to admit I wanted Harry for myself and that I never liked Betsy. Hated her is the way they put it."

"Denise, you told me many times that you hate her. You probably said the same thing to other people, and one of them must have mentioned it when they were questioned. But I don't understand what this is all about. Harry is the one who died, not his wife."

"They think I killed him so Betsy couldn't have him."

If the situation hadn't been so serious, I would have laughed at the melodramatic implications. "That's ridiculous," I said. "Do they think it took you all this time to make up your mind to kill him? It must be at least a year since they married."

"It was last October."

"All right. October. Do they really believe you brooded about their marriage for ten months and then decided to kill him?"

"But you see, Ruthie, they think we remained lovers and I couldn't stand it any more."

"And that's even harder to believe. Why would he marry a beautiful young woman—excuse me, I have to be brutally frank now—and continue an affair with you?"

Denise laughed and came out with the kind of impish remark that usually made her such good company. "Ask Princess Di's biographers that one."

"Yes, but you're free. If their assumptions were true, Harry could have married you any time before last October."

"I think we're both too exhausted to think straight. Let me make some coffee." I followed her into the kitchen where she quickly put two cups of instant coffee into her microwave and a plate of chocolate chip cookies on the table. I was glad to get the coffee; even instant would help tonight.

As I drank my coffee and munched on cookies, I thought about the entire bizarre story. It just didn't make sense to me.

Denise sat across the table, stirring sweetener into her coffee. "I don't understand it," she said. "Why do they suspect me when Harry's children and Betsy all have motives?"

"Maybe the police are questioning everyone the same way. Maybe that's what they do when they have no leads."

"What happened to innocent until proven guilty?"

Since I assumed the question was a rhetorical one, I didn't try to answer her. I started to worry that the police would be waiting for me at the pharmacy in the morning. But I had nothing to hide except some long ago daydreams. I was thankful I'd never said anything against Betsy, not only because of Denise's experience today, but also because she was Michael's daughter. Michael's daughter—I still hadn't come to grips with that knowledge.

I pulled myself together, realizing the selfish turn my thoughts had taken. "Did the police say anything about further questions for you?"

"No, but I'm worried. I always believed if you kept your nose clean, you'd be okay. Now I'm not so sure about that."

"Denise, you know you didn't harm Harry," I said firmly. "And I know you didn't. You can't be a serious suspect."

She was twisting strands of her hair now. "I haven't told you everything," she said. "There's something I just can't talk about."

Chapter 9.

Thursday, I was on the day shift again and half expected to see either Michael or the police when I arrived at Food Go. But it was surprisingly quiet. My first customer came in twenty minutes after I opened, which gave me time to catch up on paperwork.

Detective Frank Moreway arrived an hour or so later. I was on the phone, trying to solve a difficult problem. The patient wanted a refill of Vasotec, 5 milligrams, to reduce his blood pressure. He didn't have the original vial or the prescription number, so I looked him up in the computer. Then I pulled the hard copy, handwritten by a Dr. Thomas; but when I called Dr. Thomas's office, no one had heard of the patient. Now the office nurse had put Dr. Thomas himself on the phone, and I was listening to an indignant denial that Mr. Rosofsky was his patient.

"But Dr. Thomas, the script is handwritten on your blank."

"I don't care how it's written; he's not my patient."

At that point, a man in a dark suit, incongruous for Scottsdale in August, had stepped up to the window and shoved his I.D. at me. I recognized the name. Detective Frank Moreway was Joey's brother-in-law, and I smiled and held up my hand to indicate I'd be right with him. He glared at me, obviously not used to waiting when he wanted to talk to someone. Now I had another problem: doctors are not accustomed to being put on hold, and here was a Scottsdale police detective who didn't want to wait either.

The patient chose that moment to reappear and yell at me. "I never heard of Dr. Thomas. Just give me my blood pressure medicine. I don't need you to raise my pressure."

"Sir, I can't refill your Vasotec without the doctor's okay. He has no record of you, and now you tell me he's not your doctor."

Frank Moreway, in a deliberately polite voice, interrupted. "Can we hold off on that for a minute, ma'am? I need to get back into the pharmacy and look up some records."

"Detective Moreway, you can come back now." I indicated the door and went to open it for him. "I'm sorry, but I must finish with this gentleman before I can call up any records for you on the computer."

The customer's face had turned red and he was shouting at me again. "Don't give me excuses. I want my medicine."

I sighed. "Sir, this is the original prescription. It's handwritten on Dr. Thomas's form and signed by him. He never heard of you and you never heard of him, so we're at an impasse here." I showed him the prescription.

"I don't care what you say," he shouted. "I go to Dr. Birmann, not Dr. Thomas."

Suddenly, I saw what had happened. "Sir, both of those doctors are in the same office, and they cover for each other on vacations. Let me call the office again and see if they can find your record under Dr. Birmann."

So I did and they did. The customer admitted he'd seen some other doctor last time, apologized profusely, and thanked me for straightening things out. I filled his Vasotec, told two other people that I'd have their prescriptions in half an hour, and turned my attention to Frank Moreway.

"I want a printout of every prescription Harry Stokes got since the beginning of this year," he said. "Also, I have a list of other people whose records I want to see."

He handed me a list that included Betsy Stokes, Richard Stokes, Nancy Stokes, Sheila Stokes, and Denise Seaford. I ran all the names through my computer and saw that Harry's children were not our customers. While the computer printed out the records for Harry, Betsy, and Denise, I tried to talk to Frank Moreway.

"I don't understand, Detective. I thought Harry Stokes died of natural causes."

For someone who, at least according to Joey, gossiped so much at home, the detective was surprisingly laconic with me. "I'm not permitted to discuss the case, ma'am. Just give me the records and I'll get out of your way."

I indicated the printer and tried to lighten the situation. "If I could invent one that works faster when people are in a hurry, I'd be rich."

"What time are you off duty?" He glanced briefly at a young woman who had come up to the window. "I have some questions, and I don't want the public listening in."

I could feel the color leaving my face even though I knew I hadn't done anything wrong. Leaning over the printer as if to check it, I tried to hide my reaction from Frank Moreway. But I was sure he'd noticed. *Stop being foolish*, I warned myself. *Straighten up and act your age.*

"Detective, I'll be glad to answer any questions, but this is a retail business and there'll be people around even at five when my shift ends."

"Isn't there an office here?"

"Yes, but employees will be coming and going all the time."

He gave me a look that I interpreted as suspicious. "Then you have two choices. I can go out to your residence or you can come to police headquarters."

I dawdled with the printouts while I thought this over. Going to the police department could be embarrassing, but it might be even worse if he pulled up in front of my house in a patrol car. "I'll come to you," I said.

"Fine. Just ask for Criminal Investigations and someone will direct you."

"About 5:30?" I couldn't help making it a question and waited for his approval.

"Five-thirty," he repeated and left with the printouts.

All day, I dreaded the coming interview. Surely my private daydreams had no bearing on the case. He just wanted to discuss the prescriptions with me. But my uneasiness never subsided.

At five, I walked over to the Food Go employee restrooms, where I carefully brushed my hair, trying to neaten the wayward curls caused by the humidity, and reapplied lipstick. Luckily, I had worn my taupe and white geometric-patterned dress, which was less frivolous looking than some of my other summer outfits. I needed all the self-confidence I could muster.

When I arrived at police headquarters and was directed to Detective Moreway's desk in Criminal Investigations, my nervousness increased. *Maybe I'm just reacting to Denise's story*, I thought, and tried to calm myself.

Frank Moreway offered me a chair and sat on the edge of the desk, looking down at me. For the first time, I noticed the brown shoes and socks he wore with his dark blue suit. I considered it a sign that he didn't know everything and relaxed slightly just before he led me through a description of every drug on the printouts. Or maybe I just became more professional as we entered my own sphere of knowledge.

First, we discussed the four prescriptions that Harry Stokes regularly filled at Food Go. I explained the significance of the increased dosages of Micronase and Lopressor. "But you really should talk to his doctor," I suggested. A noncommittal grunt was his only response, which I interpreted to mean he'd already done so but wasn't going to give anything away.

"Let me be sure I've got it all," Detective Moreway said. Then he had me repeat everything. It was hard to equate this man with the brother-in-law that Joey admired so much, although I was fairly sure repetition was a ploy to see whether I changed any information.

After we went over Harry Stokes's prescription record several times, the detective began to question me about how well I knew Harry. "I knew him only as a customer," I told him.

"How often did you see him outside of Food Go?"

"Never."

"You were at his funeral," he said flatly.

Here was another dilemma, but I was not going to make things worse for Denise. "He was a very good customer; I wanted to pay my respects."

Too late I realized that Joey had heard the entire conversation when Denise urged me to go to the funeral with her. Well, this was my story and I would stick to it.

He surprised me by not pursuing the subject. Instead he went on to Denise's prescriptions, which were pretty straightforward. In addition to her regular script each month for 60 Seldane, which she took for her allergies, the record showed one for Seldane D last month when she had a bad summer cold. I'd cautioned her not to take both drugs at the same time but to use only the Seldane D until the cold symptoms eased off. I remembered thinking it would be simpler and cheaper if her doctor told her to buy Food-Fed, Food Go's brand of pseudoephedrine, a decongestant that doesn't require a prescription, and take it along with the allergy drug.

"No birth control pills?" Frank Moreway asked.

I felt my face flush. "This is the complete record. You saw me pull it from the computer."

"Couldn't the record be altered?"

"Yes, I suppose it could be, but you're welcome to look over the hard copies—paper copies—of the prescriptions. Anytime."

"I might just do that," he said and began to question me about Betsy Stokes's prescription record.

One glance at her printout and my shocked expression was enough to alert Detective Moreway. "What is it? Was she taking something unusual?"

"No. Nothing unusual. I just didn't suspect... I mean, Harry was so much older... that is..." I was silent.

"You might as well stop trying to hide things from me. I haven't been to *her* doctor yet, but I'm sure he'll cooperate."

I was too disturbed then by the prescription record and his assumption that I was holding back information to notice the tacit admission that he'd talked with Harry Stokes's physician. "I'm not hiding anything," I said indignantly.

He got down from the desk and loomed over me. "Well."

"She's taking Stuartnatal 1 + 1. The other pharmacist filled the script, so I didn't know until now."

"In words of one syllable," Frank Moreway said slowly, "I want you to explain what that means."

"Stuartnatal 1 + 1 is a prenatal vitamin."

His face still had a puzzled expression, or maybe that was a ploy, too, so I hurried to explain. "Betsy... I mean Mrs. Stokes... is pregnant."

"And why the shocked reaction? You must fill hundreds of prescriptions for prenatal vitamins."

"It's just the circumstances," I lamely excused myself.

He wasn't going to let that one get by. "What circumstances in particular? That her husband was a senior citizen?"

I winced at this term. But then again, to a young man like Detective Moreway, it must have seemed a natural distinction. My mind raced as I tried to absorb the implications of Betsy's pregnancy. Any lingering doubts about suicide were gone, and I thought the likelihood that Betsy had murdered her husband was also diminished. Then I remembered Denise. If she knew about the pregnancy, would the police consider it her motive? In view of the direction of their questions, this seemed likely. I couldn't believe she was a murderer, and I was not going to help them harass her.

"You haven't answered my question," Detective Moreway said.

I couldn't remember the question and must have looked blank. "Why does her pregnancy shock you?"

"Detective Moreway," I said firmly, looking up at him. "I'm trying to cooperate with you in every way possible." Despite the air conditioning, I could feel sweat trickling down my forehead. It was a normal physical reaction during the Arizona monsoon season, but I was afraid he'd attribute it to a guilty conscience.

He resumed his perch on the edge of the desk. Ordinarily I would have enjoyed talking to him rather than sitting home alone in front of my television. He wasn't really handsome, but his strong features and confident manner would make him attractive to many women. And how often did any young man waste more than a few minutes talking to me? I was just another one of Scottsdale's "seniors." We were as indistinguishable to most young men, and women too, as the palm trees outside.

"All right, ma'am," he said finally. "Let's look at the other prescription drugs that Betsy Stokes gets from you."

The printout showed her scripts in reverse chronological order, with the latest at the top of the page, but nothing unusual had caught my eye until I reached the prenatal vitamins. Now I started from the beginning and looked over the rest of Betsy Stokes' recent medical history for Frank Moreway.

Her first prenatal exam had probably been on July 18th because she'd gotten the Stuartnatal 1 + 1 that day. On July 24th, her doctor had prescribed penicillin and Tussi-Organidin DM. "She must have caught the summer cold that's been going around," I explained.

"Is it safe for a pregnant woman to take those drugs?"

"Her doctor prescribed them."

"That's no answer."

Why was he so antagonistic? No one had called Harry's death murder; yet he seemed to be suspicious of everyone. "The doctor writes them and I fill them," I said.

"And if you think the doctor made an error?"

"Then I call him, or her, and check it out." All at once, I was tired of acting like a victim. It was time to confront Detective Moreway. "I don't understand," I said. "Betsy Stokes is very much alive. What does her summer cold have to do with anything?"

I stood in front of him now, all my nervousness suddenly gone. "It's not what the doctors prescribe for pregnant women that I worry about. It's the nonprescription drugs people buy over the counter." I gathered the printouts and handed them to Frank Moreway. Then I adjusted the straps of my taupe leather shoulder bag, giving him time to insist on further questions. He looked surprised but said nothing.

"If you want to have a philosophical discussion on the subject some time, I'll be glad to give you my opinion. But pharmacists don't get a lunch hour at Food Go, and it's nearly eleven hours since breakfast." Half expecting him to call me back, I left the room at a carefully moderated pace and walked to my car.

Chapter 10.

I didn't recognize Richard Stokes when he came up to the pharmacy window the next afternoon. This balding man of thirty-five or so, in a forest green and white rugby shirt bore little resemblance to the conservatively dressed mourner at the funeral. He rapped on the counter even though he could see I was right there.

"In the electronic age," he said pompously, "I guess you can see everyone's prescriptions right away."

"You mean fill them right away?"

"No, I need a list."

Usually they wanted lists of all their prescriptions at income tax time, not in August. I was about to make sure that's what he really wanted when he was joined by a mousey-looking woman.

"Miss," she said in a hesitant voice. "My husband has to have a record of every one of his father's and stepmother's prescriptions."

Maybe it was the association of father and stepmother, but now I recognized Richard and Nancy Stokes. *This is turning into farce instead of tragedy*, I thought grimly. *Who's going to ask for the printout next? Let's see, Harry had a daughter and there's her fiancé. Soon we'll get the maid and the milkman.*

"Sorry, I've already given that record to the police." I don't know why I said that. Probably just tired of the pushed-around feeling.

"Don't tell me the police are finally going to do something," Richard Stokes said.

Almost simultaneously, his wife's expression showed traces of fear. "Now see what you've done," she shrieked at him.

"Will you stop it?" he said to her through clenched teeth.

"You always say that. Why don't *you* stop it?" She was crying now and pulled a wad of yellow tissues from her purse to dab her eyes.

"Wait for me outside," he said.

Like a child, she wailed, "It's too hot to wait outside." But then she turned and walked awkwardly away from the pharmacy. I didn't know what to do or say, so I busied myself at the computer, trying to act as though I hadn't witnessed the miserable scene.

"Are you getting me the records? That's for Harry Stokes and Betsy Stokes."

"Prescription records are confidential."

"I know that," he said. "But I told you they're for my father and stepmother."

"Then they have to request the records."

"Don't be stupid. My father is dead."

Just what I needed, some customer abuse. That's when I get very polite; that's when I get so polite, it's almost insulting. "Sir, we have a firm policy not to release such information." I articulated each word clearly as though I were speaking to someone with weak English skills.

"I'm getting the store manager," he said and moved quickly away.

Great, I thought. *The customer is always right, so how is my manager going to get around this one?*

I tried to concentrate on answering the phone and taking care of patients at the window while I waited to see what would happen. Meanwhile, I thought about pharmacy law: was it specific on the subject or would I have to explain the ethics of the situation to my manager and hope he'd support me. He was usually good about supporting us, but I worried just the same.

Richard Stokes returned alone about fifteen minutes later. He spoke now with the voice of reason. "I'm sorry I lost my temper," he said. "Father died last week and I'm sure you realize how upset we are."

"Yes, of course," I said, trying to sound reasonable in return but determined not to release confidential information.

"Well, his death was unexpected. You probably know that he had a few minor ailments."

Although I hadn't heard diabetes and high blood pressure called minor ailments before, I tried to keep an interested but noncommittal expression.

"Now we need the records to see what Dad was taking."

"Can't you just look at his prescription bottles?"

He hesitated. "Look, I see you're good at keeping confidences, so I'll tell you the problem. Dad remarried last year, and we can't... I mean his wife won't... That is, we don't want to disturb her when she's grieving."

"Oh, I see."

"I knew you'd understand. And we need her prescriptions because... well, she's so distraught that we're afraid she might... you know, do something foolish."

Either the family was unaware of Betsy's pregnancy or he thought I didn't know. I must have looked skeptical at his last statement, because he finished lamely, "It happens, you know."

I wasn't going to let him off that easily. "What happens?" I asked.

He put his face right up to the window, assuming a solemn expression. "Suicide," he whispered.

"You can't mean that. She's a young woman with her whole life ahead of her." I watched him as I tossed the platitude. He looked angry again and I was prepared for more nasty comments, but he controlled himself.

"All of us are concerned about her. She doesn't eat or sleep, and she never leaves the house."

That's a good story, I thought, but aloud I matched his serious tone. "I'm really surprised to hear that." I paused for effect. "Her father doesn't seem to worry about suicide."

Again, his face darkened in anger and I hastily excused myself to help another customer. When I turned back to Richard Stokes, he was ready with another tactic.

"I see you're too clever for me, so I'll have to tell you the truth, distasteful as it is to wash our dirty linen in public."

He would definitely win any cliché contest. I answered two phone calls and then waited to see what he'd say this time. He looked around to make sure no other customers were nearby.

"My wife and I, and my sister as well, believe my father was either driven to suicide or murdered."

As though this were news to me, I gave an appropriate gasp. It must have seemed realistic enough to him, for he continued. "My father was in perfect health. Yes, I know, he had diabetes and high blood pressure, but that's all the more reason why he should have lived to a ripe old age."

Definitely a cliché artist, but I listened patiently while he described a study that was supposed to show "people in our level of society" with such diseases lived longer because they sought medical care earlier and more frequently than the average person. "And my father took care of himself. He never missed taking his medications."

"Yes, he seemed careful about his health," I said.

"So, now you understand why we want the prescription records."

He's so transparent, I reflected. *If Harry Stokes had been murdered, this is one person who couldn't have done it. He had plenty of guile, but his words and body language were overdone.*

The pharmacy was quiet for the moment, so I decided to play, too. "No. I really don't understand."

Now he was exasperated. "Look here, miss," he started to say and caught himself. The voice of reason returned. "It's simple. We think Father's death wasn't from natural causes."

"Yes...?"

"So we think he took something or was given something that killed him." He folded his arms and tried for a sincere look this time. "Now you know. I can't say it any clearer."

Sure you can, I thought. *You can come right out and say you think his wife was responsible for his death. By asking for her prescriptions, you intimated it anyhow.*

"And you've already told the police about your suspicions."

Another glare was his only response.

"I guess that's why Detective Moreway came in for the records yesterday." I tried to sound as if the thought had just struck me. My acting skills probably were no better than his, but I left him no choice.

"Yes. I suppose so."

"Well, in that case, the information is in good hands." I worded all my comments to support my original insinuation that the records were no longer in my possession. It didn't work.

"Don't you still have copies in the computer?"

We had circled to the original impasse. When three more prescriptions came in, I turned away hoping Richard Stokes would give up and leave, but he waited until I was free again. "I'm sure you want to see justice done," he said this time.

Yes, and no news is good news and a bird in the hand is worth two in the bush, I said to myself. "That's exactly why I cooperated with the Scottsdale Police Department." I couldn't resist it: "The ball's in their court, now."

"Naturally, I have complete faith in the authorities," he said.

"In that case..."

"Let me finish, miss. You probably don't know this, but the Stokes are an old Arizona family. We come from pioneer stock, self-reliant folks, and I'm not waiting for the police to find out who's responsible for my father's death."

"That's strange. I understood you were the one who brought the police into this in the first place."

Now I'd done it. The rage he'd been trying to control burst like water spurting from a garden hose. "You think you're clever," he shouted. "All you ladies with careers are the same. Do you think they fire lady engineers? No, I'm the one who got axed, but the ladies kept their jobs." He glared at me so threateningly that I drew back in alarm. "Pardon me, the *women*. The *women* don't have to worry every time there's a layoff. They're needed to keep the government off the company's back."

I waited for him to run down, but he seemed to be venting the accumulated hatred of years. Although I'd had abusive customers before, this general condemnation of female professionals was something new. I thought I understood what was driving him, but I didn't know what to do. Customers came to the window, heard him shouting, and edged away. I had to calm him.

"Mr. Stokes," I said. He didn't seem to hear me but kept shouting, repeating himself without winding down. "I'm trying to help you."

Finally, he stopped shouting and looked directly at me. "You're not helping; you're part of the problem."

I wondered whether it had all been an act. If he were really so disturbed, would he be back to clichés again? "Mr. Stokes, last night I spent two hours at police headquarters going over the prescription records of your father, Betsy Stokes, and ... others. I suggest you see Detective Moreway and discuss all of this with him."

His expression became even more filled with hatred. If he had a weapon, I was sure he'd use it, and I prepared to drop to the Mexican tile floor behind the prescription counter. "Maybe we've been suspecting the wrong person," he said. "After all, you have more access to poisons than anyone else."

Chapter 11.

All day, I tried to convince myself that Richard Stokes's accusations were ridiculous; no one could possibly believe him. But I thought of Denise and the way the police had hammered at her. If they suspected Denise because of a friendship that, to their way of thinking, gave her access to the pharmacy—who would believe me? Their suppositions about her interest in Harry could apply to me, too. I thought how awkward it would be, even though they could never prove anything. And, my inner voice said, how embarrassing if Michael were to hear of my romantic fantasies.

Stop being so foolish, Ruthie, I told myself. I tried to be logical about it. Despite a prescription department full of drugs, I had no idea how to kill a person. If anyone supposed I had a motive for murdering Harry Stokes, did they really believe I could have dropped arsenic or strychnine in his coffee? I relaxed a little at this idea—we didn't even have arsenic or strychnine in the store. Not only that, I'd never had coffee or anything else with Harry Stokes.

But would Frank Moreway believe me? An accusation of murder was a serious charge and he'd have to investigate. On the other hand, Richard Stokes had already accused his stepmother. Surely, if he showed up at police headquarters today and accused someone else, he would lose whatever credibility he'd had.

I couldn't afford to let someone like Richard Stokes unnerve me. Since Bob's death, I'd become used to coping alone, and I was stronger for it. But this was no ordinary predicament; I needed advice, and I didn't know where to turn. I couldn't bother Denise; she had her own troubles. As for my other friends, I didn't relish telling any of them I might be a murder suspect. *There's Michael,* I thought. And I knew he had been in my mind all along.

When I got home from work that night, I ran through possible conversations with him. The next day, Saturday, was my day off this week. I could invite Michael for lunch or dinner. No, that might give him the wrong impression; it was better just to ask him over to talk. If he demurred, I would add details. Otherwise, I preferred to say nothing on the telephone about Richard Stokes and his accusations.

Possibly Michael had gone back to Tucson by now. I had heard nothing from him since our dinner three nights ago. But surely his daughter still needed him, and somehow I didn't think he'd leave town without saying goodbye to me.

I dialed, expecting Betsy Stokes to answer the telephone—after all it was her home I was calling—so when I heard Michael's voice, I forgot my carefully prepared words. "This is Ruthie Kantor... I mean Ruthie Morris."

He laughed and that deep, joyous sound brought back the old memories, but I refused to let myself get caught in the past again. "You didn't have to give a name," he said. "I recognized you right away."

"I wasn't sure you were still in Scottsdale."

His voice sobered immediately. "Yes, of course, I'm still here."

Why was it so hard to ask him to stop by tomorrow? It wasn't a date. And if Michael suspected an excuse for seeing him again, he'd soon discover the real reason for my call. I closed out the schoolgirl reactions and invited him.

Michael said he'd drive over as soon after eleven o'clock as possible. "I have something to do earlier, but I should be finished by then." I gave him my address and directions. Like the Stokes home, mine is on a cul-de-sac that makes it hard to find.

After we said our goodbyes, and despite telling myself over and over that this wasn't a social call, I checked to see what refreshments I had on hand. *Coffee, that's all you need to serve*, I insisted to myself. But that was an error in the opposite direction, for any friend or neighbor who came to the house would be offered cake or ice cream along with a cup of coffee. I always kept a raspberry or lemon danish log and two flavors of ice cream in my freezer, just in case. Embarrassment would come not from too much hospitality but from treating Michael less cordially than anyone else.

I fell asleep that night before I'd decided what to wear. During the long Arizona summers, I usually preferred shorts and knit shirts on my days off. Even though I still looked reasonably well in shorts, I decided on a pale blue sleeveless dress instead. The air-conditioning would be blasting away anyhow, and I'd feel more comfortable that way.

In the morning, I quickly straightened the house, trying to look at it through Michael's eyes. The Gorman prints Bob and I had bought over the years added color to the champagne walls and dark traditional furniture, and I was proud of my collection of old pharmacy beakers from Dad's store, grouped on end tables and shelves throughout the house. I knew my birch kitchen contrasted sharply with the sophistication of Betsy's starkly modern one, but I had no idea whether Michael's taste was similar to that of his daughter.

He's only an acquaintance now, I told myself. *Maybe we can be friends, but expecting anything else will only lead to disappointment. And be honest, while it's pleasant to dream of might-have-beens, we're both different people now.*

Michael arrived just after eleven, and I tried to seem calm as he followed me into my living room, but I knew my face was flushed and my eyes were too bright. We settled across the room from each other; he sat on the turquoise-striped sofa and I went to one of the turquoise-and-peach floral armchairs. I was glad he hadn't taken the other armchair, the one I still thought of as Bob's, because I didn't want to compare Bob and Michael. Michael had been my first love, but Bob had been my husband for more than thirty years.

"At least one worry is gone," he said. "I took Betsy to her doctor this morning and everything's fine."

I didn't know whether to acknowledge awareness of her pregnancy, but he continued before I could react. "She's in her third month, and she was desperately afraid of losing the baby. But, of course, you probably knew about the pregnancy before anyone else."

"Actually, I didn't know until I looked at her prescription record two days ago. Tim, he's our other pharmacist, must have filled the Stuartnatal 1 + 1."

"Yes, I know Tim Barnard," he said drily.

"That's right. He was at the funeral."

Michael didn't want to talk about Tim. "Surely, you must have guessed when you saw us buying a stuffed elephant at the mall."

"It never occurred to me."

"Didn't you think it a bit unusual for her to be buying toys at such a time?" He didn't wait for my reply. "Betsy was so unhappy that I wanted to whiz her out of that house. I'm sure you know talk and sympathy only go so far."

I could feel my eyes fill and I turned away from him. The conversation was too intense, and I looked for an escape. "Can I offer you some coffee and cake?"

Michael must have understood, for he said that coffee sounded great and followed me into the kitchen. As I stood at the turquoise Corian counter, my back toward him, he continued.

"I thought a tangible link to the future might help, so I suggested buying toys for the baby. Maybe it was a silly idea, but it seemed to work until we met you and that nosy neighbor of Betsy's."

"Denise is okay," I assured him.

"Possibly, but she always seems to be around when we leave the house or pull in again."

I had regained some self-composure now and hurried to defend Denise. "She's a good person, Michael. I value her friendship."

"Okay, forget I said that and tell me what's worrying you." He reacted to my startled look by assuring me he could still sense when something was wrong. Again, I resolutely shut out the past and concentrated on telling Michael of my encounter with his daughter's stepson. I tried to keep a neutral tone and subdue my emotions.

Michael surprised me again. He did not adopt the easy tactics of reassurance and insist that Richard would talk but not act. Nor did he make light of my unease and embarrassment.

"You're right, Ruthie. He could put you in a difficult position professionally."

"And personally," I added.

"Yes. Although I think he'd have to offer some proof that you and Harry were seen together other than at Food Go." By this time, we were seated at my kitchen table with untouched cups of coffee and plates of danish pastry in front of us.

"Harry was a friendly type. Are you sure you never did see him outside of the store?"

I got to my feet, indignation fueled by the knowledge that I would never tell him about my daydreams. "You know I'm not a liar."

"Indeed, you've always been painfully honest."

"Then, why...?

"Because I can tell that you're holding back something."

"Well, if you must know, you're right," I burst out. "He was a handsome man, and he and I were both alone, so I imagined he'd ask me out. It was a fantasy. He never noticed me as anything but his 'friendly neighborhood pharmacist.'" I phrased the last words sarcastically.

Michael jumped up, too, and took my hand. "I'm sorry," he said. "I didn't mean to push you into confidences. And it's nothing to be ashamed of. If we were all held accountable for fantasies, they couldn't build prisons fast enough for everyone." He moved away from me, picked up our two coffee cups and nodded toward the microwave. "Why don't I reheat these?"

Two minutes later, we sat at the table again, sipping hot coffee. We talked about Michael's work. He was on unpaid leave from his job as director of a busy hospital pharmacy. He managed four full-time pharmacists and three technicians, and the hospital administration was being very supportive, using part-timers to fill in for Michael.

"I'd like to hijack Betsy back to Tucson for a time, but she wants to stay here."

"Let her do it her own way," I advised. "Sometimes people mean well, but they don't realize we need to adjust to living alone in familiar surroundings. Otherwise, we face a second bereavement when we do return."

His intense look warmed me. "You had to go through it all alone, didn't you?"

"Betsy's so much younger," I said. "At least Bob and I had many years together. And these suspicions of suicide or murder—that must make it much harder."

"You've been drawn into this mess, Ruthie, and you should know what's been happening. Let me clue you in."

I refilled our coffee cups and listened, half afraid of what he would say, but glad that I'd finally hear facts instead of rumors.

"I'm sure you know from his prescriptions that Harry had diabetes and high blood pressure, so we expected his doctor to certify either one or both as the cause of death. But he refused to do it." Michael, who had always seemed so sure of himself, looked disconcerted.

"Of course, we wanted to know why, and we were told that both conditions had been under control. Neither was considered life threatening in Harry's case." Michael continued to look uneasy.

"But his physician couldn't be sure of that."

"I know, and before we could challenge him, the son and daughter claimed Betsy had driven their father to suicide."

"Why?"

"You've met Richard. Does he strike you as a rational person?"

I laughed despite the serious turn of our conversation. "You know what they say—even paranoids can have enemies."

"They've made things very difficult for Betsy. I guess it's to be expected when the stepmother is younger than the children of the first marriage."

"And even when she isn't," I said.

"That's probably true in some cases." His intent gaze was directed toward me again. "I won't insult you by asking for promises of confidentiality, but I want to tell you about my daughter's situation. Too many people have misjudged her."

I put my elbows inelegantly on the table and leaned forward. He paused for a moment as if to collect his thoughts, or perhaps he was still hesitant about revealing too much.

"After the divorce, Betsy lived with her mother from the time she was five until just after her ninth birthday. She was with me every other weekend and for a month in the summertime. And I talked to her on the telephone nearly every day.

"Then her mother remarried and moved to London, and Betsy came to live with me. But those formative years... I know what the shrinks say about needing a father figure. When she became serious about someone a little older than me, I guess I should have expected it."

"Are you saying it was a complete surprise?"

Michael took a moment to reflect, although I was sure he'd already considered the facts many times. "Before Harry, her few serious relationships were with men in her own age group, like Tim Barnard," he said. "Yes, I was surprised. In fact, I didn't expect it to last.

"Betsy always talked about a large family; she missed having siblings." He smiled ruefully. "Well, I was wrong about one thing. I told her Harry was too old to give her a child."

"Do the Stokes family know she's pregnant?"

"I'm not sure. She isn't on close terms with them. They haven't treated her very well—innuendos about marrying for money. That sort of thing."

"Even grown children find it hard to believe their parents are attractive to others," I said.

"Maybe that's part of it. But I think it's more like projection."

Michael's coffee cup was empty again, and I quietly refilled it without interrupting him. He went on, slowly, as if weighing every word. "I don't enjoy discrediting my daughter's family by marriage, even though they haven't acted like family."

I thought it was time to help him along. "What exactly happened?"

"Betsy tells me they constantly tried to get money from Harry. Not small loans, either. You may not know that Richard lost his job recently. He wanted his father to be his venture capitalist."

"He expected Harry to finance him in a new business?" Even Denise hadn't seemed aware of this turn of events.

"Yes, Richard and his wife constantly badgered him. They tried to make him feel guilty about remarrying. And the daughter was just as relentless."

"I thought she was doing well in real estate sales." I'd heard all about Sheila's wonderful career from Denise.

"But not well enough to help her boyfriend buy the jazz club where he works."

It looked like they all viewed Harry as a cash machine. I wondered whether Betsy had wanted anything special for herself. They'd certainly spent a bit on remodeling the house, but that might have been Harry's idea.

Michael again anticipated my thought. "Betsy loved him, and all she wanted from him was a family."

"Suspicion of suicide is bad enough," I said, "but now that they're talking of murder, what will happen?"

"The police are probing in all directions. If they had anything concrete to go on, something would've happened by now."

"As long as we're being frank with each other, Michael, I have to tell you I did hear suicide mentioned. But as soon as I knew about the baby, I figured they were wrong; he had everything to live for."

Michael's expression changed, a strange look that I couldn't read. He said nothing, so I went on. "And you? Do you think it was suicide?"

"I don't know."

This answer surprised me, for Michael had just told me how much Betsy wanted the baby. I wondered if Harry Stokes had reacted differently to the news.

"I guess I should tell you: when my daughter's pregnancy was confirmed, Harry wanted her to have an abortion."

"An abortion! But you just told me how much she wanted children."

"Yes, she did and she still does. On the other hand, Harry's family is grown. He has grandchildren. So, he said he was past that stage in life; he didn't want to start all over again with a baby that would be mistaken for another grandchild.

Michael's eyes seemed to ask something of me, but I couldn't decipher his meaning. He paused and then spoke in a rushed voice, as though he wanted to get the words out as quickly as possible.

"I may as well be frank with you. They argued constantly about it from the time they knew about her pregnancy until his death a couple of weeks later."

Chapter 12.

I stared at Michael. So much for my psychological insights. "I thought Harry would be happy about the baby. Some older men would be proud to have a pregnant young wife."

"Perhaps, but he should have thought of the possibility before he married Betsy. It's a mistake to marry out of your generation."

Was he sending me a message or was my imagination misinterpreting his words? I reverted to the original subject.

"You said you're unsure about suicide. Does that mean you think murder is a real possibility?"

"I don't know."

He had surprised me again. I'd expected a vehement denial because suspicion of murder would be far worse for Betsy than whispers of suicide. "Was there any evidence?"

"Ruthie, the police haven't told us much. We know there was no suicide note. And the autopsy showed no sign of poison."

"Then aside from Harry's doctor, what's the problem?"

He turned away and studied my sunlit peach-and-turquoise kitchen without expression. After a moment, he seemed to reach a decision. "I guess I'd better tell you everything."

I waited for him to continue, too unnerved to comment. The only sound in the room was the air conditioner as it cut in automatically. Without knowing why, I felt chilled enough to want to raise the thermostat temperature.

"As you know, Harry's death was sudden and completely unexpected. The reason I wanted to know what medications he was taking—there was a box of 12 Hour Food-Fed, your store's brand of pseudoephedrine, by his bedside table."

"Surely he knew enough to avoid decongestants with his heart condition."

"They weren't his tablets; they were Betsy's."

I stifled my exclamation of surprise. No wonder she was suspected of contributing to her husband's death. Food-Fed is an OTC, a drug sold over the counter. No prescription needed. It's effective in clearing cold symptoms and making it easier to breathe at night. Many people with clogged nasal passages take the longer-acting twelve-hour tablets at bedtime so they can get a good night's rest. I knew that Food-Fed, taken with Harry Stokes's other prescriptions, was contraindicated because it would act as a cardiac stimulant. Betsy also would have known because of the warning on the package.

Michael's tone was even, but I could see how troubled he was. "Betsy had the cold symptoms first, and she was taking the Food-Fed. When Harry began experiencing the same discomfort, he must have taken her pills."

"Are you sure that's what happened?"

"We don't really know. But Betsy says she only used four tablets. Then she started worrying about the baby and checked with her gynecologist. He okayed the Food-Fed, but meanwhile she felt better and decided not to use them anymore."

"How many were left in the box you found on Harry's night table?"

"One."

I winced. Each box contains twelve tablets, which meant Harry must have used seven of them. For anyone else, Food-Fed would be a good choice to relieve nasal congestion. With Harry's physical problems, it was not. His doctor should have advised him never to use that kind of stimulant, especially since the dosage of his blood pressure medication had just been increased. No wonder the police were asking so many questions. But why did they examine Denise's record if a nonprescription drug contributed to Harry's death? It didn't make sense.

"The whole thing is unbelievable," I said.

"And frightening, too. Betsy insists that she had no idea Harry was taking her decongestant. She tells me she put the unused pills in the medicine cabinet and forgot all about them."

"But when Harry's cold symptoms began, was she the one who suggested the Food-Fed?"

Michael looked uncomfortable. I thought I'd hit upon the truth, but I was wrong. He started to speak, hesitated, and then began again. "They weren't on good terms during the last weeks of Harry's life. In fact, they were barely speaking to each other except to argue about the baby."

"She must feel terrible now."

"It's been a nightmare." He met my eyes and held them. "I know I sound like a father defending his daughter, but she loved him very much. And, Ruthie, he loved her. Betsy was convinced he'd change his mind about the baby."

"This entire situation is so strange, Michael. No one could be sure that the decongestant would kill him."

"That's what I told the police, but Detective Moreway says if it hadn't worked, the murderer might have tried something else."

"Murderer!" My voice sounded hoarse to me. "Then they really believe Harry was murdered?"

"That's one of the possibilities they're investigating. There's no way to prove his heart gave out because he took or was given a cold remedy that overstimulated his heart. And there's no way to prove Betsy didn't give him her pills. On the other hand, we can't show he died of natural causes, and the uncertainty makes everything worse for Betsy."

"What are you doing to help her?"

"I haven't been able to accomplish anything. It's unbearably frustrating to wait for others to act."

"And I didn't help when I refused to give you the printout."

He smiled at me. "I wasn't trying to make you feel guilty. In any event, the printout didn't change Detective Moreway's suspicions."

"I think," I said slowly, "it's all right to reveal that Harry wasn't taking anything you don't already know about."

"That's what I was afraid of."

"Afraid of?" I echoed.

Michael gathered our dirty cups and saucers and carried them to the countertop. "You see, my daughter's trained me to an active role in kitchen duties."

I got up and stood beside him. "I'll just pop everything in the dishwasher."

"Good. I didn't really relish washing dishes."

"Okay, Michael," I said, getting back to the pertinent conversation. "Level with me."

He seemed surprised at my firm tone, but answered readily enough. "I've been hoping Harry's doctor had prescribed something that would explain his death. No, that's not right either. What I want is a discovery that will vindicate Betsy."

"And implicate someone else?"

"If that's what it takes."

"What if the 'someone else' is innocent? After all, I'm one possible 'someone else.'"

Michael took me gently by the shoulders. "No one in his right mind would suspect you."

"Now, we're going in circles. If I agreed, I wouldn't have asked for your advice."

He had the grace to look embarrassed. "Ruthie, there's no evidence against *anyone*. Anyone at all. I know this police investigation is difficult for you and Denise. Maybe for Harry's children, too. But it's far worse for Betsy. We're talking about a newly bereaved young woman, a pregnant widow."

I sympathized with Michael and his daughter, but I couldn't suppress the thought that she might be guilty after all. Fathers are not the best judges of a daughter's moral fiber and, if Betsy were a murderer, her father would probably deny it even after justice was done.

"This is all supposition," I said. "No matter how much we talk about natural death versus suicide versus murder, we'll probably never know the truth."

"I must find out whether Harry was murdered."

"How?"

"I haven't worked out the details yet," Michael said. "But I know I never wanted anything as much as I want this grandchild. And I'm not going to let Betsy suffer like this through her pregnancy."

Anxiety for Michael made me shudder. "It could be dangerous for you."

"That's precisely the point. If I can seem to know too much, the murderer will come after me."

Chapter 13.

After Michael left, I could only replay our conversation. I'd expected him to calm my fears; instead, my turmoil had increased. I changed into a bathing suit, grabbed my Mace canister, and went out to the pool, hoping some exercise would help.

As I opened the patio doors and stepped outside, a blast of hot air made me gasp. I reached for one of the beach towels hanging on the patio and carefully placed it and the Mace on the stone bench beside the pool. Some of my friends tease me about the Mace, but since Bob's death left me alone, I worry about someone climbing the back fence into the pool area.

The pebbled surface around the pool, supposedly cooler than cement, was too hot to walk on in bare feet. I ran quickly to the deep end, jumped in, and did thirty laps before I had to rest. Thirty laps sounds terrific, but for my pool size, it's not much. I once read about a 78-year-old man who swam his age in laps every day, but I've never reached my own magic number without long breaks in between.

Although the pool water must have been about 100 degrees, it revived me and I sat on the patio, more relaxed than I'd felt in days. Suddenly, my fears seemed exaggerated. The sudden death of someone in his sixties with diabetes and high blood pressure was more likely to be a natural occurrence than suicide or murder. It wasn't surprising that the police thought in terms of the latter, but I refused to go along with their scenario.

I decided it was foolish to worry about Michael. There was no murderer, so the trap he intended to set would never spring. I understood Michael's anxiety for his daughter, but it was misplaced. Nothing would happen. Police inquiries would go nowhere, and eventually Michael would return to Tucson.

That certainty stopped me for a moment. *If you want to daydream*, I told myself, *go ahead. But know that it's only a pleasant way to pass a sultry summer afternoon.*

After a time, the heat drove me into the water again, and I passed the rest of my day off alternating between pool and patio. I spent most of the evening in front of the TV, my usual Saturday night pattern since losing

Bob. Sunday was a workday for me, so I turned in early, with only a brief thought about Harry Stokes's death before I fell asleep.

At the pharmacy, Sunday was usually a quiet day. Unlike the rest of the store, it was only open from nine to five. I worked alone, but was able to catch up on paperwork and transmit a huge order to the wholesaler for delivery the next day. Mondays were always busy, and anything I could do in advance would make life easier.

I didn't see any of the people involved in the Stokes case, if you could call it a case. Denise was working the late shift in the coffee shop, and none of Harry's relatives showed up demanding confidential prescription records.

I still felt relaxed when I opened up on Monday. My first customer shattered this calm mood. The problem was her insurance plan, which wouldn't accept her card when I ran it through our machine. I sympathized with the customer until I became the target of her anger. She was a thin woman who didn't look like she had the lung power to explode the way she did.

"What do you mean it won't take?" she screamed. "I've got a sick child out in the car, and I need his antibiotic."

"Out in the car?" I couldn't contain myself. "Surely not in this heat."

"You mind your own business and give me the medicine."

I explained again that I couldn't put it on her insurance plan, but she could pay for it now and try to collect from the insurance company later. While I tried to straighten out this problem, more customers arrived at the window. Both phones rang continually, and I tried to keep sane until ten o'clock when my technician would arrive. One thing about Joey, he never wasted a moment when he came in or waited for me to tell him what to do.

The next time I glanced at the clock, it was close to eleven. Where was Joey anyhow? He was hardly ever late, and I really needed him today.

By noon, I was convinced he'd caught the summer cold that was going around, but why hadn't he phoned in? I called Greg Blackstone, the store manager, on the intercom.

"I think Joey's sick," I told him. "Can you get me one of your people to fill in?"

He promised some help and eventually sent a young woman from the cosmetic counter. She'd never worked in the pharmacy before but quickly took over the phones and the cash register, which allowed me to concentrate on filling prescriptions. From time to time, I wondered about Joey and whether I should call him at home. *Better not*, I told myself. *He's responsible enough to call in as soon as he can.*

Just before one o'clock, Denise appeared at the pharmacy. "Where's Joey? I wanted to talk to him before I clock in."

"I don't know where he is."

"Did he hear anything new from his brother-in-law?"

"I couldn't tell you," I said impatiently. "He hasn't shown up today."

"Okay, don't get upset. I recognize busy people when I see them." She turned to leave.

I assured Denise I'd see her later at the coffee shop and returned to the prescription backlog, without time to spare her another thought. When she reappeared a few minutes later, I tried to hide my annoyance. I noticed she was dabbing at her eyes with a tissue.

"Ruthie, let me into the pharmacy. Hurry!"

I unlocked the door for her and had just time enough to guess that her allergies must be acting up before she grabbed both my arms. She was sobbing now, the tears running unchecked and ruining her makeup.

"I telephoned," she said. "They told me... Oh God, I can't believe it... they told me he's dead."

Without conscious thought, I knew who she meant, but the words wouldn't form. I waited.

"He drowned in that damn fountain. How could it happen? Little children drown in swimming pools here. It's in the papers all the time." Her sobs were louder now. "But Joey was twenty years old. He couldn't drown like that!"

Even though I'd known, her words hit me so forcibly that I doubled over, holding onto the counter for support. I cried along with Denise, the customers at the window forgotten.

"When?" I whispered.

"Sometime during the night. The maintenance crew found him this morning." She choked up and couldn't continue.

I pictured that beautiful fountain at the Franklin's condominium complex. How would Joey's parents ever be able to look at it again? I thought of Joey—so eager to learn, so avid to be a part of everything.

But I couldn't grieve for him now; I had to help all the people who needed their medications. Many of them were in pain, too. I had to pull myself together.

Motioning to the relief technician, who was staring at us helplessly, I asked her to take Denise to the employees' lunchroom. Once again, I called Greg Blackstone on the intercom.

He appeared almost at once, breathing as if he had run all the way. "Ruth, what's happening here? At least three customers reported something wrong in the pharmacy."

I explained briefly, trying not to break down again. His shocked expression showed he hadn't yet heard. "Okay, I'll try to get someone here. When is the other pharmacist due in?"

He turned to the waiting customers. "Folks, the pharmacist isn't feeling well. There'll be a slight delay in filling your prescriptions, so why don't you do your grocery shopping meanwhile. We'll take care of you as quickly as we can."

Some of the customers murmured sympathetically and handed their prescriptions to the store manager, but I heard one grumble that he couldn't wait. "You go and take a break," Greg told me. "I'll stay here and run a holding operation."

Legally, a licensed pharmacist must be in the pharmacy at all times, but I didn't argue with the manager. I grabbed my handbag and ran to the customer restrooms, not wanting to see other Food Go people in the lunchroom. By now, Denise would have told everyone. I couldn't bear to hear them discuss Joey's death over and over, adding details even if they had no real information.

The shocking news and Denise's abrupt way of relaying it made me feel as if I'd been kicked in the head. And every minute my head ached more as I thought of poor Joey. I splashed cold water on my face and reached into my handbag for aspirins. After a while, I forced myself to return to the pharmacy.

"I phoned your staff pharmacist. He'll be here as soon as possible," Greg Blackstone said when I let myself into the pharmacy. He had a telephone receiver in each hand and looked more harried than usual.

"Thanks. Why don't I take one of those calls?"

He handed the nearest receiver to me, and I took down a prescription for Erythromycin, an antibiotic. "Look, I don't want you giving out drugs while you're in this shocked condition. You take the phone calls and I'll be the people person."

I was trying to regain some semblance of my professional self and at least hold on until Tim could arrive, but my mind wasn't functioning clearly and I realized Greg was right.

Tim Barnard came rushing into the pharmacy shortly afterwards. "What's wrong?" he asked. "You said we had an emergency."

"I didn't want to break it over the telephone," Greg told him. "We've had terrible news—it's Joey Franklin."

"Joey? Is the kid sick?"

"No, Tim. He's dead."

Tim looked as shocked as I felt. Maybe I should have suggested that Greg Blackstone call in a relief pharmacist from another Food Go, one who didn't know Joey. But I hadn't been thinking clearly.

"What happened?" Tim asked. "Was it a traffic accident?"

"We don't have any details, only that he was drowned."

"Those kids are always rafting on old tires. I told Joey a couple of times it's too dangerous."

"Don't jump to conclusions," Greg said quietly. "The main question is whether you feel up to taking over here. I want to send Ruth home."

"I feel terrible, too, but Ruthie is—was a lot closer to Joey. I can manage okay." He turned to me. "Can you drive yourself home? Maybe the store could spare someone to drive you."

I assured both Tim and Greg that I could get home by myself. "But I'm worried about Denise," I told the store manager.

"That's my next job. I figured the pharmacy's needs had a higher priority than the coffee shop's."

I wanted nothing more than to go home alone, crank up the air-conditioning, and burrow into the bedclothes. But I couldn't desert Denise. "If you can spare her, I'll take Denise to my house."

"Go ahead." Greg looked toward Tim Barnard, who was already at the window, talking to customers. "It looks like the pharmacy is under control."

He took my arm and walked me to the employees' lunchroom where we found Denise, crouched over one of the lunch tables, her head buried in her hands. Two other Food Go employees, a woman from the bakery and one of the meat cutters, were trying to calm her.

Greg Blackstone went to the water fountain, filled a paper cup, and walked over to Denise. "Here, drink this," he said in an authoritative voice he seldom used.

She took the cup and stared at it. I thought she must be in shock, but when Greg repeated, "Drink this," she drained the cup.

"Give her something stronger when you get her to your house," Greg said. "If she still seems dazed, call a doctor."

As disturbed as Denise was, his decisive manner produced results, and I realized, not for the first time, why he was an effective manager. Denise got up and, with one of us gripping each arm, walked out of the store.

At her first exposure to the bright sunlight, she pulled her arms away from our supporting grip and covered her eyes. "Her pupils must be dilated enough to be painful," I told Greg Blackstone. We led Denise to my car and Greg helped her in, even buckling her seat belt for her. Then he helped me into the driver's seat, asking again if I were sure I could manage. I tied my own seat belt and reassured Greg, but I was finding it hard to believe I could drive the five miles to my home.

Take it slowly and concentrate, I told myself. There won't be much traffic. You can do it. I pulled out of my parking space carefully, knowing Greg was watching, and headed for the shopping strip exit.

The drive home seemed interminable. I tried to turn my thoughts away from Joey and my friend, who sat beside me whimpering. I couldn't understand why Denise had reacted so strongly. Unbidden, the idea leaped into my mind that feelings of guilt motivated her response. Quickly suppressing that thought, I avoided questioning Denise. I really didn't want to know the answer.

When I pulled into my driveway, I wondered how I'd get Denise into the house without help. She was in the same trancelike state, but she followed me inside without resistance.

It was cooler in the house, but not cool enough and I started toward the thermostat to lower it. "I'm cold," Denise mumbled before I moved more than a few feet.

Shock, I thought. I led her to my guest bedroom, opened the sofa bed, and helped her off with her shoes. "I'll be right back with some blankets," I told her.

The blankets were packed away for the summer, and it took me a few minutes to collect two of them. I put one over Denise and told her to let me know if she was still cold. "I'm going to make you some hot tea."

"Thanks," she said.

I figured it was an encouraging sign; she wasn't completely out of it. My own shock was mitigated by the need to help Denise, and I quickly heated two cups of tea in the microwave. While the microwave was going, I found some pillows and propped her up so she could drink the tea. I added lots of sugar to both cups, put them on a tray and returned to her.

She sipped the tea, and I saw some color return to her face. "Thanks," she repeated.

"Should I try to get you to a doctor?"

"No, I'm doing better. I'm not so cold anymore."

I observed her closely. She wasn't shivering, which I took as a good sign. Her eyes seemed more focused, although she kept them closed most of the time. But they were probably still hurting; she'd been crying for the better part of an hour.

"It was the way they told me. I was so unprepared. Well, I guess you're always unprepared." She picked up the cup of tea again. I noticed she'd moved the covers back a little, so she must be warmer. The perspiration was running down my own face, and I mopped at it with a tissue, wishing I could adjust the thermostat.

"Some stranger answered the phone, not one of the Franklins. I thought it must be one of Joey's friends, and I asked to speak to him." Denise started to cry again. I silently passed along the box of tissues I was using.

"There was no warning, no attempt to lead up to bad news. 'Joey's dead,' he said. 'That's a stupid joke to play on me,' I yelled. But I think I knew. 'It's no joke, lady. I wish it was,' he said. And that was that."

I wondered if it was better to keep her from reliving that telephone call, but I realized she had to talk. "How did you get the details?" I asked quietly.

"I don't know. He must have told me."

"His parents were so proud of him," I said. The lump in my throat seemed to thicken, but I controlled the tears that threatened. It would only make everything worse for Denise.

I thought about Joey again. When Bob died, my world had fallen apart. But in its own way, this death was as devastating. A young man of twenty, and one that I would have been delighted to have as a son. I felt bad when Harry Stokes died, but he was really only a casual acquaintance. Joey and I had worked side by side for nearly two years.

Something flashed into my mind when I thought of Harry Stokes. Was it too much of a coincidence for Joey to die so soon after Harry? I pushed the thought away, convinced there was no connection. Harry's death, as far as anyone had been able to prove, resulted from natural causes. From what Denise had discovered, Joey's death was a terrible accident.

The connection between Harry Stokes and Joey was too tenuous. *Now, if Michael had been the victim of a drowning accident,* I told myself, *that would be suspicious.* Michael had been setting himself up to trap a nonexistent killer. His death would have made murder a plausible assumption.

Chapter 14.

Eventually Denise fell asleep. She didn't hear the phone when Greg Blackstone called to see how we were doing, and she didn't awaken when Tim Barnard called to ask about a prescription that had come in earlier that day. I looked in on her from time to time, but mostly I sat in my kitchen drinking iced coffee and thinking about Joey.

My mind kept returning to thoughts of murder even though I'd already decided there was no rational basis to connect the deaths of Joey and Harry. One possibility kept nagging at me. If Joey's brother-in-law had been right, if Denise... No, I refused to consider it.

But I couldn't drive away the suspicion. I would have to think it through. Frank Moreway had questioned Denise and then me about the possibility that she got something from the pharmacy and used it to kill Harry. He knew Denise and I were friends and surmised that gave her access to the pharmacy.

I had no doubts about my own actions: Denise couldn't have gotten any such drugs from me, either overtly or covertly.

Now I had to consider Joey. Was it possible he had allowed Denise into the pharmacy? Again, I was certain this had never happened when I was on duty. And Tim never let anyone into the pharmacy, not even the store manager.

We did have a few relief pharmacists who filled in for days off and vacations. But it hardly seemed likely they'd even know Denise, let alone invite her into the pharmacy.

And my thoughts careened head on into the same wall they'd hit days ago. We had nothing for a murderer to use. The times when someone could buy arsenic to kill mice or weeds or whatever were long past—if they'd ever existed outside of fiction.

I suddenly felt ashamed of my suspicions, but I knew I had to work them through before facing Detective Moreway's inevitable questions. A detective who refused to accept Harry Stokes's passing as a natural occurrence would be relentless in probing his own brother-in-law's death.

Now I'd come full circle. After convincing myself the two deaths were unconnected, why was I so sure Frank Moreway would take the opposite view?

I went to the refrigerator and got more ice. The house was hotter than I liked it, but I was afraid to cool it down. Denise was still asleep, wrapped in the blanket, and I figured she would have kicked it off if she were too warm.

No one else telephoned. Twice I started to call Michael but hung up after pushing two or three numbers. I considered phoning one of my friends just for someone to talk to, but there was no one else I wanted to share my worries with.

At about 5:30 in the afternoon, Denise came into the kitchen. Her eyes looked swollen, underlined by dark smudges where her makeup had run. With her uncombed hair and creased dress, she seemed very different from the impeccably turned-out woman I was used to seeing.

"I'm sorry, Ruthie. It must be awful for you to have me on your hands right now."

"Stop apologizing. You would do the same for me."

"That's just the point. You were even closer to Joey." Her voice shook when she said his name, and I was afraid of another crying jag. She clenched her teeth and went on. "I should have been helping you over the shock, not the other way around."

"You did help me. You gave me someone else to think about."

Denise shook her head but was quiet. I offered her a sweater if she still felt chilled, but she insisted she was better.

"What can I fix for dinner?"

She started to protest. "Denise, the best thing we can do is spend some time together and talk it out. Otherwise, we'll each eat alone and be even more miserable."

"Then let me pitch in. I make a great salad."

"Okay, just take whatever you need from the fridge. I've got oil, vinegar, and cans of tuna and anchovies in the cabinet by the window."

I took out the gray placemats; they matched my mood. On second thought, I added napkins with a peach and gray floral design. No reason to make dinner any gloomier than I expected it to be.

While Denise tore apart a head of lettuce she found in the crisper, I arranged slices of cheese and rye bread on a platter. Then I started a fresh pot of decaffeinated coffee. We took our time over the light meal, not saying much at first.

Denise suddenly put down her fork. "We've been avoiding the subject. We need to talk."

"There isn't much to say."

"Yes, there is. I was awake for a while before I came out to find you. Going over everything." She stared across the table as if wanting to pull words from me.

I obliged. "Everything?"

"Let me ask you, Ruthie. Haven't you noticed how strange it all is?"

There was no way I could tell her about my suspicions since she was their object. So I played dumb. "What do you mean?"

"Two deaths in less than two weeks."

"People die every day. Every hour. Even more often."

"These two people knew each other."

I let my eyebrows show skepticism. "It's the shock, Denise. You're still not thinking clearly."

"I'm thinking very clearly. First Harry, then Joey. It can't be a coincidence."

It was hard to contradict Denise when I'd considered the same possibility. But I felt it necessary to dispel her morbid ideas. "They only knew each other casually."

"You'd be surprised. They talked a lot."

"Joey and Harry Stokes?"

"Why do you think Joey wanted to tag along with us to the funeral?" She stopped for a moment, and I knew she was thinking we'd be going to another funeral now.

"I don't know. I figured he wanted to pay his respects because he knew Harry as a customer."

"Ruthie, twenty-year-old boys don't worry about paying their respects."

"Well, maybe he was curious."

"Curious about what?"

"He probably overheard us talking about Harry and Betsy and that whole situation."

Denise helped herself to more salad and reached for the pepper, covering the entire surface of the salad. I'd seen people in the southwest eat this way since my childhood in Tucson but had never picked up the habit. She seemed to be marking time while deciding how much to tell me.

"A few times when Joey was on the late shift, he'd have lunch in the coffee shop first."

"Well, that's nothing unusual. Many Food Go people do that."

"Yeah, but why would he have lunch with Harry Stokes?"

I thought over this piece of news. What did the two of them have in common? It was an unlikely combination. "You tell me, Denise."

"Joey was trying to get money from him."

"What?"

"You don't have to shout at me. I'm not trying to say anything bad about Joey—not blackmail or anything like that."

I forced myself to laugh. "You do have a vivid imagination."

She was angry now. "You always say that. But I've been right before, and I know what I'm talking about. Maybe I don't have much education, but I..."

"Please, Denise, I wasn't trying to put you down."

"I'm sorry. It's hard to make sense of what's happening, but I need to tell someone. You know how small the coffee shop is, so I couldn't help overhearing them."

"You don't have to apologize. Just tell me, and I promise not to interrupt again."

Denise, when she got down to it, gave the details concisely. She had forgotten about those lunches until this afternoon, but she was sure they represented a connection between the two deaths. "Joey wanted a loan to help with his college expenses. He said it was too hard to work so many hours at Food Go and get good enough grades for medical school."

"Yes, he did talk about medical school all the time."

"His family lives comfortably, but Joey's always had to help out with tuition and his other expenses."

"I know that. But why would he expect Harry Stokes to finance him?"

"It was supposed to be a business deal. They would have a lawyer draw up a note and Joey would return the money with interest to Harry or his heirs."

"Why didn't he just get student loans the usual way?" I asked.

"That was Harry's question, too. Joey said student loans are more difficult to get nowadays."

"And how did Harry react to all this?"

"It was hard to tell, Ruthie. I heard him turn Joey down, but they continued to lunch together and discuss it."

"You and I must be the only ones who didn't want money from Harry Stokes," I said.

Denise's summer tan suddenly turned an unbecoming reddish brown. I looked at her in surprise. "You, too?"

Her eyes wouldn't meet mine but were fixed on the last bits of lettuce and diced tomatoes on her plate. "I wanted to become a dental hygienist," she mumbled.

"You never told me."

"I got the idea from Joey. I mean, I had the dream for a long time but no money to make it real."

I didn't know what to say. All I could do was thank God that Detective Moreway didn't know about this aspect of Denise and Harry's relationship. He was digging for information, suspecting an affair, but here was another strong motive for revenge.

"Maybe it sounds tacky when I put it this way. But I kept thinking that I'd known Harry for years. If he was going to help anyone through school, it should be me."

"Yes, but why should he? He had his own family to think of." I nearly mentioned the expected baby but stopped myself in time.

"It would have been strictly business. I made the same offer as Joey— a legal note, interest, the works."

I sighed. It seemed a lot of people were playing Harry like a private Arizona lottery. "Why not take an equity loan on your house and use that money?"

"There's no way I could make the extra payments."

"Then how could you have paid Harry back?"

"The arrangement would have been to start paying back as soon as I finished and got a good job," Denise said stiffly.

It sounded unrealistic to me. As far as I knew, dental hygienists didn't make all that much. "What did Harry say?"

"He told me everyone was after his money."

"I guess they were."

"His children never paid back. They got money from him for years. Called it a loan each time, until he finally got wise and refused to give them more."

"Denise, did you and Joey approach him recently?"

"You don't have to be so tactful. Why not ask me straight out if it was before or after he married Betsy?"

"Okay, was it before or after?"

"It was two months ago." She refilled our coffee cups, acting as hostess in my kitchen, or maybe she was just used to refilling coffee cups.

I found it hard to meet her eyes. "Does anyone else know all this?"

"Maybe."

"What does that mean?"

"I think he told Betsy. She started avoiding me around that time."

In this, my sympathies were with Betsy, but I couldn't say so. I wondered whether hearing about her from Michael's point of view had influenced me. "I don't know what to say, Denise. If Detective Moreway questions you again, it might be better to tell him the truth before he hears it from someone else."

She looked even more upset. "That's what worries me."

"Let's sit in the living room and talk. And if you're warm enough now, I'd like to lower the thermostat."

Denise started to clear the table, but I insisted it was more important for us to talk without interruption. So she followed me out of the kitchen and waited while I detoured to the thermostat, lowering it to 68 degrees.

"Give me your opinion, Ruthie."

"I just did."

"No, not about telling Detective Moreway. About what's been happening."

I tried to keep my voice as calm as possible. "We can't have an intelligent opinion until we know more about how Joey happened to drown in that fountain. There may be a simple explanation."

"Let's check the local news tonight. Maybe they'll have something about it."

So we talked of other things until it was time for the news. I turned on the TV, and we watched world and national news, sports, the weather. I really didn't expect to hear about Joey, but it was the first local item. And the police were investigating his death as a suspected murder.

Chapter 15.

Neither of us said a word. We sat and watched the screen, mesmerized by the police spokeswoman who explained that it was impossible for an adult to fall into the fountain accidentally and drown. We saw a closeup of the familiar fountain and watched her point to the height of the curved edging.

"What if he were sitting on the edge and fell in?" the reporter asked.

"You can't sit on the edge. Look at the design." A well-known Scottsdale architect now appeared on screen to explain the fountain was deliberately scalloped, to keep children from hopping onto the rim and walking it.

"Could he have hit his head and fallen in?" the reporter asked.

"The matter is still under investigation," the police spokeswoman said stiffly. "We have no further information at this time."

Hints about caring for your pets in the monsoon season came on next, and I turned off the set. We stared at each other. Although it was Denise who had talked of murder, she now seemed more surprised than I was.

"It can't be," she said over and over.

"It didn't sound like they have much to go on. Maybe that was just TV hype."

"The Franklins live in a gated complex." She went on as if I hadn't said anything. "You saw the security guard; no one could get by him and kill Joey."

"We don't know what really happened."

"Yes," Denise said. "It's too soon."

We were both silent for a time, until Denise asked me to run her back to Food Go so she could pick up her car, assuring me she would have no trouble driving. She was over the first shock.

I did as she asked. We had very little to say to each other as we rode to the store. At the parking lot, I let her out alongside her car, said good night, and hurried away. All my suspicions had returned, and I wondered if trying to get money from Harry Stokes was what Denise had avoided telling me that day the police questioned her. In any case, I could find no rational explanation for her contradictory behavior.

Trying not to think about Joey or Denise, I drove slowly home to find Michael's silver- and-gray Lexus in my driveway. He was leaning against the side of the car, his hair silvery in the moonlight. I was so glad to see him that I had to concentrate very hard on parking my own car.

"I was afraid one of your neighbors would suspect me of burglary and call the police."

"Are burglars driving Lexuses these days?"

He grinned at me. "I'm glad you're okay; I was worried about you."

We walked into the house together and settled in the living room after Michael refused my offer of coffee. "How is your daughter?" I asked him.

"About what you'd expect until today's news hit."

"Yes. I figured you were here because of Joey." I tried to keep my voice steady, but it caught as I said his name.

Michael took my hand and held it for a moment. "It must be very tough for you. Have you... had you worked together long?"

"Nearly two years. He was a good kid." Despite what Denise had revealed about his attempt to borrow money from Harry Stokes, I still believed this. *Then why are you so hard on Denise for the same thing*, I asked myself. *She's a mature woman; she should know better*, I thought.

Continuing to argue with myself, knowing that I'd never had her money worries, I missed what Michael was saying. "I'm sorry. My mind keeps wandering."

"That's understandable." He was so comfortable to be with, not judgmental like some of my friends. "I asked if the police contacted you."

"No," I said and paused. "Not yet." I told Michael how few details we had and how Denise had broken down at the news.

"I whizzed back to Tucson yesterday and stayed overnight. Picked up my mail, checked that my job was still waiting. Other errands like that. This afternoon, when I heard the news on my car radio, the name didn't mean anything. But then I picked up a Phoenix station, and they said he worked in a Food Go pharmacy."

Michael reached for my hand again. "Ruthie, they're calling it murder."

"Do you think there's a connection?"

He didn't have to ask the kind of connection I meant. "Remember what I said the other day, that I want the murderer to think I know too much. Maybe Joey really did know too much."

I wondered if Michael also suspected Denise, but assured myself he didn't know enough about her. "Who do you think...? My voice trailed off.

"Either Richard Stokes or Sheila's boyfriend."

To hide my relief at not hearing Denise's name, I jumped up and turned toward the kitchen. "I need something cold to drink. What about you?"

He said he preferred water, so I filled two glasses with ice cubes and filtered water and brought them back into the living room. Michael was standing by the white baby grand piano, looking at the two framed photographs I keep there—my wedding picture and another of Bob and me on our silver anniversary.

"You both look very happy," he said and moved back to his seat on the sofa.

I sipped the cold water, but was silent, thinking about the contrast between his own marriage that had ended in divorce and mine that had ended in death. I could see Bob so clearly, sitting in this room, an audience of one, eyes closed and expression absorbed, as I played his favorite piano concertos. For all the piano lessons I'd had as a child and teenager, I was only mildly competent. But Bob always enjoyed my playing and wouldn't allow me to criticize myself.

I forced my thoughts to the present. "Why do you suspect those two?"

"They're the most likely candidates. I told you they were after Harry's money."

"Yes, but murder..."

"Someone did it. I thought so all along, but now with Joey's death, I'm convinced."

"Michael, remember that course in logic we both took when we needed credit in the humanities? Just because one event follows another, it doesn't mean they're connected." I tried to concentrate on the Latin expression for faulty causation, but couldn't think of it.

"This is not a case of 'post hoc, ergo propter hoc,'" Michael said without a pause.

"After this, therefore because of this," I translated. "That's what I meant."

"Can you think of any other reason for Joey's murder?"

"Robbery."

"I know we have muggings in Arizona just like anywhere else. But I really doubt this was one."

"You may be right. I'd guess most muggers would avoid an area with guarded gates."

"Was he involved with drugs? I mean illegal ones?" He saw my look of astonishment and backtracked. "That was a stupid question. You'd never have kept him as your technician."

"That's probably the first thing that comes into people's minds these days when a young person is murdered," I said. "When I think of his parents, I'm just overwhelmed."

"Did he know Harry?"

I hesitated. No way was I going to destroy Joey's reputation by repeating secondhand information. "Harry was often in the store. We all knew him."

"Only as a customer? Are you sure?"

Now I was angry. "You sound like Detective Moreway. There was no reason for anyone to kill Joey."

"Don't get so upset. I wasn't implying anything wrong."

"You weren't implying anything wrong," I echoed. "First you suggest drugs, then... then I don't know what else." My voice faded. *Take care*, I warned myself; *you're on dangerous ground.*

"Okay, let's look at it from another direction. Is there something Joey could have learned that placed him in jeopardy?"

"I don't know," I answered truthfully.

"Whatever the reason for Joey's death, I'm more determined than ever to trap the killer."

"Why put yourself in danger? If the two deaths are connected, you don't have to worry about the accusations against your daughter; she's out of the picture now."

"What do you mean?"

"Even Detective Moreway wouldn't believe a pregnant woman could sneak out in the middle of the night and drag a strong young man into that fountain."

Michael rose from the sofa and paced across my living room. "Unfortunately, Betsy has no alibi, since I was in Tucson last night."

And that means you have no alibi either. The thought leaped into my mind without conscious deliberation. I wondered how I could suspect someone who had once been so important in my life.

Chapter 16.

After Michael left, I went over our conversation. He'd made it clear he was only trying to anticipate how the police could interpret the situation. He still seemed to believe he had to find the murderer to remove suspicion from his daughter–*and from Denise and himself,* I thought. *And from me, too.*

If I had these crazy ideas, what did other people think? Michael was right; we couldn't fully trust anyone until we learned who was responsible for the two deaths.

Now I realized I no longer doubted. If Joey had been murdered, he was not a random victim. Somehow he'd acquired dangerous information, and it had to be about Harry Stokes. Nothing else made sense.

I turned this over. What could Joey have learned? The police had investigated the prescription records of Denise and of everyone in the Stokes family. *But not his father-in-law's,* that persistent inner voice said. Michael's pharmacy record would be down in Tucson.

Be logical, I cautioned myself. *If they're in Tucson, Joey wouldn't have had access either. And besides, Michael had probably been in Tucson until his daughter needed him, which wasn't until after Harry's death.*

But what could Joey have found out that no one else knew? He was a technician, not a pharmacist. Well, that didn't mean anything. A good technician, and he'd been one, could pick up quite a bit. After two years at Food Go, someone with Joey's inquiring mind probably knew more about the practical aspects of pharmacy than many a senior-year pharmacy student. But I still couldn't see how Joey would be the only one with knowledge dangerous to the killer.

Exhausted though I was, I tried looking at the problem from different angles as I got ready for bed. Because I desperately wanted to believe in the people I cared about, I assumed Denise, Michael, and Betsy were all innocent. *Yes,* I admitted to myself. *I care about Michael and about his daughter, too.* And Denise was my best friend. That left Richard Stokes, his wife Nancy, Sheila Stokes, and Sheila's boyfriend—whatever his name was. What could any of them have done that Joey discovered? I finally dozed off with the same questions spinning in my mind.

Although I had the night shift on Tuesday and could sleep late, I awoke at six, drenched in perspiration despite the air-conditioning and the ceiling fan over my bed. Even on the hottest nights, I liked to sleep under a light cotton sheet. This morning, one end of the sheet was twisted round and round as if I'd transferred my confused thoughts to the bedclothes.

It was during breakfast that I decided Joey's parents might know something. I couldn't just barge in and ask questions, but as Joey's manager, I should visit them. It would be easier to ask Denise to come along, but I decided to make this condolence call alone.

Here was another thought to be examined. Was I mistrustful enough of Denise to exclude her? *No*, I assured myself; *I just didn't want distractions.*

At eleven, I passed the fountain and pulled up to the guarded gate at the Franklin's complex. The guard took my name and telephoned for clearance before he raised the electronic arm and let me drive through.

Following his instructions, I made two right turns and pulled up in front of a two-story pink condo with roof tiles of a paler pink. Just beyond its wrought-iron fence, also pink, I could see Joey's motorcycle in the side yard. A Ford pickup and a late-model sedan were visible in the carport, but no other cars were parked outside. It looked like I was the only visitor, and that's what I'd been hoping for.

Ordinarily, I'd have wanted other visitors to help with the small talk. I dreaded this condolence visit to Joey's family, but it could be my only chance for some insight into why Joey was killed. And I needed to remove suspicion of the people I cared about.

A heavy-set woman in a sleeveless housedress opened the door. I'd met Joey's parents several times. Although this woman looked familiar, I knew she wasn't Mrs. Franklin.

"I'm Ruth Morris, the pharmacy manager at the Food Go where Joey worked," I told her.

"I know," she said. "Don't you remember me? I get all my medicine from you."

I looked at her again, trying to put a name to the face, but it wouldn't come. For a minute, I was tempted to try a social lie, but I was never good at lying. "I'd like to see Mrs. Franklin," I said.

The flabby face took on a hurt expression. "I'm surprised you don't recognize me. Dr. Ellis calls in all my medicines to you." We stood in the entry hall while I waited for her to ask me in, but she hadn't finished with her grievances. "Because of Joey, I always drove all the way to Food Go.

Five other drug stores. That's how many I pass every time. Well," she added plaintively, "I guess I won't bother any more."

Just what I needed, I thought, as she moved away from the door and I followed without invitation. The pink slate tiles of the entry met deep-pile mauve carpeting in the living room, and I wondered if Joey's mother liked pink or if a previous owner had chosen the exterior and interior colors. I tried to recall how long the Franklins had lived here, focusing on irrelevancies to avoid thinking of what I must do.

Both of Joey's parents were seated on a rattan sofa covered in a floral chintz, the style of furniture I associated with Key West and Ernest Hemingway. Mrs. Franklin's eyes were red-rimmed. She clutched a handful of tissues and, as I walked into the room, she was reaching for another one from a box on her rattan and glass coffee table. Her expression seemed unfocused, and it didn't change when she saw me. I wondered what drugs they had put her on.

"Ruth Morris," I said into the silence, and shook hands with her and the dour-looking man beside her. "I wanted to tell you how sorry we all are. Joey was the best pharmacy technician we ever had at Food Go," I added so she could place me.

"Oh, yes. Food Go. Ruthie. Joey always called you Ruthie." The words were choppy and seemed to be forced out of a mouth that trembled when she said her son's name.

"I used to tell him to have more respect," Mr. Franklin said. "Who ever heard of calling your boss 'Ruthie'? I always call mine 'Mr. Williams.'"

Although they were my contemporaries, the Franklins seemed older, which was surprising for a couple whose son had barely passed his teens. On the other hand, their daughter, Detective Moreway's wife, was eight or nine years Joey's senior. I looked around the room, surprised not to see her.

After an awkward pause, they introduced my ex-customer as their next-door neighbor, which explained why there were no extra cars parked outside. I wondered whether I could outstay her and, if so, how I could get the Franklins to talk.

The neighbor offered to make coffee for everyone and bustled off to the kitchen. I could hear her rattling cabinet doors and thought uncharitably about this opportunity for her to examine the contents of every closet.

I waited, very self-conscious, not sure what to say. The Franklins waited, too. When the silence became unbearable, I remembered how people had seemed afraid to talk to me about Bob after his death. Yet, I would have preferred reminiscences to stilted conversation and awkward pauses.

"Joey had such a quick mind," I said. "He absorbed information so fast I sometimes thought he knew more about pharmacy than some of our new graduates."

"He wanted to be a doctor," Mrs. Franklin said and reached for her tissues again.

"I told him to become a druggist," her husband said. "We don't have money for medical school. All those years, and studying so hard he wouldn't be able to earn."

"Joey could've done it." Mrs. Franklin turned to face her husband. "You know he could. Once he made up his mind..."

"Well, he liked working in the drugstore. So, I told him to become a druggist."

"He would've been a wonderful doctor."

They seemed to be repeating an old argument, one that saddened me immeasurably. I had to speak. "Joey was good with people. He really cared about them."

"He was always like that," Mrs. Franklin told me. "If I had a headache, if his sister had a cold, he'd wait on us hand and foot. Hand and foot. Most boys aren't any use around a sickroom. But Joey felt real bad if someone was hurting."

"Druggists help people, too." Mr. Franklin wasn't giving up.

"Do you like your coffee black?" The neighbor asked me. Despite her hurt feelings or maybe because of them, she'd taken pains to arrange slices on a tray—something that looked like banana bread interleaved with a darker bread I didn't recognize. She handed cups and saucers to each of us and poured the coffee.

The coffee occupied us for a few minutes, making it unnecessary to search for topics of conversation. I concentrated on my slice of banana bread, noticing the pink rose pattern of the dishes. The neighbor spoke first. "I have to get home, Edna. I'll look in again later to see if you need anything."

She made no move to leave but sighed as she helped herself to a second piece of the darker bread. "I keep thinking he's going to walk in and tease me to bake zucchini bread for him."

"Yes," Mrs. Franklin said. "Joey always loved your zucchini bread."

I had taken the last forkful from my plate, and it suddenly thickened into a lump that I couldn't swallow. How awful for the Franklins if I choked up here. I made an effort, aided by a quick sip of coffee, and managed to swallow after all. "Did you bake this?" I gestured toward the tray. "It's delicious."

She looked directly at me for the first time since I'd disappointed her at the door and, at that moment, her name burst into my mind. Stephenson, Alice Stephenson.

"Don't you like my zucchini bread? You only had the banana bread."

"Thanks, Mrs. Stephenson." I reached for another slice, thinking of the old joke about the mother who bought her son two shirts for his birthday. He put one on right away only to hear her ask, "What's the matter? You didn't like the other one?"

My mind was playing tricks on me again because I didn't know how to bring the conversation around to the things I wanted to know. And it would be even more difficult with the neighbor listening.

"Alice has been so good to us," Mrs. Franklin said. "I don't know what we'd do without her."

"No more than anyone else would do for you," the neighbor mumbled. She walked over to the sofa, hugged Joey's mother and father, gave me a brief wave, and left the house.

One obstacle out of the way, I thought. As I considered my next move, Mr. Franklin returned to our previous conversation. "Joey would've been a wonderful druggist."

"He knew just how to talk to our customers," I said. "They all liked him."

"That's because he cared about them," Mrs. Franklin said.

We were going in circles and I was afraid we'd say the same things over and over no matter how long I stayed. And what would I do if their daughter walked in with Frank Moreway? I was trying so hard to figure out how to get information from them that I nearly missed it.

"Really cared about people. Not like most boys his age," Mrs. Franklin was saying. "That man who died a couple of weeks ago. You wouldn't believe how upset Joey was."

"Do you mean Harry Stokes?"

"Yes, that's the one."

"And Joey was upset?"

"He said the man came into Food Go all the time. Of course, it bothered Joey. I told you he cared..."In my impatience, I cut off the flow of words. "I know he was a caring person, Mrs. Franklin. But how could you tell he was so upset? What did he say? What did he do?"

I was afraid the Franklins would wonder at the strange turn in the conversation, but they didn't seem to find anything odd in my questions.

"He wasn't eating right," Mrs. Franklin said.

"And he talked about the old guy all the time," her husband, who wasn't much younger than Harry, added.

I tried to think back to the day we'd learned of Harry's death. Joey had seemed excited. Then he'd surprised me by wanting to go to the funeral. Had he been upset or worried? I'd been aware of Denise's mood, but I didn't remember consciously observing Joey. After I left the Franklins and had more time to think, I would try to reconstruct those two weeks.

"What did he say about Harry Stokes?" I asked, and held my breath. They'd surely find this question strange.

"He talked about the summer colds or flu or whatever that was going around," Mrs. Franklin said. "When I think how I used to worry about Joey being exposed to all those sick people, and now..." Her voice trailed off and she reached for another tissue.

"This old guy had the flu, but he came in for his other medicine." Mr. Franklin made a croaking sound that could have been a laugh and patted his own bald head. "You probably know he was taking something to grow hair."

So much for patient confidentiality, I thought, but nodded and quietly waited for Joey's father to continue.

"Someone on television or in the movies, I could see it. But to spend so much money every month. And that other stuff, too." Mr. Franklin flushed and stopped talking.

"I never like to take anything unless I have to," his wife added. "Joey said the more you take, the more careful you have to be. Some drugs are okay by themselves, he told me, but they can kill you if you mix them." She looked squarely at me for the first time. "You probably know all that."

"That's why we keep patient records in the computer. Patient profiles we call them." Now or never, I thought, and just as I told myself I had to be more direct to find out anything, the telephone rang. Ordinarily, I might have used the ringing phone as an opportunity to say goodbye and escape, but I was determined to learn more from Joey's parents.

Mrs. Franklin excused herself and went into another room to take the call. She was one of those people who pitched her voice higher for the telephone than for in-person conversation. "You don't have to rush over here again. Just rest up." She paused. "Okay, if you want to." She paused again. "No, we haven't been alone. Alice came by. And now Joey's boss is here." Another pause. "Okay, I'll tell Dad."

As I'd guessed from Mrs. Franklin's end of the conversation, Joey's sister would be here soon. "She's expecting again," her mother explained to me. "I don't want her to get overtired."

Now I knew I would only have Joey's parents to myself for a short time. I had to find out as much as I could and as quickly as possible. But what could they tell me that the police, including their son-in-law, hadn't already asked? On the other hand, I had no way of knowing if the police saw a connection between Harry Stokes's death and Joey's. Maybe they weren't asking the right questions. The trouble was I didn't know the right questions either.

I'd learned that Joey was concerned about drug interactions, but so was Detective Moreway when he interviewed me. And Joey's interest might have been awakened by his brother-in-law, rather than the reverse. This family certainly revealed professional information to each other. I wondered whether Joey's sister knew of her husband's suspicions about me and what her reaction had been to the news that I was at her parents' home.

"So you don't really know why Joey wasn't eating right?" I raised my voice at the end to make it a question rather than a statement.

"He cared about people. That's why."

"Yes, of course." I tried it differently. "Did his appetite change all at once or did it happen gradually?"

This time, Mrs. Franklin did look puzzled, but she answered nonetheless. "No, it didn't happen right away. He talked to us about the man that died just the way he told us about a lot of the customers. We liked to know what Joey was doing at work. And he made it interesting."

I said nothing although I blamed myself for not emphasizing confidentiality to Joey. Had he talked about the customers to all his friends, too?

Mrs. Franklin still seemed uncertain, but now I suspected it was because she was trying to recall when Joey's eating habits had changed. I waited, hoping I could get out of there before their daughter arrived. Not knowing how long it would take her to drive over, I shifted uneasily at the sound of every passing car.

"Don't you remember?" Mr. Franklin asked his wife. "It was the day of that funeral. You thought he was just late for work when he rushed off without dinner."

"That's right. He didn't eat anything before work, so I had hamburgers waiting for him. On those nice onion buns. The ones we buy at Food Go. Joey loved burgers on onion buns, but he said he was tired and went right to bed."

Maybe he was *tired and I'm being foolish*, I thought, remembering how exhausted I'd felt the night of the funeral. But I was quite a bit older than Joey, and talking to Michael had drained me emotionally.

"Joey said you never had children, so you probably don't know how much a teenage boy eats. Well, he wasn't a teenager anymore." Mrs. Franklin pressed a tissue to her face and was silent, while I sat there hating myself for doing this to her. "But he still ate like one. I used to make all his favorites. He was always rushing off to school or work. And I wanted to be sure he had regular meals."

Mrs. Franklin seemed so obsessed with Joey's eating habits, I couldn't tell how much of her concern was justified. "And he was oversleeping and cutting classes," she suddenly added.

"That's because he was walking around all night," her husband told her.

"You never said."

"I didn't want to worry you. A couple of nights, when I got up for the bathroom, Joey was sitting here with the television. Just the picture—no sound."

"Why? Did he say why?"

"He said he was thinking. Listen, I figured it was that girl he broke up with last winter. You know, he wanted to keep seeing her and she wanted to date other boys. Joey was miserable."

"But he got over that," Mrs. Franklin protested.

"They act like they're over it, but it's just an act. I know he wanted to get back with her again. She wouldn't have him."

"She wouldn't have Joey!" His mother was outraged.

"What's the use of talking about that now?" Mr. Franklin rose suddenly and left the room.

I listened to their conversation and suddenly remembered that I, too, had thought Joey wasn't sleeping enough. But I couldn't sort out the details now. It was time for me to leave and I got up, trying to rationalize my terrible intrusion because I was there to help find Joey's murderer. *And to clear my friends and myself from suspicion*, I said silently.

Before I could take Mrs. Franklin's hand, say goodbye, and go, I heard the front door open and then sharp steps on the entry tile. Joey's sister, whom I'd met once or twice at Food Go, rushed into the room and hugged her mother. Despite my dismay at not getting away before her arrival, I felt some relief that she was alone.

"And you're Ruthie," she said. "It's so nice of you to come."

"I was just leaving."

"No, please don't. It does my folks good to have people to talk to."

So I sat down again, thankful that at least her husband, the police detective, hadn't accompanied her. Carolyn Moreway took the armchair across from mine. "Joey really loved working for you," she said.

I half expected to hear that he should have been a druggist, but Mr. Franklin had not reappeared. "And I was telling your parents he was the best pharmacy tech we ever had."

Carolyn sighed. "You'd think people would be safe in a gated complex. Guard service twenty-four hours a day. And it costs my folks plenty for that."

"Did Frank find out anything?"

"They're still trying to trace all Joey's movements on Sunday. Frank is questioning someone right now."

"I told Frank he was with his friends all day."

"Yes, Mom. Frank talked to all of them. They were hanging out at Bill Reed's, mostly playing volleyball in the swimming pool."

"Did the Reeds invite him for dinner?"

I was trying not to seem too interested in the conversation between mother and daughter, but I wondered again why Mrs. Franklin was so worried about food. Maybe she was right and I didn't appreciate how normal her concerns were because I'd never had children.

"Bill's parents weren't home. The boys sent out for pizza, but Joey only had one slice. He was meeting someone later for dinner at the Sizzler."

"A girl?"

"That's what Bill Reed and Joey's other friends figured. But it was a man. They didn't remember his name, only that Joey was talking about a customer who died. And this was the wife's father. Frank thinks he was the last person to see Joey alive, and he's questioning the man right now."

Chapter 17.

I must have gasped, for both women turned toward me. "Sorry," I said and stood up again. "I just realized I'm late for an appointment." With a minimal exchange of polite words, I left Joey's mother and sister. His father still hadn't reemerged, so I asked them to say goodbye for me.

Hot as it was outside, I was glad to get back into my car. The key was unsteady in my hands, but I put it into the ignition on the third try and slowly made my way out of the complex, shuddering as I passed the fountain. I turned into the first side street and pulled over, letting the motor run so the air-conditioning would work.

It couldn't be Michael, I told myself. *He had no reason to kill them.* But I remembered his eyes when he told me he wanted Betsy's happiness and the grandchild-to-be more than anything else in the world. And Michael had kept after me about the prescription record. Was it to find out how much I knew? Could he have been pursuing the same information from Joey? Maybe he was after Tim Barnard, too. I would have to warn Tim.

Warn people against Michael? I couldn't believe the turn my thoughts had taken. But I knew I must tell Tim discreetly to be careful about revealing professional information to anyone except the police.

This was getting worse all the time. First the police had suspected Denise and, I admitted to myself, at one time I had wondered about her. Now it was Michael.

I gripped the steering wheel but left the car in neutral. *Frank Moreway questioned you, too*, I told myself. *Why are you so disturbed about Michael?*

But this was different. Michael had invited Joey out to dinner on the eve of his murder, and I couldn't think of any legitimate reason. As far as I knew, they had never even spoken to each other, although Michael might have noticed Joey at the funeral and at Food Go.

This could all be part of Michael's scheme to bring the murderer into the open by appearing to know too much. But that didn't make sense either, because it meant he'd suspected Joey, which was absurd.

It's only absurd now that someone murdered Joey, I thought. I considered what Denise had told me about Joey's attempts to borrow money from Harry Stokes. What if Joey had been responsible for Harry's death and Michael had found out? Then, in a rage, Michael had drowned Joey.

Michael didn't have rages. He had a very even disposition. *Thirty years ago*, that inner voice said. *How do you know what kind of a man he is today*? And there was something else; something Michael had said was bothering me, and I was too upset to figure out what it was.

I forced my hands to a normal position on the steering wheel and moved into drive. Avoiding the heavy traffic on Scottsdale Road, I kept to side streets as much as possible and drove slowly home. My answering machine showed calls from Denise and Tim. Nothing from Michael.

Denise, I knew would be at Food Go at noon, so I didn't bother returning her call. Her message asked me to see her at the coffee shop before I clocked in, so I'd have to leave for work soon.

I called Tim at the store. He wanted to be sure I would be there on time, because he had an appointment. After reassuring him, I decided to get to Food Go early enough to eat lunch at the coffee shop and see what Denise wanted. Then I'd still have a chance to sound out Tim and try to urge caution. As for Michael, I wouldn't be able to contact him today, but maybe he'd come into Food Go later. If he had nothing to hide, he might even tell me about his dinner with Joey.

Now I remembered what was bothering me. Michael and I had already talked about Joey's death, but he'd never mentioned the dinner. I tried to think of a reason for Michael's reticence, but each idea that came to mind was more sinister than the one before.

When I arrived at Food Go, the coffee shop was still busy with the lunchtime crowd, but it was past one o'clock and I knew they'd be thinning out soon. Denise brought over my usual tuna salad and iced tea but couldn't stop to talk. I dawdled over the food, waiting for her to have some free time.

After a while, the tables occupied by twenty- and thirty-somethings from nearby office buildings emptied out. Four senior citizens at the nearest table to mine stayed on, but they had finished eating and only wanted their coffee cups refilled from time to time.

Denise walked over with the iced-tea pitcher. "I'm glad you're here. We need to talk." She stood with her back to the seniors and mouthed the words. I could barely hear her.

I shrugged toward the other table. "They're too busy talking to each other to pay attention to us."

"Maybe."

"What's happening, Denise?"

"I'm worried."

That didn't surprise me. Who wouldn't be worried after a co-worker was found murdered, especially since Denise also lived next door to another possible victim?

She remained at my table with the pitcher in her hand, continuing after a quick glance to be sure her manager wasn't in earshot. "I have no alibi."

"You're being silly now. How could anyone who lives alone be expected to have one for the middle of the night? I don't have an alibi either, but it never occurred to me that I'd need one."

"Well, it should have occurred to you," she told me firmly. "All of us will be questioned. When I think what they put me through when Harry Stokes died... And this will be worse because this time there's no longer any doubt. A killer is walking around."

"You're melodramatic again."

"And you're an ostrich with your head in the sand."

I didn't want to quarrel with Denise. And far from worrying about her whereabouts Sunday night and early Monday morning, I could think only of Michael and the contradiction between where he'd said he was and where he really had been.

"Let's not argue, Denise. I just can't understand why you seem to want the police to suspect you."

"I don't *want* it. In fact, I'm terrified." Her voice was still so low that I had to strain to hear the words. "But it's not the police I'm afraid of. What if the killer thinks I saw something Sunday night?"

"At the Stokes's? What does that have to do with Joey?"

"They always hang around there. All of them—Richard and Nancy, Sheila and her boyfriend—I see them come and go."

"What about Betsy?" I hesitated and added, "And her father?"

"Oh, I didn't remember telling you about her father. Did you know he's that good-looking older guy we saw with her at the toy store?" Her disappointment showed as she put the question to me.

"Yes, I know. Someone else told me," I said, without elaboration.

"He was gone all weekend. As soon as he wasn't around to protect Betsy, the others started arriving. First Richard and Nancy. I can always recognize that leased Mercedes of his. Typical of Scottsdale—the guy has no job and he drives a sixty-thousand dollar car."

I was impatient with her. "What are you trying to tell me?"

"Just that they were arguing with Betsy. She came running across the two driveways to my door to get away from them. And they followed her. It was terrible."

Two young mothers, each with a toddler by the hand, entered the coffee shop, and Denise had to seat them and take their orders. I thought about her story. Although she hadn't had a chance to give me the details, I doubted whether any confrontation of Denise with the Stokes family related to Joey's death. Now, if one of their family had been killed that night...

I looked at my watch. Time to check in, especially since I wanted to talk to Tim Barnard before he left for the day. As I retrieved my time card and put it into the machine, I wondered whether Denise had seen Michael at all that weekend. Was she really sure he had been away the entire time? Even so, it wouldn't be much of an alibi. If he'd returned quietly from Tucson on Sunday night, he could have easily avoided his daughter's home and the people who knew him.

And then there was Denise. Was she telling me about all the people she'd observed over the weekend to give the impression that she'd been home all the time? Was it a ploy to defuse suspicion about her own whereabouts? More confused than ever about the murders, I unlocked the door to the pharmacy and walked in.

"You're early," Tim said. It was the way he usually greeted me when I was on the late shift.

"You said you had an appointment."

"Yes, well. I do have to leave on time today."

The pharmacy seemed quiet for the moment. Better say what I had to before the telephones started ringing and people lined up at the window for their prescriptions. Still, I hesitated because it was never easy to talk to Tim, and I knew he'd take offense now.

"People have been asking me what we filled for Harry Stokes."

"What kind of people?"

"You know, relatives, the police." I tried for humor. "Sometimes it seems like everyone and his sister."

"Well, you're the manager here. Why would they talk to me?"

It was a sore point with Tim that I was the pharmacy manager; he had made it clear on more than one occasion that he felt he could do a better job. He wanted to set the schedules, and he wanted to attend store meetings with managers from the other departments. That was one reason why I never asked him to change shifts with me unless I absolutely had to.

"I'm not here all the time."

"Well, neither am I."

"Tim, this is important. I think Joey was killed because of something he found out about Harry Stokes, and I don't want you to put yourself in danger."

"I can take care of myself."

Despite his brave words, I could see that Tim's jaw was clenched. I wanted to make sure he'd be careful. "Joey probably didn't feel threatened either," I told him. "Listen, Tim, I'm trying to figure out what's happening, but meanwhile I felt I had to warn you."

"And the police? Why haven't they warned me?"

"I don't think they've made the connection."

"If the police aren't worried, then neither am I," Tim said.

I turned away to help a middle-aged man at the window. He handed me a prescription for 30 Mevacor, informing me that it was to lower his cholesterol.

"This cholesterol business is nonsense," he said. "My doctor is overreacting."

I wondered what his count was but decided I had no right to ask. He was still complaining as I turned to the computer. Both phones had started ringing, but Tim had already removed his white jacket and was studiously ignoring them. I answered the phones and returned to my customer, who was tapping on the window to get my attention.

"How much will it be?"

I looked it up and gave him the price–"Ninety dollars for thirty tablets."

"No way am I going to pay that much when my doctor just wants me to try them. Give me ten."

"Ten will be thirty-five dollars."

"That's outrageous. Can't you do simple division? Ten should be only thirty dollars."

"Sir, a larger size of most things you buy costs less per unit. The Mevacor is three dollars a tablet when you get thirty, but it works out to three-fifty a tablet when you buy ten."

"Highway robbery," he muttered. "Give me back that prescription!"

As I went to help several more people who'd appeared at the window, I was thankful he wasn't shouting his displeasure. Too bad he hadn't showed up during Tim's shift. I thought about how much I missed Joey, who would have remarked cheerfully that it takes all kinds, a comment I'd heard so often from him. Joey was gone, though, and now I'd antagonized Denise, too.

But Denise didn't stay angry for long. During her break, she came by just long enough to invite me to her house after work. "Some people who want to talk to you will be there," she said. She wouldn't give me more information, and I was too busy to press her. So at nine o'clock, I went through my closing procedure, clocked out, and drove to her house.

I suppose I expected to see Michael and his daughter there, but instead found Denise's other neighbors, Verna and Raymond Branden, the ones I'd met at the funeral. Verna Branden was a thin, white-haired woman who seemed to take as much interest in the Stokes family as Denise did. She explained to me that she and Raymond were block-watch captains. I could see they were serious about the job.

"So much crime today, you know." She peered expectantly at me, and paused until I nodded in agreement. "We had two burglaries in the neighborhood so far this summer. Of course, both houses are owned by winter residents, so no one was around at the time. Why, if Raymond and I hadn't noticed the broken windows, I don't know what would have happened." This time she looked toward her husband for confirmation.

"The police won't catch them anyways," her husband said, lips curving down in a sour expression.

"Burglary is bad enough, but to have a murder on the block... And that Richard Stokes had the nerve to tell me to my face that we're in the block watch because we're nosy." She waited for a reaction from Denise and me, but we said nothing. "Everyone knows we're supposed to check up on all the houses in this cul-de-sac. I don't see other people volunteering to do the job."

"Don't worry, Verna. The rest of us are glad to know you're looking after things," Denise said. "Especially when we have to be at work."

"Everyone thinks when you're retired you have nothing else to do. I can tell you Raymond and I have plenty to do with our time. We're just trying to help our neighbors."

I thought of my own neighbors. Jean and Jerry Flint live just west of me in a territorial-style home. Despite the high block fences separating houses on our street, occasionally we walk outside to our mailboxes at the same time and exchange a few friendly words.

To the east, Gloria and Ken Woodman have added Spanish archways and bay windows, giving their house a distinctive look. The Woodmans aren't home much, but we wave to each other whenever we happen to pull into or out of our driveways simultaneously.

Unlike Denise's neighbors, only Jean and Jerry walk around our street—and that's because they own an Irish setter. I don't often meet them because they walk Justinian in the early mornings and late evenings. Yet, even though we rarely socialize—both couples are busy with grown children and grandchildren—I know I can count on the Flints and Woodmans in an emergency. They were so good to me during Bob's last illness.

"They don't appreciate our help," Raymond was saying when I tuned back in. "They're all so afraid we'll gossip about them. I don't know what they have to hide."

Denise brought over dishes of chocolate-swirl ice cream with peanut butter cookies on the side. It was now past ten P.M., and I accepted mine gratefully, remembering that I hadn't had anything to eat since lunch.

"I know you don't want to get involved with the police," Denise said to the Brandens, "but I'd like Ruthie's opinion about what happened Sunday night."

The Brandens looked at each other in surprise. I wondered why they thought Denise had asked all of us to her house at this late hour, if not to hear their story. They seemed in no hurry to speak; yet I could tell that Verna was bursting with her news.

"Denise said she told you about the big argument over there." Verna nodded toward the Stokes house.

"Just that Betsy rushed over here to get away from the others."

"Who knows what might have happened if Raymond and I weren't passing by? We kept them from following her into this house. I tell you the way Richard Stokes looked, I wouldn't be surprised if he tried to strangle me."

"I was right there, wasn't I?" Raymond asked.

"It was like a lynch mob," she continued without acknowledging him. "I never had much use for Betsy, marrying poor Harry for what she could get out of him. But four against one isn't right. She didn't know what to do, but I said, 'Just go on over to Denise's, and I'll take care of these bullies.'"

"Did they hurt her?"

"Not when they saw those big flashlights Raymond and I carry. I held mine up like a club. And they stood back, I can tell you."

"What did they say?"

"They didn't dare say another word. The son and his wife got into their Mercedes, and the daughter got on her boyfriend's motorcycle, and that was that."

"Betsy should have called the police," Raymond said.

"I wanted to call them, but she wouldn't let me," Denise told him. Their comments lacked the intensity I would have expected, which convinced me they had all been exchanged before.

"What were they arguing about?"

"She didn't want to talk," Denise said. "But Verna and Raymond heard enough to guess the rest."

"We were just making our rounds. About ten-thirty, it was. Most people are watching TV at that hour or asleep. We never hear conversations. And hardly ever arguments."

"These houses were well built," Raymond added.

I suspected if the Brandens missed anything that went on in the neighborhood, it wasn't because of negligence on their part. But unwilling to put ideas into their heads, I couldn't ask what I most wanted to know. Did they see Michael on Sunday night? Instead, I listened to their story.

"They must have been in the front room because we could hear them shouting. I mean, we couldn't tell who it was or what was happening—it could have been a burglary in progress—so we went up the front walk to make sure everyone was okay."

Denise interrupted. "Did you know that Betsy's pregnant?"

I acknowledged that I knew and waited to hear more. Verna appeared to be gathering her strength by cramming one cookie after another into her mouth. I wondered how she stayed so thin.

"It was awful," she said. "Richard kept asking whose baby she's carrying. 'You killed Dad so he wouldn't find out the truth about the baby. I know it's not his.

"'You're crazy,' Betsy shrieked at him.

"'If you think you can get away with this, you're the one who's crazy. We'll see to it that you don't get a cent of Dad's money.'"

"That was the first we heard about a baby," Raymond said.

Verna picked up the story again. "I was afraid for Betsy. Richard was accusing her of murder. But he sounded so violent, I'm sure he's really the one who did it."

"Anyways, I rang the doorbell," Raymond said, "but no one answered at first. Then Betsy called out to wait a minute. It all happened so fast; the daughter-in-law opened the door a crack, and Betsy pushed her aside and ran. That's when Verna and me kept them from following her."

"Where was her father when all that was going on?" I asked. Although Denise had already told me he wasn't around, I wanted to see if the Brandens would corroborate her information. I waited, wondering what they would say about Michael, afraid that Betsy had said something to implicate him in Joey's death.

"I asked her that first thing," Verna said. "She told me he had a dinner appointment and he never came back."

"Dinner appointment," Denise said. "I thought he was in Tucson."

"Maybe the dinner date was in Tucson," I said, but this new discrepancy between Michael's account of his whereabouts and Betsy's words when she was at her most distraught hit me like a blow to the head.

Chapter 18.

On my drive home that night, I decided to see Michael as soon as possible. I would not rely on Betsy's neighbors for information but would approach him directly. Clearly, her neighbors suspected Richard Stokes, and I wanted to believe they were right. But although I hated to doubt Michael, I had to know why he lied about Sunday evening. Since I was on the late shift the next day, I decided to call him in the morning.

I didn't sleep well again that night. Vivid pictures of the Stokes family chasing Betsy flashed through my mind. Even though I knew her pregnancy wasn't that far advanced, I saw her as big as if she were at term, clumsily running from the others. Only in my dream, Michael was one of those chasing her.

Immediately after breakfast I telephoned. Betsy answered. "It's Ruth Morris," I said. "Is your Dad there?"

"He went out for a while, but I expect him back soon. Would you like to come over and wait for him?"

I was surprised at the invitation but decided to take advantage of it. Maybe Betsy didn't want to be alone in the house after the events of Sunday night.

When I pulled into their driveway, I saw Michael's silver-and-gray Lexus through the open garage door. This encounter would be awkward no matter what happened, but I was relieved not to have to make small talk with Betsy.

He opened the door for me and I followed him into the entryway, past the two white fluted columns, and stepped down into Betsy's living room, all sharp angles in black and white. It looked different today without the crowd who'd filled the house after the funeral.

I had dressed carefully in an off-white pleated skirt with a black and white blouse. If my blouse had been a geometric rather than a paisley print, I'd have fit right into the room. Michael, wearing white tennis shorts and a navy pullover, looked bright and cheerful, if a bit flushed. I wondered if he'd been out playing tennis despite the heat.

He led me to one of the black wrought iron armchairs, which I would have mistaken for outdoor furniture if not for their overstuffed white cushions. I sat down but Michael remained standing. He had picked up a small terra cotta coyote from the lamp table next to me and was turning it round and round in his hands. I thought of the stone coyotes circling the fountain where Joey died. But this was foolish. I knew well enough that coyotes were popular in southwestern art now and, in fact, could see them pictured in an oil painting over the sofa and an alabaster sculpture in front of the windows. It was probably Betsy's way, or an interior decorator's way, of reconciling the southwestern exterior of the house and its sleek, ultramodern indoor look. Watching Michael, I wondered if he also associated the coyotes with Joey's death.

"Are you off today or are you on nights?" he asked.

"Nights." One advantage of being with other pharmacists is not having to explain our odd work schedules.

"I'm glad you stopped by, Ruthie."

Realizing this was his polite way of finding out why I wanted to see him, I plunged in. "I'm worried. Betsy's neighbors told me what happened here Sunday night, and I think it may be connected with the two deaths."

"I'm sure my daughter appreciates your concern," he said drily, a touch of coldness in his tone.

This was not going as I'd anticipated. "It's you I'm worried about right now, not Betsy," I blurted.

"Let me get this straight. You're worried about me because Harry's children are being nasty to my daughter."

His words did make me sound ridiculous, but I would not be sidetracked. "You know what I mean. Twice now you've said you intend to act as bait to trap the murderer. Have you considered that those accusations by Richard and the others may be smokescreens to hide their own complicity?"

"Yes, and that's exactly what I had in mind when I revved up my campaign."

"But it's dangerous."

"It's more dangerous to have a murderer on the loose."

We had both raised our voices, and Betsy now appeared in the doorway between living and dining rooms. I was surprised to see her in an off-white maternity dress with red and black vertical stripes. Surely she was in the third month at most. But maybe this was her way of announcing the pregnancy to friends, family, and nosy neighbors. I wondered whether Betsy had worn maternity clothes Sunday night, and if that had precipitated the quarrel with Harry's children.

"Will you have some cold juice?" She was carrying two glasses filled with crushed ice and orange juice, and held one out to each of us.

"What about you, hon?" Michael asked her.

"I had some while you were at the tennis courts."

"You may as well join us instead of wondering what we're talking about." Michael's voice had softened as he spoke to his daughter.

She walked over and took the coyote figure out of his hands. "Look at you," she said. "And you keep telling me to be calm."

"I'm not the pregnant one."

"You could have fooled me." She was flippant with her father, but I saw that she was concerned about him, too. I didn't know how frank I should be about Sunday night with Betsy in the room, but after a moment she turned to me.

"My neighbors used to annoy me. I thought they were always prying, so mostly I tried to avoid them. But the other night, I found out how much it means to have good neighbors."

"Denise really is a caring person," I said.

"I know that now."

"You have to admit she can be intrusive at times," Michael added. "She's been over here just about every day."

"When Harry was alive, she only came by when he was home. I used to think she had a crush on him. But I guess I was wrong."

I sipped my orange juice and said nothing. Denise must have been pretty obvious.

"For a while, I suspected her of somehow causing Harry's death. But Sunday night, she was so good to me that I changed my mind. Now after that young man's murder, I don't know what to think. Especially since he worked at Food Go with Denise."

Like carousel rides, suspicion kept spinning round and round. No wonder the police seemed to be baffled. I decided this wasn't the right time to remind Betsy that Joey had worked in *my* department at Food Go.

"What happened Sunday night?" I asked since she had brought up the subject.

Betsy looked embarrassed and I doubted she'd tell me anything. But I was wrong. "It was very unpleasant," she began and hesitated.

"You may as well tell Ruthie the details before she gets a distorted story from someone else," Michael said. He was still standing, twirling the juice glass in his hands now.

"Harry's children have always been cold to me, but they didn't dare confront me while he was alive. They mostly talked to him and ignored me."

Michael's expression had hardened. "I warned you that would happen if you married a man with grown children."

"Yes, Dad. And you didn't want me to marry Tim Barnard before Harry, and you had something against everyone else I ever went out with."

That was interesting news. I wondered whether I should add Tim to my list of suspects, but all the vengeful ex-husbands and boyfriends I'd ever read about went after the woman who threw them over. Sometimes they killed the men who supplanted them, too, but surely Betsy would have been the primary target. *And*, I thought, *he wouldn't have waited all this time, either.*

Michael hadn't answered his daughter. She paused a moment and continued. "After... afterward, Dad was here, so they couldn't say too much. They managed to get some digs in. Mostly Richard. I think the others might have accepted me if he weren't so... so negative."

"You've probably heard gossip that Harry was a rich man," Michael said. "Well, the nosy neighbors were right this time; he was quite successful in real estate and the stock market. But Betsy would have been better off if he hadn't done so well financially. It's the money that keeps his children steamed up."

"They all think I married him for it. Couldn't they recognize his zest for life? Couldn't they see how attractive it made him? Age doesn't change that." Her voice lowered as she tried to control her emotions.

Her words made me think again of Yeats's poem, and I could understand Betsy. It wasn't only Michael whose compelling personality could not be diminished by age.

"Anyhow, Dad had to go to Tucson for the weekend." Did I imagine that she hesitated over the name of the city? I certainly didn't imagine the way she shifted in her chair or the way Michael's eyes would not meet mine.

"I don't know how they found out I was alone here. Maybe they came by and didn't see Dad's car in the driveway."

"Maybe one of your wonderful neighbors called them," Michael said sarcastically.

She ignored the remark. "When they all arrived at the same time, I knew it was prearranged. I guess I was foolish to let them in, but they *are* Harry's family.

"Richard wanted me to divide everything equally between him and Sheila—she's his sister—and sign it all over to them. He said he'd 'let me' keep the house if I did that.

"I reminded them that Harry had changed the beneficiaries of his Living Trust because they were into him for so much money. He told me he was tired of supporting his grown children.

"Richard started shouting at me. It was dreadful..."

"Okay, hon, it's over," Michael said. "They won't bother you while I'm here."

"And what happens later?"

"We get a restraining order if they won't stay away from you."

Betsy turned toward me again. "It got worse. Richard said if I didn't sign over everything, he'd go to the police. He said he had proof that I killed Harry."

"What kind of proof?"

"He said Harry died because I gave him my medicine, and he knew it was deliberate."

"You should know that he accused me, too," I told her.

"And me," Michael said.

"You've told me that before, Dad, but it's not the same. They always suspect the spouse. And all of them—Richard and his wife and Sheila and Scott–each one said they'd testify that Harry and I fought constantly."

I remembered Michael's words about the quarrels over the expected baby, but couldn't bring up that subject unless one of them did first. "Many husbands and wives argue, but that doesn't mean they murder each other," I said.

"Yes, but they did find my Food-Fed on Harry's night table."

"And the police have known that from the beginning," Michael reassured her. It sounded like something he'd told her before. "There's nothing Harry's children can do to harm you."

"The situation has changed now," I said. "If you have an alibi for the time that Joey died..."

"Unless it happened earlier than what they're saying on the news, I don't have one."

"It's a shame your Dad was gone that night," I said. I avoided looking at Michael, but I could hear him move toward the armchair next to mine and heard the chair shift as he sat down.

"You ought to tell her," Betsy said.

"Yes, I was just about to." Michael rose and began to pace again. "The police already know I was here Sunday night. I had dinner with Joey."

"I know. Joey's parents told me."

His eyes held mine as if he were trying to reach beyond them into my thoughts. "So you're here because you suspected me, not because you're concerned about me."

I tried to ignore the cold tone that had returned to his voice. "Wouldn't you be suspicious of me if you discovered I lied to you?"

"No, Ruthie. If I didn't trust you, I'd be probing to find out whether you gave Harry something that wasn't prescribed for him. After all, you were his pharmacist."

"You think I..." My voice trailed in disbelief.

"That's not what I said. *I* trust *you*."

Now I was angry enough to shout at him. "I'm not the one who claimed to be in Tucson when Joey was killed. And all the time you were with him."

"I wasn't with him."

"Make up your mind." I was still shouting.

"It looks like you've made up yours." His voice was icy now.

Betsy intervened. "Calm down both of you. You're acting like children."

"I'm sorry," I said. "I'm not myself today."

"We've all been upset the last few weeks. Let's start over." He moved his chair closer to mine. "Joey and I met at the Sizzler at seven-thirty Sunday night. We were there, eating and talking, for about an hour and a half. Then he went off, and I hurried back to Tucson."

"You drove to Scottsdale and back to Tucson just to have dinner with Joey?" I couldn't keep the skepticism from my voice.

"You really don't trust me," Michael said.

"What would you think if someone told you that? Supposing Richard or Denise kept changing stories?"

"It would depend on what I thought of that person to begin with."

"I see," I said. "I'm supposed to take it on faith because we knew each other all those years ago."

"No," Betsy said. "You don't have to take it on faith. I was there, too."

Chapter 19.

Michael's face paled as he turned to his daughter. "We agreed never to tell anyone."

"What's the use, Dad? When the police check your story, someone will remember seeing me there."

"No one will remember. That's why Joey picked the Sizzler in the first place."

I looked from one to another, not knowing whether this development exonerated both father and daughter or implicated them further. "Would one of you tell me what's going on?"

"First of all," Betsy said, "let me assure you that Dad really did go to Tucson on Saturday night, and he intended to return here late on Monday."

"I had doubts about leaving Betsy alone, but she said she wanted to get used to it gradually."

A spontaneous spasm of pity gripped me and, for the first time, I felt more than superficial identification with Betsy. I remembered the indescribable loneliness of those first weeks and months of widowhood, and I wanted to comfort her. Now I understood that trip to the toy store. If buying a stuffed elephant for the expected baby provided a few moments of solace, Denise and I were wrong to criticize.

"If only I hadn't told him about Joey's call when Dad phoned Sunday morning to see how I was doing," Betsy said.

"Joey called you?"

"He said he had something to tell my father."

"But who suggested dinner? Joey was comfortable talking to people, but I can't see him inviting Michael to dinner at the Sizzler."

"Why not?" Michael asked.

"For one thing, he didn't know you." I said lamely.

Betsy laughed. It was a musical laugh with an underlying sweetness that destroyed once and for all the golddigger image implanted by Denise. I knew I was foolish to judge her by that sound and the brief change in her expression. But I suddenly thought that Betsy could have been my daughter, mine and Michael's. Fighting a sadness that threatened to overwhelm me, I asked as calmly as I could, "Did the two of you know the Franklins socially?"

The musical laugh was softer this time. "That's a tactful way to phrase the question. No, I didn't even realize who he was when he phoned." Her face became serious now. "When he said he was the pharmacy technician, I thought he meant at the hospital down in Tucson. I was terrified that something had happened to Dad."

Ashamed of my suspicions, I decided to listen without comment. Surely, Betsy would not be telling all this to me if she or Michael had anything to do with Joey's death. It seemed absurd to link either of them to the murder. Yet someone had killed Joey and, because of the Stokes connection, the chances were that I knew the person. I could not eliminate Betsy or Michael or Denise from suspicion just because I liked them.

"Joey said he wanted to meet my father at seven-thirty Sunday night, and he repeated that he had something very important to tell Dad and only him."

But Michael was already in Tucson, I thought, and nearly interrupted to ask why Betsy hadn't postponed the dinner appointment until his return. Betsy answered my unspoken question.

"I was afraid to tell Joey that Dad was away, so I said I'd give him the message. Actually, I was going to meet Joey instead."

"Then I called and hit the ceiling when I heard about it."

I was outraged. "Surely Joey wasn't one of your suspects, Michael."

"You have to understand that I didn't really know Joey. At that point, I suspected everyone until I could logically eliminate them."

"Joey was eliminated all right," I said bitterly. "Do we all have to be killed before we get off your list?"

"And what about your list?"

"Truce," I said. "I promise to listen quietly from now on."

Betsy continued. "I refused to break the appointment, so Dad insisted on joining us."

"Tucson is not in outer space," Michael said. "It took less than two hours to race back up here."

"Dad told me he'd meet us at the restaurant and I shouldn't leave before he turned up no matter what happened."

This reminded me of those suspense novels where the murder suspect gets the heroine to rendezvous in some dark, forbidding place without letting anyone else know. But in this case, the person who was killed was the one who arranged the meeting. If Betsy and Michael were telling the truth, I reminded myself. Their story sounded plausible so far; I would try to reserve judgment until I heard it all.

"The truth—and we are telling you the truth, Ruthie—is that I wanted to give them a chance to sit down and start eating before I appeared. Betsy was going to assure him that I'd be there any minute."

"What did Joey say?"

"That's the problem," Michael said. "He dropped hints, but he didn't reveal much. "He told me Detective Moreway was his brother-in-law, so he knew all about the case. That's what he called Harry's death—the case." Betsy's voice was tightly controlled. I guessed from the quick glance she gave her father that she was more concerned about worrying him than breaking down in front of me.

"Joey was only twenty years old," I said. "To him, the drama and mystery overshadowed the human beings whose lives were touched."

"A nice enough young man, but at that age they think everyone over thirty is too old to feel anything," Michael said drily.

"I know you've heard all this already, Dad, but let me tell it to Ruthie from the beginning. Since she knew Joey so much better than we did, maybe she can figure out what was behind it all.

"Joey was in cutoffs and a T-shirt, but so were half the people in the restaurant. We went up to the salad bar first, and he filled his plate with spaghetti and meat sauce. No salad. I tried to make a joke about it, asking didn't his mom ever tell him salads are healthy. He was very polite, but I could see he didn't appreciate the remark.

"Joey said he wanted to talk to Dad first and then his brother-in-law. He explained that if he told everything to Detective Moreway, he was afraid it would become part of the official record. He didn't want to get anyone in trouble, but something was bothering him.

"Then he began a long explanation about how helpful Denise had always been to him. I guessed the two ideas were connected and it was Denise he was afraid of hurting.

"He asked whether I knew that Denise had wanted my husband to finance her education. Actually, I'd never heard that, but I tried to be noncommittal. I was embarrassed to have him think Harry kept things from me."

"Denise told me all about it," I said, figuring there was no longer any reason to keep quiet. It could be important to emphasize that Denise herself had told me, that it was not a secret. I didn't like what I was hearing, and I wanted to balance the scales. "It wasn't the way it sounds. Denise wants to become a dental hygienist; she would have drawn up a promissory note and started paying him back as soon as she got a job."

"She had a job," Michael said in that cold voice that made me so uncomfortable.

"Everyone has dreams," I said. "Maybe Denise had unrealistic ones, but I don't believe she'd ever harm anyone."

"Joey said she was furious when Harry turned her down."

"Are you trying to say that Joey implicated Denise?" I felt queasy, almost as sick as when I first heard from the Franklins about Joey's dinner appointment with Michael. "Let's be logical about it. Why would she kill Joey if he'd already told you what he knew about Harry's death?"

"That's the problem," Michael said. "He didn't reveal what he knew. When I joined them that night, my daughter insisted on hearing what he had to tell me, and Joey wouldn't say another word."

"Did you ask Denise about it?" I turned to Betsy, hoping for a negative response.

"Yes," she said, looking miserable. "The same night. The night Joey was murdered."

"What are you talking about? Denise didn't know anything about his death until Monday afternoon." She couldn't be that good an actress, I thought.

"Don't you see the point we're making?" Michael asked. "We were in the Sizzler with Joey until about nine o'clock. Since Betsy and I'd come in separate cars, she drove home from the restaurant and I rushed right back to Tucson."

"Dad wanted to follow me home to make sure I got there safely. But I told him I'm a big girl now." She smiled at her father.

"And then Harry's children came here that night and started playing their little games with Betsy. When the neighbors, and that includes Denise, tried to help her, it must have been close to eleven."

I didn't want them to know the Brandens had already told me it was ten-thirty. And who knows? That nosy couple could have been outside this house listening to the argument for some time.

"Denise and I talked for a while. I told her everything Joey had said, as tactfully as I could. She seemed embarrassed, but was very kind and walked me back to my front door to make sure the others hadn't returned."

"And that must have been around midnight," Michael said.

I knew what he was implying. According to the TV and newspapers, Joey had been killed between midnight and five-thirty in the morning. Reporters had gotten to the man who'd been on duty at the guard gate that night. In response to their questions, he said he'd walked past the fountain just before his shift began at midnight. "Everything looked the same as always," he said. "The fountain was still lit up—it's on a timer—and I could see it was okay."

During the summer, like many people who had to work outdoors in the Arizona heat, the groundskeepers for the complex began work at five-thirty. Probably the medical examiner could narrow the time, but I no longer had a pipeline to information from Frank Moreway. *Poor Joey*, I thought. *I wonder if those insider details he got from his brother-in-law somehow led to his death.*

The timing didn't eliminate anybody. If Michael really had left for Tucson at nine, he wasn't a suspect, but we had only his word for it unless someone in that city corroborated his story. A painful possibility leaped into my mind. Was Michael living with someone in Tucson? Would she vouch for his arrival there and give him an alibi for the early morning hours that followed? I certainly couldn't ask Michael, but the police probably had already done so.

In the old days, Michael's deep blue eyes had often seemed to penetrate my thoughts. He hadn't lost the knack. "If you're wondering whether anyone saw me in Tucson that night," he said, "no such luck. So if you're still suspicious of me, I have no alibi until the next morning when I popped into the hospital pharmacy where I work. And, of course, that doesn't mean anything. I could have driven there directly from Scottsdale that morning instead of spending the night at my home in Tucson."

I found I was more interested in the fact that he lived alone than in the lack of corroboration for his story. *This won't do*, I told myself, and was about to try to find out the details of Michael's interrogation when the doorbell rang. Betsy went to answer it. I half expected to see Denise follow her into the living room, but the newcomers were Sheila Stokes and her fiancé, Scott Robbins.

Sheila was wearing the "Scotty's Groupie" T-shirt again, but the letters were an iridescent green this time. I wondered if she had a whole wardrobe of shirts proclaiming her status as Scott's girlfriend.

Michael was on his feet, a torrent of angry words beginning to erupt, but Betsy took his arm and quieted him with a look. "Dad, Sheila and Scott came to apologize for Sunday night."

"That's right," Sheila said. "We didn't want you to think we agreed with Richard."

"It took you long enough to decide. Why didn't you support Betsy when she needed you?"

Sheila stood in the middle of the living room, looking awkwardly from Betsy to Michael. No one had invited her to sit down and, considering that she must have grown up in this house, I thought it an unfortunate oversight. "I've known since childhood it's no use reasoning with my brother when he's in that kind of mood."

"And he ignores *me*," Scott added without a trace of embarrassment. He was wearing black bicycle shorts that left nothing to the imagination and a Hard Rock Café T-shirt. "He won't even give me credit for trying to better myself. Why does he think I'm over there in Tempe every day, taking classes at the University?"

"I told you not to take it personally, Scotty," Sheila said. Their exchange reverberated with the echo of countless repetitions. I didn't want to miss the confrontation that was about to take place but felt I had to be polite. As I was the only one still seated, I got up and mumbled something about leaving.

"You sit right down, Ruthie," Michael said loudly. "You're the only one who was invited here."

"Dad!"

"I'm tired of being courteous to people who've treated my daughter shabbily from day one."

Sheila looked as if she'd been slapped. "I didn't mean to be rotten to Betsy. It was the shock of Dad marrying again. And someone so young."

"You're trying to tell me that an older stepmother would have been all right. Don't make me laugh! It's been the money all along."

"He was my father," Sheila said.

"And I'm Betsy's father, and no one is going to hurt her again."

"Now just a minute," Scott said. "Sheila is not out to hurt anyone. She cares about people, not money."

"You think we don't know how much Harry gave his children. A hundred and fifty thousand to each of you over the last few years, and still you and Richard always had your hands out for more."

"Richard thinks we deserve what's in the trust. I'm sure my father didn't want to cut us out. Why, there's more than two million."

"And a good part of that is tied up in this house. You're not going to get your hands on it. Betsy and the baby need a place to live."

"Dad, please." Betsy was tugging Michael's arm, trying to get him away from Sheila and Scott.

Sheila looked as if she were ready to cry. "You heard what Richard said. We wouldn't touch the house. It's the rest of the money."

"Oh, yes, you want my daughter to turn everything but the house over to you."

"That's what Richard wants. I think we should divide it three ways."

"How generous of you," Michael said, and I could hear the sarcasm in his voice.

"Hey, man, there's enough for everyone," Scott said.

"Evidently one hundred and fifty thousand dollars wasn't enough for Sheila or Richard."

"Money goes fast when you're out of a job; my brother has to have enough to tide him over until he finds something else. If Betsy would only be fair, Richard might even be able to start his own business."

"Just like me," Scott said.

"Look, Scott, I remember you from Tucson. You've never kept a job for more than two or three months."

"And I remember you from Tucson, too. I remember how you talked your daughter out of seeing me, and how you objected to Tim and everyone else she ever dated. You always treated her like a princess. No one was good enough for Betsy Loring."

He turned to Sheila. "You know what, I'm going to talk to that cop about him. He probably killed your father so his own daughter would get all the money."

Chapter 20.

Round and round we go, I thought. I wanted badly to step off this merry-go-round, but it was my own fault for getting so involved. I waited to hear Michael's reaction to the accusation, but he said nothing. Instead, he walked past the white fluted columns and into the small entryway. A rush of hot air mingled with the artificially cooled atmosphere of the house. I knew he'd opened the front door even though I couldn't see it from where I'd just reseated myself.

Sheila looked toward the door and then at Scott. He shrugged his shoulders in a gesture of noninvolvement. "I'm sorry," she said to Betsy and the two of them left the house. A moment later, I heard Scott's motorcycle start up. I couldn't tell if he were gunning the engine in defiance or if that was how he always drove, but the noise faded and Michael returned to the living room.

"Well, now you know what it's been like for Betsy," he said to me.

"Everyone's accusing everyone else. That won't catch the murderer."

"The police questioned me for more than three hours yesterday." Michael sighed heavily and sat down again. "If they had evidence against anyone at all, I don't think they would have wasted so much time on me."

"Maybe they don't consider it wasted time." I could have bitten my tongue for saying that.

Michael considered me impassively. "You still don't trust me."

"That's not the point. What happens when they find out you lied?"

"Are you going to tell them?"

I wanted to cry out that I wouldn't be the one to turn him in even if he'd killed Joey, but I just shook my head. "I suppose Detective Moreway will question me again," I said.

"You have no first-hand information about Sunday night," Michael told me. "Only hearsay, and that's not evidence."

Now he was throwing legalisms at me. I wondered how long it would be before he hired an attorney for himself and Betsy. Ironically, I'd come there to find out what really happened Sunday night so I could stop suspecting Michael. Instead, when I left the Stokes house and got back into my car, I was no closer to the truth, and still suspicious of him.

At home, I slathered mustard on two slices of rye bread and sliced some salami to go with it. I didn't feel up to lunch in the coffee shop, where I'd have to talk to Denise. There was nothing about this morning's visit that I wanted to discuss with her, so I was careful to clock in and go straight to the pharmacy. Detective Frank Moreway, neatly dressed in a white shirt, red-figured power tie, and lightweight blue pants, the fabric of which looked like seersucker but wasn't, was waiting for me. I looked quickly at his shoes to see whether they were black or brown. Brown would mean that he was not infallible.

"I tried to see you at home this morning," he said.

"I was out."

"So I discovered. Where can we talk?"

Tim's and my shifts overlapped on Wednesdays, so the pharmacy was covered. I turned around and walked over to the employee lounge with Frank Moreway, hoping we could find a quiet corner. One of the bakery clerks was on break, reading a movie magazine, but she didn't even look up when we entered the lounge. We sat as far across the room as we could get from her. When he crossed his legs, I saw that he was wearing navy blue socks and brown shoes. He was not infallible after all.

"The other pharmacist told me when to expect you." He looked around. "I wanted to talk to you privately."

"Then it's either after nine-thirty tonight or about five tomorrow afternoon."

"Yes, he said you're on early tomorrow. Tell me, how do the shifts work? I thought you worked one late week and one early week, but now I see that doesn't necessarily follow."

Why did I feel so nervous around this man? He was doing his job, and I should be glad to help him track down Joey's killer. I studied his face. He had dark circles under his eyes and seemed different from the self-confident policeman who'd questioned me before. I wondered if he could be objective about the case now that his brother-in-law was a victim, and why they hadn't put someone else on it.

A produce clerk and one of the meat cutters walked into the room, and Frank Moreway must have realized a private conversation was now impossible, especially when the meat cutter took a seat at our table.

"Is this cop pestering you, Ruthie?" he asked.

"No," I said. "Not at all."

"Well, we want you to catch the turkey who did Joey in," he said to Detective Moreway. "But if you're going to waste time questioning my favorite pharmacist here, you'll never find him."

Frank Moreway looked annoyed at the interruption, but told him politely that this was just routine. He waited awhile, evidently trying to decide whether to continue despite the lack of privacy. After some minutes in thought, he asked me more about my working hours. "I take it you have a definite schedule. It doesn't just change from day to night to day randomly."

"No, of course not. We have to be able to plan things if we want to go out with friends or go to plays or ballgames or whatever."

"So, how does it work?"

"Basically, it's a two-week schedule, with every other weekend off. I have it posted in the pharmacy, if you want to see it."

"That's retail for you," the meat cutter said. "Terrible hours."

Frank Moreway ignored him. "Were you off this past Sunday?"

Until that question, I hadn't realized what he was leading up to. I looked straight at him. "Detective," I said, "why don't you just ask me where I was that night. It doesn't matter what my schedule is here because the pharmacy closes at six o'clock on Sundays. I worked from opening to closing and then went home, so I have no alibi."

"And how did you know what time you need the alibi for?"

"Give her a break," the meat cutter said. "We all saw it on TV."

Now Frank Moreway turned to him. I could see he was holding in his anger, whether because of the interruptions and lack of privacy or because television news had interfered with his job, I didn't know. "Don't believe everything you see on TV," was all he said.

The meat cutter winked at me and got up. "Break's over. Gotta go."

"What was the time of death?" I asked.

"Just what you heard. Between midnight and five-thirty in the morning."

"Then why are you wasting time asking about my work schedule? Are you trying to intimidate me that way?"

"I told you, this is routine questioning. Anyhow, Food Go is open twenty-four hours a day. I didn't know the pharmacy hours were different."

"They're posted."

"Yes, I suppose they are." He looked so unhappy, I suddenly regretted arguing with him. After all, if I hadn't been worried about implicating my friends, I would have cooperated fully. I decided to do so unless the questions veered toward them.

"I'm sorry," I said. "It's been a strain for all of us, but I'm sure it's worse for you. Ask me whatever you'd like."

"You worked with Joey for a long time, and I know he had only good things to say about you. I need to know if he said anything at all these last few weeks that seemed odd."

"Odd," I echoed.

"Let's say out of character, unusual, surprising. Anything at all that I should know."

"I've been trying to think along those lines, too, but I haven't found anything. His folks told me he'd been different since the Stokes funeral, but I never noticed."

"Yes, the Stokes funeral. Why did Joey attend?"

"I don't know."

"He went with you and Mrs. Seaford?"

"That's right."

"Tell me how that happened."

I tried to remember the funeral. It was only nine days ago, but it seemed like a month or more had passed. Joey had invited himself a few days beforehand. Although I didn't want to reveal Denise's plea that I go with her, I told Frank Moreway she had offered to do the driving and Joey had asked to join us.

"And where did she pick him up, at Food Go or at his home?"

Uh, oh. I was on the merry-go-round again, and Frank Moreway was searching for the one who had the brass ring. I decided this was too easy to check and told the truth.

"So you were both familiar with the complex. And you couldn't help seeing the fountain when you drove in."

"Just a minute," I said. "Thousands of people must have seen the fountain. What are you trying to do?"

"Just routine," he insisted again. "Why are you so upset?"

"I'm not upset."

"Then why are you raising your voice?"

"You're making me sound like a suspect. First you questioned my work schedule and now you're asking if I'm familiar with the place where Joey died."

"I told you, this is routine. We're asking the same questions of everyone who knew Joey or worked with him. And we're also going back to those who knew Harry Stokes."

"So you have connected the two deaths," I said.

"Not officially, but we can't rule out a relationship. I take it from your comment that you see a connection?" His tone alerted me that this was a question and, as he waited pointedly, I knew he expected a response from me.

"Coincidences do happen, but I thought all along there was something strange about Harry Stokes' death. And together with what your in-laws said about Joey's behavior since then..."

"That's too vague. Do you have any concrete reason to suspect the Stokes death wasn't from natural causes?"

When I admitted that I had only vague suspicions, he was silent for a minute, staring at the door to the employee lounge. I twisted in my seat to find out the reason and saw that Denise had walked into the room. She was wearing her green Food Go apron with the patch pockets over an electric blue skirt. Her blouse was green, too. The colors should have clashed, but on Denise they looked interesting.

She sent one startled look our way, seemed to be on the verge of rushing off, hesitated, and came over to our table. "Have you found Joey's murderer yet?" she asked.

"We're working on it."

"Well, you won't find anything here. You need to check out all of Harry Stokes's family, including the ones related by marriage."

"What makes you say that?" he asked her.

"Isn't it obvious?"

"Maybe it's not to me. Why don't you sit down and explain what you mean?"

Denise took the seat across the table from Detective Moreway and proceeded to tell him all about the quarrel at the Stokes house Sunday evening. I was sure he'd had all the details from Michael on Tuesday, but I kept quiet. I was hearing the story for the third time, and I wondered if it would be exactly the same. Although I thought Denise was dramatizing the details for Frank Moreway's benefit, her basic story hadn't changed.

"And what did you do after Betsy Stokes returned to her own house?"

"After all that commotion, I was exhausted. I went right to sleep, Detective," she said.

I couldn't figure Denise out. When she discussed the situation with me, she seemed to relish her role as a possible suspect. But now she had opened her eyes wide in a parody of innocence. Maybe Frank Moreway didn't know her well enough to recognize that this pose wasn't Denise's normal look, but I did. It was as though she were playing a game with me or with the police.

Detective Moreway stood. "Thank you both for your cooperation," he said. "And Mrs. Morris, will you do me a favor and send the other pharmacist over here for a few minutes? I'm sure you can spare him once you're back on duty."

Denise left with me, although I knew she hadn't used up her break time. "What do you think?" she asked as soon as we were out of the room.

"I think he has no hard evidence at this point."

"That's not what I mean. Does he suspect me?"

I realized for the first time how self-centered Denise could be. Usually, this aspect of her character was hidden beneath her concern for others, but now I wondered which was the real Denise. And how far would that person go to get what she wanted. "You see that he's talking to everyone. If you hadn't walked in, he wouldn't have asked you those questions."

"He would have come after me next. After Tim, anyhow." She lowered her voice. "Why Tim? He hardly knew Harry Stokes."

I remembered some of the comments Scott had made, remarks to which I hadn't paid much attention. "It seems to be routine, but it may be because Tim knew the family down in Tucson."

"Be serious," Denise said. "Tim may have a negative personality, but murder two people?"

"I'm beginning to think we can't rule out anyone," I told her.

"You suspect me, too. I know you do."

"Denise, please." We had just reached the pharmacy and several people were waiting at the window. I excused myself, gave Tim the message, and took over at the computer.

Greg Blackstone, the store manager, had promised me some help from other departments until we could find and train a new technician, but so far no one had materialized. I filled the prescription Tim had been working on, handed it over to the young woman who was waiting, and braced myself for a busy afternoon. I recognized the other two people at the window, a middle-aged woman and her elderly mother, although I didn't remember their names.

"I need a refill, but I don't have the prescription number," the daughter said timidly. "Is it okay?"

"No problem," I assured her, even though it meant more work for me. "What was the prescription for?"

"Thank you so much," she said. "It's for those nicotine patches. Now that Mother is with us, I'm worried about her emphysema. I've just got to stop smoking."

What a pleasure to help an appreciative customer, I thought, as I asked her name and looked the record up in the computer. I refilled her

Nicoderm and handed it over, to a chorus of thanks from daughter and mother.

For the next half hour, I was too busy to worry about Harry Stokes and Joey Franklin, but when Tim returned looking sullen, I tried to find out about his interview without overt prying. He was unforthcoming at the best of times, and I tried to be tactful.

"Detective Moreway doesn't seem to have anything definite," I said. "I think he's on a fishing expedition."

Tim just grunted and busied himself at the computer, leaving the telephones and the window to me as usual. Knowing I would have to be more direct, I tried again at the first lull. "Someone told me you used to date Betsy Stokes."

He compressed his lips into a thin line and was quiet for so long, I thought he wasn't going to respond. "It's no secret," he said finally.

"I suppose not. Scott Robbins seems to know all about it. He seemed to think her father caused the breakup." I was guessing here, because Scott could have been exaggerating. "That surprised me. After all, she's not a teenager."

"She's thirty-one. Same as me."

I persisted, knowing I had no right to ask. "And both of you were willing to listen to her father?"

"That shows how much you know," Tim said. "We went on seeing each other long after that phony intellectual tried to interfere."

Chapter 21.

I looked at Tim, trying not to show my astonishment at his outburst. "And then what happened?" I dared to ask, holding my breath.

"You want to know what happened?" he asked in a loud voice. I glanced nervously at the window, but no one was in sight. "She loved me; she always loved me. But when she had the chance to marry money, she couldn't resist."

"You make a decent salary."

He laughed, but it wasn't a pleasant laugh. "Decent, sure. The same as her Dad. Well, Betsy grew up in a middle-class home, on a pharmacist's income, and she wanted more." His voice took on an earnest tone, as if he wanted to convince both of us. "You know how pretty she is; she deserved more, and I didn't begrudge it to her. I wanted her to have a beautiful house and nice things, so I didn't stand in her way when she married that old man."

Not so old, I automatically said to myself. But there were more important things to think about. Could Tim have killed Harry Stokes for revenge?

"I can see exactly what you're thinking," he said to me. "And it's stupid. If I wanted to get rid of that old guy, why would I have waited so long? I told you. I knew she married him for the beautiful home and all the other things he could give her, and I agreed."

"You agreed? I don't understand."

"If you must know, Betsy moved up here a few months before I transferred to Scottsdale. She used to come into the pharmacy and tell me all about him. All the things he could do for her. It was a marriage of convenience."

What an old-fashioned phrase for someone of Tim's generation to use, I thought. Whether or not he realized it, he was echoing the slanders of Harry's children, and I no longer believed them.

"Marriage of convenience," I said before I had time to consider the implications. "Not when Betsy is pregnant." But he knows that, I realized as I spoke. His initials had been on the computer printout as the one who filled her prescription for Stuartnatal 1 + 1, the prenatal vitamins.

To my dismay, I saw Tim's face redden and braced myself for another outburst. But he turned away, took off his white jacket, carefully hung it up, and abruptly walked out of the pharmacy. It wasn't the first time he'd left for the day without saying anything, but I couldn't shake my uneasiness all afternoon and evening. I wondered whether Frank Moreway was aware of the relationship between Tim and Betsy. *When I get home tonight, I'm going to think this through and decide whether it's important enough to tell the police*, I promised myself.

Just before closing, I had a prescription for Retin-A, 0.01%. We were out of that strength, so I called some of the other Food Go stores and then two or three of our competitors. "No one has that strength in stock," I told the customer. "But I can catch tonight's order and have it here tomorrow."

"My son needs it to clear up his acne," she said. "I can't wait for you to order it."

"Then, I'll be happy to return the prescription," I told her. "You can try other pharmacies on your own, but you heard me check around."

"What will I do? It's an emergency."

Terminal acne, we called it among ourselves. We were always surprised how unconcerned some people were for drugs like penicillin that they really needed immediately and how upset they could become if we were out of acne medicine. After thinking it over, the customer left the prescription to be picked up the next day, but I was twenty minutes late closing up.

I was half afraid to see Tim lurking in the parking lot and clutched my Mace canister tightly, but it was Denise who waited for me outside the main exit. She was still wearing the green blouse she'd had on earlier but had changed her skirt for a pair of white shorts. "What are you doing here?" I asked. "I thought you were on days."

"I came back to see you."

"Shall we go inside?"

"No, not here. The Village Inn on Indian School is open late. Will you meet me there?"

I sighed inwardly but she seemed so desperate; I couldn't refuse her. During the ten-minute drive to the restaurant, I anticipated another dramatic encounter. Funny, I thought, none of the detective stories I've read reveal how exhausting it is to be in the middle of a murder mystery.

Denise was waiting just inside the entrance to the Village Inn. Only two tables were occupied in the nonsmoking section, and the hostess tried to seat us between them. "No, we want to be over there," Denise told her and pointed to a booth at the opposite end of the place.

"Why do restaurants always try to put everyone in one area?" I asked after we were seated.

"That's because it's easier for the help. You'd be surprised, though, how many people won't take the table I want to give them in the coffee shop."

"Somehow I've never had the nerve to ask for a different table," I admitted. Denise was tapping her long fingernails against the menu and her obvious nervousness was making me uneasy. We both ordered coffee and cheesecake, and I waited for her to speak. She said nothing for a long time.

"It's getting worse, Ruthie."

"Not another confrontation at the Stokes house?" I knew she'd been at work during the morning visit of Sheila and Scott, but perhaps they'd returned later.

The waitress brought our orders to the table, and we were quiet again. Denise looked down at her cheesecake and started mashing pieces of the crust, without eating anything. "I'm scared," she said suddenly.

My stomach tightened and I lowered the forkful of cake I'd just picked up. It looked like neither of us was going to eat anything tonight. "Why?"

"I lied to Detective Moreway."

"Are you sure you want to tell me this?"

"I have to tell someone," she said. "That Sunday night when Joey was killed, he called me just after midnight. His voice was strange. I didn't even realize it was Joey at first."

I stared at Denise. "You've got to tell the police he telephoned you. What did he say?"

"He said something was bothering him about Harry Stokes and he was trying to get answers."

"And what did he ask you? How long did you talk? It could narrow the time frame for the murder."

"You don't understand, Ruthie. He didn't tell me anything on the phone. He wanted me to meet him in front of the fountain."

"My God," I said. "You mean you were there?"

She must have realized how shocked I was. "You believe I did it. You think you're sitting here talking to a double murderer."

"I'm sure you realize it must be someone we know."

"So you suspect me. Well, I know I'm innocent, so maybe *I* should be suspicious of *you.*"

I smiled uneasily. "I'm not the one who was at the fountain when Joey was killed."

"How do I know who else was there that night. But I do know Joey was expecting to meet someone after me."

"Tell me what happened," I said, hoping I could put Denise's information together with everything I'd heard so far and figure out who the murderer was. After all, I knew all these people better than Frank Moreway did; I should be able to determine which one was lying. But I was too close to most of them. Denise was my friend, I worked with Tim, and I was—I guess emotionally involved was the best way to put it—with Michael and his daughter. I even sympathized with Sheila and Scott. With my personal feelings obscuring things, it wouldn't be that easy to look at all of them dispassionately. The only one I'd disliked at once was Richard Stokes. How neatly it would tie together if Richard, who was going around accusing everyone else, had killed his father and Joey.

Denise had paused while the waitress refilled our coffee. She lifted her cup, and I did the same. It burned my tongue, and I wondered how she could drink it that hot. Then I noticed she didn't seem aware of the heat.

"Joey asked me if I thought it was murder if you gave someone a drug that was harmless to most people but not the one you gave it to."

"But that can describe so many medications," I said. "Maybe even all."

"I asked if it was done deliberately." She stared at me defiantly. "I guess I should apologize for getting angry at you a little while ago. The truth is, I thought Joey meant that he was the one who'd made a mistake."

This was a new angle, one I hadn't considered before. Could Harry Stokes have been killed in error? But if the mistake had been my technician's, who profited from Joey's own death?

"Who made the mistake?" I asked Denise.

"He didn't say it was a mistake."

"Then what did he say?" I was getting tired of people talking around the subject. If we were going to put the pieces together and solve the puzzle, we had to know all the details.

"He said he knew I used Food-Fed decongestant for my allergies, and he wanted to know if I'd ever recommended them to Harry or given any to him."

"And?"

"I told him I never had." Her look was still defiant. "Whether you believe me or not, I had nothing to do with Harry's death."

"Do you think Joey was seeing all of the people who were close to Harry that night?"

"Why? Who else did he meet?"

I didn't want to tell her about Betsy and Michael, so I said nothing. But Denise wouldn't let it rest.

"Did he make an appointment with you?" she asked me.

That started another train of thought. *If Joey was conducting an investigation of his own, why hadn't he called me, too? Did he think the error was mine? Maybe he intended to talk to me the next day, but had been killed first.*

Denise was waiting for my reply. "He did see others," I told her, "but it was before your appointment." I backtracked to something that was bothering me. "How is it the guard at the gate didn't see you?"

"No one was at the gate," she said. "I just drove right in, and about ten minutes later when we finished talking, I drove right out again."

"Did you park and get out of your car?"

"Ruthie, are you trying to trip me up? You've been there and you know there's no place to park by the fountain. I had to pull into the visitor's parking area and walk back to the fountain to talk to Joey."

"Weren't you afraid to be there alone at night?"

"I saw Joey waiting at the fountain as I drove in, and I certainly wasn't worried about him."

The coffee had cooled somewhat and I sipped it, wondering what else Denise had to reveal. She didn't wait for more questions, but continued in a high, excited voice. "He kept looking around, as if he thought someone might overhear us. But the place was deserted. Maybe he was watching in case the gate guard came along."

"And no one else showed up."

"No one. But we did hear a rustling noise about where the oleanders border the driveway."

"I suppose someone could have been hiding there. You wouldn't see anything even in the daytime."

"Joey got more nervous when we heard the noise. He wouldn't say another word."

Just what had happened at the Sizzler with Betsy and Michael, I thought. In a way, each of them had verified the other's story. If they were telling the truth, I reminded myself. And that would indicate that Joey had been seeing people all evening. Could the earlier ones be discounted as suspects, or did one of them decide Joey was too close to the truth and return to kill him?

"Ruthie, you've got to believe me," Denise said. "When I drove away, Joey was standing by the fountain. He must have been waiting for someone else."

"I don't suppose the real murderer would be telling me all this," I said, half to myself.

Denise seemed to relax and her voice lowered to its normal pitch. "Should I go to the police?"

My first impulse was to answer affirmatively. Even though I couldn't decipher the significance of Sunday night's events, the police had more experience with crime. They might see something that Denise and I were overlooking. But what if I advised her to go to Frank Moreway and he arrested her for murder.

"I really believe it's best to be honest with them, but there are no guarantees. It could be hard for you to prove Joey was alive when you left him."

"I'm not just being selfish," Denise insisted, as if I'd accused her of it. "I keep thinking if they concentrate on me again, the murderer might get away with it completely."

"Denise, everything we know about murder cases comes from newspaper stories and from fictional accounts in books and on television. Probably distorted in both cases. We need to let the people with real experience have all the facts. All the facts we're aware of," I amended.

She put her head in her hands and murmured something I couldn't hear, so I asked her to repeat it. "You still don't get it," she told me, lifting her head and staring fixedly at me.

All at once, I did understand because I could see the fear in her eyes. "I know it's a tough decision," I said, intending to comfort her.

"That's not it, Ruthie. The murderer saw me with Joey that night and may think I know too much. I'm afraid I'm in danger."

Chapter 22.

I wanted to credit Denise's imagination with working overtime again, but I thought about Joey. Suppose he had said the same words last week. Would anyone have believed him? It was time for amateurs like us to stop taking risks. Yet I was sure the answer lay in my prescription files, the files just about everyone had wanted to see. If I could figure out who the killer was, I could clear Denise from suspicion. And Michael most of all, I added, acknowledging in that moment how important he still was to me.

"Then you should go to Detective Moreway immediately," I told her firmly.

"That's easy advice, but I could get into a worse mess that way."

"Call it easy advice or whatever you want. It's the only sensible thing to do." I tried hard to convince Denise without letting her see that I was afraid, too. "Let's look at the worst case. If you go to the police and they jail you, at least you'll be alive and able to prove your innocence. But if the murderer really is after you, you won't get that chance."

Denise didn't respond and I couldn't recognize any other emotion through the fear that still predominated. "I'll have to think about it," she said.

"Meanwhile, maybe it would be better if you tell me what you suspect. Did you catch a glimpse of the other person? Or see a familiar car when you parked yours? Did the noise you heard suggest who could have been there?" I fired my questions at Denise, waiting for answers but getting only a shake of her head after each one.

"You can't exactly wear a signboard saying, 'I know nothing about it,'" I told her.

"Let's get out of here." She scooped her handbag and the check and started for the cash register. The cashier waited patiently while we added the tip and divided the check between us. Denise dropped all the loose change out of her wallet as we left the register and walked into the Village Inn parking lot.

Her nervousness was so obvious that I offered to help. "Why don't I follow behind you in my car?" I asked her. "I'll wait until you're safely inside the house?" *Too bad neither one of us has a car phone*, I thought. But I could make plenty of noise and rouse all Denise's neighbors if anything went wrong.

My offer seemed to calm her somewhat, but I saw her look into the back seat of her car before she opened the doors. I did the same with mine.

When we pulled into Denise's driveway, I watched carefully as she made her way inside. No one appeared to be around and about in her neighborhood. My own neighborhood was also quiet, with no lights showing at the Flints or the Woodmans when I arrived home. My hands were shaking when I unlocked the door leading from the garage into the kitchen.

* * * *

The next day, Thursday, my schedule changed to the early shift. I found it hard to get started that morning. My beige- and coffee-colored print dress seemed lifeless, and I added a coral-and-gold necklace and matching earrings to feel more cheerful. I barely made it to Food Go to open on time, dreading what the day would bring, convinced I'd hear terrible news about Denise. The morning was a quiet one, and I was thankful for it. For once, customers and phone calls alike came one at a time. Before Tim arrived at two o'clock, I was completely caught up with my work.

I wondered if he'd refer to yesterday's conversation, but he mumbled a greeting and stationed himself at the computer. This was normal behavior for Tim, and I felt a surge of relief that he, at least, was acting the way he always did.

Denise didn't approach the pharmacy during her breaks and I had neither breaks nor lunch hour to spend in the coffee shop, even if I had wanted to. When my shift was over, I debated with myself about heading there but went directly home instead.

I popped a frozen ravioli dinner in the microwave, quickly changed to my bathing suit, and jumped into the pool to cool down. It felt wonderful. I didn't even bother drying off but went right into my kitchen to turn the cardboard tray around in the microwave. During the remaining three minutes of cooking, I poured ice cubes into a glass and added a diet cola. Even when eating alone, I sometimes dressed the table with a pretty placemat and matching cloth napkin. Today, I ate directly from the cardboard tray on a piece of paper towel. I felt like I was waiting for something to happen, but I didn't know what.

When the doorbell rang, I quickly threw a housedress over my bathing suit, and looked through the decorative glass inset of the front door. It was Detective Moreway. I felt a sharp twinge of fear at the sight of him, certain that something had happened to Denise.

He followed me into the kitchen and apologized for interrupting my dinner. Dinner hardly seemed the right word for the remaining bits of ravioli cooling in the cardboard microwave tray, sitting on a paper towel that was now spotted with tomato sauce. I was embarrassed but tried not to show it, offering Frank Moreway a can of diet cola, too. He asked for ice water instead.

I thought of all the detective stories I'd read in which the police refused drinks from suspects. Did ice water count, I wondered. On the other hand, it must still be over 105 degrees outdoors and he looked as though he needed the ice water.

"Please finish your dinner," he said.

"I'm done," I told him as I scraped the remaining ravioli into the disposer and threw tray and paper towel into the trash container that I keep under my kitchen sink.

We both sat at the kitchen table. All the fizz had left my diet cola, but I drank it anyhow. The silence was unbearable, and I found it hard not to ask him what was uppermost in my mind.

"Were you off today or on an early shift?" he asked.

"You must have checked with the store before you came out here." *That's a stupid answer*, I thought. *Why do you want to antagonize him?*

"I'm asking because I did call the store, and they said you weren't there." I could tell he was making an effort to be patient.

"I was on the early shift, nine to four."

"And what about Mrs. Seaford? Was she at work today?"

"I didn't see her."

"And when did you see her last?"

"Yesterday." I hoped he would assume I'd seen her only at Food Go and wouldn't try to pin down the time, but he was persistent.

"Can you give me some details?"

I told him we'd gone out for coffee after work. It was not up to me to reveal our conversation. He listened carefully but wanted to know more.

"I understand Mrs. Seaford was on the day shift and came back to the store to meet you. Wasn't that unusual?"

"Not when you consider what's been happening."

"So her purpose was to talk about the murders?"

"Of course. We talk about them all the time. Isn't that normal?"

He didn't answer. "I also understand you were at the Stokes house yesterday before you went to work."

Now I was getting annoyed. "Are you following me around?"

"Why? Do you have something to hide?"

That remark angered me, but I forced myself to remain calm. "Tell me what this is all about, please. I can cooperate better if you don't play games with me."

"Suppose you give me a rundown of your visit to Betsy Stokes."

"You're still not revealing your reasons for these questions. I don't want to repeat private conversations without knowing what's going on."

"Will knowing my reasons change what you have to say?"

"No, but it will help me focus on what's important. I'm sure you don't want all the trivialities."

"I'll be the judge of that," he said, then relented enough to tell me that he wanted to hear about Sheila Stokes and Scott Robbins.

I wondered how he knew about their visit to Betsy and Michael. Or mine, for that matter. Perhaps he's already questioned some or all of the people involved, I thought. Five people had been present during the visit he was asking me about, and I supposed he would compare our stories. This must be the basis of police work. I nearly asked Frank Moreway if he'd ever seen *Rashomon*, the Japanese film in which each eyewitness gives a different version of the same crime. Could any group of people ever agree on what they'd seen and heard?

Although these reflections passed through my mind very quickly, they didn't solve my problem. I decided to be frank about Sheila and Scott's visit, omitting only Scott's accusation at the end.

Detective Moreway listened, taking notes from time to time. When I finished, his eyes held mine for a moment. "And what exactly did Scott say that caused Michael Loring to kick him out of the house?"

"He didn't kick Scott out," I said indignantly.

"Maybe not physically. But wouldn't you agree that holding the door open until Scott and Sheila left was the psychological equivalent?"

"They could have ignored Michael. It's not even his home."

"And if that led to physical action?" Frank Moreway asked.

"I don't understand what this is all about. Did Scott and Sheila file some sort of complaint? Are you trying to say that it's against the law to hint that you want unwelcome visitors to leave?"

"Mrs. Morris, you're evading the original question. I asked what Scott said directly before the confrontation."

"I don't remember," I said stubbornly.

Frank Moreway flipped back a few pages in his notebook. "I've been told Scott threatened to speak to me about Michael Loring. And he intended to claim that Michael killed Harry Stokes so Betsy could inherit."

He waited then, but I was silent. "Does that jog your memory?"

"Detective Moreway, everyone has been accusing everyone else. Either I ignore the accusations or I will never be able to trust my friends again."

"And is Michael Loring your friend?"

Another tough one. I decided to follow my advice to Denise and tell the truth. "We went to school together many, many years ago. Until recently, I hadn't seen him since that time."

I was afraid the next question would relate to the strength of that relationship, and who in today's society would believe Michael and I had not had an affair? But Frank Moreway changed the subject again.

"What vehicles do you own?"

The question was so unexpected, I hesitated for a fraction of a second. "I only own one car, a Honda Accord."

"Model year? Color?" He was writing in the notebook again.

"A ninety-seven, white."

"What about your friend, Denise?"

I jumped up and rushed to his side of the table. "You must tell me what's wrong. What happened to Denise?"

"Just answer the questions, please."

"She drives a black Ford. An older one. I don't know the year."

"Does she have another vehicle?"

"Not that I know of."

He continued questioning me about other people and their cars. I remembered Michael's Lexus but had no idea what the others drove other than Scott, who had some kind of motorcycle. Then I recalled the Brandens had mentioned Richard Stokes's Mercedes but this was not first-hand information. Again, I asked what it was all about.

"Would you like to tell me why you're so concerned about Mrs. Seaford?"

"Because she's very nervous. I guess I picked up on that." I had no intention of revealing what Denise had told me last night at the restaurant. Thank God, no one else was present during that conversation.

"When did you first meet Scott Robbins?"

I was really bewildered now. His questions didn't seem to have any purpose. I wondered whether he was disorganized or trying to trip me up in some way.

"The first time I saw him was at the funeral. Harry Stokes's funeral. I didn't really meet him until yesterday."

"But Denise knows him well?"

"I have no idea."

"What about Michael Loring?

"I've already said that Michael turned up here the other week, and it had been years since I last saw him." I knew my voice sounded plaintive, but the strain was beginning to show. No wonder they say people will confess to anything after relentless questioning.

I tried again. "Isn't it about time you told me why you're asking me these ridiculous questions about people's cars?

"These aren't ridiculous questions, Mrs. Morris. Scott Robbins was seriously injured this morning. He was on his motorcycle; it was a hit and run."

Chapter 23.

My first thought, relief that it wasn't Denise, was followed immediately by gratitude that I had been at work all morning. Dozens of customers and Food Go employees must have seen me there. Then I realized I didn't know the time of the accident.

"When did it happen?" I asked.

"Don't you want to know his condition?"

"Of course, I do. But the way you've been questioning me, I guess I want to be sure you don't suspect me."

"Nine-thirty this morning, near the university campus in Tempe. I suppose people can confirm you were in the pharmacy?"

He phrased it as a question and I nodded my head in agreement. Knowing I was in the clear made me feel better than I had in days. Then I remembered his questions about the various vehicles other people owned.

"You think it was deliberate, not an accident," I said. Nothing else made sense in view of his questions.

"We don't know," he admitted.

Belatedly, I asked about Scott's condition. "Will he be all right?"

"He might have been if the helmet law was still on the books. Right now, he's in intensive care. Head injuries."

I thought about Sheila, the caressing lilt to her voice when she called him "Scotty," and the way her eyes followed him. Not another widow to join the crowd, I hoped. But she would not be a widow in any case, at least not in the legal sense.

"Why would anyone want to run him down?" I asked.

"It isn't much more than twenty-four hours since he was accusing a specific person of murder. I'm not saying there's a connection, you understand, but we have to check into every possibility." He looked at the pages in his notebook again. "Will you confirm that Scott accused Michael Loring of murder yesterday?"

I remained quiet for a long time. Too long, but maybe he'd think I was trying to visualize the confrontation. "I don't remember," I repeated as firmly as I could.

"Let me help your memory," he said. "They were talking about money. About Sheila and her brother sharing in their father's estate. She wanted the money to start a business with her fiancé." Detective Moreway read from the notebook, "I remember you from Tucson. You can't keep a job, Scott." He looked expectantly at me. "Do you remember those words?"

"Those weren't his exact words." Too late I realized I'd fallen into his trap.

"So, you do remember the conversation."

"Sheila's a lot younger than me. Her memory is probably better."

Detective Moreway laughed and, while his manner remained polite, it wasn't a pleasant sound. "Good excuse," he said. "In that case, assuming she's the source of my information, would you be willing to confirm the rest of it?"

"I can only tell you what I remember."

"Scott's words were addressed to Sheila." As Frank Moreway read them from his notebook, I hoped they'd be slightly off, too. Then I could honestly say I hadn't heard them. But Sheila, if she had been his informant, and I supposed she had to be the one, had been only too accurate. "'He probably killed your father so his own daughter would get all that money.'" Detective Moreway quoted.

Is it possible, I wondered. *Thank God, the police were unaware that Michael had another strong motive, wanting to safeguard his daughter's expected baby.* I was silent.

"We need your help," Frank Moreway said. "You can't protect people under a mistaken notion of friendship. If your friends are innocent, nothing you say will hurt them. But have you thought about the alternative? Are you willing to take a chance, even a slight chance, that you're shielding someone who's killed twice and is ready to kill again to protect himself or herself."

"If I knew anything to help you, I'd say it."

"How will you feel if someone else gets killed? I'm convinced you have information that could make the difference. Maybe not about the conversation that took place yesterday morning. You may not even be aware of the information you hold. But you know something." His eyes darkened as he stared intently at me. "You could be in danger, too," he told me.

I laughed uneasily. "You're trying to frighten me."

"And I hope I'm succeeding."

I remembered how nervous Denise had been the night before, convinced of her own danger. It wasn't pleasant to find myself in the same situation.

He was watching my face and must have understood my reaction. "If you have anything to add, now's the time."

I shook my head and he got up to leave. At the front door, he turned and told me to contact him when I changed my mind. *He seems so sure of himself*, I thought, as I locked up after him. *But he couldn't be right. Whatever I knew, others knew as well. The murderer could gain nothing by coming after me.*

Despite the air-conditioning, I felt uncomfortably hot and perspired. I was still in my bathing suit, so I removed my wraparound housedress and went out through the patio doors and into the pool to cool down. The swim calmed me only for a short time, and when I got out and dried off, I realized how agitated my thoughts were. I sat in front of the television the rest of the evening, but I don't remember what I watched, only that the local news had nothing about Scott Robbins and his motorcycle accident.

* * * *

By morning, I still had no thunderbolt of revelation. Maybe it was just too hot to think straight. Fridays were always busy because people wanted their medicines before the weekend. I was on the day shift again, and I was glad to keep occupied. Without a technician, it was even more difficult to keep up with the flow of customers. Luckily Greg Blackstone passed by when the lineup of people at the window was beginning to get out of control. He was a good manager, and immediately brought over one of the clerks from the film department. Karen was a high school student, but she looked older. She was wearing shorts and a T-shirt, which wasn't good for the pharmacy's image, but I was desperate enough to appreciate any live body.

"Karen can help for a few hours," Greg told me. "What is she allowed to do?"

I explained to both of them that under my supervision, state law allowed her to take prescriptions from patients at the window. She could answer the telephone and write down the prescription number for a refill and the name of the person okaying it. But she must call me over for new prescriptions.

"I can see you're too busy to train Karen now," Greg said. "Isn't there something simple she can do to ease things for you?"

"Answering the phone would help most, Karen," I told her. "But call me over unless it's a refill."

"No problem," she said.

Although she seemed alert and happy to be away from the photo center, I was careful to keep tuned to the way she handled phone calls while I took care of everything else. Just having her to field the calls helped tremendously, and she needed no reminders to take down the numbers and prescribers' names. The first three calls were for refills, and I listened as I worked to see what would happen when a new script was called in.

"One minute, please," I heard her say. "The pharmacist will be right with you."

Maybe Greg would allow her to replace Joey, I thought. If she's computer literate, I can teach her our system, and she can enter information and do the labels. Then we can get to the more difficult tasks. Verifying the completeness of scripts, taking drugs off the shelves, counting or pouring. Joey had seemed to have a natural affinity for the pharmacy, and I remembered Mr. Franklin saying over and over that his son should have been a druggist. It was selfish to miss Joey because of his work in the pharmacy but, then again, I also missed his cheerfulness and his patience with customers.

Between phone calls, Karen asked if she could do anything else and I soon had her at the window. She was polite and efficient and, after a while, wanted to hand out the finished prescriptions. I explained that state law didn't allow anyone but a registered pharmacist to hand out new prescriptions.

"Why?" she asked. "If you're the one filling it, what difference does it make who gives it out?"

"I'm supposed to communicate with patients as I hand the medicine to them," I explained. "To tell them the name of the drug, its strength, the directions, and any cautions."

"Cautions?"

"Not to take it on an empty stomach or with milk products or that it might make them sleepy so they should try not to drive. Whatever they need to know to avoid problems."

She was listening to me wide-eyed, and I felt like some sort of guru. I remembered how fascinated I'd been at the same age when I helped in my Dad's drug store. Fascinated enough to go to pharmacy college as soon as I finished high school.

Pharmacy college reminded me of Michael and now, busy as I was, I could no longer postpone thinking of what I'd resolutely put out of my mind last night after Detective Moreway had left. Michael seemed to be the only one with a motive for trying to kill Scott Robbins. Scott had accused him of murder and, the next day, someone had gone after Scott. No matter how hard I tried to come up with another reason for the accident, nothing else fit. Combined with Michael's antipathy toward his son-in-law and evasions concerning his whereabouts on the night Joey died, this seemed like strong circumstantial evidence. I shut my eyes and tried to explain it all away, but I couldn't do it.

Somehow I got through the morning. For a person who'd always loved her work, I was finding it increasingly difficult to concentrate in the pharmacy. These days, my mind was like a computer with insufficient disk space. And I couldn't seem to retrieve the data I needed.

Tim arrived at two o'clock and stared at Karen. "Are we running a kindergarten now?" he asked me, waiting until she was off the phone and couldn't miss hearing him.

"Karen's been invaluable and, if she's willing, I'm going to ask Greg if she can train as a technician."

"Fine, as long as you do the training."

Typical of Tim, I thought. *He wanted to replace me as pharmacy manager but would never do any of the tasks that went with that job.* Unfortunately, I hadn't warned Karen about him, an awkward business anyhow. I couldn't denigrate a colleague to her, but I should have told her not to worry about his outward manner. A caution like those on prescription bottles!

Karen was on the telephone again, carefully taking down information about another refill. Since Tim had stationed himself in his usual position at the computer, I spent my time at the window, trying to catch up with paperwork whenever the flow of customers eased. I watched to see Karen's reaction to Tim's gruffness, but she simply avoided him as much as possible in the confined space of our small area. When she left to return to her own department, she agreed to put in as many hours in the pharmacy as Greg Blackstone allowed.

As soon as Karen was gone, I rounded on Tim. "You know we need a replacement for Joey. Please try to get along with her."

"I get along with everyone," Tim said.

To see ourselves as others do, I thought, and changed the subject. "Did you hear the latest about the killings?"

"They caught him?"

I was afraid to ask which "him" he meant. "No, it's something else. Scott Robbins was in a motorcycle accident. Hit and run."

Tim did an exaggerated double take. "Are you going to find connections between everything that happens to any of those people?" His skepticism showed in his voice and raised eyebrows.

"There is a relationship," I insisted.

"Sure," he said, with the same tone of disbelief.

I wasn't surprised. It was pointless to argue with Tim. His opinions were always the only right ones, so I don't know why I wanted to convince him. Maybe because I was avoiding Denise and needed to talk it over with someone.

We both got busy, but I was determined to continue the conversation. Since Tim's knowledge of Michael was more recent than mine, I had to find out what I could about the Michael Loring of today.

Just before my shift ended, we had another quiet spell and I brought the subject up again. "You may not believe it, but there's a definite chain of events." I didn't want to say anything about the conflicting reactions of Michael and Harry Stokes to Betsy's pregnancy, but I felt the pregnancy was an important factor.

"I think that chain begins with Betsy Stokes's visit to her obstetrician. You know I don't gossip about customers, but I think this is important. I keep going over the sequence in my mind. Betsy finds out she's pregnant. Next thing, her husband's dead. Maybe it's natural causes, maybe suicide, maybe murder. But then Joey, who works in the pharmacy where Betsy and Harry both get all their medications, is killed. And now Sheila Stokes's fiancé, a young man who knew most of the key players in Tucson, is seriously hurt in a hit and run." I said "key players" deliberately, to avoid mentioning Michael by name. I looked at Tim, wondering if he realized which key player I meant.

"You want to ramble on, it's okay with me. But what makes you think you're smarter than the police?"

"I never said that," I protested.

"Obviously, you have a suspect. Who is it? Betsy? Her father?"

He was getting too close now, and I didn't want to answer. But he persistently added names. "Harry's kids? Me? Denise?" He grinned at me. "What about you?"

"Now you're being ridiculous," I said.

"Why should you be any less of a suspect than anyone else?"

"And what's my motive?" I asked tartly, although I didn't mind the game if it led him away from Michael.

"Unrequited love."

I laughed uneasily. "For Joey or for Scott?"

"For the old man," he said and turned back to the computer screen, too quickly to see me wince at his words.

Don't be a fool, I told myself. To Tim, Harry Stokes *was* an old man, and the epithet helped him to belittle Betsy's choice. I wondered if I should tell him about my alibi for the time of Scott's accident, but decided his accusation hadn't been serious; there was no need to defend myself.

Although Tim was finished with the subject, I wasn't. Just before my shift ended, I began again. "Tim, you know these people better than I do. Seriously now, who do you think is responsible for what's going on?"

"I told you. Nothing is going on. You know as well as I do that Harry Stokes had all sorts of health problems. He died of natural causes."

"That's what we were supposed to think, but I know better."

His set expression showed his disagreement, but that didn't stop me because I was used to Tim taking the opposite point of view to mine on every possible occasion. "As for Scott," he went on. "Do you know how many motorcyclists land in Tempe emergency rooms every day?"

I persisted. "And how will you explain away Joey's death?"

"That's easy. When you stop trying to connect three distinct events, Joey's death will turn out to be a mugging that went wrong. Or maybe a gang killing."

"If he'd been shot from a moving car rather than drowned, I might agree. But I don't believe in this kind of coincidence, and the way the police have been questioning all of us, I can see they don't either."

"What do they know?" he muttered and reached for the stack of new scripts I put next to the computer. I reminded him to transmit the order to the wholesaler before closing. To make sure he didn't forget again, I put the order machine where he couldn't miss it, and left for the day.

* * * *

Sundown was more than two hours away, and it was at least 110 degrees outside. I'd been early enough to find a parking spot under a bottlebrush tree, and my car was hot but not unbearable. Even so, I was ready for a few laps in the pool before dinner.

Determined not to spend another agitated evening, I considered going to the movies. Only two weeks ago, I'd been at the mall with Denise and seen Michael for the first time since college. But I didn't want to call Denise even though I knew she probably had the same shift as I did today.

As to my other friends, sometimes they included me in family outings, but I felt uncomfortable as the proverbial third wheel.

There was always television. It hadn't helped last night, but I turned on the set and mindlessly watched reruns for hours. At nine-thirty, I put on a dry bathing suit, turned on the patio lights, and went back to the pool. I was just drying off when someone knocked at the back gate.

This is such an early-to-bed city that I never expect late visitors. But it was Friday night and, although I had to work the next day, most people were off for the weekend. *It must be Michael*, I thought. A variety of emotions surged through my mind with that certainty. I wanted to see him again, but would it be safe to open the gate for him? I reminded myself that this was Michael, the man I had nearly married. Wrapping the huge beach towel over my bathing suit, sarong fashion, I walked over to the gate and looked out. I was surprised to see Tim but somewhat relieved that it wasn't Michael.

"I tried telephoning, Ruthie, but no one answered."

"It's hard to hear the phone when I'm swimming," I explained as I unlocked the gate. "What's happening?"

"I need your advice about a strange conversation I had with Greg Blackstone tonight. He sounded like he's ready to transfer me."

This was surprising. I couldn't remember Tim ever asking my advice before. In any case, I was glad to have this opportunity for a talk with him away from the busy pharmacy. Our conversations in the store had left me edgy, because I couldn't shake the feeling that some things he'd said should be followed up and clarified.

Tim sat at the glass-topped patio table across from me and refused my offer of iced tea, while I thought about this development. I'd been hoping for months that Tim would transfer out. From a selfish point of view, this wasn't the right time because I'd have a new technician and a new staff pharmacist to contend with simultaneously. Surely Greg was aware of this problem, so why would he suddenly try to send Tim to another Food Go store? I wondered if Karen had complained to the manager about him.

"If you want to make a change, I wouldn't stand in your way," I told Tim, giving him a chance to put a positive spin on the transfer. Now I sound like a politician, I thought. Why does Tim always make me feel like the old-fashioned, stereotypical female boss?

"You were asking me about Betsy Loring tonight," he said. "Why?"

"Why?" I echoed and hesitated. I certainly was not going to tell him my suspicions about Michael.

We heard the click as my pool cleaning system started up. I realized it was ten o'clock, the hour I'd set the timer for. Tim stood and sauntered over to the pool. "What kind of cleaner is that, anyhow?"

It was an odd change of subject, but I was used to friends watching my little robotic system in action. I walked over and joined him, ready to point out the pros and cons of the new pool cleaner, wondering why I felt so uneasy.

Suddenly I sensed the terrible danger I faced. But before I could react, Tim grabbed me. I could feel his arms tighten painfully around my body. He was edging me closer to the pool. The shock was so intense, my mind refused to accept what was happening. My thoughts were jumbled from pain and terror. I was afraid I'd black out. I could feel his relentless grip as he dragged me along the pebbled pool deck. They would find me floating face down in my own swimming pool. Despite the overwhelming fear that engulfed me, I realized I must act quickly or face certain death. I knew that Tim was younger and stronger than I, but desperation drove me. I was determined to save myself.

Chapter 24.

He kept dragging me along to the deep end of the pool. I could feel his rough hands. The pebbled deck hurt my bare feet as the ground rushed by. Thoughts tumbled through my mind, incredibly fast. I foolishly wondered why he didn't simply hold my head under water at the shallow part. *But this time he has to be sure it looks like an accident. He can't drown me in shallow water, and he can't leave any unexplained marks on me. That must be why he isn't trying to choke me.*

He was behind me, one hand over my mouth to keep me from screaming, the other wrapped around my abdomen, inexorably forcing me closer and closer to the deep end. My arms were free, but I couldn't reach him. It was no use even if I had the strength to fight him. Then I remembered reading about protesters. They let their bodies go limp to make themselves more difficult to drag. I tried to deaden my weight. If only I had the Mace spray in my hand. It probably wouldn't stop him for long, but it could buy me time. I could run out of the gate and over to Jean and Jerry's house.

The spray would be where I always put it when I swam, on the stone bench alongside the pool, next to my bathing cap and swim goggles. I had to get the Mace. *Oh, God, if only we haven't already passed the bench*, I prayed silently. But as I reached my hand out to check, I felt my legs scrape along its base. This was my only chance. I was going to make the most of it. My heartbeat speeded up as I got ready to grab the canister, lift it in Tim's direction, and squeeze the nozzle before he knew what was happening. In a sudden flash of desperate insight, I realized the spray would affect me, too, but it would be worse for Tim.

If only we haven't passed the Mace, I thought again. *I have to get it!*

As all this flashed through my mind, I felt my bathing cap on the bench. I was afraid it was too late–that I'd passed by the Mace. But I wasn't going to give up. There... there it was! A fraction of a second later, I had the canister in my hand, aimed it behind me, and pressed. We were both coughing, but the attack shocked Tim long enough to slacken his hold on me. I ran to the gate, released the spring lock, and was out in the driveway so quickly that I hadn't even decided where to go. I only knew I needed help, and I could hear myself screaming for it as strongly as I could between bouts of coughing.

No one will hear, I thought in despair. *They'll all be watching television or sleeping.* I didn't dare look back to see whether Tim had recovered enough to come after me. Then I heard the gate click and knew he was close behind. Someone grabbed my arms and I screamed loud enough to bruise my throat before I realized it couldn't be Tim. This person was in front of me, and he let go immediately.

"Ruthie, it's all right. You're safe."

It was Michael's voice, and I stopped screaming although I still couldn't stop the ragged coughing or control my shaking knees. There were no racing footsteps behind us. "Tim," I said. "He's trying to kill me."

"Yes, but he may as well give up," Michael said, shouting so Tim would hear him. "I called the police on my car phone as soon as I saw his car in your driveway."

Michael's Lexus was slanted across the driveway, blocking Tim's green Riviera. We couldn't see Tim, but we could hear him coughing. The sound told us he was running across my lawn to the street. "He can't get far," Michael said. "I'll let the police be the heroes."

We heard the sirens then. Within minutes, two Scottsdale patrol cars pulled into the driveway. Somehow, because he was so closely connected in my mind with the investigation, I expected to see Frank Moreway. But I didn't recognize any of the four patrol officers who approached us, and I was afraid we'd waste valuable time explaining, while Tim got away.

Michael immediately called to them that he was the one who had telephoned, and I vouched for him. We pointed out the direction Tim had taken. One officer stayed behind to talk to us.

Before I could begin my story, my legs started to shake so violently that I had to sit on the grass at the side of my driveway. Michael sat beside me, offering his shoulder for support.

After my first few sentences, the officer left us and went back to his patrol car to use the radio. And by the time I finished telling him exactly what had happened, another patrol car pulled up. Detective Moreway got out.

By this time, too, the Flints, the Woodmans, and other neighbors had gathered on the sidewalk in front of my house. I wondered why the arrival of the police had brought them out but not my screams. Then again, I could be misjudging them; they could have waited just inside their front doors, ready to provide a haven for me.

I'd always preferred neighbors who minded their own business, but perhaps it was better to have people like the Brandens living next door. They would have been outside at the sound of my first scream. *None of this matters*, I thought soberly. *If I hadn't reached the canister of Mace on my own, it would have been too late.*

I expected to see the police hauling Tim to one of the patrol cars by now, but they returned without him. One of them must have radioed for the police helicopter, for it was soon overhead spotlighting the area. Local television and newspaper reporters soon arrived on the scene. I didn't want to talk or allow them into the pool area, but I didn't have the strength to resist. Denise told me later that she saw me on the morning news, sitting on my front lawn, wearing only a pink bathing suit. That must have been a sight, a fifty-five-year-old pinup.

The questions and the commotion finally stopped. One patrol car remained outside the house, and the two police officers in it assured me I was safe. The front door was still locked. There was no way Tim could have passed us and reached the back door through the driveway. Michael checked out the house anyhow and poured a glass of Mogen David wine for me, the only alcoholic beverage I had in the house.

"I'm going to leave now, Ruthie. Lock up after me, get some rest, and we'll talk in the morning."

As he spoke, an idea struck with the force of a blow to the head. "Michael, I forgot. Betsy is the key to everything. He could go after her." I was pulling at his arm, trying to make sure he understood. "You've got to call and warn her not to open the door for him."

I didn't know how much time had elapsed since Tim's escape, but since his car was still in my driveway, he couldn't have reached the Stokes home quickly. Michael's face paled and he ran to my kitchen phone. He gripped the receiver fiercely as he waited. The phone rang unanswered for a long time, and his grim expression haunted me. When she picked up the phone, he started to relax but I saw his brows knit as he talked to her.

"Are you alone, Betsy?"

He waited, tension in every line of his face. Then the lines softened, but he warned her not to let Tim Barnard in the house no matter what excuses he gave her.

She must have wanted reasons, because I heard him explain that Tim had just tried to kill me. "I'll be there as quickly as possible," Michael said and hung up the telephone.

"Can't we get the police to watch her house, too?"

"It will take too long to convince them. I've got to be there myself."

"Call those neighbors," I told him. "The Brandens. They can keep watch until you arrive. No, you go. I'll call them. Will you phone me when you get there?"

He nodded and dashed to the front door, stopping only long enough to be sure I locked up behind him. I tried unsuccessfully to reach the Brandens, wishing I'd thought about the danger to Betsy earlier.

If the police hadn't been busy trying to capture Tim, Michael would surely have gotten a ticket for speeding. I watched him from my dining room window as he shot out of the driveway and raced up the street. Then there was silence. The neighbors had drifted away and so had the reporters, and the men in the remaining patrol car were quiet shadows.

I waited for Michael's call. It should take him about twenty minutes to drive to his daughter's home, maybe only fifteen the way he was going. When he hadn't called at the end of half an hour, I began to worry.

My thoughts were wild. What if Tim had been lurking at Betsy's and used her father as a hostage to get into the house? I paced from room to room, holding my portable phone so I could answer the instant Michael's call came through.

All the news items I'd ever seen about rejected lovers who killed family, friends, and anyone else they blamed for the breakup flashed through my mind. I realized I couldn't bear the thought of losing Michael, and couldn't believe I had ever suspected him of murder. During these few weeks, I had grown used to his warm smile and vibrant personality again. Even if we were only to remain friends and see each other occasionally, that would be enough for me. And surely he'd call now and then when he came up to Scottsdale to see Betsy and his grandchild. With all my foolish suspicions behind us, we could reminisce lightheartedly and enjoy each other's company.

I continued to pace, wondering if I should go outside to the patrol car and ask them to check on the Stokes house. Michael had always been dependable. Surely he couldn't have forgotten to call and reassure me that his daughter was safe.

Just as I made up my mind to approach the police, the phone rang. At Michael's "Hello, Ruthie," I sat on the floor right where I was and leaned against the wall, weak with relief.

"I'm sorry for the delay," he said. "We had some excitement here, but we're both okay."

"Tim was there?" I could barely get the question out. "He was at Betsy's house?" I remembered the terror of that scene by my swimming pool and grieved at the thought of a pregnant young woman going through similar violence.

"He was hiding by the front door, behind one of the pillars. I was unlocking the door, when he came up and tried to force his way into the house."

I was glad I had the wall for support. It was too easy to imagine the scene as Michael described it.

"Luckily, I was able to reverse direction and back into him," Michael continued. "We both landed on the walk and had a bit of a fight, but it didn't last long. I was so furious with him for trying to kill you and for going after Betsy, that the police had to pry me off him when they arrived."

"Are you really all right?" I asked, my voice shaky with relief that Tim must now be in police custody.

"Absolutely. Would you believe Betsy had gone back to bed after my call from your place and slept through it all?"

"Then who called the police?" I asked. But I knew my earlier conjecture about neighbors like the Brandens was accurate.

Michael gave me a few more details about Tim's arrest. "They'll probably recall the patrol car at your house," he said. "Do you think you'll be all right?"

I assured him that I'd be fine and repeated my assurances to the officer who came to the door to tell me what I already knew about Tim's arrest. But even though I knew I was safe, I spent what was left of that night with my canister of Mace on the pillow next to me.

Chapter 25.

It would have been wonderful to stay home the next day, but that was my Saturday on. Even if it were my day off, though, they'd have needed me to open up the pharmacy because Tim would never be available again.

I had to force myself to shower and dress. Breakfast was out of the question, but I got into my car and, wilted from monsoon humidity in the brief interval before the air-conditioning kicked in, headed to Food Go. By the time I arrived at the pharmacy, I didn't know how I'd make it through the day.

Greg Blackstone, who'd heard the news on his car radio, was waiting for me at the pharmacy. "Fill me in, Ruthie. I can't believe what they're saying about Tim Barnard."

"It's true. He tried to drown me last night."

Greg's usually placid expression creased into a rubbery mask of horror, but before I could give him details, my first customer of the day approached the window with three prescriptions in her outstretched hand. "I don't think you should be working today," Greg said as he walked away. "Call around and see if you can get someone to fill in."

Coming from my store manager, this request meant I could have the day off, provided I found a replacement. Before taking care of customers—they were now starting to line up—I got on the telephone, searching for an available relief pharmacist. Luck was with me. I made contact with a recent pharmacy graduate, Louise Rettenberg, who was working as a floater for Food Go, filling in where needed. She had nothing scheduled and would be there within the hour.

Greg sent Karen to work in the pharmacy, and I was energized enough to take care of all the waiting customers before Louise arrived. She was a little shorter than me, with dark hair that she wore in one neat braid. It reached just below the back collar of her store jacket. I was pleased to see her shake hands with Karen when I introduced them. Some pharmacists are condescending toward technicians, which destroys the harmony in our small workspace. *If Louise is willing to work full time*, I thought, *maybe she can replace Tim.*

Even though she was familiar with the basic Food Go layout and methods, I spent some time showing Louise the peculiarities of our pharmacy. Since Karen was also new, I didn't feel I could leave right away, but at least the pressure had eased for me.

Just as I was preparing to hand over to Louise, I looked up to see Betsy and Michael at the window. "I hoped you'd be home today, resting up after your ordeal," Michael said.

"It's arranged now," I told him. "I'm about to go."

"We're all meeting in the coffee shop," Betsy said. "Will you join us?"

If I'd given any thought to the people she included, I would have guessed at Denise, so I wasn't surprised to see her when we walked into the coffee shop. The others, sitting where Denise had moved two tables together, were the unexpected ones. Richard Stokes and his wife, Nancy, sat across from Sheila and Denise. Verna and Raymond Branden were at the other table, and Michael held out chairs at that table for his daughter and me. He carried over another chair, placed it at one end of the joined tables, and sat with us.

No one spoke. Ellen, the waitress on duty, took our orders. The others wanted only coffee, but I suddenly realized I was starving and asked for French toast and iced tea. We waited silently for our orders and when they came, Michael gave me just enough time to cut the French toast into bite-sized pieces and eat one or two of them.

"Ruthie, we all need to know what happened," Michael said. "Not just last night, but what led up to it. I thought I was dangling myself as bait to catch the killer and, all the time, you were the one in danger."

Richard spoke up, too, sounding no less petulant now that he knew none of those present had harmed his father. "I don't even know that guy. How did he get into the picture?"

I was too tired to match clichés with him again. "Betsy or Michael can tell you about that."

"Tim and I used to date before I met your Dad," Betsy told him. "He was possessive. I guess that's the best word. He didn't want me to go anywhere or do anything without him, not even with the friends I grew up with."

"I never liked the way he treated Betsy," Michael added. "But I didn't recognize that he was dangerous."

"He could have killed all of us," Richard said. "You should have warned us about him."

We all looked at Richard, wondering if he would ever understand. His sister put her hand on his arm. "Do you think Michael would have endangered his daughter if he'd suspected anything?"

"Not everyone who shouts is dangerous," Nancy Stokes said. We all understood she was referring to her husband, although it wasn't clear whether he realized it.

"I moved up from Tucson to get away from Tim," Betsy continued. "It took him a few months to find me. One of my friends who didn't know about our problems gave him the address."

"And meanwhile you met Dad," Sheila said.

"Yes, meanwhile I met Harry." Betsy's voice had softened. "He seemed so safe. And self-confident enough not to be possessive. The opposite of Tim in every way."

"You really did care for Dad." Sheila's voice held a note of surprise.

"Sheila," Richard said warningly.

"Oh, give it up. Betsy and I have both been through enough." Sheila turned to Betsy. "I didn't understand what it was like for you until I nearly lost Scott. I'm sorry for adding to your unhappiness."

Betsy nodded her thanks and continued. "When Tim found me, I told him it was over. He didn't believe it." She turned to me. "That's why he transferred from Food Go in Tucson and moved up here."

"But that must have been at least a year ago," Denise said. "Before you married. I don't understand why Tim waited so long to kill Harry."

"That's why Betsy and I never suspected him," Michael said. "He remained friendly; he never threatened her or Harry."

Betsy's face reddened slightly. "He'd convinced himself that it was nothing personal, that I married Harry for his money. I don't know what changed his mind about that."

It was time for me to explain, but I asked for Betsy's permission before I talked about her prescriptions. "Everyone's been asking the wrong question all along," I told her. "Detective Moreway, your Dad, Richard. All of them wanted to know what prescriptions the various people in the Stokes family were taking."

"That was the wrong question?" Richard's voice was surprisingly quiet.

"Yes, the question should have been, 'Who knew what medicines all of you were taking?'" I turned to Betsy again. "When you went to your obstetrician and learned you were pregnant, you came here with the prescription for Stuartnatal 1 + 1, the prenatal vitamin. That was on July eighteenth, a Saturday. It was my day off, and Tim filled your prescription."

"How do you know that?" Richard demanded.

"His initials were on the computerized record. I never gave it a thought, but Tim knew immediately what that prescription meant. Until your pregnancy, he could convince himself he was a self-sacrificing lover. He even told me he'd 'agreed' to a marriage of convenience so Betsy could have all the material things she deserved."

"That's just what he said when he met Harry last year," Betsy said.

"Tim had no trouble believing you still loved him. In his eyes, Harry was an old man and no threat. Maybe Tim thought you'd come back to him one day. The baby changed all that. It probably made the marriage real for the first time. I'm convinced that's what drove him over the line."

"He never said anything to me," Betsy told us. "We'd known each other for so many years, I was foolish enough to think he'd congratulate me. That young man took the written prescription from me. Joey, the one who was killed. I could see Tim by the computer, but he never came over to the window."

"He must have handed you the filled prescription," I said.

"No, Joey brought it to me. Tim just stood there and never even glanced up."

Michael and I looked at each other. We were the only ones there who knew that Arizona law required the pharmacist, not the technician, to physically give a new script to the patient. Well, that was the least of Tim's legal incursions.

"So Joey knew something was strange even then," I mused aloud.

"Surely Tim didn't risk killing him just for that," Michael said.

"No. But Betsy caught the summer cold that was going around and a week later, she brought in prescriptions for a cough mixture, Tusssi-Organidin DM, and for penicillin."

"He talked to me that time," Betsy said. "My throat was sore, I was terribly congested, and I was coughing. Tim seemed very sympathetic and recommended the Food-Fed decongestant." She thought for a moment. "He even asked after Harry."

"Did he ask whether Harry was sick, too?"

"Yes, he did."

"That must have been when the idea first took shape in Tim's mind," I said. "Harry filled all his prescriptions here, so Tim knew Harry had high blood pressure and diabetes, and that it was dangerous for him to take decongestants. All he had to do was wait for Harry to come in and recommend that he take his wife's Food-Fed."

"But surely that's not a foolproof way to kill someone," Raymond Branden said.

"No, not guaranteed but Tim knew if it worked, no one could ever prove foul play. And when Harry came in on the twenty-seventh, he had new prescriptions—increased dosages for his high blood pressure and diabetes medicines."

"Yes." Betsy's voice had a tinge of sadness. "He was so upset emotionally because of the baby and our arguments, it must have thrown him off balance physically as well."

"Your dad and I discussed all of this before, but we were looking at it from the wrong angle." I wasn't going to admit that, like the police, I'd suspected Betsy of giving the decongestants to her husband. Her eyes met mine and I could see she understood.

"But why did Tim kill Joey," Denise asked. "And why did he go after Scott and you?"

"It would have been a perfect crime if he stopped after Harry's death," I said. "But Joey was a bright young man who wanted to go to medical school. He was always asking questions and reading package inserts." At the Brandens' blank looks, I explained that package inserts are information sheets that tell all about the drug and its possible side effects.

"Joey knew more about medicine than most pharmacy technicians," I continued. "He would have realized something was wrong when Tim wouldn't hand Betsy's prescriptions to her and didn't discuss the drugs with her. But we were both accustomed to Tim's attitude problems. Joey would have known the omission was illegal, but I doubt if he gave it much thought at that point."

"Then why did Joey want to see Denise and my dad?" Betsy asked.

"We know Joey was aware of the various precautions for different drugs. He certainly heard us talk to patients over and over during the two years he worked at Food Go. And he always asked why some drugs couldn't be taken with others. Joey's parents told me something was bothering him after Harry's death, something that affected his eating and sleeping habits. He must have heard Tim recommend the Food-Fed and it must have been on his mind."

"If Joey hadn't been killed, I'd suspect he was the one who recommended the decongestant and that he did it by mistake," Michael said.

"Impossible," I told him. "The first month Joey worked here, he would suggest over-the-counter remedies for customers. I caught him at it and warned him never to do that again. He argued with me, complaining that I underestimated him, that he only recommended drugs he was familiar with. I had to explain the state pharmacy board's views on consultations to him. And I told him even *I* don't recommend specific over-the-counter drugs because we can be sued if something goes wrong. I always show customers where things are and name two or three possibilities. And then I advise them to check with their physicians."

"And did that little lecture stop Joey?" Michael asked with a smile.

"After he heard it two or three times, yes. It's a long time since Joey did anything of the sort, and I'm sure he didn't with Harry."

"Besides," Sheila said. "If the recommendation to take that decongestant came from Joey, he'd still be alive."

Richard was ready to argue again. "Only if you assume my father's and Joey's deaths were connected."

"I admit it's an assumption," I told him. "But remember the night Joey was killed, he had met with most of the principals in this case. I think it's a valid assumption that he saw Tim, too."

"But why did that awful person try to kill Scott and then you?" Nancy Stokes spoke up for the first time. I saw her husband glare at her and watched her shrink back in her seat. But the question had been asked, and despite Richard's reaction to his wife's mild attempt at independence, I was going to answer her.

"My questions about his relationship with Betsy and his feelings when she married someone else were getting too close. I even told him I was convinced Betsy's pregnancy had initiated the chain of events. Then he slipped up when he claimed to have heard nothing about Scott but knew the accident happened in Tempe. I didn't realize it at the time, but he must have figured I would remember his words later on. So, he came to my house to see how much I really knew. He might have left without the attempt on my life." I looked apologetically at Betsy. "But I hesitated when he tried to find out the reason for my questions about you."

"And Scott?" Nancy asked again.

"Scotty regained consciousness this morning," Sheila told her. "He's not thinking too clearly yet. But he confirmed that when Betsy first left Tucson, Tim had threatened to get anyone who took his place in her life."

"I wish I'd known that," I said.

"You wouldn't have wasted time suspecting me," Michael said.

Startled, I turned too quickly toward him, giving myself away. But his eyes had that teasing brightness I remembered so well. I managed a light smile, embarrassed at being understood.

"Detective Moreway told me about your lapse of memory," Michael continued. The others looked puzzled, but neither one of us explained.

"The part that bothers me," I said, "is having to get the details from TV and the papers. In books, the police come around and wrap up everything for the participants."

"You expected Tim to confess?" Betsy asked.

"I don't know what I expected, but it feels unfinished."

"Tim will never admit he's wrong about anything. The police will have to rely on your testimony and on Scott's."

"But that's only *attempted* murder." I could hear the dismay in Denise's voice. "Harry and Joey deserve vengeance."

Everyone was quiet. I know I was thinking how doubtful it was that Tim would ever be implicated in Harry's death. But there was Joey, and Detective Moreway was married to his sister. "Don't worry," I assured Denise. "Now that the police know where to look, they'll surely find evidence linking Tim to Joey's murder."

This seemed the signal to break up. The Brandens were the first to leave, and then Richard pulled his wife away without saying goodbye. Sheila shook hands with the rest of us, and I was pleased to hear the warmth in her voice when she told Betsy she'd call soon.

After a few awkward moments while Michael picked up the check and paid at the register, Denise said she'd better be clocking in for work. Betsy and I stood in the doorway of the Food Go coffee shop.

"I want to thank you, Ruthie. Dad told me you were the one who realized I might be in danger last night."

"We were both lucky."

She smiled at me with that same sweet expression I'd first noticed at her house a few days before. Then she looked toward her father, who was approaching the doorway. "Dad, let me have your car keys and I'll get the air-conditioning started."

We both looked after Betsy as she walked out into the Food Go parking lot. "I think she'll be all right now," I said.

"Yes," Michael agreed. "But I'll be coming up from Tucson every few weeks to check on her." He took my hand and the blue eyes looked steadily at me. "And on you, too," he said.

—End of Book 1—

Book II: Deadly Rx

Ruthie Kantor Morris, R. Ph.
Pharmacy Sleuth Series
created and written by

Renée B. Horowitz

MEDICAL CENTER

NAME _____ AGE ____
ADDRESS _____ DATE ____

Rx

2
Deadly Rx

DISPENSE AS WRITTEN   SIGNATURE
REFILL 0 1 2 3 4 5 PRN NR

Deadly Rx (#2 in the Pharmacy Sleuth Trilogy)

Copyright © 1997 by Renée B. Horowitz. All Rights Reserved.

The Rx Pharmacy Sleuth Trilogy
Copyright © 2016 by Renée B. Horowitz. All Rights Reserved.

Dedication

For Lorraine, David, and Alexis Horowitz; Steve Horowitz; Myron "Mike" Braunstein; and Arthur, of course

Author's Note

To the best of my knowledge, there is no supermarket chain called Food Go. Many drugs that required prescriptions as the time of this novel (such as Pepcid and Zantac) no longer require prescriptions but now can be bought "over the counter." Others may have been discontinued. Such changes in status are a pharmaceutical constant and may affect other drugs before you read my Rx series. Some of the restaurants mentioned in Deadly Rx, as well, are no longer in existence in Scottsdale.

This Deadly Rx is an update of an earlier edition, published by Avon Books.

Chapter 1.

"Have you noticed how many more prescriptions we've been filling lately?" Louise asked. Her question surprised me. Although she's only worked here since August, my new staff pharmacist rarely wants input from me.

"It's seasonal," I explained. "We'll be even busier as more and more winter visitors arrive."

"I've never seen so many women with the same three scripts," she said. "An antibiotic, a blood clotting agent, and a pain pill. And always on Wednesdays and Fridays."

I looked at Louise Rettenberg, trying to gauge whether she was concerned about her ability to work in a busy store. She's a recent pharmacy school graduate, but until now I'd considered her to be self-assured and efficient.

"They come from the clinic on E. Arizona Street," I said.

She looked puzzled. "I know that."

"Abortions," I added–and waited.

"Oh!" She tugged on the neat dark braid that reached just below the collar of her white lab jacket, a nervous gesture I'd seen before.

"Does it bother you?" I asked bluntly.

"Only because most of the women seem so young."

I suppressed a smile. Louise is at least thirty years younger than me. But she was right, and my amusement died quickly as I remembered how frightened and teary-eyed many of these patients look. Some have boyfriends or husbands along; others are with their mothers. But too many seem to be alone, and they're the ones I worry about.

"Don't get me wrong," she added. "I can handle it."

She sounded upset and I hurried to reassure her. "I wasn't doubting your professionalism. Since I'm the pharmacy manager, though, I need to know about potential problems."

Although I'm the pharmacy manager, Louise has never confided in me during the two months we've worked together. She seems to talk more to our young technician, Karen, but the only personal conversation I ever overheard centered on Karen's latest boyfriend.

Louise, Karen, and me—Ruth Kantor Morris. More than half of today's pharmacy graduates are women, but our all-female pharmacy is unusual enough to invite comments from customers and other pharmacists.

Louise was right; we were busy. People seemed to arrive in Scottsdale hourly from the East and Midwest. I had even noticed a few Canadian license plates in the parking lot. Although most Arizonans call these seasonal arrivals "snowbirds," I prefer the polite term, "winter visitors." After all, many of them are my customers here at the Food Go pharmacy.

Compared to the weather they're escaping from, our October days are warm. After surviving another Arizona summer, however, I feel chilly in the early mornings and evenings. That's why I arrived at the pharmacy a little while ago carrying my white cotton cardigan—too warm to wear now, but I'm on the night shift. I'll need the sweater when I leave work this evening. Now, I put on my professional jacket and started to help Louise clear the backlog of prescriptions. We had no time to talk.

Louise's shift ended about an hour later. Karen, our technician, was off today, so I'd be working alone until closing. I tried to move fast to keep up with the flow, but as quickly as I filled prescriptions, they kept coming in. At one point, at least four people were at the window. Others took the opportunity to shop while they waited, which was one advantage of a supermarket pharmacy.

"Is my prescription ready?" A thin, thirtyish woman with dark eyes that darted from side to side and never looked directly at me was next.

I took her name and looked through the "will call" stack. Nothing. The Rx's we were keeping "on hold" for a doctor's telephoned okay also yielded nothing. The only other place to look, the stack waiting for incoming inventory, was another miss. I rubbed my forehead, wondering what I'd overlooked and checked the computer.

"Nothing here for you," I told the customer.

"Has to be. Didn't my doctor call you?"

"No. I'm sorry." I looked at the screen. The computer showed that we filled a script for Toradol, the non-narcotic pain reliever, for this patient on the 10th of October and refilled it on the 12th. Today was the 14th of the month.

"Toradol, that's right," she said when I gave her the details. "That's the one I want."

"I'm sorry," I repeated. "You got it already."

"How can you tell?"

That was an odd question, but I showed her the original written prescription with the stickers that the computer generates when we fill each script. By this time, five or six other people had lined up behind her. I would never catch up.

"Somebody else got my medicine," she announced to the crowd. "I never did."

"Would you like me to call your doctor?"

"Never mind. I'll take care of it myself." She turned again to the people behind her. "I didn't even see the doctor until today."

"That's strange," I countered. "Right here, in the doctor's own handwriting, it says October 10th."

I saw some of the other customers trying not to laugh, but a waiting teenager seemed lost in her own thoughts, and the older woman with her looked grim. Before walking away, the woman threw one parting dart at me. "Well, I don't care what you say. You made a mistake."

This was a serious accusation, and I glanced quickly at my other customers to see their reactions. I intercepted a few sympathetic looks, and the next woman in line even reminded me that it takes all kinds. I smiled at her, but thought it would be unprofessional to agree.

Working as quickly as I safely could, I finally got to the last of the line of waiting customers and saw that no new ones had approached. Maybe I'd have some breathing space to do paperwork tonight.

The last people in line were the teenager I'd noticed before and her dour companion. The younger woman handed me prescriptions for an antibiotic, a blood clotting agent, and a pain pill. I felt a surge of sympathy, knowing she'd probably just had an abortion.

Although the young woman wasn't alone, she was the kind of patient I worried about. She was wearing jeans and a pink T-shirt that advertised a popular amusement park. A typical teen at first glance, but her eyes were bloodshot with dark smudges below, and she seemed to be making an effort to hold herself together. She was thin enough to appear emaciated, and her face was pale. I looked at the first script again. Her name was Amy Brookman. She was sixteen.

"It'll take about ten minutes," I said.

"Okay."

"Can you make it faster?" the older woman demanded. Her voice was deep, but I couldn't tell whether it was an emotional huskiness or her natural tone. She was about sixty, with well-shaped features and short white hair. I thought she looked too old to have a teenage daughter. Neatly dressed in a black and white herringbone suit and crisp white blouse, she seemed to have just stepped out of one of the office buildings across the

street from Food Go. I wondered if Amy had been left to face the surgery
alone while mother went to work. That was unfair, I reminded myself. Not
everyone could afford to lose a day's salary.

Usually, I hate it when people try to rush me. They can't really think I
take my time deliberately. Amy, however, looked as if she couldn't stand
up much longer, so I buried my annoyance.

"I'll do my best," I answered mildly and moved over to the computer.
While the labels for the three scripts were printing, I pulled the bottles
from the shelves and counted out the dosages. She was getting the usual—
10 Doxycycline, the antibiotic, to be taken one capsule twice a day. Then,
her 20 Vicodin pain pills for the cramps. I used the generic here to save her
money. And, finally, the 12 Methergine to control the bleeding.

Taking the labels from the printer, I checked each vial before labeling
them. Amy and the older woman hadn't moved or spoken to each other. I
reached across the pharmacy window and showed each vial, in turn, to
Amy before bagging them. "The blue capsules, the Doxycyclines, are the
antibiotic. You have to take one capsule twice a day for five days. Be sure
to take them all." I paused a moment and added in my most professional
tone, "That's very important."

She wasn't meeting my eyes, and I wondered how much patient
counseling was getting through. At least her mother seemed to be
listening.

"The purple ones are to stop the bleeding," I continued. "Take one
tablet four times a day for three days. Be sure to take them until they're all
gone, too."

Now she looked at me. I could see the sudden realization that I knew
what her medications were for.

"The last ones, the white tablets are for pain," I said, keeping my
voice as detached as possible. "Take one every four hours if you need
them. That will help with the cramps."

"Did you understand, dear?" The husky voice was solicitous, and I
was glad to see the girl's mother was supportive. Sometimes when a
teenager is involved, the mothers humiliate their daughters by berating
them right in front of me and any other customers who might be listening.
And when boyfriends or husbands accompany the young women, their
attitudes range from tenderness to abusiveness.

"Yes, Auntie."

Well, I had guessed wrong. As they left the pharmacy area, I
wondered momentarily where her mother was. I would never know the
girl's story, but she seemed so fragile that my heart went out to her. Both
telephones in the pharmacy began to ring just then, and I forgot all about

Amy. By the time I took care of the call-ins, more customers were at the window. The next prescription I filled was for Clomid, a fertility pill, but I was too busy to reflect on life's ironies.

Chapter 2.

My memory of Amy Brookman revived with an unexpected jolt two days later when I recognized her picture under the headline, "TEEN DIES FOLLOWING ABORTION." Either stories of local interest were scarce that day or the newspaper was using scare tactics to support its anti-abortion stand and its campaign against teenage pregnancies. In any case, I stared at the photo. Amy looked even younger than she had in person. Perhaps it was an old picture. She wasn't smiling but had the same serious expression I remembered.

I read the article. Amy had hemorrhaged and gone into shock before she could be helped. There were few details. The reporter said that the girl's parents were separated, and Amy had been living in Scottsdale with an aunt, her mother's older sister. The story served as a departure point for statistics about deaths from abortions per thousand procedures. Both pro-life and pro-choice activists were interviewed, but the doctor who performed the operation could not be reached. Nor would anyone in Amy's family comment.

"Did you read this?" I asked Denise Seaford after ordering my lunch at the Food Go Coffee Shop. Denise was a waitress there, and we'd become friendly after my husband's death two years ago. During the summer, Denise and I had suffered through the ordeal of a murder investigation. I still felt guilty when I remembered that, for a while at least, I had thought she was the murderer.

Denise, who'd been smiling when she seated me, turned pale. "I wonder sometimes what would've happened if Craig and I had kids," she said.

"Did you want children?" I never had the nerve to ask before.

"Yes, but we were always saving for something or other. The time just got away from us, I guess."

I knew what was coming and braced myself. "What about you?" she asked.

"No luck."

"Didn't you see a doctor?"

"Of course, I did! We both were tested and retested, but there weren't so many options then."

I thought about Bob and myself in the first years of our marriage. In those days, women expected to marry and have children. And I was no different even though I'd become a pharmacist at a time when few of us were in that profession. It took three miscarriages before I gave up.

Denise left to turn in my order, but I could see our conversation had to wait because two men had seated themselves at the opposite end of the coffee shop. I watched as she handed them menus, filled their water glasses, and took their beverage orders. They were in their forties, wearing white shirts and ties, but no jackets. I figured they were attorneys from one of the nearby office buildings. Engrossed in conversation, they paid little attention to Denise; but I noticed the way she looked at the one with thinning dark hair and old-fashioned horn-rimmed glasses and guessed she was interested in him.

Denise sometimes dated her customers, but I could never understand why these men faded from her life so quickly. She looked younger than her forty-five years, with a zest for life that showed in her flair for color combinations in her makeup and clothes. Today, she was wearing a lime green blouse with splashes of old rose that would have looked unfashionable on anyone else. Her skirt matched the rose in the blouse and so did her makeup. With the dark green aprons supplied by Food Go for their coffee shop waitresses, the effect was surprisingly attractive.

Denise soon returned with the tuna salad and iced tea I always ordered. When the weather cooled off a little more, I would switch to coffee or hot tea. At this time of year, I preferred hot beverages in the mornings and evenings, iced tea during the day.

"Do you know him?" I asked.

One of the things I like about Denise is her lack of pretension. Another woman might have asked what I meant.

"He comes in for lunch a couple of times a week. When he's alone, we get to talk, so I know he's divorced."

"Do you think he's interested in you?"

"I don't know. Maybe I started daydreaming about him because I get so lonely sometimes."

"Yes," I said. "No matter how busy we are, the nights are long."

"You have Michael now."

"I don't *have* Michael."

"Please don't think I'm envious, Ruthie. It's just harder for me now. I feel like I'm the only one who's alone."

I thought about Michael Loring. He had come back into my life with overwhelming impact when he had wanted access to some prescription files. Michael was sure the records would prove his daughter had nothing to do with her husband's sudden death.

"He just comes up from Tucson to see his daughter," I assured Denise.

"Could be, but he takes you to dinner whenever he gets to Scottsdale."

"We're old friends," I said.

Denise looked skeptical although I'd never told her that many years ago, Michael and I had planned to marry as soon as we both graduated from pharmacy school. "I don't know about that. You've been a widow for two years now. It's perfectly normal to date an attractive man."

"Men in their fifties aren't interested in their contemporaries," I said, knowing I sounded cynical, but unable to completely hide my uncertainties "They prefer younger women."

The two men at the other table signaled for coffee refills, and Denise hurried across to their table. Then, she had to detour to seat a middle-aged, casually dressed couple, and took their order before coming back to me.

"I know you won't talk about your patients," Denise said, "but I can guess this Amy who just died was one of them. Otherwise, you wouldn't be so shook up."

"Am I upset?"

"Maybe you can fool other people, Ruthie, but not me."

The light above the counter was flashing, which meant an order was ready. Denise left to deliver it to the two men. Meanwhile, a group of high school kids came into the coffee shop, and I knew she would be too busy to talk for quite a while. I finished my lunch and went to the office to clock in.

My night shift shouldn't be too hectic this time, I thought. Louise wasn't scheduled to leave for a few more hours and our technician, Karen, would be in after school. I entered the pharmacy and, seeing at once how busy Louise was at the computer, waded into the fray.

"Have you been helped yet?"

Mrs. Wilmer, a white-haired woman in her seventies, handed me her prescription. She was a feisty one, despite the many ailments that frequently brought her into the pharmacy, and I always enjoyed helping her.

I saw immediately that the physician had checked off "Dispense as written," which meant I could not legally fill the script with a generic drug.

I remembered, however, that we charged $43.55 for 30 capsules of the name brand, while the generic equivalent would cost her considerably less—under five dollars. I took the time to explain the price difference to her.

"Then, of course, I prefer the generic," she said.

"There's just one problem," I told her. "Your doctor always writes for the brand name. We've asked him to use generics before, but no luck."

"Let me try." The customer's tone was firm. "That is, if I may use your telephone."

I handed the phone to her through the window. "Yes, I'm sure *Doctor* is busy, but I want my prescription changed to the generic," I heard her say. A long pause followed. "Please go back again and tell him I can't afford the extra money. It's close to $40 more."

This time the wait was longer. "Fine," she said. "Maybe *Doctor* would like to pay the difference."

After a moment, the customer handed the phone to me. I took down the change in the script and replaced the receiver. "I guess you got his attention."

She laughed. "Would you believe it? He said he didn't know I felt so strongly about the cost."

A heavyset man in gray came up to the window as she walked away and placed his open wallet on the counter. I expected to see a card from some insurance plan. It was an ID from the Arizona State Board of Pharmacy.

"One moment," I said and unlocked the door for him. Periodically, someone from the State Board arrives unannounced to check on each pharmacy in the state. The examiner looks for outdated drugs, makes sure the pharmacy is clean, checks that the licenses of the registered pharmacists on duty are displayed, and audits Schedule II drugs—the ones the government considers most likely to be abused. These routine inspections are supposed to help pharmacists comply voluntarily with state and federal laws. As pharmacy manager or, as the State of Arizona puts it, "pharmacist-in-charge," I'm responsible for any violations the inspector may find, and I always feel slightly nervous until he fills out his report and hands it to me.

Karen, who had arrived just before the examiner, and Louise both stopped what they were doing and watched the man as though they expected him to perform magic tricks. I figured a State Board visit must be a new experience for both women. And although I'd been through so many of them during my years in pharmacy, I felt a sudden chill. My records were always in order; I couldn't understand why I was so much more apprehensive than usual.

After the examiner introduced himself as Jim Dalton, I waited for him to begin inspecting the pharmacy. Instead, he asked me to call up Amy Brookman's records on the computer.

Not a routine visit, I thought. For some reason, though, my nervousness increased as I busied myself printing out the information Dalton wanted.

"Her visit on the 14th was the first time here?"

I nodded. My throat felt too dry to speak.

Louise and Karen, still ignoring customers at the window, moved closer. "That's the young woman who died, isn't it?" Louise asked. "I didn't realize she was one of our patients. She must have come in after my shift ended."

Louise sounds like she's giving herself an alibi, I thought. What's going on here?

Dalton was looking at the printout. "Did you counsel her?" he asked.

"Of course, I did." I knew I sounded defensive.

"Do you remember what you said?"

"I always say the same things to abortion patients."

He was silent, waiting for me to continue. I cleared my throat, willing my voice to sound natural. "As you see, she got the usual three scripts," I began.

"And you personally handed them to her."

"I was the only one here."

"How *busy* were you?" He emphasized the word "busy," and again I felt defensive.

"It doesn't matter how busy I am. I hand every vial to every customer separately, naming the drug, and mentioning the color as an added safeguard." My stomach was in knots. Why did I always feel guilty even when I knew I hadn't done anything wrong?

"Then I tell them the dosage, and I stress how important it is to follow the full regimen—to take the medications until they're gone."

He looked down at the printout. "And you filled the script for 12 Methergine to control the bleeding."

Now I understood why I was reacting so tensely to Dalton's visit. Before conscious thought, my body had known the danger I faced and had gone into fight or flight mode. I remembered the newspaper account. Amy Brookman had bled to death.

"How could she hemorrhage when she was taking Methergine?" I asked the question as it leaped into my mind.

"That's exactly what we're trying to determine," Dalton said. "We're analyzing the contents of the vial with the Methergine label. The tablets are purple all right. But I have to tell you, to the admitting doctor at the hospital, they looked more like Coumadin."

"Coumadin," I whispered. "No, that's impossible." Coumadin is an anti-clotting agent, a blood thinner. It's probably saved innumerable lives of people who may be prone to heart attacks or strokes. But if Amy had taken a drug that prevented clotting after her abortion instead of one that aided it... No, it didn't bear thinking about.

"We were terribly busy that afternoon," Louise said. Now she sounded like she was trying to give *me* an alibi. I didn't want an alibi. There was no way I could have made such a mistake.

Dalton turned to her. "Didn't you say your shift had ended?"

"That's true. But when I left, we were way behind. I would have stayed and helped Ruthie clear the backlog, but I had an appointment."

What is she doing, I wondered. *She's trying to protect herself, but now she's making it worse for me.* Even though my physical distress was increasing by the minute, I had to say something.

"Mr. Dalton, it's not possible that I could have substituted Coumadin for the Methergine, if that's what you're implying. We don't shelve them anywhere near each other. And even though they're both purple, you know they don't look alike. Besides, no matter how busy we are, I always double check medications before I hand them to the patient."

"I'm sure you do," he said, but his tone didn't match his words.

Years ago, I'd attended an assertiveness seminar. It was time to make use of the techniques I'd been taught. I took a deep breath and spoke forcefully. "You'll find I'm very professional in everything I do. I think we should wait for the analysis before we continue this discussion."

He gathered up the printout, thanked me for my help, and left the pharmacy.

Karen looked like she was about to cry. I patted her shoulder lightly. "Don't worry," I said, not knowing whether I was talking to her or trying to reassure myself. "It will be okay."

Out of the corner of my eye, I saw Louise shrug. "Are you sure you didn't make a mistake?" she asked.

"Louise, don't even joke about something like that."

Chapter 3.

I stared at Louise, unable to believe she had so little confidence in me. It's true we've only worked together for two months, but surely she could see by now that I'm methodical and careful. Because there were so few women pharmacists when I graduated from pharmacy school more than thirty years ago, I had known I must excel to prove myself. I had worked hard during those early years to be accepted as a capable professional. And the habits I developed then had never changed.

"Every pharmacist makes mistakes," Louise said in a low voice so the waiting customers couldn't hear her. "One of my professors told us that. What you have to do, he warned us, is minimize your legal liability. Cover yourself."

This was a new Louise. I was surprised at her cynicism and wondered what they were teaching in the pharmacy schools nowadays.

"Listen to me, Louise," I said as firmly as I could. "You know there's no way I could have made such a mistake. The Methergine is a coated tablet with white printing, not embossing like Coumadin. And Coumadin is flatter, uncoated, and a much lighter shade of purple."

"And if you just registered that the tablets were purple?"

"No. It's impossible. They don't look alike at all." I wanted to suggest that she transfer to another Food Go pharmacy if she had so little confidence in my abilities, but a customer was tapping on the counter. I didn't blame the young man. He'd waited patiently for at least ten minutes.

I walked over to the window and took his three prescriptions. "They're for my friend," he said, his expression daring me to comment. Doxycycline, Vicodin, and Methergine. His "friend" must be another abortion patient.

The scripts seemed to burn my fingers. I stood staring at them for a moment and, suddenly unable to cope, handed them to Louise to fill. At least the next customer, a middle-aged woman, would need some other medications.

I looked down and saw the same three prescriptions. This was becoming nightmarish. How could my head be burning this way when I felt so cold?

"It's for my daughter," the woman said. "I don't know what to do with her. Two abortions already, and she's only eighteen."

I'd heard this lament before and tried to look sympathetic. Any comment would be unprofessional. Karen was at the computer, doing the labels for the previous customer while Louise took down a prescription over the telephone. I would have to pull myself together and retrieve these medications from the shelves.

My fingers felt clammy as I took down the three bottles. I looked at their labels and compared them to the scripts. Then I checked again. When I counted out the Methergine, my hands shook, and I took four or five deep breaths to steady myself. The tablets were coated and darker than Coumadin. Methergine, without a doubt.

I gave the prescriptions to Karen to do the computer work. Louise was at the window, handing out the young man's medications. "And you must tell your friend to take these purple tablets four times a day for three days. Otherwise, she can bleed to death."

Good God, I thought. What kind of patient counseling is that?

Karen had the labels ready and I attached them to the scripts I'd just filled, checking each vial again. This time, I also rechecked as I told the woman how her daughter should take each one.

"The instructions are on the labels, but be sure to go over them with her and be certain she understands," I said.

Louise was now behind me, looking over my shoulder. "Did you double check everything?" she asked.

The customer couldn't miss her words, and I felt my face flush from combined embarrassment, chagrin, and anger. "Louise," I said softly. "I've been a pharmacist since before you were born."

Now why did I say that, I wondered. I don't have to justify myself to her. What's happening to me?

Louise gave another expressive shrug and went to help the next customer. I wanted to talk about her scare tactics with the young man but couldn't bring myself to confront her. I walked into the back room. Ordinarily, I would ask Karen to unpack the order that was waiting. I started to do it instead, knowing I was hiding back there. I couldn't help myself.

Nothing like this had ever happened to me. I'd had encounters with addicts who presented forged prescriptions. Only two months ago, I escaped from a murderer who tried to drown me in my own swimming pool. But this was different.

In the quiet back room of the pharmacy, I thought about Amy Brookman. *Could I have made a mistake? Not one like that*, I told myself. I probed to see if my reaction was wishful thinking or self-delusion. If I'd done nothing wrong, why was I so upset?

Louise left about an hour later, and my own shift continued with no further problems until I finished at nine o'clock that night. The next day, my Saturday to work, was uneventful except for a call from Michael.

"I meant to dash up from Tucson sooner," he said. Michael's vitality showed even in his word choices. When we were in school together, I never heard him plan to do homework problems or write a paper. He was always going to tackle the assignment or race by the library. "I hope it's not too late to ask you out for Sunday brunch."

His voice turned the telephone wires into a lifeline. I wondered if I could tell Michael about Amy Brookman and my self-doubts. When we had been in love, all those years ago, I wouldn't have hesitated. Even now, if we were alone... On the other hand, if his widowed daughter, Betsy Stokes, was going to join us, I knew I could say nothing. I would have to wait and decide tomorrow.

* * * *

Saturday evening, after I arrived home from the pharmacy, I found myself regressing to my coed years, to the young woman who so joyously dressed for dates with Michael. I remembered one special evening, a Sunday night dance at our synagogue. My parents had argued with me for days.

"You can't take that one to a dance at the *shul*."

"His name is Michael."

"I know his name. Michael this and Michael that. It's a household word around here."

My family had moved to Tucson from New York before I was born, so I was that rarity—a native Arizonan. I lived at home—no dorms for Ruthie Kantor—and my mother was always in the kitchen when I returned from classes at the University. She usually helped Dad in his drugstore for a few hours during the late mornings and early afternoons. No matter how busy the store was, Mama was waiting with a snack for me. In some ways, she was the stereotype of the Jewish mother–not the kind some people joked about or vilified in recent years. Instead, she was the "yiddische mama" of song, the one whose jewels were her children. In this case, child, because I was the only one she had carried to term.

"Ruthie, you know we want only good things for you."

"Mama, I'm not marrying him. I just want to take him to the dance."

"What's wrong with Bernie Levine? What's wrong with Stanley Harris?" When my mother followed this track, she could continue indefinitely. I once counted 17 names before she ran out of steam.

"I enjoy talking to Michael. We're in class together. With other boys, I never know what to say."

Although I was a university student, my mother insisted I have milk and cookies every afternoon before I went to take her place at the drugstore. Milk for strong bones. Well, that medical insight turned out to be surprisingly accurate. I wondered if Mama was also right about Michael. Would we have been happy if we'd married or would it have ended in divorce the way his eventual marriage to Betsy's mother had ended?

"*My yiddische mama, I need her more than ever now.*" The words of the song ran through my mind as I thought about Michael and how much I still cared for him. It was the first time since he'd come back into my life that I'd admitted those feelings, even to myself.

As I remembered that dance so many years ago, I was rummaging through my closet, trying to decide what to wear tomorrow. The weather forecast was calling for just over 100 degrees. Temperature in Arizona is relative, however. In Spring, we make bets as to when the thermometer will first hit that 100-degree mark. And despite our air-conditioned environments, we suffer when the temperature begins to climb.

Now, in Fall, it was different. "It's just perfect today," people tell each other. "Only 101 degrees."

* * * *

When Michael turned into my driveway, Sunday morning, I was sitting in the dining room where I could see the street from my bay window. I had decided to wear a rust and white print dress with a matching short-sleeved jacket. Now that the winter visitors were returning to Scottsdale, the restaurant probably would have the air cranked to their needs. For residents, that could be too chilly.

I watched as Michael walked up the path to my front door, knowing I couldn't be seen from the street. In the sunlight, his hair looked more white than blond, but the vigor of his stride denied the years that had passed. Before the door chimes sounded, I had time enough to register that he was wearing tan slacks, an off-white shirt, and a tan and navy tie. He looked wonderful to me.

"Ruthie." His tone was warm, but he made no attempt to kiss me. In this age of casual acquaintances who never hesitate to peck each other's cheeks, I could only guess he was deliberately avoiding a gesture that I might misinterpret.

We had only seen each other twice since August, when his son-in-law's murderer had nearly drowned me. Both times, Michael had taken me to dinner. Brunch seemed more casual somehow—not what we would have called a real date when I was young.

He held open the door of his silver-and-gray Lexus for me and waited while I seated myself and buckled my seat belt. Since I had ceiling fans throughout the house, I was no longer using my air conditioner at home, but cars could still heat up quickly. Even in the short time Michael's car was parked in my sunny driveway, the interior had become uncomfortably hot, and I was thankful when he turned the motor on and the air kicked in.

We were awkward with each other for a few minutes. I asked after his daughter and whether she would be joining us at brunch.

"Betsy wanted to sleep late. But she told me to be sure and whisk you back to her house."

I knew his daughter was having a difficult pregnancy. She must be in her fifth month, I calculated. Several times, Michael had driven up from Tucson to be with her when she'd sounded despondent over the telephone. He had called me those times, too, but hadn't wanted to leave Betsy alone. I knew he worried about her.

"She tries to sound cheerful," Michael told me. "But I understand how much she misses Harry."

Despite an initial negative reaction to Betsy, my feelings toward her were sympathetic now. *At least her inheritance from Harry Stokes and her father's support will see her through*, I thought, relieved for her sake.

Many of the young women I saw in the pharmacy seemed to have far less going for them than Betsy. I shivered as I remembered Amy Brookman and determined to tell Michael about her. He was a pharmacist, too; he would understand.

Michael had made brunch reservations at one of the luxury resorts on Scottsdale Road. We were seated in a corner near the windows, and I wondered if he'd requested that quiet table. I decided to wait until we'd taken the edge off our appetites and then confide in him.

A waitress brought champagne and we sipped it slowly, in no rush to join the crowd at the buffet tables. Michael told me a few stories about the hospital pharmacy he managed, not naming the patients, of course. I had no idea what he did when he wasn't at work or whether he was seeing anyone in Tucson. As far as I could tell, he lived alone, but I wasn't even certain about that.

How did one find out? I was new to the jargon of the singles scene but supposed I could ask if he were involved in a relationship. What was the term nowadays? Significant other. I could just hear myself saying that!

Not wanting to talk shop yet, I toyed with my champagne glass. Today, talking shop meant telling Michael about Amy Brookman and, although we were alone, I was strangely reluctant to broach the subject. "Let's get some food," I said finally.

We walked over to the omelet bar and gave our orders to the chef. While we waited for him to make the omelets with our choice of ingredients, Michael stood close beside me. "Your hair is longer than it was in August," he said. "Now you look just the way I remember you."

"I've been letting it grow since summer's over."

For a moment, I thought he was about to put his arm around me, but he suddenly moved away to take the plate the chef held out. "Mushrooms, cheese, and salsa," Michael said. "This must be yours."

His own omelet, which came up next, was topped with ham. As we reseated ourselves, he glanced at the meat and back at me. "This wasn't too sensitive on my part. Does the ham offend you?"

Michael had told me back in August, the first time we had dinner together, that he would have encouraged me to keep my traditions, even though our religions were different. "No," I said. "I think I told you Bob wasn't observant. We never had pork or shellfish in our own home—I couldn't bring myself to do that—but he ate it elsewhere."

"Do you realize, Ruthie, we never discussed how to make it work? You and your parents were so insistent that you could never marry a non-Jew."

I wondered why he was bringing that up now. It had been so many years ago, and we were very different people today. So different that two months ago, I'd even suspected Michael of murder. I looked down at my plate and ignored the question.

"For a while, I was rather bitter," Michael said. "Please don't misunderstand; I'm not criticizing."

He wasn't eating much, but I deliberately concentrated on my omelet to avoid replying. The salsa suddenly seemed too spicy to bear.

"Over the years, I gathered up every book I could find about Judaism, and I thought for a time I had some idea why you wouldn't marry me. But I don't think I really understood then."

"Let's not dwell on the past, Michael."

"This is something I feel compelled to tell you," he continued. "Have you been to the holocaust museum in Washington?"

"Not yet."

"I flew over to D.C. earlier this year for a hospital pharmacy convention. It was just before we met again."

He concentrated on me with that vitality I remembered so well. The waitress came by to refill our champagne glasses, but now neither of us was eating or drinking. I had lost my appetite but, at the same time, wanted to cram food into my mouth so I wouldn't have to respond to Michael's words.

"I couldn't believe it when we met again. I'd been thinking about you for months."

Now I was afraid he'd ask whether I'd ever thought about him. I didn't want to reveal my vulnerability. This was going to be worse than the first time. It would take me much longer to recover from Michael than when I was twenty years old.

"You've probably read how they create empathy at the museum. Each visitor takes on the identity of someone who was caught up in the holocaust. At the end, you discover what happened to your person."

He paused and I was surprised to hear the catch in his voice. "My person died at Buchenwald. I cried when I found out."

No longer worrying about my own vulnerability, I reached out and put my hand on Michael's. I suddenly felt incredibly alive as he turned our hands so that mine was enveloped in his larger one.

"Yes, it makes you appreciate being alive," he said, as though he'd read my mind.

"And I wanted to tell you then, but I didn't know how to reach you."

The moment was too intense. I was glad when the waitress came by and asked if we wanted clean plates. We returned to the buffet tables and filled our plates, seemingly absorbed in our own thoughts, but they must have been following parallel lines.

"How young we were," I started to say as we walked back to our own table. At almost the same moment, Michael said, "We were too young to rush headlong into life."

"My parents kept telling me we were too young. We should wait and see if we still felt the same way later on."

Michael held out my chair for me. "And did you still feel the same way?"

I hesitated for a moment, then decided to be honest. "By that time, it was too late. You had already transferred from the U. of A."

"But I hurried away from the University of Arizona because you told me it was hopeless, that we could never marry."

"Michael," I said and repeated, "Let's not dwell on the past." I tried to erase from my voice traces of the despair I'd felt all those years ago. "It doesn't do any good."

We both had heaped our plates with the usual Sunday buffet food, but neither of us had tasted any of it. I picked up my knife and spread cream cheese on the two halves of a small onion bagel. Then I speared some Bermuda onion rings and a slice of tomato, added them, and topped it all off with smoked salmon. The smoked salmon looked delicious, a much better quality than I usually found in the Food Go deli. When I tried to eat, though, everything tasted like cardboard. I put the bagel down.

"I think we do need to talk about the past," Michael said. "If we're going to remain friends, and I'd like to, we have some cobwebs to brush away."

"Maybe, you're right."

"For a long time, I was overwhelmed with resentment. I jumped past that years ago, but I need to understand some things." He had chosen a croissant instead of a bagel, and I watched as he broke it and slathered it with strawberry jam and butter—but he wasn't eating either.

"Go ahead, Michael. I guess it is time to take our memories out of storage and look them over once more before we throw them away."

"Since we met again last summer, I've thought about something you told me before we broke up. It was about intermarriage not being fair to children." He turned the full intensity of those blue eyes on me. "But you never had a child, Ruthie."

My eyes filled with tears, but I couldn't cry in front of him. I concentrated on rearranging the food on my plate until I could control myself. "It wasn't intentional."

"Another irony," he said. This time it was Michael who reached out for my hand. "Ruthie, I'm sorry. I didn't intend to hurt you, but I just had to know. "

"The early years, when Bob and I wanted a child so badly—that was when it hurt. Women would come into the pharmacy with their new babies, and I'd wonder why not me. But it's a long time since I felt that way."

He was silent, but I could sense his doubts. I hurried to be absolutely truthful. "Lately, since Bob's death, I've thought about children again. About how wonderful it would be to have family now."

At Michael's expression, I hurried to add with a little laugh for emphasis, "Don't worry. These bouts of self-pity don't happen very often." In reality, I despised myself when self-pity took over; and I couldn't understand why I'd revealed so much to him. "It's just lately with the abortion clinic sending so many patients to my pharmacy."

"Abortion clinic?"

"Yes. The way it affects me is strange, Michael. Some of them... some are just girls. And it hurts to see them discard what I wanted so badly."

"Did you and Bob consider adopting?"

I thought back to the early years of my marriage. Bob Morris was the son of a family friend. His name was one of the many Mama used to mention when she wanted me to go out with a nice Jewish boy instead of Michael. I didn't marry Bob on the rebound, though. When I finally agreed to meet him, it was more than two years after Michael had transferred to an eastern school.

I liked Bob right away. Although we were the same age, he had a serious air that made him seem older. We dated every Saturday night, as young people did in those days, and we might have drifted apart if Bob hadn't been drafted during the Vietnam War. It was while he served overseas that I realized how much I missed him. And when he returned, we decided to marry.

We lived in Tucson because I still worked for Dad. Immediately after I graduated from pharmacy college, Dad had enlarged the drugstore to make room for his only child. I enjoyed working with him, and I learned faster and smoother ways to make ointments, how to sell over-the-counter items, and other things that had never been taught in school.

The pharmacy was an old one, with paneled walls and thick shelves that still held many old-fashioned medicine bottles. We had no computers in those days, just an old manual typewriter, and if I made a typo in a label, I had to redo it completely.

Bob and I alternated Friday night dinners between my folks and his parents and, no matter which home we were at, we heard the same question each week, "Well, when do we get a grandchild?"

After a few years, the pressure mounted. Our families convinced us that I would carry to term if only I stayed at home and didn't work so hard—not an uncommon belief in those days. So I left my profession and bustled around the small house we had bought in Tucson, looking for things to occupy my time. And nothing happened. Meanwhile, one of the dreaded supermarket chains had opened across the street from Dad's drugstore. Their pharmacy drained customers from us, and when I wanted to return to work, there was no longer enough business to keep two registered pharmacists busy.

At about this time, Bob was invited to work at a start-up company in Scottsdale. We decided the time was right to leave Tucson and, especially, to put 120 miles between ourselves and the parental nagging that, gentle though it was, never stopped.

I went back to work, this time at a pharmacy in a small medical building in Scottsdale and stayed with them until I transferred to Food Go sometime later. We bought the house I still live in and were a comfortable couple until Bob's death just over two years ago.

My retreat into the past had taken only moments, but I realized Michael was waiting for an answer to his question. "Yes," I told him. "We talked about it, and then we made the mistake of mentioning the possibility to our families." The ensuing uproar had been a major factor in our decision to move from Tucson.

Remembering how much parental approval or disapproval meant to us then seems unreal in today's world. Thinking back to the social climate in those days and trying to comprehend why it affected us so much is nearly as difficult as reading Jane Austen and understanding the way Emma catered to her father's wishes. Even after we moved, we were unable to ignore their opposition to adopting children.

I told Michael, and he wanted to know why they opposed adoption. "If they ever gave us reasons, I don't remember them." It was the truth. Either I'd repressed the memory, or they had felt reasons were unnecessary.

"And what happened after you moved up here?"

"I don't know. There were no more pregnancies. We spent some time going to fertility specialists and found out the problem was with Bob." I smiled ruefully. "Ironic, isn't it? I gave up pharmacy for more than a year because of an old wives' tale."

"You haven't eaten anything," Michael said. "I'm sorry I brought up such a painful topic."

"It hasn't been painful for a long time now. I guess what happened last week is affecting me more than I realized."

"Let's get some dessert and talk about it," he said.

We walked over to the dessert table and looked at the array of cakes and pastries. I chose a slice of pecan cheesecake and waited while Michael decided on a double chocolate layer cake. My appetite hadn't improved, but I tasted the cheesecake to avoid talking. *You're foolish*, I told myself. *This is the opportunity you wanted. Michael's a pharmacist, too. See what he thinks about the Amy Brookman situation.*

"Michael," I said hesitantly. "Have you ever dispensed the wrong drug?"

He rose quickly and came to my side of the table. "What pharmacist hasn't?" he asked.

"If I really did this, it was a fatal error."

I told him about Amy Brookman's prescriptions and about her death. Then I recounted the visit by the State Pharmacy Board inspector. Michael listened quietly, but he seemed to crackle with barely constrained energy.

"What I'm hearing," he said finally, "is that there's some connection in your mind between your own miscarriages and childless marriage and the way you react to women who undergo abortions."

"No, I don't think it has any bearing on this case."

"Are you sure?" Michael's words sent a chill through me that had nothing to do with the air-conditioned restaurant. "Could it have disturbed you enough to substitute an anti-clotting agent for the Methergine?"

"But that would be murder," I said, barely able to get the words out. That was when the doubts really took over. First Louise, and now Michael. I felt betrayed.

Chapter 4.

Although Michael tried to apologize, we had very little to say to each other after that. And nothing more was mentioned about going on to his daughter's house. I tried to tell myself that Michael's questions were natural ones. There was no reason to take it so badly. Others would be asking me tougher questions; I could not be so sensitive about my professionalism.

Disappointment with Michael and expectation that the Pharmacy Board inspector would reappear at any time made for a miserable work week. Each day, I read every news item in the *Arizona Republic* and the *Scottsdale Tribune*. I could find nothing about Amy Brookman, which heightened my nervous state.

By Thursday, I was too tense to carry on a normal conversation. To avoid Denise, I had lunch at home instead of the coffee shop and arrived at Food Go just before the start of my night shift. As I entered the supermarket and turned toward the pharmacy, one of the meat cutters stopped me. Jeremy Douglas is a big man with a soft voice that contradicts his girth and the shrewdness of his expression.

"Ruthie," he said. "Just the person I'm looking for."

I was accustomed to this opening from friends and acquaintances, usually on social occasions, and wondered what medical advice he wanted.

"Can we go to the lunchroom?"

The employee lounge, where many Food Go people prefer to have lunch instead of the coffee shop, was empty at this hour. Jeremy led the way to a table in the farthest corner of the long, narrow room and we sat down. He peered around as if expecting to find someone hiding under another of the tables. I decided he must need information about contraceptives or maybe something like Antabuse, which is a drug used to prevent alcoholics from drinking.

"How's my favorite pharmacist?" he asked. He always calls me that, and I remembered how he came to my defense back in August when Detective Moreway questioned me in this same employee lounge.

I managed a weak grin. "Fine," I told him, but the words seemed to stick in my throat.

"It's like that, is it?"

His comment didn't make sense to me. I hadn't been sleeping well and thought I must have missed some nuance.

"My little niece was buried today," he said suddenly.

What is he getting at? Did he want Prozac without a prescription?

"Hell, I'm not doing this right. Listen, Ruthie, you know they're not just empty words when I call you my favorite pharmacist. I don't forget how you telephoned just about every drugstore in Arizona to get Ritalin for my boy when there was a shortage." He leaned forward, and his voice was soft but sincere.

"I could see how busy you were, but you kept on until you found it. And then you had to convince that pharmacy I was legit, that my kid really is hyperactive."

"That's my job," I said, although I was pleased to be appreciated. Periodically, we experience shortages of Ritalin, which is the main treatment for hyperactivity in children, or attention-deficit-disorder as it's called today. What happens is that the Drug Enforcement Agency establishes quotas for Ritalin manufacture. When demand exceeds supply, parents of children with this disorder find it very hard to cope.

"Sure. But not everyone cares about people the way you do. That's what I told all of them. I said 'Ruthie Morris wouldn't make such a terrible mistake. Something else must have happened to Amy.'"

I froze. The cuddly bear had been replaced by a canny animal, whose acute gaze never left my face.

"Amy Brookman was your niece?"

"That's what I'm trying to say."

"But the aunt who was with her. She's not your wife."

"No, no. Not Lupe. I mean the mother's sister. Me, I'm from the father's side of the family. Amy's father and I are half-brothers. That's why my name's not Brookman." He got up suddenly. "You look like you need a cup of coffee. Sit here, and I'll bring some back for both of us."

Jeremy walked to the opposite side of the employee lounge where management had provided a microwave, small refrigerator, and 40-cup percolator. Coffee was available all day long, and employees paid a quarter a cup on the honor system.

I preferred iced tea but sipped the hot coffee without protest while I waited for him to continue his story. He wrapped his big hands around his cup but didn't drink.

"Ruthie, I didn't want to be the one to tell you. But I think you should know, so you can be prepared. Maybe hire a lawyer."

"A lawyer?"

"The family is going to sue you. I couldn't talk them out of it."

"No, it can't be." I could feel the rising hysteria, but I couldn't seem to modulate my voice.

"Don't you carry some kind of insurance? You know, like the doctors," he said. "What do they call it? Malpractice insurance, that's it."

Like most pharmacists in today's litigious society, I do carry malpractice insurance, just in case—but it would never cover the kind of award juries make nowadays. And that wasn't the point, anyhow. I pride myself on my professionalism and couldn't bear to be publicly accused of a fatal error. Despite the way my confidence plummeted when Louise and Michael doubted me and despite what Jeremy was telling me now about his family, I was sure I had not given Amy the wrong drug.

I thought about her, so young and so unhappy that day. What a terrible death and how frightened she must have been. If only I could relive the day she handed me her three prescriptions. No, I must stop wavering or they'd convince me that I caused her death.

Jeremy was still speaking, peering at his coffee cup and avoiding my eyes. "You probably know that Amy's doctor called the Pharmacy Board. And now the police may be looking into it."

"The police?"

"Didn't they question you?"

I shook my head, unable to speak. My world was crashing down around me, and there was no one I could turn to.

"The family doesn't want to wait for them to investigate. They got hold of a lawyer. Actually, he's a distant cousin of mine." Jeremy suddenly looked up at me and stood, slamming his coffee mug on the table. "You're not going to pass out on me?"

His bulky figure loomed over me, cutting off the light. Or maybe he was right, and the darkness was a physical reaction to his news.

I made an effort to pull myself together. "I'm okay. Tell me the rest of it."

"You know how people think nowadays. Anything happens and they want to sue everyone in sight." Jeremy returned to his seat. "They're going to sue you and also Food Go. I couldn't talk them out of it," he repeated.

I wanted to find out more from him, but the wall clock showed me I was nearly twenty minutes late. I had to get to the pharmacy. "Could we talk more about this?"

"Maybe I shouldn't have said anything. I didn't want to upset you."

"It's better for me to know," I told him.

"I guess we both gotta get to work now. But the wife said I should bring you to the house to discuss the situation. We want to help you."

Until now, we'd been lucky to avoid interruptions, but I saw Denise in the doorway with one of the young women from the bakery department. Denise came right over to our table.

"Your other pharmacist is complaining bitterly because you're late," she told me.

"I'm on my way," I said.

"Are you off this Saturday?" Jeremy asked. When I nodded, he said he'd be working until two o'clock. "Why don't you come here and I'll drive you?"

I saw Denise raise her eyebrows. "It's not what you think," I said as I left the employee lounge.

Like many workplaces, Food Go with its hundred or so employees was one huge gossip mill. I was sure I could trust Denise not to say anything, but the young woman from the bakery looked as if she couldn't wait to dish out this interesting tidbit. Well, I had more important things to worry about. And I faced one of them as soon as I reached the pharmacy.

Three customers were standing at the window, and Louise and Karen each had a phone to her ear. Karen smiled at me as I came through the door, but Louise grimaced.

Don't let it get to you, I told myself. *After all, you're the manager here.* A persistent inner voice reminded me it might not be for long.

I went to help the person who was first in line. He was a tired-looking man in his seventies who handed me a bottle with the original label on it. It was for 100 Pepcid, dated nearly two months earlier.

"This is my stomach medicine that I got a while back," he told me. His tone was mild, and I waited to see whether he had a complaint or merely wanted information. The bottle was empty, so I assumed he wanted a refill and started over to the computer to look him up. He called me back.

"I want to show you this," he said. He had a smaller prescription vial for 30 Pepcid, filled three days earlier. I looked inside and felt my stomach lurch. Two large, white pills—definitely not Pepcid—and the label had my initials on it.

It couldn't be a mistake. If I had made this error at a time when I was rechecking every prescription even more than normal procedure called for, then I could no longer trust myself. I stood there holding the vial, wondering what to do.

"Sir, did you have a question about this prescription?"

"Why did I only get 30 pills?"

"But where are they? I just see two here," I said, knowing I couldn't wait much longer to tell him about the error. To add to my distress, Louise had finished her telephone call and joined me at the window, about to help the next customer. She would hear every word.

The man smiled at me. I remembered him as one of the pleasant customers. At least, he probably wouldn't get nasty when I told him I had given him the wrong pills. That was beside the point, though. My professional integrity was at stake.

"These two pills don't mean anything," he said. "This here's my wife's medicine. I just needed somewhere to carry them."

The relief was so intense, I wanted to cry out. I quickly pulled myself together. "I don't understand, sir. What's the problem?"

He pointed to the original bottle. "I told you. Last time, I got 100." Then he lifted the smaller vial and repeated, "This time I only got 30 pills for the same seven dollars."

I walked over to the computer and looked at his record. His doctor had called in the prescription for 30 tablets with four refills, but his insurance company required a copayment of seven dollars for each script. It didn't make any difference if the prescription was for 30 Pepcid or 100 Pepcid. Rather than argue, I redid his prescription, using the allowable refills, and checking twice to make sure they really were Pepcid.

Louise and Karen were chatting while I filled the next prescription. Although I was disappointed at Louise's reaction to the Amy Brookman catastrophe, I had always appreciated my new pharmacist's friendliness toward our young technician. The contrast with my previous staff pharmacist, who had considered himself too superior to treat technicians like human beings, still surprised me.

When Louise's shift ended shortly afterwards, I continued to work the window while Karen fielded telephone calls. After a while, business slowed down enough for me to come out from behind the pharmacy and straighten shelves in the health and beauty area. I don't often have time to "face" the shelves, but unlike some pharmacists, I enjoy the chance to do it. For one thing, I can keep track of these items for customer information. Often, the pharmacist is the only person they can find to ask when they can't locate vitamins or suntan lotion or whatever. Also, I can think while I "face," and I badly needed to think.

I started at the far end, knowing I could depend on Karen to call me if she needed me. The hair care displays were a mess and I moved along, pulling bottles and boxes forward in an even line, beginning at eye level with Food Go's own label shampoos. As I worked, I tried to solve my problem.

In reality, I had two areas of concern, but they overlapped. I feared I was losing my self-confidence, so much so that a few minutes ago, I'd been ready to believe I was making basic errors and couldn't trust myself to fill prescriptions correctly. I understood the cause. Not only had a patient of mine died because she took a blood thinner instead of a clotting agent, but I had also been accused of substituting that drug for the one her doctor prescribed.

And now, Jeremy Douglas had told me that Amy Brookman's family was planning a malpractice suit. Unless I could be sure that I'd filled Amy's prescriptions correctly, I could not cope. Yet, how was I to convince myself? Worse, without a firm belief that I hadn't contributed to her death, how could I convince anyone else?

I'd already tried to reconstruct that afternoon dozens of times. It was impossible to remember exactly what had happened. Suddenly, however, a calm feeling enveloped me for the first time since the Pharmacy Board inspector had come in. I reminded myself that checking my work was automatic, a habit so ingrained that there was no way I could have mistaken Coumadin, the blood thinner, for Methergine. No matter what anyone else believed—the inspector, Louise, Michael—I knew there had to be some other explanation for Amy Brookman's death. And when I met with Jeremy on Saturday, I would do my best to discover what really happened.

Chapter 5.

On Saturday, I dressed as carefully as I had for brunch with Michael earlier in the week. This time, I concentrated on achieving a professional look. I knew that Jeremy Douglas and his wife believed in me. The two-piece gray dress, its short sleeves banded in white to match the white notched collar, was to bolster my own newly regained assurance.

Just after two o'clock that afternoon, I followed Jeremy's white Ford pickup to his home. Jeremy and Guadalupe Douglas lived in an older section of the city, which in Scottsdale meant the house had probably been built in the early 1960s. The neighborhood boasted many grapefruit trees, and I could see the huge crates of the citrus pickers along the curbs. At the Douglas home, however, two large mulberry trees dominated each half of the lawn. We parked in the driveway and walked along a brick path to the front door.

It was a concrete block house, beige, with a brown shake roof and brown shutters. Only the paint colors distinguished it from the other houses on the street and, in fact, every third or fourth house was also beige and brown. Because these were older homes, I could see individual touches of ownership in the landscaping and add-ons like bay windows and brick planters.

Lupe opened the door as we approached it. Like her husband, she had a large frame, but she, too, was tall enough to carry her weight. If he resembled a teddy bear, she looked like the mother figures in R. C. Gorman's lithographs.

"Come in, Ruthie. Welcome."

Since her husband usually picked up any medications for the family, I had only talked to Guadalupe Douglas a few times at Food Go. I remembered when I met her because Lupe had handled a potentially embarrassing incident with grace. She had come in with a prescription for her son's Ritalin. We have a number of Hispanic customers, and Food Go computers are programmed to translate into Spanish. So when I saw that the patient's name was Manuel and heard her speak to the little boy in Spanish, I asked if she wanted the label in that language.

Ritalin is usually prescribed to be taken "Tabs i qd," which means one tablet each day. To create a Spanish label, I could simply place the letter "S" in front of my entry. For Manuel's medicine, the label would read "*tome una tableta cada día*."

Lupe had laughed softly and said in barely accented English, "That won't be necessary."

"I guess I shouldn't jump to conclusions."

"Nothing wrong with that. It was thoughtful of you to ask."

I always enjoy the pleasant customers and, when I found out she was Jeremy's wife, I looked forward to seeing Lupe and Manuel at the pharmacy. Now, despite her warm greeting, I felt uneasy at what I might learn today from Jeremy.

He led me into a living room that mirrored the exterior beige and brown with walls of the former color and a brown and gold striped sofa. I sat in a comfortable armchair covered in a floral pattern of rust, gold, and taupe. The earth tones added to the relaxed atmosphere, and I marveled at finding one Scottsdale home that had escaped the "mauving" of America. Jeremy took the other armchair while Lupe sat on one of the sofas.

A marble cocktail table was laden with a platter of vegetables and chips arranged around a guacamole dip, and Lupe urged me to try some. I hesitated. This wasn't really a social visit, and besides I didn't want to crunch veggies while we talked.

"Let me fill a plate for you."

I agreed rather than be rude. We chatted about the weather until each of us balanced a gold cloth napkin and a plate of vegetables and chips, with a mound of guacamole in its center.

"You need to know about Amy's family first," Jeremy said. "On her father's side, Quentin and I are the only ones. But even though we're brothers, we don't see much of each other. I'll tell you about that later."

"If you're afraid to upset me, don't worry. I made peace with that one's bigotry long ago," Lupe said.

"Bigotry?" I asked.

"My folks didn't want me to marry Lupe. They considered her a foreigner even though her family's lived in Arizona more than a hundred years. Anyhow, Quentin sided with the folks. After they passed on, Quentin and I made up. Amy even used to babysit for us."

His features softened when he mentioned her name, and I thought he really cared for his niece. Lupe seemed on the verge of tears. I quickly looked away from the two of them and concentrated on dipping celery and chips into the guacamole on my plate.

"Quentin and Amy's mom split up, about two or three years ago I guess it was. Amy couldn't seem to settle down afterwards. She lived with her mother at first. You probably know what sometimes happens. Whenever they argued, Amy threatened to move out, to go to her dad. And she did, off and on. Then she'd argue with him and move back with Leila." He looked at Lupe. "Do you remember what they argued about?"

"The usual teenage tug-of-war, I think. But when the parents are divorced, it seems to be worse. The children can play one off against the other."

Jeremy had eaten some of the veggies on his plate while Lupe spoke; he cleared his throat before he continued. "Next thing you know, Amy wasn't getting along with her dad or her mom. So her aunt Virginia, her mom's sister, took her in." He looked at me. "She's the one you met."

"I didn't exactly meet her. She was with Amy that day."

Lupe nodded. "The day of the abortion."

Confidentiality obviously was not a problem here. Anyone who could read a newspaper knew about Amy's abortion.

"How did Amy die?" I asked. "Was the story in the paper accurate?"

They looked at each other. "We all knew," Lupe said. "About the baby, I mean. Quentin wanted us to talk her into marrying the baby's father."

"Was the father willing?"

"He's a high school kid. Like Amy was. Neither one was ready for marriage."

"He wasn't with her when she went to her doctor?" I made it a question, but I was pretty sure I knew the answer. If he'd been with her, I would have seen him at the pharmacy, too.

"No. Virginia took off from work that afternoon," Lupe said. "She made a big fuss. Said her office was very busy this time of year. Wanted me to go instead. I would have, too, if I had a sitter for Manuel."

Lupe bit at a fingernail. "No, I guess that's not true. I wouldn't go with her because I don't believe in abortion."

"We offered to adopt the baby even though Manuel's a handful with that attention deficit or whatever they call it now," Jeremy said. "We used to call them hyperactive kids."

"I can't have more children," Lupe told me. "And Amy's child would've been a blood relation to Manuel."

I'm always amazed at the personal things people tell me. Maybe because they usually see me in my white jacket with the badge that says, "RUTH KANTOR MORRIS, PHARMACY MANAGER."

"And she turned down your offer?"

"She was confused. She didn't know what she wanted," Jeremy said.

"I figure she would have agreed," Lupe added. "But I think her mother talked her into the abortion."

"They still saw each other?"

"Yeah," Jeremy said. "And never stopped arguing."

"What is Amy's mother like?" I needed as much information as I could get about this family who were going to sue me for malpractice.

"Frivolous. Just the opposite of her older sister."

"You probably noticed that Virginia's kind of like the maiden aunt you see in old movies."

"Frivolous in what way?" I responded to Lupe's comment first, but it was Jeremy who answered.

"She was only interested in going out to dances. Quentin met her at a dance, but then he settled down and she never did."

Lupe leaned forward and spoke in a near whisper even though we were the only people in the room. "She was running around on him. That's why Quentin wanted a divorce."

"Amy wasn't like her mother at all. She was a serious kid. Studious. And then after her folks split up, she changed."

"Oh, yes. Amy was perfect," Lupe said. "She..."

Jeremy didn't raise his voice, but his anguished tone stopped Lupe in mid-sentence.

"Lay off. She's passed on."

"Sorry." She seemed upset, too. Whether for Amy's sake or Jeremy's, I didn't know.

"She felt they'd let her down," Jeremy said. "It was like she'd do anything to get their attention."

"You think that's why she got pregnant?"

"I don't know." Jeremy shrugged his big shoulders. "I just don't know."

"But," I mused aloud, "surely if her purpose was to get attention, she would've wanted to keep the baby."

"Some young girls don't realize how much time a child needs. But Amy babysat here. She had a more realistic outlook."

"She had to cope with Manuel, and he's a handful sometimes." Jeremy sounded proud of his son's problem behavior, and I wondered if Lupe— who spent more time with the boy—would agree.

"This isn't helping Ruthie," Lupe said. "Let's tell her what the family is up to."

I listened carefully. My professional future could hang in the balance. It wasn't a question of losing my livelihood. Between our savings and Bob's pension and insurance, I could manage even if I stayed at home. My work, however, had been important to me all my life and since widowhood, it had taken on greater meaning.

Jeremy explained that the family had met at Quentin's place. "Even Amy's mother was there with her current boyfriend. Also, her Aunt Virginia and the two of us: Uncle Jeremy, and Aunt Lupe. And we had invited the young man who was responsible for Amy's pregnancy.

"It was a free-for-all at first. Everyone blaming everyone else. But Leila, that's Amy's mom, got them to listen to her."

I pictured the scene as Jeremy continued his story. Leila had reminded them that pointing the finger wouldn't bring Amy back. "Nothing will bring her back," the young man had said. "Why wouldn't she marry me? I would have taken care of her and the baby."

"That's just what I mean," Leila told him. "We have to stop blaming ourselves. Amy would be alive today if they didn't give her the wrong drug."

"We can't be sure of that," Jeremy said.

Leila ignored her brother-in-law. "Luckily, we're talking about a big supermarket chain. We can sue the pants off them."

"That won't bring Amy back either," the young man insisted.

"No, but it will make them pay."

Virginia, who usually took the opposite view in any discussion between the sisters, agreed. "I was there with Amy. They were too rushed to give her proper attention."

"You told me the pharmacy manager was the one who filled the prescriptions," Jeremy said. "That's Ruthie Morris. She wouldn't make such a mistake."

"What's the good of having a lawyer in the family, if we can't call on him for help now," Quentin said, ignoring his brother's comment. "Let's get Eric on this right away and see what he can do."

"You mean that cousin of yours?" Leila asked. "I must say he helped you during the split. My lawyer didn't have a chance."

Quentin jumped up and started to shout at her. "You got more than you deserved. If I had my way..."

"Forget all that now," Jeremy told his brother. "I think we should talk to the pharmacist and find out what happened."

"Yes, it's too soon for lawyers," Lupe said.

Leila turned on her. "Easy for you to say. If it was Manuel lying there in his grave, you'd want a lawyer, too."

"You're wrong. I'd want to know what happened. But I wouldn't be trying to make money off my child's death."

"Quentin, that woman insulted me."

"Look, Leila, I'm not going to argue with my brother and his wife no more. We made up our quarrel, and it stays made up."

"Mr. Brookman," the young man said. He was a scrawny teenager who looked younger than his seventeen years. "We need to remember Amy."

He sounded like he was holding back tears, and Jeremy paid attention to him for the first time. "Of course we're considering her," Jeremy assured him. "That's why we're here, John."

"Tommy."

"That's what I meant. Tom."

The discussion continued aimlessly for a time. First Lupe, then Jeremy again, tried to get the family to wait before calling their lawyer. The family outvoted them, however, and Quentin was delegated to get in touch with their cousin Eric.

"And tell him we don't want him to drag things out the way lawyers always do," Leila said. "We want him to find out exactly what happened. Take those depositions or whatever they do. And if we can sue Food Go and this Ruthie, let's get right on it."

Lupe and Jeremy stood up to leave. Lupe was crying. "You're monstrous," she said. "Why do you want to hurt the woman just to line your own pockets?"

"She killed my daughter, and she's going to pay."

As I listened to the end of Jeremy's account of this family meeting, I shuddered. It was even worse than I'd expected. If the girl's mother saw her death as a money-maker, there'd be no way to convince her that I had filled the prescriptions correctly.

"Did they call the lawyer? What did he say?" The words emerged so indistinctly that Jeremy asked me to repeat them.

"Quentin's supposed to let me know."

Right on cue, the doorbell chimed. Lupe went to respond and returned with someone who looked so much like Jeremy that they had to be closely related, although Quentin—for I assumed this must be Jeremy's half brother—was heavier than the meat cutter and clean-shaven.

I wanted to run, anything rather than meet Amy Brookman's father. This was a situation I'd never faced before but, I told myself, face it I must.

And I knew I'd be up against much worse before I could prove I hadn't caused Amy's fatal hemorrhage.

"Eric thinks we've got a good case," Quentin said as soon as he entered the living room. Then he saw me and stopped.

"This is Ruthie Morris," Jeremy said and added with a defiant note to his voice, "my favorite pharmacist."

"What is *she* doing here?"

"She's here because I invited her."

"How can you have this woman in your house after what she did?" His glance took in the food on the marble table and the half-emptied plates on our laps. "And you're treating her like any other guest."

"I see that Leila won you over to her view," Jeremy said.

"You leave Leila out of this. I know damn well it's your wife who fixed the guacamole and all that other stuff."

"Are you trying to tell us what we can serve a guest in our own home?"

"I shouldn't have to tell you. You ought to know better than to invite her here after what she did to Amy."

"And I told you I don't believe she had anything to do with it."

"Then you explain to me how it happened." Quentin's voice rose as he turned in my direction. "Or maybe she can tell me."

I recoiled as I looked into eyes that seemed dark with hatred. "No, I don't know what happened."

"That's what I figured you'd say. You wouldn't admit you made a mistake."

"One thing I do know," I said. "I did not make a mistake."

"Maybe you can convince these two that you're innocent," Quentin told me. "But when our lawyer gets done with you, it will be a different story. Eric will make you wish you never saw Amy."

I shivered as Quentin raised his right arm and dramatically pointed his forefinger at me. I knew I must not start to doubt myself again, but I felt as though I were already on trial and wondered how I could ever clear myself.

Chapter 6.

Although I was miserably unhappy, I couldn't get up and leave. An argument had broken out between Jeremy and his half-brother. They looked even more alike as they faced each other, lower lips thrust out and fleshy jowls quivering.

"You know Leila only cares about money. How many times did you complain to me about that over the years?"

"It's not the damn money."

"You know it is. She said so right there at your place the other night."

"Okay, maybe money drives Leila. But I'm looking for justice."

"It's not justice to do this to Ruthie," Lupe said. Until now, she had watched the brothers without saying a word.

Quentin suddenly sat on the sofa, all the anger rushing out of him like a balloon deflating. "Let's say you're right. Eric will get at the truth. He won't play games with us if there's no case."

"It wouldn't be the first time people've been sued because they had deep pockets," Jeremy said.

His brother appealed to me. "Don't you want to know what really happened? You should be the person who wants that more than anyone."

I didn't answer him but, for the first time, realized I couldn't sit by passively and wait for things to happen. If I was going to save myself, I must discover the cause of Amy's death. The problem was that I had no idea how to go about it.

All the way home, I operated on automatic pilot and, for the rest of the day, I tried to plan. Only a few months ago, I had helped to catch a murderer when police suspicion fell on me and people I cared about, friends like Denise Seaford and Michael Loring. For an accidental death, I told myself, it should be easier to get information. I was sure Lupe and Jeremy would help.

* * * *

Although the next day was my Sunday to work and I needed my sleep, I tossed restlessly that night, the same way I often did during the hottest part of the summer, the Arizona monsoon. It was a cool October night, though; the weather had nothing to do with my insomnia.

"You look terrible, Ruthie," Denise said when I made my way into the Food Go coffee shop for breakfast. I hadn't been able to cope with making it for myself.

I tried to brighten up. "That's a great way to greet a customer."

"I'm just not used to seeing you like this. You always dress so neatly and professionally and look at least ten years younger than your real age."

I glanced down at my pleated black and gold striped skirt. That at least was a polyester blend and looked fresh. My long-sleeved silk blouse, on the other hand, had crease marks from being stored in the closet during the hot weather, and I hadn't had the energy to press it this morning or to choose something else to wear.

"And that blouse always brings out gold highlights in your hair. But today it makes you look sickly," Denise continued. She handed me a menu without her usual flourish. "I'm worried about you."

"Thanks," I said, unable to keep a sarcastic note from my voice.

"If you pretend nothing's wrong, I can't help."

Denise had been there for me after Bob's death, and she had helped me to regain my equilibrium without encouraging self-pity. We found we enjoyed each other's company, something my other friends couldn't understand because she was "only a waitress." I no longer bothered to defend that friendship; in fact, I had gradually pulled away from those who judged people by their occupations.

I did need to talk to someone, to voice the fears that were keeping me awake nights. "Let's meet after work, and I'll tell you about it," I said.

Since the coffee shop opened hours before the pharmacy, Denise's shift would end earlier than mine, but we agreed to meet at 6:30 at a Thai restaurant, Malee's on Main, where we could sit and talk quietly over dinner.

On Sundays, I worked alone because the pharmacy was rarely busy when all the doctors' offices were closed. I caught up on some paperwork between prescriptions, transmitted a large order to our wholesalers, and was ready to leave only a few minutes after our six o'clock p.m. closing time.

When I arrived at Malee's, Denise was standing just inside the front door. She had put our names on the waiting list, which was a short one since Arizona's winter visitors were not yet here in full force, and we were shown to our table about ten minutes later.

We talked about innocuous subjects until our salads arrived. Denise had met someone new, through Food Go like most of the men she went out with. "Actually, he's a driver for our bread and roll suppliers. He's always been friendly, but last week when we were talking, I found out he just got divorced."

"They say that's either the best time or the worst time to start seeing someone."

Denise laughed lightly. She looked very attractive in her aqua and navy sunburst print, eye shadow that was one shade darker than the aqua, and costume jewelry that picked up both colors, interspersed with silver beads. "Could be. Well, I'll find out, won't I?"

She always went into these relationships so hopefully. Most of the time, the men seemed defined by her own romantic fantasies. The relationships never lasted long, and I still couldn't figure out the reason.

"Well, let's hear what's bothering you, Ruthie. Maybe I can help."

Denise was the most helpful person I knew. She bought Girl Scout cookies from every Food Go employee whose daughter was trying to sell them; she was the first to stop by with a covered dish when someone was ill or flowers if they were hospitalized. What she did best, though, was to listen to our troubles. I knew Craig Seaford had divorced her to marry someone else, and I thought he must be a fool.

Since Amy Brookman's story had been in the newspapers and my information wouldn't breach patient confidentiality, I told Denise what I knew about Amy's death and the possible mix-up of her medication. "At first, I blamed myself," I admitted. "But I'm sure I didn't give her the wrong prescription."

She took me through some of the main points again, especially the difference in appearance between Methergine and Coumadin. "I've watched you in action," she told me. "Not only when you're behind the pharmacy but in other things you do. You're always so exact, so careful. I know you couldn't have made a mistake like that."

"Denise," I said sincerely. "I do appreciate your confidence in me."

"Well, it's the truth."

"But I've gone over it so many times, and I can't figure out what else could have happened."

"If it wasn't an accident, Ruthie, then it had to be murder."

"Denise!"

"Well, I was right last time, wasn't I?"

She was referring to something that happened during the summer when her neighbor, who was also a customer of mine, had died suddenly. Denise was always so melodramatic about everything, a habit I usually laughed off as the result of too many late night movies on television. Suddenly, however, my sleeplessness and nervousness coalesced in a burst of irritation. This time she was dramatizing my professional life.

"Denise, please don't do this to me," I shouted.

An elderly couple at the next table glanced at us, then politely turned back to their own conversation. Denise's eyebrows contracted and she looked pained at my outburst.

"Ruthie, I'm sorry. Sometimes, I have an unfortunate way of saying the first thing that pops into my mind. It's spoiled a lot of relationships for me, but I don't want to lose your friendship."

"I shouldn't have shouted at you. I'm not myself."

"Let's forget that part. But we have to look at every angle."

I thought for a moment. Murder sounded far-fetched, although I hadn't been able to come up with any reasonable explanation after the Pharmacy Board inspector talked to me. If I didn't dispense the wrong drug to Amy Brookman, how then did it get into the prescription vial I gave her? When normal means didn't seem to apply, maybe it was time to examine other possibilities.

"It never occurred to me."

"That doesn't mean it couldn't happen. Tell me, what is this other drug—whatever you called it—used for?"

"Coumadin. It's what's known as an anti-coagulant. It thins the blood to prevent clots from forming. People take it who have heart conditions or have had heart attacks or strokes."

"A lot of people?"

"Quite a few," I said.

"And why would Amy die from taking Coumadin instead of the other medicine?"

"After an abortion, doctors prescribe a drug to stop the bleeding. Coumadin does exactly the opposite. I reviewed the literature after the State Board man told me what happened. Coumadin is a powerful medication; it's very effective. Like any other drug, however, it must be used carefully. And where there's any possibility of hemorrhage, Coumadin is contraindicated. Either it shouldn't be taken at all or it must be closely monitored."

"So you don't think the drug was prescribed for Amy."

"It's possible that she was taking it for some other purpose and didn't tell her doctor, but it's unlikely. She was much too young."

"Well, then, why are they trying to blame you, Ruthie?"

"Because that doesn't explain how Coumadin was found in a prescription vial with the Food Go label and my initials on that label."

Denise was silent. And although I usually loved the tasty peanut dressing on Malee's salads, my appetite was gone. I pushed some lettuce around on my plate until the waitress brought our entrées and I could let her remove the salad plate. Meanwhile. I thought about Denise's questions and my answers to them. Maybe it took someone who wasn't knowledgeable about pharmacy to make sense about what had happened to Amy Brookman. I was too close to the day-to-day practice of filling prescriptions to understand how other people would see it.

"There's only one other possibility," Denise said. "Someone else who takes Coumadin deliberately substituted it for the drug Amy was supposed to get to control the bleeding."

I felt as if my lungs would burst with the effort it took to keep from shouting at Denise again. Most of the time, the dramatic sense that underlined her vivid personality was charming; but now, when I seemed to be embroiled in a hopeless situation, her insistence that someone had deliberately murdered Amy only added to my feelings of futility. I wanted to believe, but on the one hand, it was too easy a solution. And on the other hand, if it were true, how could I ever prove it?

"You don't have to tell me," Denise said. "You think it's an off-the-wall solution, and you're trying not to be upset with me."

I admitted that she was right and silently wondered why I had told Denise all my doubts and fears. It was pointless to lean on people. I had tried with Michael, and he hadn't trusted me enough.

"Why don't you start by finding out if any of the people close to Amy had access to Coumadin?" Denise said. "At least it will give you something to do instead of worrying about lawsuits."

"It's not only the lawsuit that worries me. The State Board of Pharmacy could revoke my license."

"That's all the more reason for you to find out what really happened."

Again I thought over the possibilities Denise had raised. "There's one catch," I said.

"Probably more than one. But it gives us a starting point."

"I'm not sure it does after all," I said, choosing each word carefully. "Let's try to follow this through. Amy was young but certainly old enough to realize the pills looked different."

"Did she know what the first drug was supposed to look like?"

"The Methergine. Yes, I handed it to her, and I said..." I stopped, trying to visualize the scene. "At first, I didn't have Amy's full attention. But that changed as I told her about each medication."

"What did you say?"

"What I always tell them. After an abortion, patients get the same three prescriptions. I fill them and put the directions on the labels. Then, I explain how to use each one as I hand them over."

"But what do you say?" Denise repeated.

"I tell them the purpose and how to take the medications."

"Ruthie, this is like pulling teeth. It's so familiar to you that you do it automatically. Try to think of the exact words you used when you gave her that drug."

I closed my eyes and said in a hollow voice, not really believing it would make a difference, "The purple ones are to stop the bleeding. Take one tablet four times a day for three days. Be sure to take them until they're all gone."

Denise gasped audibly. "That's it!"

"Please," I started to say, not wanting more drama. And then I saw it, too. Amy knew only that she was supposed to take the purple ones four times a day. Aside from their color, she could have no idea what they were supposed to look like. For the first time, I acknowledged that Denise's scenario was possible.

Chapter 7.

"Let's assume you're right, Denise. Suppose someone deliberately switched Amy Brookman's medication and that's how she died." I tried to keep the despair from my voice. "I'm not a private investigator or on the police force. There's no way for me to question people."

"You've already started," Denise said, the excitement in her voice having the perverse effect of calming me. "You've talked to her father and her aunt and uncle."

"And what did I learn? Only that I'm going to be sued for malpractice."

"You learned quite a lot about the family dynamics."

"Nothing that points to a murderer."

"What about the boyfriend? Don't the police always look at boyfriends or spouses when a woman dies mysteriously?"

"I doubt whether the police see anything mysterious about it, Denise. They're more likely to assume negligence on my part."

"Think about it." She appealed to me as if I could do anything I put my mind to. And, for the first time, I started to examine the situation objectively. There were measures open to me instead of waiting passively for the other shoe to fall. For one thing, I could get a lawyer of my own, someone to cope with cousin Eric.

"I need a good lawyer," I said aloud.

"Have you ever been in the Cactus Plaza building across the street from our Food Go? Lots of legal offices there."

"That would be convenient, but I can't go to just anyone. I need an attorney who knows what he's doing."

"Or what she's doing," Denise added. "Maybe a woman would understand you better."

"It doesn't make any difference to me," I said. "But male or female, I'd still better ask around and get one who's highly recommended."

Denise was quiet; I guessed she was thinking it over. After a moment, she asked whether I'd noticed the dark-haired man with horn-rimmed glasses who often had lunch in the coffee shop.

"His name's Sterling Harraday. He's with Davis and Harraday."

"But I don't know anything about him or even what type of cases he handles."

"He's very intelligent," Denise said and blushed.

I smiled for the first time in days. "Could do worse, I guess."

"Just talk to him. If he thinks you need some sort of specialist, I'm sure he'd recommend one."

I decided I would call Sterling Harraday the next morning. Maybe that would be better than asking around. Certainly, I should avoid telling too many people about Amy Brookman, and I was thankful that nothing more had appeared in the news.

This respite turned out to be short-lived. The next morning's local TV news featured Amy. A group campaigning against abortion was using her death to organize a demonstration. A spokesperson for the group appeared on the program. She wore a well-cut turquoise dress with an antique-style lapel pin and either had a fresh permanent, or her light brown hair was naturally very curly. It was the sign she carried, however, that attracted my attention: "NO MORE AMY BROOKMANS." In the background, other would-be demonstrators had unfurled a banner with the words, "WE WON'T ALLOW MURDERERS TO GO FREE."

My pulse raced as I thought for a moment that they were accusing me. Then, as I listened to the interview, I realized the group equated abortion with murder. It sounded like they intended to exploit Amy's death to promote their own agenda. I wondered what her family thought about it and, in fact, I couldn't help thinking about Amy herself. This group was using her. Her death would frighten those who had no knowledge of the peculiar circumstances surrounding it, which was probably the intent of the demonstrators. Although I knew many people were concerned about teenage pregnancies and abortions, I felt it was unfair to exploit a dead girl.

As I listened, I could follow the path the group intended to take. Sixteen-year-old Amy had all the right qualifications to be their symbol. And bleeding to death, as the group's spokeswoman graphically described the hemorrhage, was a particularly horrible fate.

Denise had watched the same TV news and called me the minute the reporters went to another topic. "You can add Faith Sommers to our list of suspects," she said excitedly.

"Who?"

"You said you saw the news. I mean that woman. Didn't you notice the look in her eyes?"

"No, I was concentrating on what she had to say."

I could imagine a grimace on Denise's expressive face. "That news report just pinpointed someone with a serious motive for murdering Amy. The kind of person you should be looking for."

"That's rather far-fetched."

"Make life easier for yourself, Ruthie. This couldn't be a better opportunity."

After another nearly sleepless night, I felt too tired to cope with this latest happening. "All I could think of was the publicity," I told Denise. "I was hoping there'd be nothing more about Amy in the media."

"But this is good news for you."

I couldn't agree. The only good news would be that Amy was alive, which was impossible. "I'll tell Sterling Harraday about it," I said. "He's going to see me during his lunch hour today."

"That's great!" She paused. "Look, Ruthie, don't tell him, but I think you and I should go to that demonstration Wednesday morning."

"And what do we do about our jobs?"

"First of all, this is more important. Anyhow, I already changed my shift so I can go there with you."

I thought how typical it was of Denise to act impulsively in support of a friend. "You're unbelievable," I blurted and then realized she might take my comment as a criticism. "I mean that as a compliment," I added.

Denise laughed. "Could be. I'll consider it one."

She was right about the demonstration. It was surely better than sitting at home and worrying. Besides, I would be working on the night shift and wouldn't even have to change my schedule.

After Denise's phone call, I felt surprisingly optimistic. This morning, although I put on an outfit I often wore to work, I pressed it carefully before I dressed for my appointment with the lawyer. I sat at my kitchen table and wrote out the main points concerning Amy Brookman so I could present them coherently and concisely to him. At 11:30, I got into my white Accord and slowly drove the three miles from my home to the Cactus Plaza Professional Building.

Although the temperature was only about 84 degrees, I automatically looked for a parking space under a tree. They were all occupied, so I unrolled my sunshade and placed it on the windshield. At least, I no longer needed to wrap a towel around the steering wheel the way most of us had to do during the Arizona summer.

The offices of Davis and Harraday were one flight up. I took the elevator and thought with a pang how different it would be if Michael were with me. He'd had no patience to wait for elevators when we were at the University. Then I wondered why I was thinking of Michael rather than Bob. If Bob were alive... No, I wasn't a helpless female who needed a man at my elbow. I was certainly capable enough to meet with the lawyer on my own and discuss the situation.

* * * *

At Davis and Harraday, a middle-aged receptionist occupied a desk placed at right angles to the doorway. She was absorbed in the words on her computer screen but looked up and smiled when I appeared.

"You must be Mrs. Morris. Please have a seat and I'll buzz Mr. Harraday."

I sat in the kind of chair we used to call Danish Modern, gripping the teakwood arms as a spasm of nervousness suddenly went through me. *You're doing the right thing*, I told myself. *Stop worrying*.

Sterling Harraday came out to the reception area to usher me into his office. As I'd assumed, he was the slightly balding, dark-haired man I had noticed in the Food Go Coffee Shop, although I didn't remember ever seeing him at the pharmacy. I decided this wasn't the right time to mention the coffee shop.

His office was furnished in the same teakwood as the reception area with a huge desk in front of the picture window. Two armchairs flanked one side of the desk, and he motioned me to one of them. Instead of taking his own seat behind the desk, he walked around to the other armchair and turned it to face me, a posture that disconcerted me at first. I quickly realized that this gesture was designed to make our talk seem less formal and to put me at ease.

"When we spoke on the phone, I believe you mentioned you work at the Food Go supermarket across the street. Can you tell me what your job is?"

"I'm the pharmacy manager," I said. "In fact, that's the reason I'm here."

"Let me tell you up front that we don't handle labor-management disputes. I can recommend several firms that do."

"This isn't a labor-management situation," I said.

He apologized for jumping to conclusions, but his words had reassured me. I now knew that if he felt the case to be beyond his expertise, he would refer me to another attorney. "Tell me in your own words why you're here." His smile was warm, and I could see why Denise was attracted to him. "I'll try not to interrupt unless I have to clarify something."

I began the story of Amy Brookman, explaining how I filled prescriptions, what I remembered of the day of Amy's abortion, and what I had learned from the State Board inspector and from Jeremy Douglas. He took me back over some of the details, especially my description of Methergine and how it differed in appearance from Coumadin.

"And you are sure you filled the prescriptions properly."

"Yes, sir, I am," I said as firmly as I could.

"You realize it could mean someone changed the tablets in that vial."

I was surprised he had reached that conclusion so quickly. It had taken me days to arrive there and only at Denise's insistence. "I've thought of that," I said, "but I don't know how we could possibly prove it."

"We don't have to prove it. Only raise a doubt."

I gripped the arms of my chair. "But it would look very bad for me."

"Cases involving medical professionals usually come down to whether the person's acts would be considered reasonable and prudent." He looked at me. I could see he was waiting for my reaction.

"Yes, I've read that in the pharmacy magazines, but I've also seen that pharmacists have been sued even when they did nothing wrong."

"Anyone can sue anyone else. That doesn't mean the case has merit."

The wood was biting into my hands and I made a conscious effort to relax them. When I remembered and told him of cases I'd read about, however, I became more agitated and my command of language broke down. "One case. The pharmacist used a childproof cap. Someone voluntarily removed it. Afterwards. After he brought the medication home. A child ingested the drug and died. The family sued." I looked across at the lawyer. "And a jury awarded them millions of dollars."

"It happens," he said calmly. "But let's consider your situation. I need to ask you some questions."

"I'm sorry," I said and wondered why I was apologizing.

"Did you get the full name of this cousin Eric they mentioned?"

"No, but I can find out from Jeremy Douglas."

"That might be a good idea, but try to be casual about it. I don't think you want to let them know at this point that you've retained counsel." His face reflected a warmth that lessened some of the tension I felt. "That is, if you do want to retain me."

"I've never been in a situation like this before," I said. "I'm not sure what to do."

"Why don't you think about it? If nothing further happens, you won't need me. But if they do initiate a lawsuit, I'd be pleased to represent you."

He told me his hourly fee was $145 plus expenses. If we went to court, costs would increase, but he would try to keep this from going that far.

"There's one other thing," I said as he was showing me to the door. "We've only talked about a civil suit, and that's bad enough. But what if the police decide to prosecute me?"

"Do you have reason to believe they will?"

"I don't know."

"Is there something you haven't told me?" he asked. The genial expression was still there, but his voice had hardened. It seemed a hint of his courtroom manner.

We were still standing in the doorway, but he motioned me back to the armchair. I didn't know where to begin. No matter what I said, I'd sound like the legal profession's equivalent of a hypochondriac. Sterling Harraday waited patiently, although I realized he probably still hoped to salvage part of his lunch hour.

"A few months ago, the police questioned me about a murder," I began hesitantly.

"Another murder?" His tone was sharp.

Pull yourself together, Ruthie, I told myself. You can communicate better than this.

"That murder was solved," I said, "but not before I nearly became a victim." Keeping my tone light, I added, "I didn't mean to cause more conclusion jumping."

The warm smile returned and he leaned forward, encouraging me to continue. "Sometimes I think I was more frightened when the police suspected me than when the murderer came after me."

Sterling Harraday couldn't hide his astonishment. "But why?" he asked.

Maybe I should have looked for a woman attorney after all, I thought. A woman might understand how I'd felt when Detective Frank Moreway questioned me, suspicion in every word and gesture, making me feel guilty even when I knew I'd done nothing wrong. And this time, as far as I know, I'm the only one they suspect of supplying Amy with the wrong tablets. If Sterling Harraday says, "There, there," I decided, I'll look for another lawyer.

He said nothing for a few minutes. Then it was my turn to be surprised. "I guess police routine is overwhelming when you aren't accustomed to it," he said. "As bewildering as it would be for me to face the array of drugs in your pharmacy." My expression must have given me away because he quickly added, "And that's meant sincerely, not condescendingly."

"I'll accept it that way," I said, "but you still haven't answered my original question—what if the police decide to prosecute me?"

"To your knowledge, had you ever seen Amy Brookman before that day?"

"No."

"I doubt whether the District Attorney's office could consider any charge other than involuntary manslaughter and, as it stands now, there doesn't seem to be enough evidence for that charge."

As it stands now, I thought. He had hedged his words and, although I knew he'd intended to reassure me, I felt only despair at the phrase "involuntary manslaughter."

"That's a worst-case scenario," Sterling Harraday hastened to add. "I don't believe you will ever be indicted on that charge."

"Isn't there some way we can find out what happened?" I could hear my own desperation.

He took time to think this over, too. "We could hire someone to investigate the backgrounds of the people involved," he said finally. "My professional opinion, however, is to wait. If we do anything at all now, we indicate that we expect legal action."

I agreed that a conservative approach was best but left the offices of Davis and Harraday determined not to wait. Even an insect struggled to free itself when caught in a spider web. I would do no less to help myself.

Chapter 8.

Denise called for me on Wednesday morning, and we drove to the abortion clinic in her old black Ford. The clinic was located in a one-story building, concrete block surrounded by more concrete in the form of a large parking lot. I remembered at least two restaurants and several other businesses had tried to succeed in that location. The large sign—blue letters on a white background, reading *Women's Center*, covering most of one window—startled me for a moment because I was accustomed to hear people call the place an abortion clinic.

Whenever I'd happened to drive past the area, I had noticed two or three pickets and no onlookers. Today, a huge chain cordoned the driveway, and police stood guard at its entrance. We could see them questioning anyone who tried to get into the parking lot. Dozens of people blocked the sidewalks, most of them waving signs toward two vans with the call letters of local TV stations that were pulled up on the street in front of the lot. We decided to park on a side street and walk back.

We circled the neighborhood and eventually found a parking space two blocks away. "I'm spoiled," Denise said. "I figured it would be crowded and warm, but I never thought about having to walk."

I looked down at her slingback shoes with their three-inch heels. She was wearing a sleeveless print dress in shades of green that I recognized as one of her favorites. With eye makeup that matched her bronze shoes and handbag, Denise looked as she always did, well-coordinated. I guessed, though, that walking in those shoes and then standing around to watch the demonstration was going to be painful for her.

As we neared the women's center on foot, we realized people were shouting, "No more Amy Brookmans," words that we hadn't heard through the car windows. I steeled myself. If I were to learn anything today, I had to mingle with people and try to talk to them.

I noticed a few women standing somewhat apart from the sign bearers, watching the television crews. They seemed to be onlookers rather than demonstrators, and we decided to join them first and then work our way along the sidewalk.

Denise approached a chunky-looking woman about her own age. "What's going on?" she asked innocently.

"It's a demonstration." The woman seemed eager to talk. "I saw the TV trucks. Figured maybe some celebrity was here. But it's really nothing much."

"How can you say that?" a younger onlooker asked. "Some teenager died because she had an abortion here."

As she spoke, the shouting died down, and I realized we were close enough for the demonstrators to have overheard. A tall woman moved closer to us. She was wearing a nondescript rust-colored shirtdress, but I recognized the antique lapel pin I'd noticed in the TV close-up. Faith Sommers, their spokesperson, stood before me. She carried the sign that read "NO MORE AMY BROOKMANS." With her other hand, she held onto a boy about four or five years old. *If she had him late in life, Faith Sommers could be the child's mother*, I thought. *More likely, she was his grandmother.*

She seemed rather young for that role, but perhaps Faith herself had been a teenaged mother, which could explain her reforming zeal. I wondered whether his mother knew the boy was out here. A moment later, I realized he wasn't the only child in the crowd. It was hard to imagine anyone taking children or grandchildren along to a potentially explosive situation. Well, the little boy would make it easier for me to begin a conversation with Faith Sommers.

Denise must have had the same idea. She bent to the child's level and smiled at him. "Hi, there, what's your name?" I had watched her charm children at Food Go and knew she genuinely liked them. The boy looked up at Faith Sommers as if he wanted her permission to answer. At her slight nod, he told us he was Bobby. This accomplished, Denise turned to the woman and ingenuously asked, "Didn't we see you on television?"

Faith Sommers inclined her head graciously. "I'm so glad my interview made you ladies aware of our crusade here." Her voice was soft and had a trace of a southern drawl.

Everyone wants to raise our consciousness these days, I thought. I looked closely at the woman, wondering if Denise could possibly be right in calling her a murder suspect. Faith's speech sounded cultured, she was well-dressed, and she certainly wasn't the stereotypical fanatic I had expected to find. On the other hand, she had said "crusade," a word with loaded connotations for me. And despite her refined voice and appearance, she'd been shouting with the others only a short time ago.

To find out what I needed to know, I couldn't afford to be squeamish. "We wanted to learn more about your cause," I said shamelessly.

The other demonstrators had begun chanting slogans again, but Faith Sommers remained with us. "You heard about the little girl who died?" she asked.

For a moment, I was bewildered. "Little girl?"

She waved her placard at me. "Amy Brookman. She was only sixteen."

"Yes, I know," I murmured.

"Of course, you might call it retribution because she murdered her baby first," she said. "But I forgive her. She really didn't know what she was doing."

I found it hard to meet her eyes when she spoke of Amy Brookman, but I glanced up in time to see her expression. It made me revise my opinion again. Faith Sommers glowed self-righteously. She was ready to "forgive" a teenager who had the misfortune to die after an abortion. And since I now wanted to believe Denise was right, that someone deliberately caused the hemorrhage, I had to control my anger at Faith Sommers' attitude.

"But how did the girl die?" Denise asked.

Faith nodded toward the clinic. "Those butchers killed her."

"What do you mean?" Denise gasped, looking properly horrified.

"First they killed her baby. Then they killed her."

"She died in there?" Denise knew as well as I did that Amy died the day after the abortion.

"No, but they were responsible just the same."

Swallowing nervously, I forced myself to say the words that were important to me. "Didn't I hear she took the wrong tablets... I mean pills..." I could sound just as naive as Denise. "They were supposed to clot the blood or something, but they made her hemorrhage instead."

"Where did you hear that?" Faith Sommers demanded harshly.

The little boy, Bobby, looked ready to cry. "Grandma, can we go home now?"

"Soon, honey. You go on over there and hold Miss Virginia's hand till I finish speaking with these ladies."

She pointed to one of the chanters and, for the first time, I recognized Amy's aunt among the demonstrators. Despite the warm October day, she wore a dark suit. She seemed thinner than I remembered, almost gaunt, but when she half-turned to reach down for Bobby's hand, I saw that her dark clothes were softened by a frilly white blouse.

Faith Sommers must have caught me staring at the woman, for she suddenly whispered, "I see you recognize Virginia. She wanted to bring the entire family to join us today, but Amy's parents were too distraught to come along."

I realized Denise didn't understand but before I could explain, Faith continued. "She blames herself, poor thing, for Amy's poor judgment. But I told her it's not her fault; it's the peer pressure." She stared at the women's center again, her expression venomous.

"She's the aunt?" Denise asked. "Didn't I hear she was with her niece during the abortion?"

Good for you, I thought. *I would never have had the courage to ask that question.* But I knew we must extract as much information as we could get from every possible source. Watching Faith Sommers purse her lips, I expected her to turn from us. I could see her struggle between wanting to cut off our impertinent questions and wanting to gain converts to her cause.

"Yes, she was here with Amy. She doesn't believe in abortion but she wasn't strong enough to change Amy's mind. That's the saddest part."

Privately, I thought the saddest part was Amy's death, but I listened without argument. I could tell by the expression on her face that Faith Sommers was about to use this conversation for moral instruction. "Virginia was once like you ladies. She didn't give much thought to girls whose lives are in jeopardy, but now we have a staunch supporter. Now we have someone who stands here with us to keep these foolish young girls from going into that place."

I knew I was on rocky ground, but I had to get back to the most important point.

"Yes, I see what you mean," I said, "but if Amy died because she took the wrong medicine..." I let my voice trail off.

"That's a lie." Faith Sommers' tone had changed from the voice of the patient moral arbiter of a moment before. This was the second time mention of the real cause of Amy's hemorrhage had flustered her calm demeanor. I wondered what she really knew about the young woman's death. Maybe Denise was right about Faith's complicity.

"Are you reporters?" Faith Sommers suddenly asked.

"No, of course not."

"You certainly have peculiar questions. Well, I'm not here to gossip."

A few more people had joined the onlookers, and now I could see that one TV camera was panning the crowd. Faith noticed, too, and squared her shoulders and raised her placard so the camera could pick up its words. The other demonstrators also had observed the camera and went into a frenzy of slogan shouts.

This action didn't last long. Within moments, the camera was placed in the van, and the TV crew got in and drove away. The other van had already left. Now the demonstrators pulled their signs into their own vehicles and prepared to leave, too. Amy's aunt walked over to return Bobby to his grandmother. I waited, half expectantly and half fearfully to see whether she'd remember me. Even frequent Food Go customers usually don't know me outside of the pharmacy. Most of them never look beyond that white professional jacket with its name tag: "RUTH KANTOR MORRIS, PHARMACY MANAGER."

Virginia didn't pay any attention to Denise or me. "You are ready for lunch, young man, aren't you?" she asked as she released the boy's hand to his grandmother. Her words had a rusty quality as though she wasn't used to talking to children.

"Can we go now, Grandma?"

"Soon, Bobby," Faith said. "Remember, I explained we have to help little babies so they can grow up to be big boys like you."

I looked at Amy's aunt and willed her to recognize me, afraid of her reaction but knowing I couldn't clear myself without understanding more about these people who were using Amy's death to further their cause. She was about to leave; soon it would be too late.

Before I could say anything, Denise acted. "Ruthie," she said, her voice louder than its normal pitch. "You're going to be late getting back to the pharmacy."

Amy's aunt stared at me. "I thought I recognized you," she said. All of her features seemed to darken as she took a step forward and pointed her forefinger at me. "How do you have the nerve to show up here?"

"This is a public street," Denise said.

"I was not talking to you." Amy's aunt came closer to me. Her pale face was ashen as she looked down from the slight advantage her greater height gave her. I knew I had to control my fear and make her talk.

"What do you mean?" I asked, trying to keep my voice steady.

"Don't pretend with me."

"Who is she?" Faith Sommers asked. "I knew there was something fishy going on."

"This woman killed Amy."

I gasped at the stark words. Jeremy Douglas had warned me that Amy's mother was ready to accuse me because she saw a way to make some money, but why was the aunt denouncing me, too?

"She works in that place?"

"No, Faith. Not the abortion clinic. This woman is the druggist who gave Amy the wrong pills."

Faith Sommers looked surprised. "What does that have to do with anything? We're here to put those butchers out of business."

"You do not understand," she said, her words stiffly formal. "They started it, but this woman is the one who killed my niece."

Anyone could raise her eyebrows to appear surprised, but Faith Sommers really seemed stunned. Either she was a terrific actress or she had known nothing about the substitution of Coumadin tablets for Methergine.

"Amy died from pills? Not from the abortion?"

"The abortion was a contributing factor. That is why I'm here with you today." Virginia spoke earnestly to Faith Sommers. "The family tried to keep it quiet because we intend to take legal action. But we know the real reason Amy died. The doctor gave her some prescriptions. One was supposed to stop the bleeding."

I felt glued to the spot even though she was pointing to me again, her expression malicious. *This is what you wanted*, I told myself. *Let her talk*; but my stomach churned, and a headache was beginning behind my eyes.

"This woman is a druggist at Food Go. She gave Amy the medicines, but she gave her the wrong ones."

It was essential for me to stop this attack. I moistened my lips and forced myself to speak. "I check over every prescription very carefully. There is no way I could have made such a mistake."

"That is just what I told my sister," Virginia said.

"Then why are you attacking me this way?"

"You gave Amy a blood thinner instead of a drug that stops bleeding. And I agree that you could not have done it accidentally."

Denise came to my defense again. "Are you crazy?" she asked. "You can't talk this way. Why, you're libeling Ruthie."

"I am not worried about libel. The facts are clear. Even though Amy was bleeding so badly, I thought to take along all the pills so the emergency room doctor could look at them. He called in the hospital pharmacist, and they explained everything to me. They showed me what the pills were supposed to look like."

Ignoring Denise now, Virginia swiveled her head from Faith to me and back again. "No, I do not think you made a mistake," she told me, her voice thickened with emotion. "You deliberately switched those pills to kill my niece."

Chapter 9.

This couldn't be happening. It had to be a nightmare. I stood there, while Amy's aunt vehemently accused me, feeling like someone had taken me out to the desert and stranded me. I couldn't say a word. Soon, I realized Denise was talking again, but she sounded far away.

"What possible reason could Ruthie have to kill your niece?"

"We'll all find that out soon enough."

My mouth parched, my voice cracking, I made myself speak. The words seemed to be coming from someone else. "I didn't even know your niece. I only saw her that one time."

"We know all about you."

"Know what? What are you talking about?"

"I cannot say anything else now." She turned and walked swiftly away, leaving Faith Sommers, Denise, and me all staring after her.

"This requires an explanation," Faith said. "I can't have our cause damaged."

"*You* want an explanation!"

"I think I'm owed one."

"Grandma." Bobby tugged on Faith's hand. "I'm hungry. You promised."

"All right, dear. We're leaving now." She and Bobby started to walk toward a gray Buick Riviera, one of the few cars remaining in front of the clinic. Faith unlocked the door. As she put Bobby into his car seat, she looked at me over her shoulder. "We have unfinished business," she told me. It sounded like a threat.

I had worried about Denise walking around in her three-inch heels, but I was the one who felt as if my legs couldn't carry me back to our parking spot. Denise gave me her arm, and I leaned on her as if I'd suddenly aged twenty years.

"She must be the one," Denise suddenly said.

"That's why we came out here in the first place. Because you thought it was Faith Sommers."

"Not Faith, the aunt. Why else would she accuse you?"

"But they're all accusing me. They'll do anything to get money from me." I knew my voice had risen, but I couldn't control it. "That's why I went to see the lawyer. Because Jeremy from the meat department said the family plans to sue me."

"That was for a supposed mistake. But this woman's talking about murder."

"So were you."

We had reached the car, and I sank back against the seat as soon as I opened the door and got in. I wasn't sure I'd ever get up again.

"It's early," Denise said. "I'm taking you back to my place for some food before we both have to go to work."

I was too drained to protest, too wrapped in my own thoughts even to be aware that we'd pulled into Denise's driveway until she cut the motor and removed her keys. She came around to the passenger side and opened the car door.

"Are you okay? Can you make it into my house?"

You can't fall apart, Ruthie, I told myself. With a day's work in the pharmacy ahead of you, this won't do. I made a determined effort to pull myself together.

My mind was so preoccupied with the accusations of Amy's aunt that I didn't notice the silver-and-gray Lexus pull into the driveway of the house next door. Denise's neighbor was Michael Loring's daughter, a young widow whose husband had been murdered a few months ago. Michael called to me as I started up the path to Denise's front door.

Although I was trying to walk without help, Denise was supporting me as she had when we left the demonstration. Michael must have realized that something was wrong. He bounded across the two driveways, his energy contrasting sharply with my own depleted stamina.

"Ruthie, are you all right?"

"Yes, yes. Of course I am." I tried to force conviction into my tone.

"She's not all right at all," Denise told him.

"What's wrong?" Michael tried to hold my eyes with his own, but I looked away. He turned to Denise and repeated his question.

"Some loony woman just accused Ruthie of deliberately—"

"Denise," I interrupted. "Let's not discuss it now." I remembered Michael's intimation that I might subconsciously have wanted to harm Amy Brookman. His words hadn't been as vicious as those of Amy's aunt, but I couldn't bear to stand in the driveway discussing one of the worst moments in my life.

He directed that intense gaze toward me again. "I know I don't deserve your confidence after our last meeting, but I see that something's troubling you. Please let me help."

"Thanks, but I'm really okay now."

"Why don't you come inside?" Denise asked Michael, gesturing toward her house. "I think we need another opinion. Especially since I heard you're also a pharmacist."

I frowned at Denise to show that I was against the idea. Although I knew she was adept at reading people's expressions, she refused to acknowledge my body language.

Michael glanced back toward his own car, and now I noticed he hadn't been alone. At first, I thought the woman who emerged from the passenger side of the Lexus was his daughter, Betsy Stokes. During the summer, when Michael and I met again after so many years apart, he had seemed so solicitous of Betsy and so much a part of her life, that I'd assumed a romantic interest until I had learned they were father and daughter.

Betsy's blond hair was styled differently, I realized, fuller with crimped curls. When this woman got out of the car and crossed over toward us, I saw that her hair was short and nearly straight, ending in a soft curl just below her ears. Unlike Betsy, who was expecting her first child, this woman was svelte. And she was closer to my age than to Betsy's.

The distance between the two driveways wasn't that great. In any case, she would have reached us quickly because she strode along with a brisk, no-nonsense step. Betsy, who seemed to have an unlimited wardrobe of expensive-looking casual fashions would now be wearing maternity clothes. Michael's passenger also was dressed casually, but looked chic and attractive in well-fitted beige slacks and a cream-colored, long-sleeved blouse.

I waited for an introduction, but Michael said nothing. We stood there awkwardly for a few moments until Denise introduced herself.

"I'm Patricia Donleavy," the woman responded and shook Denise's hand formally.

"Ruth Morris," I said when she turned toward me.

"Ah, yes, Ruthie."

For a moment, I thought she must be one of my customers at the pharmacy. Perhaps she was another of Betsy's neighbors, and Michael had given her a lift. Then she touched Michael's arm to get his attention.

"Why are we all standing out here?" she asked. "Let's invite everyone next door."

I didn't want to jump to conclusions again, but this woman was obviously more than an acquaintance. *Well, what did you expect*, I asked myself. *Michael is still an attractive, vital man.*

Denise renewed her own invitation, and we all followed her indoors. Although she lived next to the Stokes house, Denise's home was more modest. The Stokes house had been built by the original owner of all the land in the cul-de-sac and had been extensively remodeled since that time. I'd heard that the latest renovation, completed just before Harry Stokes's death, had cost quite a bit. Harry had been wealthy, however, unlike Denise who struggled to make the mortgage payments since her divorce.

I saw the look of surprise on Patricia Donleavy's face as we walked through a small tiled entry hall into the living room. Seeing it through another woman's eyes this time, I noticed that Denise's favorite throw pillows with the sand painting motifs couldn't quite cover her sofa's shabbiness.

Michael and Patricia sat on opposite ends of the sofa, but he put his arm across its carved wooden back as though reaching out to her. I took one of the armless chairs that made up the group, while Denise excused herself and disappeared in the direction of her kitchen.

I could think of nothing to say to Michael or his companion. Patricia spoke first. "Betsy's architect did such a superb remodeling job for her. Perhaps she would recommend him to her neighbor."

At least, this was a neutral topic. "Remodeling is rather expensive," I said, astonished to hear the curtness in my voice.

Michael seemed surprised, too. "Ruthie," he said again. "Please tell me what's wrong."

"Nothing," I insisted, "but I did mean to ask you how Betsy is feeling." He must have interpreted my quick glance at Patricia, for he went along with the change of subject.

"Much better now that she's well into the second trimester," he said.

"I don't think she looks like herself at all," Patricia contradicted.

Here was interesting news. It told me this wasn't Patricia's first visit to Betsy Stokes. To make conversation without resorting to weather reports, I was about to ask Patricia if she lived in Tucson, but I was saved from trivialities when Denise reappeared with a tray of refreshments. We helped ourselves to mugs of coffee and chocolate chip cookies.

"Do you both have the day off?" Michael asked.

"Night shift," Denise said.

Michael replaced his coffee mug and stood up. "Then we'd better run along."

"No, no. We have time," Denise assured him. I could have kicked her, but I sat there quietly, hoping she wouldn't reveal my problems in front of a stranger. It was too much to expect. Denise, who thrived on drama, couldn't be discreet when she had new listeners. I was unable to think of any way to silence her.

"We went to watch a demonstration at the abortion clinic," she said and quickly filled them in. "And that woman dared to accuse Ruthie of deliberately murdering her niece," she finished with a flourish, waiting for their reactions.

I saw that Denise could talk about the accusation because she didn't take it seriously, but I knew it could ruin me nonetheless. *Bad enough for Michael to doubt me*, I thought, *but for this woman to hear it... this attractive blonde whose eyes were not on Denise while she spoke but moved from Michael to me and back again.*

Patricia Donleavy surprised me. "How utterly abominable!" she said in ringing tones. "Some of these people are quite mad."

Denise agreed warmly, but Michael and I remained silent. "I remember years ago," Patricia continued, "when I miscarried. Before Roe vs. Wade allowed doctors to legally do a D and C on a pregnant woman."

Her words were clipped, and a look of pain crossed her face as she relived the experience. I saw Michael's sympathy reflected in his eyes and realized that this woman was important to him.

Patricia spoke again after a moment's pause that seemed necessary to gain control. "I knew something was wrong with the pregnancy, so I visited my gynecologist. He told me the fetus was dead, but he couldn't do anything about it. I must wait for nature to take its course.

"So, I went home and waited. And that night I hemorrhaged—not fatal in my case, but nonetheless a rather traumatic experience," she finished coolly.

Michael had reached for Patricia's hand while she told us the story, and I noticed how unhappy he seemed. She let him hold her hand for a few seconds after she stopped speaking. Then she removed it with a natural gesture, as poised as everything else about her.

"I wasn't angling for sympathy," she said. "I just get so furious with people who lack empathy." She turned back to me. "But now, what can we do to help you?" she asked.

Her concern for others was evident, and I could understand her attraction for Michael. I warmed toward Patricia despite my disappointment in seeing him with this lovely blonde.

"That's just it," I said. My voice sounded somewhat hoarse to me. "I don't know what can be done." *And I've never felt so helpless in my life*, I added silently.

She turned to Michael. "You're a pharmacist, too. Surely you can help."

"Of course, I want to help. But how?"

"You can find out if any of the people connected with Amy Brookman take that blood thinner—Coumadin," Denise blurted suddenly. "Someone close to her had to make the substitution. That's what I told Ruthie days ago, and I still think it's the only possibility."

Michael seemed startled by the outburst, and I knew he would never agree to Denise's suggestion. He already had voiced his doubts about me during that Sunday brunch, and I saw no reason to expect a change of mind. I had lost all chance of receiving the kind of understanding he had just shown to Patricia.

Well, it was my own fault. We had been apart too long, and our breakup had destroyed whatever feeling he'd once had for me. I was a fool to think we could be close again, even as friends, misled by that temporary closeness after his son-in-law's murder and my own brush with death last summer.

"I'm sorry, Ruthie. I did mean to race over and apologize for sounding as if I didn't have confidence in you," Michael said, "but I've been tied up." I intercepted a glance at Patricia as he spoke. "I should have realized what you're going through and been to see you sooner."

"I wasn't expecting a knight in shining armor to rescue me," I said.

"And I'm not trying to play that role, but I spoke impulsively the other day and I want to make up for it." He turned toward my friend. "You're right, Denise. I can call other pharmacies and see what we can learn."

Chapter 10.

I stared at Michael, feeling my face flush. "That's not necessary," I told him. "I can do it myself."

Michael hesitated. "It's better if another pharmacist makes those calls." He spoke slowly, as if he were choosing his words carefully this time instead of rushing headlong into conversation the way he usually did.

"Why?" I asked but suddenly understood what Michael hadn't wanted to say. If I were unable to clear myself and went to trial—either civilly for accidental substitution of one drug for another or criminally for deliberate substitution—making such calls myself might be incriminating.

The others seemed to realize I now knew what Michael had left unsaid. "We need to discover as much as possible about anyone closely involved with Amy Brookman," Denise repeated.

"I suppose we can look up each of their addresses and call pharmacies in their neighborhoods."

"Let's also try to find out where they work. Perhaps they drop off prescriptions on the way in or on the way home." This was Patricia's suggestion, and I thought it sounded like a sensible one.

"We can do better than that," Denise said. "I'll talk to Jeremy Douglas, Amy's uncle. The one who works for Food Go. I'm sure he can give us addresses and workplaces for most of Amy's family. And maybe for other people—like her boyfriend."

"I'll be happy to coordinate the list and look up all the telephone numbers," Patricia offered.

Michael smiled at her. "If this weren't so serious, I'd say it sounds like we're planning an amateur show."

I decided it was time to tell them about the attorney I'd consulted. "I should talk to him before we go ahead," I said.

We agreed that I would contact Sterling Harraday and call Michael at his daughter's house as soon as I got the lawyer's advice. Meanwhile, Denise would try to save time by seeing Jeremy for the information we wanted from him.

Patricia and Michael refused more coffee. They left, first reassuring us that they would stay in close touch. I stood in the doorway with Denise and watched them cross the two driveways to Betsy Stokes's house.

"That was unexpected," Denise said.

I couldn't pretend to misunderstand. "We never made any commitments."

"Obviously he didn't," she said drily, "but what about you?"

Gathering up the dirty coffee mugs, I walked quickly into Denise's kitchen with them. My ploy to avoid discussing Michael and Patricia didn't work. I hadn't thought it would.

"Ruthie, if you really care about Michael, you'll have to fight for him."

How typical of Denise, I thought. She was scripting scenes from an old movie for me to play out, determined to link Michael and me romantically although she had no idea we'd dated all those years ago. Denise was a good friend, but I couldn't talk about the time back in pharmacy college. And who today would believe that our love had never been consummated?

I wanted to tell Denise to follow her own advice, not to give up so easily when she met someone she liked—but I would never hurt her that way. Instead I tried to deflect any suspicion that I was interested in Michael.

"Patricia seems like a very decent person."

"Very attractive, if you like skinny intellectual types."

My laughter was genuine. "Intellectual?"

"Didn't you notice her way with words? And her suggestions were very clever."

"Patricia did seem intelligent," I agreed. "I'm glad Michael's found someone like her. He's had enough problems."

"Everyone has problems," Denise said. "Speaking of which, let's get to the store early so I can try to question Jeremy."

I put the mugs in the dishwasher while Denise replaced the leftover cookies in their original box. *Yes*, I thought, *you have a lot more to worry about than Michael taking another woman to meet his daughter.* But it hurt to know he had someone else.

I remembered my own visits to the house next door. When I first knew Betsy, I'd stereotyped her as a "dumb blonde," a gold-digger, who had married an older man for his money and was after Michael even before her husband's funeral. Later, knowing her as Michael's daughter, seeing how vulnerable she was, and realizing she had loved Harry Stokes, my attitude changed. Now, whenever I saw Betsy, I could think only that she might have been my daughter if Michael and I had married, but I couldn't admit any of this to Denise.

She didn't pursue the subject. Instead, on the way back to my house to pick up my car, we went over the information she would try to get from Jeremy Dalton. "What do I say if he wants to know why?"

"Tell him the truth, Denise."

"I wasn't going to lie."

"Sorry, I didn't mean it that way."

We were stopped for a red light at Camelback and Hayden, and Denise turned to look at me. "You've really been hit hard from too many directions at once, haven't you?"

"I can cope," I assured her. Privately, I wasn't so sure. Although I'd made a determined effort to avoid self-pity after the first shock of widowhood, sometimes the battle still raged. These days, it was escalating to all-out war. My resistance had been lowered by too many sleepless nights since Amy Brookman's death. Now, despite the discovery that any fantasies about Michael were just that, I couldn't afford to feel sorry for myself. I must concentrate on clearing my name. If Patricia and Michael were willing to help, that was all that mattered.

Denise dropped me off. The morning had been so debilitating, I felt I needed a quick shower and change of clothes before starting on my late shift at the pharmacy. Something bright, I thought, as I looked through my closet. I didn't want to look defeated.

I chose a floral print in shades of rust and gold. Once I arrived at the pharmacy and put on my white jacket, no one would see the dress. Customers would glimpse only the top third of my body when they approached the pharmacy window with their prescriptions, but I could look down and see the cheerful colors whenever I needed comfort.

* * * *

The pharmacy was busy. Louise looked up from the computer screen when I came in. "You can take over here," she said by way of greeting. "And I'll get the people at the window."

Why did my staff pharmacists always want to displace me as pharmacy manager, I wondered. Louise had changed during the last two weeks, acting almost as if I were incompetent and she must guide me. I still found it difficult to be assertive but knew I must force myself before things got completely out of hand.

"That's okay, Louise," I said. "I'll get the window." Before she could answer, I quickly grabbed my white jacket and walked over to help the first customer in line.

She was a short, dark-haired young woman who handed me a birth-control prescription. It was a new one, not a refill, and I passed it to Louise to enter into the computer while I went to the shelves to find the Ortho Novum. When the paperwork emerged from the printer, I started to place the label on the hinged lid of the compact but noticed the customer was trying to get my attention.

"I forgot to ask how much it will cost," she said.

I looked down at the computer-generated receipt. "It's $30.35."

"So much!" She seemed dismayed. "I don't know if it's worth it."

Just then, as if on cue, we heard a child howling elsewhere in the store. We grinned at each other. "I guess it is worth it," she said.

It was the kind of incident that made me enjoy my profession. Even today, with all the unshakeable worries in the forefront of my mind, I found myself smiling again as I helped the next customer. He was a middle-aged man who came in for a Zantac refill every month but never had the vial or the prescription number.

"Number?" I asked, although I already knew the answer.

"It's in the computer."

"Okay, I'll look it up and fill that for you, sir."

He turned away but came back to the window before I reached Louise at the computer. "Isn't my Zantac ready yet?" he asked.

"Sir, we need to look it up and make sure you still have refills. Then we'll try to get you out as soon as possible. So give us about 15 minutes." *Instantaneous service would be wonderful*, I thought, *but even if he were the only customer in the place, it would still take time to fill his prescription.*

I could see there was no way I'd have time to call Sterling Harraday. Louise's shift was due to end soon, and it was Karen's day off. Once Louise left, I'd be busier still. In any case, I didn't want her to overhear my conversation with the lawyer. I'll wait until tomorrow, I decided. I would be opening up and could surely find time to make the call.

The rush of customers continued. Louise suddenly walked away from the computer and removed her white jacket, signaling that she was ready to leave. "Mrs. Jackson will be in later, but we never got an okay to refill her Ventolin Inhaler," she told me.

"Couldn't you reach her doctor?"

Louise shrugged. "He's been out all day."

"All right. I'll explain it to her. Anything else I need to know before you leave?"

"No, but there's something I'd like to ask."

She probably wants to exchange hours with me, I thought. Tim, my previous staff pharmacist, always was reluctant to swap when I needed to change shifts, but I'd be glad to oblige Louise. I waited for her to continue.

"Have you heard anything more about that mistake?" she asked. "Are they going to prosecute you?"

I should be beyond shock at Louise's bluntness, I thought, but couldn't repress a shudder at her callous words. She could easily have framed the question differently, something like "I hope that nonsense about the so-called mistake has been dropped." Maybe that was wishful thinking, though. Louise seemed to believe not only that I was capable of making such an error but also that I had done it. I couldn't understand her attitude. From the beginning, when she first came to fill in at Food Go, I'd tried to be friendly with her. But she had remained aloof.

Louise would make a great witness for the prosecution, I thought unhappily. Well, I would just have to prove that she was wrong. Even Michael, who had seemed unsupportive when I first told him about Amy Brookman's death, was now actively trying to help. Although it hurt to find that someone else now had Michael's love, I told myself it was more important to learn that he did believe in me after all.

Louise was staring at me, tugging on her long braid, large dark eyes unreadable.

She waited expectantly, looking older than her twenty-three years, more like the cartoon figure of a woman ready to hear a juicy bit of gossip over the back fence.

"There was no mistake, Louise," I said as firmly as I could.

"You can't just wish it away."

"I'm saying that I made no error."

Louise didn't even try to hide her disbelief. "Well, I hope you have a good lawyer," she called over her shoulder as she left the pharmacy for the day.

Surprisingly calm, I continued to help my waiting customers. This time, I didn't have to depend on the years of professional experience to carry me through. I knew I had friends who believed in me even if my staff pharmacist did not. Buoyed by this knowledge, I worked on, feeling more like myself than I had for some time.

This precarious self-confidence got an unexpected boost from my next patient, a young woman who dropped off an Amoxicillin prescription for her nine-year-old daughter. When she returned to the window, I had the antibiotic ready. "You probably know the school nurse can't dispense anything unless it's fully labeled," I said. "Would you like another label and a small vial for her to take to school?"

"What a great idea!" she said. "That way, Michelle won't have to bring the entire bottle back and forth every day."

I attached a second label to an empty vial and added it to her package.

"That's really thoughtful of you," the woman said. "I can't tell you how much I appreciate your help."

I suppose I could have called my attorney instead of taking time for this woman and for some of the others who needed extra attention that afternoon, but Dad had taught me well.

Patients need that little human touch, and I wasn't going to neglect my professional responsibilities no matter what happened.

The evening went by quickly as I tried to keep up with periodic customer rushes and do paperwork during any slight lull. I didn't have much time to worry about my situation but did wonder why I'd heard nothing from Denise. It was impossible for me to take a break and walk into the coffee shop since I was alone in the pharmacy. The waitresses, on the other hand, had regularly scheduled breaks; and I kept expecting Denise to come by and tell me what was happening.

I knew the meat cutters began work hours before we did. Maybe Jeremy had an early shift today. Or he could have the day off. No point guessing. Denise would surely let me know as soon as she had some information. Closing time came, however, without any word from her.

When I left the store, though, I found Jeremy waiting just outside the doors nearest the pharmacy end of Food Go. "How's my favorite pharmacist?" he said, but the words sounded forced this time.

"Fine," I assured him. "Is everyone okay at home? I can reopen if you have a prescription."

"No, I don't need anything." He hesitated for a moment, fiddling with the bolo clip on his western tie. "Denise caught me as I was leaving this afternoon."

"I knew she planned to talk with you."

Jeremy spoke as if he were measuring his words. "I wasn't sure if it was okay to give all those names and addresses out. But after I got home from work, I thought about it all evening. And I talked it over with Lupe."

I waited, trying not to think how much depended on Jeremy's cooperation.

"We decided it was better to make one more try first. I mean to get the family to drop everything."

"The lawsuit?" Even if they dropped the civil action, I still needed to find out what really happened in order to clear my name.

He nodded. "You saw that I couldn't convince my brother—Amy's father. But it's really his wife, ex that is, who's pushing the lawsuit. And that boyfriend of hers smells money, so he's egging her on."

Two customers, pushing a grocery cart, passed us on their way out of the store. They nodded to me and looked curiously at Jeremy. Although I was one of the most visible Food Go employees, the meat cutters were rarely seen by customers. I knew they were wondering about him and our earnest conversation.

Jeremy also noticed their interest. He waited until they passed out of earshot. "We can't talk here," he said. "Why don't you follow my truck? I want to take you to see Leila."

My earlier self-confidence plummeted at the thought of meeting Amy Brookman's mother. If she were anything like her sister, Virginia, I was in for a terrible time. A rapid mental argument followed my first "can't do it" reaction. *You know you didn't cause Amy's death*, I told myself. *Let's not revert to that scenario. This is your opportunity to know more members of the family. And Jeremy could be right. Maybe we can change his sister-in-law's mind.*

"Okay," I said. "Let's go!"

He showed me where his pickup was parked and walked me to my car. I eased out of my space and waited just behind his parking spot until he pulled out.

Why didn't I take down the address, I wondered as I followed. What if I lose him?

Jeremy drove slowly, however, carefully waiting after each stop sign and traffic light to make sure I got through. Traffic was thin at this hour, and his white pickup was easy to follow.

We drove about twenty minutes before pulling into a driveway on the Scottsdale side of the Salt River-Pima Indian reservation. The neighborhood was a modest one, negating the common assumption that only wealthy people live in Scottsdale. I couldn't see much of the house in the dark, but its white exterior and avocado trim looked freshly painted.

Jeremy had emerged from the pickup and walked back to my Honda. I let down the driver's window, suddenly afraid to leave the comfy blanket of my car. "Does she expect us?" I whispered.

In the dim light from a street lamp at the corner, I could see his embarrassed expression. "I couldn't take a chance on calling, Ruthie. She might have told me to go to hell."

This was getting worse by the minute. Leila Brookman didn't sound like someone who would listen to reason. I sat there, ready to back up and flee.

"I'm trying to help," Jeremy said.

He was right. If I wanted to stop the threat to my self-esteem and professional reputation, I had to take advantage of this opportunity. I got out of the car and followed Jeremy to the front door, trying not to hang back too noticeably as he rang the bell.

A harsh voice, male, called out, "If you're selling something, we don't want any."

Oh no, I thought, but forced myself to ignore the impulse to run. Jeremy, undaunted, gave his name in a firm voice. When the door opened, he nodded encouragement and pushed me gently forward.

The man framed in the entry light was not as tall as Jeremy but looked like someone who worked out regularly. Muscles bulged below the sleeves of his purple and orange Phoenix Suns T-shirt, and I thought if he decided to throw us out, even Jeremy couldn't stop him.

"Who is it, Nick?" a woman's husky voice called out.

"Your brother-in-law and some broad."

"My ex-brother-in-law. And don't call Lupe a broad. You're as bad as Quentin."

He muttered to himself as he led us through a cluttered family room into the kitchen. I didn't catch anything he said, but from the tone was glad I couldn't hear the words. "It ain't Lupe," he said as we walked into a brightly lit kitchen that must have been a holdover from the sixties. Everything in it was avocado green—appliances, counter tops, linoleum, and curtains.

Leila Brookman didn't look at all the way I'd pictured her from Jeremy and Lupe's comments. I guess I expected someone flashy and brassy. Leila, however, except for the obvious age difference, resembled her sister. Like Virginia, she was tall and thin, with the same well-shaped features. The similarities ended there. I had only seen Virginia twice but both times, she wore dark suits with white blouses. Leila was casually dressed in black T-shirt and checked slacks. The main difference was her facial expression. Even when Leila frowned at Jeremy's introduction of me, she showed none of Virginia's grimness.

"What do you want?" she said, but it was as if she were reading lines in a bad play. The words had no force.

"And this is Nick Kenmore, Ruthie," Jeremy continued blandly, as he nodded toward our escort.

Nick's scowl was more intimidating than Leila's words. I dug my heels into that avocado linoleum and stood fast.

"If you've come to apologize, forget it," Leila said. "It won't do any good."

"No, I didn't come to apologize. I'm sorry, of course, that your daughter died, but I had nothing to do with it."

"Let's go sit in the front room," Jeremy said. No one paid attention to him. We remained in that avocado kitchen, under bright fluorescent lights and glared at each other; that is, Leila and Nick glared at me. I tried to look concerned (the easy part) and relaxed (the impossible part).

"Why did you bring her?" Leila asked Jeremy.

"I want you to listen to her story."

"Story is right," Nick said. "I'll bet it's a good one."

"Just give Ruthie ten minutes," Jeremy pleaded.

"Sure thing. It's your five million we're going after, so talk."

"Five million! I don't have five million."

This confrontation was completely different from anything I'd expected. Instead of trying to convince them of my innocence, I was now sidetracked by sheer incredulity at the magnitude of their claim.

"You got that kind of insurance that the doctors have," Nick said.

"You mean malpractice insurance? But pharmacists don't carry large amounts like that."

"Well, the supermarket can make up the difference."

I looked at them, not understanding for a moment. "You didn't tell me you're suing Food Go, too," Jeremy said. "You know I work for them."

"So what! They won't go out of business because of one lousy lawsuit. Every company gets sued these days."

Their greed made them seem like ambulance-chasing caricatures. Surprisingly, after my first incredulous reaction, their preposterous claim fortified my resolve. "You have no case," I told them. "Neither I nor Food Go had anything to do with Amy's death."

Nick moved closer, invading my space as he hovered over me. "We don't have to prove anything. All the jury needs to hear is how Leila lost her beautiful daughter. They always side with the little people against big companies."

"Ruthie isn't a big company," Jeremy said. "You're going to ruin a decent person's life just to make some money. Blood money!"

"We deserve that money," Leila told him. She moved closer to Nick so that both of them hemmed me in.

"No, you don't," Jeremy said. "Amy couldn't even bear to live with the two of you."

Nick's voice turned ugly. I ducked involuntarily as he raised his fist. I had already noticed the black and blue marks on Leila's arms and didn't want to be his next victim. "And just what are you trying to say?"

Jeremy became the peacemaker again. "Let's sit down and talk this over like sensible people," he said. Without waiting for an answer, he took my arm and propelled me away from Leila and Nick to a wrought-iron chair at the kitchen table. He seated me and pulled out another chair for himself. "I could use some coffee," he said to Leila. "We are guests here, even though I admit we weren't invited."

He must have known how to deal with his former sister-in-law because she smiled and busied herself with a jar of instant coffee. She filled four cups with tap water and put them in the microwave. All of us waited without speaking until the coffee was ready. The coffee was bitter. Everyone else that I knew used bottled water or had a reverse osmosis system to filter the terrible tasting city water. I was grateful for the coffee, though, realizing for the first time how much this confrontation was affecting me.

Leila and Nick seemed an odd couple. Each time they started to fit one stereotype or other, something shifted. I had expected Nick to pull a can of beer out of the refrigerator, but he drank coffee with the rest of us. And Leila certainly didn't seem like a grieving mother. Not only because she wanted to profit from her daughter's death, but also because she showed no signs of sadness. I thought of her sister, Amy's aunt, who had seemed shattered by the girl's death.

I remembered another murder last summer. The parents had been inconsolable, wanting to talk nonstop about how wonderful their son had been. Leila, on the other hand, still hadn't said a word about her daughter.

The four of us sat at the table, making the coffee last, as if reluctant to begin speaking again. It was Jeremy who returned to the subject we had come there to discuss.

"The reason I brought Ruthie here, Leila, is that I wanted you to see what kind of person she is. She's a good pharmacist. Real professional. Helps people all the time, like she helped when we couldn't get that medicine for Manuel. What you're trying to do is gonna ruin her."

He paused, eyes fixed on Leila, waiting for her to react. For a long time, she said nothing. Then she turned to me.

"Look," she said. "I'll level with you. I got nothing personal against you. Maybe you made a mistake and maybe you didn't."

"I didn't!" I said with as much energy as I could muster.

"That don't matter. I'll bet you got a nicer house than this. Well, you're my ticket outta here. I'm gonna have a house in Paradise Valley.

And I'm gonna shop in Saks and Neiman Marcus." She smiled dreamily at Nick. "And Nick wants a boat, so I'm gonna buy him one."

I couldn't believe what I was hearing. She was admitting things that would damage her in court. As if she read my mind, Leila said, "And don't think you can tell the judge what I just said. I'll deny it all, and Nick will be my witness."

Chapter 11.

I looked at Jeremy. Didn't Leila realize he could corroborate what we heard here tonight? She followed my glance.

"Jeremy's still family," she said. "When push comes to shove, he won't forget Amy was his favorite niece."

"Don't be so sure I'll back you," Jeremy contradicted.

"I am sure."

"I can't let you treat Ruthie this way. Not when you just admitted you're deliberately going after the deepest pockets."

Leila stared at him and then at me. "I never knew you liked older women," she said. "Tell me, does Lupe know you got something going here?"

Even though I realized the purpose behind her ridiculous accusation, I could feel my face flush. She grinned at me. "Well, why not? He's a handsome guy. I got to admit, I always liked him better than Quentin. After it was too late, anyways."

Nick slammed his fist into the kitchen table so hard he rattled the coffee cups. "Stop fooling around, Leila. I'm not gonna tell you again."

This wasn't getting us anywhere. It was definitely time to leave. I turned to tell Jeremy I wanted to go, but the doorbell interrupted me. *Now what?* I wondered.

Leila said the same words aloud as she went off in the direction of the front door, returning with a thin, dark-haired boy who looked about fourteen years old. "Hello, Tommy," Jeremy greeted him, and I realized he must be Amy's boyfriend.

I saw Nick's face harden as he looked at the boy. "What do you want?" he asked. "Didn't we tell you not to come around here no more?"

No one answered Nick, but Leila had walked over to the kitchen counter and was already filling another cup with instant coffee and tap water for Tommy. I glanced at him curiously, knowing from Jeremy that the boy was older than he looked—seventeen, in fact—and that he'd wanted to marry Amy.

Jeremy, in that easygoing way of his, asked Tommy how he was getting along, while Nick glared at each of us in turn. Leila, at least, could keep occupied. She motioned to the boy to take her own seat, brought over the cup of coffee for him, and resupplied the rest of us. Despite her negative, greedy side that I'd just witnessed, I had to admit Leila was a conscientious hostess to all her uninvited guests.

"Who did you want to talk to?" Jeremy asked.

The boy fidgeted in his seat, without answering. He was wearing a blue flannel shirt and unfrayed jeans, his light brown hair neatly combed. Either he worked at a place that enforced a dress code or had taken care with his appearance before coming here.

"Yeah, what do you want?" Nick repeated.

"Amy's mom."

Leila looked surprised but told Nick to let the boy have his coffee in peace. She went and stood behind Nick's chair, her hands massaging his shoulders. He made no move to offer her his seat or to bring one from elsewhere in the house. It was Jeremy who rose and said he'd get another chair from the master bedroom.

Tommy gulped down his coffee so fast that he must have scalded his mouth. "I think about Amy every day," he said suddenly.

For the first time that evening, I detected a trace of sadness on Leila's face. "So do I," she told him. I could see the sudden tightening of the hands that had been caressing Nick's shoulders and the corresponding strained look on his face, but there was no way to tell whether he was feeling sympathetic or annoyed.

Jeremy returned carrying a brass stool by its rim, three legs protruding outward. It was the kind some women used with their dressing tables or bathroom vanities. Under one arm, he gripped a cushion—the color we used to call hot pink. He put the chair down next to Leila and carefully replaced the round cushion. She nodded her thanks but remained standing.

Tommy cleared his throat a couple of times. "I've been watching the house most nights," he said to Jeremy, "trying to see Amy's mom alone. But he's always here, and I was afraid to come in."

With a quick movement, Nick started to get out of his seat. Leila pushed him back and even though he could easily have shaken her off, he subsided. "Sure, I'm always here. I live here."

"You must go out sometimes," Tommy said. "I've been waiting for days." He looked toward Jeremy again. "Then, I saw the two of you arrive tonight, and I figured he couldn't do anything to hurt me while you're both here."

"Hurt you, you creep. You'll be lucky to get out of this house alive." This time, Leila couldn't restrain Nick. He jumped out of his chair and rushed to confront Tommy. The boy leapt from his own seat and turned to Jeremy for protection in a scene that would have been farcical if the situation were not so serious.

Now Jeremy was out of his chair, too, blocking Nick. "Are you crazy? Leave the kid alone. He's got a right to talk, and I want to hear what he has to say."

Tommy seemed too frightened to speak. "I'm leaving," he said. "You gotta let me go."

"Don't worry, kid. No one's going to hurt you."

"He's going to kill me, like he killed Amy."

Leila looked stunned. I think Jeremy and I shouted at the same time, asking Tommy what he meant. The surprising part was Nick's reaction. I expected him to make a more determined effort to get at the boy and shut him up. Instead, he sat down again and laughed.

"You think this is funny?" Jeremy asked.

"Sure, I do. The kid don't know what he's talking about. This ain't the first time he's been saying things against me. Why do you think I told him to stay away from here?"

"You didn't tell me about it," Leila said.

"There wasn't nothing to tell."

"Then why was he watching the house? Why is he here tonight?"

They stood, arms folded, glaring at each other, voices harsh—in complete contrast to the loving tableau they had presented only a few moments before. "I didn't want you to hear his lies," Nick said.

"You let me be the judge of that."

"Can't you see he's got some crazy idea in his head? He's just looking for someone to blame because Amy wouldn't marry him."

"Why would he blame you? You didn't try to stop them from marrying."

Nick softened his body language and his voice. "Look, honey. Let's throw everyone out. We don't need to talk in front of them."

I waited, expecting to be ejected along with Jeremy and Tommy, thinking it would be more dignified to leave first. Never having met Leila or Nick before, I couldn't assess the likelihood of being thrown out, so I watched Jeremy, figuring he knew these people. He made no move to go, so I settled back in my chair. After all, more than anyone else, I needed to know what Leila and Nick were up to and whether Tommy had real knowledge of what happened to Amy.

A rapid exchange of meaningful looks followed. Leila seemed upset, but Nick continued as the voice of reason. "You just got over the bad time, honey." He spoke to her seductively, as if they were alone in the room. "Let's not start all over again just when you been doing so well."

She moved forward and leaned into his body. "Okay, I guess you're right."

"Don't let him con you the way he conned Amy," Tommy cried out.

"Shut up and get out."

"You think you can scare everyone because you lift weights. I know you're twice as big as I am, but so's he." He pointed to Jeremy. "I pleaded with Amy to go to him for help. See your uncle, I told her, but she was afraid. And now she's dead."

I wondered how much of the boy's words came from his grief over losing Amy and how much could be true. There didn't seem to be any motive for Nick to kill her. She didn't even live with her mother and Nick.

"She's dead because you couldn't keep your hands off her," Nick said.

Tommy choked back a sob. "That's not true. I loved her; I wanted to marry her."

"That's your story."

"What's the use of talking about it now?" Leila asked. "It's too late."

"You have to know what really happened. You have to know what kind of man you live with."

"Wait a minute," Jeremy said. "I don't get it. Why are you blaming Nick?"

"You don't understand."

"Then tell me."

"I said to get out!" Nick shouted.

"And I want to hear what the kid has to say," Jeremy countered. I said nothing, still wanting to run but unwilling to miss what was happening.

Tommy spoke to Leila. "Mrs. Brookman, I don't want to hurt you..." He hesitated, seeming to search for the right words, as she turned to face him.

"Shut up!" I thought Nick's rage would frighten the boy into silence, but it had the opposite effect this time.

"It was his baby," Tommy said.

I sat there frozen for long moments before I could look at the others to judge their reactions. Leila's mouth was open in a wordless "Oh," and I saw Jeremy move quickly to block Nick from going after the boy.

"That's a damn lie," Nick bellowed. "You're just a troublemaker."

"It's the truth, and you know it." Tommy appealed to the rest of us. "Why do you think she couldn't bear to keep the baby? Or even to let you have it," he said, turning to Jeremy.

"I always wondered why she wouldn't marry the kid," Jeremy muttered, half to himself. He seemed to be turning Tommy's words over in his mind, trying to pinpoint their accuracy. Suddenly, he made his move, grabbing Nick's T-shirt with both hands and facing him down.

"It's bad enough when it's two kids who think they're in love. But if I find out you went after Amy, a sixteen-year-old, for God's sake... I'm gonna kill you." He released Nick's shirt and turned toward his former sister-in-law.

"And you, Leila. Her own mother. You must have known what was going on." He didn't touch Leila but looked murderously at her, too.

"That's why she went to live with her Aunt Virginia," Tommy said. "She couldn't stand being in the same house with him."

Leila looked as if she, too, were weighing the boy's words. "Nick...?"

"Damn it, Leila. You know me better than that. You're not gonna believe this punk."

"Why did she move out?"

"She was restless; you know that. Remember how she moved in with Quentin for a while."

Leila seemed relieved. I could see that she wanted to trust Nick.

"I knew he'd talk you around." The boy's tone was anguished. "That's why I was trying to see you alone."

It was hard to come to grips with what I was hearing. I wanted to get out of there and take the time to sort things over in my mind. If Tommy's claims were true, it would put an entirely new slant on the pregnancy that led to Amy's death. But how could anyone prove or disprove his story?

Chapter 12.

Tommy had made two accusations against Nick: that he had impregnated Leila's daughter and, then, that he had killed her. If the first charge were true, the second could have resulted from it. Suppose Amy threatened Nick. She was only sixteen; he was more than twice her age. Not only would such an accusation have ended Nick's relationship with Leila but, since Amy was underage, it also could have led to prosecution and a long prison sentence.

Although it was obvious that Jeremy wanted to stay and shake the truth from Nick, Leila abandoned her hospitable manner, urging us to go, insisting she would find out what really happened.

"Okay," Jeremy agreed. "I'm leaving it up to you for now, but I won't drop this."

"Don't worry. I won't drop it either." Leila looked hard at Nick.

"Come on, kid," Jeremy said. "You'd better come with us."

"Just a minute." Leila grabbed the boy's arm to get his full attention. "Tommy, if it turns out you just wanted to make trouble, you'll have to deal with me."

"It's the truth, Mrs. Brookman. Amy made me swear not to tell anyone, and I kept my promise all this time. But I couldn't stand it anymore. I had to tell." He walked behind me and just ahead of Jeremy to the front door, using us for protection. I could sense his fear, and I was frightened, too.

When we reached the door, I pulled it open, hurrying onto the front walk to escape this house as quickly as possible. But Tommy stopped in the narrow entry and, blocked as he was by Jeremy's large frame, shouted at Leila and Nick.

"She didn't have to die. I won't let him get away with it."

Jeremy propelled him out through the doorway and into the cool October night. For a moment, I recoiled inwardly, expecting Nick to come barreling after us; but there was no sound at all from the house, and the only acknowledgment of our presence was a negative one. Before we had taken more than a few steps along the front walk, the outside lights were switched off and we were in darkness. Again I felt that touch of fear, knowing how many Arizonans are proud gun owners. Maybe Nick was planning to shoot at us. No, I reminded myself. We would have made better targets with the lights left on.

Tommy had parked about half a block away from the house. We walked him to his car, an old blue and white Colt, and waited while he unlocked it and climbed in. He rolled down the driver's side window. "What I said," he told us, "was true. I couldn't make up a story like that."

Jeremy stood there, seeming to think things over. "How did you find out?"

"She told me. We never..." He hesitated. "I knew it couldn't be my baby." His voice became an anguished cry in that quiet street. "We loved each other. She wasn't seeing anyone else. Then he came along."

"When did she tell you?"

To me, it sounded like Jeremy was pressing for more details because he doubted the boy's story. I didn't know what to believe, but I had a sickening feeling that Tommy was telling the truth.

"Not when it first happened. She just got very quiet and kind of sad and went straight from school to her aunt's house one afternoon. She didn't even try to get her clothes and stuff from her mom's. I couldn't understand it."

In the moonlight, I could see that Tommy looked uncomfortable. "I mean, her aunt was much stricter than her mom. We couldn't see each other on school nights anymore and things like that."

"Did she tell Virginia?"

"No, she was afraid to."

"Well, what did Amy say to you? And why didn't she speak to me or her father so we could take care of Nick?"

I wondered if Jeremy believed him or whether he was leading the boy on to trip him up. Tommy remained silent for a few seconds.

"She was flattered and she was willing at first. Then when she tried to break it off, she didn't think anyone would believe her."

"God damn it!" Jeremy exploded. "At least we would have checked it out when she became pregnant. There's ways now to be sure. Blood tests."

"Amy wasn't acting like herself. All she could think of was getting away from him."

"We'll never get Nick to admit anything now," I said, surprised at myself for breaking into their conversation.

"Leila won't let it rest. If there's any truth to this story, she'll get it from him."

"He certainly won't admit to murder," I said.

"Murder?"

"Yes, Jeremy. You're outraged that he'd seduce Amy. And I agree that's unconscionable. But think about it. If Tommy's right, he may have killed her."

"What are you talking about?" Jeremy asked. "I thought he meant that Nick was responsible for her death because the pregnancy was his doing."

"And I think someone murdered Amy. If the baby was his, who had a better motive?"

Jeremy turned to Tommy. "Tell us exactly what you meant. But first, let's find someplace where we can talk without hanging out the car window."

"I won't go back to their house."

"Okay, I have a better idea. Quentin needs to hear this."

"Amy's dad won't listen," Tommy said. "She didn't get along with him. He was too strict."

Maybe nobody was strict enough, I thought, but didn't say it aloud. I was nearly two generations older than Amy and Tommy, and I knew my views were different. If not, I might have been married to Michael all these years. *And then again*, I told myself, *you would have missed your life with Bob.*

Tommy agreed to drive to Quentin's and wait for us in front of his home. We backtracked to Leila and Nick's driveway, my nervousness increasing the closer we approached to their place. It was very quiet. Either their house was too solidly built to expose arguments or they had settled their differences.

"Do you think she believes Tommy?" I asked Jeremy. "Do you?"

"I don't know."

"That young man was terrified of Nick."

"He'd probably be as scared if he made up the story."

I thought about it. Maybe I was just looking for a way to clear myself. Yet, Tommy's story seemed to make sense. I wondered whether any of us were safe if Nick had deliberately killed Amy.

"Do you want to leave your car here and ride in the truck?" Jeremy asked.

I didn't ever want to return to this house, so I told Jeremy I'd follow him. We would have made a small cortege if Tommy had waited, but he had taken off quickly and was out of sight before we reached our own vehicles.

* * * *

Quentin lived in an older condominium not far from his ex-wife's house. I pulled into a visitor's parking lot next to Jeremy's truck and looked around. Although the landscaping featured desert plantings, tall palm trees and salmon-colored oleander bushes gave it a lush appearance. As I got out of my car, I noticed that Tommy's Colt was already in the lot.

"Leila got the house when they divorced," Jeremy told me when I reached his truck. "This condo is nothing fancy. He got just enough together to make the down payment."

"How can we drop in at this hour? Won't he be asleep?" Arizonans are early risers. People think nothing of telephoning at seven in the morning, but apologize for calls after nine in the evening.

"I don't care if he is asleep. This is important."

"Well, he's your brother."

"Half-brother," Jeremy corrected. "Listen, he's got no complaints. I'm the one who has to be at work early tomorrow."

I said no more but it was now after 11:00 pm, and I was still dubious about arriving unannounced at this hour. Tommy joined us at the front door of a one-story condo that, from the outside, seemed to be all garage. We could hear chimes echo through the house, but no one responded to the doorbell. Jeremy rang again, holding his forefinger on the bell. This time, a voice thick with sleep, sounded through the door.

"Who the hell's there?"

"Jeremy."

"What the hell do you want?"

It wasn't an auspicious beginning. And he didn't know that Tommy and I were there, too. Not for the first time that night, I wished I were safely at home. I took a deep breath and steeled myself for what was to come. Too much was at stake to worry about Quentin's reaction to our visit.

"I hope you've got some clothes on," Jeremy said. "I'm not alone."

"Hold on a minute."

We waited at least five, but Quentin finally opened the door. He grunted a greeting to the other two but just stared in my direction. I could see he didn't remember me.

Quentin led us to his living room, flopped into a brown recliner that took up a good part of the small room, and grunted to us to sit down. The place had an untidy look, with clothes and copies of *USA Today* strewn around the floor. There was a green sofa that looked like a Salvation Army reject, and not much other furniture.

I brushed aside some of the mess and, without waiting for an invitation, cleared enough space for Jeremy and myself to sit on the sofa. The cushions felt uncomfortably hard, and there were no throw pillows. I figured Leila must have gotten most of the furniture.

Tommy pulled over a rickety-looking folding chair and sat across from us. *We certainly wouldn't get any hospitality here*, I thought. But I reminded myself I wasn't there for coffee.

No one spoke for a while. "Well, you must've had a reason to come and wake me up," Quentin said finally.

"I don't know how to tell you this," Jeremy said. "Maybe you should just listen to what Tommy here has to say."

"Well, spit it out, kid." Quentin obviously didn't have a clue to what was coming.

"Tommy, tell him what you told us over at Leila's," Jeremy prompted.

"You're coming from there? What's going on?"

"Just listen, Quent. We need your advice."

"That's a new one."

Tommy looked as if he wanted to get up and run out of the house. I could sympathize with him. "See, everyone blamed me," he said. "But Amy and I never did anything."

"Say what you mean," Jeremy told him. He turned to Quentin. "The boy claims they never made out. That it was Nick's baby."

Quentin zoomed out of the recliner so fast I couldn't suppress a scream. He grabbed Tommy, yanking him out of the folding chair so forcefully that it tipped over. "Is that the truth? Are you telling me the truth?" He didn't wait for an answer. "I'll kill that miserable animal. And Leila, how could she let him touch our little girl?"

He suddenly let go of Tommy and collapsed on the floor, turning away from us as he wept, gasping and wheezing in a futile effort to control himself. I saw Jeremy start to go to him and then change his mind. We waited, not making eye contact.

After a few minutes, Quentin got up and left the room. He returned with a bottle of Jim Beam and some paper cups. "Here, we can all use this."

"Tommy's underage."

"What are you, a cop now?" There were no end tables or coffee table in the room, so he sat on the floor, pulled over a sheet of the discarded *USA Today*, and put the whiskey and cups on it. We all joined him, sitting cross-legged on the floor and helped ourselves. No one spoke.

The alcohol did help. At least, it kept me from giving up and running ignominiously out the door. Quentin started to speak, stopped, and began again. "Tell me what you know," he said to Tommy.

"She was acting so strange those last few weeks. Crying all the time. And she wouldn't tell me why." The boy stared at the floor as he spoke. "Then after she moved to her aunt's, she wouldn't hardly talk to me."

"If it wasn't your baby, why was she mad at you?" Quentin asked.

"She wasn't just mad at me. It was everyone and mostly herself. Maybe I'm not explaining it right." He suddenly looked up toward me. "Do people get like that when they're depressed?"

"Maybe. If they feel they have no control over their lives."

"That's it," he said. "She kept telling me she couldn't go on. Couldn't face things, is how she said it."

I hated myself for the surge of hope, but I couldn't help it. They say soldiers on the battlefield feel this way, sad for the ones who died but unable to control the joy of survival. It sounded as if Amy had committed suicide, and that would exonerate me.

Jeremy was the one who pursued the idea. "Are you saying that Amy killed herself?"

"No. She said she thought about it but couldn't do it. And then she told me what happened." He helped himself to some of the Jim Beam, grimaced as though he wasn't used to alcohol, and continued. "We were sitting in the park over near the high school. She was crying so hard, I couldn't understand her right away. I wanted to beat Nick up, but I knew I didn't stand a chance with him.

"Why didn't you come to me?" Quentin demanded.

"She didn't want anyone to know. I told her it wasn't her fault, but she kept blaming herself. She said she should have moved out when he started coming on to her. But at first she was flattered; she thought it was really love."

Quentin got up and paced around the tiny living room, nearly knocking over the bottle and cups. "And where was her mother? Why didn't Leila help her?"

"Amy and Nick got together back in August, that time her mom went to San Diego for a few days to cool off. He said he had some kind of deal in the works and couldn't leave town, so Amy's mom went by herself."

"That selfish woman," Quentin yelled and pounded his fist on the wall. He stood there, massaging his reddened knuckles, seeming unaware of what caused the pain.

"Stop it, Quent," Jeremy said. "Leila couldn't know what would happen. And she doesn't even believe it. Right this minute, Nick's probably talking her around."

"She loved her daughter," I said. "Anyone can see that."

For the first time, Quentin Brookman seemed to notice my presence. "And who the hell are you?" he asked. He turned to Jeremy. "Why is she here?"

"This is Ruthie. You know, the pharmacist."

"What?" he bellowed, and I was afraid he'd take his rage out on me. "Are you crazy, Jeremy? She's the one who killed Amy."

"Now just sit down and listen to the rest of Tommy's story," Jeremy said. "He thinks Nick killed Amy to keep her quiet."

I expected another explosion from Quentin, but was surprised he said nothing at all.

"She was afraid of him. He said he'd kill Amy if she told anyone it was his baby."

"It does make sense in a way." Quentin spoke very slowly. "It explains why she refused to marry Tommy and why that old battleaxe, Virginia, was so enraged."

I thought of Amy's aunt that day at the pharmacy. She did look grim, but so do many relatives of the young women who come in after an abortion. This morning at the demonstration—was it really only this morning?—she certainly seemed implacable. *On the other hand*, I told myself, *she didn't come across as an opportunist like her sister. If Virginia really believed me responsible for her niece's death, I couldn't blame her for those dour looks.*

"If you want me to take a lie detector test, I will," Tommy suddenly said.

"You've been watching too much TV, kid," Jeremy told him, not unkindly.

"Well, what do you think?" Quentin asked his brother.

"I don't know."

"That makes two of us. I've got half a mind to go over there now and take Nick apart."

"You won't get anywhere with him. He's too slick," Jeremy insisted.

"Well, I'll get somewhere with Leila," Quentin said. "I can always tell when she's lying to me."

"That's assuming she knows."

"I'll give her a day or two. If there's anything to find out, she'll know by then."

Quentin walked over and grabbed the boy's arm in a gesture almost identical to Leila's earlier in the evening. "And you, Tommy, if I find out you're the liar..."

"I just don't want him to get away with what he did."

"You stay out of it now," Quentin said. "I'll take care of the two of them."

Chapter 13.

Quentin spoke with such icy force, I was nearly as frightened of him as I'd been of Nick. I looked at Jeremy. He seemed the only rational one I'd dealt with that night. Yet, I knew he and Lupe had cared about Amy, too.

We didn't stay much longer, and I was glad to leave all of them. Reminding myself that Jeremy was not the only one with an early shift the next morning, I slid into my car to drive home.

After all the confrontations that evening, and despite my weariness, I anticipated an uneasy night with little or no sleep. Exhaustion took over, though, the moment my head hit the pillow.

I don't know what I expected the next day. All the threats that were voiced the night before made me jump every time the telephone rang. And in a busy Food Go pharmacy, the phone is seldom quiet. I worried about Tommy. He was the only one with direct knowledge about Nick and Amy; he'd make a prime victim. *Maybe I should warn him*, I thought, and realized how ridiculous that would be. I didn't even know how to reach him, and I couldn't bring myself to ask Jeremy.

Nothing relating to Amy Brookman or her family happened during the next few days. I would be off on Sunday and Monday this week, and I wanted to phone Michael to see if he had new information. Good excuse, I told myself. You know he'd call you if he learned anything. Probably too busy with Patricia, I thought, and wanted to kick myself for succumbing to the old self-pity bug that I'd worked so hard to exterminate after my first months as a widow.

On Sunday, Patricia called me. Her telephone voice was low and throaty, but with a sparkle to it. I guessed men would consider it sexy. "We were planning to see the Duck Race yesterday," she said, referring to an annual fund-raising event during which tens of thousands of rubber bathtub ducks are launched into Tempe Town Lake. Each duck has a paying sponsor, and the sponsors of the fastest rubber ducks are awarded prizes.

"But Michael had to drive back to Tucson," she continued. "Something about the relief pharmacist coming down with a 24-hour virus."

"Oh," I said, thinking my response didn't sound very bright. If someone were recording this conversation, Patricia would win hands down in the personality department. Then I reminded myself I wasn't in competition with Patricia. I had let Michael go too many years before.

"He's been calling every pharmacy contact, and he planned to keep trying from Tucson." She paused. "Most important, Michael wanted me to get your schedule for tomorrow; he expects to be back up here in the morning."

So why didn't he just call me and ask? I wondered. *Don't be a fool, Ruthie. He wanted to talk to Patricia. Why make two long-distance calls?* I resolved again to restrain feelings that kept getting in the way of the more pressing issues at stake.

"Tomorrow's my day off," I told Patricia.

"Brilliant! When and where would you like to meet?"

"Can you come here? Any time that's convenient for both of you."

We made an appointment for eleven the next morning, subject to Michael's arrival from Tucson in time. "But he said he'll probably be here tonight," Patricia told me.

Sure, I thought. *He won't want to miss spending the night with you.* And I couldn't blame him. She was everything I was not—sophisticated, elegant, cosmopolitan. I knew I envied her, but I liked her, too.

Since I'd been trained to be meticulous in my father's pharmacy, my house was always neat. I vacuumed the carpets, anyhow, and went to the nearest supermarket for some pastries. *Patricia's probably a world-class baker*, I thought, and gave myself another mental kick for regressing.

I spent time carefully choosing my clothes for the next day, rejecting any silk dresses first of all. It wouldn't do to look overdressed. Besides, with a sunny and warm weather forecast, we might sit out on the patio. Slacks, I decided, stifling the image of Patricia Donleavy in her well-tailored beige slacks and cream blouse. My hair had lost much of its natural ginger color and I now depended on my hairdresser, but I was no more than five pounds over my college weight. White slacks with a black and white striped blouse would do. They'd look neatly crisp, just right for a visit that really wasn't a social call.

Too bad I couldn't control my thoughts as easily as I did my wardrobe. For months now, I'd been denying how much Michael meant to me. Now, even though Patricia would be with him, I couldn't ignore the soaring feeling, the anticipation that always took over when I knew I'd be seeing him.

Monday morning, they appeared promptly at eleven. I suggested the patio, and they both agreed. Patricia also wore white slacks, but her blouse was cocoa, which set off her blond hair. She stretched out on one of the padded lounges and sighed. "This is heavenly. But I mustn't relax too much. We need to be serious."

Michael laughed. "When are you ever serious?" He'd taken one of the white wrought-iron chairs around the table, partially shaded by the turquoise umbrella I'd made sure to open that morning. He was wearing khaki pants with a navy and khaki shirt. The combination looked great on him.

I did my best to be a gracious hostess, but they waved away offers of refreshment. "Maybe later," Michael said, pulling out a chair for me next to him. "Let's not get distracted now. There's too much to discuss."

"You found out something?"

"Not enough, Ruthie. But we can build on it."

I tried to hide my disappointment. After all, what could I expect in just under a week. They had their own lives to lead.

"Since you couldn't get much information from the girl's uncle, we had to work with whatever I was able to pull up."

"We may be able to get more cooperation from Jeremy after all. I'll tell you about it later."

"First thing I did, I ran through all the connections I've built up with other pharmacists over the years—people I know from continuing education seminars and state conventions." He paused, as if unsure that he wanted to continue. "Some of them were concerned about the ethics of revealing patient information, the way you were when I needed to know about Harry's prescriptions."

I understood his hesitation, remembering how he had reappeared in my life after the death of his son-in-law, Harry Stokes. I'd refused to give Michael the computer printout he wanted to help prove his daughter hadn't killed Harry.

"After I explained," Michael continued, "I did get some results."

I was shocked. "You told them about the accusations against me?"

"No, of course not. I just gave a general picture without using your name or revealing where you work."

"Why don't you tell Ruthie exactly how you went about gathering information?" Patricia said.

His expression showed his approval of her suggestion. "By the way, Patricia stayed up and organized my notes last night. She started a database with all the material I was able to gather."

"A database?"

"You know, a list of every pharmacy I called, the telephone number, the contact person, and brief remarks about what they did or didn't tell me."

"I know what a database is, Michael. I was just surprised."

"It didn't take long," Patricia added, as if she wanted to downplay her contribution. "I have a laptop computer with me."

I smiled at her. "Thanks, Patricia," I said and realized I meant it. She was a stranger, but she believed in me.

"What I did," Michael said, "was list every pharmacist I know personally. Especially the ones who work for chains. I figured they'd have access to the records of patients who fill their scripts anywhere in the chain."

"And they were willing to divulge prescription information?"

"Well, I went about it as indirectly as possible. First I had to get the right person. Some of them were actually off for the weekend."

I laughed despite my tension. It's a standard complaint of pharmacists that we often have to work nights, weekends, and holidays.

Michael continued, telling me that he knew at least one pharmacist in each of the chains. "The first one I called refused to give me any patient information, so I changed my tack. From then on, I began by saying that I only needed to know two things."

"Two things?" I echoed.

"Yes. Was so-and-so a patient and was he or she taking Coumadin?"

"Didn't they ask the reason?"

"Some did. I told them I wasn't at liberty to say."

"And they bought that?"

"Ruthie, you have to realize these are pharmacists who know me. They understand I wouldn't ask for information idly. I suppose they figured it involved some kind of court case, but they don't know about you."

"Not to sound ungrateful, Michael, but how can it help me if you contact pharmacists in Tucson?"

"That's why I started with the chain stores. Their computers are networked, so they can punch in the patient's name and check chain-wide."

"I can't believe I didn't think of accessing Food Go's computer database," I said.

"No problem. You can hit theirs on your next shift." He removed a neatly folded sheet of paper from his pants pocket. "I listed everyone I could think of—her mother and father, Leila and Quentin Brookman..."

I interrupted Michael. "Didn't the other pharmacists recognize the name Brookman?"

"If they did, they never said anything."

Patricia, silent until now, spoke up. "When people aren't directly involved, they usually don't remember things like that."

"Then there's Lupe and Jeremy Douglas."

"Oh, no," I said.

"We have to consider everyone," Michael insisted.

"But Jeremy's been helping me. That's part of what I want to talk to you about later."

"He could be helping you to avoid suspicion, Ruthie. Let's keep him on our list along with the others—the aunt, Virginia Rowland. The demonstrator you told me about, Faith Sommers. And Amy's boyfriend, Tommy."

"There's one more person we didn't know about," I told him. "Leila Brookman is living with someone."

"Nick Kenmore," Michael said.

"How did you know that?"

My astonishment seemed to please him. "There's some surprises left in the old boy."

"Indeed!" Patricia said.

I tried not to look disconcerted, but her smile, quickly concealed, seemed too knowing. *This is no time to get sidetracked*, I told myself. *It's more important to hear the details of Michael's investigation.*

"Were any of our suspects taking Coumadin?"

"Only three of them shopped at the chains I called so far, Ruthie. Neither Faith Sommers nor Nick Kenmore filled Coumadin scripts."

"They could go to other pharmacies for that particular drug."

We both knew that was possible. Many people shopped around for prescriptions just as they comparison-shopped for other commodities. Besides, stores often offered promotional coupons for as much as $10.00 off new scripts. At Food Go, we tried to counteract this trend by accepting any other store's coupons. I sometimes griped about the bother of transferring prescriptions from store to store for people I privately considered to be "coupon abusers."

I felt discouraged. With more than three million people in the Phoenix metropolitan area, which includes Scottsdale, Phoenix, Mesa, Tempe, and other adjacent cities, I didn't see how we were going to find out which of our suspects had access to Coumadin, the blood thinner that Amy Brookman shouldn't have taken.

Patricia seemed to sense my mood. "Couldn't you try the uncle again, the one who works at Food Go? He may know who has to use Coumadin."

"You mentioned three people. Who was the third one?" I asked.

It was getting warmer now as noon approached. Michael shifted his chair into the shade. "Patricia, would you like something cold to drink?"

"Water would be fine."

My impatience to hear about Michael's discoveries had to wait while I went into the kitchen and took down a turquoise enameled tray from the top shelf in one of the cabinets. I stifled the realization that I hadn't used this tray since Bob's death. Quickly filling two pitchers with crushed ice, I added the iced tea I always kept on hand for myself to one of them and filtered water to the other. The tray was too heavy now, so I removed the pitchers to carry them out separately, placing napkins, silverware, plates, and a platter of small pastries on the tray.

I carried the tray out first, planning to return immediately for the two pitchers. As I approached the sliding French doors to the patio, I could see Michael and Patricia framed through them. He had moved from his seat at the table and was perched on the edge of her chaise. Leaning toward her, in earnest conversation, he was unaware of my return. I imagined I could almost see the charged air between them.

For a moment, I had to move away and put the tray down. I couldn't bear to go outside and face the two of them. Although I'd been warning myself that Michael felt only friendship for me now, this scene put everything into perspective. I realized, even with Patricia's arrival, I hadn't abandoned romantic images of the young Michael and Ruthie on the campus in Tucson all those years ago and my hope that we could somehow recapture those days. Didn't I occasionally read such stories in newspapers and magazines? Couples who had been separated in their youth and eventually found each other again to live happily ever after.

I smiled ruefully. Did I really believe in that sort of destiny for myself? It was more important to think about saving my professional reputation. Michael's private life hadn't been my concern for more than 35 years, and it was pointless to allow regret to take over when I needed to direct all my energy to discover what really happened to Amy Brookman.

Gathering up the tray again, I balanced it on one arm and slid open the patio doors. I carefully set the tray on the table, my eyes deliberately avoiding Michael and Patricia. Then I went back in and reemerged with the two pitchers. This time, I found that Michael had returned to his seat at the table. I busied myself passing around beverages and pastries, trying to appear unruffled.

Michael chugged down a full glass of ice water before continuing his story. "Faith Sommers gets her scripts filled at Walgreens," he said. "No Coumadin. Nick Kenmore and Leila Brookman are both Osco customers. No Coumadin for him." He paused and delivered the next bit of information in staccato tones that only served to underline their importance. "Leila Brookman is on Coumadin, one tablet, 2 milligram strength, every other day."

"Two milligrams," I shouted. "Those are the purple ones."

"Let's not jump to conclusions," Michael said. "You know as well as I do that Coumadin is heavily prescribed."

"And if Nick Kenmore lives with her, he'd have access, too," Patricia reminded us.

"I could believe it of him. He looks like a thug."

"That doesn't make him a killer. What about motive?" Michael asked.

I remembered that Michael and Patricia knew nothing about my visits with Jeremy. It was time to fill them in. "If anyone had a reason to kill Amy Brookman, it was Nick," I finished.

"That's not enough to convict anyone. It's not even enough to try him."

"What a horrible man!" Patricia said.

"Not only that, but I'm sure he abuses Leila. She had bruises..." I stopped.

"Of course," I said.

They both looked surprised but waited politely for me to continue.

"Nick seems like such a brute that when I saw black and blue marks on Leila's arms, I made the wrong assumption."

Now Michael's face registered understanding, but Patricia still looked bewildered. "Coumadin is prescribed for people with heart conditions," Michael explained to her. "It's a blood thinner, and when the blood is thinned, people bruise very easily. So it often causes black and blue marks on their arms and legs."

"But Leila seems young to be taking Coumadin," I said.

Michael looked thoughtful for a moment. "Consider the dosage," he said. "Every other day sounds like there's a family history of heart disease. It was probably prescribed as a preventive measure."

I nodded agreement. "It does give us something to work with."

"Too dangerous and too soon."

"I have to act. Do you expect me to just sit and wait for a civil or criminal action against me?"

"No, of course not. But we haven't checked everyone out. Wait until you look up all of our suspects in the Food Go computers."

"I didn't recognize any of them as Food Go customers."

"What about Lupe and Jeremy Douglas?"

"You can't suspect them!"

"Ruthie, be realistic. We have to suspect anyone connected with Amy. Anyone who could have switched her medications."

"What about the young man?" Patricia asked. "Perhaps his parents are patients of yours even if he's not."

I hadn't considered Tommy's family either. I remembered that a few months ago, someone I thought I knew had come close to killing me because I hadn't suspected him until it was nearly too late. If I were to gather enough information to take to the police, I must not be so trusting this time.

Chapter 14.

My schedule, odd for most people but typical for pharmacists, put me on the night shift Tuesday after my Sunday and Monday off. I came in early to have lunch in the Food Go coffee shop. Denise was standing at a corner table, order book in hand, talking to a customer. She was wearing one of her most becoming outfits—a multicolored lavender, violet, and orchid skirt with a long-sleeved orchid blouse. The weather was still warm by tourist standards, but most Arizonans had put their summer things away.

Denise's expressive face seemed to glow, and I looked more carefully at the customer. Dark-haired, slightly balding, horn-rimmed glasses—my attorney, Sterling Harraday. Denise didn't notice me, but Sterling gestured to the empty chair at his table. I saw her face fall and then brighten when she realized who was joining Sterling.

If only she's not hurt again, I thought, as I walked up to them. Denise's happy-go-lucky attitude masked a vulnerability that I'd become aware of only recently. *Stop worrying about Denise*, I told myself; *she's friendly with all of her customers.*

"Mrs. Morris," Sterling said, pulling out a chair for me. "You're just the person I wanted to see."

"Can I get iced tea for you, Ruthie?" Denise asked.

"Please. And my usual tuna on rye bread."

She turned to go, but Sterling stopped her. I read anticipation in her face and wondered if she expected him to invite her to join us. "Could you top up my coffee, please?" he said.

"Yes, sir. Right away." I could see the light go out of her eyes, and her voice was toneless. It seemed I hadn't imagined her interest in the lawyer. Thinking of Michael and my own disappointed hopes, I ached for her.

"I was in court most of the morning," Sterling said, "but I was planning to call right after lunch and fill you in."

Denise returned with the coffee pot in one hand and a tall glass of iced tea in the other. Sterling waited until she put the tea in front of me, refilled his coffee, and walked away. "I had a call yesterday from an Eric Manning, the attorney for Amy Brookman"s family."

"Yes, I heard of him. He's a cousin of theirs."

"That's not the issue here," Sterling started to say, sounding pompous for a moment. Then he laughed at himself. "Sorry," he said. "I tend to forget that things may seem important to my clients even though they don't really affect the case." Now, I could see something of his appeal for Denise.

"I guess I'm the one who should apologize," I said. "You're the expert in this area, and I need to rely on your judgment." I waited, wanting to tell Sterling of my own findings, but knowing I should hear him out first. He paused, sipping his coffee, but I was too nervous to touch my iced tea.

"They haven't filed a civil suit yet," Sterling said. "It seems they're willing to settle out of court for..." He broke off as Denise returned with my tuna salad sandwich.

"It's okay," I told him. "Denise is a close friend of mine. I don't have anything to hide from her."

He looked surprised, and I wondered if he was one of those people who couldn't see beyond Denise's waitress job and the frilly green apron that hid the front of her colorful skirt. *If he is, Denise might as well take her daydreams elsewhere*, I thought. And then I remembered that mine would never materialize either.

Despite my assurances, Sterling waited for Denise to walk away before continuing. "They're asking for $250,000," he told me.

"That's absurd," I said.

"You do have malpractice insurance," he reminded me quietly.

"I didn't commit malpractice."

"But you need to consider all the possibilities. No one can predict how a lawsuit would turn out."

"Why are they suddenly willing to settle for $250,000? They were talking about millions."

"I gathered that they don't want to wait for the money. If we agree to settle now, they won't file the suit. So unless there's a criminal action—and I very much doubt there's enough evidence to get an indictment—you're home free."

"You don't seem to understand," I said. I tried to match his quiet tone, holding my indignation in check. "Settling would mean admitting I gave Amy the wrong medication."

"Not settling will mean publicity first of all. And once it goes to court, anything can happen."

"I realize that," I said. "But I can't do it. They just about admitted they're only after money." I told him about my visit to Leila's house and the conversation there.

"Will the girl's uncle testify in your behalf?"

"I don't know," I said, miserably.

"We have to consider that they may be right about his attitude. Family loyalties can be overwhelming."

"But that isn't the point," I insisted. "I'm sure now that Amy was murdered, and they're claiming I made a mistake to cover it up and also to get some money out of the situation."

He listened without interruption while I recounted the rest of last Wednesday evening's events. "I'm not trying to talk you into settling with them," he said when I had finished. "You're the one who'll have to make the final decision. But I'd be remiss if I didn't present the pros and cons."

"Do you think I have enough to take to the police?" I asked.

He paused so long this time that I nearly repeated the question. "That might be wise, after all. Would you like me to accompany you?"

I tried to think whether I'd look guilty if I brought along my lawyer, but I didn't know enough about the way the system worked. I'd have to go by instinct, and my instinct—or maybe it was my fear, which had returned tenfold—insisted I'd be safer with Sterling at my side.

We were both unavailable the next day, but we agreed to try for Thursday morning. I told Sterling about Detective Moreway and how I'd helped find his young brother-in-law's murderer. "For a while, he suspected me," I said. "But I think he knows me better now."

"I'll have my secretary make an appointment for us," Sterling said. He picked up my check and his own, left a three-dollar tip for Denise and walked away. Despite my own turbulent emotions, I watched to see whether he'd take the opportunity to talk to her. Instead, I saw him pay the cashier and leave the coffee shop without a backward glance.

Denise approached my table a few minutes later, saw the three dollars and winced. "I wish they'd abolish tipping," she said.

"Then they'd have to raise salaries."

"Most of the time, I don't mind because the money comes in handy and Lord knows, I work hard enough here."

I looked up in surprise. Denise never complained. "I know it's easy for me to say, but don't take it personally," I told her.

"But it is personal sometimes. He had a sandwich and coffee. You had a sandwich and tea. This is only a coffee shop, not the Phoenician. A normal tip would have been about two dollars, but he threw in the extra dollar just because we talk a lot."

"Denise," I started to say and stopped abruptly.

"I know," she said, holding up her hands. "I'm being foolish, but he's the most interesting man who comes in here."

That was a side to Sterling I hadn't noticed, maybe because I only cared about his competence. "Are you on break yet?" I asked. "Can you join me for a bit before I have to check in at the pharmacy?"

She went behind the counter to tell her manager she'd be taking a break and returned to sit at my table, first removing the green apron to show she was off duty. I gave her all the news as quickly as I could.

"Then that settles it," she said.

"We'll find out when your friend Sterling and I meet with Frank Moreway."

She made a face at the word "friend." "Maybe you're satisfied to be Michael's friend," she said, emphasizing the last word, "but I'm looking for something more than friendship."

"We don't always have much choice."

"No, not if you just give up."

"I'm not giving up. I just told you we're going to get the police to investigate Amy's family and whether one of them murdered her."

"I wasn't talking about Amy Brookman, and you know it. If you really care for Michael, you have to fight for him."

"You know we're..."

"Yes, I heard all that before. But I don't believe it, and I'm sure you don't believe it either. Betsy let slip that you and Michael were going together way back when."

I kept forgetting that Denise and Michael's daughter were neighbors. "I was twenty years old then. That ended a long time ago."

"Only if you want it to be over."

"Denise, please don't dramatize. This isn't a soap opera."

She started to laugh. Denise didn't exactly giggle, but her laugh had an infectious quality that always made me join in. "It's sure beginning to sound like one. Will Ruthie and Michael get together again after thirty-something years apart? Thirty-something. Now there's a good title."

"That's not what it means."

She ignored my comment. "Will the handsome attorney realize that the waitress with the heart of gold is meant for him?"

I joined in. "Will the police find the real murderer of sixteen-year-old Amy before our dedicated woman pharmacist loses her professional standing and goes to trial?"

We were both nearly doubled up with laughter. I suppose it was the release of tension because I realized now that some people did believe in me. And I knew I was ready to act to counteract accusations that had haunted me for weeks.

"Denise, your break was up five minutes ago." The coffee shop manager stood over our table, frowning at us. "Maybe you think it's funny to keep people waiting, but I don't." For the first time, we noticed an older couple who had come in and taken a table at the far end of the room.

Denise jumped up, said she'd see me later, and put her apron back on. I watched her rush over to wait on the people, reflecting that even though my customers could be demanding at times, at least I wasn't accountable to anyone else in the pharmacy.

I had reason to remember that after I signed in and put on my own insignia of service, the white jacket with the name tag, "RUTH KANTOR MORRIS, PHARMACY MANAGER." My staff pharmacist greeted me with an injured tone. "I was hoping you'd get here earlier today," she said. "It's very busy."

I found myself making excuses about the things I'd had to take care of. Then, looking at my watch, I discovered my shift didn't actually begin for another twenty minutes. I turned to tell Louise, but she was at the window, helping a customer.

Why is she so antagonistic toward me, I wondered. Everyone else seems to believe in me now, but Louise still thinks I made a mistake in filling Amy Brookman's prescription. I hoped I would soon prove she was wrong to doubt me.

My first customer drove all thoughts of my own problems away. She was a blonde in her late twenties with a prescription for 100 Tylenol #4 with one grain of codeine and another for 60 Valium, 10 milligrams. That seemed excessive to me, so I looked more closely at the scripts. The physician was in Las Vegas. I tried to call him but found it was his afternoon off. The office was closed, and I got his answering service, so I left a message for him to return my call to check the dosages.

My instincts screamed "drug abuse," and I looked up to see where the patient was. She stood about ten feet back from the pharmacy window watching me. When she caught my eye, she returned to the pharmacy. "Is there a problem?" she asked.

I decided to ask her for an ID. "It's not for me," she said. "It's for my grandmother." Trying to make it sound like routine, I insisted on seeing her driver's license. "But I'm paying cash," she said.

I never find it easy to lie, but something seemed wrong here. "Yes, but for out-of-state prescriptions, we need to see ID's."

She seemed startled, which didn't surprise me. "Oh, okay. It's out in my car. I'll be right back."

Now I knew. Over the years, the only patients whose driver's licenses were "out in the car" never returned. A phony prescription was the only explanation.

Louise had finished with her customer and heard this last exchange. "What in the world is wrong with you, Ruthie? I think that girl's death has affected your ability to deal with customers."

For a moment, I stood still, unable to answer her. Why couldn't I get a staff pharmacist who believed that my years of experience meant something? Why couldn't I get someone who looked up to me as a mentor? Why couldn't I at least get one who treated me as an equal? I smiled to myself ruefully, knowing I was not alone in facing what I thought of as careerism. Even in this pharmacy, one of the least busy in the Food Go chain, with only two full-time pharmacists, the number two person wanted to replace me as manager.

The thought made me smile in earnest. My job must be better than I'd realized if Louise wanted it so badly. I forced myself to speak casually. "Watch," I said. "Maybe you'll learn something."

I knew I sounded smug, but I felt it was deserved when fifteen minutes and then a half hour went by without the customer returning. "This is the way it works, Louise. If you suspect a phony script and you stall or do anything out of the ordinary like I just did, they fade away as quickly as the Cheshire cat."

"But you should report phony scripts," she said indignantly.

I might have known. How could she be so self-righteous at her age? "I had no way of being sure until she disappeared. I couldn't reach the doctor."

She turned away and, since both phones were ringing, I didn't pursue the point. We were both too busy to talk much after that. The few hours that we worked together flew by until it was nearly time for Louise to leave for the day. As she walked to the back of the pharmacy to hang up her white jacket, someone approached the window and began tapping on the counter. I hate when customers do that and looked up, trying not to show my annoyance. It was Jeremy Douglas.

"Ruthie," he called. His voice was hoarse and when I got closer to the window, I saw how haggard he looked. *So that's it*, I thought. *He needs some medication in a hurry.*

"Aren't you feeling well, Jeremy?"

"It's not me," he said.

Either Lupe or the little boy must be sick then. I should have realized he'd be more impatient for his wife's or son's needs than for his own. I waited, expecting him to hand me some scripts. He just stared at me.

"What can I do for you?" I asked to break the silence.

And big, teddy-bearish Jeremy put his hands over his eyes and silently wept. I reached across the pharmacy window and awkwardly patted his shoulder. Louise had come up behind me, wearing her own denim jacket now instead of the white pharmacy one. I knew she was ready to leave for the day, but curiosity had probably drawn her back to the front counter.

"Come on now, Jeremy," she said. "You'll scare away the paying customers."

Doesn't that woman have any empathy for other people, I wondered. But even as I stood there, wanting to respond angrily, her remark had its effect. Jeremy slowly brushed his hands away from his face.

"I don't know why these things are happening to our family," he said.

"What things?" Louise asked.

Jeremy looked at me. "Ruthie knows," he said. "First my sixteen-year-old niece got pregnant and had an abortion. Then she died. And we found out the father was..." He stopped, unable to say what we had learned—that the father was her mother's live-in boyfriend.

"Did the police arrest Nick for Amy's murder?" I asked. "Oh my God," I blurted suddenly. "Surely her mother didn't blame Amy and kill her for it."

"No, the one thing we know for sure is Leila didn't do it." His voice broke when he mentioned her name. My thoughts took another leap. Could Jeremy be in love with Leila? I quickly reviewed their behavior toward each other that night I'd met Leila. He had brought the chair for her when Nick hadn't cared enough to bother, but surely that was just Jeremy's polite way of doing things. On reflection, I couldn't believe Jeremy felt anything other than family loyalty toward his former sister-in-law.

"How do you know?" I asked.

The hoarseness in his voice was even more pronounced, and I could see how red his eyes looked. "Because someone murdered Leila this morning," he said.

Chapter 15.

At least two of our phones were ringing, but I ignored them. I could hear Louise gasp, but I fought to stay calm. "What happened?" I asked Jeremy. "Was it Nick?"

"I don't know. The police just notified Quentin, and he called me." He started to cover his eyes again but quickly forced his hands away from his face with an abrupt gesture. "I'm going over there now, but I thought I should come by and tell you first."

"Why would the police call Quentin?" I asked. "Aren't Leila and he divorced?"

"No, not really. We say so in the family because it sounds better now that Nick's living with her. Quentin and Leila are legally separated, not divorced."

"I know you want to be with your brother. But Jeremy, before you go, could you just tell me how she was killed?"

"Quentin said they won't be sure until after the autopsy. What it looks like..." He stopped, and I could see his throat move as he swallowed hard before continuing. "They found the chair from her dressing table lying next to her. The police think she was knocked unconscious with it first and then choked to death."

I could picture that pink-cushioned brass stool and felt the blood draining from my face. What an awful way to die. Then again, any murder was horrible.

"I'm not sure I understand," Louise said. "Are you talking about the mother of that girl, the one who died from the wrong post-abortion medication?"

Jeremy gave an almost imperceptible nod, turned without saying another word, and walked rapidly out of the Food Go supermarket. Louise stared after him. "I must say that was rude. After all, he does work here with us."

Yes, I thought to myself. *And you and I work together, too, but that doesn't stop you from rudeness even though you have less provocation.*

Aloud, I said, "Have a heart, Louise. She was his sister-in-law. You can't expect him to stand around and gossip with us about her murder."

"I never gossip." She barely paused before she said slowly, as though underlining each word, "Well, it's certainly good news for you."

This was a new low, even for Louise. I was appalled. "I don't know what you mean," I said, although I was afraid I knew exactly what she was driving at.

"The family'll be too tied up in knots to think about suing you now."

Before I could form an answer, she tossed her braid over one shoulder, picked up her purse, and left the pharmacy. I wanted to run after her, to convince her that I felt terrible about Leila's death, that any advantage to myself had never occurred to me. Both phones were ringing now, however, and a patient had just stepped up to the window.

I told the white-haired gentleman that I'd be with him in a minute and picked up each receiver in turn, asking the customers to please hold. Then I returned to the window, took the man's two prescriptions, promised I'd have them ready in twenty minutes, and went back to the phones. There was no time at all to think about Leila Brookman's murder.

Several times during the evening, the prescription rush quieted enough for me to visualize Leila as I'd seen her less than a week ago in that bright avocado kitchen, playing hostess to her unwelcome trio of guests. I pictured the brass stool from her vanity for a moment and shuddered, not wanting to carry the image further and think about the way Leila had met her death. Toward eight o'clock that night when business slowed longer than usual, I remembered Louise's words. It wasn't that they'd be too busy to consider suing me. This murder proved that something was wrong, something that had nothing to do with the prescriptions I'd filled for Amy Brookman. Saddened as I was by Leila's death, it represented one more piece of evidence to present to the Scottsdale Police Department on Thursday.

As if my thoughts had conjured him, Detective Frank Moreway appeared at the prescription window. The last few times I'd seen him, he'd been cordial. Tonight, his manner reminded me of that time, only a few months ago, when he suspected all of us—myself, Michael, Denise, Michael's daughter—of involvement in a couple of murders and an attempted murder.

"Ms. Morris," he said. "I need to talk to you."

"Didn't my attorney make an appointment for us to meet on Thursday?"

"This can't wait for Thursday."

"Oh, is it about Leila Brookman?"

278   Renée B. Horowitz

"And how do you know about that?" His voice was heavy with suspicion.

Not again, I thought, but explained it to him. "Her brother-in-law works here at Food Go."

"Yes, I remember him," he said drily. "The one who thought I was harassing you the last time you got mixed up in a murder investigation."

"I hope you're not implying I'm involved this time. I didn't even know the woman."

"You were at her house only last week."

"I didn't say I never met her."

"You're quibbling now," he said. "People usually don't invite casual acquaintances to their homes."

"She didn't invite me," I said.

He stared hard at me, and I realized how that sounded. For once, I was happy when the phone started ringing. "Excuse me, please," I said and went to answer it without waiting for his approval.

By the time I finished with the caller, two more customers were at the window. Frank Moreway looked at them and evidently thought better of continuing our conversation. "When you close up, I'd like to talk with you," he said. "I'll expect you at my office about 9:30 tonight."

"I don't think I should see you without my attorney," I said, while the heavy-set woman in bright red slacks and a red turtleneck, standing just behind Detective Moreway leaned forward to listen.

"That's up to you," he said. "But I'm not waiting until Thursday."

"I'll try to reach him."

"You do that. But remember, 9:30 sharp."

I glared after him, thinking of the private eye stories where the police always suspect the P.I. first, even after they've been proven wrong in case after case. *You'd think by now he'd trust me*, I told myself. And I'm not a private investigator, holding back information to protect a client. Then I remembered that I had once tried to keep things from him to protect Michael and Denise.

I took a prescription for Ortho Novum 35's from the woman in red. It figured. As soon as they start thinking about bed, they remember they're out of birth control pills. She smiled at me. Actually, it looked more like a knowing smirk.

"You be sure to have your lawyer with you, dearie. Otherwise, your ex will keep it all," she said. "I just about let my old man get away with murder. But I know better now."

For a minute, the word "murder" startled me. Then, I realized she was using the term figuratively. *If you only knew what I need* MY *lawyer for*, I thought. I smiled back as I handed the filled prescription to her. "Thanks for the advice." I nearly added "dearie" but stopped myself in time. Smart-aleck answers don't go over well when serving the public.

I thought about her advice, misapplied as it was, while I finished with my final customer and began my closing routine. As I waited for the computer to print out a copy of that day's Rx record, I looked up Sterling Harraday's home telephone number and debated whether to call him. *He probably wouldn't come out this late anyhow*, I told myself. Besides, I had nothing to fear from Frank Moreway. It wasn't like the first time I'd gone to his office with computer printouts for everyone in the Stokes family and for Denise, too. Clearly, Leila's live-in boyfriend had killed her. None of my friends was in danger of being falsely accused of *this* murder.

I took off my white jacket, put it neatly on a hanger, locked the door to the pharmacy, and went to sign out as I had done thousands of times before. The sign-out process was so automatic after all these years, I rarely resented having to punch a time card. At Food Go, it didn't matter if you were a professional or a clerk. Everyone who worked for the supermarket chain signed in and out.

Pima Road was the best route to Police Headquarters on Via Linda, and I couldn't help thinking of Leila when I passed her street and hoped she hadn't known she was about to die. I pulled into the Police Headquarters parking lot at exactly 9:35 pm. Not nervous this time, I congratulated myself, remembering how tense I'd been back in August.

Frank Moreway was waiting for me at the reception desk and led the way to his office without saying anything. This would have terrified me once, but I felt calm and relaxed, knowing that I had nothing to worry about now.

He motioned me to a seat in front of his desk but stood to the side, looking down at me. "Leila Brookman was about to ruin you professionally and financially," he said without preamble. "Is that why you killed her?"

I was so astonished, I couldn't say a word. When I recovered from the initial shock, I found I was angry rather than frightened. "What is this?" I asked him. "Every time you can't find a murderer, you accuse me."

"If you read the papers, you know we've had other murders since the last time I questioned you."

"Probably drive-by shootings. Even *you* wouldn't suspect me of those." I was surprised to hear my flippant responses. It wasn't my usual style, but I just couldn't take his accusations seriously.

He suddenly stopped hovering over me and sat down behind his desk. "Suppose you tell me why you visited Leila last Wednesday evening."

"You obviously have the whole story from someone else."

"I want to hear what you have to say."

"That's why my lawyer and I made the appointment to see you the day after tomorrow," I said. "Don't forget, we contacted you. We think we know why Amy Brookman was killed, and now I believe the same person murdered her mother."

I went on to tell him about Wednesday night in detail. He didn't interrupt until I got to the part about Tommy's charges against Nick. "Did Leila believe her boyfriend was responsible for the daughter's pregnancy?" he asked.

I winced at the phrasing. "I'm not sure. She didn't want to believe it, but after we all left and she had time to think about it, she may have."

"Had she contacted you since that night?"

"No."

"Did you call her or see her?"

"I never had anything to do with her before or after that evening."

"And what were you planning to do about the lawsuit?"

"Her lawyer contacted mine. He wants to settle out of court." I told Frank Moreway about the terms. "So you see, they knew I had nothing to do with Amy's death. They never hid their reasons for blaming me. They were after as much money as they could get from me and from Food Go."

"No one else has confirmed that part of your story."

So my lawyer was right about Jeremy. He was protecting his dead sister-in-law and wasn't going to talk about her greed. "It's true," I insisted.

"We only have your word."

"And my lawyer's. He'll tell you about the offer to settle."

"Which doesn't prove anything. People may settle for all sorts of reasons."

I looked at him—the neat navy-blue suit, the pale gray shirt, the darker gray tie. Then, I glanced down at his shoes. Once before, when I'd noticed he wore brown shoes with his blue suit, I'd realized he wasn't infallible. It had given me courage then to deal with his questions. Tonight, I wasn't the same easily intimidated person. Maybe it was because I'd outwitted a murderer and survived his attempt to drown me. Or it could have been because I was convinced Leila's murder, beyond any possible doubt, meant that I had not given Amy the wrong medication.

"Do you seriously believe I bashed this woman over the head and then strangled her?" I asked him. "And before you demand how I knew the way she was killed, let me tell you it was from Jeremy Douglas."

He didn't exactly smile then, but the crease between his eyebrows deepened and his lips turned up slightly. "I have to question everyone with motive and opportunity. You did have a motive. Now let's get to the opportunity part. Where were you since last midnight?"

"Home."

"Alone?"

"Of course. You know I'm a widow."

This time the smile was unmistakable. "You can't be that naive."

I don't often blush, but I could feel my face redden. Michael's image came into my mind so clearly it was almost as if he were in the room. Just think, I told myself, if you were having an affair with Michael, he could be your alibi. "Let's just say I was alone and forget the rest of it."

"Did you have any telephone calls? Anyone come to the door? Run any errands?"

The questions were thrown at me so fast, I barely had time to digest them. That was probably his intent, but since I had no reason to lie, I answered "no" to all of them.

"What time did you leave for work?"

"About 11:30 this morning."

"You work a nine hour shift now?"

"No. I usually come in early when I'm on nights and eat lunch in the coffee shop. And today," I added, "at least two people can vouch for that."

"As you'll discover when you see the news, by that time, the police had already been called in."

He continued to fence with me for another hour, several times making me repeat the conversations of that evening at Leila Brookman's. Suddenly, he asked what I did after leaving Leila's house.

"Didn't anyone fill you in on our visit to her ex-husband?" I still thought of Quentin that way.

No response. So, I told him everything I remembered. He stopped me to ask whether I saw any indication that Quentin blamed his wife for Nick's actions. Although I was convinced Nick murdered Amy to keep her quiet, I thought carefully before answering. It was possible that Quentin killed Leila, but I didn't know of any reason for him to kill his daughter. It seemed highly unlikely to me that we had two murderers operating here.

All of this went through my mind very quickly but took longer to explain to Detective Moreway, especially since he remained skeptical. "On the other hand, *you* had a motive for both deaths," he said.

"Here we go again. Look, I don't mean to be flippant, but I know I didn't go anywhere near Leila or Leila's house except for that one time last Wednesday evening."

"Nevertheless, we do need to take your fingerprints," he said.

"I don't mind. But how can you tell when fingerprints at the house were made? After all, you know I was there last week."

"Were you in the master bedroom at all? Did you handle that chair?"

"No, of course not."

"Then you have nothing to worry about," he said.

Fingerprinting took only a few minutes, and I was soon on my way home. I couldn't stop thinking about Leila Brookman, though. Unlike the two murder victims last August, she was a relative stranger to me. Yet, I was involved with Leila and her family because of Amy and because of Jeremy and Lupe.

I had met Amy herself, her mother and father, and her aunt Virginia. Then there were Nick and Tommy, each of whom had accused the other of responsibility for Amy's pregnancy. *More than that*, I thought. *Tommy believes Nick killed her. And I agree with him, but I don't intend to do anything further about it. This time, it will be up to the police to identify the murderer.*

I suddenly realized I hadn't told Detective Moreway about Michael's Coumadin discovery and decided that if our appointment for Thursday was still on, I could give him the information then. We no longer had to find out who had access to Coumadin. Now it was a job for the police. I wondered if Sterling would be upset with me for talking to them without him, but we could fix that on Thursday, too.

I didn't believe Frank Moreway seriously suspected me. If he did, I was sure the facts about Nick's possible access to the blood thinner should deflect him. I could think of no logical reason why anyone but Nick would have killed both women, and I realized now that my earlier suspicions of people like the demonstrator, Faith Sommers, were ridiculous.

My schedule called for an early shift the next day, but when I arrived home, I was too keyed up and too hungry to turn in right away. I found some of the pastries I'd bought to offer Patricia and Michael the day before and had two of them with decaf. Then, feeling very tired after all, I set the alarm and went to bed without even preparing my clothes for the morning.

When I hit the pillow, I deliberately avoided thinking about Leila Brookman's murder. Just before I fell asleep, though, a picture came into my mind of Jeremy carrying the brass stool from the master bedroom into the kitchen for Leila to sit on.

Chapter 16.

The image was still there when my alarm woke me at seven the next morning. This time, I realized its importance. Jeremy's fingerprints would be on the rim of that stool. I wondered if I should call and warn him. Maybe I'd wait and talk to him at the store. Then I realized Jeremy surely wouldn't be coming to work today. *I must telephone*, I thought frantically, and then decided it was too early. I would call him just before leaving for Food Go.

Lupe answered the phone on the first ring. Her voice sounded breathless and strained. "Jeremy..."

"It's Ruthie Morris. From the pharmacy." Although I knew it sounded foolish, I couldn't ignore the conventions. "I was sorry to hear about your sister-in-law."

People usually make some kind of polite reply to such comments, but Lupe was silent. "I need to speak to Jeremy," I told her. "It's very important."

"I'm sure it is." She sounded so different, cold when she had always been friendly.

"Well, thanks to you, Jeremy's at the Scottsdale Police Department, not here. They came to question him early this morning, and he had to go with them." Now her voice sounded as if she were trying not to cry.

"That's just routine," I assured her. "Detective Moreway questioned me last night, too."

"Really, and what did you say that made him come after Jeremy?"

"Nothing," I insisted. "I told Frank Moreway I'm sure Nick is the killer."

"Then why did they want to see Jeremy again? And why did they come for him instead of asking for a statement at his convenience like they did yesterday?"

I was too upset to conclude right then that Jeremy was probably the one who told the police about my visit to Leila's, leaving out essential facts like the purpose of the lawsuit. "Oh my God, Lupe. Did they say anything about fingerprints?"

"No, but they took his fingerprints yesterday."

"I know the reason for that," I said. "When we were at Leila's house the other night, Jeremy carried a brass stool into the kitchen for her to sit on." I could picture Jeremy as I described the scene to Lupe. "He had a three-legged stool in one hand and a pink cushion in the other," I told her. "It had to be the same brass stool the murderer used."

"It's pretty bad when the police can suspect a person because he was brought up to be polite to women."

I knew she was oversimplifying in her distress, but I didn't contradict her. "I'm sure he'll be home soon," I said.

"Why did you want to talk to Jeremy?"

"I wanted to remind him about what I just told you."

"So you put the police on him and now you're feeling guilty enough to want to stop them," she said.

"Lupe, it never for one moment entered my mind that Jeremy could murder anyone. And I certainly would never give the police any reason to doubt him."

"Not even to save your own skin?"

"My own skin is not in danger."

"It should be. We all know she was going to ruin you."

I was upset. Even considering Lupe's worry for her husband, it was an unpardonable accusation. "I don't understand you. Doesn't what Nick did to your niece bother you? Why are you blaming me instead of him?"

"Sorry," she said. "I'm upset right now. Deep down, I know it wasn't you and I'm ready to kill that animal myself." She was quiet for a moment. "Now if Nick had been murdered, any of us might have done it. Quentin, Tommy, Leila, Virginia, Jeremy, me. But why would anyone want to kill Leila?"

"That's why I'm so sure Nick did it. Maybe she confronted him. Said she was going to charge him with seducing her underage daughter."

"I suppose that's possible," Lupe said, "but Nick's not the type to stay around and wait for the police to pick him up. If he did it, he'd have drifted away."

"Who found Leila?" I asked.

"Nick."

"Maybe he thought he'd look innocent that way—if he stayed and reported the murder."

"That just doesn't sound like Nick."

"Why wasn't he at work? Was Leila supporting him?" *Another minute and she'll tell me to mind my own business and hang up*, I thought; but after a brief silence, Lupe continued.

"Nick's a mechanic. He was at work, but he had to take a car out to test drive. Something about a loud engine noise. He told us he forgot his lunch, so he figured he'd stop by the house and get it. That's when he found Leila."

"And the police believe him?" I asked.

"I don't know. Look, I have to get off the phone. What if Jeremy is trying to reach me?"

"I'll be at the pharmacy, Lupe. When Jeremy gets home, please ask him to call me."

She didn't respond, and I heard the click as she hung up. I could only hope she'd give him the message. At least, she didn't ask why I wanted to talk to him, since it was too late for my warning. I wasn't sure myself. Certainly it wasn't idle curiosity—not when I was also a suspect.

I was going to be late opening the pharmacy, so I rushed off without trying to call Sterling Harraday. As soon as I finished my opening procedure, I'd try to contact him and let him know about last night's police interview. Unfortunately, three customers were waiting when I unlocked the door, keyed in the alarm code, and rolled up the metal shutter that protected the pharmacy.

My computer, which stayed on all night, was already spewing out messages. I read that we'd be getting price updates early the next morning and that the pharmacies would be open only from 9:00 am to 1:00 pm on Thanksgiving Day. Then I took the first of the prescriptions. It was a refill for E-mycin, acne medicine for the customer's son, a quick one to do.

The next patient was one of my favorite customers, a woman in her eighties who was always cheerful even though she was on Tamoxifen. I knew from her prescriptions that she must have had breast cancer because Tamoxifen is a maintenance drug to prevent recurrence of the disease.

"I need my poison," she said and smiled at me. It was a running joke between us. When she had first started taking the drug, she asked me whether there might be any side effects.

"Everything in here has possible side effects," I'd explained to her. "What we need to do is weigh them against the benefits."

"That makes sense," she said.

I gave her the package insert, the sheet that drug manufacturers must provide to give chemical formulation, usage, warnings, precautions, and so forth. Some doctors don't want patients to see the package inserts. I guess they're afraid people might develop side effects through power of suggestion or maybe decide not to take their medicine at all.

As I half expected, when I did reach Sterling Harraday, he was furious that I'd submitted to questioning without insisting on my right to an attorney. "But I know I had nothing to do with Leila's death," I said.

"That makes no difference. I can't look after your interests if you don't bother to contact me when something like this happens."

"I never expected to be treated like a suspect."

"Well, it would have occurred to me immediately. And I'd have kept the police from fishing expeditions."

"I'll bet Jeremy doesn't have a lawyer, and he's in more danger than I am." I told him about the meat cutter and how he'd handled the brass stool. "Maybe you should call his wife."

"I'm not an ambulance chaser. They'll probably contact Eric Manning." He paused and said in a matter-of-fact way. "This may stop the family from going through with the lawsuit."

I was furious. "Why do people think that way? This is much worse than a lawsuit. You have no idea... this woman... she was decent to us despite everything. I couldn't dislike her even though I wanted to."

"All right. I understand. But we have to be practical," he said. "Just before Manning's settlement offer expires, I'll call him. We should be able to get an extension in view of this death."

Callous as it seemed, I had to admit he was right. Nothing we did to fend off the suit would bring Leila back to life. "Are we meeting with Detective Moreway tomorrow?"

"I think it would be wise even though you seem to have told him everything we planned to go over."

The appointment was for 10:30 the next morning, and we agreed to meet at the Scottsdale Police Department. "And please follow my lead. I don't want you to answer anything that could be self-incriminating."

Again, I felt indignant. "If you don't believe me..."

"My beliefs have nothing to do with your legal rights," he said and ended the call with a polite reminder to wait for him before going into Detective Moreway's office.

Great, I thought. *Now my own lawyer doubts me.* I managed, however, to maintain my new confidence and went about my work efficiently, filling prescription after prescription.

When Louise arrived to begin her shift, she was friendlier than she'd been since Amy Brookman's death. Instead of taking over the computer right away, she planted herself in front of me, too invasive of my space for comfort.

"What's the latest on that woman's murder?" she asked. "The morning paper didn't say much."

I hadn't had time to look at the paper, but I should have known they would carry the story. Despite all the recent drive-by shootings, a murder like this one would be front-page news. And especially since the victim's young daughter had died under mysterious circumstances only three weeks ago.

"I don't know any more than you do," I said.

"Sure you do."

"Why are you so interested, Louise?" It wasn't so long since my last staff pharmacist had turned out to be a killer. For one wild moment, I was afraid Louise had somehow been behind the two murders. Maybe that was why she'd been quick to blame me for Amy's death; but, I admitted, I knew of no connection between Louise and the Brookman family.

"The mother of one of our customers was murdered. Of course, I'm interested."

"I really don't know anything more," I repeated. Her words reminded me that I wanted to check my computer records to see whether any of the other people involved in this case filled their scripts at Food Go.

It'll have to wait, I thought. *No way am I going to do that in front of Louise.* Tomorrow, I'd be on the night shift again. Karen, our technician, would be working, and she could take over the window and phones while I did a computer search.

I got through the rest of my work day, trying not to worry about Jeremy. He hadn't called, but that could mean Lupe never gave him my message.

Just as I was ready to check out, Denise appeared in front of the pharmacy. "Come on," she said, "I'll buy you a late dinner."

"Thanks, Denise, but I really want to get away from the store."

"Do I look like that kind of cheapskate? I mean a real restaurant, not the Food Go Coffee Shop. We'll go where the presentations are dazzling and the service is by anyone but Denise Seaford."

I laughed for the first time that day. "Not Denny's either?" I asked. When we were both on the same shift, we often went to Denny's or the Village Inn after work.

"Not even Taco Bell."

We both walked into the office and checked out. The parking lot was crowded, but since we were employees, it didn't make any difference. Even on slow days, we had to park toward the back, leaving the close-in spaces for customers.

"Okay, I give up. Where to?"

"I'll tell you what. Leave your car and let's ride together. That way we'll have more time to talk."

"You just don't want to admit we're going to some fast-food place."

We kept up the banter until we were rolling along Scottsdale Road. "The Backstage," she said, naming a popular restaurant on the Scottsdale Mall. Then she turned serious. "Is that okay, Ruthie? I know it's been rough for you, and I thought you needed a cheerful place for dinner."

We found a space a block away from the park-like mall that adjoins Old Town Scottsdale and walked upstairs and through the colorful terrace. The restaurant was buzzing with people, many of them seated at the outdoor tables, but we agreed that an early November evening was cool enough for indoor dining. I looked around at the brightly dressed servers and the chattering crowd and did feel my mood lighten.

"What do you think of Sterling?" Denise suddenly asked as we studied the menu.

"This isn't the right time to ask that question. He got pretty upset with me on the phone this morning." I told her about our conversation.

"He's right, Ruthie. I remember what it was like when Frank Moreway questioned me last summer, insinuating that I had an affair with Harry Stokes."

I knew that Harry Stokes had figured prominently in both of our daydreams before he married Betsy. Although they were customers of mine, I hadn't known Betsy was Michael Loring's daughter. And when I'd seen Michael with her right after Harry's death, I'd been convinced she liked older men and was ready to replace her departed husband with Michael.

Too bad Patricia couldn't possibly be another daughter, I thought, but I had seen the closeness between her and Michael. This time, I couldn't be mistaken.

"Sterling will be with me tomorrow when I see the police again."

"If you get a chance... I mean if it comes up naturally... Can you bring me into the conversation?" Denise suddenly seemed transfixed by the menu in front of her, as if she were looking for the one perfect entrée.

"What do you want me to say?"

"You know. Try to find out what he thinks about me."

"Okay, I'll just casually ask when he's going to take you out."

"Ruthie," she said and then realized I was teasing her. She smiled. "Who knows? Maybe the direct approach would work. We're not teenagers, after all."

"I'll try," I promised, "but don't be disappointed."

"I won't."

I knew she really believed she could be casual about his reaction, but I was afraid for her. Sterling Harraday seemed like a decent human being, but I didn't know him well enough to understand whether his occasional pompous air was just a surface mannerism. I hoped it wouldn't keep him from seeing beyond Denise the waitress to Denise the person I knew, the one who was warm and helpful whenever people needed her.

"We have to talk about that young girl," she said, changing the subject. "We can be sure now that I was right—Amy was murdered—and we need to find the motive."

I told her about Nick, that he was responsible for Amy's pregnancy. She was silent for a long time. Meanwhile, the waitress took our orders. It seemed too late in the evening for a full meal, so I ordered a vegetarian sandwich called "The Earthquake" on rye bread with potato salad and cole slaw.

I waited impatiently for the server to leave, curious to hear what Denise would say. She toyed with her water glass as though she were distracting herself from her thoughts.

"Doesn't it seem ironic?" she said finally.

"What do you mean?" I asked, but something told me what Denise was going to say, because I was childless too and sometimes felt the same way. I knew she loved children. Often enough, I'd seen her in the coffee shop, helping to quiet a crying baby or praising the pictures children drew while waiting for their food. She had told me once that her ex-husband never wanted children.

"He always said we should wait to have a family; the time wasn't right." She looked up at me, and I could see the glint of tears in her eyes. "But the time never was right. I think he just didn't like children. I always thought he'd change his mind, but he never did."

Betsy Stokes' problem had been similar, I remembered. Her husband, much older than she was and with grown children from his previous marriage, hadn't wanted a baby either. I wondered how that child, whose father had died during the first months of Betsy's pregnancy would fare. On the other hand, Betsy could easily support her baby emotionally and materially. Denise, on the other hand, had all she could manage to take care of herself. Her dream of going back to school to become a dental hygienist, the dream that led her to try borrowing money from Harry Stokes and then made her a suspect when he died, seemed perpetually out of reach.

"No one but the people involved can say what was right or wrong," I told her. "You did the best you could at the time."

"I know that," Denise said. "And until all this happened with Amy Brookman, I hardly ever let it into my mind. Now, I think about Amy all the time and how her baby was unwanted even before the abortion. Knowing that her mother's boyfriend was the father, I understand the reason for her decision. I want to kill that man with my bare hands."

"Too bad he wasn't the victim instead of Leila, but maybe they'll get him for her murder."

"Much as I hate to say so, Ruthie, I don't believe he did it."

I was surprised. "What do you mean? Surely you don't think it was Jeremy... or me," I finished, just as our sandwiches arrived.

"Of course not. Nick just seems too obvious."

Denise's main fault, it always seems to me, is a tendency to confuse fiction with reality. I tried not to sound as exasperated as I felt. "This isn't a movie. In real life, the most likely person usually is the murderer."

"Not always."

"I'll grant you that. Now tell me who you suspect and why."

"Faith Sommers."

"An interesting choice, but don't forget the 'why,'" I reminded her.

"Ruthie, you saw her that day. The way she looked. Those people are fanatics."

"But why would she murder Amy?"

"Those people think they're saving lives by killing people."

"But why would she murder Amy? Why not go after the clinic people?"

"What better way to scare women out of having abortions?"

"I'll mention her to Detective Moreway tomorrow. He's in a better position to check on her than we are." Then I remembered Leila. "Why the second murder?" I asked.

"Don't forget, we saw Faith with Amy's aunt that day. It's very possible that she knew both sisters. Maybe Leila found out something that pointed to Faith."

"Denise, I know your dramatic sense zeros in accurately sometimes. But this is too far-fetched, even for you."

"We'll see," she said.

"Anyhow other than talking to Frank Moreway, there's nothing we can do."

"We can turn up at her next demonstration. She has them all the time."

I bit into my sandwich and tasted avocado and melted cheese. Denise sat there without eating, obviously waiting for my response. "Aside from everything else, it wouldn't do one bit of good now that she knows us."

"You could say you're repenting. That you may stop filling prescriptions for the abortion clinic." Her eyes, shadowed in electric blue today to match her blue and white striped dress, opened wide as she tried to convince me.

"Denise, you know women legally have the right to choose, and I won't imply that it's wrong for me to fill post-abortion scripts."

"I didn't say you shouldn't fill them. But I can't think of any other way to see more of Faith Sommers than to pretend you need advice from her."

By this time, we had both stopped eating. "I understand what you're trying to do," I told Denise. "It's just not something I can carry out."

"Now that I think of it, you're right. You never could lie convincingly."

I laughed. "You make that sound like an insult."

"You're such a straight arrow, Ruthie. In books, the sleuths are always breaking into people's houses or offices. And they lie like crazy when it's for a good cause."

"Real people don't do that," I said.

"Could be they don't break into places, but you'd be surprised how much lying goes on." She shook her head at me. "You deal with the public all day long, same as I do. Don't tell me you haven't been lied to over and over."

I thought of the times customers tried to get their prescriptions ahead of other people, claiming they had to catch a plane. Or the ones who brought back half-used bottles of pills insisting that I'd miscounted. But those were in the minority. Most of my customers were decent people, wanting only to get well quickly.

"And what about the really nice customers you have at the coffee shop?" I asked. "Surely you see more good ones."

"Yes, but at the coffee shop, I'm not involved in life and death situations. You're involved in one, and I think it's okay to fib for a worthy cause."

"No sense getting into the ends versus the means debate, Denise. People have never been able to agree on that one."

"Okay, closed subject. I see I can't change your mind."

I realized she probably would attempt to contact Faith Sommers on her own. Since I was convinced the murderer was Nick and not Faith, I decided not to worry about it.

We paid for our food and left the restaurant, talking about inconsequential things on the way back to the Food Go parking lot to get my car. As we pulled into the lot, I saw Lupe Douglas framed in the entrance lights of the supermarket.

"Stop the car," I yelled to Denise.

She pulled up to the no parking zone in front of the store and we both jumped out. "Lupe," I said. "Where's Jeremy? What's happening?"

"You're the one I came to see," she said. "They arrested Jeremy for murder, and it's all your fault."

Chapter 17.

We stood there in the parking lot, next to the open doors of Denise's old black Ford and stared at Lupe. I'd never before seen her look so distraught, not even when her little boy's attention deficit disorder was at its worst.

"Impossible," I said. "No one could really believe Jeremy killed her."

She was rubbing her hands over her cheeks, pulling them down in a grotesque pattern, and I could tell now why her face looked so strange. "Easy to say. You're probably the one who did it."

"Pull yourself together, Lupe. Ruthie would never harm anyone."

"I'm sorry. I don't know what I'm saying anymore."

"Why don't you get in, so we can talk without being overheard?" Denise said and gestured to her car. It was a good suggestion, considering I'd already noticed Food Go customers staring at us as they pushed shopping carts out of the supermarket. I just hoped Lupe wasn't too overwrought to go along with it. But she got right into the front passenger seat, and I reached around to open the back door, getting in so Denise could drive to a more secluded part of the lot.

While she parked the car, I wondered about Jeremy. Aside from the fact that I knew and liked him, I had seen how shocked and miserable he looked when he told me about Leila's death. Unless he was a terrific actor, and I'd never noticed such talent before, I was sure he couldn't have murdered her.

"Tell us what happened," I said to Lupe.

"You already know he handled that dressing table stool. You're probably the one who told the police."

"We've been through that already," I said and then realized I should be more patient with her. "Lupe, I don't for one minute believe Jeremy killed her. And I'll do anything I can to help convince the police." I leaned closer toward the front seat, trying to make her understand I was sincere.

"What can you do? Eric can't even get him out on bail."

"We've got a good lawyer..." Denise started to say.

What a time to drum up business for Sterling, I thought, and then decided I was being unfair to Denise. She was just trying to help.

"We already have one," Lupe said. "And Eric's a cousin. If anyone will look out for our interests, Eric will." She moved sideways on the front seat and looked back to face me.

"I'm sure you know that."

I ignored the comment, but the bitterness in her voice unsettled me. *She's terrified for Jeremy*, I thought. *No one can blame her for lashing out at other people.*

"Don't you see, Lupe. I'm the main witness... the main willing one," I corrected myself, "to say that Jeremy had a reason to handle that chair and did it openly. And Tommy will have to back me up even if Nick won't."

"Tommy has disappeared," she said.

"What?" This opened up an entirely new line of reasoning. "Then why did the police arrest Jeremy? If Tommy ran off, that's surely suspicious."

"His folks say he disappeared before Leila..." Her voice broke here, which surprised me because I had the impression she wasn't fond of her sister-in-law.

"I'm sure the police are looking for Tommy," Denise said. "Even if he ran away first, that doesn't let him off the hook."

Lupe calmed down a bit then. We talked a little while longer, and I promised I'd contact her immediately after we saw Detective Moreway the next day. Denise offered to drive her home, but she didn't want to leave the pickup in the lot overnight.

We watched her walk to the truck, get in, and drive away. "She seems to be handling the truck smoothly enough," Denise said. "I'm sure she'll get home okay." She turned back to me. "What a mess, Ruthie. We've got to find the real murderer."

"I don't think we can do it. It's a job for the police."

"You did it before."

"And nearly got killed in the process. Whoever it is—Nick, Faith, Tommy—has killed twice."

"Are you afraid?" Denise asked.

"Of course, I'm afraid. If you think accusing me of fear will change my mind about seeing Faith Sommers, it won't work."

"I'll call you as soon as I find out when she plans to hold her next demonstration," Denise said, and dropped me at my car.

* * * *

The next morning, I met my attorney as planned at the Scottsdale Police Department. He looked very lawyerly in a navy suit with a fine pinstripe and a red-and-navy striped power tie. I was sure he'd never wear brown shoes with such a suit and, despite my worry about Jeremy, glanced down to see highly polished black ones. It was probably a foolish generalization, but I decided he'd be a match for Frank Moreway.

We were led to the same office I was interviewed in earlier. The men introduced themselves to each other and we were motioned to seats in front of Frank's desk. As usual, he remained standing, hovering over us.

"Please be seated," Sterling Harraday told him. "I find it hard to crane my neck when I speak to people."

Frank hesitated momentarily. "I certainly wouldn't want you to be uncomfortable, counselor," he said.

How much more easily Sterling handles Detective Moreway than I do, I thought. I wondered if it was male bonding or Sterling's legal training and experience that made the difference.

"My client insists on making a statement that she hopes will help Jeremy Douglas," Sterling said carefully.

"Fine, but before we get to that, I want to go over one or two things in the statement she made Tuesday night."

"And why wasn't she advised to secure counsel that night?"

"She came here voluntarily, counselor," Frank Moreway said.

"Hereafter, Mrs. Morris will not be interviewed unless I'm at her side," Sterling told him blandly. "I hope that's understood."

"I don't know what the problem is. We certainly don't suspect her of any crime. As you well know, someone else is under arrest at this point."

"At this point," Sterling said, "but that was not the case Tuesday evening."

Detective Moreway didn't dispute his words, but began going over the same questions he'd asked me that night. He brought up the brass stool several times, and I described how Leila had given Tommy her own chair and remained standing until Jeremy got the dressing table stool for her.

"How did you know it was from a dressing table?" Frank Moreway asked me; it was a new question.

"Any woman would recognize it. You see them all over. This one had brass legs and a pink cushion. It couldn't have been from anything but a dressing table—or I guess some people call them 'vanities' nowadays." I thought for a moment. "Besides, Jeremy told us he was going to the master bedroom to get another chair," I remembered.

"And why did Jeremy get it? Why not the boyfriend, Nick?"

"Jeremy has good manners," I said coldly. "Nick is a brute."

Sterling coughed warningly. "I don't care," I said. "Nick is the one you should be arresting."

The detective ignored my comment. "So Jeremy knew his way around his sister-in-law's bedroom?"

I stared at Frank Moreway. "What are you implying this time? Back when Harry Stokes died, you tried to prove that either Denise or I or both of us had affairs with him. Don't you know any decent people?"

"Mrs. Morris," Sterling was warning me again.

"You're supposed to me on my side," I said to him, and then realized how childish I sounded. "I'm sorry. I guess indignation doesn't do anyone any good."

Detective Moreway smiled for the first time. "Accepted. I'm trying to get an impression of the various people involved and their relationships with each other." He looked through the notes on his desk. "I'll rephrase the question."

"Please do," I said.

"You've already let me know that you believe in Jeremy Douglas. The best way you can help him is to stop trying to protect him. If he's innocent, he doesn't need your protection, and you may be doing more harm than you realize." He stopped and looked intently at me. "You're an intelligent woman. You must have formed some impressions about these people."

"I'll try to fill you in," I said.

"Let's start with Leila's husband. You told me he threatened to get Nick."

"I also said I don't know him well enough to judge whether he meant it. Any father would explode under the circumstances."

"That may be, but we're not guessing about violence here. We have a body."

"Detective Moreway," I said. "We're not getting anywhere. If Nick were the victim, I'd probably suspect Quentin. But what motive did Quentin have to kill Leila?"

"What if he blamed his wife for everything?"

"That's really reaching."

"You'd be surprised what sets people off."

Sterling interrupted here. "This is pointless, Detective. You're wasting my client's time. She came here to give you evidence, not to conjecture."

"On the contrary. I have great respect for Mrs. Morris' insights. Has she told you how she helped us in the past?"

"If that's the case, why did you treat her like a suspect the other night?"

I was surprised to see Frank Moreway look uncomfortable. "Occupational hazard," he told us.

"Maybe it would help if I knew more about the crime," I said, surprising myself.

"You know I can't do that."

"Why not? Reporters always manage to get the details."

"I will tell you this," he said. "The only fingerprints on the chair other than Leila's were Jeremy's. They were on the rim of the seat, which is consistent with the way you say he handled the chair that night. But the murderer held the chair by the legs and wiped all the prints off them. And that's all I'm going to tell you."

"Why weren't any of Nick's prints on the stool? After all, he lived there."

He continued as if he hadn't heard me. "What about the young man, Tommy? How did he act toward Leila?"

"Leila was the one he wanted to talk to."

"But you told me he was waiting to see her alone. Did he blame Leila for her daughter's problems?"

"Problems?" Now I was really annoyed. He was minimizing Amy's seduction and the resultant pregnancy.

I looked at my $145 an hour attorney and then at Frank Moreway. Neither one of them responded. "Tommy was afraid of Nick," I told them. "I think that's the only reason he was trying to see Leila alone."

"Look," I continued, "none of them threatened Leila, and I don't know of any strong motive—unless she found out who exchanged the pills that killed Amy."

"Obviously, that conclusion is to your advantage."

Sterling Harraday interrupted. "We won't discuss that now, Detective. It may be prejudicial to my client if the civil lawsuit materializes."

Frank Moreway allowed his surprise to show, perhaps deliberately. "I can easily ask the girl's father. This is your client's chance to tell her side of the story."

"Go ahead then," Sterling advised me.

"I told you about it the other night, Detective Moreway."

"Let's have all the details this time."

I explained again what had happened. "This second murder makes things very clear," I insisted.

"And gives you an opportunity to exonerate yourself of having made a fatal mistake," Frank Moreway said.

"There was no mistake. That's why we made this appointment in the first place. I wanted to inform you that Nick had every reason to kill Amy. And Leila's murder makes it even more certain."

"Are you trying to tell me you've never made a mistake in filling a prescription?"

"This is beginning to sound like a fishing expedition," Sterling said, rising from his chair. "If you have nothing new to ask my client, I believe it's past time for us to leave."

"She needs to give an official statement about that dressing table stool so we can release Jeremy Douglas," he said.

I was so relieved for Jeremy and Lupe's sakes, I barely heard Sterling caution me to confine my words only to that brass stool. Frank Moreway called someone in to take down my statement. Before he allowed me to sign, Sterling read it over slowly and carefully.

"That's all for now," Detective Moreway told us. "But Ruthie," he said, dropping his more formal manner, "if you think of anything else, I want you to contact me immediately. No more amateur attempts at solving murder."

"Don't worry," I told him. And it was at that precise moment that I decided to check on Faith Sommers, provided Denise would then come with me to talk to Nick.

Chapter 18.

Sterling Harraday and I walked out of police headquarters into the bright sunlight of Scottsdale in early November. "It's customary," he said, "when you hire someone to represent you, to follow his advice."

His dark eyes were alert behind the horn-rimmed glasses, but his expression was mild. I thought I could detect a smile trying to break through the slight pomposity I was determined to overlook.

"I'm worried about Jeremy," I said.

"That does you credit."

Not his air so much, I decided, but the choice of words made him seem pompous. Although I couldn't believe he and Denise had much in common, I had promised to sound him out. If he went back to his office now, I'd never have the opportunity again. I tried but couldn't find an excuse to detain him.

"We should discuss our strategy," Sterling said.

"Yes."

"My other morning appointment canceled, so I'm free until one o'clock. When do you have to be at the pharmacy?"

"At two."

"Then let's get lunch somewhere," he said. There was that flash of humor finally coming through. "I promise I won't bill you for the time."

"In that case, let lunch be on me."

"Why don't we take both cars so we won't have to come back here? Shall we go to Jacqueline's?" he asked, naming a Scottsdale restaurant that specialized in salads, quiches, and delicious baked goods.

Sterling arrived there first. *He has that in common with Denise*, I thought, as I joined him. *They both drive much faster than I do*. It was somewhat early for lunch, and the restaurant wasn't too crowded. We requested patio seating and were shown to a brightly covered table amid the greenery, an oasis that effectively screened out the adjacent parking lot. The waitress took our orders—iced tea and a vegetable quiche for me, coffee and a Caesar salad with chicken for Sterling.

I thought of an opening that would provide me with the means to mention Denise and try to discern whether he was at all interested in her. "This is more relaxing for me than the coffee shop at Food Go."

"I guess you find it convenient to eat there," he said.

This was it. "Also, Denise is a good friend. I enjoy talking with her."

"She seems very concerned for you."

"Denise is that kind of person," I told him. "She always cares about people." It was his move, and I waited to hear whether he'd change the subject.

The waitress returned with our beverages. No frilly green Food Go aprons here. I saw that she was an attractive blonde with short, curly hair—much younger than Denise. Sterling didn't seem to notice her at all.

"And you socialize outside of work?"

I felt myself stiffen. If he revealed any hint of snobbery, I was prepared to tell him off. Then I would find another attorney.

"Denise has been divorced for some time. I was widowed about two years ago. She was wonderful when Bob died, and I got to know her better." I decided to go further. "It may sound corny to say so, but I think of Denise as one of those rare people who are good through and through. I don't mean that she's perfect," I added, thinking how her penchant for melodrama sometimes irritated me, "but I value her immensely as a friend."

The waitress appeared with our food, and Sterling was silent for a time. I decided I wasn't going to speak first. If I wanted to discover whether there was a chance for Denise and Sterling to get together, I must hear what he had to say.

My quiche was moist and herbed just right. I ate slowly, waiting, and saw that Sterling also was using his food to postpone further conversation. *Funny*, I thought, *if I were interested in him, I wouldn't be able to keep quiet and wait. But for someone else's sake, I could play the game.*

"I'm divorced, too," he said. "More recently than Denise."

"Were you married long?"

"Fifteen years. I have two children, a boy of twelve and a girl of ten." He cut his salad carefully and began eating. "They're with me on weekends."

I wondered if Denise knew all of this. Perhaps Sterling was using me to transfer information as I attempted to do the same. "That's difficult," I said.

"It's worked out so far." He stopped as if wondering how much to tell me. "She remarried almost at once."

That seemed to be a coded message, a way to let me know that the divorce hadn't been his idea. "But you haven't remarried," I said, more as a statement than a question. Since I was probably about ten years older than he, I figured I could probe without any possibility of my motives being misunderstood.

"No," he said. "I've been afraid of the rebound effect."

This surely was meant to be passed along to Denise. I could think of no other reason for his confidences. I cut into the crust of my quiche, the part I liked best. Sterling also had started to eat more steadily, and neither of us spoke.

After a while, he changed the subject and asked why I was so sure of Jeremy's innocence. "Even if his fingerprints on the stool can be explained, that doesn't preclude later prints that he wiped off."

"Yes. And he certainly knew where to find it if he wanted to use it as a weapon." I put down my fork and met Sterling's reflective gaze. "But he doesn't have a motive," I said.

"You mean, he doesn't have one we know about."

"Look," I explained patiently. "Jeremy has a wife and son he treasures. Why would he kill his niece and sister-in-law?"

"How well do you know him?"

"Mostly from Food Go."

"And you think that's enough to judge how he'd act under pressure? Do you see him socially?"

"What are you driving at?"

"I'm merely trying to understand the situation," he answered blandly.

"And I'm good at catching nuances," I said. "You're hinting at some sort of relationship. Even Frank Moreway didn't go that far this time."

"This time?"

I found I had to tell Sterling about Harry Stokes's death and the detective's suspicion that I'd had an affair with Harry. "Of course, he was completely wrong," I finished. "But Harry was older than I am; you surely know that Jeremy is much younger."

"Experience has taught me to disregard age when I'm trying to understand motivation," he said. "All right, I admit I wanted to see your reaction. If I'm representing you, I need to be sure I know why you haven't kept me informed or followed my advice."

We'd come full circle. "It's precisely because I have nothing to hide," I said and ignored him while I stopped a passing server for an iced tea refill.

"How does Jeremy get along with the rest of the family? I understand Leila's husband is only his half-brother."

"There's no 'only' to it," I said. "He refers to Quentin as his brother."

"You didn't answer my question."

I thought about what I'd learned, that the family hadn't accepted Lupe because of her Hispanic heritage. Surely Jeremy had indicated that was in the past. "They seemed fairly close," I told him. "Amy babysat for their little boy."

As soon as the words were out, I regretted them. Maybe it was better not to emphasize that particular closeness.

"And I understand they wanted to adopt her baby," Sterling said.

Who could have told him that, I wondered. *Surely not Denise.* "I don't see what that has to do with anything."

"On the contrary," he said. "I can come up with some interesting motives. It wouldn't be the first time someone killed because the other person thwarted his wishes."

"You're really reaching now. Maybe if Lupe and Jeremy were childless and this was their only chance at adoption, but..."

"I've thought this over carefully," Sterling said. "There's a very good possibility that the wrongful death suit will be dropped if we can link the two deaths. Or, worst case, we go to court and I raise enough doubts because of Leila's murder to win the suit." He stopped as the waitress returned to clear our plates.

"Some dessert today?" she asked.

Sterling looked inquiringly at me. I shook my head. "We'll pass," he said, "but we'd like more coffee and iced tea, please."

"You don't understand," I told him. "Naturally, if we have to go to court, I prefer to win. But even if we win, it will ruin me professionally."

"Then, we must get serious about this. You can't afford sentimental objections to pinpointing Jeremy—or anyone else, for that matter."

"I wasn't being sentimental," I told him. "But surely you can see that Nick Kenmore is a much more likely suspect."

"Or the young man who disappeared. The police are looking at both of them. Meanwhile, you've been trying to clear a viable candidate."

"So, you're telling me I should have let Jeremy stay in jail. Don't you realize how distraught his wife was?"

"And that's exactly my point about sentimentality."

Our beverages were refilled and the waitress, obviously well-trained, put the check midway between Sterling and me. I picked it up.

"What I'm saying," my lawyer told me, "is that Detective Moreway is right. The police don't need amateurs muddying the waters."

Sterling was the second person this morning to try and keep me from doing what I knew I must do. I took my wallet out of my handbag and extracted a credit card, making the process last as long as possible, afraid that if my lawyer looked closely at my face, he would guess my resolve to do exactly the opposite of what he'd just advised. Although I was paying this man $145 an hour for his counsel, I knew I couldn't sit back and wait. I must prove I had not been professionally negligent.

Chapter 19.

I was sure Tommy's disappearance rather than my evidence about the fingerprints led to Jeremy's release from jail, but I didn't say that to him or to Lupe when I dropped in on them after work that evening. Both of them thanked me for going to the police to support Jeremy's story about the prints.

If anything, Lupe seemed more haggard than she had the night before. Her eyes were red-rimmed, but she was neatly dressed in a flowered housecoat. They kept looking at each other and smiling, and I was ashamed of thinking even for a moment that Jeremy had been infatuated with his sister-in-law.

Lupe insisted on making coffee, but I told her I couldn't stay. "I have to open up tomorrow, and I know you're both early risers, too."

"Thanks for coming by to see how things are," Jeremy said.

Now I felt worse. "Actually, I had another reason. Denise and I want to check out some things about Nick and about that woman who tried to make an example of Amy."

"I'll go with you," Jeremy said.

"No, we won't discover anything that way. But I need you to figure out some plausible excuse to meet with Nick. He knows me, of course, so I can't pretend to be anyone else, even if I wanted to. But there must be some way."

Lupe was always the practical one. "What will you accomplish?"

"I certainly don't expect him to confess to us. I just want to shake him up."

"That's not very smart if you think he's a murderer." Lupe said.

"The police aren't doing anything about Nick. I can't bear to see him get away with murder and besides, I still have to prove I didn't give Amy the wrong pills."

Jeremy grinned. "So, if anything happens to my favorite pharmacist, we'll know it was Nick."

"Or Faith-whatever-her-name," Lupe said.

This was small consolation although certainly better than keeping knowledge about my plans from everyone. Since I wasn't foolhardy enough to see Faith or Nick alone, though, I had no reason to be afraid.

"You could tell Nick you need to talk to him about the lawsuit," Lupe suggested. "It sounds plausible to want to know if it's still on."

"But if I call him, he'll just say a few words on the telephone, and that will be the end of it. I won't get to sound him out."

"You really expect to trip him up, to somehow make him confess to you?"

I could hear Jeremy's skepticism as he voiced the question. He was forcing me to realize how naive my approach was. "No," I said slowly. "But even Detective Moreway wanted my impressions of the people involved. I need to be clearer in my mind about them. Right now, I keep thinking I should know what happened, but I can't quite get at it."

"If you're serious about talking to Nick, just go over there unexpectedly again."

"I can't watch the house the way Tommy did on the off-chance of catching him at home."

"The funeral..." Jeremy's voice broke and he started again. "The funeral is Friday. After that Nick'll probably go back to work. I know I will." He fingered his reddish beard, which looked rather scruffy tonight. "What's your schedule this weekend?"

"Off Saturday, on Sunday."

"Okay, he works half days on weekends. If you and Denise get over there Saturday after two o'clock or so, I think you'll find him home."

"Thanks, Jeremy."

"If that doesn't work, let me know and I'll run interference for you. I can call and act like I need to see him. Then once I have his schedule..." His voice trailed off, and he looked so exhausted that I said my goodbyes and hastily left.

* * * *

I was afraid Denise would be working on Saturday. Impatient though I was to talk to Nick, I would not go alone. For once, however, our schedules did coincide.

"We should really go to Leila's funeral and observe all of them," she said.

"No way. We have no reason to be there. I only met Leila once, and you never met her at all."

"So what? Lots of people go to funerals after a sensational murder."

"Denise, this was only sensational for the family. Otherwise, it's just another crime that people read about in the newspapers—and a fairly ordinary one at that."

"I'll bet the police will be observing everyone."

"All the more reason for us to stay away."

When she realized I wouldn't change my mind about the funeral, Denise said she'd pick me up just before two o'clock on Saturday to try and see Nick, but this wasn't until I told her I agreed we should meet with Faith Sommers again, too.

Meanwhile, I made time to check the Food Go computers but could find none of the names I was looking for. And early Saturday morning, Michael called again from Tucson to tell me he hadn't found any other Coumadin leads either. "You realize it could be someone we haven't even heard of."

"No," I said. "Jeremy told me he checked it out. At first, the family wasn't supposed to know about the abortion. But Amy didn't seem to be doing well, and her aunt decided to call Leila. That night and the next day, all of them were at Virginia's house at one time or another."

"Then, I'll keep trying. I don't always get people I know or people who'll talk, so it takes quite a few calls to each chain of pharmacies. And the independently owned pharmacies are another problem. Luckily for our purpose, there aren't too many of those left."

I thought of my father and what his reaction would have been to Michael's casual disposal of the former backbone of the profession. Even though I now worked for the chains my Dad had hated, I could still be saddened that so few individually owned drugstores had survived.

Michael didn't mention Patricia and, unwilling to hurt myself further, neither did I. I didn't tell him about the plans Denise and I had made. No one was going to talk me out of doing whatever I could to get at the truth.

After we said goodbye, I stepped outside to check the weather. It was overcast, which in November meant a chilly day by Scottsdale standards. I decided to dress casually in my turquoise jogset and a short-sleeved blouse in a deeper shade of turquoise. If the sun did come out later, I could always take off the jacket to the jogset and still be comfortable.

I was determined not to be nervous about the meeting with Nick, but I found it hard to stay calm. Usually, I tried to avoid working around the house on Saturday. Even though so many years had passed, and I was no longer an observant Jew in most respects, those early restrictions were hard to relinquish. Not for the first time, I thought how ironic that I had given up Michael for reasons that turned out to be transitory. Well, it was too late now.

Denise arrived on time, and I directed her to the house where Leila had lived with Nick. I assumed he hadn't moved since Jeremy would have let me know about any change. We planned our strategy.

"I guess I'll do the talking," I said, more nervous than I cared to admit at the prospect.

"And I'll flirt with him."

I looked at Denise. She also wore a jogset, but hers was black and, despite the cooler weather, I could see she had on a bandeau top. Even wearing the jacket, she exposed a great deal of tanned flesh. "Are you serious? I told you, he's a brute."

"Could be. But he's surely not going to attack me. I just thought it would be a good idea to try and get him interested. Maybe meet with him later on and see what I can find out."

I looked dubious. Despite her lovely grey eyes and slim figure, Denise didn't interest men that easily.

"Ruthie, I know what you're thinking. But I never have trouble attracting the wrong ones. It's only the guys like Sterling that I can't seem to make any progress with."

That reminded me I had talked about Denise to him and had gathered some information about his personal life. I told Denise what I'd learned. "Do you really like him that much?" She nodded, so I asked, "Why?"

"Probably because he doesn't come on to me. You have no idea what it's like working as a waitress. Some men seem to think that makes you fair game."

She rarely complained, and I kicked myself for not realizing how unpleasant some of her customers must be. Her job made mine seem wonderful, even though I sometimes had to placate angry patients. And many of mine are there because they're not feeling well, I told myself. Or they may be in pain. You'd think people would be in a better mood when they drop in for a snack at the coffee shop.

* * * *

I nearly didn't recognize the house. Even though it had been dark when Jeremy and I were there, I had an impression of a modest but well-kept home. Today, I saw that much of the Bermuda grass had died, but no one had planted a winter lawn. What was left of the summer lawn looked like it hadn't been mowed recently. Leila had struck me as house-proud, and I couldn't believe that so much had changed in so short a time.

"Where should I park?" Denise whispered, as if someone could overhear her.

I found myself whispering back. "Go up a few houses. Over there. By that palm tree. He won't be able to see the car from his windows."

"Was that his van in the driveway?"

"I don't know. Let's just go up and ring the doorbell." Anything was better than sitting in the car, worrying what I would say and how Nick would react.

The same harsh voice I remembered repeated the words I'd heard that other night. "If you're selling something, we don't want any."

I wondered about the "we." Maybe it was habit.

Denise pushed the doorbell again, and this time Nick Kenmore opened the door. "What do you want?" he said.

All the carefully rehearsed excuses fled my mind, and I found myself gaping at him, unable to say a word. He stared back at me but didn't shut the door in our faces as I half-expected him to do.

"May we come in?" Denise asked politely. "We want to talk."

Again I anticipated rejection, but he held open the door and waved us in. "You interrupted my lunch," he said. "You got something to say, talk while I eat. Maybe I'll listen."

We followed him into the kitchen. I looked around, expecting to find dirty dishes piled up everywhere, but it was surprisingly neat. Nick took a seat at the far end of the table, which was set with an oval placemat. I could see one half-eaten sandwich and a mound of potato chips. No plate, which explained the clean countertops. Without waiting for an invitation, we pulled out chairs and sat down, too.

"Okay, what can I do for you girls?"

I winced, but my prepared script suddenly came back to help me. "First, of course, we want to tell you how sorry we are about Leila. I only met her that one time, but she was decent to me despite everything."

"Despite everything," he echoed. "Why don't you come out and say what you mean?"

"I was planning to."

He picked up a handful of chips and crunched on them. "You want to know if I'm still gonna to sue the pants off you."

Again I winced, wondering how Amy had let this insensitive man sweet talk her into a relationship, however briefly. I guessed a psychologist would have found a rivalry issue with her mother or something along those lines.

"Yes, my friend does want to know your plans," Denise said.

"And Jeremy thinks you're so smart," Nick said to me. "Don't you know only the lawyers are supposed to talk to each other? I bet yours don't know you're here today."

I suddenly felt chilled. Was this a clever way to find out if anyone was aware of our visit to Nick's place? Don't be foolish, I told myself. Even a double murderer would hesitate to kill two more people when anyone might know we'd been to see him.

"Lupe and Jeremy know where we are."

He laughed and took a bite of his sandwich. "If you're afraid of me, why didn't you just use the telephone? Why pop in here?"

We were prepared for that question. "It's easier to discuss something like this in person."

"So discuss. I'm listening."

Denise and I looked at each other. "You never did answer the question," she said.

"And I ain't about to."

"Does that mean you haven't decided?"

"It means whatever you want it to mean. I suppose your shyster told you we offered to settle. Take it. You'll never get a better deal."

If I wanted to see his reactions, I would have to be direct. "I don't believe you have any possibility of a lawsuit anymore."

"Lady, anyone can sue anyone else. It's the American way." He scarfed more potato chips and got up to refill his supply from a bag on the countertop.

"Don't try to tell us that Leila's murder had nothing to do with Amy's death. Both of them were murdered, and you know it."

He slammed his fist on the table, and I forced myself not to react. This man was used to bullying people, and I didn't intend to let him frighten me the way he had the last time I encountered him. I continued, keeping my voice even. "When we find out who killed her mother, we'll know who killed Amy."

"If you're trying to pin it on me, you just cleared me. I can prove I was at work when Leila... when it happened." For the first time, his voice showed emotion, and I began to see that he might really have cared for Leila.

"Yes, but I happen to know you have the kind of job where you can take off and ride around during the day, testing the cars you repair."

"Sounds like you been getting an earful from Jeremy. Remember, he's the one they arrested—not me."

"And they released him right away. If you're so innocent, why didn't you tell them how Jeremy's fingerprints got on that chair."

"Why should I?"

I was horrified to see Denise remove the jacket to her jogging suit. *Not now*, I thought. *You're only going to distract him.*

He was staring at her and suddenly got up. The abrupt movement startled me. I found myself perspiring with suppressed anxiety but kept my own jacket on. He walked over to the refrigerator, took out some cans of soft drink, and handed one to each of us. "This house is always too warm," he said.

It was such an ordinary gesture and such a considerate one, it was hard to sustain my image of him as villain. I pulled the tab on the can and slowly sipped the cola. At least it gave me time to think. This visit wasn't going to accomplish anything unless I confronted him directly.

"You say you have an alibi," I told him. "But alibis don't always mean anything. You had motives to kill both of them, and I told the police all about you."

I expected a violent reaction, but he laughed. "You're such a busybody!"

My face felt flushed. He was right in a way, but I had every reason to try and prove Amy had been murdered. And right now, it seemed the best way to do that was to discover what really happened to Leila.

"Did you also tell the police about that kid's motive? Don't you think it's strange that he ran away?"

"What motive?" Denise asked.

"Your friend here is so busy trying to pin something on me that she believed every word he said," Nick answered her. He stared at each of us in turn, his face sullen and angry at the same time. "I don't know why I bother to talk to you."

"If you think Tommy's the murderer, then don't stop now. Give us your reasons."

"And..." he taunted.

"And we may believe you." Denise said.

"So what. Why should I care what you girls think?"

"You deal with the public in your job. Suspicion isn't good for you," Denise told him.

"Are you threatening me?"

"No," I hurried to say. "We're just trying to get to the bottom of this."

"In that case, talk to Amy's father. He came around here after Leila's funeral, threatening to beat me up." Nick stopped to finish the remains of his sandwich. "I'd like to see him try. A guy who couldn't even hold onto his wife."

"All very macho," I said surprising myself, "but you still haven't told us anything concrete."

"You want concrete. Here's concrete—back when Amy lived at her father's place, Quentin had to get a restraining order to keep that kid away from his daughter." He looked pleased with himself when he saw our startled expressions.

"I don't believe you. That young man loved her."

"That young man," he said, his voice mimicking me, "is a con artist."

Chapter 20.

"Don't think we won't check this out," I said, although I was beginning to wonder about Tommy despite my earlier convictions. His disappearance, coupled with this new information, certainly seemed suspicious. If only I could discover whether he also had access to Coumadin. I decided to redouble my efforts at locating the pharmacy his parents patronized.

Even though there seemed to be no point trying to find out more from Nick, I made a last effort. "You're trying to implicate Tommy, but we know you're the one who had access to Coumadin."

"Lady," he said, his voice serious rather than taunting this time, "before Amy died, I never even heard of that drug."

"You expect us to believe you lived here with Leila and didn't know she was on Coumadin."

"I don't expect you to believe nothing."

"So why are you claiming you didn't know about the blood thinner?" Denise asked.

"Leila once said there was heart disease in her family. I knew she took something to head off that kind of trouble, but we never talked about details." He stood now and loomed over us, a stance that would have seemed menacing on anyone's part but was more threatening coming from Nick.

"I got better things to do than waste time with you girls," he said and led us through the house to the front door.

There didn't seem to be any reason to avoid following him, so we left. Back in Denise's car, we discussed the visit. "What do you think?" Denise asked. "Are you still convinced he's the one?"

"I'm more confused than before," I admitted. "Do you see him as a murderer?"

"Could be."

"On the positive side, the police probably didn't check his alibi that thoroughly once they arrested Jeremy. And now they have Tommy to look for." I leaned back against the headrest and closed my eyes. "Also, despite his claims to the contrary, we know Nick had access to Coumadin. It still makes sense to figure Leila realized what happened once she saw he had a motive to kill her daughter and access, through her, to the drug that did it. Maybe she even noticed some of her medication was missing and that tipped her off."

"How do we prove it?"

"We can't. But I can keep hounding Frank Moreway so that he has to investigate Nick more carefully. The trouble is I'm not sure anymore." I opened my eyes again and turned toward Denise. "Did you get the impression he really cared for Leila despite everything?"

"Hard to believe, but it could be."

"And he didn't act like a guilty person."

"How does a guilty person act? No one realized who killed Harry Stokes until it was nearly too late," she reminded me. "Let's go to see Faith now." She inserted the ignition key and started her car, gunning the motor in her haste to interview our next suspect.

I had expected someone in the public eye to have an unlisted number but, surprisingly, we had found Faith Sommers in the phone book. She lived in North Scottsdale in one of the newer areas, marked by houses with terracotta tile roofs in contrast to the ubiquitous red tile of the older neighborhoods. Again, we took the chance of finding our quarry at home. We didn't dare risk refusal by telephoning for an appointment.

The streets curved in disorienting circles, some of which led to dead ends. Denise, who was more confident in her driving and her sense of direction than I, continued searching, unflustered. Despite the richness of the homes, the area seemed barren to me. Even the desert vegetation failed to disguise its newness. Many of the owners had planted citrus and palms, but they were small compared to the full-grown trees I was accustomed to seeing in my older Scottsdale neighborhood. In keeping with the desert look and the need to conserve water, no one had planted lawns.

After losing our way a few times, we found the house. It looked just like all the other homes we had passed, the front dominated by a three-car garage, but the landscaping was more distinctive here. Someone had planted yellow flowers that I couldn't identify around the cactus and decorative rock groupings. And the front walks were bordered with yellow thevetia bushes.

Since the area was so new, I thought for a moment of passing ourselves off as neighbors but couldn't bring myself to lie about it. We walked up to the front door, rang the bell, and waited to be observed through etched glass panels.

Chimes announced our presence, and Faith Sommers herself answered the doorbell. Today, she also wore a jogging outfit, which was standard for Arizona in November, but hers was a dark green silk set. She smiled at us, and I saw no sign of recognition.

"Won't you step in?" she said graciously.

I was surprised. When I was growing up in Tucson, this was exactly the way we responded to people on our doorstep. We would've been considered very rude to react in any other way. Nowadays, though, most people had long since become wary of strangers; we usually found out their business before opening the door and inviting them in.

Denise and I followed her through a large entryway and down two steps into a living room furnished like some of the upscale model homes I'd seen in magazine ads. Carpets, drapes, and furniture were all off-white. Color in the room came from flowered cornices over the expanse of windows and matching throw pillows on the white sofas and chairs. Through the windows, I could see a rectangular swimming pool like mine, but this one had rock gardens on three sides giving it a lagoon-like appearance.

"What a lovely pool," I said spontaneously and with absolute sincerity. Swimming pools were no novelty in Scottsdale. Our long, hot summers made them a necessity and even relatively inexpensive homes were built with in-ground pools, but this one was obviously custom-designed.

"Thank you. We enjoy it." She seated us on one white sofa and, poised and waiting to hear our business, sat on an identical one at right angles to us.

When we'd planned this visit, Denise and I had discussed telling Faith we wanted to join her anti-abortion group. I couldn't bring myself to lie, however, no matter how important our purpose.

"Do you remember us?" Denise asked.

She looked closely at both of us. "I hope you'll excuse me. My memory for faces has never been very good."

"We were at that demonstration about ten days ago."

She seemed pleased. "You're interested in our movement."

I was tempted to agree but didn't. "If you'll bear with us, Mrs. Sommers, we want to talk about Leila Brookman."

"Sorry, I don't think I know anyone named Leila."

I had been watching closely to see her reaction but could detect no evidence of guile. Even Denise had to see that this woman wasn't implicated in Leila's murder, I decided. Unless Faith had been on the stage, I couldn't believe she knew what we were talking about.

"Surely you remember that last name," Denise said. "Brookman. The girl who died after an abortion."

"Oh yes. Amy Brookman. Such a tragedy, and one that should have been avoided."

"It certainly should have been avoided," I agreed. "She was deliberately murdered."

This time, Faith lost some of her poise and gave a slight gasp. I tried to assess whether her reaction was too theatrical to be real but concluded it wasn't overdone. In fact, it sounded quite normal to me.

"I haven't come across anything about that on the news."

"It's only a matter of time," I said.

"Now that her mother's also been murdered," Denise added.

"Are you saying that this Leila was the girl's mother and that she's dead, too?"

"Murdered. You must have seen *that* on TV." Denise's words were so sharp that I realized her suspicions remained alive.

"I never connected the two deaths. Surely it's a coincidence."

"Very unlikely, don't you think?"

"I don't know what to believe." She collected herself. "But why are you here?

This was the moment of truth. We couldn't say we suspected her, but we had to find out if she was involved. I decided the only way to handle this interview was to say exactly what I wanted to know and why.

"Let me tell you what we think happened," I said. "I'm a pharmacist. You probably heard that her family believes I gave Amy the wrong drug."

"I remember now. Virginia Rowland said you did it deliberately, but she seemed overwrought from the tragedy, so I put it out of my mind."

"Virginia was right in saying it couldn't have happened by accident. But I'm not the one who made the substitution. You heard Amy's aunt say she was supposed to take a prescribed drug to prevent excessive bleeding. Instead, she took a blood thinner called Coumadin." I paused and asked one of the crucial questions. "Are you familiar with Coumadin?"

"As a matter of fact, my husband is on that medication."

Denise and I looked at each other. Faith was quick to catch and interpret our reaction. "Surely you're not accusing me," she said.

"I'm not accusing anyone," I told her.

"Then why are you here?"

This was it. She might throw us out, very politely of course, or she might help willingly. And we would have to interpret her reaction, for either course could hide guilt.

"As far as we know, the police don't believe Amy was murdered. Even now, when there's no doubt someone killed her mother, the detective I talked with doesn't seem to connect the two deaths."

"And you have a decided interest in making that connection."

"Well, yes, I do."

"I agree that it does seem rather a coincidence. You still haven't told me why you're here if you don't suspect me of somehow..." Her voice trailed off as if the idea was too ridiculous to be voiced.

"We need to talk to everyone who might have information. Then, maybe we can piece it all together."

"I think you've been reading too many mysteries." She smiled to take the sting out of her words, and I was surprised to find that I rather liked Faith Sommers. Despite some negative experiences in a profession that few women entered in my day, I had never been a political activist. And I guess I stereotyped women like Faith as fanatics.

"Did you ever meet Amy?" Denise asked.

"Yes, I met her," Faith said slowly. "I could deny it, but I have nothing to hide. If there's any possibility she was deliberately murdered, then I, too, want that person to be caught."

"Could you tell us the details of your meeting?"

"Her Aunt Virginia brought her to see me."

"Here?"

She nodded. "At the time, Amy was talking about an abortion. Virginia wanted me to show her some of the pictures we have, to talk her out of going through with it."

"Could you tell us exactly what happened?"

"I don't see how that visit could have anything to do with her death, even if it turns out she really was murdered."

"Please," I said. "At this stage, we don't know what's important. We're trying to learn everything we can about Amy and the people who knew her."

I waited, uncertain again as to Faith's reaction. She seemed doubtful, too, pausing for a long time. I could see Denise restlessly crossing and uncrossing her legs, and I knew she also was worried.

"Let me think," Faith said. "Amy sat right where you are, and her aunt was over here next to me. I always prefer this sofa because it's closer to the kitchen if I want to bring out any refreshments."

She looked rather embarrassed for a moment but made no move to offer anything to us. *How different from Leila*, I thought, with a pang. Leila, whose modest home had probably cost far less than this one, hadn't hesitated to offer hospitality to her unwelcome guests.

Faith continued. "The girl looked much younger than her age, and she was very quiet. Virginia and I did all the talking."

"Had you known Virginia before?"

"We met once or twice. She supports our movement."

"What did Virginia say to you?"

"She called first to make an appointment." Faith looked pointedly at us. "So I knew why they had come. Virginia told me the girl was adamant, which made me decide to approach things carefully."

"Did she tell you why Amy wanted an abortion?"

"That was what I was supposed to find out."

"Weren't you surprised she was with her aunt instead of her mother?" I asked.

"I already knew the mother was a flighty type, not to speak ill of the dead, of course. The girl was living with her aunt, couldn't get along with the mother's boyfriend, I gathered." She pursed her lips and turned back into the stereotype I'd originally expected her to be.

"Then Virginia didn't know that her sister's boyfriend was the baby's father." I made it a statement, not a question.

Faith gasped once more. "Some families are so dysfunctional today. I don't know how we're going to cope with their children."

"Maybe that's why Amy wanted an abortion," Denise said drily. I gave her a look that was meant as a reminder not to antagonize Faith.

"There are other alternatives."

"And did you discuss those with Amy?"

"Of course. That was the point. I understood another aunt was willing to adopt the baby."

So, Lupe's offer to adopt was known before the fact. I had wondered if she and Jeremy had really committed themselves or simply said so after Amy's death. Faith continued without waiting for my questions to prompt her.

"She was such a pathetic girl, so thin, so unhappy. Now that you've told me about the baby's father, I can understand why she seemed so sad. At the time, I thought she was unhappy about her decision. I was sure I could change her mind." Faith's hands were clasped as if in prayer.

"When I showed her the pictures, she started to cry. But we couldn't make her change her mind. Her aunt put her arms around Amy and tried to console her."

I couldn't picture that unyielding woman consoling her niece, but it wasn't the first time I'd misjudged people. And her aunt was the one who took her in, no questions asked, for she obviously had never learned about Nick.

"Sometimes, after I talk to them, they think things over and keep the babies. Or give them up for adoption," Faith said. "I prayed Amy would do that, but Virginia called the next day to tell me the girl wouldn't reconsider."

"Was Virginia upset?" I asked. *Maybe she's the one*, I suddenly thought. She had seemed so supportive of her niece, I'd never suspected her before.

"Of course, she was upset. Who wouldn't be?"

"That's not what I meant. Not upset in general, but upset with Amy."

Faith's glance at me seemed contemptuous, and I flinched inwardly, but I told myself I couldn't afford to eliminate anyone from my list of suspects. She was quiet for a few moments, and again I worried that she would freeze us out.

"If you had seen the two of them together, you'd bite your tongue before accusing Virginia."

"I did see the two of them together," I told her, hearing the stiffness in my tone and knowing it was because I was thoroughly ashamed of myself. We'd come here because Denise had pegged this woman as a murderer, and now I was mentally condemning another woman. And I hadn't even given that one a chance to speak for herself as we had with Nick and now were doing with Faith.

"Virginia has a very responsible position. She's administrative assistant to an executive at an electronics company in Tempe. Since she never married or had children of her own, she told me Amy was like a daughter to her."

I remembered my first impression—that they were mother and daughter. But I wasn't naive enough to cross Virginia Rowland off my list for that reason, especially since she did have opportunity, and I didn't know who else besides Nick had the chance to substitute the pills. On the other hand, I could think of no motive for her to kill Amy and even less of a reason for her to murder Leila. For that matter, Denise's suspicion of Faith, resulting from the latter's attempt to use the death politically, seemed rather farfetched to me as I sat in Faith's attractive home. By stretching our imaginations, we possibly could find motives for people like Lupe, Jeremy, and Quentin. I was becoming convinced, however, that only Nick and Tommy had substantial reasons to get rid of both victims.

Faith seemed to be waiting for me to say something, so I obliged. "And that was the last time you saw Amy?"

I observed two spots of red suddenly appear on Faith's high cheekbones, and I began to think I'd dismissed her from my list of suspects too soon. She seemed reluctant to speak.

"You did see her again?"

"Yes." The word was spoken so softly I nearly missed it. "I was at Virginia's that night. She called me."

"I understand why Virginia brought Amy to see you beforehand, but why would she call you to come over after the abortion?" I asked.

Faith really appeared flustered now. Finally she sighed and continued. "I know how this is going to sound to both of you in the light of what happened to Amy. Hindsight is a wonderful luxury."

We waited. She rose and stood looking out through the wall of windows, her back to us. I saw now that French doors were set into that glass wall, their panes matching the window panes. She turned and faced us, looking miserable. For one wild moment, I expected a confession.

"I went there to take pictures."

"Pictures?"

"You have to understand how much it means to me to keep women from going for abortions." She paused. "Amy seemed so frail when I met her. I knew she'd look a lot worse after the abortion." Faith's poise had deserted her, and she gazed almost pleadingly at Denise and me.

Suddenly, I understood and I was furious. "You planned to use Amy's photograph to frighten people. How could you invade her privacy that way? I suppose you also took pictures of her in her coffin," I finished.

"One person's privacy isn't as important as countless lives."

"We've heard that line before," Denise said.

"You don't understand..."

"I understand only too well," Denise told her.

Faith Sommers had collected herself and was calm again. "It's done. We'll have to agree to differ. Just remember—I had her aunt's permission."

"And what about Amy's consent?"

"Amy was in no position to consent. She didn't seem aware of much that was going on at the time."

It seemed to that made it worse, but I could see no point in arguing. Faith had convinced herself that she was right, and nothing I said would change her mind.

It was Denise who caught something I'd missed. "What did you mean about things going on at the time? Was anyone else there?"

"Virginia's house was crowded with people."

Here it was at last. Until now, since I couldn't question everyone about their whereabouts the way the police could, I'd been limited to looking at motives. Faith Sommers, however, was about to reveal who had the opportunity to switch medications that night. And the more I considered it, the clearer it was to me that the change had to be made the first evening. Once Amy began taking the real Methergine, she couldn't have missed the differences in shade of purple and in shape between that drug and Coumadin, the blood thinner.

"Who else was there?" I asked, trying to keep the excitement from my voice, afraid she'd refuse to discuss it further.

"Let's see now. I told you I don't have a good memory for people." She seated herself again and appeared lost in thought.

My suspicions of her were reawakened, and I wondered if she'd try to implicate other people to dilute the impact of her own visit on our suspicions. I debated whether I should try to prompt her by asking about individuals connected to Amy.

"I didn't see everyone. The father was just leaving as I arrived. And I guess I did meet the mother after all. She was with another man—must have been the one you mentioned, the one who lives with her."

I waited, nodding slightly at Denise to keep her from interrupting, afraid we'd lose this source of information. Already, I could see how difficult it would be to pinpoint the murderer if so many people had been to see Amy that night.

"There was a boy about Amy's age. I remember thinking he was her brother, but the way he spoke to her, I thought he... you know," she finished delicately. "I could see he was in love with her."

"Then, just as I was leaving, two more people came in. I'm not sure I caught the relationship," she said almost apologetically. "I didn't stay long enough to talk to them."

"What did they look like?"

"My dear, I'm hopeless at that sort of thing. I meet so many people when I speak and when we demonstrate..."

They could have been neighbors, friends, anyone. I thought about all the people I'd already met who were involved with Amy. This was going to be a lot more difficult to figure out than Harry Stokes's murder. And I certainly didn't want to put myself or anyone else in danger this time.

"Were they men or women?" Denise prompted. "Young or old?"

"Let's see now. A big man. Oh, yes, the woman was Mexican."

"Hispanic," I corrected automatically.

"Amy's aunt and uncle," Denise said.

"Maybe. I just don't remember."

It seemed indisputable, and I was surprised neither Lupe nor Jeremy mentioned they'd seen Amy the night of her abortion. What else were they hiding? Perhaps, because I liked him so much, I'd been too quick to explain away Jeremy's fingerprints on the brass stool.

Chapter 21.

We thanked Faith Sommers and she graciously told us she was happy to help, but I could see how eagerly she waited for us to go. She had, however, given us important information that we might never have learned elsewhere. Now I had to figure out who was implicated by Faith's story.

Denise was quiet as we left the house and got into her car. To avoid interrupting her thoughts, I waited to speak until I couldn't stand the silence.

"Do you still think Faith is the one?"

"Could be. But I have to admit I'm confused. Tell you what, Ruthie, let's go back to my house and talk it out."

I remembered the last time I'd been to Denise's, the day of the demonstration. That was when I'd first seen Michael and Patricia together. My automatic impulse was to avoid Denise's house now, since she lived next door to Michael's daughter, but I decided the chances of anyone noticing our arrival were slim. Besides, I'd heard nothing from either of them all week, which probably meant they had no new information.

"Good idea," I said. "We do need to sort out our impressions. I keep thinking I'm overlooking something important."

Twenty minutes later when we pulled into Denise's driveway, I tried to be inconspicuous as I scanned that other driveway. No one was in sight.

The air was heavy with the unpleasant odor that permeates Scottsdale every autumn when people put in their winter lawns, overseeding with rye grass. The problem isn't the grass itself but the animal fertilizer, which is used to speed germination. Winter lawns do best here after nighttime temperatures fall below 60 degrees, which is usually late September or early October. Since some homeowners begin planting early and others do so at the last minute, we usually have about six odorous weeks, but I guess it's worth it to have green lawns all year round. I often wish, though, that everyone would get together and decide on a day to plant rye grass, so we'd get it all over with at once. When my own neighbors fertilize, I avoid the outdoors or else try to pretend it's springtime—March with its wonderful perfume of citrus in bloom.

"Let's get inside quickly," Denise said. "Betsy had her winter lawn put in yesterday."

"Did Michael do the work for her?" I couldn't help asking.

"With all the money Betsy inherited from her husband? She has a lawn crew, of course."

"Come on, Denise. You know how commonplace lawn crews are out here. If they had to depend only on wealthy people to employ them, they'd starve." Denise, attracted to Harry Stokes herself, had been convinced that Betsy married for money. After Harry's death, when I came to know Betsy, I realized how much she had loved Harry and was suffering as a young widow, left alone to carry his child. I'd only partially convinced Denise, for I couldn't bring myself to tell her how strongly I wished Betsy were my child instead of the daughter of Michael and his ex-wife.

As usual, we sat in Denise's cheerful kitchen. "I'll get paper and pen," she said. "That's the way they always do it in books."

I took the small telephone notepad Denise handed me and suggested we use one page for each person, at any rate those we knew had been with Amy Brookman after her abortion. "I've got Virginia, Faith, Lupe, Jeremy, Quentin, Leila, Nick, and Tommy," I said. "Can you think of anyone else?"

"No, but we're sure now that they all had opportunity."

"In the right place at the right time, yes, but that's not the whole story." I drew thick lines under each name while I thought about it. "As far as we've been able to find out, only Faith, Leila, and Nick had access to Coumadin."

"First of all, we can eliminate Leila. I can't believe we have two murderers."

"So we're back to where we started this afternoon—Faith or Nick," I said.

"Let's look at motive next. That should help."

"Now that we've talked to her, do you still believe Faith had a strong enough motive, just to use Amy's death as a deterrent?"

"I can tell from the word 'just' what you think. But Ruthie, the woman seems so nice. Then, all of a sudden, she does something monstrous like taking that poor girl's picture when she was probably completely out of it."

"That's not in the same class as murder."

Denise got up and filled a pitcher with ice cubes. She added iced tea concentrate and water and brought it over to me with a tall plastic glass and a napkin. "I know you drink this stuff all year round."

I thanked her and waited while she reheated some coffee in the microwave for herself. Before she joined me at the table, I pulled out the page with Leila's name. Unfortunately, that loosened the rest of the pages. *Why doesn't this ever happen in books*, I thought, and then decided I liked loose pages better. This way, we could move them around and try to arrange the various suspects in order of probability.

"Whoever killed Leila must have done it because she found out he or she caused Amy's death," Denise said.

"That seems pretty obvious. But if it was Nick, there may have been a terrible fight after Tommy revealed his affair with Amy."

"Could be. If Nick changed the pills, he probably did it to keep Amy from telling her mother about him in the first place."

"We're back to Faith and Nick again," I said. "I can't figure out a reason for any of the others to want Amy dead." I drank some of the iced tea. Maybe the caffeine would help me see what I was missing. The word "missing" made me think of Tommy, and I reminded Denise about him.

"If we pinpoint the same person the police are looking for, we may as well leave it in their hands," Denise said.

"This isn't a competition."

She looked embarrassed. "I didn't mean it that way. But, as far as we know, the police seem interested only in Leila's murder. If you're going to clear yourself and prove you didn't make a deadly mistake, we have to discover who switched the pills."

I knew she was right. Although I'd heard from Nick, and no one else, that the family still planned to go ahead with the wrongful death lawsuit, he probably had inside information. Now that Leila was dead, I couldn't see how he would gain from the civil lawsuit, but maybe he was her heir. I'd have to ask Sterling Harraday whether Nick could expect to claim any part of a possible settlement.

We sat in Denise's kitchen for another hour, brainstorming, finding only the most farfetched reasons for any of the others to have killed Amy.

"Maybe her death was an accident," I said.

"Ruthie, you know you wouldn't make a mistake like that."

"I didn't mean that kind of accident. But what if someone wanted to make her condition worse, not expecting the hemorrhage to be fatal?"

"Why?"

I had no answer for Denise. It didn't make sense, except perhaps for Faith Sommers, and I couldn't bring myself to believe that fastidious woman would kill two people to validate her point of view.

324   Renée B. Horowitz

Finally, I gathered the pages together, borrowed a paper clip, and placed them carefully into my handbag to study later. I put on the jacket to my jogset and asked Denise to drop me back home.

"Are you in a hurry?" she asked.

"It depends what you have in mind," I said. "But I'm not going back to Faith's place."

"Not there. But could you direct me to Quentin Brookman's? I think we should talk to him."

I considered demurring but then decided we might as well do it. Timidity was not going to clear my name. Besides, I wasn't afraid of Quentin.

In case I couldn't find his condo again, we checked the address in the phone directory and started out to see Amy's father. Unable to think of a stronger excuse, we decided to use the same one we'd given Nick. The more I thought about it, I did want to know whether they still planned to file a wrongful death suit against me.

We arrived at Quentin's condo just before six o'clock that evening, much earlier than on my first visit. Here, there was no fertilizer odor because his complex had desert landscaping, rocks and cactus, rather than green lawns.

In answer to our ring, he pulled aside the drapes and looked out from a front window, motioning to us to wait. We waited a long time for him to open the door, and I wondered what could be keeping him this time.

"Is he hoping we'll just fade away?" Denise whispered.

"If he is, he's very much mistaken."

We were the mistaken ones, however, for Quentin suddenly opened the door and greeted us politely. I introduced Denise, and the three of us stood in the doorway and talked about the weather. *This is silly*, I thought. *I have to get us inside. We need more time to talk about something other than trivialities.*

Denise tried to rescue us. "Can we come in?" she asked. "We want to discuss some things with you."

"You can say whatever you have to say right here."

Even Nick had been willing to sit down and talk with us, I thought, *but Quentin is acting like a person with something to hide.* On the other hand, maybe Nick gave that impression precisely because he was trying to appear innocent. I decided to begin by telling Quentin how sorry we were to hear of Leila's death, trying not to consider the incongruity of offering condolences first to the live-in lover and then to the husband, not even ex-husband, according to Jeremy. Although I watched closely, his unyielding expression showed no reaction to my words.

"Thanks," he said and reached behind us to open the door again.

"We're trying to find out who murdered her," I blurted, knowing I had to get his attention before we were ushered out of his condo.

"Look, Jeremy told me you helped get him out of jail, but that doesn't make you a detective."

"I know, but my professional reputation is on the line."

He stared at me. "I don't get it."

"If we can all sit down and talk..." Denise said.

Quentin's reluctance to invite us in remained obvious, but he must have realized we would not be easy to get rid of. He led the way to his living room, which looked even messier than the time before. All the drapes were tightly drawn, holding in the daytime heat even now that the sun was down and the temperature had dropped. The only light in the room came from a single floor lamp.

I decided to try the positive approach. "Of course, you know now that I had nothing to do with your daughter's death."

"I don't know any such thing."

"The same person who murdered your wife killed Amy," I said bluntly.

He looked like the idea was new to him, but I couldn't judge whether his surprise was genuine. "The police never said a word about that." He paused and stooped to make room for us on the sofa by moving some newspapers to the floor. "Neither did Jeremy."

"And that's exactly why we're trying to get information."

Quentin's expression suddenly took on a shrewdness I hadn't noticed in him before. "Sure," he said to me. "You're trying to get off the hook."

"I'm trying to prove what I knew all along—that I had nothing to do with Amy's death."

"Maybe it's the other way around," he said. "Maybe you killed Leila, too."

I could understand Frank Moreway's suspicions of me. It was his job to suspect everyone. But I wasn't going to take it from Quentin. "Let's be realistic," I said. "Who do you think had a motive?"

"Don't look at me. The police already asked me enough questions."

"Like where you were at the crucial time?"

It didn't work. He simply nodded without revealing what he'd told them. I tried another tack. "We talked to Nick Kenmore this afternoon," I said.

The name caused the explosion I was anticipating. "That miserable creep," he yelled. "Did he confess that he killed them?"

From a purely selfish point of view, I regretted I didn't have a tape recorder with me. It seemed unlikely that Quentin could go through with the lawsuit if I could have recorded that last statement.

"Did you blame Leila for not preventing Nick's pursuit of Amy?" I asked, trying to sound matter-of-fact.

"Of course, I blamed her," he said. "What kind of mother would be so oblivious to what was going on?"

So, he did have a motive after all. Quentin's strong temper was obvious, but would he have admitted his anger so freely if it had led to murder?

He must have understood what I was thinking, for he hurried to add, "But I didn't kill her. And anyhow, I can prove I was at work."

"What do you do, anyhow?" Denise asked. I guessed she was trying to find out if he had the kind of job that Nick did, one he could be away from for a time without causing any particular notice or comment.

"I work in a video store and, for your information, lots of people must have seen me that day."

"Which video store?" Denise asked.

"None of your business. I told that police detective, but I'm not having anyone else hang around asking questions."

I resolved to check it out with Jeremy as soon as possible, but I really couldn't see how we'd discover anything Frank Moreway missed.

"Let's discuss some of the other possibilities," I said. "You must have your own ideas about who did it."

"Nick," he said flatly.

"He seems to have an alibi."

"I never said Nick was stupid. Naturally, he was sure to think of saving his own skin." Quentin riffled through some of the newspapers he'd piled on the floor. "You're an educated woman," he said, his tone making it sound like an insult. "If you read the papers, you must know how many murderers are never caught."

"That's why we're trying to discover this one. And I'd think you would be at least as interested as we are."

"Just what do you expect me to do, go gunning for him?"

"Of course not. But if you really believe he's the one, you can think back to how he acted the time you were all at Virginia's, the night before your daughter's death."

For the first time, I saw sadness replace the angry expression in his eyes. He looked grim. "How do you know we were all there?"

"You're wasting time," I said, as firmly as I could. "Just try to remember anything you noticed, especially anything out of the ordinary."

He seemed to try, taking on a look of intense concentration, like a child trying to remember where he lost his newest toy. "It's hopeless," he said after a while.

"Where was Amy?"

"Lying down on the living room sofa, covered with some kind of throw thing—an afghan, I guess you call it."

"Did you see any medicine vials?"

He closed his eyes and concentrated again. "I don't know. Maybe. Virginia had set up a tray table with stuff on it for Amy, so she didn't have to get up."

"And was Nick alone with her at all?"

"Not while I was there."

This wasn't doing any good, so I decided to try something else. "What about the boy? Tommy?"

Quentin suddenly seemed uneasy. "Why bring him into it? I thought we agreed it was Nick."

"We can't be sure. You know that," Denise told him. "And Tommy could have been upset enough with Amy to want to punish her by changing the medication. Maybe he didn't expect to cause a life-and-death situation."

"And you have to admit his disappearance is suspicious," I added. "Even the police are looking for him."

Quentin was absolutely still except for his eyes, which seemed to dart to the doorway leading to the back of the condo. I had just time to wonder what he was hiding when Tommy walked into the living room, holding a large kitchen knife.

Chapter 22.

My first shocked reaction was to blurt out, "You're in it together." Then I tried to hide my fear, knowing Denise and I were no match for the two of them. My forehead glowed with perspiration, but I didn't dare move to pull a tissue from my pocket.

"Aren't you being rather silly?" Quentin asked. "Tommy had nothing to do with the murders. And neither did I," he added almost as an afterthought.

"Then why the knife?" I asked, trying to control the shakiness in my voice, "And why are you hiding Tommy? You know as well as we do that the police want to question him."

"So they can make another mistake like they did with Jeremy? My brother's a big guy. He can handle himself in any situation. But look at Tommy. How long do you think it would be before he'd confess to anything so they'd leave him alone?"

I turned to Tommy. "But why did you run in the first place?"

He was wearing jeans and a clean white T-shirt that must have been Quentin's because it was much too big on him. Rubbing the back of his neck with a nervous gesture, but still holding the knife in one hand, he stood there, not making eye contact with us.

Quentin sighed. "Now that you showed yourself, you might as well tell them everything."

"I was afraid," he said slowly.

"Of the police?" Denise asked.

"No. That came later when he," Tommy pointed at Quentin, "when he told me about Amy's uncle getting arrested."

"Then who are you afraid of?" I asked.

"The one who killed Amy and her mom."

"You know who it was?" I wondered why I was buying into his story and added, "That doesn't explain why you're pointing a weapon at us."

He reached back to the nearest corner of the room and put the knife down on the floor. I heard myself sigh in relief, but the warmth in the room and my own nervousness made me unbearably uncomfortable. I took off my jacket and tried to appear calm in order to gain information from Tommy.

When he turned to face us again, I realized for the first time that he was more nervous than we were. "None of you listened to me when I told you that other time, and now Amy's mom is dead, too."

I remembered how he insisted Nick had killed Amy. But there was no proof, and I didn't see how there could ever be proof. Whoever switched the tablets would have been careful to avoid being seen. And now, with Faith's recollections, we knew they all had opportunity.

"You can't simply accuse him," I said. "Did you see anything out of the ordinary that night at Virginia's house?"

"Why was he even there?"

"Tommy, we talked about this the other day," Quentin said. "He had to go there with Leila or it would have looked strange."

"He could've found an excuse. No, I tell you he needed Amy out of the way so she wouldn't tell her mom about him."

"You didn't answer the question, Tommy," I said. "Did you notice something? Was Nick alone in the room with Amy at all?"

"I never let him out of my sight," the boy said.

"Then you've just given him an alibi."

"He must have changed the pills before."

"When?"

There was no answer. Tommy looked at each of us in turn and then back to the corner where the knife lay. "Are you going to turn me in?"

"No," I said and was surprised to find I meant it. "But tell me, Tommy, were you still watching Leila's house after the night we met you there?" I could only hope that he'd continued his surveillance and could tell us something he'd kept from the police when he decided to hide instead of talking to them.

"I never went back," he said; but he looked away from us, and I was almost sure he was lying.

I turned to Quentin. "Wouldn't it be better for Tommy to turn himself in? If the police find him here, he'll really look guilty."

"And you'll be an accessory," Denise added.

"The boy and I've discussed this over and over. I misjudged him once, and I'm not making the same mistake again."

"Misjudged him?" I asked.

"You know," Tommy said. "The baby."

"He's okay here, and he'll stay until the cops find the real murderer. I know he's innocent."

"The only way you could be sure is if you did it yourself," Denise said.

I glanced nervously at the knife in the corner of the room. Quentin noticed and smiled for the first time. "Don't worry. I'm not a mass murderer. And besides..."

Whatever he intended to say was cut off by the doorbell. Tommy immediately turned and disappeared toward the back of the condo, while Quentin moved the drapes slightly and peered out. "Jeremy and Lupe," he said and went to let them in.

"Why's it so stifling in here, Quent?" I heard Jeremy say as he walked into the living room.

"You know why I have to keep everything closed up."

"No one's going to look for..." Jeremy stopped in midsentence as soon as he saw Denise and me.

So Jeremy knew where the boy was and hadn't told Detective Moreway either. I wondered if we could all be considered accessories to a crime even if Tommy really was innocent.

"It's okay," Quentin said. "They know."

"What's the use of hiding him if you're going to tell everyone?"

"Look, Jeremy, don't pull the big brother act. I know what I'm doing."

"Why do you think we came over? To talk you out of this harebrained stunt you're pulling."

While they argued, Lupe sat down next to Denise and me. She looked much better than she had on Thursday, with more color in her face and a calmer expression in her eyes. "Did you learn anything from Nick?" she asked.

We told her about our talk with him and also our visit to Faith Sommers. By this time, the others were listening to us. Jeremy started pacing the length of the narrow room. "Unfortunately, you've come up empty," he said.

"Have you any ideas?"

"My advice is for Tommy to give himself up. Right now, the police are wasting time looking for him when they could be searching for the real murderer."

Tommy had reappeared, and we all turned toward him. I could see how frightened he was at the idea of turning himself in, but I couldn't interpret whether it came from guilt or innocence.

"How can you say that after what they did to you?" he asked.

"Listen kid," Jeremy said. "I don't know what you expected, but they didn't beat me or torture me or do anything other than question me over and over again. I guess they were trying to trip me up. Maybe get me to change my story."

"But you didn't run away."

"That's why turning yourself in is the best thing to do. Otherwise, when they find you—and you can't hide here indefinitely—it will look far worse."

We all waited for Tommy's response, but he was silent. Finally, he said, "I have to think about it."

"Okay, kid, but don't take long to decide. The more people who know where you are, the sooner the word will get out."

I wanted to assure them that we wouldn't say anything but thought better of it. Maybe it would be smarter for Tommy to go to the police. And if he was hiding something, they could discover it more easily than we could. So far today, while we'd picked up bits of information, the solution to the murders was still tantalizingly out of our reach.

"Jeremy," I said, "and Lupe, too. According to Faith Sommers, you were both at Virginia's house at the crucial time."

"Now just wait a minute," Jeremy said.

"I'm not accusing you. But I've been asking everyone who was there to think back, to recall if they saw anything unusual that night."

"That woman was leaving just as we arrived," Lupe said. "Don't you remember, Jeremy."

"What woman?"

"The one we always see on television talking about abortions. She was wearing a cerise silk pantsuit and long pearl earrings."

"You expect me to remember what a stranger was wearing that night. I don't even know what you were wearing."

"That's not the point," I told them. "But what you just said matches Faith Sommers' story, and that is important."

Lupe smiled at Jeremy, and he put his arm around her. For a moment, I wondered whether one of them would kill to protect the other. "Who else was there?" I asked.

They had nothing to add to the facts we'd already gathered even though they'd stayed on for some time talking to Virginia and Leila. I was convinced if I could only find the right questions, we'd be able to discover who'd had the opportunity to change Amy's medication.

"What room were you in, and where was Nick while you three women were together?" I asked Lupe.

"I don't know." She turned to her husband, "Was Nick with you?"

"He was with both of us," Tommy said.

It seemed as if he had given an alibi to Jeremy now, too. And since the women were together, no one had opportunity. The more I considered it, however, the more I realized anyone could have managed time alone in the room with Amy without the others thinking anything about it. Aside from Nick, that is, since Tommy had shadowed him. Even Quentin, who'd left early, could have made the substitution, especially since fewer people were around when he was there.

In desperation, I asked, "Can't any of you remember if somebody was alone with Amy, even for a few minutes?"

"Listen Ruthie," Jeremy said. "Consider everything that's happened since that night. We need more time to think about it."

"Just try to visualize where people were."

"Maybe we should get someone to hypnotize all of you," Denise said. "That's supposed to help people recall things they didn't even realize they knew, like after a hit-and-run accident. They can describe what a car looked like and..."

"I'd be willing," Lupe said. No one else responded.

It all seemed so futile. We'd talked to most of the people involved, and we had discovered very little. "Right now," I said aloud. "It looks like everyone and no one had opportunity. And let's face it, the two people with the strongest motives were never out of sight of each other."

"Sometimes a negative can be a positive," Denise said.

Before I had a chance to ask what she meant, the doorbell chimed again. "What is this, the State Fair?" Quentin said as he pushed the curtains aside again.

"Be firm," Jeremy told him. "Don't let anyone else in."

"I don't have much choice. It's Virginia."

This is a lucky break, I thought. She's the only person we haven't been able to question about the crucial time period.

Virginia walked into the living room, looked at the littered floor and made a sound that signaled her distaste for the mess. "Aren't you ever going to clean this place up?"

"Some of us aren't so uptight about neatness," Quentin answered her.

This was only the third time I'd seen Virginia, but it was obvious she took considerable care with her appearance. Although Denise was well-coordinated in a trendy way, and I always strived to look professional on work days, Virginia's style seemed rather formal for the casual chic that was the norm in Scottsdale. And despite the uncomfortable warmth in the condo, she kept on the jacket to the slate gray suit she was wearing.

She must have a wardrobe of crisp white blouses, I thought, for she was wearing still another one today. At first, she didn't seem to notice Tommy; she was so intent on what she had to say to Quentin.

"I came to tell you I think it's disgraceful you allow that worthless man to live in my sister's house. You own the house now, and it's up to you to get rid of him."

"Eric tells me I can't just throw him out. There's all kinds of legal stuff involved."

"Then get another lawyer."

Jeremy joined the argument. "We can't change lawyers. You know Eric's a cousin."

"Much good he did with the other business."

Both Jeremy and Quentin glanced nervously in my direction, and Virginia followed their gaze. I expected her to comment; in fact, I thought she'd be as vehement as she'd been at the demonstration, but she said nothing. She merely continued to look around the room until she noticed Tommy for the first time.

"Don't say it," Quentin told her.

"Maybe you could tell my sister how to think, but no one tells me what to say. Leila would be alive today if she didn't let men run her life."

"So you also believe Nick killed her," I said.

"Or him." She pointed to Tommy, but before anyone had a chance to challenge that statement, she turned to Quentin. "I intend to stay until I get some answers from you. So you may as well find me a chair."

Jeremy and Tommy were both standing, while Lupe, Denise, and I had the sofa. Quentin, who had returned to his recliner, jumped up and went out of the room, coming back with the rickety folding chair Tommy had used the last time we were at Quentin's condo. He opened it carefully and placed it next to Virginia. She brushed off the seat, making sure we all noticed, and sat down.

I decided I wasn't going to lose the opportunity. "We've been trying to place all the people who were at your house the night before Amy died," I said. "So far, no one seems to have been alone in the room with her long enough to have switched her medication."

"You are still trying to deny your responsibility, I see."

"Let's be realistic, Ms. Rowland," I said. "Your sister's murder changed the scenario."

"And whom do you accuse?" she said, sounding like a long-forgotten high school English teacher of mine.

"I'm not accusing anyone. I just feel if we learn everything possible about that night, it will start to make sense. One thing we need to know is when Amy began taking her medications. She came into my pharmacy so late in the day that..."

"You are entitled to do what you want with your time. But I am here to get something settled with my brother-in-law."

"Ex," Quentin said.

"That's exactly the point. You and Leila were never legally divorced, so the house will belong to you."

"Virginia, this isn't the time to discuss the house. We have more important things to consider," Jeremy told her.

"Such as?"

"I agree with Ruthie. We have to reconstruct what happened the night before Amy died." Jeremy stopped for a moment, and I could see he was still having trouble controlling his grief. To me, he seemed of all the family to have taken his niece's death the hardest. *Either that* I thought suddenly, *or he's reacting to his own guilt.*

"Also," he said, "we're trying to get Tommy to turn himself in."

"Let us take the two things in order," Virginia said. "A constant stream of people came to the house that evening. Amy was exhausted, and I made her comfortable on the davenport in my living room." She paused. "All of us were in and out of that room."

"But was anyone alone with her?" Denise asked.

"I cannot be sure. It seemed so obvious to me that the wrong medication came from the pharmacy that I never considered anything else."

"And now?"

"What you say seems logical, unless Leila was killed for an entirely different reason."

"What reason?" Denise persisted.

"My sister did not have much other than her house. She looked at Quentin. "He inherits that and everything in it."

"Maybe she left it to you," Quentin countered.

"I happen to know she did not have a will, so with Amy gone, too, you are the one."

"Are you trying to say I killed two people... my wife and daughter... for a house." He was so indignant that the words tumbled out. "... not even an expensive one... and with a mortgage besides."

"You bought that house before Amy was born. I happen to know the mortgage is nearly paid off."

"If that's what you think of me, why did you come in here urging me to take the house over?"

"I wanted to see your reaction," she said calmly.

We'd all seen his reaction, but now I wondered if his supposed lack of interest in the house was a cover-up. And I remembered, too, the night I'd been here with Jeremy, when Quentin had threatened both Leila and Nick.

"Now let us talk about this young man." She turned to face Tommy, who started fidgeting when she looked at him. "If you are innocent, why are you hiding here?"

Quentin began to explain what he'd already told us, but Virginia interrupted him. "He can speak for himself."

"I dunno. I was afraid Nick would kill me, too."

If we stayed here long enough, I thought hearing the slight change in Tommy's story, I'd suspect everyone all over again, but maybe we'd eventually reach the truth.

"Then the safest place for you is in police hands," Virginia said.

Tommy suddenly looked like a boy whose teacher had threatened to keep him after school. "I guess you're right," he said.

Virginia wasn't through organizing everyone. "You had better go with him," she told Quentin. "The rest of you can clear out. And don't think I'm finished with you, Quentin. I will wait right here until you get back."

Chapter 23.

Virginia Rowland crossed her arms and sat back on the folding chair as if she were in a comfortable armchair, a pose meant to signal that she really intended to wait him out. The rest of us looked from her to Quentin. He said nothing at first, then sighed, and leaned forward to pick up his keys and a baseball cap from under one of the newspaper stacks.

"Okay, everyone," he said. "I guess we may as well do what the lady says."

I felt dazed as Denise and I walked to the front door. Quentin opened it and stood there while everyone filed out. Once outside, he handed the cap to Tommy.

"Here, put this on, so no one recognizes you before we get to the police."

We watched as Tommy and Quentin got into the latter's pickup truck. Lupe and Jeremy had parked their pickup in the driveway, and they left a minute later.

"Do you think one of them is the killer?" Denise asked as we continued on to her car. "I'm more confused than ever," I said, "but let's sit in the car and add what we just learned to those pages we filled out at your house."

Denise stopped walking abruptly. "Did we take them with us?"

"Oh, no," I said.

"Well, don't worry. If you left the lists at my house, we can drive over to work on them there."

"That's not it. I left them in my jacket and it's back there." I nodded in the direction of Quentin's condo. "I really don't want to face that woman again. I'm sure *she* never forgets anything."

"It's no big deal. I'll go with you."

We retraced our steps and pressed the doorbell again. Virginia opened the door in immediate response to the chimes. "Well?" she asked.

"Ruthie needs her jacket."

"And this is the woman who claims she does not make mistakes."

"I don't make professional mistakes," I said.

"I have been straightening up this pigsty," Virginia said. "Not that he will appreciate it."

"Then you found my jacket?"

"I did not get to the living room yet. The kitchen is in worse shape."

She led us out of the dark hallway into the living room, and I saw that she had removed her own jacket and rolled up the sleeves of her blouse to work in the kitchen.

I stared at her arms as she walked ahead of us. They were covered with bruises.

For one wild moment, I thought Nick had assaulted her and then I understood. This was the elusive fact I'd been trying to pin down. If Leila, the younger sister, was taking a preventive regimen of Coumadin because of heart disease in her family... My heart beat crazily as I finished the thought. Of course, Virginia also would be on Coumadin.

What could her motive for murder be? I wondered. Maybe she had to get rid of Leila because Leila knew about the Coumadin, but what possible reason did she have to kill Amy?

Virginia scooped my jacket off the sofa, turned, and handed it to me. I couldn't take my eyes from the black-and-blue marks on her arms in time. And I saw immediately that she was aware of my discovery. We stared at each other. Then in one swift movement, she reached down and picked up the knife Tommy had dropped.

"So, you are quite the knowledgeable pharmacist after all," she said.

I knew Denise was behind me, out of Virginia's reach. "Run, Denise. Get out of the house and call the police."

"Oh, no you don't," Virginia said. "If one of you tries to leave, the other will be dead before she reaches the front door."

"We'll be dead anyhow. Go on, Denise. Don't listen to her."

Denise didn't move and, in a moment, it was too late. Virginia took a few steps to the side to position herself so she could lunge at either of us, and I knew that even though there were two of us, we were no match for a determined woman with a large knife.

"I want you both to walk very slowly to the sofa and sit down."

We searched each other's faces, looking for a way out but realized we had to follow her instructions for now. My mind was darting frantically over the possibilities. Could we both rush forward simultaneously, one grabbing the knife hand and the other holding on to her? How could we coordinate such a move when she was standing only two feet away and could hear any word that passed between us?

I thought of the Mace canister in my handbag. It had saved me from a determined murderer once before but, although my handbag was still on my shoulder, there was no way I could open it and extract the Mace while Virginia Rowland watched us.

She seemed to be deciding what to do next, and I forced myself to appear calm and make her realize she would be caught if she tried to kill us. No, that wasn't the way to go about it. I had to treat all of this as some inexplicable mistake.

I saw Virginia reach for the folding chair she'd occupied before and use one foot to pull it toward herself. Denise started up.

"Get back there," Virginia shouted at her, waving the knife. Denise obeyed.

Even seated, now only a foot or so in front of us, Virginia looked formidable. "Too bad you were so careless to leave your jacket behind. Or was that just an excuse?"

"I don't know what you're talking about," I said. "It was so warm in here, I forgot all about needing the jacket until I got outside."

She stared at me without speaking, and I tried again. "Look, I know you think I was to blame for Amy's death, but let's allow the courts to settle it. You don't really want to harm the wrong person. Besides, Denise had nothing to do with it one way or the other."

"Good try," she said with what sounded like a choked-off laugh. "I saw your face when you noticed these." She used the point of the knife to indicate some of the larger bruises. "Coumadin side effects. You know all about them, but you never saw me with my arms uncovered until now. No one ever does."

"I don't understand," Denise said.

"She doesn't know what you're talking about, Ms. Rowland," I added. "Let her leave."

"You underestimate my intelligence."

"No, I'm sure you're very bright," I said. "I saw how well you organized everyone tonight."

"That was easy. I wanted to give the police every opportunity to question Tommy. And if they let him go, there is always Quentin and his claim to the house." She was still enunciating each word clearly, although I guessed her stress must be nearly as great as my own. How could she kill two more people and get away with it?

As if she knew exactly what I was thinking, she said, "The hard part is arranging your deaths. But I will figure it out."

"We never even suspected you," Denise said. "Every time your name came up, we didn't have a motive for you."

"So now you want to keep me talking. I told you not to underestimate me."

"I should have known it was you. You're the only one who heard me tell Amy to take the purple pills four times a day to stop the bleeding."

"You are right," she said, as if she were a teacher praising her student for giving the correct answer to a difficult problem. "That is exactly when I realized I could exchange those pills for my blood thinner." She waved her knife hand at me in an admonishing gesture. "It was all your fault. You should not say 'purple' when you mean 'lavender.'"

"Not everyone knows what I mean if I say 'lavender' or 'orchid.' So I just use 'purple' as an all-inclusive color," I said and then realized how ridiculous it was to defend myself this way. Virginia's rational tone was so at odds with the absurdity of the words that I had tried to respond logically.

"Then it is your job to educate them."

"I don't want to argue with you, Ms. Rowland."

"Then be quiet."

"Sooner or later, the police will figure out you take Coumadin," Denise said.

Virginia made that choked-off substitute for a laugh again. "The police will never even think to check on that. They are not familiar with drugs like your friend here. Legal drugs, that is."

"For your information," Denise told her, "Ruthie's very good friend, who's also a pharmacist, is checking on Coumadin prescriptions. He'll catch on and tell the police."

"Denise," I said, horrified at the idea that Virginia would go after Michael next.

"Don't worry, Ruthie. She doesn't know who he is or where to find him."

I understood what Denise was trying to do, but I could see it wouldn't work. We were an immediate threat, whereas Michael, and she couldn't be sure he really existed, was a far-fetched supposition. Since Virginia wanted quiet so she could plan, we had to keep her talking.

"What I can't understand is why you killed Amy. Everyone said she was like a daughter to you."

Her face softened into blurry lines, but the knife never wavered. "That's why," she said. "She killed my grandchild."

I gasped. "But you went with her. You helped her."

"I never helped," Virginia shouted. "Yes, I went with her to that place. Until the last minute, I thought I could change her mind."

"You thought it was Tommy's baby, didn't you?"

"What difference does it make? It was Amy's too. I would have treasured it."

Despite the terror of our situation, I thought of my own mother singing that her jewels were her children, and I pitied Virginia. All three of us were childless, I reminded myself, but that wasn't a license to kill.

"And Leila?" Denise asked.

"When I found out about Nick and Amy, I confronted her. I should have waited until I was calmer to talk to her."

"She guessed?"

"I argued with her. If she had been a good mother, none of this would have happened."

"You can't know that," I said.

"When Amy lived under my roof, I took good care of her."

Until you killed her, I thought, but didn't allow the words to escape. I started thinking again about ways for us to free ourselves. She was only one person and we were two. Surely, even though I knew rage would give her additional strength, we could overpower her. I looked carefully at the knife, trying not to give myself away. It was a heavy-duty meat knife with at least a six-inch blade. If I did try to take it away, she could plunge it into me before I succeeded. I decided to see how she planned to dispose of us first. Maybe if she took us somewhere by car, we could get away more easily. She'd have to let one of us drive and wouldn't dare knife that one or the car would go out of control.

Although I wanted to keep her talking, my throat had dried, and I felt that I couldn't get more words out. I would give her a chance to think, to realize we had to leave the house.

Her eyes moved from Denise to me, but they weren't quite focused. I knew, however, that as soon as one of us made a move, she'd be on us with the knife. When she finally spoke, I nearly gave up hope.

"You two will be victims of a fire," she said. "When I finish burning this place down, no one will know how you died."

I conquered my fear enough to speak. "They can tell," I assured her. "And they'll know you stayed on here."

"Ah, but I will be the only one left to tell what happened. And I can assure you, I will have a solid story ready."

Chapter 24.

Her intention to dispose of us right here in Quentin's condo meant I'd have to figure out another escape plan. I stared at Virginia, trying to gauge whether she would kill us first or depend on the fire. The horror of being burned alive engulfed my mind so that I couldn't think of anything else. Then I realized if she were not too far gone, if she had any sense of self-preservation left, she couldn't trust that the fire would burn long enough to be fatal.

"You're crazy." Denise hurled the words at Virginia as if she were firing them from a weapon. I knew it was the wrong thing to say, but there was no way to stop her. Now, I was sure Virginia would lose control and kill us at once.

"Too bad you will not be around to see how far I am from craziness," she said.

It seemed impossible that such a cold, calculating woman could have killed because she wanted to be a surrogate grandmother. I thought of something else to try. "If you let us go, you can say Amy's death was an accident."

"Go ahead, talk," Virginia said. "We have plenty of time. It will take the others hours to make their statements to the police." She now sat so far back on the folding chair, I prayed she would overbalance. "Besides," she continued, "the later it is, the less likely anyone will notice the fire and interfere."

"You had no way of knowing the blood thinner would cause a fatal hemorrhage."

"Well done, madam pharmacist."

I could see she was toying with us now, enjoying her power and not wanting to cut short her triumph over us. "You can still claim it was an accident."

"Perhaps I could. But then again, they will ask why I did not get medical care for Amy before it was too late."

"I'm sure you could come up with a good reason. Maybe you were out of the house when her condition became critical."

"Maybe I was."

I leaned toward her eagerly. "Then let us go. You have a better chance that way."

"But you forget my dear sister."

I hadn't forgotten Leila at all, but I'd hoped she would—at least long enough to let down her guard. "Wasn't that an accident, too?" I asked, trying to sound guileless.

"Hardly."

"But a good lawyer can..."

"That is not a risk I care to take," she said with finality.

Think, I told myself. If she's going to start a strong enough blaze, she's got to use something like gasoline or lighter fluid. She won't be able to sit here and hold that knife pointed at us. When her preparations force her to divide her attention, that will be the time to break away.

I realized almost immediately that I was wrong. She would kill us beforehand; she couldn't watch us and start the fire at the same time. We would have to save ourselves very quickly or it would all be over. Only her need to wait for the neighborhood to settle down was keeping us alive.

I glanced sideways at Denise, wondering if she also was trying to devise a way for us to escape. She was pale, but only her eyes, blinking unusually fast, betrayed her nervousness.

"How will you explain the fire?" Denise asked.

"Are you worried for my sake or for your own?"

"Curious."

"I changed my mind, if you must know."

Hope leaped into my heart even though I knew she couldn't let us go. "What did you decide?" I asked.

"Does it really matter to you? You will both be just as dead."

I found I had to clear my throat again before I could speak. "What are you going to do with us?"

"This is an older complex. Lucky for me, unlucky for you—the kitchen is not an all-electric one."

She was playing with us again, still savoring her power. I could picture her at work, running the office with petty restrictions and needless paperwork to control the secretaries. I shivered involuntarily, because I suddenly could see the way her mind was working.

"An explosion," she said.

"What about you?"

"Concerned about me? How touching."

"Curious," Denise said again.

"I will escape miraculously."

Although I knew her plan was absurd, that the police would be able to reconstruct what happened, it was no consolation. She'd be caught, but we'd be dead. Again, I tried to find a way to escape.

I had an idea, but the timing would be critical. I wasn't sure I could pull it off. After all, I was fifty-five years old. My reflexes weren't what they used to be. But then again, she wasn't that young either, and I was the more desperate of the two of us.

Virginia was still talking, describing how she would kill us first and then take her time setting up the explosion. "Everything is just right for me. The range is gas-powered, and the back door to this condo is in the kitchen. I can let the place fill with gas and toss a match in from the doorway."

"You'll kill yourself, too," I said.

She gave that harsh laugh again. "No need to worry about me. I know how to take care of myself."

She was sitting close, so she could keep both of us in full view. I did notice, though, that she turned her head slightly toward whichever one of us was speaking. *The next time Denise talks to her*, I told myself, *I'll try. We have nothing to lose.*

I flexed my right foot carefully and waited, mentally practicing the maneuver I planned. No one spoke.

Come on, Denise, I prayed silently. Ask her a question. But Denise was quiet. I would have to make it happen. "What do you think, Denise?" I asked. "Will anyone believe in two accidental deaths?"

Virginia was furious. "I do not care what you think," she yelled, leaning forward and waving the knife.

"And what about the police?" Denise asked.

All my senses shouted to do it now, and I threw my jacket at Virginia. At the same time, I quickly stretched my right leg out and hooked it around the bottom rung of the folding chair, forcing it to fall over. I expected the chair to collapse and throw Virginia forward, but I hadn't figured it out right. She and the chair went over backwards.

I didn't wait to hear the knife drop but assumed she still held it. As she fell, I grabbed one of the sofa cushions and threw it over her. She was struggling violently and, for a moment, I was afraid I hadn't succeeded; but Denise followed my lead. We now had two heavy cushions shielding us from the knife. I quickly placed one foot squarely on Virginia's upper right arm, so she couldn't move it. "Call 911," I yelled.

Denise pulled the phone across the room, ready to rush to my side if Virginia tried to dislodge me, but I could tell that the fight had gone out of her. She lay there unmoving, unresisting. I looked down to make sure the fall hadn't killed her.

Only her dark eyes moved. They gazed at me so piteously that I recoiled and nearly walked away. In my entire life, I'd never knowingly inflicted such continuous and deliberate injury on another person. I knew, though, that I had to keep my full hundred and twenty-five pounds on Virginia Rowland's arm until the police arrived. Otherwise, Denise and I would be endangered again. I'd have to come to terms with myself later.

Denise finished the telephone call and stood by my side. "They wanted me to stay on the line," she said, "but I explained that you might need help."

"It will be all right," I said, and I didn't know if I was reassuring myself or Denise.

"Is she dead?"

"No." And to myself, I added, thank God. As the adrenaline rush that I'd needed to overpower Virginia receded, I wanted only to bury my head in the one remaining sofa cushion and cry.

Chapter 25.

When the police pulled the two cushions off Virginia Rowland, we could see that the knife point had gone clear through the lower one. She was still holding the knife handle so tightly that they had to pry it away from her, but she offered no other resistance.

We told them our story, and then we drove to the Scottsdale Police Department to tell it again before a police stenographer. Although I'd put the jacket to my jogsuit back on, I couldn't seem to stop shivering.

Detective Moreway arrived just as Denise and I finished signing our statements. He looked grim as he read them over. "We would have gotten to Virginia Rowland sooner or later," he said. But I didn't believe him, especially when he quickly called to someone to release the three people he'd been questioning.

I didn't see Quentin, Jeremy, or Tommy because the police kept us a little longer to go over some of the points in our statements again. I wondered what Quentin would think when he found his condo even messier than he'd left it. Then I realized the condo was now a crime scene, and he'd have to find somewhere else to stay. *Maybe he'll room with Nick,* I thought and began to laugh.

"She's hysterical," Frank Moreway said.

"No," I told him and quickly fought to control myself.

"It's better than crying," I said to Denise as we were finally allowed to leave and walked to where she'd parked her car.

"As far as I'm concerned, Ruthie, you can laugh or cry or whatever you want to do. You saved my life."

"We did it together," I said. "You were ready when the moment of truth came."

"That's because I trusted you to act in time."

Both of us were quiet, absorbed in our own thoughts, until we pulled into Denise's driveway. This time, because I wasn't expecting Michael at all, I could see him standing on the lawn between the two houses. He seemed to be waiting for us, and I wondered how he knew what had happened.

"Where did you get to, Ruthie?" he asked. "Your car's been parked here for hours, but I haven't been able to track you down."

Then he must have noticed how bedraggled we both looked and started asking more questions. "Are you okay? What's wrong?"

"Come inside," Denise said. "We can talk there."

I saw Michael glance toward his daughter's house, motioning in the direction of Denise's front door. Almost immediately, Patricia came out and joined us. She was wearing beige slacks again with a long-sleeved tailored blouse in beige and black. I looked down at my jogsuit. The pants were grimy, and the jacket had a long tear where the knife must have caught it. I knew most of my makeup had disappeared, and my hair needed to be brushed away from my eyes.

We all followed Denise into her kitchen. "Coffee?" she asked. "Or do you want something stronger?"

"Decaf, please," I told her. The others said they'd had a late dinner and didn't want anything else, thank you.

"Why were you looking for us?" Denise asked as she measured out the coffee into two cups, added bottled water, and put them in her microwave.

"We found another Coumadin patient." Michael seemed rather pleased with himself. "Someone we never thought about."

"Virginia Rowland," I said.

"You knew?" Now he sounded disappointed.

"I know now."

"We should have realized it sooner," Michael said. "Here we are, two pharmacists, and it never occurred to us that if the younger sister was on the drug, it had almost certainly been prescribed for the older sister as well."

"Don't blame yourself, Michael." Patricia placed her hand on his arm. I noticed the colorless polish on her nails and decided to get a manicure first chance I had.

"It looks like you were thinking more clearly than I was, so no harm done," he said.

Denise and I exchanged a rueful look. "Yes, no harm done," I agreed.

"Now tell us what you've both been up to."

We told them. Patricia was the one who turned pale and gasped. "I would have been completely at sea," she said.

"Not at all," I assured her. "You'd be amazed the way danger crystallizes your thinking."

"Or else paralyzes one," she said.

I didn't tell them how I felt when Virginia, literally underfoot, lay there powerless. It would be a long time before I could talk about that to anyone.

Michael said nothing for a while, but a grave expression I remembered from the day we parted thirty-five years ago deepened his blue eyes and showed lines in his face I hadn't noticed before.

The microwave buzzer sounded. Denise took the coffee cups out and handed one to me. I sipped gratefully. No one spoke, and I wondered why Michael was so quiet. I looked up to find him staring at me.

"Sometimes you're very different than the way I remember you," he said finally.

"I guess I am. It was a long time ago."

"Self-sufficient."

"Most women have changed, Michael. We've had to."

"No, that's not it," he said. "You gave me up then because your family insisted on it. Today I think you'd follow your heart."

I looked at Patricia to see her reaction. She sat between Michael and Denise, looking poised and faintly interested in the conversation. *Why is he bringing this up now*, I asked myself. *I had never even told Denise how and why we'd parted.*

"Twenty-year-old women were different then. We were girls. But you forget. I was more independent than most, or I couldn't have made it through pharmacy college." Trying to defuse the situation, I looked across the table at Patricia. "Pharmacy schools were just about all male in those days," I explained.

"Yes, Michael told me that."

What else had he told her? I felt betrayed.

Denise looked at my face and changed the subject. "At least, they'll have to drop the lawsuit now."

"That must be a great relief," Patricia said.

I knew I should be overjoyed that I could no longer be accused of a deadly error, and I was thankful. Although my personal life hadn't worked out the way I'd hoped, my professional reputation was now secure. It was time to appreciate what I had and hide my other disappointment.

"Let me thank the two of you," I told Patricia and Michael. "You really did help. I never would have suspected Virginia if you hadn't discovered her sister's medical record."

"Yes, but you would have avoided tonight's close call," Patricia said.

I started to protest that it was better this way, but the doorbell interrupted me. Denise went to answer it and returned with Betsy Stokes.

She looked lovely, and I felt a sharp pang because she wasn't my daughter. Her face had rounded with the softened look I often saw in pregnant women. And though I knew that Betsy had been having a difficult time, she seemed serene.

"Hi, everyone," Betsy said and then focused on Patricia.

I watched as Patricia took her hand. "Are you all right, dear?"

"Stop worrying, Mother. I just came over because there's a long distance call for you."

I sat at Denise's kitchen table, trying not to let the others see my stunned expression. It had happened again. I remembered when I first realized Betsy was Michael's daughter. Although I'd never admitted it, even to myself, I had felt overwhelming joy to learn that she wasn't a romantic interest.

This, however, was different. Knowing now that Patricia was Michael's ex-wife offered no relief at all. It was worse to see him involved with her than in a casual relationship. Back with his ex-wife, Betsy's mother, both of them looking forward to their first grandchild—it was too strong a tie to allow any hope for me. And as that realization took hold, I understood myself. Finally, I had to admit how much Michael meant to me.

Betsy remained with us while Patricia left for her call. "It's my stepdad on the phone," she explained to us. "Might as well give them some privacy. That is, if you don't mind my staying here for a while, Denise," she added politely.

We went through the events of the evening all over again for Betsy. By this time I could feel myself starting to fade, and I wanted only to get home and try to get some rest. Despite my better judgment, I had felt a faint glimmer of hope at Betsy's words, but I tamped it down. No way was I going to let myself go through that again.

Betsy was all the audience one could hope for, exclaiming in horror at the appropriate moments. "Dad," she said to Michael. "You're right about Ruthie. She really is someone special." Then she turned to me. "Mother and I think he's like a teenager these days. All he does is talk about you, Ruthie."

—End of Book II—

Book III: Rx Alibi

Ruthie Kantor Morris, R. Ph.
Pharmacy Sleuth Series
created and written by

Renée B. Horowitz

MEDICAL CENTER

NAME _____ AGE _____
ADDRESS _____ DATE _____

℞

3
Rx Alibi

℄LABEL   SIGNATURE
REFILL 0 1 2 3 4 5 PRN NR

Dedication

For Arthur, once again

Acknowledgments

I would like to thank the following people who patiently answered my questions:

Charlene Law, R.N.; Diane Sullivan; Cecil Emmel; Melissa (Missy) Urlaub; Rich Schooler, M.D.; Detective Kim Pound, Criminal Investigation Division, Salt River Pima-Maricopa Community; Bill Dimpfel, physical therapist; Jim Beeby, physical therapist; and also the staff at Canine Companions for Independence (CCI), Santa Rosa, California for the fascinating demonstrations of what companion dogs can accomplish.

Author's Note

To the best of my knowledge, there is no supermarket chain called Food Go. Many drugs that required prescriptions at the time of this novel (such as Naproxen, Naprosyn, and Benadryl) no longer require prescriptions but now can be bought "over the counter." Others may have been discontinued. Such changes in status are a pharmaceutical constant and may affect other drugs before you read my Rx series. Some of the restaurants and a department store mentioned in *Rx Alibi,* as well, are no longer in existence in Scottsdale.

Chapter 1.

I took little notice of Andrea Felder's murder; but had the news reports mentioned her ex-husband's name, I would have paid attention. My friend Denise Seaford was the one who enlightened me about the victim's identity.

When Denise appeared at the prescription pick-up window, my pharmacy in the Food Go supermarket was busy. I'd just filled a script for naproxen, an anti-inflammatory drug, and was counseling the patient, a thin man in his early twenties. "This is for your sore elbow, Mr. Welles," I told him. "Be sure to take it with food or milk so it doesn't bother your stomach." I handed the prescription to him. "And if you need something for headache or pain, Tylenol would be safest while you're on this medication."

"Thanks for cluing me in about the generic," he said before he walked away. "I really appreciate the savings."

His doctor had authorized Naprosyn, the brand name drug, but had signed on the "substitution permissible" side of the prescription form, meaning the patient could request a generic. I knew my customer was still paying off his student loans, so I'd mentioned the less expensive generic equivalent.

Looking down now at the badge pinned to my white jacket, "Ruth Kantor Morris, Pharmacy Manager," I felt more like a professional than I did when simply counting out pills. Then again, I reminded myself, I'd studied many years to learn which pills and how they should be used. And, of course, those early years were difficult because I'd become a registered pharmacist at a time when few women entered the profession.

I noticed that Denise could hardly wait for my customer to leave before she began to speak. "Ruthie, something terrible has happened."

Accustomed to her flair for melodrama, I wasn't too worried by Denise's words. As always, her clothes today reflected that dramatic streak: a black and white geometric print dress and, pinned to one shoulder, a scarf in several shades of green. Matching eyeshadow lent a greenish tint to her gray eyes, and dangling earrings repeated the various greens of the scarf.

Denise worked in the Food Go coffee shop where the waitresses wore bright green aprons. Although I couldn't see her apron from where I stood behind the pharmacy counter, I had no doubt it also matched the scarf. I smiled to myself. Then I looked more closely at Denise and realized how agitated she seemed.

"Is something wrong?"

"Ruthie, didn't you hear about the murder?"

"Which one?" Even in Scottsdale, murder is no longer a singular occurrence.

"Sterling's wife, of course." She hesitated for a moment. "I mean ex-wife."

"I didn't see anything about a Harraday murder. Come to think of it, didn't his ex remarry?" I asked. "The name would be different."

"She's always used her maiden name. Andrea Felder."

"Felder! But that's the name of the man you help care for."

Denise had recently taken on this second job as part-time caregiver for Sterling Harraday's former father-in-law. I'd wondered at the time whether it would work out, but I knew she was determined to save money for training as a dental hygienist.

Suddenly, with the news about Sterling's ex-wife, I felt apprehensive for Denise without quite knowing the reason. Despite her obvious interest in Sterling, she'd never mentioned Andrea Felder. Sterling himself, however, had once talked to me about his former wife, telling me that the divorce was her idea and that she'd remarried immediately afterwards.

"Where was Andrea Felder murdered?" I asked now.

"I'm not sure, but I have a terrible feeling it happened where I work—at her father's home."

"Why? Did you see her there?"

"No, not yesterday—that's when they found her. But I did work there the same morning before my shift in the coffee shop. Amos—that's Mr. Felder—told me not to prepare lunch. He said his daughter would be taking him out to eat."

"Who else would have been there?" I asked. "Someone must have cared for him when you weren't available."

"Excuse me." The speaker was a heavy-set woman with two chubby children in tow. "This is all very interesting, but I need my medicine."

I apologized and took care of the customer while Denise waited. The flow of people continued, making it impossible for us to talk. "I'll come to the coffee shop as soon as my shift is over," I told her, and we both returned to work.

When Louise Rettenberg, my staff pharmacist arrived, I was nearly caught up. "I'll get the window," she said. "Or would you rather I worked at the computer?"

I still marvel at the way Louise has changed over the past few months. For a time, she'd been barely civil, convinced that her new pharmacy degree made her more knowledgeable than an oldtimer like me. She now was tacitly atoning for her previous lack of confidence in me, especially for her belief that I'd made a deadly mistake. She had seemed so cynical and aloof at one time, but I'd come to realize most of that was a pose to hide her own want of assurance in this, her first full-time pharmacy position.

"The window is fine," I said. She tossed her long dark braid over one shoulder and went to help an elderly woman who'd just walked up to the pharmacy.

We worked together until it was time for me to hang up my white lab jacket and leave. It was early March and, in Scottsdale, that means cool mornings and warm afternoons. I was wearing my navy print, a short-sleeved silk dress, and looked down to check whether it had become too wrinkled during my workday. *Not bad*, I thought. *That's one advantage to a job where I must stand, even at the computer.* I decided to leave my sweater on the coat rack. Tomorrow, I'd be on the late shift and wouldn't need it until it was time to go home.

Denise was busy at the other end of the coffee shop when I took my usual seat at a corner table. I smiled to see that her green apron did pick up one of the scarf colors. The smile faded, however, as I thought about the murder. I remembered how happy Denise had been when she announced her plans to work for Amos Felder. It was at her New Year's Eve party, only a couple of months ago.

"I'm planning a small gathering," she'd said by way of invitation. "Bring Michael if he can come up from Tucson."

Michael Loring and I had been in love many years ago when we were both pharmacy students at the University of Arizona in Tucson, but we'd lost track of each other after I made it clear that I couldn't marry a non-Jew. Meanwhile, Michael had married and divorced. My own marriage to Bob Morris, a happy one, had left me widowed more than two years ago.

When Michael's son-in-law was murdered last summer, Michael and I were thrown together again. At first, I'd tried to hide my reawakened feelings for him from Denise and especially from myself. It was now understood, though, that his frequent drives from Tucson to Scottsdale were to see me as well as the daughter who lived next door to Denise and was expecting her first child.

Michael did join us on New Year's Eve and so did Sterling Harraday, the attorney I'd hired after being accused of a fatal prescription error. "I'm finally going to earn enough money to train as a dental hygienist," Denise had told us that night.

"Doesn't the new job require nursing experience?" I'd asked after hearing the details.

Sterling Harraday had shifted his horn-rimmed glasses closer to his eyes. "That's no problem," he'd said in his slightly pompous way. "You see, I suggested Denise. The patient is my former father-in-law. He's wheelchair-bound."

These reflections evaporated now as Denise appeared at my table in the coffee shop. "I'll get your food and then take a coffee break," she told me. "Do you want the usual?"

I'd had no chance for lunch and suddenly realized how hungry I was. The usual, a tuna salad sandwich and iced tea, arrived quickly along with a mug of coffee for herself. Denise removed the green apron, to signify she was off-duty, and placed it on the back of her chair. "Where were we?" she asked.

"You were about to tell me who looks after Mr. Felder when you're not there."

"A nurse's aide and another caregiver divide the time. Also, he has one of those dog companions." She smiled as if remembering something humorous. "You'd have to see that dog in action to believe it. He even turns lights on and off for Amos."

"What about Andrea? How often was she around?"

"Andrea is—was—very good about being there whenever he needed her."

"Did she know about you and Sterling?"

"Could be. We never talked about him, but I think so." She was looking at the coffee mug in her hand and not at me. I knew she wasn't telling me the whole story.

"Denise, unless the police solve this right away, they'll surely question you."

"You don't have to look at me that way. I didn't kill her."

"I know that."

She got up quickly and went to refill our beverages. I thought about Denise's reaction. It wasn't like her to be so defensive and, yet, I meant what I said. Last summer, I'd briefly suspected Denise of murder. Two things had happened since then to keep me from doubting her again. We'd been through so much together that I felt I knew her better as a person and, after having been unjustly accused myself, I was now less likely to jump to conclusions about other people.

"What do you know about Andrea?" I asked when Denise returned to the table. She held the iced tea pitcher in one hand and the coffee pot in the other, carefully filling first my glass and then her mug. Without answering, she moved away to replace pitcher and coffee pot.

"Okay," I said as she sat down again. "If I'm being too nosy, say so, and we'll change the subject."

"That's not it," she insisted. "After all, I'm the one who brought it up in the first place."

"I thought you looked upset; that's why I asked."

"Not for myself. For Sterling."

"Denise! You don't seriously think he..."

"It's just that they've been quarreling lately. I'm afraid it will look bad for him when that gets out."

"But their divorce was old news. Hadn't things settled down?" I thought about it. Sterling, as the victim's ex-husband, would surely be a prime suspect; but Andrea's current husband seemed a likelier one. Didn't the police always look at the surviving spouse first?

"The divorce was a bitter one," Denise said. "She was having an affair with this guy, the one she married right afterwards. Sterling trusted her; he didn't have any idea what was going on."

"And since the divorce? Doesn't he have the children every weekend?" I knew that Denise had met Sterling's son and daughter but not how much they saw of each other.

"They're terrific kids," she said. "But the divorce was tough for them."

"Denise, something is wrong with this picture. Sterling's kids surely visit their grandfather, and they know you've been seeing their father..."

"Okay. I'll tell you." This time she didn't try to avoid my eyes. "We had words."

"You argued with Andrea?"

"She wanted her dad to fire me. When he refused, she tried to get me to quit."

"Because of Sterling?"

"Naturally."

"Why should Andrea care...have cared? If the divorce was her idea and she married again, why should she interfere with you and Sterling?"

Denise sighed, another unusual reaction from her. She looked toward the coffee pot on the counter and started to stand up. I put out my hand to stop her. "No more excuses," I said. "Just tell me about it or tell me it's none of my business."

"I want you to know. Maybe you can help me figure out what's happening." She was silent for a moment but made no further attempt to leave the table. "Andrea didn't object to the fact that Sterling was dating. She objected to *me*."

"To you? What could she have against you?"

Denise reached behind her and pulled the green apron forward, thrusting it toward me. I could see the effort it cost her to continue. "You always wondered why I'm so set on becoming a dental hygienist. Well, I'm tired of being labeled 'waitress.' It's okay for people working their way through school. Or professionals who work at upscale restaurants." She crumpled the apron into a ball. "But a woman of my age, working in a coffee shop, tells people that's all she can do."

"That's sheer ignorance. Why should it matter to other people if you're doing an honest job and doing it well?"

"You're different, Ruthie. You look at me as a person, but others only see this." She took the balled-up apron and flung it on the table between us.

I had known that Denise viewed her occupation as a dead-end job, but she'd never spoken so strongly before. For the first time, I understood the desperation that drove her first to try borrowing money and then to save for more schooling.

"What exactly did Andrea say?" I asked quietly.

"That if Sterling was going to expose her children to other women, she wanted them to be people they could look up to."

"She sounds like someone who could incite murder."

"Just self-centered."

"What I mean," I told her, "is other people were probably on the receiving end, too. Maybe where she worked, where she lived... It's unlikely you were the only target for such cruelty."

"But Sterling and I were the ones with opportunity."

"Sometimes, you can be your own worst enemy," I told Denise.

"Just trying to be realistic."

"What about her father?"

"He can't get out of his wheelchair unaided," Denise said.

"Well, there's sure to be others that we don't know about." I started to ask Denise whether she'd ever met Andrea's second husband but was interrupted by the store manager's voice on the Food Go loudspeaker system.

"Ruth Morris, please return to the pharmacy. Ruth Morris, you are wanted in the pharmacy."

Chapter 2.

Although this wasn't an unusual occurrence, I was surprised to be paged after I had finished for the day. I paid for my food, told Denise I'd see her later, and hurried to the pharmacy. My first thought, that Louise needed more information about some prescription that had been called in during my own shift, was far from the reality I discovered upon walking back into the pharmacy.

Louise—solid, dependable Louise—was standing in front of the drug-filled shelves. To any customer waiting at the window, she would appear to be searching for some medication, ready to fill a prescription. When I got closer, though, I saw the tears running down her face and heard the gasps as she tried to control herself.

"What's wrong? Are you sick?"

"Thank God you're still in the store," she said, swallowing hard with the effort to stop crying. "I called the front office to page you because I have to leave."

"Now?" I knew the question was foolish, but her words were so unexpected, I didn't know how to react—and I'd just finished an eight-hour shift on my feet, with no breaks at all.

"I know it's a lot to ask, but I need you to take over."

"Are you sick?" I repeated.

"Something happened. I can't talk about it now, but I must go home."

"Okay. I'll stay."

Louise pulled off her white jacket and ran out of the pharmacy. I stared after her, wondering what could have happened. Over the years, emergencies have arisen. Pharmacists or their children have become ill. And during Bob's last illness, I'd been called to the hospital several times before I took a leave of absence to be with him all the time.

There was no opportunity to speculate. I looked at the counter and at the computer screen trying to figure out just where Louise had been in her work. A patient record showed on the screen, and a script was lying next to the computer. The printer showed no evidence of typed labels, so I checked the screen more closely and continued keyboarding data where

Louise had obviously left off. I took care of that patient and one other before the phone started ringing.

"Food Go Pharmacy. May I help you?"

An angry male voice cut in roughly. "I told you to get over here, Louise, and I mean it. I'll give you fifteen minutes, and then I'm coming after you."

"Louise has left for the day," I said as calmly as I could. "Is there something I can help you with?"

"Good. I guess she knows I mean business this time." He broke the connection.

I continued working in the pharmacy, thankful I'd had time to sit down and eat before Louise had called me back to work. Knowing we have no scheduled lunch hour, I usually make sure to fix a big breakfast whenever I'm on the day shift; however, I didn't think breakfast alone could have seen me through from opening to closing. At fifty-five, I'm an active woman in a demanding profession, though even someone half my age would find a 12-hour shift rather daunting. I tried not to think about tiredness and concentrated instead on helping my customers, but I was glad when the time finally came to begin my closing procedure.

First, I had to connect the order machine to the telephone and transmit about 45 items from the order book to the wholesaler. These were drugs we were running low on or were completely out of. Then, I took off my white jacket for the second time that day and was ready to leave. I knew I'd need my sweater now. At this evening hour in early March, the temperature would have dropped considerably.

As I left the store, I wondered for the tenth time about that telephone call for Louise, what had happened to upset her so much, and whether I should contact someone to fill in for her the next day. She was supposed to open the pharmacy, but I decided to arrive early in case she didn't show up. Then, I could call around and find a relief pharmacist to work my own evening shift. If Louise was there in the morning, however, I'd simply leave and come back at my scheduled time.

* * * *

When I returned just before nine o'clock the next morning, I found the pharmacy shutters rolled up and the lights on. I turned around, ready to retreat before Louise caught sight of me, but it was too late. She called to me.

"Ruthie, I want to apologize."

I looked at Louise. Her long hair, always so neatly braided, hung over one shoulder as always; but I could see some ends had escaped the braid, and the effect was less tidy than usual. Her eyes were red and swollen.

"Don't worry about it," I said and added that I hoped everything was okay. Under the circumstances, I thought my words sounded ridiculous, but I couldn't think of anything else to say.

"It's my friend," she said and stopped.

I waited quietly for Louise to continue.

"His background is so different," she said. "He doesn't understand about professionalism."

I was still outside the pharmacy, leaning in at the window to talk to Louise.

Any minute now, customers would start arriving. For the moment, though, it was quiet. "Someone telephoned for you after you left last night," I told her. "He seemed upset."

"Oh, no!" Then in a calmer voice, she continued. "What did he say? I mean, I hope he... he wasn't nasty to you."

"No. Until I spoke, he thought I was you."

Louise looked so anxious that I repeated the conversation. She relaxed somewhat. "It's just that..." Her pause was longer this time. "It's just that he needed me at home."

"You don't have to explain," I assured her.

"I'll give back the time, Ruthie. Whenever you need an extra night off, just let me know. Or a morning off." Her words came out in staccato fashion. "Yes," she said, half to herself. "A morning would be better."

Louise wasn't married, but I hadn't heard about her friend before. And even though her personal life had affected me last night, it really wasn't any of my business. I tried to rein in my curiosity and make light of the whole thing.

"Okay, you owe me. I'll take you up on it and sleep late one of these mornings."

"I appreciate it," she mumbled as I stepped aside to make room for the first customer of the day.

As long as Louise was here and I didn't have to be in the pharmacy before late afternoon, I decided to head over to the Fashion Square mall and add to my spring wardrobe. Shopping for clothes had once been a pleasant distraction, but I no longer enjoyed it. Somewhere along the way, the styles had left me behind. I didn't think of myself as old, and I didn't want to dress that way. On the other hand, I wasn't about to buy the short-skirted outfits that were fashionable now. Dresses with longer hemlines seemed to feature long slits, which didn't appeal to me either. The alternative, pant suits, were all right for colder days, but we didn't have so many of those at the lower altitudes of Arizona.

I parked at the east end of the mall, walked into Robinson's-May, and took the escalator to the second floor. My dress-buying strategy these days was to look toward the bottom of the racks and pull out only the styles that seemed long enough for my taste, so I wasn't at all aware of other shoppers until someone spoke to me.

"Now why didn't I think of that," an older, rather thin woman said. "You can eliminate all the short dresses right away, can't you?"

I looked up and smiled at her. Then, I continued searching the clothes racks.

"You don't remember me, do you?"

That question always stymies me. I meet so many people at the pharmacy that I can't always recall who they are when I run into them elsewhere. The same thing happens in reverse. Customers realize they know me but aren't sure who I am when they see me without my white professional jacket. I hesitated.

"I'm Verna Branden. My husband and I are the block watchers in Betsy Stokes's neighborhood."

I knew her now. The Brandens had been very helpful last summer after the death of Betsy's husband, Harry Stokes. I'd never figured out whether their help resulted from neighborliness or nosiness.

"Yes, of course, Mrs. Branden," I said. "Denise Seaford introduced us."

"Call me Verna," she said and added immediately, "We haven't seen Denise in a long time. I can tell you she never seems to be home these days."

I wasn't sure if Verna knew about Denise's second job, and I didn't want to gossip with her. "Well, she's probably busy like everyone else."

The woman looked pointedly at me. "I thought you were a pharmacist at Food Go. Are you retired now?"

This is another question I've become accustomed to hear. Since I alternate between morning and evening shifts and varying days off, some customers question why I'm never there. When I think of the others who ask, "Don't you ever go home?" I can only laugh.

"Not yet retired," I told Verna and smiled again. "My working shifts keep changing."

"That's what Denise always tells me. But now she's gone day and night. I guess she's with that new boyfriend, the lawyer."

She waited, obviously expecting me to fill her in. I wondered if it was better to let her think Denise spent all her spare time with Sterling or to tell her about the second job. I hesitated.

"Don't get me wrong. We're happy for her."

"So am I," I finally ventured, figuring that was noncommittal enough.

"Yes," she continued. "The lawyer seems nice enough. It's the other fellow who worries me."

"Other fellow?" I asked before I caught myself.

She looked triumphant. "He's real handsome, tall and dark, but he's got that sleek look I don't trust."

I couldn't connect anyone to the description but tried to sound casual. "Did Denise introduce him to you?"

"Well, no, but we get around the neighborhood a lot. Being block watchers, you know. Raymond and I take it seriously. And, if I do say so myself, since we volunteered, there aren't so many burglaries." She took a step nearer to me and, although I didn't see any other shoppers near us, whispered, "We keep our eyes open."

"I'm sure you do."

"When we saw that fellow pull into Denise's driveway a few months ago, we waited. Not too obviously, you understand. Just like we were taking an evening stroll." She edged even closer. "Of course, when Denise opened the door and threw her arms around him, I can tell you we walked on."

"Of course," I echoed. I started to look at the dress on a lifelike model near us, half hoping Verna would go about her own business and half ashamed because I wanted to know more.

"He's been there in the daytime, too."

"Must be a relative," I said.

She made a soft huffing sound. "I met all of them. And it wasn't her ex either."

"Why don't you just ask Denise about him?"

"People can be funny," she said. "Sometimes they don't understand that we have to size up strangers in the neighborhood."

I'll bet, I thought. On the plus side, I knew the Brandens really were performing an important community service. Although I had nothing to hide, I also knew I wouldn't want my own comings and goings so closely observed, and I felt it was an invasion of Denise's privacy to discuss her in this way. Nevertheless, I couldn't help wondering who the man was. Not a salesperson if Verna really had seen Denise embrace him. I stood there lost in thought, trying to figure out why Verna didn't trust him.

As if she'd read my mind, Verna Branden asked, "You want to know why I don't trust him?" I pretended to read the price tag on the display dress. She didn't wait for an answer.

"That sleekness," she said. "That's how they look on television when they're up to no good."

I nearly laughed aloud in relief. If that was all Verna had against this new man in Denise's life, I wouldn't worry. When Denise was ready to confide in me, she would tell me about him the way she'd told me about Sterling. Tall, dark, and sleek didn't necessarily spell "villain" in my dictionary.

Chapter 3.

After a few minutes of conversation about the weather, I made my escape from Verna Branden. I spent another hour at Fashion Square, desultorily examining dresses in a few of the specialty shops, but without buying. When I passed the mall food court, I decided to stop for lunch, choosing a salad, raisin scone, and herb tea—a nice change from my usual Food Go coffee shop routine.

Verna had started a train of thought that I followed from Denise's male friends to the mysterious man whose summons had called away my staff pharmacist last night. I'd begun to feel closer to Louise Rettenberg and wondered if I could do anything to help her. Then there was Andrea Felder's death. Surely, her current husband would be the primary suspect. It was foolish to worry about Denise and Sterling—or Denise and this new man for that matter.

I finished the last crumbs of the scone, stowed my tray, and left the mall. When I reached the front entry to Food Go a little later, I found an elderly customer at my side.

"I'm so glad you're here," she said. "You're the only one I trust to give me my medicine."

I smiled down at her. She was at least a head shorter than I, and I'm only 5 foot, 6 inches tall. "You know any of us would be happy to fill your prescriptions," I assured her.

"Yes, I do know that. But you're always so nice and patient when I don't have the number for refills."

Only when we're not too busy, I thought to myself. Aloud, I reassured her. By that time, we'd reached the pharmacy, and I heard Louise counseling a patient as I walked through the door. "This might make you sleepy," she was saying, "so don't drive for at least three to four hours after taking your muscle relaxant."

"My doctor didn't warn me about that," the customer said. "I don't want anything with side effects." She was a short woman with straight brown hair, dressed in an ankle-length, paisley print dress. "Can't I get some herbal drugs instead?"

I listened, surprised, as Louise talked to the young woman. "You might look for arnica in a health food store," she said. "Many athletes use it for strains and sprains."

"Do they teach herbal medicines in pharmacy school now?" I asked after the customer left.

"Not really. I'm just interested in natural remedies."

"I'd like to learn more about them," I told her. "Even the pharmacy journals are beginning to run articles on homeopathic and other alternative medicines."

Louise looked pleased at the idea of teaching me about natural drugs. I realized that would go a long way toward compensating for the recent blows to her self-confidence. She sounded less brusque and more caring in her patient counseling these days, and I was glad that our professional relationship had also improved. I didn't think it would develop into the kind of friendship Denise and I had. On the other hand, Louise's improved attitude made work more pleasant for both of us.

Louise suddenly spoke as if in answer to my thoughts. "Your friend from the coffee shop was looking for you this morning. You should give her a copy of your schedule so she won't bother me when you're not here."

So much for improved civility, I told myself. Then I realized Denise might have interrupted during a customer rush. Maybe it would be a good idea to exchange schedules with her. I didn't have time to wonder about Denise, though, because the pharmacy remained busy right up until closing.

Denise was waiting when I left the Food Go store. "They questioned me all morning," she said. "It was horrible."

"Let's go to my house and talk," I suggested.

We walked to the far end of the lot where employees were supposed to park and got into our cars. When I pulled into my own driveway, Denise, who always drove faster than I did, was waiting. She followed me into the house and to the kitchen where we usually sat.

"I'm going to brew decaf and make turkey sandwiches. What will you have?"

"Just decaf," Denise said. "I've already eaten, but you go ahead."

I'd roasted a small turkey a few days ago, packaging the leftovers into single portions and freezing them. It was convenient on nights when I arrived home hungry after working the late shift.

My peach and turquoise kitchen was clean and tidy. I filled the coffee percolator and quickly started it perking. Meanwhile, I punctured the plastic wrap on one of the frozen turkey packages and put it into the microwave. Then, I excused myself for a minute to change to slippers from the shoes I'd been standing and walking in all day. When I returned to the kitchen, Denise was staring out the window that overlooked my pool and patio. I hadn't turned on the outside lights and knew she could see nothing in the darkness.

"What's out there?" I asked.

She turned quickly at the sound of my words. "Nothing. I was just thinking."

"Well, sit down and tell me about it."

I added catsup and the turkey to two slices of rye bread and put placemats, napkins, and silverware on the table. The coffee was ready, and I filled cups for both of us.

"How do I get involved in these things?" Denise asked.

"It's not surprising. We both have jobs where we interact with hundreds of people every week. And because we work in Scottsdale, with all the winter visitors and other tourists, all of our customers aren't regulars." As usual after an eight-hour shift in the pharmacy, I was very hungry. Even concern for Denise didn't affect my appetite, and I started on the turkey sandwich immediately.

Denise barely sipped her coffee. Either it was still too hot or she was too preoccupied to drink it. "Andrea Felder wasn't a tourist. And I've never seen her in Food Go."

"You know what I mean."

"I guess I do, but it doesn't make me feel better. They questioned me for hours."

"Detective Moreway?"

"No, someone else. I never caught his name, but he was short and had a dark mustache."

"Maybe you should have asked for Detective Moreway," I said. "At least he couldn't seriously suspect you of murder after you helped catch Amy Brookman's killer."

"New situation this time. There's no doubt Andrea Felder was murdered. And they know I had reason to dislike her."

"Denise, you didn't tell them she wanted you fired?"

"They knew." Her voice was flat, and I wondered if Sterling was the one who'd given that information to the police. *If only he's not using Denise to divert suspicion from himself,* I thought. Although Sterling seemed like a decent type, I knew from experience that I wasn't the best judge of people.

I was never good at hiding feelings either. My face must have revealed my doubts because Denise stared out the window again. "Sterling may have told them; it doesn't matter," she said, but I could tell from her bleak tone that it mattered very much.

"What did the police ask you?"

"About working for Andrea's father. How I got the job and all that."

I waited, knowing there was more, and concentrated on my sandwich. Denise's gaze had turned from the window and was focused on her coffee cup. "They wanted to know all about Sterling and me. Our relationship."

She suddenly looked directly at me. "It's not right," she said. "Last year when they accused me of having an affair with Harry Stokes, of course I was scared. It was so ridiculous, though, I couldn't worry for long."

I remembered that I'd harbored the same suspicions about Denise's complicity in her neighbor's death. Then again, that time, the police had questioned me, too.

"You don't realize how important the Felder job is to me, Ruthie. I've been able to save close to $100 a week since I started working for Amos. But I wouldn't kill to keep the job."

"I know you wouldn't." And though I'd doubted Denise in the past, I had no reservations about her now.

"It's the personal angle. The police think Sterling was going to drop me because of Andrea's interference."

Was he going to drop you, I wanted to ask. Maybe she'd be better off if he did—but I couldn't add to Denise's unhappiness by voicing those thoughts. "You must have an alibi," I said instead. "Weren't you at work when she was killed?"

"They seem to think I had enough time before getting to Food Go or even afterwards, on my break."

"Aren't they sure?"

Denise sighed. "The one who questioned me was cagey. He wouldn't give me details. Only that the murderer used a kitchen knife."

"A kitchen knife! Did someone bring it to Mr. Felder's home?" I asked, knowing he was wheelchair-bound.

"I really get angry when people make those assumptions about Amos," Denise said. "He does know how to cook and, besides, he wasn't always disabled."

"Okay, I'm sorry," I said, realizing I'd been insensitive. I paused. "Did they identify the knife?" I was excited at the idea. "Was it from his own kitchen?"

"No one will say."

"Anyhow, that would let you out."

"Ruthie, I know you're tired, but think! Anyone can get hold of a kitchen knife. And if it did belong to Amos, it would've been easy for me or whoever else was familiar with his kitchen."

"Were you familiar with his kitchen?"

She looked steadily at me. "If you don't trust me, who will?"

"That wasn't meant the way it sounded," I defended myself hastily. I'd wanted only general information about the Felder kitchen to find out who had access to the knives. "I'm just trying to make a point," I added, unsure whether Denise believed me.

"More coffee?" I asked to cover my embarrassment.

"Don't worry about what I just said, Ruthie. I think I'm getting slightly paranoid."

I refilled both our cups although Denise had barely touched her coffee. No matter how I looked at the situation, it seemed loaded with problems for my friend. Even if neither she nor Sterling had anything to do with the murder, suspicion would fall on them until the real killer was discovered—and no one could be certain if that would happen.

"Could you try to find the murderer?" Denise suddenly asked.

"Me?"

"You've done it twice now. Why not talk to Detective Moreway? Offer to help."

"Denise, that only happens in books. The Scottsdale police aren't going to listen to any offers of help from me."

"You won't know until you ask."

There was a long silence while I finished my turkey sandwich and slowly drank my decaf. In many ways, Denise could be quite practical and down-to-earth; but her melodramatic streak, harmless when it affected only clothes and makeup, was potentially dangerous at times like this.

"I'll see Frank Moreway, if you want me to," I said finally. "But don't be disappointed when he refuses to take me into his confidence. It just doesn't work that way."

To avoid further promises, I changed the subject. "I met your neighbor at the mall today."

"Betsy Stokes?"

"Your other neighbor. The block watcher."

"Oh, Verna Branden. I haven't seen much of her lately."

"That's just what she said about you." I wondered whether I should mention the "sleek" visitor Verna had noticed. Curiosity was pulling me, but reluctance to pry held me back. *Another personality trait that would keep me from emulating fictional sleuths*, I thought, and wanted to tell

Denise so; but I'd already promised to speak to Detective Moreway, and I would keep that promise.

"Some of the people on our street think the Brandens became block watchers so they could be in on everyone's doings," Denise said.

"Maybe they just want something to occupy their time."

"Could be."

We were both quiet for a few minutes. Denise started to speak and seemed to change her mind. I watched her lift the coffee cup and put it down again without drinking. She didn't seem aware of her reluctance to speak, but it was so unlike her usual manner, I started to worry.

"Did Verna say anything else about me?" she asked finally.

Now it was my turn to hesitate. "She mentioned a tall, dark, and handsome stranger." I tried to keep my tone light and teasing.

"That's what I was afraid of," Denise said.

I waited for her to continue but she was quiet. "Anyone I know?" I asked in the same light tone.

"Probably not, but I don't want to talk about him now. Some other time."

"No problem," I said.

"He's someone who turns up in my life every now and then. I never know how long he'll be around."

"It's okay, Denise," I assured her.

"The trouble is, he came to see me at Amos Felder's house yesterday. And I don't know whether to tell the police."

Chapter 4.

Now I understood why Denise was so troubled; but when I considered her words, I realized they raised more questions than they answered. Was this man connected to the Felders in some way? Did Denise really suspect him, or was she trying to keep the law away from him for another reason?

"Won't the police hear about it from someone else?"

"I don't think anyone else saw him."

"What about Amos Felder?"

"He was resting. I looked in on him right after Tony left, and I saw that he had dozed off."

"Your friend's car?" I tried to word the question tactfully.

"That could be a problem. He drives a white Corvette. Someone may have noticed it in front of the house."

"But from what you've said, Andrea arrived after you left for Food Go. Why would the police be interested in someone who came to see you earlier?"

"That's why I didn't say anything when they asked me about visitors to the house that day."

Now I wondered again why Denise was protecting this "friend." Was he someone who'd evoke police interest? All sorts of ideas leaped into my mind. Maybe he turned up in Denise's life only "now and then" because he'd been in prison.

I shook my head mentally. That was too far-fetched. And then I remembered reading about all the women who correspond with serial killers and even want to marry them. Not Denise, I told myself firmly.

She suddenly pushed back her chair and stood. "I *will* tell you all about Tony soon; I promise. But right now, I'd better get home. There's too much to think about."

I walked Denise to my front door. "You know I'll do anything I can to help," I told her.

"Just let me know what Detective Moreway says."

After Denise left, I cleared the table and put everything in the dishwasher, thinking all the while about her situation. I wondered if Sterling Harraday knew about Tony.

From Denise, my mind turned to my staff pharmacist, Louise. It seemed odd that the two women I spent most of my time with were both having trouble with the men in their lives. That led to thoughts of Michael, and I was thankful that we now seemed to understand each other. Not too long ago, I'd mistaken his daughter for a romantic interest. After that situation was clarified, I'd met Michael's ex-wife and misunderstood her role, too. I was grateful that my recent doubts about Michael had proved to be without foundation and hoped Denise's and Louise's problems could be solved as easily.

Before I leave for work tomorrow, I told myself, I'll call Frank Moreway. As to Louise, I'll just make sure to be there for her whenever she needs me to fill in. And I can let her know I want to help.

* * * *

Early the next morning, before my misgivings could take hold again, I called the Scottsdale Police and asked for Detective Moreway. He was expected later in the day, so I left a message asking for an appointment and went on to work.

At Food Go, every time the telephone sounded, I expected to hear from Detective Moreway. Between customers, I rehearsed what I would say to him. He was sure to ask why I wanted the appointment. If I gave him the specific reason, I was afraid he'd be unwilling to see me.

My original intention had been to tell him I wanted to talk about the Felder case. The more I considered it, however, the more I realized that wouldn't do. He'd probably ask whether I had new information for him, and any hint that I wanted to play amateur sleuth would be rejected out of hand. I needed to come up with something plausible, but unlike fictional detectives, I couldn't bring myself to lie.

A tap at the pharmacy window turned my attention to another patient. She was tall, with well-shaped dark hair, and wore a raspberry-colored suit that was a standout among the casually dressed Food Go customers. "I don't want you to fill this until you call my doctor," she said, handing me a prescription for tobramycin, an eyedrop.

"What's the problem?" I asked.

"I have an earache."

"Yes," I said. "But I'm wondering why you want me to check with your doctor."

"Can't you see?" Her tone was impatient, and she snatched the script from my hand, pointing to the name of the drug.

My puzzled expression seemed to annoy her. "I've had nurse's training," she said. "And I know tobramycin is an eyedrop."

"Well, yes," I agreed. "But very often, eyedrops are prescribed for earaches."

She was not convinced. "I've never heard that."

"Some antibiotics are available in eyedrop form but not as eardrops. Because the eye-drops are water-based, they can be used in the ear."

"I guess I'll have to accept your explanation."

"Not at all. I'd be happy to call your doctor."

"I can't wait around for her to get back to you. Just fill it," she added ungraciously.

She's probably in pain, I told myself, as I moved over to the computer. Some people do take it out on others when they're not feeling well. At least, she'd distracted me from worrying about what to say to Frank Moreway. Maybe an idea would come to me if I stopped thinking so much about it.

When the Scottsdale detective returned my call about an hour later, though, I still hadn't arrived at a convincing reason to meet with him. His first words dispelled my nervousness.

"I'm glad you telephoned. I want to talk to you."

"You do?" I asked, and mentally kicked myself for sounding surprised.

"About your friend Mrs. Seaford and the latest situation she's involved in."

I hesitated, unable to believe I could keep my promise to Denise so easily. "You want to talk to me about Andrea Felder's murder?"

"Is your friend mixed up in any other murders right now?"

"Denise isn't really involved in this one," I insisted. "She just happens to work for Andrea's father."

"Your friend does have the knack of being in the wrong place. For that matter," he added, "so do you."

With people starting to line up at the pharmacy window again, I couldn't continue to spar with Frank Moreway. I hastily made an appointment to see him at six that evening, which would give me about half an hour after the end of my shift to grab something to eat.

Now, I had to hope Louise wouldn't need me to substitute for her again.

You're not being fair to her, I told myself. *It's only happened once.* Nevertheless, I was relieved to see her arrive for work that afternoon. Together, we swiftly took care of our customers, so I could leave right on time with a clear conscience.

Although the Food Go coffee shop was the ideal place to eat when I wasn't going directly home and hadn't much time to spare, I didn't want to see Denise. It was too soon to tell her I'd be meeting with Detective Moreway. Instead, I decided to stop at the Blue Burrito on Shea Boulevard before continuing to Scottsdale Police Headquarters.

My timing was good enough to get me to Detective Moreway's office at exactly six o'clock. He came out to greet me and lead the way into his office, and his manner seemed friendlier than it had ever been before. Maybe it would be possible to get information from him after all.

"I'm starting to feel like a regular here," I said, attempting an icebreaker.

He unbent enough to smile. *We must be on a different footing indeed*, I thought. Maybe he was starting to view me as a person with specialized knowledge that could help the police. I had to admit, however, that I couldn't see a pharmaceutical connection to anything in Andrea Felder's murder. As far as I knew, she hadn't even been a Food Go customer.

Frank Moreway indicated the same chair at the side of his desk that I'd been offered on my previous visits. This time, though, he didn't hover over me but seated himself behind the desk. I waited for him to begin.

"I don't know how you and your friend do it," he said.

"You must realize that each of us comes in contact with hundreds of people, Denise in the coffee shop and me at the pharmacy. It's not surprising at all that we meet so many different types."

"On the contrary, it's very surprising to me." He shuffled some papers aimlessly—at least, it looked aimless to me.

I decided not to belabor the point. "What did you want to ask me?" I said instead.

"Have you ever met the Felder family? What were your impressions of them?"

"As far as I know, I've only met Andrea's ex-husband, Sterling Harraday. And Denise can tell you more about him," I said and then wanted to bite my tongue. If he didn't know Denise and Sterling were seeing each other, I didn't want to be the one to tell him.

He must have assessed the look on my face. "Don't worry," he said. "We know all about your friend and Mr. Harraday."

"You make it sound like something wrong. Denise and Sterling are both free and old enough to see anyone they choose."

"Of course," was the noncommital reply.

"Did you ask Denise her impressions of the family?"

"I want *your* opinion. Tell me about Mr. Harraday."

"He's an attorney. Quiet, not flashy. Sometimes he sounds stuffy, and I noticed he can jump to conclusions. To be fair, though, he often thinks things over and revises his opinion."

"Reading between the lines, I gather you like him."

"Yes, I guess I do."

"And how long have you known him?"

"Just a few months. I went to Sterling for legal advice when Amy Brookman's family blamed me for her death." A vivid memory of my despair at that time intruded and silenced me for a moment. Sometimes it was hard to believe so much had changed since last October.

"You hadn't been his client before?"

I shook my head. "That was the first time I ever needed an attorney."

"Then how did you decide on Mr. Harraday? Did someone recommend him?"

I'd realized where the questions were headed even before we reached that point but saw no reason to avoid answering them. "Denise suggested I see him."

"They were friends?" His slight emphasis on the last word irritated me.

"He was a customer at the Food Go coffee shop."

"And that was their only relationship?" Again, he made a question of his statement and stressed the last word. I decided it was time to take a stand.

"What is the point of all this? I'm sure you already asked Denise about Sterling Harraday."

"And if two people tell me the same thing independently of each other, don't you think it carries more weight?"

"I'm perfectly willing to answer your questions. Otherwise, I wouldn't be here." I felt myself flush, knowing I had a second motive for being there.

"Fine. Then let's do it my way. You tell me about Mrs. Seaford and Mr. Harraday."

"As far as I know, they only started seeing each other outside of Food Go about the time you wound up the Brookman case. Sterling was horrified to hear how close Denise and I came to being killed, and he discovered he cared for her."

"But they maintain separate homes?"

"Look, Detective Moreway. They're both in their forties, both had previous marriages that ended before they got together, and their relationship is none of *our* business." I deliberately copied his way of emphasizing words, stressing "our" when I really wanted to say "your."

"I'm not asking questions for the fun of it. When a man's wife has been murdered, I need to know about his current relationships."

"Ex-wife," I said. "And you know very well Denise was at work when the murder took place."

"Oh, and how do you know that?"

"Because when Denise left for Food Go, Andrea Felder hadn't arrived at the house."

"And I suppose that information came from your friend?"

"Of course."

"Which automatically means it's true."

"You can forget the sarcasm," I told him. "Tell me when Andrea was killed and I'll check the Food Go time cards for you."

"We've already done that," he said and then looked as if he wished he hadn't revealed the information. I decided it was my turn to ask questions.

"And...?"

"And what?" he asked, which really annoyed me.

"I'm sure you know what I mean. Was Denise working her shift when the murder took place?"

"Ostensibly yes, but that doesn't rule her out."

"You're still playing games with me, Detective Moreway. I know you're familiar with conditions at the Food Go coffee shop. So you can't possibly doubt Denise was there and highly visible once she clocked in."

"That's true. But the same fact also makes her highly visible, to use your words, when she *should* be there and vanishes for a time."

I was surprised. "Are you telling me you checked with her manager and found she wasn't working after all?"

"Your friend took her usual fifteen-minute break that afternoon, but the coffee shop manager says she was gone for a long time—long enough for him to be quite irritated before she finally returned." He paused, his face assuming a serious expression, and added, "I shouldn't be telling you this, but you seem to have a predisposition for trouble. I want you to be careful."

Deliberately trying to downplay my shock, I looked at him calmly. "You can't really believe I'm in any danger from Denise."

"I'm not prejudging her. And I'm certainly not accusing her of anything." He moved a stack of papers from one corner of his desk to the center and back again, not seeming to realize he hadn't changed their location.

"Then what *are* you saying?"

"I'm saying that Mrs. Seaford seems to be involved in some way. Until she levels with us, I can't make any presumptions about guilt or innocence."

I thought about his words, convinced Frank Moreway was using me. Perhaps this information was calculated to send me to Denise in order to discover where she'd been during the crucial time. If that's true, I told myself, I must make him acknowledge his strategy so that I can take advantage of it.

"Detective Moreway," I said, "you know that Denise and I are close friends. If you want me to sound her out, I need more details about the murder."

"Just read the *Arizona Republic* or watch the local news."

Now I was really infuriated. I tried not to grit my teeth as I got the words out. "In that case, why not tell me now."

"All you amateur detectives think we can pinpoint time of death to the minute." His voice had taken on an edge that I didn't care for. "We know only that Andrea Felder probably was killed between three and five o'clock. She had taken her father to lunch; they returned sometime after two. He usually napped in the afternoons, so she helped him from his wheelchair to the bed just before three."

"Did he discover the body?" I asked, thinking how awful it must have been for Mr. Felder.

"No, they have a nurse's aide who comes in at five every afternoon to go through his physical therapy routine, prepare his dinner, bathe him, and get him settled for the night."

"There must have been a struggle. Didn't Mr. Felder hear anything?"

"I'm not at liberty to tell you. And don't give me that reproachful look," he added. "We can't let the information out because we have to keep it from the murderer."

"All right," I conceded. "But some of the neighbors must have noticed what time Denise left the house and whether she returned later on."

"I don't intend to say anything about that either."

"Let's be straightforward about this, Detective Moreway. No matter how unwillingly on your part, we've worked together before. So, tell me exactly what I can do to help."

I noticed his frown, but it was quickly erased. He seemed determined not to acknowledge my help in cornering two previous murderers. "You misunderstand. I don't want you to play detective. Quite the opposite."

"Yes, you have to say that."

This time he moved two file folders to the center of his desk and carefully aligned them. Then he lifted one of the folders and tapped it on the arm of his chair. "I'm trying to be patient, Mrs. Morris."

"So am I."

"Murder is serious business. Trained professionals are working on this case, and we don't need or want amateur involvement."

"Amateurs are involved in every murder," I told him. "Think about it. Victims, murderers, witnesses—they're all amateurs."

"Very nice reasoning. But it doesn't change anything."

"Sarcasm is easy. What's harder is learning all there is to know about the people who may have wanted to kill Andrea Felder."

"And you think you can accomplish that better than the Scottsdale police?"

"No, I'm not claiming I can do that. What I can do is keep an open mind. You're ready to assume Denise is guilty. I know she isn't, so I can look in other directions."

"That's where you're wrong. We can't rule out Mrs. Seaford or her ex-con boyfriend."

Chapter 5.

My stunned expression must have given me away before I could summon the will to control it. "Are you saying that Sterling Harraday is an ex-con?"

"Of course not. If he were, he couldn't be practicing law." He stood and walked toward the door of his office, an obvious signal that the interview was over.

"Then who are you talking about?"

Now he looked smug. "So your friend *has* been holding out on you."

I was silent but determined at that moment to see Denise and find out at least as much as the police had learned. Although I hadn't wanted to pry, the situation was now too serious for such niceties. I still had no doubt about Denise's innocence, but if I were to do as she'd asked—if I were to find the murderer—she had to level with me.

"You're making a big mistake," I told Detective Moreway and left before I revealed how little Denise had trusted me. The next day, Saturday, was my day off. I decided to use the time to plan an approach rather than try to see Denise immediately.

* * * *

Pharmacy is not a nine-to-five, weekends off, type of job. My two-day weekend happened every other week, and it meant a free Sunday and Monday. On alternate weeks, I had only Saturday off. I'd been looking forward to this particular Saturday because I'd been invited to the baby shower for Betsy Stokes. Her mother, Michael Loring's former wife, had arranged a luncheon at The Other Place restaurant. Patricia had just returned to Scottsdale to await the birth of her first grandchild, due later this month. Her earlier visit last fall had caused some uncomfortable moments for me until I'd finally come to understand the family dynamics. Unlike Michael, Patricia had remarried but they'd remained on friendly terms since their divorce, many years before. Now, content with her second husband and their more cosmopolitan lifestyle in London, Patricia's visits to Arizona were no threat to me. On the contrary, I'd come to like her and looked forward to seeing her again.

Although I knew baby showers were usually all-female events and Michael wouldn't be there, I dressed carefully for the party. Back in November, the last time Patricia had been in the States, I'd discovered I couldn't emulate her chic style. However, I was determined to look good in my own way. This turned out to be more difficult than I thought. My navy print dress seemed perfect for the pre-spring weather. After carefully pressing it—I liked silk, but it always creased so quickly—I had a sudden flash of memory. This dress wouldn't do at all for Betsy Stokes's baby shower. I'd worn it to her husband's funeral last August.

I looked through my closet again and settled on a two-piece polyester, seafoam with white dots. *At least, this one won't require pressing*, I thought. My hair was newly trimmed, though still at its winter length, its auburn color heightened by my hairdresser and set in a modified page boy. *You could easily pass for fifty-four*, I told myself wryly, knowing my fifty-sixth birthday was rapidly approaching. Well, I might feel twenty years younger on good days but Michael, who'd dated me all those years ago in pharmacy college, certainly knew my exact age.

My gift for Betsy's baby was a yellow and white coverall and matching T-shirt. The coverall legs had teddy bear appliqués, and I'd also found a stuffed teddy bear that exactly matched them. Although I'd learned to wrap all types of packages in my Dad's drugstore, the bear defeated me, so I bought a decorative shopping bag for the gifts.

I knew Denise was also invited to the baby shower. Ordinarily, we'd have driven to the restaurant on Lincoln Drive together, but she was on the six a.m. to noon shift at the coffee shop and would be going to the shower directly from work. I still hadn't planned what to say to Denise. *It's no use*, I thought. *There's no way to disguise such an intrusion into her privacy.*

When I arrived at The Other Place, ten or twelve women were already milling around the small room that was reserved for private parties. Betsy and Patricia stood at the entry, in an informal receiving line with a young woman I didn't recognize at first. Michael's daughter looked radiant, happier than I'd ever seen her. She wore a royal blue maternity dress that appeared to have reached its outer limits, and I wondered what we'd all do if Betsy suddenly went into labor. Both she and her mother hugged me warmly and I told them the truth, that I was delighted to be there.

Patricia seemed cool and somehow regal in a silk pantsuit that I was startled to find was the same seafoam color as my own dress. She smiled at me. "May I compliment you on your taste in color."

No wonder she appeared so sophisticated to me. For a moment, my doubts about Michael returned. How could I ever hope to compete with this admirable ex-wife of his. Then, I remembered we weren't competing. She'd given him up and married someone else. I smiled back at Patricia. "And let me return the compliment."

"You remember Sheila Stokes." Betsy indicated the third woman.

"Of course," I said, pleased that Sheila had come to her stepmother's baby shower. Not too long before, Harry Stokes's grown children had vehemently denounced Betsy as a fortune hunter who'd married their father for his money. They'd accused Betsy of everything from driving their father to suicide to murdering him. Sheila's presence here today must mean she had accepted Betsy and the coming half-brother or -sister.

I looked around to see whether Nancy Stokes was there, too. Sheila seemed to understand. "My brother wouldn't let Nancy come with me," she whispered. "He won't have anything to do with Betsy."

"That's a shame," I said. "But I'm glad you're here." I continued in a more normal tone of voice. "How is...?" My mind refused to come up with his name

Sheila laughed. "If you mean Scott, that's over. I guess I outgrew him."

We were interrupted as more women arrived, and I was introduced to a group of Betsy's friends from Tucson. I drifted away and soon noticed a table in the corner, trimmed with white satin ribbons and piled high with gift-wrapped packages so I headed that way to deposit my own bulky package. Nearby, a smaller table held place cards. I located mine and went to find my seat.

As I walked around the room, the only other person I recognized was Verna Branden, and I remembered she was Betsy's neighbor as well as Denise's. We were not assigned the same table, which didn't disappoint me at all. I found my own place and sat down.

Denise arrived shortly afterwards. She lingered for a few moments, talking to the three women on the receiving line and then continued on, taking her own present to the designated table. From where I sat, I could see it was an exceptionally large package and I wondered what she'd bought for the expected baby. *How strange*, I thought. *Normally, we would have shopped for gifts together.*

Evidently Betsy or her mother had placed me next to Denise, knowing we were friends. Under ordinary circumstances, I would have appreciated this arrangement. Today, I wasn't so sure. *Then again,* I thought, *we can't talk about Andrea Felder or the mysterious Tony here. We'd have no privacy.*

As Denise approached our table, dressed in a bright cerise dress I hadn't seen before, her expression was so serious that she seemed almost a different person. Her first words contradicted my earlier assumption that we wouldn't talk about Andrea's murder.

"Did you speak to Detective Moreway?" Denise asked even before she sat down.

So much for the respite I expected this afternoon, I told myself; but maybe it was just as well to deal with the subject and then enjoy the party. I looked around hurriedly to see whether anyone could overhear us. Only two other women were at our table so far, and they were engrossed in a conversation about computer courses for beginners at Scottsdale Community College.

"He didn't reveal much," I said.

"Then you *did* talk to him—was it on the telephone or in his office?"

"In his office."

"That's great, Ruthie. I knew he'd appreciate your help."

I laughed. "Hold on a minute. It was just the opposite; he wanted me to butt out."

A waitress appeared at my elbow to take beverage orders. And a new arrival joined our table. She was a young woman, about Betsy's age, and also very pregnant. "Hi, I'm Jennifer Hoffman," she said and reached across the table to shake hands with everyone in turn. Her smile was warm, a laugh bubbling just below the surface.

The computer discussion halted briefly and then resumed, leaving Jennifer with only Denise and myself for conversation. I sighed with relief and asked the newcomer whether she'd known Betsy long.

"Oh, yes. I'm the one who introduced her to Harry." She lowered her voice and some of the bubbly tone disappeared. "Wasn't that a terrible shock? I feel so sorry for Betsy, having to raise the baby alone and all that."

"She'll manage very well," I assured Jennifer and changed the subject. "When is your baby due?"

"Any minute now," she said and laughed aloud this time.

"That soon?" Denise asked, and I was glad to see something other than the Felder murder capture her interest.

"Oh, I know I don't look as big as Betsy but believe me, I can't wait." She suddenly spoke to me in a subdued tone again. "Tell me, are you the pharmacist Betsy was talking about, the one who solved all those murders."

Good God, I thought. *Not another one!*

Denise turned to me with a smile that looked ironic. "You're getting a reputation, Ruthie."

"I just happened to be involved in a couple of murder cases," I said.

Jennifer's voice was even lower now, almost a whisper. "I thought I recognized your name," she said. "The reason I ask is because I went to law school with that woman who just got killed."

"Andrea Felder?" The name burst from Denise and me in unison.

"Yes, Andrea."

"But she had to be at least ten years older than you," Denise said. Although I would have tried for more tact, I also was wondering how they could have been classmates in law school.

"Don't you know? Andrea was a late bloomer. She went to law school quite a few years after her undergraduate days."

"You mean she decided on law school because she married an attorney," Denise said. She was staring at Jennifer, but I couldn't read her expression.

"Now that's a sexist remark." The bubbly note was back as if it had barely been suppressed. "As a matter of fact, she was pre-law but put her own career on hold to help Sterling through law school first."

"And then she divorced him."

The bitterness in Denise's voice both surprised and discomfited me, and I was glad to see the server approach with salads. Despite the empty chair at our table, I guessed someone else was expected because the place was set. I hoped she'd arrive and enable us to change the topic.

Jennifer passed around the rolls, and one of the other women offered the butter dish. All of us stopped talking momentarily and began eating, and I hoped it would be some time before conversation resumed.

"Feta cheese and walnuts," one of the computer novices said. "What an elegant salad!"

"And raspberries," I added, happy for an excuse to make light conversation.

"Betsy's mom chose the menu," Jennifer told us. "She has wonderful taste."

Yes, I thought. She had chosen Michael; but then again, she'd also given him up.

I wondered whether Michael was in town. We hadn't made any commitment, still seeing each other casually and infrequently. Since I'd turned him down so many years before, he could be waiting for encouragement from me; but it was difficult for someone of my generation to take the lead in... My musings were interrupted.

"I already told the police it was that ex-husband of hers." Jennifer leaned toward me, her hands outstretched in an oddly imploring gesture. "It wasn't bad enough he dumped her, he just couldn't stand to see her married to someone else."

"Just a minute," Denise said, so piercingly that one of the other women at our table threw her a startled look before turning back to her own friend. "I don't know what you heard, but she was the one who wanted the divorce. And the proof is her immediate remarriage."

"Maybe she got tired of his philandering."

"Philandering!"

Denise sounded so outraged, I was afraid she'd attack Jennifer. The server, reappearing at that moment to remove the salad plates, defused the situation. We were handed our entrées, vegetable quiche surrounded by baby squash and small roasted potatoes.

After the server left, Jennifer began eating with gusto. "I seem to be hungry all the time now," she explained. "It's a wonder I'm not twice as big."

Denise refused to allow the change in subject. "What did you mean just now? How could you call Sterling Harraday a philanderer?"

The younger woman politely finished chewing her food before replying. "Because he is one."

"You can't possibly know that. And if Andrea said so, she was probably justifying her own affair."

"On the contrary," Jennifer said. She held another forkful of quiche inches away from her mouth and seemed to assess Denise. "I know because I was one of the women he went after."

Denise was silent, filling in the time by toying with her food. I looked from one to the other, not wanting to meddle but feeling sorry for my friend. Jennifer's expression had changed now, showing a shrewdness at odds with her rotund appearance. She, too, was quiet for a few moments.

"You must be his latest," she said finally.

Denise's face flushed, then turned pale. "Yes, Sterling and I are seeing each other. But..."

The younger woman didn't give her a chance to finish. "Are you proud of yourself, breaking up a family and tempting him to kill Andrea?"

"Wait a minute," Denise said, getting to her feet.

"No, you wait. You don't want to hear it, but you obviously need someone to tell you the score."

All other conversation at our table had stopped, and some of the women at the next table also seemed to be straining to overhear. I reached up and pulled on Denise's arm. "Sit down. This isn't the time or place to talk about it."

She hesitated and then took her seat again. I turned to Jennifer and said quietly, "I don't know what you've heard, but my friend here didn't even meet Sterling until long after his divorce and Andrea's remarriage."

"Is that her story?"

"It's the truth," I insisted. "And now I think it's time to change the subject. Betsy's about to open her gifts."

Two restaurant employees had moved the gift table to the center of the room, and seated Betsy alongside. Patricia was handing the packages to her, one by one. As Betsy unwrapped the first present, a crib mobile of colorful butterflies, the roomful of women reacted with a prolonged "oooh."

Denise and I had moved our chairs around to face the center of the room, and I could see her twisting her hands in her lap. I reached out and patted her shoulder. Her look of absolute misery contrasted sharply with the scene around us and the happy comments of the crowd of women as each gift was shown and each greeting card read to us.

"It's true," Denise suddenly whispered to me. "I did know him before."

"You mean at the coffee shop—as a customer. That's nothing to worry about."

"No. We went out a few times before."

"Before what? Are you saying you got together while he was still married to Andrea?"

"I didn't know he was married," Denise said. "When I found out, I stopped seeing him."

"You never mentioned him to me?" I said, making it a question.

"It was a couple of years ago. You and I hadn't become friends yet."

I thought about it. We'd had a working acquaintanceship for many years, since we were both at the same Food Go supermarket, but our friendship didn't begin until after my husband died. I knew she met many men through the coffee shop—she'd even been interested in Harry Stokes before he married Betsy—but I'd been so sure Sterling was the first serious one.

A loud sound, more like a squeal, interrupted us. Betsy had just held up a tiny white kimono, trimmed and sashed in green. I sat there, trying to hide my agitation. If Frank Moreway learned about this, and he surely would, his suspicion of Denise would intensify. *What about you*, I asked myself. *Are you still certain she had nothing to do with Andrea's murder?* But I was determined nothing would deflect my belief in my friend this time, and I'd do whatever I could to help her out of this mess.

Betsy was looking toward Denise now and smiling at her. I realized she'd just opened Denise's gift—tiny red cowboy boots. *This is what the police should see*, I thought. *How could anyone believe she went shopping for red cowboy boots in her spare time, when she wasn't busy murdering someone?*

Now my mind drifted to Sterling. It was hard to credit Jennifer's picture of him as a philandering husband, but Denise's words just now had seemed to support that view. I didn't know what to believe.

As I saw Patricia reach for my gift, I quickly pasted a smile on my face. Like the other presents, mine brought forth an "ooh," but the sounds of approval intensified when Betsy held up the teddy bear and showed everyone that it matched the coverall appliqués. *Too bad it isn't as easy to pick out a murderer as it is to choose an appealing baby gift*, I thought.

Jennifer was trying to attract our attention. I realized Denise was deliberately ignoring her now, pretending to be absorbed in the show of presents. Turning to the younger woman, I raised my eyebrows in a questioning movement.

"To my way of thinking, your friend's the most likely suspect after Sterling. You need to ask her whereabouts when Andrea was killed."

"You're an attorney," I said. "Surely you know better than to go around accusing people."

"Let's assume I'm wrong," she told me. "The way to prove it is to find the real murderer. And I think you're the only one who can do it."

Chapter 6.

I stared at Jennifer. "That's ridiculous," I said. "I'm not a trained investigator."

"And you weren't one when you solved the other murders, but you did it anyhow. I know all about you from Betsy."

"Those cases happened to hinge on various medications," I said. "As far as I know, I haven't any professional information that could illuminate this one."

"It's obvious, though, that you have an analytical mind. So do I. And I know that people like us, if we put our abilities to work, can do almost anything."

I laughed. "If only I had your self-confidence," I told her.

"It's generational. Younger women are more self-assured than women from your day," Jennifer said, making me feel ancient. "But you'll never convince me you're a typical middle-aged woman. If you were, you couldn't have become a pharmacist when you did."

Although I know that technically anyone over forty is middle-aged, I never think of myself that way. For a moment, my reaction to the term blotted out the rest of Jennifer's comment. Then I realized she was right. Women pharmacists, in the majority now, were a tiny minority when I graduated from the University of Arizona more than thirty years ago.

"Exactly what do you think I can do?"

"I leave that up to you," she answered.

Denise still seemed absorbed in the ritual of gift display. I glanced from her to Jennifer. What worried me was the way Denise had been caught up in such damaging circumstances. And I knew that when the relationship between her and Sterling became public, even if my own faith in them remained strong, Jennifer would not be alone in her suspicions. No wonder Frank Moreway was so interested in Denise's actions that day. Possibly, the police already had discovered an earlier relationship between Sterling and herself.

On the other hand, while it was easy for Denise and now Jennifer to ask me to find the murderer, I had no idea where to begin. I'd never even met Andrea Felder or her father, Amos.

* * * *

It was Sterling Harraday who provided the opening I needed. He came up to the pharmacy a few days after the baby shower. I'd been trying to help a customer with a script for her husband. The husband was having cataract surgery, and the medication was Tylenol with Codeine #3.

"Mrs. Jamison," I said. "We have a notation in our computer that your husband is allergic to codeine. And that's what this prescription is for."

"No, I don't think he's allergic to codeine. I think Percocet is the problem." Since she seemed rather upset, I didn't want to press her; but I had to straighten this out.

"Why don't you check with your husband when he comes out of surgery? Meanwhile, I'll try to reach his doctor."

"I appreciate that. It's very thoughtful of you."

At that point I looked up and noticed Sterling waiting to see me. "I'll be just a few minutes," I told him.

"That's fine. Take your time."

When I finished with Mrs. Jamison, I half expected Sterling to hand over a prescription or two. Instead, he simply asked when I'd be free for lunch. "I'd like to talk to you," he explained.

"Unfortunately, I don't have a lunch break. I work straight through until five o'clock." He seemed puzzled. "But don't I sometimes see you having lunch in the coffee shop?"

"When I'm on the late shift, I often eat there—but that's before I begin work."

"In that case, may I take you to dinner tonight? I'd like to talk about this situation I'm in," he added hastily as my next customer stepped up to the window, leaving me no chance to voice polite regrets over the death of his ex-wife.

I agreed, wondering what I was getting into. Despite Jennifer's allegations, I wasn't worried about Sterling's intentions; I knew my "middle-aged" charms hadn't prompted this dinner invitation.

Karen, my young technician, arrived at the close of her high school day and took over the computer. We were busy as usual, but her help allowed me to catch up and together we smoothly filled prescriptions, cutting customer waiting time to a negligible amount. The day moved so quickly that I was surprised to realize Louise had arrived to work her night shift. She'd come into the pharmacy very quietly, and the first I knew of her arrival was Karen's exclamation.

"Oh, Louise! What happened to your eye?"

Evidently, she had tried to conceal it with makeup because she was wearing more than she usually did. It was impossible, though, to miss the raccoon look of her left eye.

"Oh, Louise," I heard Karen say again. "Did he do that? When *are* you going to throw him out?"

"Shh," Louise said, and I felt rather than saw her look toward me. She continued in a low voice, but I was worried about her and concentrated on listening. "He has a lot on his mind right now."

"That's no excuse."

"Maybe not. But I love him."

I thought of that phrase, "But I love him." How many women were in destructive relationships because of those four words? And I started to wonder about Denise and Sterling. Even more upsetting was the thought of the mysterious Tony, who'd visited Denise at Amos Felder's home the morning of the murder.

The immediate problem, however, was Louise Rettenberg. My first instinct was to offer the sympathy I would to any injured friend or acquaintance, but I was sure Louise would prefer me to ignore her black eye as well as the words I'd overheard. I couldn't do it.

"Are you feeling all right?" I asked her, a nice compromise that left much unsaid. "Do you need me to fill in for you tonight?"

She tugged on her one long braid, a nervous gesture I'd noticed many times before. "I'm fine, Ruthie. You go on home."

That was when I remembered Sterling. We'd been so tied up, Karen and I, filling prescriptions as though we were on an assembly line, that I hadn't thought about him. I removed my white lab jacket and hung it in place of my sweater—a black one today to accentuate my black and white print dress. It would be better to wait outside, I decided. Food Go gossip was bad enough when it was true; I didn't want any unfounded stories to get back to Denise.

Sterling drove up in his Volvo just as I reached the Food Go entrance, and I got into the car. "Do you like seafood?" he asked. "I was thinking of Landry's; you know, the restaurant that used to be called Famous Pacific."

"That sounds good to me," I said, trying for a gracious tone to hide my unease. I still couldn't figure out why Sterling wanted to talk to me. As for Denise, I hadn't told her about Sterling's invitation, and I worried that my friend would be unhappy with me when she found out about this meeting. It seemed devious somehow, because I was afraid she would be our topic of conversation.

We turned into Scottsdale Road and drove south toward the restaurant. Although it was March and many of the winter visitors had returned to their home states, traffic remained heavy. Sterling pulled up in front of the valet parking area and handed keys to the attendant, while another young man opened the passenger door for me. This was a service I'd once associated only with the wealthy. Now, however, I'd grown accustomed to use valet parking myself at times, rather than walk alone in deserted parking lots.

The restaurant was crowded for a weekday evening, another indication that many winter visitors remained in Scottsdale. Perceived wisdom claimed that Arizonans ate out so much because the hot summers discouraged cooking, but I'd often noticed restaurants were crowded even at other seasons. Many of them had outdoor dining patios that sported both heaters for cool days and misting devices for warm weather.

Sterling had called for a reservation, and we were led past the open kitchen with its mesquite grills and seated immediately. We both declined drinks, asking for decaf instead. Sterling was very quiet, seeming to hide behind the menu. I ordered a salad and grilled salmon; he wanted spicy chowder and the seafood platter. The server left, but Sterling remained silent.

I decided I couldn't ignore the murder, only a week ago, of his ex-wife; it was time to express my sympathy. Wondering if there was a better way to convey them, I voiced the conventional regrets hesitantly, "I was sorry to hear about Andrea's death."

"You knew her?"

"No. We never met."

He seemed puzzled. After a moment, I realized why—not wanting to say "your ex-wife" or "your former wife," I'd settled on "Andrea."

Our coffee arrived in time to defuse the awkward moment. "It's Andrea I wanted to talk to you about," Sterling said.

I looked at him. It was hard to read any expression behind the horn-rimmed glasses, but his tone was subdued. "I'm sure it must be hard on the children," I said, reduced to platitudes but meaning them nonetheless.

"Very hard. First the divorce and a stepfather. Now this."

His manner was so unlike the confident attorney I remembered, the one who'd helped me when I'd been accused of a deadly prescription error, that I wondered whether his unease was caused by the death of his ex-wife or his own role as a suspect. Even so, I could understand why some women might be attracted to Sterling. The combination of strength and need could be irresistible. Denise, who was a nurturer, must have found the neediness in ascendancy when she started seeing him after his divorce. Then I remembered they'd dated before the divorce. Well, they were both adults and I wasn't going to judge either of them—unless he was responsible for Andrea's death.

As though Sterling had been able to follow my train of thought, he picked up at that point. "The police have questioned me extensively. For the first time since I began legal practice, I understand how you and my other clients—the innocent ones, anyhow—felt when you were under suspicion." He spoke softly, without a trace of the courtroom manner I'd noted on occasion.

Sterling's chowder arrived now together with my salad. As we began to eat, I thought about his words. He'd been at pains to tell me, at least indirectly, of his innocence; but I couldn't be sure of him, particularly after Jennifer's denunciation. *If he's guilty*, I told myself, *Denise will be dragged into it. Even if he's the only one who's accused, she won't be able to escape the notoriety. And some people will remain convinced she was an accessory.*

"I have to assume you believe in Denise and me," he said suddenly.

"You know I trust Denise."

He laughed, but his usual warmth was missing. "That's a pointed answer. I can't say I blame you, though. You don't know me as well as you know her. But I have no motive," he assured me. "Even the police haven't come up with one."

"Did *anybody* have a reason to kill her?"

"Obviously, someone did. It could've been a client who blamed her for losing a case. Maybe even for a prison sentence."

"How would a client find Andrea at her father's home?"

"Followed her," he said succinctly.

"That doesn't sound too plausible."

"No. I'm grasping at straws, and I know it. All right. Let me tell you why I wanted to talk."

Our entrées arrived, steaming hot, and tempting me to eat first and listen later since I'd had no lunch, but Sterling's reluctance to get to the point had vanished. He looked down at his food without seeming aware of it and then stared at me as if trying to see into my mind.

"I want to hire you to discover who killed Andrea," he said.

I gasped. "You're an attorney," I said. "Surely you can find a professional to take on the job."

"Of course, I can. But Denise and I both have more confidence in you."

"Denise," I murmured. "I can understand why she'd want me to do this. We've already talked about it; but you know better."

"Don't sell yourself short. You've succeeded in the past when the police were headed in the wrong direction. And, besides, you have a personal reason to want to find the truth."

"And being personally involved is usually considered a minus, not a plus."

"Perhaps for doctors or attorneys. This is different. I don't want to hire a stranger, whose cynicism will stand in the way."

"From what you said before, you do realize I haven't decided about you."

His look was rueful. "I'd like to believe you have an open mind."

I thought about it calmly, enjoying my grilled salmon despite the tension I could feel coming from Sterling. "Anyhow, all that's beside the point. You can't possibly expect me to solve this murder when I never even met Andrea."

"Detective Moreway never met her either. Nor, as far as I know, did anyone else on the Scottsdale police force."

"You're an attorney," I repeated. "You must know better ways to go about this."

"Okay, I'll confess I was dramatizing. Must be a trait I picked up from Denise." We both smiled despite the serious tenor of our conversation. "I'll also admit that I know very well that anything you do will have to be informal, since you're not licensed as a private investigator."

I hadn't thought of that—knowing I wouldn't take payment to help Denise in any case. Now I wondered in earnest how much I could trust Sterling. He seemed to be saying whatever came into his mind, trying different angles until he found one that might work.

"That's unfair," I said stiffly.

"Yes, it was."

We were at an impasse now. I decided on shock treatment of my own. "Someone else that you know asked me to investigate."

"Yes, Denise told me she urged you to see Detective Moreway."

"I'm talking about Jennifer Hoffman."

"Jennifer!" he said and nearly knocked over his water glass. He quickly recovered and tried to change the movement into a smoother attempt to sip some water.

I remembered that this man was trained to hide his emotions except when he deliberately wanted to parade them before a jury. "She had some unflattering things to say about you, Sterling. In fact, she seems convinced that you held a grudge against Andrea." I stopped short of telling him that Jennifer had accused him of murder.

"More likely she's the one with the motive. Did she tell you that Andrea married her former boyfriend?"

"No, she didn't. And furthermore, you don't help your cause with wild accusations. Am I expected to believe a woman who's ready to give birth any day now managed to commit murder?"

"Do you know how Andrea died?"

I admitted I hadn't heard many of the facts. The server came to take our plates away, mine nearly empty, Sterling's hardly touched. A busboy refilled the coffee cups and water glasses. We had to wait again while the server flourished a dessert tray, until he saw that we weren't to be tempted and left.

"She was knifed in the back." He winced as he said this, and I was sure he pictured the scene as he spoke. "The weapon came from a butcher block holder in my father-in-law's, I mean my former father-in-law's, kitchen. There was no struggle, and he heard nothing."

"Detective Moreway told me your former..."

"Just call him Amos," Sterling said.

"Amos was napping at the time?" I made it a question, although I already knew the answer from Frank Moreway.

"Yes. He never knew what happened until the nurse came in and found Andrea's body."

"But it would be impossible to check Amos's story," I said. "Isn't he a suspect, too?"

"Why would he kill his own daughter?"

"To my way of thinking, he's certainly as much a possibility as Denise or anyone else." I said.

"Amos Felder is the most honorable man I've ever known," Sterling told me. He glanced quickly at the check that had just been placed midway between us on the table, removed a credit card from his wallet, put it in the holder, and was silent while the waiter took it away. While we waited for the credit slip, he seemed to be deep in thought and, when it arrived, he added the tip and signed it almost absentmindedly.

Sterling stood and politely helped me on with my sweater. "I hate to intrude on him," he said. "But I think you need to meet Amos Felder."

Chapter 7.

"Sterling, I'd rather not do this," I said. "The man just lost his daughter; it would be cruel."

"Didn't you imply that he killed her?"

"I didn't mean it; I shouldn't have said what I did."

"You meant it, all right," Sterling insisted. "I want you to meet Amos Felder so you can see how absurd that suspicion is."

"Forget it, please."

"I'm not planning to kidnap you, Ruthie, but will you please reconsider? I think it's very important that you two meet, and I know he'll welcome you as a friend of Denise's."

"Forget it," I repeated. "I'd be there under false pretenses."

We were waiting for the valet attendant to return Sterling's car. As we stood in front of the restaurant, I shivered. It could have been due to the normal evening drop in temperature or because I didn't like the predicament I'd gotten myself into.

"Would you like my jacket?" Sterling asked.

"I'll be all right."

"That's my Volvo coming along now." He held five dollars ready for the attendant and in less than a minute, I was in the car, waiting for Sterling to walk around to the driver's side. He followed the curve in Scottsdale Road, past the defunct Galleria Mall, and made the first right turn out of traffic and into Shoeman Lane, a quiet side street, where he pulled into the curb.

"Will you reconsider?" Sterling asked quietly.

I didn't answer right away. First, I thought about Denise—how she'd been there for me after Bob died. If there was any chance that a visit to Amos Felder could help my friend, then I couldn't refuse to go.

Sterling was smart enough to wait without saying a word. *Probably learned not to oversell in law school*, I thought cynically. I'd been looking straight ahead, peering through the windshield without seeing anything. Now I turned toward Sterling, trying to see his face, but the street lamps didn't cast enough light for me to read his expression.

"Okay," I said.

He surprised me by reaching for my hand and shaking it as though we'd reached an important agreement. "We'll go now before you change your mind."

"Don't you want to telephone first?"

Sterling's smile was warm. "He's expecting us."

Before I had a chance to resent his highhandedness, he explained. "I simply told him I'd be over this evening and that I might have someone interesting with me."

After a U-turn, Sterling was back on Scottsdale Road, heading north. We rode for a while in silence while I thought uneasily about the coming visit. Since I'd agreed to meet Andrea's father, maybe I should've waited and gone there with Denise. At least, I could be sure she wouldn't repeat my suspicions. I wasn't so certain about Sterling.

When we reached the McCormick Ranch subdivision, he drove in. I could smell the wonderful perfume aroma of citrus trees in bloom as we took a few more turns before parking in front of Amos Felder's house, one that looked like so many other Arizona homes with its white block exterior and red-tiled roof. The garage was to the left of the front entrance, projecting past the building line, but there were no cars in the driveway.

Sterling pulled a key ring from his pocket and unlocked the door. I couldn't contain a slight intake of surprise. "Those of us who often visit here have keys," he explained. "Even though Amos moves around pretty fast in his wheelchair, he finds it more convenient to have us come right in without ringing the doorbell."

"How many others have keys?"

"See, you're beginning to think like a detective."

"That's a normal question. Anyone would wonder."

"Well, come on in. I'll introduce you to Amos, and we can ask him about the keys."

We walked through double front doors into a wide hallway and then into the living room. With its dark oak wainscoting and striped wallpaper, it was the kind of room I thought of as "masculine" or, at least, what I imagined an interior decorator would design for a man who lived alone.

No one was in the room. Sterling invited me to be seated and went off to find his former father-in-law. I was too nervous to sit down but walked around, examining the many framed pictures on the walls. They were all seascapes—some serigraphs, two oils, and a lithograph—interesting choices in a desert city filled with western art. None of the artists' names were familiar to me but then again, I'd never before met anyone who collected seascapes. I wondered if they represented escape for the wheelchair-bound man or if they predated his accident.

Sterling reappeared, followed by a stocky figure wheeling himself into the room, a golden retriever alongside him. When he was halfway into the room, he commanded the dog to sit.

"Amos, this is Ruthie Morris, the pharmacist Denise and I told you about."

I walked over to shake hands with Amos Felder. His grip was firm, and I realized he must use considerable strength to propel himself around in the wheelchair. He was one of those people whose eyes seem to communicate his intelligence. They were so alive, you could almost see the thoughts moving behind them

"How do you do, Ruthie Morris," he said formally. "And this is Trafalgar." He patted the retriever's head gently as he spoke.

"I hope we're not intruding. Sterling assured me we were expected."

"No, no. I'm always delighted to meet new people." His expressive eyes flickered in agreement with the words. "Please do sit down." He gestured toward one of the brown leather armchairs and, after I sat down, moved his wheelchair alongside.

"Mrs. Morris and I have been discussing the realities of the situation," Sterling said.

"Ah, yes. But before we get to that, my caregiver—it was Maxine today—left some refreshments in the kitchen." He glanced toward Sterling, signaling his request.

"Please don't," I said hurriedly. "We've come here straight from dinner."

"It's a bowl of fruit," Amos said. "Just the thing to complement your meal."

"Where is Maxine tonight, anyhow? Why are you alone here?"

"Sterling, sometimes you treat me like an invalid," Amos said Then he laughed, a rich deep one that made both of us smile. "You know I can manage to do quite a bit on my own. And with Trafalgar here..." He reached down and patted the dog again. "I don't need full-time care."

"But someone is supposed to be here from five to midnight every evening," Sterling said.

"And someone *is* here. She simply went out to replenish my food supply." He reminded his former son-in-law again about the fruit, and Sterling quickly left the room.

I wondered whether Amos's purpose was to talk to me privately. Perhaps I should offer condolences, but it seemed awkward at best. I expected him to set the conversational tone, but the alert eyes examined me while their owner remained silent.

It was difficult for me to wait without speaking. I thought of several openings, comments about the room or the artwork, but these topics seemed trivial. So we simply waited for Sterling.

He returned carrying a cut glass bowl laden with tangerines, apples, strawberries, and grapes. A knife protruded from the center of the bowl, and I gasped when I saw it.

Sterling looked startled. "Surely, you don't think this..." His voice trailed off.

"The police have the one that killed my daughter. It was nothing like this knife," Amos said. His voice was steady although I could hear the suppressed emotion behind his words.

"I'm sorry... I wasn't thinking... A few months ago... I had a close call..."

Anything I say can only make it worse, I thought. "I'm sorry," I repeated lamely.

Sterling came to my rescue. "You remember Ruthie's narrow escape. I told you all about it at the time."

"Of course." Amos reached across and pressed my hand. "All of us find it increasingly difficult to disassociate knives from the trauma they can inflict. But the old cliché is true; life does go on."

"It would go on more easily if the police weren't underfoot," Sterling said. His tone was bitter.

"I expect it would." Amos turned to me again. "What makes you think you can help us?" he asked.

"Sterling, did you give Mr. Felder the impression that I initiated this visit?"

I watched as the younger man plucked some red grapes from the fruit bowl and began to nibble. I remembered he'd eaten little of his dinner, but I was too upset to wait calmly for him to straighten out the misunderstanding.

Before either of us could say anything, Amos spoke. "I see now. This was your idea, Sterling. Well, perhaps it was a good one after all."

"Mr. Felder, I've been trying to convince Sterling you need a trained investigator, not me. I'm truly sorry about your daughter, but I'm not the police. And I'm not a private detective."

"Your friend Denise has a great deal of faith in your abilities."

"Denise is a wonderful person, but she's not always realistic."

"Nevertheless, she's told me about the other murders you solved," Amos said.

"I knew those people, and I was aware of the medications they were taking," I told him. "In fact, their prescriptions had a bearing on the cases."

"But from all I've heard about you, your logical thought processes can help here even though no prescriptions are involved," Amos said.

"Ruthie, I know the police wouldn't give you any further details than they released to the media. Why not let Amos tell you exactly what happened and see what you think?"

I worried that reliving the day of the murder would be painful for Andrea's father but, before I could voice my doubts, he seemed to understand them and rushed to reassure me.

"It *is* difficult for me, but this is important," he said. "Each time I visualize that day again, I hope to remember some fact to explain it all."

"The police probably asked you this, Mr. Felder. Did your daughter have any enemies?"

"Yes, they put that question to me. When I told them I knew of no one who'd want to harm her, you can guess which names they threw my way." He glanced at Sterling and then back at me so quickly that I would have missed the implication had I not already known Sterling was a major suspect.

"Mrs. Morris is aware I'm under suspicion—and that Denise is, also."

"Denise!" He laughed aloud. "She can't even kill spiders. We have to wait until I can manage to reach them or just let them go."

I decided to plunge right in. If they didn't like what I asked, maybe they'd release me from any obligation to help. "Your daughter wanted you to fire Denise?" I raised my voice to make it a question.

"But I didn't fire her, did I?"

"I don't know."

"Denise still works here in the mornings whenever she's on the late shift at the supermarket."

"That might make it worse for her. The police could take it to mean she benefited from Andrea's death."

"*Cui bono?*" Sterling murmured. "Who benefits?"

"Exactly. Unless we can show other people who benefited, I'm afraid Denise will remain a suspect."

"That's just the trouble," Amos said. "We've tried, but we can't pinpoint advantages to anyone at all."

"Inheritance?"

"Andrea did inherit a considerable sum of money from her grandmother—my wife's mother—and my wife as well."

"Who does that money go to now?" I asked.

"Probably her new husband," Sterling said.

"No," Amos told him. "The children inherit everything, not Douglas Payson."

"But surely it's in trust for them, which means Douglas will have control for a number of years." Sterling turned to me. "My children are only 10 and 12. And don't get any ideas; they attend private school, and neither one was off campus at all that day."

I wondered why Sterling was so quick to give his young children an alibi. It had never occurred to me to suspect them despite some of the terrible crimes committed by children that we hear about nowadays.

He seemed to follow my thoughts. "The police did check on them," he announced drily.

"That's routine," Amos said. "You're an attorney. I'm surprised to find you taking everything personally."

"If *you* were a suspect, I'm sure you'd take it personally, too."

"At last my accident is good for something." There was no trace of self-pity in Amos's voice, and I respected him for it.

"We'd better explain," Sterling said.

Amos turned toward me. "Andrea was stabbed with a carving knife from this kitchen. My daughter was a tall woman, about 5 feet 9 inches, and the knife entered her back at a downward angle." His voice faltered for a moment. "So the killer had to be standing, which lets me out."

"And you heard nothing?"

"Nothing at all." He seemed disconcerted but went on. "I take Percocet for the pain. It knocks me out, and I sleep rather heavily."

The drug is a powerful pain reliever and acts as a sedative. I could understand why he hadn't heard anything. Knowing it was necessary, I still hesitated to ask my next question. "Was there a struggle?"

"No struggle at all. She never even turned around."

"Doesn't that mean she knew her killer?"

"I hardly think Andrea would have let a stranger into the house," Amos said. "She was very security conscious, knowing I couldn't do much to help if a burglar did get in."

"Quite a few people have keys, though."

He glanced quickly at Sterling again. "Just the various caregivers, Denise, my son-in-law, and Andrea, of course."

"And Sterling."

"I didn't include him because I knew you saw him use his key this evening."

"Is there anyone else you haven't bothered including?" Although I didn't intend to be sarcastic, I realized my question sounded that way and tried to soften it after the fact. "What I mean is, I need to have all the facts if you want me to help."

"I realize that, so let me start at the beginning and tell you everything I remember about that day. Do you want to take notes?"

He didn't wait for a reply but wheeled himself over to a small oak table occupied by a telephone and answering machine combination, opened its single drawer, and produced paper and pen for me.

Despite having solved several murders, I'd never systematically taken notes during an interview before. I listened carefully to Amos, jotting down my reactions in parentheses so I'd be able to distinguish between his comments and my own thoughts later on.

He spoke quietly but sounded to me as if he were reliving the day while he told me about it. "That morning, my daughter called and asked if I'd like to go out to lunch."

"Did she do that often?"

"Maybe once or twice a month. With all the restaurants in Scottsdale, we were able to try different ones each time." His mouth curved in a reminiscing smile.

"Anything unusual in the way she sounded?"

"Hard to tell," Sterling interrupted. "She always sounded breathless even when she was talking about the most ordinary things."

"I didn't notice anything different," Amos said.

"Was Denise here when your daughter called?"

"No, she arrived a little later. I told her Andrea would be coming over at about 12:30 because I knew it would be better if Denise left beforehand."

"So you were aware of the problem."

"I told you—it wasn't a problem. Denise knew I had no intention of letting her go, but I was afraid she might feel uncomfortable around Andrea."

I felt a warmth toward this man for his considerate treatment of Denise. She'd already mentioned to me several times how much better she liked working for Amos than for her manager in the Food Go coffee shop.

He continued in a matter-of-fact tone. "Denise left a little after noon. Then my daughter arrived and helped get the wheelchair and myself into the van. I have a minivan that was converted for wheelchair accessibility, so we took it to the restaurant rather than Andrea's sports car."

"And no one else was here?"

"No one. We locked up the house. And, yes, the door from the garage to the house was also locked. I remember because I asked Andrea to check it for me." He was obviously trying for a staccato tone to mask any emotional reaction. "When we got back from lunch, we locked it again. Andrea and I usually play gin rummy for a while, but she told me she had an appointment, so I took my Percocet, and she helped me settle in for my afternoon nap." His voice did break now. "That was the last time I saw my daughter alive."

If I'd known Amos better, I would have reached out in a comforting gesture at that moment. I liked this man and hated to see him suffer.

"You said you heard nothing while you were napping. What about just before or just after?"

"This is a quiet street. Most of my neighbors are at work during the day, and there are very few children in the area."

"I live in a similar neighborhood," I said. "But when I'm on the night shift and home in the daytime, I find the area is bustling with activity— lawn care people, cleaning services, deliveries, all sorts of things. Isn't it the same here?"

"Yes, of course; but surely, none of them could have killed Andrea. I've already told you she wouldn't open the door for a stranger."

"Your own service people?"

"We weren't expecting anyone that day."

Sterling spoke up. "Let's not dismiss what Mrs. Morris is saying too quickly. There may be some merit to her suggestion."

I wondered why he was so eager to pinpoint an outside suspect. As an attorney, he was surely aware that most victims know their murderers. On the other hand, it would certainly be convenient for him if this one turned out to be a random killing.

"There was no sign of forced entry into the house," Amos said.

"And I assume the police figured the murder wasn't premeditated since the killer used a weapon from this house."

"That's what they told me, Mrs. Morris."

"Please call me Ruthie," I said. I'd been waiting for the opportunity to change to a less formal basis. Sterling and Amos replied in kind, so I could begin addressing them by the names I used when I thought about them.

"Is it all right if I look at that knife holder?" I asked.

"Of course. Feel free to do anything that may shed light on this terrible thing." He turned to Sterling. "Why don't you show Ruthie to the kitchen?"

I was perfectly capable of finding it myself but was too polite to say so. Determined to get a good look at the room where Andrea was murdered, I quickly followed Sterling into the kitchen.

The room was bright and airy in contrast to the dark decor of the foyer and living room. Its color scheme, a throwback to the style I called "the mauving of America," was dominated by shades of mauve with gray and turquoise accents. In fact, the wallpaper sported those three shades, with mauve predominating, in a geometric pattern. Cabinets were painted pale gray, and the granite countertops were a deeper shade of gray.

"I need to ask you where her body was found," I said to Sterling.

"Right here." He pointed to an area just in front of the French doors leading to the patio. "Amos tells me they figure she was facing the doors, looking out at the backyard."

"Were the French doors unlocked?"

"No. They were exactly as you see them."

I looked closely at the doors, although I was certain the police had done so as well. They were locked and bolted. "What about the door to the garage?" I asked. "Amos said they locked it when they returned from lunch. Was it still locked when they found Andrea?"

Sterling nodded. "There was no sign whatsoever of forced entry. That's why the police are so sure Andrea knew her killer and let him into the house."

I nearly automatically added "or her" but kept quiet because I was afraid to sound as if I were pointing to Denise. Sterling also was silent for a few moments. I followed his glance and saw him staring fixedly at the floor. Whoever had cleaned up after the murder had done a thorough job. I saw no trace of blood. Even the grout between the turquoise, gray, and mauve ceramic floor tiles looked fresh and clean. I remembered reading about a new type of service company that specializes in cleaning up once the police are finished with a crime scene. *It's incredible to think of the things we quickly accept as normal occurrences nowadays*, I told myself.

"Here's where the knife block always stands." Sterling pointed to an empty space between a four-slice toaster and an electric can opener. "I moved it when I took the fruit knife out."

It didn't require much ingenuity to assume the killer saw the knives close at hand and made use of one of them. I thought how hopeless it was for me to try to solve this murder. Anything I learned would have been known by the police days ago; and while I could understand Denise's championship of my murder-solving abilities, it was hard to believe Amos Felder and Sterling Harraday could be so naive.

"Sterling," I said. "What's the real reason for bringing me here? You know I can't possibly do anything the police haven't already accomplished."

"Accomplished! Do you call it an accomplishment to blindly hit out at Denise and me and even my children?"

"You heard what Amos said. It's routine to question everyone."

"My rational self knows that. But I can't stand by and see this happening to the people I love."

Despite the seriousness of the situation, I couldn't help thinking about those words. I wondered whether he included Denise in that description, and I hoped he did love her. Even more fervently, I hoped he was innocent of his ex-wife's murder.

"Was there anything else you wanted to see in the kitchen?" he asked in a calmer tone of voice.

"No, we may as well return to the other room. I'll have to explain to Amos that I don't see any way to help."

As I spoke, I glanced about the kitchen one last time. A gray enameled tray blended into the countertop next to the refrigerator, and I saw that Amos's medications were neatly laid out on it. Professional curiosity, or perhaps just nosiness, took me over to examine the contents of the tray.

I saw carisoprodol, the generic of Soma, a muscle relaxant, to be taken two or three times a day and at bedtime; Percocet, a strong pain reliever, to be taken up to four times a day; temazepam, the generic of Restoril, to be taken as needed for insomnia; and a can of fluori-methane, to be used as needed. *He must be in constant pain*, I thought, *but you'd never know it from his positive attitude. No wonder Denise likes working for him.*

I did want to help. Not only had I exempted my friend from suspicion; but when I was with Sterling, I also found it nearly impossible to suspect him. As for the comment I'd made about Amos during dinner, it now seemed absurd. I could understand why Sterling was so insistent that I meet his former father-in-law.

Let the police suspect everyone, I told myself. I can't believe Amos Felder had anything to do with his daughter's murder. Before I was halfway out of his kitchen, however, I realized the significance of that can of fluori-methane.

Chapter 8.

I returned to the living room, mulling over what I'd just seen. Over the years, I've had a number of prescriptions for fluori-methane, which can provide temporary mobility for spastic muscles. However, I hadn't thought of fluori-methane in connection with Amos's disability. I wondered just how much mobility that prescription spray could give him and for how long. Then I tried to decide whether I should say anything about my discovery. It was unlikely that the police would realize the significance of that particular drug. As a professional pharmacist, was it my duty to give such information to Detective Moreway?

Amos looked up expectantly as we reentered the living room. I forced myself to meet his eyes, but I still hadn't decided what to say.

"You seem disturbed," he said. "Sterling, we're asking too much of Ruthie."

"She seems to think so, too."

"No, it's not that," I said.

"Please be frank. I'm not a sensitive plant; I can't afford to be." He glanced quickly down at the wheelchair.

I marveled that he was so matter-of-fact about his disability. I'd heard people complain more about a toothache. Yet, I could tell from the painkillers he was taking that he suffered. And now, his daughter—someone whose visits he obviously enjoyed and looked forward to—was dead. How could I bring myself to question him about the fluori-methane or worse, go to the police?

Instead, I tried to say what I'd intended to tell him before I scrutinized his medicine tray. "Mr. Felder—Amos—I don't think this is a job for an amateur detective..."

He interrupted. "You don't give yourself enough credit. From what Denise has told me, I wouldn't call you an amateur."

"The police certainly would disagree with you on that."

"Let me approach this a different way," Amos said. "I'm accustomed to observing people closely, and I saw your face when you walked back into this room just now. Something more than looking at the so-called scene of the crime disturbed you."

Sterling had been motioning toward the sofa, but I was anxious to leave and didn't want to sit down again. Now I realized he was too polite to seat himself while I remained standing, so I retraced my steps to the armchair I'd taken before. The wheelchair was positioned alongside it, and I wanted to watch Amos's expression when I told him what I'd observed.

"All right," I said. "I'll tell you what's bothering me."

Sterling seemed surprised. "I thought Amos was imagining things."

"Didn't you see me reading the prescription labels?" I asked the attorney. "We've all taken something for granted that may not be true."

"See that!" Sterling said to his former father-in-law. "I told you she could help us."

"I'm not so sure you'll want to hear this."

"Go ahead," Amos urged. "We need to know everything, no matter who's affected by what you observed."

I still hesitated, unwilling to voice the words. "That's easy to say, but I have no right to meddle."

"You have every right. We invited you to help."

"To help, yes. But …" I took a deep breath. There was no reason to be coy now; I had said too much to back away. "You made quite a point about the entry angle of the wound, that your disability eliminates you from suspicion."

"Of course it does," Sterling said.

"Only if your father-in-law cannot stand unaided."

"Why do you keep on about that?" Sterling sounded impatient now.

"Fluori-methane," I began and stopped to watch Amos's reaction.

That reaction enhanced my growing respect for him; he didn't pretend to misunderstand. Those eyes that so clearly reflected his intelligence brightened in sudden comprehension. I couldn't believe he was acting.

"Ah," he said.

Sterling looked from one to the other of us, obviously puzzled. "You've lost me," he muttered, half to himself.

Neither of us bothered to explain. "How much mobility does the spray give you?" I asked.

"They use it on my legs before physical therapy. The idea is to keep them from atrophying." He smiled at me and added, "Conceivably, with that spray, I might have been able to stand up long enough to..." Amos stopped speaking and made a visible effort to control his emotions.

"You must be demented," Sterling said. He spit the words out through clenched teeth. "I brought you here to help Amos, not to accuse him."

"I didn't want to do this."

"Please don't blame Ruthie. We asked her to investigate, and she's doing exactly that." Amos turned toward me. "All I can say is that I didn't do it."

"I never accused you, but you must realize if the police figure out the purpose of your prescription..."

"Are you going to tell them?" He seemed to be challenging me, which didn't fit his previous words. It was almost as if he wanted the police to know his alibi wasn't airtight. This change in attitude didn't make sense to me, unless he was protecting someone else, and I had no idea who that could be.

I thought how easily I could lie and say "no." In the mystery novels I love to read, the detectives—both amateur and professional—always seem to think the end justifies the means, but I couldn't bring myself to believe that.

My pause was a long one. "I don't know," I said finally.

Sterling's reaction was predictable. "Surely you're not going to tell them."

"Aren't there laws about withholding evidence?"

"Your discovery isn't really evidence. No one in their right mind would suspect Amos of killing his daughter."

"You can't forget your legal training just because there's a personal connection here," Amos told his former son-in-law. Again I thought, *this man wants the police to add him to their list of suspects.*

Amos spoke to me now. "I'm impressed, Ruthie. Although it's more convenient to be eliminated from suspicion, I prefer to have every possibility explored. Note that I said 'possibility' not 'probability.'"

"Amos, please don't play word games," Sterling said.

"You know what my *devoted* daughter was really like." Amos suddenly looked acutely miserable, as if he'd been playing a part until now and had finally decide to reveal the person behind the mask.

"We agreed not to talk about that."

"The pretty picture won't hold up, Sterling. Too many people knew the real Andrea."

I sat there, trying not to stare as the two men discussed Andrea Felder. Not speaking ill of the dead is so ingrained in most of us that her father's words shocked me.

"It was an accident." Sterling's usual mild voice was nearly a shout.

My God, I thought. *He's the killer after all, not Amos and not some mysterious outsider*. And then I reminded myself that Denise loved this man and wished I were anywhere else but in this room.

"Yes, it was an accident," Amos was saying. "You know I never blamed Andrea for my injury. It's what happened afterward that I hold her responsible for."

I'd known from Denise that Amos's disability resulted from an accident, but I'd never heard the details. Now I hesitated to intrude further; yet it seemed this information could have a bearing on the case.

Amos sighed. "I didn't want to discuss my daughter's character with anyone. As far as the police were told, Andrea was a perfect wife and mother. How much of that nonsense they believed, I don't know, but..." Trafalgar gave a short bark and stood up, seeming to wait for a command from Amos. A moment later, we could hear someone at the front door.

"It's us, Grandpa," a girl's voice called out. She bounded into the room, hugged her grandpa and then Trafalgar. For Sterling, she had only a "hi, dad" before she sat on the floor next to Amos's wheelchair.

"Hello, Jessica," Amos greeted her. "Where's your brother?"

"He's helping Doug carry the groceries we brought you." She reached over and petted the dog. "I ran in because I couldn't wait to see you."

I saw Sterling wince at the girl's words but couldn't tell if it was the prospect of seeing the man who'd supplanted him or the contrast between his daughter's casual greeting to himself and the much warmer one she'd given her grandfather.

Denise had told me all about the children and their stepfather, Douglas Payson. I knew that Jessica was ten years old, but she looked like a petite teenager in her jeans and sweatshirt. She was a pretty child with blond hair, dark eyes, and just a touch of baby fat that added an appealing roundness to her face.

"This is Mrs. Morris," Amos told her, nodding toward me. "My granddaughter, Jessica." She got quickly to her feet and shook hands with me.

Someone, probably her grandfather, had taught this child manners, I thought, and then realized I was buying into the negative words I'd just heard about her mother. As curious as I was to meet the children and their stepfather, I rather wished they'd delayed their visit long enough for Amos to have finished telling me about Andrea.

I had no further time for such reflections, however, because Robbie Harraday and his stepfather entered the room. The boy, like his sister, wore jeans and a sweatshirt. His purple and orange shirt sported a Phoenix

Suns logo. I watched to see how he'd greet his family and was pleased to see him shake hands with both father and grandfather.

He was two years older than his sister, with slightly darker hair, and he moved with athletic grace. Neither child resembled Sterling or Amos. Since Denise had once described their mother to me as willowy, blond, and very attractive, I guessed they had inherited their mother's looks.

Andrea's widower also shook hands with both men. *All very civilized*, I thought, and wondered what was going through their minds at that moment. Andrea's second husband seemed younger than Sterling and, for the first time, I realized she must have been at least ten years Douglas Payson's senior. Denise hadn't told me that; perhaps she'd never met him.

Unlike Sterling, Doug had a full head of dark hair and, if he needed corrective lenses, they were contacts. He was one of those people who smile a lot, but I noticed that the smile vanished when he first noticed Sterling. Judging by appearance alone, Doug Payson probably outclassed Sterling, but I was too prejudiced against this man to view him favorably. He'd broken up a marriage and a family. *How convenient it would be if he turned out to be the murderer*, I thought, *and my friends could be exonerated.*

I looked at him closely, trying to gauge his character, but I knew from experience that I couldn't pinpoint a killer so easily. Twice now, I'd suspected everyone but the guilty parties.

"The kids wanted to see their grandpa," he said as if he needed to justify his visit.

"And they insisted on grocery shopping."

"We knew you didn't have any ice cream in your freezer, Grandpa," the girl explained. Jessica had resumed her seat on the floor, tightly hugging the dog as she spoke. Her brother sat next to her, trying to switch Trafalgar's attention to himself. Knowing these children had just lost their mother, I was sure the dog helped to comfort them.

"Have you children been back to school?" Sterling asked.

I saw them glance quickly at their stepfather. "Doug said we could stay out for the rest of the week," Robbie told his father. The words seemed to remind the boy of his mother's death, for I could see him blink rapidly as though trying to hold back tears.

Because the horn-rimmed glasses partly concealed his eyes, I couldn't interpret the look on Sterling's face. It could have been contempt or even hatred, but it was so quickly veiled that I wasn't sure if I'd imagined it.

"Don't you think they'd be better off back in school?" he asked, but he addressed the question to his former father-in-law, not to Douglas.

No one responded, and I found the silence uncomfortable. I couldn't resume the conversation we'd been having before the newcomers' arrival, so I tried to think of something else to say. The children broke the stillness first, clamoring to watch television.

"Not in here," Sterling said, as if to assert his authority. "Turn on the set in Grandpa's study."

There was another awkward hush after the children left the room. Douglas Payson looked at me, waiting to be introduced. The smile had returned, but superficially; it didn't reach his eyes. "Are you a family friend?" he asked. "I'm afraid I don't remember hearing your name before."

"Ruthie's going to help us find the murderer," Sterling said flatly.

Douglas started. I was sure Denise would have interpreted his reaction as a sign of guilt, but I could understand how the bald statement might surprise anyone.

"Are you with the police?" he asked. His tone was incredulous, which didn't win him any brownie points with me.

"I'm a pharmacist."

He looked at Sterling. "I don't see the humor here."

"No humor," Amos said. "As a matter of fact, just before you arrived, Ruthie made an interesting discovery."

"Are you mad?" Sterling asked. "Why would you want to tell *him*?"

"Why not? He's at least as interested in what happened to Andrea as we are."

I watched the three men closely as Amos told Douglas Payson my observations about the fluori-methane, thinking their interplay was peculiar at best. Was Amos playing one man against the other? And if so, why? I couldn't understand the dynamics of the situation but realized if I were to make any progress in helping my friends, I must quickly discover what was happening here. I might never have another chance to see these people together.

"Amos, just before everyone arrived, you started to tell me about your accident," I said, wondering how he'd respond.

"It's no secret, " he began. "Douglas and Sterling know all about it." Although he'd been facing me, he suddenly looked away, as if he wanted to avoid seeing my reaction to his words. "I've always been thankful the children weren't with us when it happened. Andrea was driving," he said and stopped.

"How can you blame Andrea?" Douglas asked. "You know it was an accident."

"She'd been drinking," Amos said.

I was surprised at the bitterness in his voice. Until now, I'd thought he had come to terms with his disability and was surprisingly stoical about it. I wondered whether the investigation into Andrea's death had uncovered deeper feelings.

"You considered your daughter responsible for your injury?" I asked, wanting to make sure I understood the situation.

"No, I told you before that I didn't blame her. I knew how many drinks she'd had, and I offered to drive. But when Andrea refused, I didn't push it. I got into that car of my own volition, so I can't deny my share of responsibility. Believe me, I've had three years to think about all this."

"Then why do you keep talking about it if you don't blame Andrea?" Douglas asked.

"Because for three years now, I've been terrified for the children. She didn't stop drinking heavily—you know she didn't. If anything, it got worse."

"You can't be serious," Douglas said. He stared fixedly at Sterling, as if daring contradiction. "She was a social drinker, nothing more."

"So, she managed to fool *you* until the end," Sterling said, underlining the word "you" with a contemptuous thrust of his forefinger.

From their body language, I was afraid the two men would come to blows. I looked from Douglas' clenched fists to Sterling's compressed lips, wanting to defuse the situation but not sure what to say.

Amos spoke first. "There's no point arguing now. Andrea's gone, and it's more important to find out what happened to her than to dwell on the past."

"I won't stand by to hear her maligned this way," Douglas insisted.

"You're welcome to go at any time," Sterling told him. "And you can leave my children with me."

"Both of you are my guests," Amos said. "So let's behave like adults. And Sterling," he added, "you know we agreed not to uproot the children now."

"I'm not so sure about that anymore."

"You'll have a fight on your hands," Douglas said. "The children want to stay with me, and any intelligent judge will consider their wishes."

"We'll see about that..."

"This isn't getting us anyplace," Amos interrupted. "The only reason I brought up Andrea's problem is because I think it may have led to her death."

"She was knifed in the back, and you blame alcohol?" Douglas' tone was incredulous. "And I always gave you credit for a great deal of intelligence."

"Now he's insulting *you*," Sterling said.

Amos acted as if he'd heard neither man's comments. "When Andrea was drinking, she sometimes wasn't too careful about the company she kept," he said.

"Why don't you come right out and say what you mean?" Sterling asked him. "She picked men up in bars."

"You're a liar!" Douglas exploded.

"Am I? Tell me, where did she meet you?"

"That was different. We already knew each other from the office."

"Yes, I know you both worked for the same law firm; but that doesn't change anything. My wife picked you up in a bar."

"The only reason you're making these claims is to clear yourself. You had motive, you had opportunity, and you killed her."

"And the reason *you* say so is to hide your own motive. She was running around on you the way she stepped out on me. Only your colossal ego couldn't take it."

Amos suddenly wheeled his chair between the two men. "Stop it!" he shouted. "I know my daughter was no angel. Probably, I was more aware of the real Andrea than either one of you. But digging up this dirt isn't getting us anywhere."

"On the contrary," Sterling said. "We don't want the police to know what she was like, but we need to find out who she was seeing. I'm convinced that's the only way we'll discover her murderer."

"I agree that Ruthie needs to know the truth about Andrea," Amos said. "Otherwise, I wouldn't have brought it up at all."

It was time for me to enter the discussion. "Surely, you can't expect me to question people about her private life. Only the police can do that."

"That's true; but the main person you have to question is him." Sterling pointed at Douglas. "Don't forget, I was married to the woman for fifteen years. She made certain I'd know about her affairs, and I'm sure she left clues for him, too."

Chapter 9.

We all stared at Douglas Payson. At first he looked back at us defiantly, but suddenly the expression on his handsome face seemed bleak. "I only know his first name," he said. "Tony."

The name reverberated in my mind, and I couldn't help repeating it aloud. I knew there must be hundreds of Tonys in Arizona. On the other hand, it was surely too much of a coincidence that Denise had met someone named Tony in this house on the day of the murder.

"Yes, Tony," Douglas repeated.

"What does he look like?" I asked, remembering Verna Branden's description of the man she'd noticed at Denise's home.

"I have no idea," Douglas answered.

"Obviously, we need to find him," Amos said. "Can you tell us anything at all about this person?"

"If I could, don't you think I would?"

"Did you tell the police?"

Douglas stared at the Navajo carpet beneath his feet as if he could extract information from the Two Grey Hills pattern. "I didn't want anyone to know what Andrea was up to."

"I don't understand you people," I said. "You've all been withholding information. How do you expect the police to find the murderer?"

"That's why we need you," Sterling told me.

Douglas' words cut through the end of his sentence. "Do you think I want Jessica and Robbie to know about their mother?"

"Don't pretend you're concerned about the children," Sterling said contemptuously. "Andrea found a new man less than a year after your marriage—that's what you can't stand to have people discover. You're afraid they'll see how little she cared for you."

"I'm sure it helps your ego to believe that. Well, let me tell you, she *did* love me."

"Please stop this right now," Amos said, raising his voice just enough to sound determined. "Andrea's actions had nothing to do with loving or not loving and everything to do with alcoholism."

He turned the wheelchair to face me. "However, I do agree with Douglas. I don't want our dirty linen to be washed in public, and I'd like you to promise to keep quiet about what you heard here tonight."

Before I had a chance to answer, we heard someone else at the door. *Another person with a key*, I thought, as a large woman wearing a dusty pink jogsuit entered the living room. She was balancing two grocery bags. "I'm glad you have company, Amos, especially since I had to wait so long at the checkout. Just let me set these down and put the perishables away; I'll be right back." She never paused for breath and bustled from the room before anyone could speak to her.

"That was Maxine Peabody, one of the people who looks after me," Amos said. "When she comes back in, I'll introduce you. Maxine's the one who found..." He stopped, unable to go on.

"She found Andrea," Sterling said.

Maxine returned just then. "Looks like I could have saved a trip. Someone else brought groceries and Amos, you've got enough ice cream to last a good while. Why don't we all have some now?"

"A little later, Maxine. I want you to meet Ruthie Morris."

She walked over and shook hands with me, then patted Trafalgar and belatedly greeted Douglas and Sterling. "Are the kids here, too? I'm sure they'll want ice cream."

"Please sit down, Maxine. I'd like you to talk to Ruthie about what you saw last week." Amos paused. "You know what I mean."

This time, Maxine really looked at me, and I studied her as well. Her hair was graying in an unbecoming way, not quite pepper and salt but rather sprinkled with yellowish-white tufts. Her Hershey-brown eyes, which were her best feature, narrowed as she examined me. "Are you some kind of detective?"

The question embarrassed me. "No, I'm a pharmacist."

She continued to stare at me. "And..."

"And we've asked Ruthie to help us out," Amos told her.

"I don't get it," Maxine said.

Here is an honest woman, I thought. *She'd never pretend to see the emperor's new clothes.* I was about to dust off my disclaimer and tell Maxine that this wasn't my idea, but Douglas got there first.

"Just what I said. The police are the only ones who should be investigating Andrea's death."

"Not so. Ruthie's already made some discoveries the police are unaware of; that is, unless you've already told them about the fluorimethane, Maxine?" Amos's voice rose on the last syllable of her name, making it a question.

"Mr. Felder," she said, suddenly becoming formal. "I didn't tell them, and Hank didn't tell them. Me and Hank, we thought about it. We discussed it, and we decided it was none of their business."

"Hank helps me out on weekends," Amos explained to me.

"Yeah, and both of us know you had nothing to do with—with what happened."

Two more who are withholding information from the police, I thought. Loyalty was a wonderful trait, but this was beginning to sound like a farce. Instead of everyone hiding in different parts of a stage set, they were hiding what they knew.

"Is there anything else you haven't told the police?" I asked and realized I'd made a mistake the minute the words were out.

Maxine turned and walked toward the kitchen. "I'll get the ice cream," she called over her shoulder.

"I'm sorry, Amos," I said.

"Let her think about it while she busies herself with dessert. We'll get back to this later."

Again I talked about leaving and again Sterling and Amos persuaded me to stay. Meanwhile, Douglas went to summon the children for their ice cream. I found the dynamics of the situation interesting; Sterling was their father, but Douglas evidently had assumed the paternal role. He seemed to play it well, for Jessica and Robbie came bounding into the room with him.

"Grandpa," Jessica said, going over to the wheelchair and hugging him, "if you let us, Doug says we can have our ice cream by the TV."

"Come in here, kids, and tell me what flavors you want today," Maxine called.

It took some time for the children to choose their desserts and return to Amos's study, so we talked about how perfect the weather was this time of year and how wonderful the citrus blossom aroma was—unless you had allergies. Then Maxine opened up several tray tables and brought in plates of Neapolitan ice cream for us. Evidently, the adults didn't get to choose.

"My favorite, Maxine. Thanks," Amos told her as she placed a burgundy cloth napkin in his lap first and handed the ice cream to him. "You will join us?"

"If you want."

"Most definitely. And I'd still like you to tell Ruthie about that day."

Maxine disappeared even longer this time but eventually returned and took a seat close to Amos's wheelchair. I noticed that her plate held three scoops of chocolate ice cream. Unlike the rest of us, she used a soup spoon to eat her dessert. *That's one way to add calories in a hurry*, I thought.

After waiting a few minutes for Maxine to enjoy some of her ice cream, Amos pressured her again. "Maxine," was all he said, but his voice was stern.

"I'm just gathering my thoughts."

From where I was sitting, I could see Amos roll his eyes, but he said nothing.

Evidently Maxine had decided to talk and, once she began, she spoke in the same breathless way I'd noticed before. "You won't get any clues from me. I told the police everything. All I did was walk in the way I usually do—I come in five afternoons a week. I take two days off, and Hank covers those nights. Five to midnight. That's the time he needs someone; he doesn't need twenty-four-hour..."

I interrupted the flow. "Was the door locked? Did you use your key to come in that afternoon?"

"Sure I did. I said it was the same as always. I unlocked the door and walked into the kitchen, carrying some groceries for Amos's dinner. When I saw her—his daughter—on the floor with the knife in her back, I just dropped everything and ran to see if she was still alive."

"Was she?"

"Didn't anyone tell you?" Douglas asked me. "The police say she was dead at least an hour, maybe longer."

"But does the timing work out? Andrea took her father out for lunch at 12:30." I looked at Amos. "When did you get back?"

"I didn't really notice, but I'd guess it was about 2:30. Then it probably took another fifteen minutes or so until I was settled in for my nap."

"That leaves a very short time frame."

"One police theory suggested the murderer was already in the house when we returned," Amos said. "And maybe still there when Maxine arrived. Then when she ran out of the kitchen to check on me, he left."

"That doesn't sound logical," Sterling insisted. "Why would he hang around for an hour or more?"

"Was anything disturbed? Was he searching for something?"

"Nothing was out of place," Amos said.

"Just the knife," Sterling mumbled, then looked embarrassed when he realized Amos had heard. "Maybe he didn't have time to rob the house," he added.

"Did you see any strange cars outside?" I asked Maxine.

"Not a one. Besides, where would he hide, and I would've heard if someone went running out of here."

"Why don't you let Maxine tell the story in her own words," Amos said. "Since you're suspicious of me, she needs to tell you where she found me."

"I'm not suspicious of you," I assured him. "Just covering all the possibilities."

"I didn't know what to expect," Maxine continued. "Scared stiff I was that I'd find Amos dead, too, but he was sound asleep when I looked in on him."

"Maybe I was faking it," Amos said, obviously determined to play devil's advocate.

Maxine snorted derisively. "I wasn't born yesterday," she said.

I would've laughed if the situation hadn't been so serious. "So you called the police and then looked in on Amos."

"No, ma'am. I ran to Amos's room first thing. I was so afraid for him. And even to this day, I'm sure if he hadn't taken a Percocet and been out of it, he *would* be dead now."

"Did you waken him before you called the police?"

"Of course, I did. Wasn't it his daughter who was murdered? I figured it would be less of a shock if I told him before the police came."

"How long did that take?"

"Just a few minutes and then I telephoned."

"From which room?"

"Amos's room. I was right there, wasn't I?"

Amos interrupted her. "And in case, you want to know that, too. Maxine helped me into my wheelchair, and I wheeled into the kitchen to see for myself. So when the police came, they found both of us in the kitchen."

"How did the police get in if you were both in the kitchen?" I asked.

Maxine looked surprised. "I told them Mr. Felder is wheelchair-bound and they should just come right in the house."

"But how did they get in?" I repeated.

"Oh," Maxine said. "I never did lock the front door. When I got here, I had the groceries to set down first and afterwards, when I found her..." I guess I forgot all about it."

"So someone could have slipped out," Sterling said.

My ice cream had melted into a multicolored puddle, and I noticed no one else was eating either. I didn't feel my questions were getting us anywhere at all. Once more, I wanted to tell Amos and Sterling that I couldn't help them. The information I'd learned might make a difference if they leveled with the police, who could then add it to whatever facts they already had.

"Amos, I have to tell you what I said before. You need to rely on the police or to hire a private detective."

"And I thought you understood by now. We don't want the things you heard tonight to get out. Just before Maxine arrived," Amos continued, "I asked for your promise. Do I have it?"

He suddenly looked sunken into the wheelchair although his body filled it completely and, despite knowing intuitively that he'd hate it, I felt sorry for him. It was going to be a difficult decision.

Chapter 10.

I thought about all the information being withheld from the police: most important, possibly, the temporary mobility Amos could achieve with fluori-methane. I was well aware that my major discovery so far would make him a murder suspect. On the other hand, in the short time I'd known Amos, I'd come to respect him. Could I bring myself to implicate him this way?

Then there was the identity of Denise's visitor as well as Andrea's latest lover—both of whom may have been the same man. I'd need time to think about the significance of what I'd learned and whether those facts would help or harm my friend, Denise. Although many people now wanted me to investigate Andrea's murder, could that role justify my silence—a silence that might jeopardize official inquiries into her death?

"I can't promise," I said finally.

Amos's eyes held mine as if he wanted to hypnotize me into making the commitment, but he said nothing further. It was Sterling who argued with me as he drove me back to Food Go to retrieve my own car. When we reached my white Accord, I still had not agreed to a promise I wasn't sure I could keep. However, I did make one decision without informing Sterling—to see Denise the next day and find out more about Tony.

* * * *

That night was not a sleepless one, but I tossed so restlessly that it may as well have been. By morning, I was thankful to be back on the night shift so that I didn't have to rush into the pharmacy. Determined to see Denise, I thought about her schedule, remembering she'd requested as many late hours as possible at Food Go to work mornings for Amos Felder. I decided to take a chance and arrive uninvited at her home, something I'd never done before. If she'd already heard about last night's disclosures from Sterling or

Amos, I was afraid advance warning would lead to excuses not to see me.

By 12:15 that afternoon, I was parked in Denise's driveway on Ocotillo Place waiting for her to appear. I knew she might have gone directly to the coffee shop, but I was too restless to wait and see her there. Luckily, Denise pulled up in her old black Ford only a few minutes after my own arrival.

"Ruthie," she said. "This is great!"

She hasn't heard anything, I thought. Then I wondered what kind of person would treat a friend this way. *I'm trying to help her*, I rationalized.

"Come in," Denise said, opening her front door and standing back for me to precede her. "Have you had lunch?"

"I just wanted to talk."

"Well, you can talk and eat at the same time. And we won't be interrupted here the way we are at Food Go."

Since this was exactly why I'd dropped in on Denise, I walked ahead of her into the sunlit kitchen. She was wearing her coral and navy sunburst print and looked just right for spring even though, according to the calendar, that season was still ten days away. Then again, in Scottsdale spring comes early, and the pundits already were placing bets as to when the first 100-degree day would occur.

"I can make you a tuna salad sandwich," Denise said. "Or would you like something different for a change."

"Just relax. As you said, we're not at Food Go now."

For a moment, Denise looked angry, as if by referring to her waitress job, I'd somehow demeaned her. Then she smiled. "You're right. But I'm fixing lunch for myself, so why not have something with me?"

Rather than a pointless and insincere "don't bother," I agreed to tuna and iced tea, waiting to begin serious conversation until she put together sandwiches and beverages for both of us.

"I heard you met Amos last night," Denise said as soon as we were seated. "What did you think of him?" Without waiting for my reply, she continued, "Isn't he an inspiration?"

I agreed and added a few words about his obvious intelligence. "I never did hear what kind of work he did before the accident," I added.

"He was an attorney, too. They're all in the same profession: Amos, Andrea, Sterling, and even Andrea's second husband."

"Yes, I got to meet him; but I'm surprised Amos doesn't continue to practice. I wouldn't expect the wheelchair to hold him back."

"I'm sure it wouldn't have," Denise said. "Only the accident had nothing to do with his retirement. Amos made a killing on that big class-action suit a few years ago and decided he'd had enough. He always loved the sea, so he bought a boat, kept it at one of the marinas in San Diego, and spent a good part of the year sailing. I think that's what he misses most of his old life," she said reflectively, as if she'd just come to that conclusion.

"I'd already guessed he loves the sea—the artwork, his dog's name ... But why does he stay in Scottsdale?"

"The grandchildren," she said simply.

"I met them last night, too."

"Aren't they great?" Denise asked. "Now that Andrea can't interfere anymore, I'll be seeing a lot more of them."

"Good God, Denise. Don't let anyone else hear you say that."

She laughed. "I suppose you think that gives me a motive for murder. Could be, but a rather thin one, don't you think?"

"What I think doesn't matter. I don't suspect you for a minute."

"You believe in me and so do Sterling and Amos. That's all I care about," she said.

"Fine. But you still need to be careful."

We sat quietly for a few minutes now, nibbling at our sandwiches and sipping iced tea. "You didn't believe that woman?" Denise made it a question.

"If you mean Jennifer Hoffman, no; I didn't believe her. I didn't credit anything she said until you informed me that some of it *was* true."

"Let's start at the beginning, Ruthie. I told you I did go out with Sterling a few times until I discovered he was married. I didn't break up his marriage, though, and I didn't murder his ex-wife."

"We're friends, and I trust you; but if you're protecting someone else, you could be in danger."

"You think Sterling killed her," Denise said, jumping up and upsetting her iced tea. She ran quickly to the sink, picked up a sponge, and wiped the table before the tea could spread to the floor. Meanwhile, I pulled my placemat out of range and used a napkin to dab at the spill, thinking about what to say next as I worked.

"I don't know Sterling well enough to judge whether he's capable of doing it, but he isn't the one I meant." I looked up at Denise, who had remained standing. "You must realize I wouldn't pry if this weren't so serious," I said earnestly.

"You want to ask about Tony."

Maybe this won't be so difficult after all, I thought. "Let's sit down and talk calmly," I said aloud. Since I was already seated, the plural sounded more like the stereotypical "How are we feeling today?" hospital query. Denise did sit down, however, and quietly waited for me to continue, but I said nothing.

"Okay, I guess it is time to tell you about him," Denise began, and then she paused so long that I was afraid she'd changed her mind. She concentrated on finishing her sandwich, got up again to refill both glasses with iced tea, and sat silently once more.

"You've known him for a long time," I prompted.

"I never mentioned Tony to you before for a couple of reasons. Mostly, I was ashamed to admit being involved with a man who was in jail for fraud."

"When did he get out?"

"Maybe a year ago."

"And he's driving a Corvette. That was a quick recovery."

"He's always known how to make money but not always honestly. That's what landed him in prison."

"Were you together before the jail term?"

"Like I told you the other day, on and off. He came by when he felt like it. I always knew I wasn't the only one, but I loved him."

There it was again, the refrain that could cause so many problems when the word "but" prefaced it. For a minute I thought about Michael and wondered if I had any "buts." *I did when we were young*, I reminded myself. I'd never dared say the words to my mother, "He's not Jewish, but I love him." And so, I'd given Michael up. Did I still need to qualify my feelings for him? That was something I'd have to examine another time.

Denise seemed to be waiting for a response from me. "If this man is important to you, you didn't have to be ashamed to tell me about him. I hope you don't think I'm that judgmental."

"I wasn't sure you'd understand. See, I met him right after Craig dumped me, and at first he made me feel wanted again." She twisted her silver and coral necklace. I'd noticed before that Denise, who seldom mentioned her former husband, always showed signs of stress when his name did come up.

I felt a surge of sympathy for my friend, whose life had been so much more difficult than my own. She deserved a chance at happiness, and Sterling had seemed good for her. Why couldn't things go smoothly without all this mess?

"What about Sterling? I thought you really cared for him," I said aloud.

"I do. It's just that Tony makes me crazy. When he shows up, I forget about everyone else."

"Do you still love Tony?"

"No!" she said emphatically, her voice so vehement that I wondered whether he had killed Andrea and Denise knew or suspected it.

I reached across the table and squeezed her hand for a brief moment. "I'm glad. He doesn't sound like a healthy fixation."

"A fixation," Denise echoed. "That's just what he's been. Almost like an addiction, but I'm cured now."

We were both silent again. Then I remembered she had more than one reason for not telling me about him. I prompted her again. "You said you never mentioned Tony for a couple of reasons."

"The other one is even harder to talk about because it shows what a fool I've been."

"Don't tear yourself down, Denise. You're not the first or the last woman to be taken in that way."

She suddenly grinned. "You're telling me!"

As I waited to hear more, she became serious once more. "Tony showed up again a few months ago. I knew it was stupid to start with him this time when Sterling and I were seeing each other, but I couldn't resist."

"Does Sterling know about him?"

"I don't think so. Anyhow, I knew Tony wouldn't stay around very long; I just couldn't be the one to break it off." The pause was longer now.

"So what happened?" I asked finally.

"He came to pick me up at the coffee shop—we were going to the Suns game."

"And..." I prompted.

She took a deep breath and visibly forced herself to continue. "Your pharmacist—Louise—came off work and walked into the coffee shop."

No, I thought to myself, guessing where this chance meeting led. *It can't be.* But somehow it sounded plausible.

Chapter 11.

"He started chatting with her—Tony has a way with people. I didn't know for a long time," Denise said, her voice breaking. "He kept on seeing me but less and less often. And then, he moved in with her."

"I'm sorry, Denise."

"There's nothing to be sorry about. I think that's what finally woke me up."

"But you were still seeing him as of last week."

"You mean the day Andrea was killed," Denise said.

"That's right. And you're protecting him."

"Ruthie, if I thought for one minute that he could be capable of murder, I'd tell the police he was at Amos's house that day." She spoke earnestly, meeting my eyes with something like a plea in her own.

"You can't be sure." I wondered if Tony was the one who had blackened my staff pharmacist's eye. If he had a violent streak, surely Denise would be aware of it.

"I tell you I know. He didn't kill Andrea."

"You said he was in prison for fraud, not for any violent crime?" I made it a question.

"It was what they call a white-collar crime," Denise insisted. "No violence."

I tried to think of a tactful way to phrase my next question. There wasn't any. "Has he ever been abusive to you?"

At the look of pain on Denise's face, I wanted to take back the words. She went to her refrigerator for the iced tea pitcher even though our glasses were virtually untouched since the last refill. I knew she was buying time.

"Only since he got out of prison. He drinks too much these days."

"Then you don't know what he's capable of now," I said. I was thinking of Louise again but didn't want to gossip about her troubles with her boyfriend, the one I now assumed was Tony.

"He was always kind of possessive," Denise said. "This last year, though, it got much worse. He'd disappear for weeks at a time, but I was always supposed to be there when he came back. And he'd check up on me at work, too."

"How did you manage to see Sterling?"

"It was mostly when Tony didn't come around." She smiled ironically. "After the first shock, I was sort of relieved that he'd taken up with Louise. I figured now he'd be checking into her whereabouts instead of mine."

"But he came to Amos Felder's to check up on you," I said and was interrupted by the door chimes.

Denise left the kitchen so quickly I knew she was reluctant to continue the conversation. I half hoped and half feared the visitor would be Tony, wanting to form my own opinion of him but not knowing how he'd react to my presence. And if Denise's infatuation with him really had ended, would he go out of her life quietly, I wondered. He didn't sound like the type of person who'd let her leave him for someone else. When he found out about Sterling, he could be dangerous.

I heard Denise returning to the kitchen and looked up, determined now to support my friend if the heavier footsteps behind her belonged to Tony—but it was Michael Loring who surprised me, walking into the room and greeting me with a quick hug.

"I dashed over as soon as I saw your car in the driveway," he said. "I'm not intruding, am I?"

"Of course not. We're delighted," I said, including Denise in the buoyant turn my spirits had taken.

Denise pulled out a chair for Michael. "Iced tea, coffee, a coke?" she asked.

"Nothing, thanks. I just had lunch at my daughter's."

"Betsy looked radiant at the baby shower," I said. "And the luncheon was an elegant affair."

"Yes, Patricia does have a talent for organizing things."

I was relieved to feel no jealous tremor at the mention of his former wife and realized I'd finally achieved a degree of self-confidence where Michael was concerned. Maybe it was the contrast between his inherent decency and what I'd been hearing about Tony, but I suddenly knew I could count on Michael to be honest with me.

"So, are the two of you off today or both working late shifts?" Michael asked. As a pharmacist himself, he was no stranger to odd schedules.

"I dropped in to see Denise before work," I explained. Then I hesitated, uncertain whether she'd be upset if I talked to Michael about the

Felder murder. I didn't have to wonder long, for Denise herself brought up the subject.

"Did you hear about the woman attorney who was murdered last week?"

"I guess I skimmed over something in the Tucson paper." The expressive blue eyes suddenly narrowed. "Don't tell me you two are involved in that one."

"You met Sterling Harraday here at the New Year's Eve party," I reminded him. "The murdered woman was his ex-wife."

"And I've been working part-time for her father," Denise added.

"I don't believe it! How do these things happen to you, Ruthie?"

"Nothing has happened to me," I was quick to say.

"I know better than that. You're going to rush headlong into another murder investigation."

"Not if Detective Moreway has anything to say about it," I protested.

"I don't think he has a chance if you make up your mind to get involved," he teased. His voice became serious. "Be careful, Ruthie."

I was pleased that he didn't try to dictate anything more than caution to me. Some women might have confused an order to stay away from the investigation with a show of affection; but I'd been on my own since Bob's death, and that was more than two years ago. I'd find it difficult to deal with anyone who presumed to control my actions.

"I have no intention of getting into danger," I said.

"You never do," Michael answered; but a grin accompanied his words. Again, I couldn't take offense.

"Denise, Sterling, and even some other people want me to look into the murder," I said.

"So by now you've probably uncovered more than the police."

"As a matter of fact, I have." Instantly, I regretted that pride had overcome discretion. "Really!" Denise said quickly. "Is that why you've been questioning me about Tony?"

"Who's Tony?" Michael asked.

Denise gave him a watered-down version of the story I'd just heard. I watched as Michael leaned forward and put both elbows on the table, concentrating on her words. Energy seemed to flow from him even in that position.

"So you think this Tony killed her?" Michael wanted to know.

"No," Denise contradicted loudly. "Why would he do it?"

"Andrea seems to have been involved in an affair with a man named Tony. Someone she picked up in a bar." I watched Denise carefully as I spoke, trying to see whether she'd known about Andrea and Tony.

"And you decided it's the same Tony," she said. "You have no proof of that."

"Denise, coincidences do happen. But I can't believe two different men named Tony are entangled here, especially since we know your Tony showed up at the Felder house the day of the murder."

"That doesn't make him guilty."

"I'm not talking about guilt or innocence now—only about the identity of the new man in Andrea's life."

"He came to see me, not Andrea," Denise insisted. "She wasn't even there that morning."

"And did you tell him when she was expected?" Michael asked.

There was no response. Denise looked from one to the other of us and then buried her face in her hands.

"I'm sorry," I said, appalled at the distress I was causing my friend; but I couldn't let it go. I had to know.

"He did question me about the family," she mumbled through her hands. "I thought it was his usual jealousy. So I assured him the man I work for is confined to a wheelchair."

"Did he have other questions?" Michael asked.

"He wanted to know what time I got off. When I told him, he acted like he didn't believe me." She was twisting the necklace again, and I wondered if there was a pattern in the men Denise chose. All of them seemed to induce anxiety.

"Tony kept saying I must be meeting someone there. I told him I would be going straight to Food Go, that Amos's daughter would be coming by to take him to lunch."

"So he did know where to find her that afternoon," I said.

"I never guessed about him and Andrea. You have to believe me."

"Then why have you been protecting Tony?"

"Because he won't have a chance once the police discover his record. He'll be the chief suspect. I see it happen on television all the time."

I sighed. Sometimes Denise's penchant for melodrama gets to me. "You didn't really want me to solve the murder," I said. "You sent me to Frank Moreway to find out whether the police know about Tony."

"That was part of it," Denise admitted. "But I *do* need you to find the real murderer. Especially if you're right, if Tony was involved with Andrea."

Michael got up and started pacing. "I don't think you should cover for this man, Denise—no matter how much he means to you."

"He's nothing to me now. I already told that to Ruthie."

"Then go to the police," Michael said. He stopped his pacing in front of Denise's chair. "Or are you afraid of Tony?"

Her head shot up, but she didn't reply. She didn't have to—I could see the fear in her eyes. And that worried me more than anything else, for Denise was not a person who frightened easily.

Chapter 12.

Michael and I exchanged glances. "You know that Ruthie and I will support you in every way," he told her. "We can go to the police with you, if you'd like; ask for protection for you."

"Or you could move in with me for awhile," I said. "Tony won't be able to track you to my place."

"It's not what you think, Ruthie. I'm not afraid of him." Her words denied the expression of fear I'd caught, but I was sure of my interpretation.

"From what you've told me, you should be. Even if he didn't kill Andrea, you could be in danger when he finds out about Sterling."

"That's one of the things I am worried about," she admitted.

"Then let us help."

"You don't understand. Tony's not some kind of monster. Maybe he hit me sometimes when he was really upset, but he's not dangerous."

"Don't you read the papers?" Michael asked. "That kind of behavior can escalate."

"Denise," I said, trying to keep my voice calm. "We don't want to harm Tony, only to keep you safe."

"I'm okay."

"You're afraid of something, and you shouldn't have to face it alone."

She looked intently at the lights over her kitchen table, tulip-shaped fixtures attached to a ceiling fan, as if she could find some answers there. "I appreciate your offers to help. Really I do. But I can't go to the police."

"You're an adult," Michael said. "It's your decision."

We had pushed her hard, but Michael was right. She alone could make the decision and, although I knew Denise usually was far less stubborn than I am, I could see she would not change her mind.

"How about you, Ruthie?" Michael asked. "Since you seem determined to be involved, can I help *you* with anything?"

Michael's probing calls to his pharmacy contacts had been invaluable a few months before, when I'd been accused of dispensing the fatal prescription. I found myself glowing with pleasure at his offer of support now.

"There is one aspect of this case I'd like to consult with you about," I said.

"Run it by me."

I smiled to myself. Michael's energetic personality came through even in his word choices. "How much mobility would fluori-methane give a person confined to a wheelchair?"

"There's no set answer to that."

"I know. But would he be able to stand up long enough to stab someone with killing force?"

"His doctor may be the only one who could tell you, Ruthie."

"That's what I thought, but no physician would release that information to me. Not about a specific patient."

"Why don't I ask around and at least determine the possibilities?" Michael suggested.

Meanwhile, Denise had jumped to her feet, a stunned look on her face. "I don't believe this," she said. "What are you trying to do? First Tony and now Amos Felder. You can't frame Amos for his daughter's murder. He's in a wheelchair, for God's sake."

"You're the one who keeps telling me that I shouldn't assume his disability keeps him from doing things."

"Cooking, not killing," she said.

"I'm not accusing Amos of anything. And I'm certainly not framing him."

"To think he trusted you and look what you're doing behind his back."

Now I was really stung. "Not behind his back, Denise. He and I discussed the fluori-methane."

"That doesn't make any difference." She was wringing her hands, something I'd never seen her do before.

"Think about it," I said. "You're one of the people who keeps flattering me about my crime-solving ability. How can I accomplish anything if I ignore possible evidence?"

"I can't deal with this, Ruthie. Please go away."

After a moment's shocked hesitation, I decided it was better to do as she asked. Michael and I quietly walked to the front door and let ourselves out of the house.

"She'll get over it," he assured me.

"But meanwhile, she's suffering, and everything I try to do for her seems to make it worse."

"It's the old 'shoot the messenger' syndrome," Michael said. "Denise strikes me as someone with a lot of common sense. When she has time to think things over, she'll realize there can't be exceptions in a murder investigation."

"Maybe she's right," I told him. "I could be showing off—hey, look what I discovered—at the expense of people she cares for." Sure it had been stimulating to catch two murderers that the police had never suspected, even though I'd nearly been killed in the process. However, now I was discouraged enough to forget about the Felder murder. *Leave it to the Scottsdale police*, I told myself.

"You're not showing off—just doing what they thought they wanted. Only now you must be getting too close."

"You really think one of them, Tony or Amos, did it?"

"I don't know," Michael admitted. "Let's go next door, though, and push all this out of our minds for awhile. Patricia went up to Sedona for the day, but Betsy will be delighted to see you."

We crossed the two driveways that separated Denise's house from that of Michael's daughter. I noticed a red Miata parked behind his silver-and-gray Lexus. "It looks like Betsy has other company," I said. "I'd better just go."

"I don't know who that car belongs to," Michael told me. "It wasn't there when I walked over to Denise's place." He peered into the front seat of the car, as if searching for a clue to its owner. "Come on in anyhow. At least, with someone else present, we won't be tempted to talk about the murder."

As soon as I entered Betsy's starkly contemporary living room, however, and saw two pregnant women sitting on the white overstuffed sofa, I knew he was wrong. Jennifer Hoffman was sipping from a tall glass of orange juice, which she quickly placed on the glass cocktail table when she saw us. She rose and shook hands politely with both of us.

"Betsy told me her dad was here," she said. "But I didn't expect our detective friend."

"I'd rather not get into that now."

"You know each other?" Michael asked.

"We met at the baby shower last Saturday."

"I didn't mean to be flippant about Andrea's murder, Ruthie. I'm really glad to see you again," Jennifer told me.

Unable to reciprocate truthfully, I said nothing.

Michael changed the subject. "You're looking great, Jennifer. When are you due?"

"About a month after Betsy." The ebullience I'd noticed before came to the surface. "We were just comparing swollen ankles."

Betsy laughed. "It could've been worse. We might've been carrying through the summer."

"Just think of it," Jennifer agreed. "Thirty extra pounds in 118 degree weather."

"Speak for yourself, my friend. I've only gained twenty-two pounds."

Their light-hearted banter helped erase some of the uneasiness I'd felt at Denise's situation and her reaction to my probings. My mind considered and rejected a harsher word—meddling—for Denise had been the first one to insist on bringing me into the case.

"Would you like some orange juice?" Betsy asked and started to ease herself out of the sofa.

"Stay there," Michael said. "I'll get some for both of us."

As soon as he left the room, Jennifer brought up the subject of the murder again. "Have you thought about what I said at the baby shower?"

"Yes, I have. But surely you realize that my options are limited; people don't have to talk to me."

"I know that. In fact, Betsy and I discussed it. She tells me you know Denise and Sterling well. They'll relax around you and reveal things they'd never tell the police."

"And you seriously believe one of them will say, 'Oh, by the way, I murdered Andrea.'"

"Of course not, but they could let other information slip."

She was right, although I wasn't about to tell her of the facts I'd already gathered, things I was sure the police didn't yet know. And that brought the ethical question to mind again. I couldn't brush away an internal voice that insisted I tell Detective Moreway what I'd learned. There was no question of using patient confidentiality as an excuse here. As far as I knew, Amos Felder's prescriptions were not filled at the Food Go pharmacy that I managed.

Thinking of the pharmacy made me remember Louise Rettenberg, my staff pharmacist. In the light of the other information I'd uncovered, I had nearly forgotten about the relationship between her and Tony—the sinister Tony as I now thought of him. Could Louise have discovered his interest in Andrea and killed her rival? *Not another one*, I thought, remembering Tim Barnard and last summer's Stokes case.

Jennifer was speaking to me again. "You need to meet Andrea's husband and also her father. They'll help."

I had to admit I'd already met them and was bracing myself for Jennifer's reaction when Michael returned, carrying two glasses of orange juice and two cloth napkins in a bold black-and-white print. "You just missed something interesting," I said to him. "Jennifer is one of the people we talked about, the ones who've been trying to convince me I can do better than the police."

"You didn't tell me your dad knows about the murder." Jennifer sounded as if she had Betsy on the witness stand.

"Ruthie and I just discussed it for the first time a little while ago," Michael told her.

"I see," Jennifer said.

I could feel my face flush. She had managed to put more innuendo into those two words than I would've thought possible.

Michael jumped to the rescue. "I don't know what you think you see," he said.

"I assume that's your Lexus I parked behind, so you walked to wherever you were. That means you weren't too far away, and Ruthie was with you." She turned to Betsy. "Isn't Denise Seaford one of your neighbors?"

"And how do you know that?" Michael asked.

"Your daughter must have mentioned it once. I'm an attorney; remembering goes with the profession." The words could have sounded smug, but her bubbly laugh accompanied them and toned down that impression.

"For an attorney, Jennifer has been rather incautious," I said to Michael. "At the shower, she accused both Sterling and Denise of complicity in the murder."

"Do you have any evidence?" Michael asked mildly.

"It was entirely off the record. I just wanted to point Ruthie in the right direction."

"And you're sure that's the right direction?"

She looked quickly at him and then at me. "It's a start."

"A start in railroading my friends," I said.

"Let me tell you something. Maybe some murderers are loners, but most do have friends and families. Just because these people are your friends doesn't exempt them from suspicion." As she spoke, her voice rose, and I saw her fold both hands across her stomach. It seemed to be an unconscious gesture, but I began to worry about premature labor.

"Are you okay?" I asked.

"What?" She looked down and unfolded her hands, reaching instead for the orange juice. "I'm fine."

"I didn't mean to upset you," I said. "Can't we talk about something else?"

"In a minute. First there are things I think you should know. I told you some of them the other day, although I know you didn't believe me."

"I don't want to hear about Denise and Sterling. She explained it to me."

"Did she also tell you about the argument she had with Andrea?"

I guess my expression revealed the answer, but I refused to give Jennifer a chance to say anything else against my friend. "That's enough." I mustered the tone I use with teenagers who want to buy hypodermic needles, claiming their grandmothers need insulin injections. "I don't want to hear it."

"Loyalty is a wonderful trait," she said. "On the other hand, wearing blinders is just plain stupid."

Michael looked at his daughter as if prompting her to intervene. She picked up her cue. "Please, Jen. Intensity is also a valuable trait, especially in your work. But Ruthie isn't on trial here; she's my guest, just as you are."

"Sorry. I guess I got carried away."

I was having a hard time understanding this young woman. She seemed to switch from the light effervescence I'd first noticed to a sharpness that was completely at odds with the former tone. For a moment, I wondered whether Jennifer's story about Sterling's interest in her was a fantasy. Maybe it was the other way around; maybe Sterling had rejected her, and now she was out to make trouble for him.

We certainly do have some unwanted suspects this time, I told myself: my best friend, her former boyfriend, her current one, and my staff pharmacist. Of course, there is always Andrea's new husband; but that's too easy. And let's not forget the very personable gentleman who's confined to a wheelchair, as well as this highly pregnant young attorney in front of me.

Although a quick glance at my watch showed me I still had plenty of time to get to the pharmacy, I was about to make my excuses and leave when Jennifer got up awkwardly from the sofa. "Take care now," she said to Betsy, who had managed to rise more gracefully, and gave her a quick hug. "Be sure to let me know right away."

Betsy laughed. "At the rate I'm going, you may be first."

"Not a chance."

Jennifer shook hands with both Michael and me. As we all walked with her to the front door, she turned to me again. "You haven't heard the last from me. I'm not going to let Andrea's murderer get away with it, and I need your help." She waved to Betsy once more and left. We watched Jennifer's struggle to fit her pregnant body into the red Miata.

"Why is she so insistent?" Michael asked as the young woman drove away. "Most people would rely on the police."

Betsy looked embarrassed. "I guess I'm to blame."

"You told her about the other murders?" Michael asked.

"She talked about all this during the shower," I said, "but I still don't understand her."

"That's just the way Jennifer operates. When she's determined to do something, she never lets go."

Michael turned to me. "How do you feel about it?" We were still standing in the entryway to Betsy's house.

"I don't know. When we talked before, I was afraid solving crimes had become an ego trip, and I'd hate to give anyone that impression. Jennifer's right, though; people do talk to me, and they tell me things they don't tell the police."

"Ruthie, don't worry about what other people think. Do what's important to you."

"And if it hurts my friends?"

He didn't have a chance to answer the question because Denise came racing across the two driveways, calling out as she approached us. "Something terrible just happened."

"Are you okay? What's wrong?" I asked.

She had reached us now and stood there gasping for breath. "How could you do it, Ruthie?"

I was bewildered at the accusation. My first guess was that she'd seen Jennifer leave and somehow thought I was conspiring with her.

"We don't have any idea what you mean. Come inside and tell us about it," Betsy said calmly.

"If it's Jennifer, I didn't even know she was here."

Denise looked at me, her face contorted with anger. "I don't give a damn about Jennifer. It's Amos I care about. And now the police are questioning him again because you told them about that spray."

Chapter 13.

I stared at Denise, wondering why she blamed me for something I hadn't done. "Not me," I insisted.

"You're the only one who could have told them."

"Just a minute," Michael said. "From what I understand, other people also heard about the fluori-methane."

"Sure, and they all heard it from her, just like you did."

"What I'm trying to ask is why you're convinced it was Ruthie? You know any of the others could have told the police."

"No one else would've gone to that detective friend of hers."

"Detective friend of mine," I exploded. "You sent me to see him in the first place."

"Not to accuse Amos."

"I didn't say a word to the police about him."

"Sterling and Douglas were the only others there last night. And neither of them would do anything to harm Amos."

"What about the nursing help? Maybe they mentioned the spray," Michael said.

"Could be," Denise admitted, suddenly sounding calmer.

Betsy took her arm, trying to lead her into the house. "Come and sit down for a while. Maybe we can clear this up."

"No," Denise said, her agitation returning. "You fooled me for a minute, Ruthie, but Maxine Peabody just called me. She said a Detective Moreway was at the house questioning Amos. That's why I'm sure you were the instigator."

"Be reasonable. It's probably Frank's case."

"He's not the detective who originally questioned me," she insisted.

"But he *is* the one who wanted to ask me about you and Sterling," I said and then literally bit my tongue in frustration at revealing information I'd carefully hidden to protect her peace of mind.

Denise stood there in front of the doorway to Betsy Stokes's home, staring at me. Then, without another word, she turned and walked away from all of us. I called after her, "Wait. It's not what you think; I just didn't want to worry you."

"Let her go," Michael said. "She's too upset now to listen to reason."

My own thoughts were in turmoil, too. It seemed as if my friendship with Denise was over, and I'd done nothing but try to help her. Unlike those days after the death of Betsy's husband, my suspicions now had never touched on Denise but, after this fiasco, I was afraid I'd never convince her of that. Maybe if I could get Frank Moreway to tell me the source of his information...

* * * *

I didn't have to wait long to see Detective Moreway, for he was there when I arrived at the Food Go pharmacy that afternoon. Despite my visits to Denise and Betsy, I was at least twenty minutes early for my night shift. Frank Moreway's first words indicated he had checked my schedule with Louise.

"Let's talk for a few minutes before you begin work," he said. "I have some questions." He remembered the Food Go employee lounge from an earlier encounter and led me toward it.

"Don't you want privacy?" I asked.

"Your friend is already in the coffee shop, and no one else will understand what we're talking about."

We sat in a corner of the room. "If it's about Denise," I said, "I have nothing to add."

"That may be true, but you do have information about Amos Felder. I want to know why you never contacted me about that prescription spray."

"Detective Moreway, you made it quite clear to me that you didn't want to deal with amateurs. As I recall, you were rather sarcastic last time we spoke."

"You don't have to take that attitude. When the public has pertinent information, it's their duty to contact us. That's not the same as playing amateur detective."

"You want a one-way street."

"What does that mean?" he asked.

"You don't want me to investigate, but you want the results of my detective work. And I'm supposed to get those results while I'm kept completely in the dark about the things *you* already know."

"What do you expect? You have no official status."

"That's true. On the other hand, who discovered two murderers for you?"

"And nearly got killed in the process. That's not how we operate."

"Getting back to your original question," I said firmly. "I have no way of knowing how much mobility that spray would provide for Amos. You surely couldn't expect me to assume he's the murderer."

"That's not the point. Once you discovered the spray and understood the possibilities, we're the ones you should have contacted to investigate his alibi."

"Detective Moreway, you had every opportunity to check on Amos Felder. Why are you blaming me for failing to do your job?"

There was absolute silence. *Now I've done it*, I told myself.

"Eventually, we would've found what that spray is for," he said through clenched teeth. "But this is your field of expertise, and I would have expected some cooperation from you. We're not talking about that friend of yours now." He nodded in the direction of the coffee shop. "We're discussing someone I hear you met for the first time last night."

"That doesn't mean I want to see him under suspicion of murder. He's suffered enough."

"So you feel sorry for him." His tone changed, as if he were playing good cop/bad cop all by himself. "I can understand that. Hell, I felt sorry for him myself. However, that doesn't change anything. If you stumble on information the police should have, I expect you to inform me next time."

"Obviously, you did hear about it."

"Not from you."

I wanted very much to ask who had been his informant, but I didn't dare. For one thing, I knew he'd never tell me. For another, despite my attempts to downplay my responsibilities, I'd felt from the beginning that I was withholding valuable information from the police. And I hadn't come to terms with that feeling. I thought about Andrea and Tony, wondering whether I should reveal what I'd learned about their relationship. However, that was second-hand, maybe even third-hand, information.

It was time for me to be in the pharmacy. I figured the detective's purpose was to impress upon me the need to tell him anything I "stumbled on." Surprisingly, he hadn't asked whether I did have other information, and when I got up to leave, he didn't try to detain me.

* * * *

Back in the pharmacy, Louise Rettenberg was helping a customer, a scrawny-looking woman whose entire body shook with the hacking cough that kept interrupting her words. "What do you recommend for this cough?" she managed to ask between bouts.

"I showed you the section out there labeled 'cough remedies,'" Louise said.

"But what do *you* recommend?" the woman insisted.

"Any one of those will help." She paused as the coughing began again. "Or you could call your doctor to prescribe something stronger."

"There are too many choices. I'm confused."

"Then see your doctor."

After another fit of coughing, the customer asked Louise which cough mixture she personally used. Louise would not narrow the field. As I put on my white professional jacket, I remembered Dad's drugstore in Tucson and the way customers used to come in and ask "doc" for a cough mixture. He'd walk out from behind the prescription counter and lead them to the shelf of over-the-counter cold remedies, pull out one, and hand it to the customer. They trusted "doc" and his experience. Today, few pharmacists would dare to make that kind of recommendation; the specter of lawsuits hovers too closely over us.

I could hear the woman coughing continuously now as she walked away from the pharmacy. My own feelings were mixed. I'd been trained, both in pharmacy college and in Dad's old-fashioned drugstore, to do everything I could to help people. On the other hand, I'd read, heard about, and come too near to the reality of our litigious society to do more than name several possibilities when a customer wanted my recommendation. Obviously, Louise refused to do even that much.

"A persistent one," Louise said. She was standing in front of the computer, filling several prescriptions for the young man who was next in line. Although she didn't look up, I couldn't miss the fresh bruises on her face.

Tony, I thought. Why doesn't she file a complaint against him? If she did, his connection with Andrea might come out. That, in turn, could lead to his arrest, and she'd be free of him. However, I suspected she didn't want to be free of Tony—the "but I love him" syndrome again.

I wondered whether I should say something or just ignore the bruises once more. *No*, I told myself. *This is no time for cowardice; she needs help.* I hesitated, though, unwilling to alienate Louise. Two people on the same day would certainly be a record, but I decided I had to speak.

"Louise," I said quietly when she had finished counseling the young man about the possible side effects of his muscle relaxant and warned him that it might make him sleepy. "I know it's none of my business, but I can't bear to see someone treated this way."

"You're right. It *is* none of your business."

"He's dangerous, and I don't want you to be his next victim."

"Next victim! What are you talking about? You don't even know him."

"I've heard all I want to know about Tony," I said.

Louise's face was flushed, but her eyes were cold as she stared at me. "How do you know so much?" she demanded. "I never told it to you."

Now I was really torn. "A mutual friend saw you together," I said. It was the truth but without revealing information that could hurt Louise.

"You think I don't know about your Denise and what she did to him?" Louise glared at me, ignoring the fact that both phones were now ringing.

I was tempted to ignore the phones, too; but professional instinct took over, and I reached for one of them. An ophthalmologist's office was calling in a script for erythromycin ointment for an eye infection. As I copied down the prescription details, I noticed that Louise had picked up the other phone. I wanted to ask what she meant, what she thought Denise had done to Tony, but it was impossible to talk now. Louise would be leaving soon—our shifts only overlapped slightly —but I was determined to continue the discussion.

While I went to the computer to enter the eye ointment prescription, I saw that she had busied herself counting out tablets for the script she'd just taken over the telephone. I finished at the computer, pulled the labels from the printer, and selected the medication from its place on the shelves. Using my peripheral vision, I saw that Louise was now at the computer. No one was at the pharmacy window, and I prayed silently that the lull would continue.

Before Louise finished at the computer, I edged over and stood next to her. "I don't understand," I said. "What are you suggesting Denise did to Tony? From everything I've heard and noticed, I'd assume it was the other way around."

"You know as well as I do that she's been unfaithful to him."

"Unfaithful! Isn't he living with you?"

"Lower your voice," Louise told me, sounding like a parent scolding her child. "Someone's at the window now."

My stance, meant to block Louise from sidling away, had faced me toward the rear of the pharmacy. I turned now and saw a couple of teenage girls giggling self-consciously. *Maybe it has nothing to do with overhearing us*, I said to myself as I approached them. The shorter girl handed me a prescription for Benzamycin, an acne lotion.

As I filled this new script, I glanced at my watch. Louise would be leaving in five minutes, and I would lose my chance to find out what she meant. Although Louise now removed her white jacket and hung it up, she made no move to go. I hurried through my work, mixing the dissolved powder into the lotion base.

"Be sure to refrigerate it," I told the girl as I handed the lotion to her. The teenagers paid and walked away, giggling again.

I replaced the alcohol I'd used to make the lotion and was relieved to see Louise walking over to me, hands on hips, dark braid hanging over the collar of her denim blouse. The bruises on the side of her face added a vulnerable look I'd never noticed before. She made no move to throw the braid over her shoulder the way she usually did when it got in her way.

"You want to know about Tony and your friend. Okay, but you'll wish you hadn't asked me." She took a deep breath and continued. "Remember last week when I had to leave and I needed you to take over for me?"

I nodded, wondering what that had to do with Denise. It seemed like I spent half my time defending her and, ironically, she had stormed away from me only an hour or so earlier.

"That was the night he found out about her new boyfriend—the lawyer."

"Impossible," I said. "Denise was working here that evening. I was in the coffee shop talking to her when they paged me to return here."

"I don't know how; I only know he's been in a rage ever since." She fingered the largest bruise, just below her right eye.

"What is this, the old double standard? He's living with you and he's seeing…" I stopped myself before I could reveal what I'd learned about Tony and Andrea. "He sounds like one of those controlling men you read about."

"He's not living with me now," Louise said. "We see each other occasionally."

"And you let him treat you like that?"

"We agreed that we weren't ready for commitment."

"That's not what I'm talking about, Louise. I tried to ignore it before, but I can't understand why you have anything to do with a man who…" The words failed me, and I simply pointed to her bruised cheek.

"You don't understand. Tony's not really like that; he's upset because your friend isn't honest with him."

"Lots of women put up with physical abuse because they think they have no choice, Louise." I spoke earnestly, trying to make her realize what she was doing to herself. "But you're not in that situation. You're an educated woman. A professional. You earn a good salary, and you can support yourself."

"I can't give him up."

The telephone rang again, but it was a customer wanting to know whether her medicine was ready. I checked quickly and assured her she could pick it up anytime. As I talked, I watched Louise carefully, certain she'd take the opportunity to leave. She waited patiently, and I suddenly realized she wanted reassurance. Otherwise, she wouldn't be continuing this conversation.

"You're young, intelligent, and attractive. You don't have to settle for someone like Tony."

"You don't even know him," she said for the second time that afternoon.

Again I was tempted to tell her about Andrea Felder, but I held back. I'd done enough to puncture her balloon. "I'd certainly like to meet him," I heard myself say.

"I'll think about it." She turned and started to leave the pharmacy.

At that moment, we heard shouts coming from the direction of the coffee shop. We looked at each other, wondering what could be wrong.

"Shoplifters," Louise said.

"In the coffee shop?"

Now we saw that people were running in that direction from every part of the store. I knew management would have handled a shoplifting incident quietly and felt uneasy. Somehow the commotion reminded me of the tragedy that had taken place in another supermarket restaurant some years before when several people had been shot by a disgruntled ex-husband, some fatally.

"We can't both leave the pharmacy," I said, hoping Louise would volunteer to stay. Without a backward glance, though, she ran out; I was left to worry and wonder as more and more customers and employees headed to the source of the shouts. No one came close enough to the pharmacy for me to question them.

I thought of calling the front office to ask what was happening, but I knew it must be serious, and they'd be too busy to deal with my curiosity. After a while, I heard sirens coming from the Food Go parking lot. "Someone must have had a heart attack," I tried to tell myself, knowing that the coffee shop attracted many older customers for their early bird dinner specials.

Restless and anxious, I forced myself to do some paperwork while I waited for Louise to return. It seemed longer but my watch showed that only ten minutes had passed before I saw her approaching, running even faster this time. She didn't wait to enter the pharmacy but paused at the window.

"Ruthie, I'm sorry to have to tell you." Louise stopped and my heart thumped uneasily at the look on her face. "Someone just stabbed your friend."

Chapter 14.

"Oh, my God! For the first time in my professional life, I forgot about my obligation to the pharmacy. Frantically pulling the door open, I raced away, not even waiting to see whether Louise would take over for me.

As I approached the coffee shop, I saw paramedics wheeling a gurney from that direction, but the crowd prevented my getting close enough to see if Denise really was the victim—and if she was alive. I pushed my way toward the store entrance where an ambulance had pulled into the fire lane and caught one quick glimpse of Denise's face as they loaded her through its back doors.

"Please let me come along," I shouted.

One of the paramedics turned toward me. "Are you a relative?"

"I'm her friend," I said.

"Sorry." He climbed into the ambulance.

"Which hospital?" I was afraid he hadn't heard me but he said "Scottsdale Memorial" and closed the doors. The ambulance sped away, red lights pulsing and siren blasting.

She's alive, I told myself. Otherwise, they wouldn't need the siren.

I heard the words "She's alive" repeated aloud and saw Greg Blackstone, the Food Go manager, standing next to me.

"How bad is it?" I asked him, unable to control the tremor in my voice.

"I'm not sure. They hooked up an IV right away." He took my arm and led me from the crowd that still gaped after the ambulance. Always so calm and efficient, Greg looked different now. His usual placid expression was gone and his brows seemed knit together.

"Was she conscious? Was she able to talk? Who did it?" My questions tumbled furiously after each other as I followed Greg to his office.

He answered the last one first, and my frantic worry took another leap. "It happened so fast that he got away. One of the customers tried to chase after him, but the guy was younger and faster."

"The police—can't they get a description?"

"They're questioning people now," Greg said.

I remembered then. Although my conscious perceptions had all been directed toward the gurney and the ambulance, I had observed two police cars pull into the curb in front of the store.

We entered Greg's small office, and he filled a paper cup with coffee from the machine on his desk, handing it to me. "She wasn't conscious when the paramedics arrived," he said soberly.

The cup in my hand shook so badly that I had to put it down. "I've got to go to the hospital," I said. "I can't wait around."

To Greg's credit, he didn't ask me who was in the pharmacy. Instead, he leaned forward and spoke so quietly that I had to listen despite my whirling thoughts. "You know Denise better than anyone else here. I think you can do more for her if you talk to the police than if you rush off to the hospital."

"But I have to see her. I have to know how bad..." I broke off, unable to say the words.

"They won't let you see her while they're working on her. You know that." He reached across and returned the coffee cup to me.

"I need to be there," I insisted, turning the cup around in my hands without drinking.

"Here's what we'll do," Greg said. "You sit down and try calling Scottsdale Memorial. Meanwhile, I'll tell the police that you're Denise's best friend and that you're waiting to talk to them." He reached for the telephone book on his desk and looked up the hospital's number, writing it down on a pink memo slip. "Will you be all right alone here?" he asked and, at my nod, left the office.

Supermarket managers are like rulers of small kingdoms. They control everything and everyone in their stores, including the several hundred employees who work in some of the larger, full-service stores. Although I'm the pharmacy manager and supposedly make my own decisions, I've worked for some store managers who were despots, concerned only with increasing the bottom line. Thank goodness for Greg, I thought, as I dialed the hospital.

"We have no information at this point in time," I was told, not very succinctly but clearly enough to convince me I wasn't going to learn anything.

"Is Mrs. Seaford alive?"

"We have no information at this point in time," the voice repeated.

"Then connect me with someone who does have information," I insisted.

"Mrs. Seaford is in Emergency. When she's transferred to a room, you'll be able to speak to the floor nurse."

"When will that be?"

"Call back in half an hour," she said, sounding slightly more human.

I hung up and sat back, reminding myself that Denise and I had parted with angry words only a short time ago. If she didn't recover, I'd never be able to forgive myself.

A uniformed patrol officer I hadn't seen before tapped on the office door and entered. He told me his name, pulled over the only other chair in the room—the one behind Greg's desk—and sat down, notebook in hand. "Mr. Blackstone tells me you're a good friend of the victim," he began.

"Please, tell me first how bad it is. Then I'll gladly answer your questions."

"I don't know," he said. "I'm not a doctor."

My face must have shown my distress because he took pity on me. "The paramedics said Mrs. Seaford does have a pulse."

"Thank God."

"I've already seen her personnel records, but I'd like to ask some other things you may be able to help us with," he said.

"Anything, anything I can do to help."

"First, tell me about any enemies Mrs. Seaford has."

"I don't know of anyone at all."

"Her records show her marital status as divorced. Is that still accurate?"

"Yes."

"And her ex-husband, does he still live in Arizona?"

I thought for a minute. "I'm pretty sure Craig lives in Chandler," I said, naming a city that's part of the greater Phoenix area, as is Scottsdale.

He was writing it down. "Craig Seaford. Is that his name or did she take back her maiden name?"

I nodded. "Yes, it's Seaford. But he remarried years ago. Why would he suddenly want to harm her?"

"Is Mrs. Seaford seeing anyone now?"

My eagerness to answer questions, determined to help the police catch whoever stabbed Denise, suddenly evaporated. How could I throw suspicion on Sterling Harraday when I was sure he wouldn't hurt Denise?

The patrol officer waited patiently as I tried to decide what to say. "You just told me you'd do anything to help," he reminded me.

"The man she's seeing now is an attorney named Sterling Harraday, but I'm positive he didn't do it."

My uniformed questioner looked up, dark eyes alert. "Sterling Harraday," he repeated, and I knew he'd made the connection. I could almost read the thoughts as they went through his mind. Andrea Felder had also been stabbed, and this man was involved with both women. And then my own brain started to work.

"Officer," I said. "The man you want is named Tony. I don't know his last name, but he was seeing Denise on and off. She broke away from him completely only a short time ago." Now there was no hesitation on my part. I refused to consider Andrea's reputation when my friend's life was at stake.

"You obviously recognized Sterling's name and his connection with the Felder case," I continued. "Well, this Tony was also Andrea Felder's lover."

"What! Have you any proof?" he studied me intently.

"It depends what you consider proof. If you don't believe me, though, you can ask Andrea's father and her widower."

I saw him write down what I'd just said. "What else can you tell me about this man? Do you have his full name, his address, a description?"

"No, but you can ask..." I hesitated. Worried as I was about Denise, I found myself unable to bring my staff pharmacist into this mess. I would talk to Louise first and convince her to see the police. Surely, now that the situation had become so serious, she would change her mind about Tony. Her bruises alone were proof of his violent capabilities.

"Ask...?"

I thought quickly. Who else could describe Tony? And then I remembered Denise's neighbors, the block watchers. "Verna and Raymond Branden," I said. "I don't know their exact address, but it's on Ocotillo Place."

"What else can you tell me?" he asked. "Has Mrs. Seaford's behavior been different lately? Did she seem worried about something?"

"Of course, she was worried. I'm sure she suspected Tony had something to do with the Felder murder."

He wrote this down, too. "I'm going to have a detective talk to you," he said. He glanced at the badge on my white jacket. "Will you be in the pharmacy, Ms. Morris?"

"The pharmacy!" For the first time since I'd heard about Denise, I remembered where I was supposed to be. I tried to figure out how soon I could get a relief pharmacist to take over for me. If I waited until the pharmacy was scheduled to close, I knew hospital visiting hours also would be over.

The patrol officer shook hands and thanked me. As he left, Greg, who must have been just outside the office door, walked in. "Any word?" he asked.

I told him the result of my call to Scottsdale Memorial. "I'll have to drive over to the hospital," I said. "That seems to be the best way to find out how she is."

"Then do it. I've already arranged with Louise to stay on in the pharmacy and take over for you."

"That was very thoughtful, Greg."

"Just promise to call me as soon as you learn anything," he said.

The sun had gone down and the temperature had plunged by the time I left the store, but I didn't waste time returning to the pharmacy for my sweater. Since I was still wearing my white lab jacket, that would help. I got into my car and, driving much faster than my normal pace, rushed to the hospital.

Denise was no longer in the emergency room, I learned after some persistent questioning. She was now in the intensive care unit and could have only family visitors for a short time each hour. Finally, outside the intensive care area, I found a floor nurse who was willing and able to answer my questions.

"Mrs. Seaford is resting comfortably," she said.

"Her condition...?"

"Her condition is serious, but that's because she lost a lot of blood." The nurse was slightly overweight, her uniform pulling tightly around her middle. Her expression seemed kind. "Intensive care..." I began, but she interrupted me.

"We have to monitor her vital signs closely tonight," she explained. "I can't guarantee it, of course, but I think she'll be upgraded and transferred out of ICU after Doctor makes his rounds in the morning." She smiled at me. "You should be able to see her tomorrow."

If all goes well, I said silently and superstitiously. "Just tell me one more thing," I said aloud. "Is she conscious?"

The nurse nodded reassuringly, but without really committing herself. I was still wearing my white jacket with my name tag pinned to it, and I saw her glance at it. "I'll tell her you were here, Ms. Morris."

I realized it was pointless to remain at the hospital but didn't trust myself to return to Food Go and fill prescriptions. First, I'd call my store manager, I decided, to tell him the few facts I'd learned about Denise's condition and then go home. Then I thought of something else and turned back to the nurse.

"Are the police guarding Mrs. Seaford?" I asked.

"There's no risk here," she said and smiled at me again. I almost expected her to say something about my having seen too many movies. "As you've discovered yourself, no one who doesn't belong there can get into her room."

"She hasn't any relatives," I told the nurse. "But I'm afraid the man who stabbed her could pretend to be one."

"We've already been told not to admit anyone."

There was nothing else I could do, so after making my phone call to Greg, I started for home. Halfway there, I reminded myself that I had to speak to Louise and convince her to tell the police about Tony. I U-turned and went back to Food Go.

Louise looked surprised to see me. "Greg asked me to stay on; he said you wouldn't be back tonight."

"I really don't feel up to working, but I need to talk to you."

"You came all the way back here just to talk to me?" Louise asked.

"Yes, and I think you know why."

She didn't respond, but she seemed nervous, tossing her braid over her shoulder and then bringing it forward again. For the moment, the pharmacy was quiet, and I used the opportunity to wait her out. Finally, she said, "I have no idea what you're talking about."

"You haven't even asked me how Denise is." I tried to sound calm and unemotional, but I could hear my voice break on the name.

Louise paled visibly. "She's not..."

"She's in intensive care, in serious condition. I didn't tell the police that you could lead them to Tony, but I will do it first thing in the morning unless he turns himself in."

"Why are you accusing him? Tony doesn't care about Denise anymore; he's with me now. He has no reason to hurt her."

"In that case, Tony has nothing to worry about," I said drily.

"He can't get involved with the police."

"Because he has a record?" I watched Louise carefully as I spoke, wanting to see if she knew about Tony's past. She showed no sign of surprise at my question.

"I know you don't think much of Tony..." she began.

Impatiently, I interrupted her. "What do you expect? I see how he treats you, and he certainly wasn't very decent to Denise when they were together." I waited while she took a phoned-in prescription and followed her to the computer, wondering if I should tell her that Tony had been at Amos Felder's home on the morning of Andrea's murder. It didn't seem like a good idea to reveal that Denise had told me about his visit.

Assuming Tony hadn't already left town, this information might send him running.

"Denise surely saw the man who stabbed her. And there were other witnesses," I said. "Don't you think it would be better for Tony to go to the police with his side of the story before they pick him up?"

"His side of the story!" Louise sounded frantic now. "What could he possibly say if that woman claims he was the one who stabbed her?"

"Claims? Are you trying to say Denise would lie about something like that?"

"Of course she would. She'll do it to protect that lawyer she's in love with."

"Sterling has no reason to want Denise out of the way. But Tony knows she could link him to Andrea's murder." In my anger at the way Louise was trying to exonerate Tony, I let the words tumble out after all.

"You're wrong," Louise said. "I saw Sterling running from the store when I rushed to the coffee shop."

Chapter 15.

For a moment, I was stunned. Then, looking carefully at the determined set to Louise's chin, I decided she was still trying to shield Tony. "I don't believe you," I told her.

"I don't care whether you believe me."

"Surely, you wouldn't make up something that outrageous to protect Tony."

"I'm glad you realize that."

"On second thought, he has you so mesmerized, I don't know what you're capable of doing for him."

"You're just envious."

"Envious of a control freak who flits from woman to woman but won't let any of them give him up?" I was incredulous at her interpretation. "Look, Louise. Even though Denise is my friend, you and I have worked together for months now. So I never told the patrol officer who interviewed me about you and Tony. I just couldn't bring myself to do it."

"Thanks a lot." Her tone was sarcastic.

"I'm not looking for thanks. I want you to help me put a dangerous man out of circulation."

"And that's exactly what I intend to do," Louise said.

I knew we were still at cross purposes. "You can't possibly have seen Sterling running from the coffee shop," I insisted. "The man who stabbed Denise must have been long gone before you were aware of the commotion and started over there."

Louise raised her chin again, looking defiantly at me. "That's my story, and no one can prove I didn't see Sterling Harraday."

It was no use. I'd made the situation worse by talking to Louise. When a moment later, I saw a young couple approach the window, several prescriptions in hand, I turned and started out of the pharmacy, leaving Louise to take care of them. My mind was made up: if Denise couldn't identify her assailant by morning, I'd see Detective Moreway.

As I let the door to the pharmacy close behind me, I saw a man approach the window. My first instinct was to go back and help Louise by filling his prescriptions while she was busy with the couple. I hesitated in the doorway and saw that this customer was trying to get Louise's attention as she worked at the computer. He was calling her by name. Although this wasn't unusual for frequent customers—after all our names are clearly printed and pinned to our professional jackets—I was sure I had never seen the man before. Only his profile was visible to me, but I was sure I'd have remembered those ruggedly handsome features. He was about six-foot tall with very dark, curly hair. I decided to take a chance.

"Tony," I called.

He turned, which didn't prove he really was Tony. Then he smiled at me, a slightly lopsided grin, and I could see what made him so attractive to women. "Yes?" he asked.

Now that he had revealed himself, I was determined not to let him get away. I could feel my heart pounding. Somehow, I'd keep him there until I could summon the police.

"Louise is busy right now," I said, trying to sound calm. Although this was contrary to normal procedure, there was only one way I could be sure he'd remain in the store. I invited him into the pharmacy to wait for her.

Without watching to see if Tony was following, I used my key to reenter the door I'd just exited. You must be insane, I told myself. What if he still has the knife? He can kill both of us and be out of here before anyone realizes something is wrong. I forced myself to walk steadily over to Louise, who was at one of the back shelves retrieving the drugs she needed for the young couple.

As we approached and she caught sight of Tony, Louise dropped the vial she was holding. "No, Tony, don't come in. It isn't safe to stay here." she said.

"What are you talking about?" His tone was mild, but I could hear the underlying note of anger.

"Listen to me for once," Louise said. "You've got to get away."

"Why are you telling Tony to run? Didn't you just try to convince me that Sterling was the perpetrator?"

"What are you talking about?" Tony repeated. "And how did this old gal know my name. You've been shooting your mouth off, haven't you?"

Tony seemed about to explode, oblivious to me and to the customers at the pharmacy window. I was afraid for Louise now rather than for myself. "She didn't tell me anything," I said. "I guessed it was you."

"Guessed! How could that be unless she talked?"

"It wasn't Louise," I insisted.

"I get it now. That two-timing waitress."

"If you're referring to Denise Seaford," I said coldly, knowing how much she hated to be identified by her job title, "she never described you either. And what's more, she's still alive and in the hospital. As soon as she can talk, she'll be able to tell the police all about you."

"Denise is in the hospital? Are her allergies kicking up again?"

He didn't strike me as a very good actor. I thought I detected a false note in his words and a smugness to his expression, but I couldn't be sure. Tony seemed like someone who would always be quick to cover his tracks. I decided to play it straight, though, and see what happened. "She was stabbed."

"You must be kidding. Why would anyone stab Denise?"

Again he seemed to be acting, but perhaps my prejudice against him made me think so. "Don't you know?"

Now the anger returned as quickly as it had dissipated. I wondered if he was toying with me. "Are you accusing me, lady?"

We were interrupted by the young man and woman who were waiting for their prescriptions. One of them had rapped loudly on the countertop. "Look, we're in a hurry," the woman said. "Isn't my medicine ready yet?"

Louise, who had stopped working as soon as Tony and I entered the pharmacy, told them it would be a few minutes more. "Why not do your grocery shopping while you wait?" she suggested.

"Just give the prescriptions back to us. We've waited long enough."

Without a word, Louise handed the three pieces of paper to the young woman. It was nearly closing time now, and no other customers had appeared. She looked apologetically at me and rolled down the shutters that closed off the pharmacy. This was an extraordinary evening, and the usual way of doing things didn't seem as important as finding out who was responsible for Denise's injuries, so I didn't protest. All I could do was hope the couple had overheard enough to be concerned and report what was happening in the pharmacy. I didn't count on it, however; they'd seemed too self-absorbed to be aware of anything other than the inconvenience to themselves.

All sorts of wild ideas rushed through my mind. Maybe I could make some excuse and leave him in the pharmacy with Louise. If I could get to the store manager's office and telephone the police, they'd have him.

"Well, I just came back to get my sweater," I said, pulling it off the coat rack and edging toward the door. "I'll see you tomorrow."

"Just a minute, lady," Tony said. He spoke quietly, but his voice sounded more menacing to me than a shout.

I tried for nonchalance. "I have to leave now, but I'm sure Louise will be happy to fill your prescriptions."

"You're not going anywhere, lady."

Cold shivers began in my shoulders and coursed through me. I tried to think what to do next. "Of course, I'm leaving. You must have noticed I was on my way out when you arrived. I only turned back to help you."

"Sure," he said quietly. His hands were in the pockets of his black jeans, and I was convinced he had a weapon. There was an ugly sneer on his face, and I wondered that I'd thought him handsome only a few minutes before.

"I don't understand," I said, but my assumed air of innocence sounded phony even to me.

"You're going to tell me what you heard about me and what you think you know."

I glanced at Louise. Her eyes appeared glazed to me, and she seemed to be in a sort of trance. Tony followed my gaze.

"She won't help you, lady; Louise does what I say."

Her name brought Louise back to what was happening in the closed pharmacy. "Don't do this, Tony," she said. Her voice was hoarse, and the hand that she put on Tony's sleeve trembled.

I saw him pull her hand away and twist it viciously before he let it fall. She stood there rubbing her wrist, and I could see a red mark where the sleeve of her white jacket ended. *More bruises tomorrow*, I thought, and was angry enough to challenge Tony.

"What do you think you're doing?" I yelled at him. "Get out of my pharmacy!"

He laughed. I knew I had to get help from our store security people and silently reviewed Food Go's emergency procedures. To signal an emergency without alarming customers, we used the day of the month as a code, preceded by the word "manager." Today was the 11th of March, so I would have to press the loudspeaker button on the telephone and call manager eleven to the pharmacy. I sidled cautiously to the telephone, but Tony pulled me away before I reached it. Now I knew how much Louise's wrists must be hurting. Tony hadn't twisted mine, but his grip had been painful nonetheless.

"Both of you stand over there where I can see you." He pushed us to the corner of the pharmacy furthest from the telephone.

"You won't get away with this," I said. "The manager is expecting us to sign out."

He ignored my attempt to get us out of this mess. "I want to hear what you know."

"She doesn't know anything, Tony."

"I'm not talking to you. Just stay over there and don't open your damn mouth again."

If his physical manhandling of Louise a few minutes earlier had made me angry, the way he was talking to her now infuriated me. "Let her leave, and I'll answer your questions," I said.

"You'll answer them anyhow."

I clenched my teeth. *Surely he can't kill both of us and expect to get away*, I thought; but I was convinced he'd tried to do exactly that to Denise and had nearly succeeded. Maybe it would be smarter to tell him what he wanted to know, stalling as much as I dared along the way. "I don't remember the question," I said.

This time, I got the lopsided grin. "Okay, lady, I'll play along with you." His voice hardened. "How did you recognize me?"

"I just took a chance."

"You expect me to believe that?"

"It's the truth."

"So all night long, every man who walks up to the pharmacy, you call out my name."

If the situation hadn't been so frightening, I might almost have grinned back at him. The picture he evoked certainly had its humorous side. "I'd heard you were tall, dark, and handsome," I said. "That narrowed it down." I thought perhaps he'd be flattered enough to lower his guard, but it didn't work.

"Okay, cut the crap and tell me where you got the description."

"I'm not sure."

He took a step forward, hands outstretched as if he was ready to strangle me. I'd faced killers before, but this seemed worse. The pharmacy was small, and we were boxed in. There was no room to move, no way to get help.

"It was one of Denise's neighbors," I said and hurriedly added to throw him off track and make sure he didn't go after Michael's daughter, "but I don't know his name."

"You expect me to believe a stranger just happened to come up to you and describe me." I was relieved to see his hands go back into his jean pockets.

"Of course not. I've seen him around the neighborhood; he lives up the block from Denise, but I'm not sure which house."

"And he knows me?"

"I didn't say that. He happened to ask me about Denise's friend; he— uh—thought he knew you." I wasn't a good liar, but I was desperate and trying my best to make it sound like the truth.

"Right! And he told you my name, too."

It was time to give some accurate information to make my story more plausible. "Denise told me her boyfriend had left her for Louise. She mentioned your name, but she didn't say anything else about you. The description I got from the neighbor, just as I said."

"I don't believe a word of it. This one," he gestured toward Louise, "works here with you all day long, so you have plenty of time to gossip about me. I suppose she went crying to you that I banged her around."

"Louise didn't tell me anything. I'd have to be blind to miss the bruises."

"I'm still waiting to hear what you know about me."

"Nothing," I insisted.

"You need to practice, lady. You're a lousy liar." He took one hand out of his pocket again and walked toward the corner where Louise and I huddled. When he got close enough, he grabbed Louise by her long braid and pulled her toward him. He was holding her with his left hand; the right one was still in his pocket, and I wondered again whether he had a weapon there.

She barely suppressed a scream. Her hands were clenched and her lips had whitened. I could see how painful the pressure on her scalp must be. "Leave her alone," I yelled at Tony.

"Sure, lady, as soon as you tell me what I want to know."

"I know all about you and Andrea Felder," I said in desperation. "And I've already told the police everything. No matter what you do to us, you'll still be their prime suspect."

"You're not going to frame me for murder. I didn't do it."

Tony seemed so outraged, shoving his clenched right fist in and out of his jeans aimlessly, that I almost believed him, but now I could see the outline of a knife deep in his pocket. Any second now, I expected him to pull it out and stab us. I tried frantically to think of a way to stop him. With the telephone out of reach, I couldn't summon help, and since Louise had lowered the shutter that closed off the pharmacy from the rest of Food Go, no one could see us. I knew, though, because a customer had once complained to management when I'd muttered unflattering words about him, that even low sounds carried from the corner of the pharmacy in which we were standing. And I also knew that if I could stall Tony long enough, someone would come by to find out why Louise hadn't cleared her register and signed out. The instant that happened, I'd be ready.

The telephone interrupted my thoughts, and I tried to move forward to pick it up. "Let it ring," Tony said, blocking me.

I tried another tack. "It's true you had already left before Andrea arrived at her father's house," I said, realizing full well that he could easily have returned, "so you probably have an alibi." Better to play stupid and see what I could find out.

"You think I'm going to fall for that one? Well, it happens I don't even know what time she was killed."

"In that case, you have nothing to worry about. So let us go."

"Yes, Tony, you're just making things worse," Louise said.

I admired her for trying, but somehow her attempt made him angrier than my own stab for freedom. He tightened his grip on her braid, and this time I saw her bite her lips to keep from crying out.

"One of these days, I'm going to kill *you*," he said. "Keep out of my business."

"If you're innocent," I protested, "why are you holding us here?"

"I told you why."

"And I gave you the information you asked for."

He stared at me searchingly. I stared back forcing myself to look him in the eyes and seem as if I had nothing to hide. Although he didn't lower his guard, he did slacken his hold on Louise. It seemed as if we'd been here for hours, but I knew that was impossible or someone would have come by to find out why we hadn't followed our normal closing routine.

At that moment, I heard Greg Blackstone's voice. "Anyone there?" he asked. "Why aren't you answering the phone? We're waiting to clear your register."

Tony released Louise's braid and clamped his hand over her mouth, looking threateningly at me at the same time. I thought of yelling for help but was afraid of what he'd do to Louise. Instead, as if to reassure Tony, I said in a stage whisper that I hoped would carry to Greg, "It's okay; it's just manager eleven" and prayed that Louise wouldn't reveal our security procedure to our captor.

"She must be in the ladies room," we heard Greg say aloud and listened to the receding sound of his footsteps.

Chapter 16.

It didn't work, I thought, disconsolately. *I would have to think of something else.* Tony had edged toward the door and opened it a crack to peer out. All at once, the door slammed back.

"Security Officer," a voice shouted. "Come out with your hands up."

I held my breath, sure that Tony would use us as hostages. The idea seemed to cross his mind for he positioned Louise in front of him but then suddenly raised his hands. Barney Johnson, the Food Go security man, is someone I work with whenever the pharmacy has problems with phony prescriptions. He's a stocky man of medium height, about my own age, who retired from one of the local police departments a few years ago. Before today's various excitements, he seemed to spend most of his time spotting and detaining shoplifters.

"Are you two okay?" he asked Louise and me.

"Yes, Barney, but be careful. This may be the man who stabbed Denise."

"Backup is on the way," he said, reaching around to handcuff Tony and leading him out of the pharmacy. Louise and I followed them. "I want both of you to get to Greg's office and wait there," Barney told us.

He pushed Tony into one of the customer chairs in front of the pharmacy. With his hands cuffed behind his back, Tony looked uncomfortable and subdued, but I noticed the same lopsided grin as he stared up at us. I supposed it was possible to read plans for revenge and all sorts of other things into that look, but I preferred not to speculate.

As I hesitated, unwilling to be shunted away after having played a role in apprehending Tony, Louise ran over to him. "I didn't tell them anything about you. I swear I didn't," she said.

"Shut up, you little fool!"

Louise's features seemed to melt, and I expected her to begin sobbing at any moment, but she surprised me. She turned and walked away from Tony without another word. *Good for you*, I thought. *You're a bright, capable woman and you'll do fine without him.*

For the first time, I noticed that Greg Blackstone had returned. "They're on the way," he told Barney. "Can I do anything else?"

"It's all under control," the security man assured him. "But you might want to keep customers away from this area."

"I've got the aisle blocked off on both ends." Greg stared at Tony for a moment, then turned to me. "You really kept your head, using the manager eleven code like that. What was he trying to do, get Percodan from you?"

"He's Denise's ex-boyfriend," I said, deliberately leaving Louise out of the triangle. Although I'd avoided accusing Tony of the assault on Denise this time, I could see that the store manager had grasped the significance of my words.

"All right. We'll let the police sort it out," Greg said and, for the second time that evening, took me by the arm and escorted me to his small office. Now, however, Louise accompanied us.

We waited in Greg's office. Louise sat staring at a potted kalanchoe on Greg's desk without saying a word. Like the other plants that decorated the supermarket, this one still sported a price tag from our Food Go florist shop.

Within fifteen minutes, the same patrol officer who'd questioned me earlier had joined us. As soon as he arrived, words whirled from Louise's mouth like dust devils in a desert windstorm and like dust devils, they seemed to go in circles.

"What a fool I've been. I want a restraining order against him. He nearly killed us. Don't let him go; he'll kill me. You have to do something."

I listened, amazed at Louise who was always so calm and who had not panicked during our ordeal as Tony's hostages. She had protected Tony and proclaimed his innocence despite verbal and physical abuse until he told her to shut up when she was the only one who wanted to help him. I didn't know if that had been the final indignity, but whatever made her snap wasn't important. What really mattered to me was this welcome change in her attitude toward him.

We were questioned for over an hour, first by the patrol officer and then by Detective Moreway who arrived on the scene looking as if he'd been hastily summoned because of the Andrea Felder connection and had dressed hurriedly to take the call.

"I might have known," he said as he walked into the office and spotted me.

He conferred briefly with the patrol officer and looked over the latter's notes. When he turned back to Louise and me, we were asked to tell our stories once more. "How do you always manage to get involved?" he asked me.

"You can't possibly believe it was anything *I* did," I said indignantly.

"So tell me," Detective Moreway asked, "why did you call Tony Warren by name and invite him into the pharmacy? Why didn't you get away from there as quickly as possible and phone us?"

"I didn't want him to disappear."

"Detective, may I talk to you again." The patrol officer and Frank Moreway huddled together once more.

"There seems to be a slight inconsistency here," Detective Moreway said when he turned back to me. "It's clear from what happened tonight that you knew about the relationship between this young woman," he nodded at Louise, "and Tony Warren when you talked to Patrol Officer Godfrey earlier. Yet you said nothing about it."

"I..." Any excuse I made would be useless, so I stopped.

"She wanted to give me the chance to talk to him first," Louise said.

"And you think that makes it better?"

"Perhaps not from your point of view," Louise admitted. She was standing now, and despite the fact that she was the shortest one in the small office, looking more like the competent professional I knew she could be. "It's easy to use hindsight now to fault her, but Ruthie did what she thought was right."

"We're not trying to blame anyone, just to discover the truth."

"I must say, you could have fooled me," Louise said.

No one spoke for a few moments. Then Detective Moreway told us we were free to go. "But I may have more questions for you later," he added, sounding to me as if he was determined to have the last word.

Greg Blackstone, who had left his office while the police interviewed us, reappeared when the door opened. "I've taken care of your closing procedure," he told Louise. "I hope the two of you can go home and get some rest now."

We walked toward the store exits. "Just a minute," Greg said. "We've had enough excitement here for one day. I'll get one of the sackers to walk both of you to your cars."

As Louise and I waited in front of the checkout lines, I saw how drawn her face was and wondered if mine reflected the same tiredness. "Would you like me to open for you tomorrow?" I asked.

"No problem. Let's stay with our schedule."

"You did take my shift tonight," I reminded her.

"Remember, I owed you." She smiled ruefully at me. "At least I won't have to rush home anymore when he demands it."

"Thanks for supporting me back there, Louise." I nodded toward the manager's office. Then I hesitated, not wanting to sound condescending in any way, but she had earned the compliment. "I'm glad your eyes are open now because you deserve better than—than what you've had."

She shook my hand as if we'd just met, and then we both followed the young man Greg had drafted for that purpose to the parking lot and to our respective cars. I drove home very slowly, trying not to think about the dangerous encounter with Tony but determined to call the hospital and check on Denise's condition as soon as I reached my house.

The same nurse I'd spoken to earlier at the intensive care nursing station assured me that there was no change and that Mrs. Seaford was resting quietly. *At least, I don't have to worry about Tony trying to silence her again*, I told myself.

Although I was on the night shift once more, I set my alarm for seven in the morning so I could call the hospital again. The evening's events kept rioting through my mind, and I passed a restless, nearly sleepless night. Something didn't make sense, but I couldn't figure out what the problem was. Before morning, I'd convinced myself that my uneasy feelings resulted from worrying about Denise. As soon as she regained consciousness, she'd be able to pinpoint Tony as her assailant. The police had him now; it was up to them to tie him to Andrea's murder as well.

* * * *

Friday morning, I called the hospital again. Denise was conscious and they expected to transfer her from intensive care after her doctor made his rounds. I was told to call back later to check whether I could visit. When I did get the okay and drove to Scottsdale Memorial Hospital, however, I found Detective Moreway questioning Denise and had to wait outside her room until he was finished.

Frank Moreway found me there. "Your friend's another one who's been impeding our investigation by holding back information," he said drily. "I suppose you also knew where and when she last saw Tony Warren before yesterday."

"How would I know?"

He looked at me without saying a word for what seemed a long time. I felt uncomfortable under that scrutiny, but although I assumed he was talking about Tony's visit to Amos Felder's house, I couldn't be sure of it. For all I knew, Denise had seen Tony since that time. Perhaps she'd threatened to tell the police about Andrea and that had led to his actions yesterday.

"You'd better get in there if you want to see Mrs. Seaford," he said finally. "She looked like she was about to drop off to sleep."

It wouldn't have surprised me if he'd stayed to listen to our conversation, so I waited to watch him get on the elevator before I walked into Denise's room. Her eyes were closed and I tiptoed quietly to a chair at the side of her bed, figuring I'd sit there until she reawakened. I don't know what I expected, but at first I was surprised to see little change in Denise's appearance. She was paler than usual, which was easily attributable to the absence of makeup, and I could see a bandage on her left shoulder showing below the short sleeve of her hospital gown. I sat there wondering what her reaction to my visit would be, not knowing if she was still angry with me.

When Denise opened her eyes a little later, I handed over some magazines I'd bought for her, using them to bridge any awkwardness between us. Her first words reassured me that our friendship was intact.

"I owe you an apology. My stubbornness made it bad for both of us."

"Don't worry about that, Denise. The important thing is for you to recover and get out of the hospital."

"I'm much better," she said. She was speaking more slowly than she normally did, and I wondered what painkillers they were giving her. "They may let me go home tomorrow morning."

"What can I do for you? Do you need anything from home?"

"I hate to ask, Ruthie, but if you could swing by my house and get me some clothes to wear home..."

"Of course. In fact, if you call me when they release you, I'll come by and drive you home, too."

Denise seemed relieved by my assurances. "Greg Blackstone called this morning. He has my handbag and keys locked up in his office; I told him to give them to you." She smiled somewhat sheepishly at me. "I guess I knew you wouldn't hold what happened last night against me."

"Did Greg tell you? I wish he hadn't added to your worries."

"Not Greg—your friend Detective Moreway." She smiled again to show me that the words weren't loaded this time.

"He would."

"Maybe I'd have been foolish enough to claim I didn't see who knifed me, but once Detective Moreway told me about your ordeal..." Her voice trailed off, either from fatigue or reluctance to remind me about last night. She lay there quietly for a few minutes, and I wondered whether she was drifting off to sleep again.

"Let me tell you what happened," she said. She used the controls to raise the head of her hospital bed to a sitting position. "You were right, you know."

"Don't tire yourself, Denise. It can wait."

"No, you need to be aware. The police think I'm still trying to protect Tony."

I was surprised. Was she intimating that someone else had stabbed her? "Okay, then. If you feel up to it, just start at the beginning," I said mildly, although I was seething at the thought that Denise could react to Tony's perfidy this way. Even Louise had finally understood his character.

"After you and I argued about Tony's involvement and whether I should go to the police, I called him."

"Oh, no." The words escaped involuntarily.

"Don't say it! I know I was a fool, but I wanted to give him a chance to explain."

"You called from home or from Food Go?"

"I couldn't reach him before I left my house, so I tried again when I got to work."

"What did you say to him, Denise? Did you mention me by name?"

"He has a way of repeating questions over and over until he finds out what he wants to know, but I kept you out of it." She was playing with the controls of the bed again, raising and lowering it as though she couldn't find a comfortable position. "I just told him that people knew I'd let him into Amos Felder's house the day of the murder and that he should go to the police. No matter how hard I tried, I couldn't seem to convince him that it would be better to tell his story before they caught up with him.

"Tony was furious," she continued. Her voice faltered. "He called me all kinds of names, threatened to get even with me."

"You should have phoned the police yourself."

"That's easy to say, but Michael was right. I was terrified of Tony."

"And with good reason, as it turned out. Thank God he didn't succeed in killing you."

"I don't think he intended to kill me," Denise said.

Not again, I thought. *She's still trying to shield him.* Aloud, I voiced my comments carefully; I wanted to make her face reality. "From what I can see of your bandages, he aimed for the left side and nearly succeeded in knifing you through the heart."

"If Tony had wanted to kill me, he wouldn't have missed."

"How can you say that?"

"Because he's not a murderer," she insisted.

Again, I tried to reason with her. "Be realistic, Denise. You know he was seeing Andrea, and you know he was on the spot when she was killed."

"That was hours before."

"But it shows he was familiar with her father's house—the scene of the murder."

"So were dozens of others. Think about how many people come to any of our homes here in Scottsdale. Before I leave for work in the morning, I see the lawn crews, the palm tree trimmers, the part-time maids, the pest control companies, the delivery trucks, the swimming pool maintenance people..." She ran out of breath.

"And most of them never get past the front door. They hand over their packages or they work outdoors. Tony was inside the house, though; you told me that yourself."

"I couldn't convince Detective Moreway either," Denise admitted.

"What did you expect? Look, I don't want to argue with you, but what you're saying isn't logical. Why would Tony try to kill... okay... knife you if not to prevent you from accusing him?"

"You still don't understand the way Tony thinks. He was afraid of being framed. Also, he'd just found out about Sterling and me." Her voice lowered and she looked away from me now. "He wanted to teach me a lesson. That's what he said when he plunged that knife into my shoulder."

"Denise, this discussion isn't good for you." I tried to change the subject. "Tell me which clothes to bring tomorrow, and I'll get out of here and let you rest."

"I am tired," she agreed. "But you have to believe me before you leave. Otherwise, you'll be in danger."

"I'll be careful," I said to humor her and refrained from saying that the danger was over because the police were holding Tony. She seemed to understand. "You think it's safe now, Ruthie, but I'm telling you the real murderer is still out there. And too many people know about the questions you've been asking."

Chapter 17.

Denise kept trying to convince me, and I continued trying to change the subject. Finally, she became so agitated that I went out to the nurses' station. I told one of the nurses that my friend seemed upset and might need something to calm her down, but I didn't give further details. As I left, I heard a clatter in the hallway and saw that the lunch trays were being delivered to the patients. I thought of returning to help Denise but decided she could manage. It was more important for me to get her keys at Food Go and also to arrange for a relief pharmacist to work for me the next day. She'd need my help more after her release from the hospital.

* * * *

At Food Go, I avoided the pharmacy and headed straight to Greg's office. He asked after Denise first and gave me her handbag when I told him I would need to get some things from home for her. He walked out to the checkout stands with me, where he handed over two large shopping bags to use for Denise's clothes.

"On second thought, why don't I follow you to Denise's house in her car," Greg said.

"It's not a good idea to leave that car overnight in this lot again. I checked earlier, and we're just lucky it's still on this side of the border."

I agreed that his idea was a good one, and we decided to set out at once for Denise's house. Greg, who'd never been there before, followed me. When we arrived, I waved him into the driveway since he had Denise's car. I parked at the curb, which is why I was able to spot the Brandens peering into the front window of a house across the street. They walked over as soon as they noticed me.

"Just looking to make sure everything's okay," Verna Branden told me. "That house is for sale, and the owners have already moved out of town."

"Doesn't their agent keep tabs on the house?" Greg asked as he joined us.

Both Brandens tried to explain at once. "We're block watchers. This is all part of the job." They seemed to be sizing Greg up as they spoke, suspicious even though it was obvious that we were together.

"If you're looking for Mrs. Seaford," Verna said, "she's not home."

"How do you know that?" I could see that Greg wasn't impressed with their credentials and didn't intend to reveal any information.

"Because there weren't any lights on last night, and her car's been gone since yesterday; that is, until you drove it up here." Raymond Branden seemed to be waiting for an explanation.

"It's okay," I said to Greg, suddenly remembering that I'd just about pinpointed Raymond as the person who told me about Tony's visits to Denise. Even though Verna had been my informant, I might have endangered these people. True, Tony was now in police custody, but there was no way to know if he'd be released on bail. If he saw Verna and Raymond nosing about the neighborhood, he might go after them. I had to warn them.

It didn't seem right to invite the Brandens into Denise's home in her absence, so we stood talking on the sidewalk in front of the house. I reminded Verna about the man she'd mentioned to me at the Fashion Square Mall.

"Oh, that one," she said. "I didn't see him around for awhile. Then the other night, he was lurking right in Mrs. Seaford's driveway. I would have called the police, except I knew he was a *friend* of hers."

Her emphasis on the word "friend" indicated what she really thought. I wondered if that was when he'd found out about Sterling. "He's not a friend anymore," I said.

"In fact, he's quite dangerous," Greg told them. "If you should see him around here again, call the police immediately."

Of course, the Brandens wanted the details. I had to weigh Denise's right to privacy with the Brandens' need to know. In the end, we gave them an abbreviated version of yesterday's happenings, omitting Louise and Andrea completely. If the police charged Tony with killing Andrea as well as with stabbing Denise, the media would have the story soon enough.

The Brandens looked horrified and fascinated at the same time. "You can count on us," Raymond said. "We'll be keeping an eye on the place. In fact, we can swing by here even more often than we usually do."

"I told you he was too sleek-looking to be trusted," Verna reminded me.

"Yes, well, we've got to be getting some things for Denise and go back to work," Greg said, dismissing the Brandens. We used Denise's keys and walked into the Mexican-tiled entryway. Greg waited in the living room, while I quickly picked out the clothes I thought my friend would want and put them in the plastic shopping bags. I was careful to choose a well-coordinated outfit, but I wasn't about to look for matching jewelry. The idea of rummaging through someone else's things was somewhat repugnant to me, which added to my sense of haste. Luckily, she had makeup in her handbag, so I could ignore all the jars and bottles on her old-fashioned triple dresser.

When I returned to the living room, Greg pointed to the telephone answering machine on one of the end tables. "She'd probably want you to collect her messages," he said.

"There might be something personal."

"Then again, we could hear a message the police should know about."

I was still dubious. "They've already got Tony."

"If there is an important message," Greg insisted, "another twenty-four hours is too long to wait for it."

When I still hesitated, Greg pushed the playback button. Now that the decision had been made, I quickly took up the pad and pen next to the machine, ready to make notes for Denise. I recognized the first voice—Sterling Harraday.

"Hi, hon, I didn't have a chance to drop by the coffee shop today. I was tied up in court, but I'll see you tomorrow night."

Thank goodness Sterling was too restrained to say anything very personal, I told myself. A hollow-sounding voice gave the time as five o'clock, which must have been yesterday afternoon.

A message from someone trying to sell mutual funds came in at five-twenty and another from a company that wanted to clean her carpets followed right after. The next caller's voice was hard to place, but the context of the message made his identity clear.

"Denise, what happened to you this morning? Did I get your schedule confused? I'm sure I can manage until the night nurse arrives, but call and let me know how you are."

That had to be Amos Felder. He'd called at 11:05 a.m., which must have been this morning, and I realized no one had notified him of Denise's hospitalization. I was surprised that the police hadn't been there to ask him what he knew of Tony Warren and decided to call Amos as soon as I could.

I didn't recognize the last caller. "Keep your mouth shut, Denise, or pay the consequences," the muffled voice cautioned and clicked off. It was impossible to tell whether it was a man or a woman. The time had been 11:42 a.m.

Greg and I looked at each other. "Tony," he said.

"How could that be? They arrested him last night."

"Maybe they let him out on bail."

"It didn't sound like Tony."

"But the voice was so muffled, Ruthie; he was trying to disguise himself."

"After last night, I'd recognize Tony no matter what," I insisted. I sat down heavily on Denise's mint-green chair next to the telephone. My first impulse was to erase the messages so she'd be spared. She had suffered enough at Tony's hands. The muffled call was too intimidating and while I realized she'd have to be told, I thought it was better for her to hear about it secondhand.

Greg grabbed my hand before I could reach the erase button. "Leave it," he said. "We have to remove the tape and take it to Detective Moreway."

"He'll just think it's Tony."

"They have the technology to analyze the voice," Greg said.

"But will they bother when they're convinced they already know who it is?"

"I think they'd do an analysis anyhow because if that's Tony threatening Denise, the tape will make their case against him stronger. And if you insist it's not Tony, they'll *have* to do one." The implications suddenly hit me and I stood up, ready to go to the police. "Don't you realize the danger to Denise?" I asked. "If that threat doesn't come from Tony, someone else may have killed Andrea."

Chapter 18.

"You're jumping to conclusions," Greg said. "That doesn't necessarily follow."

"Yes, it does," I insisted. "What other reason can there be for the threat?"

"Possibly something we know nothing about. It wasn't a death threat, after all."

"But it could be interpreted as one. We'd be foolish not to take that message seriously when one woman has died and another is in the hospital."

Greg's usually placid expression darkened, and his features suddenly seemed to knit together as he thought about the situation. "Maybe you're right. When we hand over the tape, we'll have to convince them to protect Denise."

"We can try," I said, still dubious about police reaction. From what I'd seen in the past, Detective Moreway didn't take too kindly to my suggestions.

Greg eyed the plastic shopping bags. "Do you have everything Denise wanted?" he asked.

"I think so." We locked up carefully and left in my car. Our first move was to put the answering machine tape in police hands, so we headed across Via Linda to Scottsdale Police Headquarters. As I drove, I wondered whether to hope Detective Moreway was available so fewer explanations would be needed. On the other hand, talking to someone who was unaware of my own past activities might be more comfortable. I still hadn't decided when we were ushered into Frank Moreway's office.

He walked around his desk and shook hands with both of us, making me reflect that Greg's presence improved Detective Moreway's attitude toward me. However, that impression didn't last beyond his first words.

"Well, Mrs. Morris, you're becoming a familiar visitor here."

I felt my face flush but Greg retrieved the answering machine tape from his shirt pocket and handed it over. "We took care of some things for

Mrs. Seaford," he explained. "These recordings include a threat that you should hear."

"Before we begin," I said, "we need to know whether Tony Warren is still in custody."

"And why do you want that information?"

"Aside from any other motive, the man has proven to be a danger to Mrs. Seaford, to my staff pharmacist, and to me. Isn't that enough of a reason?"

The detective agreed mildly that it was. "But I suspect you have another purpose for your question."

"I'd rather you listen to the tape before I tell you about that."

Frank Moreway was already at the door, calling to someone to bring him a machine that could play the small tape. "Mr. Warren is still being held. His initial appearance before a judge was this morning, and bail was denied," he told us.

Greg and I looked at each other, speechless for the moment. Then Greg asked, "Does he have access to a telephone?"

"Possibly. I'm surprised, though; I thought you'd be relieved to know bail was denied."

Someone tapped on the door and handed Detective Moreway a small telephone answering machine. He plugged it in and played the taped messages several times. "So you think this is Tony Warren and that he's tried to disguise his voice."

"I don't think that at all," I said.

"I'm afraid you're right. He was in court at the time this message was recorded."

"Don't you understand what that means?" I asked, disturbed by his calm tone.

"You're implying that someone else is threatening your friend."

"It's more than that. Tony had a personal grudge against Denise; he was upset because she was seeing someone else. But *this* threat can only be from the person who killed Andrea."

"That's quite a leap. What evidence do you have?"

"You heard the tape," I said.

"The caller said nothing about Andrea Felder."

"What else could he want her to keep quiet about?"

"I can think of many possibilities, including some Food Go gossip that worried the caller," Detective Moreway said.

I looked at Greg, waiting for him to support me but realized his reaction had been somewhat similar when we first heard the tape. "The person who made the threat thought Denise was at home. By this morning, everyone at Food Go had surely heard about her hospitalization," I said.

Frank Moreway, who'd been sitting behind his desk while he played the tape, got to his feet and did his looming act. "What difference does that make? The message would've been there when she got home if you hadn't taken it upon yourself to remove it."

It's no use, I thought. Although he worked at curbing his antagonism, it was quite clear that Detective Moreway resented my involvement in his cases. His resentment probably was stronger now that I'd solved two of them before the police. I shifted in my chair, but realized my discomfort wasn't really physical. "So you refuse to believe that Denise is in danger?"

This time Greg did speak up. "We think she needs police protection."

Frank Moreway was quiet for a few moments, as if he wanted to consider Greg's words. When he spoke again, however, he addressed me. "In the past, I seem to remember, you were the one who insisted that multiple deaths were not coincidences, that the same murderer was responsible."

"I knew you were influenced by those other cases!" Sorry that I'd raised my voice, I subsided, knowing it was foolish to antagonize this man.

He seemed unflappable, not even acknowledging my outburst. "And now, you want me to believe that a murder and an attempted murder— both of which were knifings, as you well know—were committed by two different people?"

Greg looked uneasy. He'd always been a decent, caring person who ran our Food Go store calmly and efficiently, but now he appeared out of his depth. I realized he was accustomed to absolute authority on his own grounds and was rather intimidated here at Police Headquarters. "Well, when you put it that way..." he started to say.

I interrupted. "On the surface, it looks like you're right, considering the connection between the victims. But talk to Denise. She's frightened, and she doesn't even know about this taped threat."

"Of course Mrs. Seaford is frightened. That's understandable considering the attack on her."

"Look, Detective Moreway, I didn't believe her either at first. I do now."

"All because of a few threatening words on an answering machine?"

"You can't trivialize that message."

"Hundreds, maybe thousands, of people receive threats every day."

"And how many of them have been stabbed and are lying in a hospital bed as we speak?" Greg demanded.

"You're arguing in circles."

"No," I said. "You're the one who's trying to fit together facts that don't agree. Aren't you even going to investigate this threat?"

"Mrs. Morris," Detective Moreway said, "this type of threat usually doesn't mean anything. If it had been possible for Tony Warren to make that phone call, we'd certainly take it more seriously and try for an analysis. Since he had no access to a telephone at the crucial time, we can rule him out." He paused and asked in a surprisingly reasonable tone, "Whose voice do you suggest we compare to the tape?"

I had no answer to that but wasn't ready to give up. "All I know is Denise has the most compelling reasons to pinpoint Tony as the murderer, but she's convinced it was someone else. Surely that should make you continue your investigation."

"We haven't closed it."

"But you're sure Tony did it, and that's bound to blind you to other possibilities."

"I'm well aware that you stumbled upon my brother-in-law's murderer, Mrs. Morris. And despite what you think, I'm grateful to you. That doesn't mean you can do a better job than the police this time. Stay out of this case."

The words "stumbled upon" were galling, but I didn't protest. Too much was at stake now because of the danger to Denise and, I suddenly remembered, she believed I was in jeopardy as well. Since I hadn't convinced Frank Moreway, I realized I must disregard his order and intensify my own investigation into the murder.

I held out a hand for the tape and put it in my handbag. "Detective Moreway, you say that Tony's initial appearance before a judge was taking place when this message came in. Can you tell me the exact time he was in court?"

He gave me a look that clearly expressed his impatience. "You never give up, do you?"

"I simply want to check that the time stamp on Denise's machine is accurate."

Frank Moreway had already pulled out a small notebook and was searching through it. "His initial appearance was set for 11:00 a.m., so he was in court at that time. The one just prior to his was running late, however. Mr. Warren's initial appearance began at 11:22 and was over just before noon. Then he was returned to his cell."

"Thank you," I said and got up to leave.

"You do understand that we're concerned about Mrs. Seaford," Greg said, evidently wanting to end on a tactful note.

"The Scottsdale Police Department is also concerned about her welfare. However, as you know, she's already identified the man who stabbed her. Further, you're aware that he's in our custody. I think you can rest easy now." He walked us to the outer door, where he shook hands with both of us once more.

"Do you really want to go back to Denise's house now?" Greg asked as we got into my car.

""I must know if the time stamp is accurate. It would ease my mind if it turns out that Tony could have made the call after all."

"Yes, that would change everything," Greg agreed.

"My own shift doesn't begin for another two hours, so I can check the answering machine clock before I go to work," I told him. "Why don't I drop you at Food Go and then go on to Denise's house."

"All right," Greg said. "I really should be getting back to the store."

When we arrived at Food Go, however, Greg seemed to have second thoughts. "Should I go back with you?" he asked. "Are you sure you'll be okay?"

"Of course." I tried to sound assured, although I was far from convinced myself. "Denise has lived alone there for many years. Don't forget that the stabbing took place at the store, not at her home. Besides," I finished, knowing what had been in my mind all along, "I have friends in the neighborhood."

"I guess those people do keep an eye on the place," Greg said. I didn't correct him, but it wasn't the Brandens I had in mind.

The drive back to Denise's place was uneventful, and the Brandens were not in evidence this time. I let myself into the house and checked the time stamp on her answering machine. It was only three minutes slower than my own watch, not enough of a difference to implicate Tony as the one who made the 11:40 a.m. threat.

I sat on the sofa, leaning against one of its carved wooden arms, and thought about the situation. My original impulse earlier that day to spare Denise from hearing the message was wrong, I decided. She had to know. Furthermore, I should replace the tape, unerased, in case anyone else called. And if the threats were repeated...? Well, we needed to know that, too. Luckily, I had the tape now, not Greg. I quickly replaced it in the answering machine, locked up carefully again, and left the house; but I didn't get into my car. Instead, I walked across the two driveways to Betsy Stokes's house.

As I approached the front door, Patricia Loring Donleavy came out, looking svelte in black slacks with a zebra-print pullover. She was carrying a small suitcase.

"Oh," I said. "I didn't know you were leaving again."

"I'm not. This is Betsy's. We're on our way to Scottsdale Memorial." She sounded very composed, and I wondered whether I'd be as calm if this were the birth of my first grandchild.

"Can I help? Do you need a ride?"

"Thanks, Ruthie. I do appreciate your offer, but I'll just drive Betsy's car."

Betsy appeared at that moment; she held the stuffed elephant I'd seen her buy shortly after her husband's death, so many months ago. That night had also been the first meeting between Michael and me since our college days.

"Hi Ruthie," Betsy said. Her voice was cheerful but her face seemed drawn. I wondered how far apart her labor pains were but didn't feel I could ask. She came up to me and kissed my cheek. Not for the first time, I reflected that if Michael and I had married... I quickly cut off the thought and hugged her silently. *She'll be all right*, I told myself. *It's only a few weeks early*. Now, however, I had one more person to worry about.

Patricia opened the garage door and pulled Betsy's car into the driveway. I helped the younger woman into the front seat; she was still clutching the toy elephant. I realized it had become some sort of talisman for her, a comfy object. "Does your Dad know?" I asked.

"He'll drive up from Tucson as soon as he can get away from the pharmacy."

That's the problem with our profession, I thought. Just about any other job, you can get away immediately if an emergency arises. But we can never leave the pharmacy untended, and we can't simply close up either. I stepped away from the car, not wanting to hold them back. "Good luck," I called awkwardly, not quite sure what to say. Both women waved to me, and they were gone.

Chapter 19.

I reached Food Go early but even though I'd had no lunch, I couldn't bear to eat in the coffee shop, knowing Denise was in the hospital. With my hand on the doorknob, I hesitated. It seemed strange to walk into the pharmacy again after all that had happened here last night. I unclenched my fists, trying to release some of the tension I felt, and wondered how Louise was coping. As traumatic as last night had been for me, it must have been far worse for her since Tony, who meant nothing to me, was someone she'd professed to love.

Louise was working at the computer. At first I thought she was talking back to the machine as we all do at times, but when I reached past her to get my white jacket, I could hear that she was singing to herself. Although I didn't recognize the tune, it sounded upbeat to me. In that moment, I realized Louise seemed happier than she'd been in weeks.

She smiled at me. "How are you, Ruthie? I hope all the excitement didn't have any lasting effects."

"I'll be okay; it's you I was concerned about."

"You know, Ruthie. I'm almost ashamed to admit it, and I didn't understand until I woke up this morning, but what I feel is relief. Intense relief."

"Thank God, you're out of that mess," I said.

"You're great, Ruthie. And not just because you were so brave last night, summoning help right under Tony's nose. What I mean is..." She looked down at the computer keyboard as if she was embarrassed to meet my eyes. "You didn't come in here with recriminations, even though I know I deserve them for causing so much trouble."

"Don't blame yourself. You're not the only one who was under Tony's spell."

"You mean Denise, don't you? I blame myself for what happened to her, too."

"Both of you were vulnerable, somehow, and he took advantage of that," I said, "but you're basically strong women. I don't think you'll ever be victims again."

"No, I won't be." Louise tossed her braid over her shoulder, but there was an indefinable difference this time. It was a defiant gesture, not a nervous one.

"After yesterday's events, do you think Tony was the one who murdered Andrea Felder?" I was anxious to hear her response, wondering if it would support my own misgivings or ease them.

"It's hard for me to see him as a murderer. Maybe I just don't want to believe he'd go that far. Threats and beatings..." Louise's voice wavered here for a moment, "but not murder."

I wasn't sure whether to tell her about the message on Denise's answering machine. Too many people already knew too many details about Denise's private life. Before I could decide, though, someone rapped on the counter. *This won't do*, I told myself as I approached the window. *I have to give the customers my full attention.*

The young man, who was still using his knuckles impatiently on the pharmacy counter, wasn't anyone I recognized. He had regular features in a chubby face with a rather worried expression. I noticed the expensive-looking casual clothes he sported. "I'm traveling," he said suddenly.

"And how may I help you?" I asked, figuring he wanted me to phone an out-of-state doctor for a prescription.

"It's my cat."

Two more people suddenly appeared behind him. One of them was waving a handful of prescriptions at me as if that would bring her faster service. I tried to encourage the young man as politely as possible to get to the point. "You have a prescription for your cat?" I asked.

"No, I just need advice."

"I'll try," I said. "What's the problem?"

It all came out in a rush this time. "I hate to do it. But last time, he was impossible to handle. I need to sedate him. Someone told me to get Benadryl."

"What does your cat weigh?"

He thought about it for a moment. "About twelve pounds."

I considered the situation. "You know, I'd feel better if you checked with your vet. I'm just not sure of the safe dosage for such a small animal."

"But my vet is back home."

"You could try the Humane Society," I suggested.

The chubby face lit up. "Thanks, miss. I'll do that. Thanks again."

He was more appreciative than the woman waiting behind him with her half-dozen prescriptions. She peered into the pharmacy while I worked and glared at me when I counseled her about the proper usage and possible side effects of her medications. I couldn't even be sure she was listening.

Karen, the high school student who worked as our technician, came in just then and took over the phones. I suddenly realized that in all the excitement last night, we'd never transmitted our order to the wholesale drug supplier and checked with Louise.

"It went out first thing this morning," she assured me.

"You must have had plenty of irate customers today wanting drugs we hadn't reordered."

She laughed. "No more than I expected."

I saw Karen look closely at Louise. "Are things better?" she whispered.

"No secrets anymore," Louise told her. "Ruthie knows all about what I've been going through."

In between customers, we filled Karen in on yesterday's events. She was glowing with excitement. "And to think it was my day off. I can't believe I missed it all."

"Be glad you did," Louise said.

The phone rang again and Karen picked it up. "Food Go Pharmacy, Karen speaking." She looked in my direction to see whether I was still free. "One minute, please," she said and handed me the receiver.

I expected to hear someone from a doctor's office at the other end of the line, calling in a new prescription. Arizona state law allows technicians like Karen to take down refills over the telephone, but only registered pharmacists may deal with new scripts.

"Pharmacist," I said, identifying myself.

I didn't recognize the woman's voice, but that wasn't unusual. Staff turnover in medical offices can be frequent. "Is this Ruthie?" she asked.

"Ruthie Morris speaking."

"You met me the other night. At Mr. Felder's house."

I was puzzled for a moment but realized this must be the nurse's aide. "Maxine Peabody?" I asked.

"That's right." She hesitated and I was surprised to hear her take several deep breaths before she spoke again.

"I need to talk to you," she said.

"Go ahead."

"No, that's not what I mean. I must see you."

"I'm here until nine p.m."

"But I can't leave Mr. Felder that long. Will you come to his house?" She paused again. "He'll be asleep by ten. You can just knock softly and I'll let you in without disturbing him."

I've read too many mystery novels to walk blithely into that kind of situation. Sure, on the surface it looked like Tony was the killer, and he was safely locked up; but I'd heard the message on Denise's answering machine, and it was impossible to tell whether that threat had come from a man or woman. I wasn't going to take chances.

"What is it about?" I asked.

"I said I can't discuss it over the phone. But there are things you should know if you want to find out what really happened here."

"Why don't you go to the police?"

"I can't tell them," she said.

We were at an impasse now, and I had to think before I spoke again. "I won't sneak into Amos's home that way," I said. "He has to invite me."

"That's impossible. He mustn't discover what I know."

"Then we'll have to meet somewhere else—when you're not at work."

"No, wait a minute. I have to think," Maxine said.

I waited impatiently, watching while Karen picked up the other phone, and knowing I could be asked to take that call at any moment. Some businesses, I'd read, limit the amount of time their employees are allowed to spend on the telephone with each customer. I wonder how they can possibly keep their customers when so many people feel no urgency to get to the point.

"Suppose I tell Mr. Felder there's someone I need to see and I invited her to stop by after I help him to bed. Is that okay?" She sounded as nervous as if my reply was a life and death matter to her. "I know he won't mind because I've done it before," she added. "Will you come?" It was my turn to think, but she filled the silence almost immediately. "If you don't trust me, tell other people where you'll be," she said.

I was embarrassed that she'd understood my doubts so easily but determined to do exactly as she suggested. "Okay, I'll be there at ten o'clock tonight," I told her.

Maxine Peabody, obviously relieved, thanked me profusely. "Maybe closer to eleven o'clock would be better," she said. "He's not always asleep when he's supposed to be." She hung up, and I went back to work, wondering what I'd let myself in for and whether I really needed to tell someone about my appointment with her. With Denise in the hospital, Louise was the logical confidante, but by the time her shift ended, I still hadn't made up my mind.

Before I closed the pharmacy that evening, I did call Denise but only to see how she was feeling and to reassure her that I'd be at the hospital in the morning to take her home. Then I drove to my own house to get something to eat before my appointment with Maxine Peabody.

I was checking my mailbox at curbside when Jean and Jerry Flint, who live just west of me, came by with their Irish setter on a leash. "Hello, Ruthie, how're you doing?" Jerry asked. His hearty manner always made him seem like the stereotypical insurance salesperson to me even though I knew he'd been in the management end of that business for many years now.

"Just fine," I told him.

"We haven't seen you in ages," Jean Flint said. "Would you like to join us while we walk Justinian? That is, if you're not too tired," she added. She was a slightly overweight woman with graying hair worn in a short, straight cut. From the time the Flints had moved into their territorial style home some years ago, Jean Flint had seemed rather aloof to me; but during Bob's last illness, she'd always offered to pick up anything I might need before going about her own errands, and she was unobtrusively ready to help in any other way. My attempts to let her know how much I appreciated this help had always been waved away. We still didn't socialize much, but I knew now that I could count on the Flints.

"That sounds a perfect way to unwind," I said and joined them.

"Just what I always say," Jerry told me.

"You sure do," Jean agreed. "Every single evening." She laughed and squeezed his arm.

I thought of Michael and felt a pang. It wasn't envy, just a wish that I could be with him. I'd had no news about Betsy yet. As this was her first child, though, I guessed she probably was still in labor. And since I wasn't a family member, I couldn't expect to join them in waiting for the baby's birth.

Jerry interrupted my thoughts. "Well, are you keeping out of trouble?" His tone was jovial, and I was sure he knew nothing about the happenings of the last few weeks; but his words gave me an idea. It was risky to meet with Maxine without telling anyone. And the thought I'd had on my drive home from work—to leave a note on my kitchen table—suddenly seemed foolish. Anyone who wanted to harm me could easily use my own keys to check the house afterwards. On the other hand, no one would know about the Flints.

"Do you really want to hear what I've been up to?" I asked, determined to tell them just enough to protect myself but, at the same time, feeling like a character in a thriller.

As I guessed they would, Jean and Jerry assured me they wanted to hear my story. I reminded them of Andrea Felder's murder, which the media had reported, and told them that I knew the victim's family. Then I added that they wanted me to see what I could discover about her murder, carefully avoiding any mention of Denise or Louise and Tony.

"Tonight, I'm going to see the woman who found the body." I stopped walking and looked at Jean and Jerry in turn. "So you can see why I want someone to know where I'll be... just in case," I finished.

Jerry pulled a small leather notepad and a silver Cross pen from his pocket. "I never trust to memory for something important," he explained. "Let me write down the name of this woman you're going to meet."

I gave him Maxine's name and Amos Felder's address. As he wrote, I could feel myself relax a little and realized for the first time just how tightly wound I'd been. I was still worried about seeing Maxine but talking to my neighbors had relieved some of the tension. "Thanks, Jerry, I feel better about this meeting now."

We had started walking again. Residential areas in Scottsdale usually have street lights only at the intersections, so I couldn't see Jean's expression clearly but her words and tone surprised me.

"I don't think you should meet this person, Ruthie." Her voice wavered and I realized she was concerned about me.

"I'm sorry to worry you."

"That doesn't matter. You're the one who's in danger, not I."

"If I really thought this meeting would be dangerous, I assure you I wouldn't go," I told her.

"Jeannie, she's just bringing us on board to be sensible," her husband said.

"No, it's not sensible. Do you think this Maxine is going to check whether anyone's been told about her? And what if another person is involved, someone who's unaware that the meeting was prearranged?"

"That's rather farfetched," Jerry said.

"I don't think so. It's more than likely that a murderer won't ask questions first. And what good will it do Ruthie if we pinpoint Maxine after she kills again?"

I was surprised. Jean Flint had always struck me as a rather unflappable woman. Now she sounded more like Denise in full melodramatic spate. "I don't expect to be in danger," I said. "This is just a precaution. In fact, if I hadn't run into the two of you, I wouldn't have told anyone about Maxine's call."

"And that surprises me," Jean said. "How can you take such chances, especially after that other murderer nearly drowned you last year?"

"I'm still here," I said and then was ashamed of my flippancy, because Jean seemed genuinely concerned about me.

By this time, we'd circled the block, pausing from time to time while Justinian sniffed at various lawns and mailboxes. They walked me to my front door, and we stood talking a little longer, but Jean couldn't convince me to drop my plans to meet Maxine and discover what she wanted to tell me.

"Don't worry," Jerry said as I unlocked my front door. He patted his shirt pocket. "I've got all the information right here. If she kills you, we'll get her." His hearty laugh rang out as I unlocked the door, and I couldn't tell whether he was genuinely unconcerned or merely trying to reassure his wife. If the latter was his purpose, it didn't work. As I walked into my house, I heard Jean protesting her husband's refusal to take the situation seriously.

By now, it was nearly 10:40. Although I'd intended to make myself a sandwich and some fresh coffee, there wasn't enough time left. Instead, I grabbed a muffin to ease my hunger pangs and headed for the car, not wanting to be late. If I'd been honest with myself, I'd have admitted that the real reason was to get the meeting over as quickly as possible.

My unease returned as I drove to Amos Felder's house. Jean is right, I told myself. What good will it do me if Jerry Flint can tell the police where I was headed and name the person I was meeting? Maybe I should have asked the Flints to come along. And Justinian, too, I added and laughed aloud at the thought.

I don't consider myself particularly brave, but I'm not a coward either. And I'd taken reasonable precautions. It was time to find out what Maxine had to tell me about the murder without allowing my imagination to work overtime.

* * * *

Maxine had left some outside lights on for me, and I pulled into the driveway behind a Chevy Corsica that I figured was her car. She had told me not to ring the doorbell—it might disturb Amos Felder—but to come to the back door, the one that opened into the laundry room and from there led to the kitchen. Either Maxine was watching for me or this door had a motion detector for that light went on as I approached, startling me. For a moment, I had to resist the impulse to turn and run back to my car.

I knocked softly and then more firmly when no one answered. I couldn't remember whether she'd told me to walk right in but, after waiting and rapping on the door for at least five minutes, decided that was probably what she intended me to do.

This is when the murderer lurks behind the door, waiting for the foolish victim to come into her parlor, I told myself; but I was determined to learn what Maxine would say, and I'd convinced myself she would have lured me to some other location if she wanted to get rid of me. So I tried the door, found it was unlocked, and walked in.

No one was in the laundry room, which was dimly lit by a night light. "Maxine, it's Ruthie," I called. I tried to keep my voice down although I knew Amos would be in the bedroom wing on the other side of the house. *That's probably where she is*, I thought. *Amos must have needed some last minute help.*

I continued on to the kitchen, brightly lit in contrast to the laundry room. Maxine Peabody was lying on the floor in front of the patio doors, a kitchen knife protruding from her back. I was too shocked to scream. While I had been worrying about danger to myself from Maxine, I saw now, she had been the murderer's target.

Chapter 20.

My first thought was to run for safety, but I suppressed the panic that threatened to engulf me. I couldn't control my shivers and the trembling of my legs but tried to ignore them. *If the murderer is still around*, I told myself, *he would have attacked me by now. I must remain calm and summon help.*

A gray extension phone hung on the kitchen wall just above the tray that held Amos Felder's medications. I dialed 9-1-1 and gave precise information when the dispatcher responded, although I couldn't refrain from urging, "Hurry, please hurry." Then I nerved myself to walk to the rear of the house and find Amos's bedroom. I suppose it was foolhardy to wander around that house after what I'd discovered in the kitchen, but I had to make sure he was all right. If Amos needed help and I failed to give it, I'd never forgive myself. Even calling immediately for an ambulance instead of waiting for the police to arrive could make a difference.

As I found the hallway leading to the bedroom wing and turned on the light, I reassured myself with the knowledge that the police were on the way. Amos's bedroom door was halfway open and I looked in, dreading what I might find. His wheelchair was at the side of the bed and Trafalgar lay next to it, whimpering softly. When I tried to come closer to the bed to look at Amos, the dog barred my way. I was deciding what to do when I heard sirens and went to the front door instead. It was also unlocked and I opened it wide and called out to the two patrol officers who were getting out of their car.

"I'm the one who phoned 9-1-1," I said.

"Stay where you are," one of them told me. He had a slight Hispanic accent. They had drawn their guns, and I put my hands in the air even though no one had asked me to do so.

"Detective Moreway knows me," I said. "He'll vouch for me."

"Why do you think you need someone to vouch for you, Ms..."

"Ruthie Morris."

"Ms. Morris, you called 9-1-1 about a stabbing victim."

I nodded my head. "I'll show you where she is."

"That won't be necessary," the officer with the accent told me. His partner had already entered the house, gun held before him in the stance I'd seen so many times on television. My legs suddenly began to tremble.

"Please, I need to sit down." I was embarrassed to hear how shaky my voice sounded.

He led me to the front seat of the patrol car, and I sank into it gratefully. Whatever strength had sustained me until now seemed to have deserted me once the immediate emergency was over, but I thought of Amos and pulled myself together.

"The man who lives here, Amos Felder, is disabled. I tried to check on him but his companion dog wouldn't let me get close enough. Could you please see if he's all right?"

"My partner will be going through the house, Ms. Morris. You don't have to worry about Mr. Felder."

"But every minute might count if he's been hurt, too."

He looked suspiciously at me. "What makes you think he's been hurt?"

"I don't know *how* he is; that's the problem."

"Right now, I need to get some information from you, Ms. Morris. My partner will take care of everything else."

I sat there and told my story, realizing as I did so how strange it must sound to the officer. In most mysteries I've read, the person who finds the body is immediately suspected of committing the murder. Somehow, though, I was completely unafraid—or perhaps I was in shock over my discovery. *Not only because of this killing*, I thought, *but also everything else that's happened the last few days*. The terrible sight of the ambulance attendants carrying Denise out of Food Go, Tony holding Louise and me at knifepoint, and now Maxine Peabody with a knife in her back and blood all over the place were enough to throw anyone into shock. I realized now the blood hadn't really registered, which convinced me that my mind had refused to cope with this latest blow.

At that point, the other patrol officer returned. I noticed immediately that he'd holstered his gun. "No one inside but an old man who seems to be sleeping it off. And there's a dog," he added. "I telephoned for the team."

The Hispanic officer, who'd taken my name and address even before the other details, asked a few follow-up questions and then told me I could leave. "But I want to be sure Amos Felder is all right," I insisted again, despite my numbed state.

Now I thought he looked at me more intently. "How well do you know Mr. Felder?" he asked.

"I've only met him once."

"Then why do you keep asking about him?" I could hear the suspicious note in his voice.

"It's only natural, isn't it?" I realized I sounded defensive. "It's his home and his nurse was just murdered. Of course, I'm concerned."

"If you mean the old man, take it from me, he's alive. I don't know how he slept through all this. May be drugged."

"He's not drugged," I said indignantly. "He takes temazepam when the pain keeps him awake."

"How do you know so much about Mr. Felder if you only met him once?"

"Because I saw the temazepam on his medicine tray in the kitchen." Now I got suspicious glances from both patrol officers. "I've already told you I'm a pharmacist," I said.

"And after you discovered the dead woman, you went and examined this Mr. Felder's medicines?"

"Of course not." Despite my numbed exhaustion, I rallied enough to counteract their obvious skepticism. "I saw the medications the one and only other time I was here."

They still looked doubtful, but the Hispanic officer told me again I could leave. I managed to thank them and got into my own car. As I started the engine, I saw two unmarked cars pull up in front of Amos Felder's home. Several men and one woman emerged and started toward the two patrol officers, and I looked quickly to see whether Dectective Moreway was among them. Since I didn't see him, I decided to leave before the police changed their minds about me. I was too tired to care that I was missing my chance to see how a police investigation really worked.

* * * *

The light on my answering machine was flashing when I arrived home and at first I was tempted to ignore it. All I wanted to do was fall into bed and forget everything for a few hours, but Michael or his ex-wife might have left a message about their grandchild's birth. My hand froze just before I pushed the "Play Messages" button on my machine. It could be a threat like the one I'd heard at Denise's house.

It was Michael. His words rushed out at me, showing how excited he was. "I raced to the phone to tell you right away, Ruthie. It's a boy! I saw him. He's the handsomest baby I've ever seen. Not even redfaced. Oh, and

Betsy's fine, too." He paused for breath here. "I'll talk to you later. Take care now."

The usual southwestern words of farewell sounded ironic to me. I was delighted to hear about Betsy's new son, though. She deserved some happiness now after being widowed during the early months of this pregnancy and accused by her grown stepchildren of murdering their father. I hoped I'd be able to see Betsy and the baby frequently, especially after her own mother returned to London. Although I vowed never to reveal these daydreams to anyone, I hugged to my heart the thought that this baby could have been my grandchild.

There were no other messages. Since it was too late to return Michael's call, I tried to get some sleep. I was exhausted with barely enough strength to walk to my bedroom, yet I remained awake for hours, trying to figure out what Maxine Peabody could possibly have wanted to tell me. I went over our telephone conversation many times, remembering how unwilling she'd been to let Amos know we were planning to meet. The obvious conclusion, that she had reason to be suspicious of her employer, seemed unthinkable to me. I still found it impossible to believe Amos could have murdered his daughter.

I replayed the conversation in my mind once again. Maxine had said there were things I should know, which must mean either that she had held some information she'd never given the police or that she'd stumbled across new evidence. Whatever she knew must lead directly to Andrea Felder's murderer or Maxine would still be alive.

She had told me something else, and I struggled to remember her exact words. Not that Amos mustn't know what she'd discovered. Those words were still clear in my mind. I was missing an important part of our telephone conversation, however, and I couldn't pinpoint what it was.

* * * *

Despite my late night and inability to sleep, I'd set my alarm early to check with the hospital about Denise's release. I spoke to a woman at the nurse's station who told me "Doctor" would make his rounds soon and if he signed her out, Mrs. Seaford would be ready to leave by 10:00 a.m. Then I asked to be connected to Denise's room to assure her I'd be there before ten o'clock to take her home.

I wanted to call Michael at his daughter's house to find out how Betsy and the baby were doing, but the doorbell rang just as I was dialing. It was Frank Moreway.

"I'm afraid I don't have much time," I told him.

"Why not? You're not due in the pharmacy until late this afternoon."

So he'd checked my schedule. I waited to feel the familiar tingle of apprehension at this realization but found I wasn't fazed at all. "Detective Moreway, a great part of my time is spent in the pharmacy at Food Go, but that's not my entire life."

"Okay, I'll grant you may have other things to do this morning, but they can't be more important than a murder investigation."

"I agree. And I'm happy to answer any questions you have, but I must be at Scottsdale Memorial in..." I looked at my watch. "In less than an hour."

He nodded. "I take it your friend is going home today?"

"Yes, and I'm worried about her safety."

"Will Mrs. Seaford be staying with you then?"

"I'll try to convince her to do that, but I don't think she'll agree." I spoke harshly to let Frank Moreway know how I felt about his previous doubts: "So you believe me now," I said. "Too bad, another woman had to die first."

I was surprised to hear the detective defend himself. "Don't you think it was natural to assume that we had the perp?"

"The perp who held Louise and me at knifepoint, yes," I said, using his jargon. "Maybe even the one who stabbed Denise Seaford, but not necessarily Andrea's killer. And now that someone else has been stabbed to death in the same way and in the same place, you finally agree that my friend is in danger."

"Not just your friend," he said, speaking slowly and evidently choosing his words with care after my outburst. "I think you may be in danger, too."

"I doubt that."

His eyebrows raised slightly in surprise but he said nothing, obviously waiting for an explanation. I obliged. "If the murderer wanted to kill me, all he had to do was wait around that house last night."

"And how did he know you were expected."

"That's easy," I said. "He had to be aware that Maxine knew something and was about to reveal it. Otherwise, there'd have been no motive for her murder."

"I see you have it all figured out," Detective Moreway said.

"No, I don't have it all figured out." I decided to challenge him. "Are you waiting for me to solve this one, too?"

There was a long pause, and I thought I'd gone too far this time. Surprisingly, Frank Moreway suddenly began to laugh.

"You think it's funny," I said.

"Despite the opinion you seem to have about your detecting abilities, the Scottsdale Police Department—and any other Police Department, for that matter—does *not* rely on civilians to solve crimes."

"Is that why you have a Silent Witness line?"

"That's entirely different. In fact, if you had made use of the telephone to relay information to us instead of going off and doing your own thing, you wouldn't have put yourself in jeopardy last night."

I was getting tired of fencing with him. Detective Moreway would never acknowledge the value of my help and, while I knew the police were more experienced and had more resources to call upon, I felt those capabilities couldn't equal my own determination to shield people I cared about from harm. And that meant not only Denise and Sterling but also Louise.

"What exactly did you want to ask me?" I said and looked at my watch again to remind him that my time was limited.

"I'd like you to go over your telephone conversation with Maxine Peabody again."

We were still standing in the entryway to my house, so I invited him into the living room where we sat across from each other on the turquoise and peach armchairs. I repeated the conversation as carefully as I could.

"And why do you think she was determined to keep what she knew from Mr. Felder?"

"I couldn't say."

"Did she seem afraid of him?"

Now I was really angry. "Don't try to pin these murders on Amos Felder. You know he couldn't possibly have committed them."

"And I happen to be aware of a muscle relaxant called fluori-methane, something you knew about but never told to us."

"It didn't have any bearing on what happened," I insisted stubbornly.

"Suppose you let us decide in future," Detective Moreway said.

I didn't fully understand why I was so determined to protect Amos Felder, but I liked him and I was certain the police would question him closely enough without my information.

"Are you sure that was all Maxine Peabody said to you on the telephone?"

"No, I'm not sure," I admitted. "I've been going over it in my mind, and I think there was something else."

"We could have you hypnotized to see whether there's anything more. Would you be willing?"

I thought about Frank Moreway's suggestion. After all, I had nothing to hide; if hypnosis could uncover information leading to the murderer, it might be a worthwhile tool to consider.

"Do you think that would work?" I asked.

"I'd certainly like to keep hypnosis in reserve as a possibility."

Detective Moreway took another ten minutes to have me describe my arrival at the Felder house and discovery of the body. "I know you went through all of this last night," he said, "but I want to hear it directly from you."

He still doesn't trust me, I thought, as I went through the details for him. I tried to be as accurate as possible and show him I had nothing to hide.

"And you're convinced Mr. Felder was asleep when you looked in on him?"

"I told you I couldn't get close enough to the bed to see."

"I'm asking for your impression here, nothing more."

Detective Moreway sounded impatient with me, and it was probably lack of sleep that made me respond sharply. "Your own patrol officers can answer that question better than I can. Surely they told you enough to eliminate Amos Felder as a suspect."

"I haven't eliminated anyone."

"Let's see now: Denise is in the hospital and Tony Warren is in jail." I paused for effect. "Are you trying to tell me I'm on your list once again?"

He surprised me again, this time with a deeper laugh. "Now that I've seen you in action a few times, I realize you simply attract trouble. And while I do admit you've helped us, the Scottsdale Police Department is quite capable of investigating and solving murders without your help. In fact, I want you to stay away from these people."

"You're trying to tell me who to associate with?" I was so annoyed, I couldn't be bothered to watch my grammar.

"Of course not!"

"Then just what are you saying?"

"I'm trying to make you understand that you've been lucky so far. This time, though, there isn't any doubt that we're dealing with someone who's already committed two murders." He lowered his voice and sounded serious again. "You told me a few minutes ago that you don't believe you're in danger, and maybe you're right; but I'm not so sure."

Detective Moreway rose and moved toward my front door. "I wish we could provide police protection for you and for Mrs. Seaford. Unfortunately, we can't do it, so I'm asking you to be careful until we find this killer."

Chapter 21.

I stared after the detective in surprise. Fencing with him was exhilarating, but I had told him the truth: I'd never really believed I was in danger. Denise was the one I worried about and was determined to protect. Yet I couldn't ignore the concern Frank Moreway had twice expressed during our conversation.

It was time to leave for Scottsdale Memorial Hospital, but I continued to think about Detective Moreway's words during the short drive there. I knew I couldn't lock myself in my home indefinitely and neither could Denise. We both had obligations to meet and, for the same reason, couldn't spend all our time together even if Denise moved in with me for a while.

By the time I arrived at the hospital, I still hadn't reached a decision. I would just have to talk things over with Denise and see whether she had any ideas. Perhaps she would want to stay with Sterling until the murderer was found.

Denise was waiting for me, already dressed in the clothes I'd brought over the day before. Although, I'd seen this turquoise and white dress with its huge gold buttons before, this was the first time Denise wasn't wearing eye shadow to match. She obviously had used some of the makeup from her handbag, but her features seemed drawn and made her face look thinner than usual.

A nurse approached to advise me that hospital rules required her to take Denise downstairs in a wheelchair. "In the meantime, you can pull your car around," she said and told me where to bring the car.

I didn't have long to wait. As I pulled up, the nurse wheeled Denise to my car and together we helped her into the front passenger seat. I could see how weak she was by the careful way she held herself as she got out of the wheelchair, and I made up my mind to invite her to stay at my house as long as she wished. Not only her safety, but also her health made that necessary. All I had to do now was convince Denise herself.

Just as I was about to get into the driver's seat of my Accord, I saw another nurse wheel a patient through the same hospital exit, while Michael's silver and gray Lexus pulled up to the curb behind me. I looked more carefully at this departing patient and, as I expected, saw Betsy. She was cradling the baby in her arms. Patricia Loring Donleavy walked alongside the wheelchair, smiling down at her new grandchild.

I stood there, unwilling to intrude but wanting desperately to go over to them. Betsy noticed me first and called out, "Ruthie, come and meet my son." By this time, Betsy's party had reached her father's car. Michael was already out of the vehicle, looking as if he couldn't contain his delight.

"Have you seen a handsomer little boy?" he demanded of me.

Betsy held the sleeping infant so I could see him. Now Patricia and I stood side by side, both beaming at the baby. He looked like most newborns but I dutifully admired him, trying not to sound wistful.

"We'd better rush him home," Michael said. "It's a little breezy today." The nurse helped to carefully place the baby in an infant car seat, while Michael handed his daughter and his ex-wife into the car.

Betsy leaned out of the window. "Come over and see us," she said.

"Yes," her mother echoed. "I'll be returning to London in about ten days, so please make it soon."

I waited to see whether Michael would add his own invitation, but he had entered his car now without saying anything further. As I started to walk toward my own vehicle, Michael pulled alongside and let his window down. "Betsy wants to know how Mrs. Seaford is feeling," he said.

I looked toward my car. Denise was leaning against the seat with her eyes closed, which made me want to kick myself for taking time out when she obviously needed to get home as soon as possible. On the other hand, this strengthened my belief that she couldn't possibly manage alone, and I knew I must convince her to come to my house for a few days.

"Denise is better, but she needs to rest," I told Michael. "I should be going."

He waved goodbye to me and drove off. I wanted to savor this meeting with Michael, the glimpse of his grandson, and the warmth of the invitations from Betsy and Patricia, but there was no time to waste. As soon as I got into my own car, I broached the subject that was uppermost in my mind.

"Denise, I'd like you to stay with me while you recuperate."

"No, no. I must get back to my own house." She sounded so agitated that I was at a loss. This wasn't simply unwillingness to create extra work for a friend; something more was behind Denise's refusal.

"Be practical," I said. "You need time to rest and recover your strength."

"I can't do it!"

"Denise, I'm not going to pressure you—but please think about it before I reach your house."

"There's nothing to think about. I need to be home."

"Okay, calm down. If you don't want to stay at my house, we'll have to come up with another solution."

I drove slowly, hoping she'd change her mind. When I pulled into her driveway, however, she was still adamantly refusing to go anywhere but her own home. Desperate enough to consider asking the Brandens to keep an eye on her, I sought a compromise.

"I'd like to come over and help out. Will you at least let me do that?"

Denise paused. "I don't want to sound ungracious. You know I really do appreciate all you want to do for me. It's just that I feel hiding out at your house will only make things worse."

"I don't get it, Denise. Why would it create problems if you stay with me until you're better able to cope?"

"I need to be home in case Tony calls me."

It was the last answer I expected. "I thought surely you'd never want anything more to do with him."

"I'm waiting to hear his apology," she said.

I was silent for a moment as I digested this information. Some studies of abused women talk about this phenomenon, the aftermath to abuse when the spouse or friend tries to make amends by promising everything will be different from now on. He "proves" he's changed by thoughtful actions like bringing gifts to the woman and treating her exceptionally well for some time afterwards.

"Denise," I said finally. "Even if he apologizes, will it really make up for what you've been through?"

"I'm not planning to take him back." Her voice was getting weaker now, and I wanted to end the conversation.

"Let's not discuss this now. If you're determined to stay here, I'll help you inside so you can rest."

We walked into the house and Denise, who'd seemed hardly able to stand a moment before, headed straight for her living room and the answering machine. She played back her messages, and I listened to them all over again with her. There were no new ones.

"Nothing from Tony," she said, sounding defeated for the first time.

I was impatient with her. "Forget about Tony. What about the threat?"

"Threat? Oh, that other message. That doesn't mean anything."

"Denise, sit down and listen to me." She took the sofa, leaning against one of its carved wooden arms while I paced back and forth. "Greg Blackstone and I were concerned enough to take that tape to the police. I didn't want to worry you; in fact, I nearly erased it. Much as I'd like to spare you, though, we can't ignore that threat. If you're in danger, we have to take precautions."

"Now I understand why you've been so insistent I stay with you."

"That's part of it," I admitted. "I also think it's too soon for you to be on your own."

"I'm not worried, Ruthie. It's just a crank call. Closed subject."

I knew from experience that Denise meant it when she used that phrase. There was nothing I could do but be there whenever she needed me. "Can I get you anything before I go?" I asked.

"Luckily, I happened to stock up on groceries before this happened. I'm just going to rest here on the sofa now."

"Then, I'll leave; but will you promise to call if you need anything?" I hesitated. "Is it all right to come by tomorrow? It's my day off."

Denise smiled at me, looking more like herself than she had since the knifing. "Of course, it is. I didn't mean to sound ungrateful, Ruthie. I truly appreciate everything you've done for me."

I hugged her very carefully, avoiding her wounded side, and turned to go. "What about locking your door?"

"I'll get up in a minute and take care of it." She must have interpreted the look on my face. "Now, don't worry," she said. "And come by whenever you'd like."

"I won't be too early; I have to catch up on some sleep." Although I still hadn't told Denise about Maxine Peabody's murder the night before, I couldn't bring myself to do so now. For a moment, I considered whether that knowledge might help me to change Denise's mind, but I doubted it.

* * * *

My shift at the pharmacy was uneventful that night, and I went through the closing procedure quickly so I could leave as soon as possible. Greg showed up and asked after Denise as did one of the women from the bakery and a man from produce. It had been a long, tiring day and I was glad to go home.

At my house, I found another message from Michael. "If I have your schedule right, Ruthie, shouldn't you be off tomorrow? Please let me know."

It's too late to call, I thought, afraid to disturb Betsy and her baby. The next morning, though, I did reach him at his daughter's house. By then, he'd had time to read the previous day's newspapers and knew about Maxine's death and my role in finding her body.

"When I saw you yesterday, I had no idea that you were involved in another murder," he said.

"Not involved, Michael. It was just a coincidence."

When I heard the smile in his voice, I could picture those blue eyes crinkling at the corners. "Okay, Ruthie. I know nothing I say will keep you off the trail. And I must admit you *do* have a knack for discovering things."

"This one's more difficult."

"I suppose it wouldn't do any good to suggest you leave it to the Scottsdale Police Department."

"Michael, I had every intention of doing that; but they don't seem to be getting anywhere, and I'm worried about the danger to Denise." I filled him in briefly about Tony and also about the threatening message.

He didn't comment at first. Then he said, "You're bright enough to minimize the risks, Ruthie, so I won't say anything more except this—if you think I can help, be sure to call on me."

I appreciated his words just as I would have resented any heavy-handed attempt to deter me from my purpose, but it was time to change the subject. "Tell me about Betsy and the baby. How are they?" I asked.

His tone, more than his words, showed how proud he was of his family. "They're wonderful. And that reminds me, Betsy wants me to be sure and ask you to visit today."

I wanted to go out and buy a gift first, so we settled on late afternoon for a visit. This also would give me a chance to stop off at Denise's house first in case I was needed to run any errands for her.

The morning was peaceful. Although I'd already given Betsy gifts for the new baby at the shower, I didn't want to walk into her house empty-handed. I bought an attractive set of bibs in various sizes, had a cup of coffee and a scone at the Coffee Plantation, and went on to see Denise. Here, too, there was no news. A number of friends and co-workers had called to find out how Denise was feeling, and she was resting as much as possible between phone conversations. Tony hadn't telephoned and she'd had no further threats, but she was worried because she'd heard nothing from Amos Felder and had been unable to reach him.

"What about Sterling? He may have taken Amos out to lunch."

"Could be. I couldn't contact Sterling either, but that doesn't worry me. He might be golfing."

I stifled the uneasiness I was beginning to feel. People don't sit around waiting for telephone calls on the weekend. It was a beautiful

March day, which in Arizona means lots of sunshine and temperature in the mid-80s. I wanted to ask whether Denise had talked with Sterling at all since she came home from the hospital but felt that would be prying. If she wanted to volunteer the information, she would have done so.

"He didn't know about Tony," Denise suddenly said. "I'm afraid he's going to dump me now."

I was indignant. "If Sterling won't stand by you now when you need him..."

She didn't give me a chance to finish. "Don't, Ruthie. You know his history with Andrea, so it's understandable. He wants someone he can trust, and I guess I blew it."

"Maybe not. Let's wait and see."

"I don't even want to think about Sterling now," she said. "I'm too mixed up."

"Okay, I'll tell you about Betsy's baby instead."

She brightened immediately. "As soon as I feel strong enough, I'm going over to see the baby. I've already put away another gift."

We compared notes about baby gifts and talked about trifles for a while. When it was time for me to leave and go next door to Betsy's house, I still had said nothing to Denise about the latest murder. She insisted on walking me to the front door this time, explaining that she didn't want to forget to lock up after me.

Just as we reached the entryway, Denise turned and put her hand on my arm. "Don't keep trying to spare me, Ruthie. I didn't get to read yesterday's newspapers, but I watched television for a while last night."

I realized then that she knew about Maxine. "You seemed so exhausted, I didn't want to make things worse."

"Poor Maxine," she said. Her voice suddenly rose in alarm. "You don't think the police arrested Amos, do you?"

"Of course not. We would have heard."

"I'm not so sure of that. Could you check with Detective Moreway, Ruthie? It would really relieve my mind."

I thought about it. "What do you suggest? I can't very well ask whether he has Amos in custody."

"Maybe you could ride over to Amos's house. But with Michael, this time. Not alone again, whatever you do," she added.

"Don't worry," I said. "Once was enough." I started out the front door. "I'll call and let you know as soon as I find out anything."

My visit to Betsy's house was a serene respite after all the recent turmoil. *Perhaps I'm only in the eye of the storm,* I thought, and then forgot about everything else when I went into the room that Betsy and her mother had decorated for the baby. Touches of blue bowed to tradition, but the two women had chosen a lemony yellow as the predominant color. It was a cheerful room, filled with stuffed animals of all kinds. I recognized the elephant Betsy and her father had been buying that evening so many months before when Denise and I came upon them in the mall. A butterfly mobile that repeated the blue and yellow hues was positioned over the crib, but I had eyes only for the occupant of that crib.

The baby still seemed to me no different than most infants. As I stood there gazing at him, though, he stirred in his sleep and I smiled involuntarily. Betsy's mother, Patricia, had come into the room behind us.

"I envy you, Ruthie," she said. "I'll be going home soon and by the time I fly back to the States again, he'll have changed so very much. But you will get to see him as he grows."

Not that often, I thought. *Perhaps they'll invite me over sometimes when Michael is up here from Tucson, but I can't count on it.* Aloud I said, "When I was a child, I used to wonder about all the families that emigrated to this country. Many of our grandparents, mine included, stayed behind in Europe and never saw their children and grandchildren again."

I suddenly realized how that must sound to Patricia. "I'm sorry," I said. "I didn't mean to minimize your own situation."

"Don't apologize, Ruthie. In fact, whenever I miss Betsy and the little guy, I *will* try to remember all the people who didn't have the luxury of trans-Atlantic jets."

We returned to the living room where Michael was waiting for us. "Before I go, I need to ask a favor of you," I said to him.

"Sure thing."

I told him about Denise's unsuccessful efforts to reach Amos Felder. "She wants me to go over there and see whether he's okay."

"Perfect timing. Betsy and Patricia can both use some space." He smiled at us. "They've been after me to take my 'restless energy,' as they call it, out of the house for a while."

"Yes, please do," Patricia said, but her tone was good-humored.

"In that case, let's drive up Camelback Mountain and watch the sunset. Then we can continue on to see Amos."

Watching the sunset is a favorite pastime of Arizona visitors and residents alike and while it isn't really necessary to do more than drive in a westerly direction to see spectacular displays, the view from Camelback is special. We decided to leave my car parked in Denise's driveway and take Michael's Lexus to Camelback Mountain. From there, it was only about a ten-minute drive to Amos Felder's home.

Michael didn't say much as we drove along, and I was thinking about Patricia's comment that I'd be there to watch the baby grow. For a brief moment, I wondered if Michael had told her anything to make her believe I'd be closer to the family. Watching the sunset did sound like an excuse for us to spend time alone together, but I cautioned myself not to be foolish and discarded the thought.

Sitting next to Michael in the car could lead to all kinds of daydreams, I decided. It was time to face reality, though. If Michael had wanted to see more of me, it would not have been difficult, for I was aware that he drove up from Tucson frequently.

We soon arrived at Echo Park, near the head of the camel-shaped mountain, and Michael parked his car. Many of the other cars there bore out-of-state license plates, and I also noticed one from Canada as we sat there, watching the sky with its feathery array of reds and pinks—streaks that turned darker as the sun dropped behind the horizon.

"Ruthie," Michael suddenly said, reaching for my hand. "You know how concerned I've been about Betsy all through her pregnancy."

"Yes, I do know. I guess we're all relieved that she and the baby are doing well despite all the trauma she's been through."

"Then you must have realized why I was waiting, that I wanted to be sure they were okay before talking to you." He paused. "What I'm trying to say is..." He hesitated and I made an effort not to let my imagination find meaning he didn't intend.

It was getting darker now; but I could still see the expression on Michael's face, and I was suddenly reminded of the way he used to look at me all those years ago in Tucson. I felt as if an electrical current were racing through me.

He began again. "Ruthie, we've been lucky enough to have a second chance. Let's take it; let's get married this time."

Chapter 22.

My breathing seemed to stop at his words, but my head whirled with inescapable memories of my parents and their reaction to Michael. *How strange*, I thought, *that a woman in her fifties—a woman whose mother and father have long since passed away–is influenced now by that long ago opposition to marriage with Michael.* As much as I wanted to say "yes," those memories held me back.

He must have sensed my discomfort. "Don't answer now," he said. "Just promise to think about it."

"I will, Michael." I felt intense relief at the opportunity to postpone my decision.

"But, Ruthie, remember this," he added. "I don't intend to give up so easily this time."

The sky had now darkened enough so that only faint rays of color showed. Michael turned on the car's motor and headlights, and we started down Camelback. "I'm sure you understood I wasn't really interested in the sunset," he said. "I just figured it was a great setting for a proposal, but I guess I should have waited. Right now, you're too worried about Amos Felder."

"No, that's not it. You surprised me."

"Surely you've realized that I've fallen in love with you all over again." His voice softened. "Ruthie, we're not the same kids we were back in pharmacy school. We've both experienced the ups and downs, the highs and lows of life. I figure we should know what we want by now."

"I need time, Michael."

"But not too much time; we've waited long enough."

I had given Amos's address to Michael, and I saw that we were approaching that neighborhood. It was time to give him more specific directions, which meant a change of subject. He didn't refer to his proposal again.

When we arrived at Amos's house and parked, the lights went on automatically as soon as they detected motion. It gave me a terrible feeling of déjà vu. "This is how it was last night," I said.

"All the more reason to find out what's happening. If no one answers the doorbell, we can call the police. They're the ones who should check this out."

I gave a shaky laugh. "Well, I wasn't planning to try the door this time."

"If he's disabled, maybe he can't get to the door or telephone," Michael suggested.

"But he's supposed to have help in the evenings."

"Let's not stand here and speculate. I'll ring the bell, and we can take it from there."

The door was opened almost immediately after we heard the echo of the door chimes. A tall man, handsome if you liked the overly muscular build that some women find attractive, stood there staring at us. "We don't buy anything from door-to-door salespeople," he said.

"We're not selling anything. I'm a friend of Mr. Felder's."

"And we don't want to talk to any reporters."

"We're not reporters either," I told him. "I'm Ruthie Morris. Why don't you ask Mr. Felder about me?"

"Just a minute." He closed the door firmly, leaving us on the front sidewalk.

"I wonder what's going on," I said to Michael.

"Probably being cautious. They must have been bothered by the media all day. I guess it's why nobody's answering the phone."

"That can't be the problem," I said. "Amos isn't a celebrity, so why would they keep after him?"

"Be realistic, Ruthie. Two murders in the same house—in the same kitchen, in fact. Of course, reporters have been swarming around."

By that time, the man had returned and opened the door. "Come on in," he said, holding out his hand to me. "Hank Overton. I help care for Mr. Felder." He looked suspiciously at Michael. "Mr Felder does want to see you, Mrs. Morris, but he asked me to find out the name of his other visitor."

"A friend of mine, Michael Loring," I said just as Amos wheeled himself into the hallway. Trafalgar, the companion dog, walked alongside the wheelchair.

"Come in, come in," Amos said.

We followed him into the living room, where Hank Overton quickly pulled some magazines from the sofa, placing them on the coffee table. Then, rather ostentatiously, Hank declared he would leave the room so we could talk privately.

"Now, now, Hank. You know I don't have any secrets from you." Despite Amos's words, however, Hank did leave.

Amos looked searchingly from Michael to me. "So this is the gentleman Denise told me about."

I could feel myself blushing, something I don't do often. Why would Denise have told him about Michael or me at a time when we were both strangers to him? Then I realized they must have had hours to fill every morning. Unless they used those hours watching daytime television or reading, they'd probably be talking. For someone who couldn't simply get up and go wherever he pleased, whenever he wanted to, conversation would be an interesting way to pass the time, especially since Amos was often alone between the shifts of his various caregivers.

"Ah, I see you don't like the fact that we talked about you."

"That's all right. I understand."

"Don't be condescending, Ruthie," he said.

"Mr. Felder, there's no reason to take that tone with Ruthie," Michael told him.

"Isn't there? Do you know the police consider me their number one nominee for the killer role?"

"Oh, no," I cried out, involuntarily.

"You may well say that, Ruthie. But *you* are responsible."

"I never said or did anything to make them suspect you. As far as I could tell, you were asleep when Maxine was murdered."

"Yes, after you'd already planted the idea of my guilt in official minds when you revealed the uses of fluori-methane."

"I never told them anything about it," I said indignantly.

"You may as well own up. You're the pharmacist who noticed it in my kitchen; Hank and poor Maxine both assured me they didn't say anything to the police. So, by process of elimination..." He smiled stiffly at me. "Who else could have reported it?"

"Sir, this is completely uncalled for," Michael said. "We came here because Ruthie and her friend Denise were concerned about you. Denise has been trying to reach you on the telephone all day."

"And why hasn't Denise shown up here the last few days? I'll tell you why; it's because her friend here influenced her to stay away."

This was too much for me. "I had a great deal of respect for you," I told him. "You seemed like a decent human being who didn't let your disability rule your life. But now I see how self-centered you are."

"You don't agree that I have a right to be upset with you and Denise?"

"Have you given any thought to the possibility that Denise has troubles of her own? Problems that have nothing to do with you."

"All right," he said quietly. "Tell me what's been happening."

I filled him in about Tony Warren's attack on Denise. He sat stroking Trafalgar as if to control his discomfort at hearing the story.

"Why didn't you let me know?"

"Denise didn't want to worry you."

"This was worse," he said. "I thought she stopped coming here because she suspected me of killing Andrea."

"Denise believes in you."

"And you?"

I hesitated a second too long. He picked up on it immediately, looking from me to Michael and back again. "I see now why Mr. Loring is here with you."

"That's hardly fair," Michael said. "You know damn well what happened the last time Ruthie came to this house alone."

"If I'm mistaken, I apologize. That still doesn't answer the main question, though: What did you tell the police to make them question me so relentlessly?"

"They're probably questioning everyone that way," I said. "What do you expect when your home was the scene of two murders?"

"Again, you're avoiding an answer to my question."

"I'm willing to repeat to you everything I said to the police."

Amos Felder seemed to relax, and I suddenly realized that was what he was after all along. I remembered he had practiced law for years and reminded myself to be careful. As soon as that thought popped into my mind, I questioned it. If I believed Amos to be innocent, why was I wary?

Michael and I had been standing all this time. Amos now invited us to be seated and called to Hank, asking him to bring coffee for us. I found the change in his attitude intriguing but had no time to speculate about it.

"I'm listening," Amos said.

I detailed everything I'd told to the patrol officers and later to Detective Moreway. Amos listened intently and I noticed that Hank, who had returned to the living room doorway, was eavesdropping.

When I'd finished my story, Amos seemed thoughtful. "I see," he said, finally.

"You see what?" Michael asked.

"Don't you realize how incriminating Ruthie's testimony is to me?"

I was surprised. "On the contrary, I emphasized that you were in bed and seemed to be asleep. Surely the police must know you couldn't physically..." I hesitated.

"Go ahead, say it. You believe my disability means I was immobile once Maxine had helped me to bed."

"Isn't that true? Wouldn't it be better for you if that were so?"

He shook his head and his expression seemed sad to me. "Ruthie, what I liked about you when we met was the way you treated me—like any other human being. Now I find your reactions as superficial as that of most people."

I was stung. "Just because I'm uncertain as to how much you're physically able to do..." I stopped because I could hear the break in my voice.

"Not that. It's because you want me to use my physical limitations as an alibi."

I understood now why Amos Felder seemed to waver between wanting to be considered a murder suspect like everyone else and wanting his disability to clear him of suspicion. Pride and common sense seemed to be warring in his mind, and this vacillation was the result. Okay, if he wanted me to treat him like anyone else, I would not mince words.

"Maybe I've been taking my cue from you. Your reactions seem to fluctuate, so what do you expect from other people?"

"Good," Amos said. "That's more like it."

"Are you going to tell us what you consider incriminating in Ruthie's story to the police?" Michael asked.

Hank came into the room carrying two cups of coffee, which he placed on an end table between the armchairs Michael and I occupied. He hadn't asked whether we wanted the coffee or whether we took cream or sugar and provided nothing but the beverage itself. He turned to go.

"You may as well stay, Hank. You should hear this," Amos said.

"I have your coffee ready, too."

"It can wait. Sit down and stop pretending you're not interested in what's going on here."

Hank sat on the sofa, in the furthest corner of the room. I tried to read his expression but couldn't and wondered if he had an alibi for last night. Surely the police had checked him out. He was certainly acting strangely, but I didn't know if this ungracious manner was his usual attitude. Worse, I had no way to determine his alibi or his background unless he volunteered the information.

"Mrs. Morris just repeated what Maxine told her on the telephone," Amos explained to Hank. "I see one significant point that we need to discuss."

"I already told you I have no idea about what she knew," Hank said.

"No one's accusing you of anything. Now just listen." He turned toward me again, wheeling himself so that he faced me directly. "Didn't Maxine's statement, 'He mustn't find out what I know' raise any flags?"

"He mustn't discover what I know," I corrected automatically.

"And who did you think 'he' meant in that context?"

"It could have meant anyone," I protested. "Maxine wasn't an English teacher. She was too excited and too upset to worry about the antecedent of her pronoun."

"Exactly," Amos said, and again I had a glimpse of the way he must have cross-examined witnesses.

I decided to turn the tables on him. "Who do *you* think she meant?"

"If I were sure, I'd tell the police. But consider this—it could have been Hank here."

"What?" Hank half rose from his seat at the end of the sofa. "You can't think I killed her."

"We can't eliminate anyone," Amos told him.

"And what reason would I have to kill your daughter and Maxine?"

Hank's words were spoken calmly, and he seemed to expect that question to remove suspicion from him; but I saw Amos grip the edges of his wheelchair and hesitate before he replied. I could almost feel him struggling between the desire to speak out and his need to keep quiet for some reason.

"I know you were seeing Andrea."

"That's a lie!"

"Denial won't help. My daughter may no longer be able to speak for herself, but Maxine knew about your relationship and so did I."

Now I understood why Amos had hesitated to challenge Hank. He was still trying to protect his daughter's reputation. I looked at the caregiver. He seemed as shocked at the revelation as I was. I'd read about a person's jaw dropping in surprise but had never actually witnessed the phenomenon before—at least not to this degree. In fact, I wondered whether Hank was exaggerating his reaction for our benefit.

"So we went out drinking a couple of times. Does that make me a murderer?"

"The police may wonder why you've been hiding the fact."

"Do I look like a fool? Why would I want to be dragged into this mess?"

"The point is," Amos said, slowly drawing out the words, "the more information the police have, the more likely they are to find the murderer."

Coming from Amos, who had withheld so much information, this would have been funny if the situation weren't so tense. Both men seemed to forget about Michael and me as they glared at each other.

"And why would I kill her?"

"I don't know, but where there's a relationship, anything is possible. She could have dumped you for someone else."

"And Maxine?"

"Maxine was an observant woman. She probably knew more about all of us than we imagined."

"That gives you a motive, too," Hank said.

"And everyone else who has access to this house."

"But she could have testified about the fluori-methane and what she knew about the amount of mobility you have."

"And you could, too. Are you the one who informed the police?"

"No," Hank answered flatly.

I didn't know whether to believe him. We kept coming back to fluori-methane. It seemed that many people knew about the prescription but hadn't realized its significance until I'd pinpointed it on my first visit here. This reminded me of something else I'd been thinking.

"With Maxine's murder, all those theories about a random killing drift away," I pointed out.

"The police are ahead of you on that one," Amos said.

"Did they tell you that?" Michael asked. He'd been listening quietly all this time, but I knew him well enough to realize he was analyzing the situation.

"They didn't have to tell me," Amos said. "I could figure it out from their questions."

"Such as?"

Amos looked at his caregiver before answering Michael. "For one thing, they asked how much I knew about Hank and had I noticed any changes in him lately."

"And your answer?" Michael persisted despite a loud grunt from Hank.

The front door slamming and light running footsteps announced Sterling's children. I remembered how their arrival had interrupted Amos's revelations about his daughter's character during my first visit here. This time Jessica and Robbie skipped into the room together, followed by their stepfather. Despite the hubbub, I tried to focus on Hank to see whether he was relieved at this break in our conversation. As far as I could tell, his expression was unchanged.

"You remember Mrs. Morris," Amos said to the newcomers and then introduced Michael. The children were polite but uninterested in anyone but their grandfather and Trafalgar.

"Grandpa, we came to take you to dinner," Jessica said. "Isn't that cool?"

Amos looked inquiringly at Doug Payson. "We thought you'd like to get away from the house for awhile," Doug told him, "but I didn't realize you had visitors."

"We're not staying; we just stopped by for a few minutes," I said.

"Why don't you join us?" Doug asked. "We're going to Sweet Tomatoes at the Scottsdale Pavilions."

"They've got frozen yogurt with chocolate sprinkles," Jessica said, pursing her lips with the word "chocolate."

"All different colors, rainbow sprinkles," Robbie corrected.

"Chocolate."

Amos laughed. "I seem to remember that they have both kinds." He seconded his son-in-law's invitation.

"I'd love to join you, but I'm expected back at my daughter's house," Michael said.

"How about you, Ruthie?" Amos asked. His dark eyes fixed upon me with an anxious expression.

Although it was clear Amos wanted me to join the group, I had to explain that I couldn't stay because I'd come in Michael's car. "My own car is in Denise Seaford's driveway."

"No problem," Doug said. "I'll drop you there on our way back."

I started to protest with the usual words about not creating extra bother but subsided at the look on Amos's face. The anxious expression had intensified, and he had raised his hands in a gesture of prayer. I couldn't refuse.

"Why don't you go on, Michael? I'll pick up my car later tonight."

I walked Michael to the door so we could have a few words alone. "Would you ring up Denise and reassure her about Amos?"

"Of course, I will. But Ruthie, I don't like to leave you with strangers." This last was said in a whisper, and I looked up quickly to see if Hank was hovering again.

"Michael, I'm with two children as well as their grandfather and stepfather. You don't have to worry."

"Two children whose mother was murdered less than two weeks ago," he reminded me.

"Well, you certainly don't think the children had anything to do with that."

"They're about the only ones I do trust."

"Surely you don't suspect Amos now that you've met him," I said.

"Ruthie, you must know from experience that you can't pinpoint a murderer by his outward manner. You'll be safe in the restaurant but promise me that you won't come back to this house tonight."

"I do have common sense. Please don't give me orders." I was sorry as soon as the words were out. Bad enough that I hadn't accepted his proposal tonight; we didn't have to argue.

He looked at me for a long moment. "I'm sorry you misunderstood my concern," he said stiffly. "I'll be running along now."

He walked out of Amos Felder's house, closing the front door quietly behind him. I wanted to call Michael back, but I stood there until I heard his car start up. Then I went to join the others.

Chapter 23.

All of them were still in the living room: Hank helping Amos into a charcoal gray blazer, the children impatiently dancing around the wheelchair, and Doug sitting quietly on the sofa looking through the magazines that Hank had moved earlier.

"Ready?" Doug asked as soon as I walked in. "We'll take Amos's minivan. It's a wheelchair conversion van."

"One minute," Amos said. "Hank, if you have anything you want to do while we're out, feel free to take off for a couple of hours."

"Just don't open the door for anyone," Doug cautioned.

Hank grunted. "With all the keys you people give out, anyone can get into this place."

"I have a key, too," Robbie said. "Only I'm not allowed to ride my bike this far."

"Me, too. Only I lost mine."

We all looked at Jessica. I knew the same thoughts that were whirling in my head must be going through their minds, too. If the little girl had lost her key, we were back to square one, the square that encompassed a host of possible suspects.

"When did you lose your key, honey?" Amos asked.

"I don't know, grandpa."

"Was it today?"

"No. I had it the last time mommy and I came here." Jessica suddenly started to cry. "Mommy let me open the door."

Amos reached out and pulled the girl closer to him. "Don't cry, honey. It's okay."

"It's not okay. It's not."

"Let's get going to Sweet Tomatoes, Jessica," Doug said. I couldn't tell whether this indicated an attempt to distract the little girl or impatience. She continued to hold onto her grandfather, but I could hear her sobs diminish to sniffles as she tried to contain them.

"We're allowed to cry. Daddy said so."

I looked at Doug in time to see him wince at Robbie's defense of his sister. He said nothing further to the children but addressed Hank instead.

"Why don't you load Amos into the van?" Doug said. "I'll have everyone outside by the time you're ready."

He certainly makes Amos sound like a package, I thought, *but maybe I'm being overly sensitive.* Amos's usually mobile face was impassive; I couldn't tell whether he found his son-in-law's words offensive.

"Let's go Mr. F," Hank said. "Is Trafalgar coming along?"

Amos thought for a moment. "I hate to leave him, but with the kids and all, maybe it would be better not to take him to the restaurant."

"Anything else you need, Mr. F?"

"Just my rain hat."

"Oh, grandpa; it's not gonna rain."

"It is so, Jessie. Didn't you see the weatherman on TV?" The superior air that went with Robbie's words seemed to infuriate Jessica, but at least it stopped her sniffling.

"Shows what you know. He said 'rain' yesterday and it was sunny as could be."

"Stop arguing, kids," Amos said. "I'd rather have my rain hat and not use it."

"It's gonna rain; it's gonna rain; it's gonna rain," Robbie chanted.

In the desert climate of Arizona's lower elevations, schoolchildren rush out to play when it rains the way they play in snow in other states. Robbie seemed more intent on teasing his sister, however, than finding pleasure in the prediction of rain.

It took at least fifteen minutes before we were finally all settled in the van. The children wanted to sit in the back with their grandfather, so Hank switched removable seats around, leaving space for the wheelchair in the back rather than the passenger side of the van. I watched as Hank pushed a button near the steering wheel to lower an electrical ramp. Then Amos wheeled himself up the ramp through the sliding door on the right-hand side of the van. Hank then retracted the ramp, which fitted itself under the van chassis, below the sliding door. He stood outside the door and reached in to attach the tiedowns that held the wheelchair securely to the floor of the van.

I rode up front with Douglas Payson. He didn't say much, limiting his conversation to passing comments on the traffic and the fact that one lane in each direction was closed.

"If it does rain, this construction area will be hazardous," he said. "Look how everyone is speeding along when the signs call for reduced speed."

* * * *

The Pavilions Mall is a large outdoor facility on land owned by the Salt River Pima-Maricopa Indian Community. It takes up two sides of Indian Bend Road. The restaurant we headed for is in a free-standing building with lots of available parking. I could tell from the number of cars, though, that Sweet Tomatoes would be crowded. That didn't matter much to me—although I was starting to feel hungry—but I wondered how the children would react if we had to wait on line for any length of time.

Luckily the line was moving at a reasonable pace, and the children were too engrossed in choosing what they wanted to balk at any tie-ups. Since Amos couldn't reach the food displays, I took a plate for him and filled it at his direction. He wanted a little of everything, which also was time-consuming.

I filled my own plate with Caesar salad, adding fresh sliced mushrooms and a few other vegetables. It may not have been a traditional Caesar with my additions, but I knew from experience that I'd enjoy it.

All of us eventually filled our plates and reached the cashier, at which point Amos and Doug both insisted on paying for the entire party. I protested mildly, but Amos surprised me with a harsh demand that the cashier take his credit card rather than his son-in-law's. The young cashier looked from one to another of the adults, at a loss.

Meanwhile, the children had carried their trays to a table and were unloading them. Jessica returned as the argument continued. "What's taking so long?" she asked. "All the yogurt will be gone."

"Don't worry, Jessie. They always refill the frozen yogurt machine." Amos suddenly capitulated and replaced his wallet in an inside jacket pocket.

We were off to an awkward beginning, and I took my seat at the table with misgivings. It had seemed like a good idea to join the family. First of all, Amos clearly wanted me to come along. Then, too, I had hoped to learn something that could help me discover who killed Andrea and Maxine.

I realized quickly that the latter expectation was unrealistic. Nothing much was happening that wouldn't take place at any family gathering. The children settled down between quick trips for pasta and yogurt. Neither their stepfather nor their grandfather seemed to mind when they opted for dessert midway through the meal. When I was ready for dessert, too, I asked Amos whether I could get anything for him.

"I'll come along with you," he said. "I want to pick out some fruit."

The yogurt and fruit bars were on the far side of the room, and Amos deftly wheeled his way between the tables. "I need to talk to you, Ruthie," he said as soon as we were out of sight and hearing of the others.

"I thought so!"

"Listen carefully because I have to talk fast. I realize now it was Doug who tried to convince the police that I committed the murders."

"But why?"

"Money."

"I don't understand. How could that mean money for him?" We had reached the self-service yogurt bar, but too many people were in the area so I said nothing more. I filled a plate with fruit for Amos and hurriedly swirled vanilla yogurt into another one for myself. If we were lucky, we'd have a brief opportunity to talk on the way back to our table.

Amos must have planned what to say in the limited time we had alone. "I'm the executor for Andrea's estate and trustee for the children. If anything happens to me, Doug is next in line."

"Not their father?"

"Andrea changed her will after she divorced Sterling. The money was from her mother's estate, not community property, so she had the power to do that."

Although we moved along as slowly as possible, we couldn't prolong our return to the others any longer. I noticed that Doug was watching us intently and, for the first time, wondered whether he had killed the two women. According to Amos, he had a motive, but so did Hank. For that matter, Sterling also had one. Thank God, Denise could no longer be a suspect; she'd been hospitalized when Maxine was murdered.

Doug gave us a tight-lipped smile. "Must have been a long line."

"Well, it is a bit crowded here tonight," I said, trying to sound calm. I wanted to ask Amos how he'd decided Doug was the one who told the police about the fluori-methane medication. Even if Andrea's husband was the informer, it was still quite a leap to assume that made him the killer.

I watched Doug wipe some chocolate sprinkles from Jessica's chin and thought it was impossible. He really appeared to care for his stepchildren, and they seemed to like him.

Surely a murderer couldn't relate to his victim's children this way; but if he'd tried to implicate Amos... I couldn't finish the thought because Doug was asking me something.

"You haven't made much progress in your sleuthing," he said.

I was surprised to hear him bring up the subject in front of the children even in that roundabout way. *We're in a restaurant full of people,*

I thought. *I'll never have a better time to test him.* "As a matter of fact, I have figured out what Maxine wanted to tell me," I said and as I spoke those words, I realized they were true. The only problem was I didn't know what it meant.

Doug looked mildly curious but Amos seemed upset at my words. For a moment, I wondered whether I was mistaken about his innocence. Then intercepting his quick glance at the children and slight shake of his head, I realized Maxine's death had been kept from them.

"Let's talk about it later," Amos said.

"No need to wait. Just choose your words carefully," Doug told me.

"Everything hinges on the word 'he.' But if we discard the idea of a random..." I stopped and looked at Jessica and Robbie, "event," I continued, "we can now limit our list to four possibilities: the two of you, Hank, and Sterling."

"And *you* know which one?" Doug asked, his tone showing his skepticism.

I said nothing for a long time.

"Well?" Doug challenged. Amos was staring at me, but I couldn't decipher his expression.

"Having fun?" The voice came from somewhere over my left shoulder. I turned and saw Jennifer Hoffman, looking so rotund that I couldn't believe she hadn't given birth yet.

"Hello Jen," Doug said. He was tearing the tops off one sugar packet after another, looking very uncomfortable. I remembered hearing that Jennifer and Doug had been together before Andrea came on the scene.

"Would you like to join us, Jennifer?" Amos asked.

"I'm with a friend. We're on the patio." Jennifer patted her stomach. "She's probably freezing out there, but I'm always warm these days."

Doug now jumped to his feet and indicated his own chair. "Sit down for a minute."

"I just came in to get some more focaccia," Jennifer said. For the first time, I noticed the two small plates she carried, one holding several pieces of the Italian delicacy and the other filled with muffins.

"Tell you what," she suddenly said, looking at the children. "Which one of you kids would like to carry these plates out to the patio? Give them to the woman in the dark green dress, and tell her I'll be there soon."

"Me," Jessica said.

"No, me."

Jennifer Hoffman handed a plate to each child. "You can both go and keep my friend company until I get back." She took Doug's seat and he pulled over a chair from another table.

"I guess you figured out by now that I know something I didn't want to say in front of the kids."

That thought had occurred to me but other than repeating her accusations against Denise and Sterling, I couldn't think of anything Jennifer might have to tell us.

"I met that nurse's aide, the one who was killed at your house, Mr. Felder," she said.

There was nothing startling about that statement; all of us waited for her to continue. I watched their faces. As far as I could see, neither Amos nor Doug showed any anxiety at her words.

"Many people met her," Amos said. "Was it the night she died?"

"The night before Andrea's murder."

I suddenly remembered Maxine's words, words that neither the police nor I had taken much notice of—"I know he won't mind because I've done it before," she had said when I'd demurred about visiting the house after Amos's bedtime.

"Why would you come to my house to meet Maxine? And why would she be so secretive about it? She knew I enjoyed visitors."

"We were discussing your daughter; she didn't want to worry you with Andrea's latest escapades."

"And you think whatever she told you had a bearing on her death? In that case, you should have gone to the police immediately."

"You're wrong, Mr. Felder. I didn't make the connection until that nurse's aide was killed, too."

"I don't think I want to hear any tales about my wife now that she's no longer able to defend herself," Doug said and started to get up and walk away.

"Wait a minute. You need to know that she was seeing the other caregiver, the hunk."

"That's old news," Amos said.

I wasn't so sure. Hank clearly hadn't realized his affair with Andrea was known to others.

"And what did Maxine expect you to do?" Amos was asking.

"She wanted me to talk to Andrea, to convince her to break up with the guy."

With those words, Amos's male caregiver become my primary suspect. It seemed to me now that he had the strongest motive to kill both Andrea and Maxine.

Chapter 24.

"Last time I saw you, Jennifer, you tried to convince me that Denise or Sterling or the two of them together were the guilty ones," I said.

"I told you—I didn't suspect anything until Maxine's death."

"And what do you suspect now? Spell it out," Amos insisted.

"That's not for me to say. I simply wanted to give you a missing piece of information. At least I thought it was new information."

"Don't be coy," I said. "You didn't hesitate to accuse people before." I found myself becoming angry at her evasive manner.

"I see that I was wrong before, so I'm being careful now."

I mulled over Jennifer's disclosure while the others tried to make her pinpoint Hank by name. Somehow from what I'd learned about Andrea, she didn't seem the sort of woman who'd have paid much attention to a lecture from Jennifer. The more I considered the situation, the less likely my assumption of a few minutes ago seemed—that Hank killed Andrea in some sort of jealous rage when she dumped him.

"What did Andrea say when you approached her?" I asked.

"About what you'd expect from her. She pretty much told me to mind my own business."

"Was that the end of the subject? Did you talk to anyone else?"

Jennifer was evasive again. "Who else would I have talked to?"

"Hank?" I ventured.

"You may have observed that I'm prone to sticking my neck out. But I do it only so far." Her voice had hardened. "No, I did *not* talk to Hank about it."

I noticed that she qualified her answer. "Then what did you speak to Hank about?"

The look she gave me seemed half-admiring and half-defiant. "Pretty good," she said. "Maybe you should trade in pharmacy for law."

"Before my grandchildren come back, suppose you tell us exactly what happened," Amos said.

Jennifer gave a little shrug and moved around in her seat, trying for a more comfortable position. "I phoned Andrea at her office that Tuesday morning, said I needed to talk to her, and suggested lunch. She told me she was taking you to lunch, Amos, and why didn't I just go ahead and say whatever I had on my mind. So I did.

"Andrea laughed at me. 'You're behind the times,' she said. 'It's really none of your business, but I met someone new.' Her voice suddenly softened and she sounded like a teenager. 'Tony's the most exciting man I've ever known,' she told me.

"Somehow Andrea always wanted me to envy her conquests, rubbing it in that she could get any man she went after." Jennifer glanced up at Doug and quickly looked away again.

"So she told Hank she was through with him, and he killed her," Amos said.

Doug seemed shaken by Jennifer's story. He had taken up the papers he'd torn off the sugar packets and was twisting them. "But why would Hank kill Maxine?"

"Because she knew about him and could tell the police."

"That can't be the reason," I said. "She wasn't the only one who knew."

"But did Hank realize that?"

It was getting too involved. I never trust complex motives for murder. According to the news stories I've read or heard about, most murderers have fairly basic motives. Either they want something the victim has or want revenge for some real or fancied slight. In fiction, on the other hand, motives are rarely straightforward.

"I'm going to confront Hank as soon as I get home," Amos said.

"Be careful," Jennifer told him as she started to walk away.

"I'll be perfectly safe. After all, he can't possibly get rid of all of us."

Although I only knew Andrea through photos, I found it hard to believe Hank was so in love with her that he killed her when she turned to Tony. If jealousy were his motive, wouldn't he have gone after her husband long before another lover appeared on the scene?

This started an interesting train of thought, and I found myself staring at Douglas Payson with sudden suspicion; but I quickly looked away when he met my eyes. *Maybe Doug hadn't known about his wife's affairs. Jennifer's story, on the other hand, seemed to put a different perspective on Andrea's relationship with Tony. What if Andrea had told Doug she wanted a divorce?*

"Why so thoughtful?" Doug asked. "Did Jen give you *the* clue to solve everything?"

I found myself stuttering. "N-no. I was just—just trying to remember..."

Luckily, the children came bounding back to our table, ending my struggle to avoid telegraphing my sudden insight to Doug. "That lady is very nice," Jessica said. "She told us all about her cat, and we told her about Trafalgar."

"But it was too cold outside. I need a cup of coffee," Robbie said, tugging on Doug's arm.

"Good try," Amos told him.

"Daddy lets us have coffee," Jessica said.

I saw Doug's eyebrows pull together. His hand twitched as though he wanted to strike the little girl, and I saw the effort he made to restrain himself. "Well, I don't and neither does your grandfather."

Without really formulating reasons for my distrust of him, I decided at that moment to call a taxi when we arrived back at Amos's house. I didn't want Doug Payson to drive me home. This was not the time to think it through logically, to see whether I believed him to be the murderer. He had already noticed when my mind drifted, and I didn't want him to be aware that I was absorbed in thought again.

"If everyone's ready to go, I'll bring the van around," Doug said.

At that point, I nearly told him I'd take a taxi from the restaurant, but I still had hopes of solving the murders and didn't want to miss any confrontation between Amos and Hank. I decided that the cliché about safety in numbers applied here and waited with Amos and the children for the van. Doug pulled up in front of Sweet Tomatoes even before we exited the restaurant since he had parked the van, with its special handicap license plates, in a nearby space.

"Hey, kids, why don't you tell Mrs. Morris about the trip we're going to take during spring break?" Doug said when we were all in the minivan again.

"I didn't know you were planning a trip." Amos not only sounded surprised, but also disapproving.

"We could use some time away."

The children began to talk about Disneyland, and I turned halfway in my seat so I could join the conversation. "We're gonna see Splash Mountain and the Haunted House," Jessica said. "And the big Electric Parade."

"You're stupid. They don't have that anymore."

"Do too."

Amos suddenly interrupted them. "Why are we on the reservation, Doug?"

I turned forward and realized that instead of heading toward Amos's home, we'd gone south. We were now driving east, further into the Salt

River Pima-Maricopa Indian Community. All my doubts about Douglas Payson crystallized, and I felt my hands become icy. The thought flashed through my mind that I could have been safely back at the restaurant waiting for a taxi to arrive. Then I told myself not to be silly. Including the children, he'd have to dispose of four of us. No one would be that foolhardy.

"The kids enjoy it. They like to spot the wild horses."

"In the dark?" Amos asked.

"Sure. The headlights illuminate them."

"This isn't a good idea, Doug. We're subject to tribal law here; it's too easy to commit a driving infraction and..."

"Nonsense, this is just a short detour."

I listened to their discussion, growing more uneasy by the minute. Close to the shopping mall and the nearby casino, there were houses and people, but we had now traveled about four or five miles east and seemed to be in one of the undeveloped areas. I'd read that the Salt River Pima-Maricopa Indian Community considers undeveloped desert land to be of prime importance and that thick mesquite groves exist not far from the border between Scottsdale and tribal lands.

Like most Scottsdale residents, I'd crossed the reservation from time to time. In fact, the Pavilions (the shopping mall where we'd just eaten) and the casino were both on Indian land. I'd never been onto the undeveloped areas, however, and didn't want to explore them in the company of a man I now suspected of murdering two people.

"I should be getting back," I said.

"Plenty of time," Doug answered. "You don't want to deprive the kiddies of their treat, do you?"

His tone was strange, even sarcastic, and I wondered if it was my imagination or whether we were really in danger. I gathered my courage and confronted him. "I'm sure Jessica and Robbie would be just as happy to see the horses some other time."

"Preferably in daylight," Amos added.

He sounded calm, and I had begun to doubt my instincts when Doug suddenly pulled the van into a thick mesquite grove and stopped. The engine remained on.

"So you want to go back," Doug said. "Don't you know there's no turning back?"

I saw that he held a wrench in his right hand and again I tried to reassure myself by counting on the fact that there were four of us. Then I heard him muttering as if he could read my thoughts.

"It will be easy," he said. "Two kids, an old woman, and a man in a wheelchair."

I had no time to resent the description; my mind was whirling in an attempt to find some way to rescue myself and the others. "This is silly. Think how many people know we're with you—Hank, Michael, Jennifer."

Amos immediately picked up on my words. "Just take us home, Doug, and we'll forget about this stunt. It's not very funny, anyhow."

"Too late. I could see Ruthie's mind working away in the restaurant just like Maxine's when she realized Andrea wanted to divorce me, so she gets added to the list."

Keep him talking, I thought. The van's headlights are still on; maybe someone will come along and check on us. "What list?" I said aloud.

"You don't think these kiddies were going to come back alive from the Disneyland trip, do you? And as for their grandfather, I tried to pin Andrea's murder on him, but it didn't work. This is a much better idea."

He suddenly turned and slapped Robbie's hand away from the doorknob. "Don't even think of it," he said and clicked the child safety lock to shut all the van's doors. "We're going to have a nice little accident—four fatalities, but one person miraculously walks away with minor injuries."

"But why?" I asked, trying to sound naive.

"Andrea's money," Amos said. "I should have figured it out long ago."

"Enough talk. I want you kids to unbuckle your seat belts. You, too, Ruthie." He gave a harsh laugh. "Too bad, I'm the only one who was buckled in. That and the air bag saved my life."

Jessica started to cry. "I want to go home."

"Be quiet," Robbie hissed. "You're too young to understand."

"Both of you shut up. I'm still perfecting my plan."

"You can't possibly make it look like an accident," Amos said. "The police will be able to tell that wrench injuries aren't consistent with a traffic accident."

I marveled that he still sounded so calm, but I was sure that reasoning with Doug wasn't going to work. He seemed well beyond rational thought. There had to be another way out.

"You're right. I need some big rocks." He pulled the keys out of the ignition and, still holding onto the wrench, got out of the van, locking the doors behind him. I could see that he was using the van's headlights to search for something to use in creating his scenario.

"Robbie," I said. "Be quick. The driver's side window is open."

The boy reacted immediately, bounding into the front seat. "Get out and hide," I told him. "He can't do anything unless he gets all of us at once."

I helped Robbie climb out of the window, holding onto his jacket as he eased himself soundlessly out of the van. Jessica started crying again, "I wanna go with Robbie," she said.

"Sh-h-h, honey," her grandfather told her. He reached out and hugged her.

I was afraid that the commotion would alert Doug, but he had moved further away. *This is a good time for Jessica and me to climb out, too*, I thought; but knew Amos couldn't escape, and I wouldn't leave him. In his rage at our flight, there was no telling what Doug might do to his father-in-law.

Doug was coming back. The headlights had turned off automatically by now, but his flashlight was still on. I could see that he was carrying several large rocks in addition to the wrench and had had to put the flashlight under one arm. He'd probably have to kill us first and then wreck the van, arranging the scene to look as though we'd all been thrown out on impact. I didn't see how he could do it convincingly, but it was clear to me that he was beyond logic now. Besides, he'd have plenty of time to figure things out before anyone came upon the wreck.

The question occupying my mind now was whether it would be safer for us if it took him longer to discover Robbie's escape, thereby giving the boy time to reach a more settled part of the reservation; or whether we could persuade him to change his mind once he knew Robbie was gone. Doug's plans had been hastily conceived and seemed full of holes, but he must have persuaded himself it was the only way out.

I started to ask Amos for his opinion, but it was too late. Doug had reached the minivan.

Chapter 25.

Doug Payson unlocked the passenger door on my side of the van. He reached across me and dropped the wrench and flashlight on the driver's seat so he could pull me from the van, but he held onto the rocks. "Sit on the ground where I can see you and fold your hands over your head."

"If you want me to sit still, you'll have to tie me up," I said, stalling for time.

"You think you're clever, don't you? Well, you can just stop trying to outsmart me. I know better than to stage an accident and leave rope burns on your hands and legs."

"If you know so much," I told him, "then you should also realize there's no way you can kill us outside the van and stage a convincing accident."

"Just shut up. I'm smart enough to make it work; I don't need advice from you." His voice was quiet and he seemed very calm, nothing to show he'd gone over the edge. I found that more frightening than if he had raged at us.

Doug now released the sliding door behind the passenger side of the minivan. "Jessica, you come out and sit on the ground next to Ruthie." The little girl obeyed him. I put one arm around her despite his order to keep them clasped over my head.

"Robbie, you know how to unhook the wheelchair tiedowns. I want you to do that now."

There was no sound from the van. "I'm not going to tell you again, Robbie. Stop fooling around and do as I said."

"Robbie isn't here," Amos told him.

"You're lying. He couldn't get out; he's hiding back there."

"Come and see for yourself."

"And leave those two alone outside. You must think I'm a fool."

"Robbie isn't here," Amos repeated. "He's gone for help, and the only way you're going to discover the truth is to come in and look."

Doug hesitated for a moment, then yanked me to my feet. "I'll get the wheelchair out myself; then I'll find Robbie. But I'm not taking any chances with you; you're getting back in the van." He lit the interior of the van by turning on the ignition without engaging the engine fully, pushed me up into the front seat and slammed the door. Jessica was still outside; he must have figured she was too young to try to escape.

I moved over to the driver's seat and felt the wrench and flashlight beneath me. This might be my chance, I thought. If I could give the ignition key one more turn, I could drive away. Anything is worth a try rather than sitting here and hoping Robbie can get help in time; but it's useless: I can't leave Jessica.

Then I remembered the button that would lower the ramp electronically. I reached under me and grabbed the wrench, then waited until I heard Doug put down the rocks and begin to undo the tiedowns that fastened Amos's wheelchair securely to the van.

His feet were on the ground, outside the van, and he was leaning into it to reach the wheelchair as he worked on releasing the tiedowns. *Now*, I thought, and pushed the button. Immediately, I flung myself over the seat, gripping the wrench, ready to bring it down on Doug's head.

Because the mechanism that released the ramp worked too gently to do more than throw him slightly off balance for a moment, I missed his head and hit his shoulder instead. I raised the wrench again; but Doug had gripped my arm, and I couldn't get enough purchase to swing again. His full attention was aimed at getting the tool away from me.

While we struggled, Amos rammed the wheelchair into Doug, forcing him to let go of me. This time when I brought the wrench down, I connected with his head. I could hear the thud as his body hit the ramp. There wasn't another sound, and I knew I'd knocked him out.

"Are you okay, Amos?" I asked, my breathing unsteady and my voice ragged from the effort I'd made to save us.

"Grandpa, did he hurt you?" Jessica cried simultaneously, running back to the van.

"I'm all right," he assured us. "Come sit with me, Jessie." The little girl clambered onto his lap, although the wheelchair seemed dangerously unstable to me.

I turned my attention to Doug, relieved to find he was breathing. As I searched for a way to keep him immobilized before he regained consciousness, the headlights of an approaching car beamed on us. Robbie had led the Tribal Police to us.

* * * *

After Doug Payson had been handcuffed and placed in the patrol car, Amos and I told our stories to the tribal detective. Eventually, we were free to go. The detective and Robbie helped to reposition Amos's wheelchair, lining it up to replace the tiedowns and storing the electrical ramp below the chassis once more. I had never driven a van before but I knew that, shaky as I felt from our close brush with death, it was up to me to get Amos and the children back to his house.

The detective offered to lead the way off the reservation, and I accepted gratefully. I drove very slowly. Jessica, sobbing quietly, sat in back with her grandfather. Her brother, on the other hand, couldn't stop talking. I understood his need to make sense of the evening.

"He never liked us. I always knew he pretended in front of Mom and Grandpa."

"Who's gonna take care of us now?" Jessica suddenly asked between sobs. At her strained voice and the heartbreaking words, I could hardly keep from crying myself.

"I'll take care of you and Robbie, honey," Amos said. "All the bad things are over."

They'll need therapy, I thought. Thank God, Doug Payson never got to take them on that trip to California. If they'd been alone with him there, no one could have saved them.

"I ran and ran," Robbie was saying. "You wouldn't believe how far I ran. Then I saw a house. I knocked and knocked on the door until an Indian lady opened it. She telephoned the police."

I was stopped for a traffic light when the boy got to that part of his story, so I reached over and hugged him. "You were great, Robbie."

"These children were wonderful," Amos called out from the back of the minivan. "But you're the one we owe our lives to, Ruthie."

"Everyone helped," I insisted. Now that it was all over, my hands were shaking so much that I had to hold tightly onto the steering wheel, and I went past the turn to Amos's street. When I finally pulled into the driveway, Hank came out to the van.

"Where's Mr. Payson?" he asked. He gave me a critical look as I got out of the van and nearly collapsed on the sidewalk. "You sure parked slantwise," he told me. "You shouldn't be driving this vehicle."

Too bad I'd mistaken surliness for a murderous disposition, I thought, as Hank wheeled Amos into the house while the children and I followed them. How certain I'd been that Amos's caregiver had killed Andrea and Maxine!

"Don't badger Ruthie," Amos said. "She can park in the hibiscus beds, and I wouldn't complain."

"The Indian policeman took Doug away," Jessica said, rubbing her tear-stained face with very dirty hands to dry it. "Doug wanted to kill us."

I didn't plan to wait around and relive the night's terrors again, but the Tribal Police had contacted Scottsdale police headquarters, and a patrol car arrived before I could call a taxi and leave. It took hours before they finished questioning all of us.

Meanwhile, Michael telephoned to ask whether I needed a ride. "I'm not rushing you, but I can see your car's still sitting in Denise's driveway."

In view of his earlier proposal, I wondered whether his choice of the word "rushing" had a double meaning. He knew me well enough to realize I wouldn't relish the idea of someone checking up on me. I'd been looking after myself since Bob's last illness, and I wasn't used to having to account for my whereabouts.

Briefly I asked myself if I was ready to give up that independence, but I was too tired to think about it now. I told him I'd be taking a taxi and would pick up my car shortly.

"I'm going to call your daddy," Amos was telling the children when I focused on them again. "Would you like him to stay here tonight, too?"

"We can't stay," Jessica told him. She was on the floor, hugging Trafalgar as if she'd never let the dog go. "We don't have our jammies."

"I've got some clean T-shirts you can wear," Amos assured her. "Tomorrow, your daddy can drive over to your house and bring back more clothes for you."

Everything had happened so fast, I'd had no time to hate Doug Payson. Now when I thought about the way he'd affected the lives of these young children, I could only rejoice that he was in police custody.

Sterling arrived just before my taxi came. I didn't wait to hear Amos and the children repeat the evening's happenings once more but stayed only long enough to see him gather Jessica and Robbie to him and hold them tightly. At least they had a father and grandfather who loved them. *And who knows*, I thought, *maybe someday Denise will be part of that family.*

As I rode back to Ocotillo Place in the taxi, I knew I'd have to go over everything again for Michael and the others. Thinking of him, I realized I had never focused on Michael's proposal. Despite my dazed state after all the evening's terrors, I began to consider it now.

Some people rationalized, insisting the spouse who'd passed away would want them to remarry and be happy again. I didn't really know if Bob would have felt that way. My mother and father were another story;

they would never have changed their minds about Michael. Now that I was past childbearing age, though, the religious difference between Michael and myself didn't seem as important as it once had.

How is it, I asked myself once again, *that I can't act without wanting to please parents who died so long ago? But I love Michael*, I thought. Then I said it aloud for the first time, not caring if the taxi driver heard me. "But I love him."

—End of Trilogy—

About the Author

RENÉE B. HOROWITZ, a retired professor of information technology at Arizona State University, has published many academic articles and conference papers during her university career. Renée also was a founding member and past president of the Desert Sleuths Chapter of Sisters in Crime. She lives in Scottsdale, Arizona. Her two sons and granddaughter live in California.

Her authentic, behind-the-scenes look at pharmacy in the Rx series is inspired not only by her late pharmacist husband Arthur, but also by both their late pharmacist dads.

Look for more information about Pharmacy Sleuth Ruthie Kantor Morris and other fiction by the author at Renée's website:

www.rxmysteries.com.

You may type in www.pharmacysleuth.com to be redirected to the above website.

On the following two pages, please see information about two other unique and exciting novels by Renée B. Horowitz. As with all of her five Clocktower Books titles, they are also available in print and digital formats.

Two Other Exciting Novels by Renée B. Horowitz

Bitter Moon Over Brooklyn

Life in the Mediterranean Arms, a luxury apartment building in Brooklyn, is at times like living in a soap opera. It's the 1970s—women were still called 'girls', and many filled their days gossiping about their neighbors.

When a beautiful young widow, Marion Davis, is attracted to dashing Neil Kramer, the attraction seems mutual. Marion believes Neil will make her life exciting again.

In true daytime soap mode, there's just one problem. Neil is married to Sandra, her best friend and neighbor.

Then there's Eddie Berg, Sandra Kramer's brother, who tries desperately to make Marion realize the difference between illusion and reality, between the superficial and the genuine.

The yentas of the Mediterranean Arms focus on Marion, betting how long it will take her to 'get' Neil? But is he worth it? And will Marion's awakening come too late to avoid disaster?

The Write Way to Murder

Expert aerospace technical writer Marlene Dreyfus is pulled into a deadly vortex of danger and murder. When a colleague engineer is stabbed and left to die in a company hallway during the busy workday at a major industrial plant, can Marlene sleuth the murderer before he or she strikes again?

Bitter Moon Over Brooklyn (Cover Image)

A Novel and Retrospective by Renée B. Horowitz

The Write Way to Murder (Cover Image)

A Mystery Novel by Renée B. Horowitz

About Clocktower Books

Clocktower Books, a pioneering e-book and Print on Demand publisher, began in April 1996 by publishing some of the world's first entire (not partial) proprietary (not public domain) novels (long works, industry standard) for reading online in HTML format (not on portable media like CD-ROM, floppies, or other intermediary media).

We have been an omnibus publisher (e-book and print) since 1996.

We have been honored since 2000 to have on board such excellent talent as Renee B. Horowitz, Ph.D., Dennis Latham, Robin Marchesi, and other fine authors.

To learn about our latest offerings, please visit the website at

www.clocktowerbooks.com

You will find at the Museum Pages on our website a detailed history of our pioneering publishing house starting from 1996, including references and documentation (ever a work in progress).

A Short History of Clocktower Books

You can read more detail about our history on the Museum Pages of Clocktower Books (www.clocktowerbooks.com).

Clocktower Books has been a pioneer in digital and on-demand publishing since 1996.Doing business as C&C Publishers, we launched our first mystery and suspense website in spring 1996, titled Neon Blue Fiction. The final iteration of this site and its content is still online at

www.neonbluefiction.com.

We followed up in July 1996 with a Dark & Speculative Fiction (Science Fiction, Fantasy, Horror or SFFH) named The Haunted Village, which is still online in its final iteration here:

www.hauntedvillagesffh.com

In December 1996, we (Brian Callahan and John T. Cullen) created the umbrella or omnibus publishing site Clocktower Fiction, which we renamed Clocktower Books in 2000 to cover nonfiction titles.

On 15 April 1998, we launched what for a decade would be the world's first and oldest Web-only (online) magazine of speculative and dark fiction, named Deep Outside SFFH, whose final iteration is here:

www.deepoutside.com

When John T. Cullen became sole proprietor of Clocktower Books in 2002, he renamed the magazine Far Sector SFFH and changed the publishing format in new and innovative ways, using Fictionwise.com as the retail outlet. This worked until December 2012, when Fictionwise ceased operations. The final iteration of this magazine is here:

www.farsector.com

More info at the Clocktower Books Museum Pages.

Click the Museum link at the main page of our website (www.clocktowerbooks.com).